BLIND YOUR PONIES

Also by Stanley Gordon West

Sweet Shattered Dreams
Growing an Inch
Amos: To Ride a Dead Horse
Until They Bring the Streetcars Back
Finding Laura Buggs

BLIND YOUR PONIES

a novel by

STANLEY GORDON WEST

ALGONQUIN BOOKS
OF CHAPEL HILL
2011

Published by
ALGONQUIN BOOKS OF CHAPEL HILL
Post Office Box 2225
Chapel Hill, North Carolina 27515-2225

a division of
WORKMAN PUBLISHING
225 Varick Street
New York, New York 10014

This is a work of fiction. While, as in all fiction, the literary perceptions and insights are based on experience, all names, characters, places, and incidents either are products of the author's imagination or are used fictitiously.

Quotations from *Man of La Mancha* used with permission of Dale Wasserman © 1966.

LIBRARY OF CONGRESS CATALOGING-IN-PUBLICATION DATA
West, Stanley Gordon, [date]
    Blind your ponies : a novel / by Stanley Gordon West. — 1st ed.
        p. cm.
    ISBN 978-1-56512-984-9
    1. Basketball coaches — Fiction.   2. High school boys — Fiction.   3. City and town life — Montana — Fiction.   4. Willow Creek (Mont.) — Fiction.
    5. Basketball stories. I. Title.
    PS3573.E8255B58 2011
    813'.54 — dc22   2010038087

10 9 8 7 6 5 4 3 2

For my father and mother

How did they keep a fire going
with the few scraps of wood they were given?

ALDONZA: You spoke of a dream. And about the Quest!

DON QUIXOTE: Quest?

ALDONZA: How you must fight and it doesn't matter whether you win or lose if only you follow the Quest!

DON QUIXOTE: The words. Tell me the words!

ALDONZA: (*speaking to music*)
"To dream the impossible dream . . ."
But they're your own words!

—from *Man of La Mancha*

BLIND YOUR PONIES

BOOK I

⮎ CHAPTER 1 ⮌

Looking back, Sam Pickett knew the trouble began that day at the state fair, when the madness winked at him. Even as a ten-year-old, he had a sneaking suspicion that, somewhere in that shrouded realm where fates are sealed, his life had been irrevocably jinxed.

ON A LATE AUGUST afternoon, while students still enjoyed summer vacation, Sam hunched over his desk, polishing details on a lesson plan for November.

Use movie version of *Man of La Mancha* for section on Cervantes's novel *Don Quixote* . . . first half of movie this period with time for discussion. Assignment: Read first 18 pages on life of Cervantes. Introduce theme: *The problem of appearance and reality.*

Sam glanced up from his dog-eared lesson plans. The sun had worked its way around and sunlight slanted in through the large, west-facing windows of his classroom, signaling the passing of another day. He was still surprised at the strangeness of his life, teaching high school in the fly-over town of Willow Creek, Montana.

A rattletrap farm truck hauling hay bales backfired as it chugged past the school, startling him. That damned muffled discharge! The feeling came over him with a choking sensation, and he fought for breath. He stared at the blackboard where the sun, coming through cottonwood leaves, left a dappled pattern.

He thought back to that day, to that Friday afternoon. He'd picked up Amy at the school where she taught. They were both high-spirited and happy, looking forward to the weekend together.

He pulled into the long line waiting for drive-up service. Amy said she could get the French fries faster at the counter, so she blew him a kiss and hurried into the building. It was a race to see who'd get the food first, and he hoped she'd win just so he could see the enchanting expression on her face and be rewarded by her childlike laughter. He felt a rush of happiness when he thought of the games they often played, like hide-and-seek in their apartment, in the dark, naked.

From the car, he heard the muffled sound, and then it came again, and again. A backfire? Not inside a building! He ran from the car and collided with terrified people stampeding out the door, fleeing the Burger King. Inside, it was bedlam, a madhouse in which people screamed, crawled under tables, and dove over counters. He frantically searched for her face, and then he saw her. With the bag of French fries still clutched in one hand, she had been hurled onto the tile floor, but not all of her. Parts of her were spattered on the wall, shrapnel from her head, small bits of brain and bone, skin and hair, sailing down the stainless steel on a sea of gore.

He knelt beside her and gently pulled her long black hair over the mutilation, as if that might heal her shattered skull. He took her hand in his, the hand that clung to the French fries she had playfully insisted on getting for him. Amid the chaos a white-haired man knelt beside him.

"She didn't appear to be afraid," the man said, slowly shaking his head. "She looked right at him and said, 'No, please.' Then he pulled the trigger."

Sam looked into the man's watery blue eyes as if asking for understanding.

"Was she your wife?" the man kneeling in her blood said.

Sam nodded. He couldn't breathe, the room was spinning. Five minutes ago his life was full of joy and anticipation. "Oh God, oh God," he moaned.

The man put his hand on Sam's shoulder.

"Why did I turn on Elliot? We could have gone another way, stopped some place else."

It was as if Amy had been drawn to the shotgun blast by some irresistible fate, and he had been helpless to prevent it. He stared at the grisly scene, the blood, the bits of flesh and bone.

The chaos continued, but he stayed beside her on the floor. He felt no fear, hoping the maniac would return and with one more pull of the trigger send him off to be with her. He heard the words from somewhere deep inside, *The Lord giveth and the Lord taketh away.* Was it God who nudged him to take a different route home? Was it God who stoked Sam's impatience with the heavy traffic? If God had any hand in this, then life was a slaughterhouse.

When the sadness erupted over his happy life, the abyss opened beneath him and he fell. In this headlong plunge he instinctively reached out and grabbed hold of something, he didn't know who or what. He hung there, trying to catch his breath, trying to restore his heartbeat, dangling over the darkness.

The city he loved turned gray: green trees, the waterfront, his classroom, friends, the concerts and plays, the lovely boulevards and buildings, all gray. The sadness overwhelmed him. He left everything and fled.

At present, he was hanging on, but he knew he had to identify what it was he clung to, and he knew he had to find some reason to continue to hang on or he would give in to it, let go, and fall into the great dark void and be lost.

"Pickett!"

The voice startled him, jolting him from the trance. Truly Osborn stood in the doorway. Sam caught his breath.

"Hard at it I see," Truly said, as he stepped smartly to Sam's desk.

"Yes," Sam responded, standing, slightly unbalanced.

"I wish a few of the other teachers were as conscientious. When I was running the school in Great Falls, well, things were different, I'll tell you."

Truly glanced at the walls Sam had cluttered with quotations and posters depicting films and books and musical plays.

"Had seventy-six teachers under me, seventy-six. Could account for every paper clip. Can't expect discipline in this outpost."

He twitched his nose as was his habit.

"Is all this necessary?" he said, waving a hand at the wall. "It's so . . . unorganized."

Without allowing a moment for a response, he turned his gaze on Sam, who had settled back into his chair, his heart still racing. He swallowed and tried to pay attention to his superintendent.

"Now then, the other night the school board nearly did away with the basketball program. John English expressed the frustration and embarrassment we all feel because of the team, but due to the persistence of that foolhardy Wainwright and his lackey Ray Collins, they decided to go one more year. Can you imagine?"

Sam glanced down at his lesson plan and his eyes focused on *The problem of appearance and reality.* He was lost. Somehow, Amy's voice came softly and calmly.

Truly continued to talk, and finally his words penetrated.

". . . However, they realize how hard it has been for you to coach these past five years, the time and travel for what, heaven knows, is little extra money. We're prepared to assign the task to Mr. Grant, our new math teacher. Hopefully it will only be for one more year. Might as well pass the misery around."

Sam wanted to protest, wanted to volunteer for another year. If nothing else, the basketball program filled many hours during the winter months, and he didn't know how he'd handle that much unscheduled time.

"Oh, and the board asked me to convey their gratitude for the way you've stuck to it, even though you never did manage to win a game."

Sam caught the not-so-subtle sarcasm. The superintendent twitched his nose like a rabbit.

"They appreciate your . . . fortitude. Mr. Grant can carry on the ridiculous comedy with the boys."

He slung a hand toward the classroom wall.

"See if you can't neaten this up a bit."

Then he turned and scurried from the room.

Pompous ass, Sam thought.

He stood, teetering slightly, still finding it hard to breathe. He pulled the shade, darkening the room. Truly's cruel reference to the team's efforts as "comic" had made him wince, and he admitted that deep inside he had wanted to win just one game, for the boys, for the town. Though the furthest he'd gone with basketball was playing on his high school team, Sam believed he was a capable English teacher. As a basketball coach he was 0–87. Wasn't that some kind of a world's record, a *Guiness Book* oddity? And even better, the team was 0–93, having lost its last six the season before Sam arrived. It would be exceedingly difficult to lose ninety-three in a row without some law of nature kicking in to bring the odds back into balance, something like an entire opposing team coming down with trichinosis in the middle of the third quarter or their eyes going crossed for all of the second half.

What Truly viewed as a ridiculous comedy actually had taught Sam something about heroism. Heroism wasn't playing hard with a chance to win, a chance to receive the acclaim and praise of victory. True heroism was refusing to quit when there was no chance to win. True heroism was giving your all in the face of absolute defeat. He thought that these boys, who were pitied by some, were learning life's lesson sooner than most, learning that life is a series of losses.

Sam gathered several folders off his desk and worried about how he would fill this new block of free time. He regarded the lesson plans for a moment, then dropped them on the desktop. He picked up his tattered copy of *Don Quixote* and left the room. He'd read the eight hundred and some pages again; that should occupy him for several days at least.

He raced down the hall and a flight of stairs, then ducked out the front door. The basketball court in front of the school stood empty in the late afternoon heat. The mountains shimmered to the west and the sweet aroma of freshly-cut alfalfa filled his nostrils as he headed toward his rental house. The town stretched along the road for about eight blocks, with the school situated on the south end, and Sam's one-story home—for which he paid two hundred dollars a month in rent—in the middle.

Rip, the oldest resident in Willow Creek, shuffled along the street toward Sam. The skeletal-looking man's suspenders appeared to be pulling him further and further down into his pants.

"Hello, Rip," Sam said, slowing as they passed.

"Hey, Coach," Rip said, flashing a toothless smile. "We're gonna do it this year, by golly, ain't we?"

"Yeah, sure," Sam said, trying to keep the sarcasm out of his voice.

It still amazed Sam that Willow Creek—with an entire high school enrollment of eighteen or nineteen students, and with a senior class last year consisting of three—somehow managed to maintain a basketball team and compete in the state-sanctioned conference. The school, whose greatest athletic achievement was fielding five standing, breathing boys, hadn't won a basketball game in over five years, spreading a pall over the lives of those who identified with the community and its team. It was a virtual bloodletting, sanctioned by the Montana High School Association.

He turned in at the walkway to his house, mentally planning the evening ahead: run and walk the loop over the Jefferson River bridge, shower, supper, an hour of television, read until he fell asleep. He stepped onto the creaking porch, shoved the ill-fitting door open, and prayed he could hold off the afternoon's vision until he escaped into the murky shadows of sleep.

Though he hated to admit it to himself, he was afraid to go to sleep, and he dreaded waking up in the morning to the memory of his relentless dreams. Somewhere in his mind, Amy's voice played back at random times throughout the day and night.

He was also haunted by the Indian legend he first heard when he came to Montana. Members of the Crow tribe were camped along the Yellowstone River near present-day Billings. Warriors, returning from a long hunting trip, found the camp decimated by smallpox. Their wives, mothers, children, were all dead. So overcome with grief, sure they would join their loved ones in another world, they blinded their ponies and rode them off a sixty-foot cliff.

Five years after losing Amy, Sam still identified with those Crow warriors who couldn't bear life without their loved ones. He would never admit to anyone that, on a daily basis, he entertained the thought of blinding his pony and riding off the cliff to be with her.

↬ CHAPTER 2 ↫

Peter Strong waited for his Grandma Chapman in front of the café that doubled as the bus depot in Three Forks, Montana. The family-shattering detonation of his parents' divorce had been followed by the anguish of leaving his girlfriend and the comfort zone he knew in St. Paul, Minnesota, and heading by Greyhound to eastern Montana, where he'd spend one dreaded school year in Willow Creek.

"Hey, Grandma. How are you?" Peter said as he watched his mother's mother amble toward him from her faded green VW bus.

"I'm cookin', sweetheart, I'm cookin'."

Having already noticed the comfortable temperature, without a touch of Midwest humidity, he figured she wasn't referring to the weather and that it must be some kind of Western-speak. She hugged him and then held him at arm's length, eyeing him like she might a newborn pup, checking to see if it had all its parts. He hadn't seen his grandmother in several years and was taken aback by her appearance and bluster. She had no left hand, but he already knew that. No, it was the clothes. Dressed in Levis, and wearing a white sweatshirt with black lettering, beat-up Reeboks, red-framed glasses, and a man's brown felt hat perched on her snow-gray hair, she reminded him of the street people he saw in Saint Paul, and he couldn't decide if he should laugh or hand her a dollar.

"Welcome to Montana!" she half shouted.

"Welcome to the end of the world," he said under his breath, glancing at the three blocks that made up Three Forks' depressed business district. "Willow Creek is bigger, right?" he asked.

"Smaller."

"That's impossible," he said, trying to swallow a sudden rush of panic and loneliness.

"You've gone and growed up," she said, hugging him and then stepping back to look at his hair. "That how the young lions wear their mane in the big city?"

"Yeah, some."

She rubbed her hand over his blond hair, cut short along the sides, long on top and back. "Looks like the barber got started and you ran out of cash. Reminds me of the bushmen in *National Geographic*."

She smiled—sadly he thought—and her face took on the look of a worn leather glove. Her figureless body slumped toward the middle: no hips, no curves, just legs and arms and a head sprouting from a slightly bent and twisted trunk. Her sweatshirt read:

This package is sold by weight, not volume.
Some settling of contents may have occurred
during shipment and handling.

"Sure got your mother's eyes; the gals'll be fluttering over you."

"I have a girlfriend."

"So I've heard. Well, better pull the shades on those gorgeous blue peepers, then. I don't want you breaking any hearts."

With the dull ache in his chest he'd carried all the way from Saint Paul, he picked up his suitcase and duffel. At least there was one good thing, he thought: he liked his kooky grandmother.

"How's your mom doing?" she asked as they walked toward her bus.

"I don't know." He wanted her to ask how he was doing. He was the one who got shipped out! "Divorce sucks."

"Don't suppose it's a picnic for you," she said.

"Some people wait until their kids are grown up—why can't they?"

"Got no answer for that."

"I can take care of myself when Mom has to travel. She's only gone for a week at a time. She thinks I'm a baby or something."

"Wants you to get the care you deserve."

"They just don't want a snot-nosed kid around anymore."

"Well, that's my good fortune then, because I'll love having you around."

A dusty red pickup rattled to the curb and stopped a short distance from them.

"Oh, Peter, come here," his grandmother said.

She walked to the passenger side of the truck. He followed and found a girl with wide blue eyes sitting beside the somber woman driver.

"Hello, Sally. Want you to meet my grandson, Peter," his grandmother said through the open window. "Peter, this is Sally Cutter." She nodded at the driver. "And this is her girl, Denise. How are you, honey?"

"Hello," the woman said without turning her eyes on Peter. He regarded the girl for a moment. Her lively eyes seemed to pick up on everything, even though her head teetered gently and a string of drool hung from the corner of her mouth. Strapped into the pickup with some special kind of seat belt, she made a guttural sound.

"Hello," Peter said and smiled. He sensed the mother was embarrassed by her girl.

Feeling uneasy, he picked up his suitcase and duffel and tossed them into the VW bus. A road-worn bumper sticker clung to the back bumper: "DO IT IN WILLOW CREEK, MONTANA," it read. Feeling ill at ease, he climbed into the passenger seat and waited while the women visited. In a minute his grandmother pulled herself up behind the wheel and turned the key. Nothing happened.

"Wouldn't you know," she said, grabbing a screwdriver out of the glove box.

"What's wrong?" he said.

"Nothing I can't fix."

In moments she was out the door, around behind the bus and out of sight. Peter climbed out and found her lying in the street on her back, only her jeans and tennis shoes sticking out from under the bumper. He knelt to peer under the bus when suddenly the engine kicked over and started. She slid out, stood up, and brushed herself off.

"Happens now and then."

They climbed in and roared down the main drag, the engine sounding as if they were doing eighty, although he knew they couldn't be doing more than twenty-five.

"What did you do?" he asked.

"Jumped it, like a hot-wire."

He had no idea what that meant, but he didn't let on, didn't want her thinking he was a stupid city kid.

"Two of Willow Creek's heroes," she said, by which, Peter finally realized, she was referring to the mother and daughter he had just met.

"They live in Willow Creek?"

"Few miles south of town, in the hills where the soil is pretty thin."

His loneliness slid up into his throat; the mother and daughter rattled him. "Why heroes?"

"'Cause they keep playin' with the hand they were dealt, not like some people I know."

"How old is she, the girl?"

"Sixteen, seventeen, about your age."

He wanted to tell her it scared the hell out of him to see someone his age like that, knowing it could be him, but he'd learned from painful experience not to share such things with anyone.

"Got a driver's license?" his grandmother asked.

"Yeah."

"Ever drive a stick shift?"

"No, we have automatic."

"Trilobite is nearly automatic," she said while laying her right hand atop the stick shift.

"Trilobite?"

"A fossil they find in rocks. As vehicles go, she's about as much a fossil as I am, so we respect each other. She's a sixty-five, twenty-five years old, so I'll expect you to drive her with respect."

"Dad says only hippies drive VW buses," he said.

"That so . . . what else does your dad say?"

"He thinks you're kind of a screwball, says you're a 'refried hippie.'"

"Well, coming from my distant son-in-law I'll take that as a compliment." They laughed.

His grandma's faded white-frame house sat on Main Street, halfway between the Blue Willow Inn and the school, where—Grandma explained—the teachers attempted to enlighten kindergarten through senior high students, and the school board annually took its stand against the inevitable, like fighting gravity, hanging onto the high school for one more year.

She introduced him to her family: a motley green parrot named Parrot—

whose cage she quickly covered before he could speak—and her three-legged cat, Tripod.

"Found him in the backyard a year ago, a stray no one'd claim. Sick and dying, his right front leg shredded by some beast or machine or steel-jawed trap. Nursed him back to life after the vet amputated his bum leg. Ever since he sticks to me like panty hose." She led him into the cozy and cluttered kitchen. "You can call him One Chance if you like."

"Why One Chance?"

"When I took him to the vet he said the cat had one chance in a million and maybe we should just put him to sleep. I told him no, that if he had one chance, let's go for it."

Peter sat in a chair by the kitchen table, and the apricot-and-white cat came to him as if with some instinctual understanding that they were orphaned kin. His grandmother slipped larger eyeglasses over the pair she wore, and stuck a piece of a jigsaw puzzle in place in the half-finished depiction of a sailing ship that sprawled across part of the table.

"I play bingo on Tuesdays and Thursdays, go bowling Wednesday afternoons, do aerobics most mornings in front of the TV, hit the garage sales on Saturday mornings with Hazel Brown, have coffee at the Blue Willow once or twice a day—that was the joint we passed comin' into town—watch *The Waltons* reruns, and we get up a game of hearts or whist whenever we've a mind to, but generally I'm just hanging around."

She found another puzzle piece that fit and thumbed it into place. "Landsakes." She looked at him. "What's the matter with me? You must be starving."

She pulled off the top pair of glasses.

"Oh, darn, forgot again." She opened a prescription bottle near the sink and popped a capsule in her mouth, washing it down with a glass of water. "I have to keep gettin' a new doc," she said.

"Why?"

"They keep dyin' on me."

His grandmother laughed and fetched a carton of milk from the refrigerator. He noticed a small hand-lettered poster on the wall: "AS LONG AS SHE SWIMS I WILL COOK." It made no sense to Peter.

She poured a glass and set it in front of him. "What kind of milk do you like?"

"Two percent," he said. "Are you sick?"

"Landsakes, no. This doc keeps wanting me to come in for checkups. Fussy old fool. Thinks my blood pressure is high." She hooted. "Just never seen a seventy-four-year-old who's still alive."

They hadn't been in the house a half hour—enough time to stuff him with milk and uncounted Oreos—when his grandmother challenged him to a game of Horse.

"What do you mean?" Peter asked, startled.

"A game of Horse. You play Horse in Saint Paul, don't you?"

"Yeah . . . but—"

"Then quit your stammering and get on your playing shoes." She opened a closet and produced a shiny new basketball, firing a snappy pass that he caught more with reflex than skill.

Somewhat astonished, he followed silently as they walked the two blocks up Main Street to the school grounds. Looking about, he realized it appeared to be the only street.

"Where's the rest of the town?" he said.

"You're lookin' at it."

"We have shopping malls bigger than this."

"Minus the Tobacco Roots," she said, waving a hand at the massive mountain range to the west, "and clean air and cutthroat trout." Attached to an old three-story brick building—which Pete at first thought must be the grade school—stood a more recently built gymnasium with HOME OF THE BRONCS AND THE BLUE PONIES lettered in weather-beaten blue on its east wall.

"Who are the Blue Ponies?" he asked.

"Girls' basketball . . . haven't had enough players for a team the past few years, though. You might say the Blue Ponies are temporarily, if not permanently, out to pasture." She nodded at the gym. "Seeing as the boys' nickname is the Broncs, some of the nasty folks around here refer to this as the glue factory."

In front of the school there was an asphalt basketball court with four baskets. His grandmother promptly made a free throw and tossed the ball at Pete. He tried a shot and missed, and she hooted with delight.

"'H'! You got an 'H,' boy!"

His grandmother actually won the first game by methodically throwing a spastic sort of hook shot, but when Peter got his bearings, he began hitting baskets, and eventually had to hold back, feeling guilty for beating her so badly.

"You'll be as popular as all get-out around here come basketball season," she said, while trying to throw the ball from outside the circle.

Peter retrieved her errant shot. "Do they have a good team?"

"Nope, haven't won a game in five years. But, lordy, I think that's gonna change."

"Five years!" He swished a long shot. "That's diseased. Think I can make the team?"

His grandmother cocked her head as if he were putting her on. "All you have to do is show up. Everyone with balls makes the team, and by that I don't mean the family jewels. I mean guts, I mean backbone, I mean heart."

Peter blushed slightly at her reference to the family jewels, and when she said she had to get home and work on the dinner, he was glad to stay and shoot for a while. The few vehicles that had drifted by showed no surprise at this seventy-four-year-old, one-handed woman out banging a basketball off the backboard.

THE ROAD FROM Three Forks made a gentle curve into Willow Creek and became Main Street, the only pavement in that end-of-the-road village. Peter could see snow-tipped mountains in almost any direction, and they looked huge. As for Willow Creek, it was hard to tell where the fields and cow pastures ended and the town began. There just wasn't anything there.

Peter tried to be positive, but he was pissed and confused and scared. He began practicing with a vengeance because he didn't know what else to do:

long shot, rebound, lay-up, over and over, breaking a sweat, trying to dunk the rebound and coming close, there on the outdoor court of a school where by some fluke of fate he would have to spend his junior year. His life had blown up on him, and he had been hurled to this godforsaken place.

As if in a dream he sent the ball on its graceful arc, and the swish of the net blended with the sounds of lowing cattle and distant children's voices drifting in the dry mountain air. He looked around him, already plotting his escape.

✎ CHAPTER 3 ✎

With only a few days before school was to start, Sam Pickett labored at his desk over lesson plans. In the background, the soundtrack from *Rocky* reverberated from the stereo in the corner of the classroom, prodding him with its beat.

He felt the floor tremble and glanced up to see Hazel Brown as she blustered into his classroom.

"Mr. Pickett, there's something you've *got* to see."

She wore a sheen of sweat on her face and labored to catch her breath, which wasn't unusual for Hazel. Sam wouldn't call Hazel obese, though he figured she was twice the size God intended. He'd call her *big*.

"What is it?" he said, wanting to finish what he was doing before going home, and anxious not to be interrupted.

"Something out in front." She giggled. "It won't take long, Mr. Pickett."

For years he had explained that she didn't have to call him mister, but she refused to pay attention. As the school cook, Hazel sometimes helped out with custodial chores, and Sam figured she always heard the students call him Mr. Pickett and felt obliged to follow suit.

"Can it wait until I leave? I'll only be another twenty minutes," he said with an intended irritation in his voice.

"It may be gone by then, Mr. Pickett. It won't take but a minute."

She stood there in enormous jeans and tentlike sweatshirt with her head slightly tilted, holding her chubby hands together in a supplicating pose.

"Oh, all right," he said and tossed his ballpoint down on his desk. He pushed his chair back and followed Hazel out of the room, urged on by the *Rocky* soundtrack. As he walked behind her down the stairs he couldn't help but wonder where she found jeans that size. When he first met Hazel, he held back, expecting some unpleasant body odor because of her enormous bulk, but instead he whiffed a sweet cosmetics-counter aroma that became as much a part of her in his mind as her heavy tread. He walked down the stairs, following the wake of that pungent fragrance, and realized that if he had to he could track Hazel in the pitch dark.

She didn't go out the school's front door but instead led him around through the gym and into the small lunchroom where they could peer out at the asphalt basketball court without being seen.

"There," she said, giggling and pointing to the court. Sam slid up beside her and gazed through the lunchroom window. Outside, a boy he'd never seen before assaulted the rim and backboard with a basketball, going at it as if his life depended on it.

"Watch this," Hazel said. The boy dashed toward the backboard, grabbed the bouncing ball and nearly dunked it. "Grandma Chapman made me promise I'd introduce you. He's her grandson from Saint Paul."

"Well, I'm pretty busy . . . maybe I can meet him some other time," Sam said, anxious to get back to work but unable to turn away as the boy hit shot after shot from the far side of the court.

"Oh, c'mon, Mr. Pickett," Hazel said, and she hauled her body out the lunchroom door toward the asphalt court.

Sam hesitated a moment and then gave in to his curiosity.

"Peter!" Hazel shouted.

The boy stopped dribbling and turned toward the approaching couple.

"Peter, this is Mr. Pickett." She turned to Sam. "Mr. Pickett, this is Peter Strong, Elizabeth Chapman's grandson."

Sam moved up beside Hazel and extended his hand. "Hello, Peter."

"Hi."

With his chest heaving and his T-shirt soaked, the boy took Sam's hand in a sweaty grip. Sam guessed him to be about six foot even.

"Mr. Pickett's our basketball coach," Hazel said, as if it were some unheard of honor instead of an ungodly indictment.

"No . . . no longer. Mr. Grant will coach the team this year," Sam said.

"Since when?" Hazel frowned, obviously hurt not to be up to the minute on what was going on around the school.

"What do you think of Willow Creek?" Sam said, ignoring Hazel's question.

"I don't know, I mean . . . there's nothing here. I never knew a town could die and people would keep on living there." He wiped sweat from his forehead with the palm of his hand and dried it on his jeans.

"Kind of like ghosts, huh?" Sam said, and laughed. "Are you going to be here long?"

"I sure hope not, my family's just getting things worked out. I plan to be home by Christmas."

"That's not what your grandma says," Hazel said with a defensive tone. "She said you'd be one more student for the high school this year."

"How many kids are there?" Peter asked.

"Seventeen," Sam said.

"*Seventeen?*"

"Eighteen," Hazel said. "We're getting an exchange student, a boy from Norway."

"Huh. Back home I have over four hundred kids in just my class."

"Well," Sam said, "it was nice meeting you. Be careful you don't turn into a ghost while you're here." Sam smiled and headed back toward the school.

"See you later, Peter," Hazel said, following Sam. She caught him halfway up the second floor stairs.

"What do you think, Mr. Pickett?" she said, panting.

Sam stopped at the landing.

"What do I think about what?"

"About Grandma Chapman's grandson. He sure has an attitude about him."

"Remember the first time *you* saw Willow Creek?" Sam said.

"She says he's going to be here for the whole school year. Do you think he'll make a difference?"

Sam climbed another step and stopped. "Do you mean will he help Willow Creek win a game? No, probably not."

"That's what I told Elizabeth. Heavens to Betsy, it'll take more than that kid. Magic Johnson couldn't win a game here."

"Oh, he looks like a player," he said. "Was he on his high school team in Saint Paul?"

"To hear Grandma Chapman talk you'd think he was going into the NBA next week."

"Well, it doesn't sound like he'll be here for the basketball season anyway."

"I don't blame you for quitting coaching, Mr. Pickett." She glanced into his eyes for a moment and then looked away. "I don't know how you stood it so long."

"Yeah, well, it was something to do."

Sam turned and climbed the stairs. He knew he wasn't in the main loop of village gossip, in fact he purposely avoided it. But after eating so many meals at the Blue Willow, the hive of town scuttlebutt, he couldn't help but gain a certain level of knowledge about everyone in town. The word was that Hazel grew up in St. Louis with her unwed mother, never married, bounced around the West waiting tables and cooking for twenty years, and then she showed up in Willow Creek ten or twelve years ago and anchored her forty-two-foot aluminum trailer as if she were making her stand. She sent out her need for approval like cottonwood seed and it stuck to everyone.

At the end of the hall he hurried into his classroom, where the *Rocky* soundtrack continued to urge him on. Ten minutes later he was up to speed, revising, polishing, and adding new material, trying to recapture the excitement he once felt in introducing students to words and language and the wonder of their magic in great writing.

But no matter how he tried to ignore it, something stuck at the back of his mind, and he couldn't shake it. Was he annoyed at Hazel Brown for interrupting him? No, that wasn't it. Was it what Peter Strong had said? Had the boy seen through the appearance of Willow Creek to its reality? If the kid stayed, Mr. Grant—with senior Rob Johnson—would have two good basketball players to work with. Even so, that was no longer Sam's worry, and he tried to shove it out of his mind and keep at his lesson plans.

It didn't work; he couldn't concentrate, couldn't prevent himself from crossing the hall and peering from the window, down to the asphalt basketball court where the unsettled boy raged against the basket as though he were fighting to stay alive, as though he were afraid he, too, would turn into a Willow Creek ghost. Sam walked away from the window, suddenly agitated, considering the possibility that's what had happened to him. Had Sam turned into a ghost?

Later that night, as he lay in his sleepless bed, having read Cervantes until nearly two in the morning, he played tricks with his mind, trying to hold off the haunting that circled his bed like silent moths. Out of the shadows of his memory he could hear his mother's voice: *You get on that elephant!*

That elephant, that little gray elephant thumped its way into his mind on the familiar memory of his mother's voice. *You get on that elephant, I paid good money.*

It had been at a fly-by-night carnival in some ragtag town in Indiana, and Sam was six or seven. When they first saw the exotic creature, circling in a small roped-off area with gleeful children on its back and parents snapping photos, Sam wanted to ride. His mother bought a ticket. Sam waited in line and eventually climbed a step or two of the platform they used for children to mount the animal. The kids just ahead of him were getting on, and Sam found himself at eye level with the unfamiliar beast. He noticed its long eyelashes and thought it must be a girl elephant. All at once the creature gazed at him, opening its eyelid slowly, suddenly presenting him with a porthole into the heart of creation itself. Startled, Sam looked into the elephant's dark watery eye.

As young as he was, he immediately recognized a sadness that matched something within him, a grief so excruciating it overwhelmed him. This wasn't a happy time with laughing children and waving parents. The elephant was heartsick! They were stealing its life! It would never be free to run across the grass, play with other elephants, wade into a lake and splash and frolic. It had been taken hostage, confined to this dreary little circle, day after day, year after year, going in endless circles so that its owner could make money. Sam suddenly sensed the great freighted sorrow of all those creatures of the earth whose lives were pillaged for human gain and satisfaction. He had seen the awful woe in the elephant's eye, and he had to turn away.

"I don't want to ride!" he called to his mother with an escalating panic. "I don't want to ride!"

"You get up there and ride, I paid good money for that ticket."

The attendant waited impatiently to help him on.

"I'll pay you back with my allowance," Sam said, near tears now.

"You'll be all right," his mother said. "The elephant won't hurt you."

"I don't—"

"The nice elephant likes boys and girls."

"But, Mom . . ."

She thought he was afraid; he wasn't afraid. He just didn't want to be a part of the elephant's murder.

"You get on *right now,* you're holding everyone up, you'll be all right."

Sam climbed on. They loaded two kids behind him. As he waited, he leaned forward and whispered in the elephant's huge ear: "I'm sorry, elephant, I'm sorry."

When he clambered off the animal he couldn't look back into that window of sorrow, as though he had participated in stealing the animal's life. From that day, he became a vigilant survivor who, at all costs, avoided looking into the elephant's eye.

Sam Pickett, English teacher and former basketball coach at Willow Creek High School, scrounged for sleep in his tangled bed. He was thirty-six years old and he hadn't a clue as to who he was or what his life was about. He bore a wound he couldn't heal.

He pulled the bedding over his head and thought back to the boy playing basketball. Sam was relieved to have severed his connection with the basketball team, yet he couldn't help harboring the inescapable shame of a traitor.

CHAPTER 4

Mervin Painter stood in the drive waiting for his wife, Claire, to get ready, something he'd grown accustomed to over the thirty-one years they'd been married. He ran his eyes over the ranch, and memories glided to him like a red-tailed hawk on the warm August breeze. The original sod hut his grandfather built when he homesteaded the land, now returning to the soil; the two-story frame house in which Mervin grew up, sitting empty; and behind him the ranch-style brick-and-cedar-sided rambler they moved into when his girls were in school.

He reflected on how well he'd covered his inner firestorm, knowing his neighbors and Willow Creek townsfolk saw him as an easygoing, patient man who faced life with a calm resolve, while inside, underneath that mellow image, he wrestled with unresolved regret and remorse and rage. He would never let on, never give his big brother satisfaction or bewilder his unsuspecting wife.

Of the two brothers, he had been the loyal son who stayed and worked the land side by side with their father. He had a sweetheart, Maggie Swanson, and everyone in the community figured they'd be married one day. They had plans. Mervin was waiting until he could build them a modest house on the ranch; he'd witnessed the disasters that happened when a couple moved in with their parents.

It was tough enough living only a few hundred feet apart.

Having Maggie, a girlfriend, was the one feat Mervin had managed better than his older brother, Carl. Carl never went with a girl more than a few weeks, couldn't seem to match up. He drank too much, picked up several DUIs, and couldn't seem to "find himself."

Rumors of brutal fights and general carousing filtered through the valley and their father was chagrined. Then, when he turned twenty-one, Carl took off, traipsing around the world, Australia, Mexico, Alaska, writing from distant ports and pleading for money, which their father always sent with the hope that Carl would eventually come home and settle on the land. Mervin prayed that he wouldn't.

Carl had not been a good big brother, no buddy or companion you could count on. Three years older, always bigger, often mean and brutal, he would beat up Mervin when Mervin didn't toe Carl's line. A punch in the stomach, a bloody nose, and on several occasions Carl had knocked Mervin unconscious. Mervin never tattled. He learned to stay clear of his combative brother, waiting for the time when he would grow big enough to stand up to Carl and, if not beat him, at least do enough damage that Carl would limp away with his own blood leaking onto the ground. About the time Mervin put on the weight and muscle to take Carl on, Carl took off on his world travels, "sowing his wild oats" as people around Willow Creek would say. Rumors circulated that his abrupt departure had to do with some serious trouble he was in, that he'd bitten off more than he could chew.

More than a year later, Carl returned to the valley but he didn't come home, stayed with friends and only came by briefly to say hello and retrieve some of his belongings, as if he feared being trapped on the land. He seemed to have money. They'd see him at the Blue Willow and pass him coming or going in his new Chevy pickup.

One day Dennis Reed told Mervin he saw Carl with Maggie in his pickup. Mervin staggered from the punch to his heart. *Maggie with Carl! His girl, his darling, his life.* Like a madman he took off looking for his big brother, prepared to tear him apart with his bare hands. He searched everywhere he could imagine, driving back roads frantically until one in the morning, but came up empty.

Racing to Maggie's family place west of town, he woke her parents and they discovered she wasn't in her bed. Mervin waited in his pickup until five-fifteen when Maggie came driving home.

Sitting in her car, she wouldn't tell him where Carl was but she got him to calm down and told him over and over how sorry she was. He had hope; he thought she wanted to make up. Then she said she still loved him, but she was going to marry Carl. The blows kept landing, his brother was beating him up again. He pleaded with her, it wasn't too late, they could put this behind them and go ahead with their plans. No, they couldn't, she was pregnant.

He couldn't find his breath. They had wrestled mightily with waiting until they were married to make love, though they'd done some pretty heavy necking and petting down by the Jefferson River bridge. She said she wanted to be a virgin on her wedding night and, though he liked the idea of it, he had often tried to persuade her otherwise without success. His big brother is home a month or two and she's lain with him in his pickup or some hayloft, slipped off her panties, opened her sweetness to him! He tried to block it from his mind and feared he'd go insane.

He never said another word to her. He drove away without looking back, his brother's fist tearing something loose in his chest. He couldn't breathe, thought he'd suffocate. The sun came up as he turned in the ranch road. When his parents asked where he'd been he didn't respond. He took a shower and went out and worked like a madman without food or drink until long past dark.

Carl and Maggie were married ten days later, and they moved onto a place with her grandparents over near Churchill. Carl knuckled down working the ranch, they had three boys, and in a few years both of Maggie's grandparents passed away, leaving their place to the young couple.

Mervin met Claire the following summer at a friend's wedding in Livingston and they married a year later. He never felt the same with Claire as he had with Maggie. He tortured himself for years for not marrying Maggie while Carl was away, punished himself unrelentingly for not swallowing his pride and telling Maggie that it didn't matter that she was pregnant, that he'd marry her and raise the child as their own. He'd always wondered what she would have said. Had she felt trapped and believed she had no option but to marry Carl? Had she been seduced in her simple innocence by his worldly brother though she truly loved Mervin after all? He'd never know.

As he stood there in the driveway, he couldn't sort out his feelings.

He knew he still loved Maggie like he'd love no one else. And he knew he would never do anything to hurt Claire, sweet, childlike Claire. Through all the cousins' graduations and weddings he'd managed to avoid any private conversation with Maggie, but he knew his brother still drank and at times he thought he caught a sadness in her eyes and the shadow of a bruise on her lovely face.

When Mervin's father retired, he willed the family place to Mervin, with Carl's share to be paid in cash when their father passed on. But what graveled Mervin to the core was that their father gave the old John Deere "D" tractor to Carl, a family heirloom passed down for three generations. Mervin believed he deserved the tractor, the son who stayed home and began working the place with his father the day he graduated from high school, the son who did everything his father ever asked. It was a birthright Carl had forfeited.

The John Deere "D" was the first tractor their grandfather ever had. He only used it a few years and then purchased a more powerful and versatile machine. Never able to bring himself to trade it in on other equipment, it had become like a faithful old work horse that had carved a soft spot in their grandfather's heart. The "D" was kept in a machine shed away from weather and sun ever since and was "a rare son-bitch" as Mervin's father used to say. Carl only displayed it in parades, antique shows and the like, a treasured family coat of arms. It should have gone to Mervin.

Mervin had come to the point where he couldn't stay in church that Sunday each year when the text for the day was "The Prodigal Son." Damn it, his father had killed the fatted calf when his wayward brother came home, only it was the John Deere "D" he gave him, as though it were a symbol that he'd forgiven him and taken him back with open arms. Mervin would pretend to be ill or find some other excuse to leave when he'd glance at the bulletin and see that Luke 15:11-32 would be the basis for the minister's sermon. He'd be damned if he'd put himself through that anymore.

Son, you are always with me
And all that is mine is yours.
It was fitting to make merry and be glad,
For this your brother was dead, and is alive;
He was lost, and is found.

Why didn't the sonofabitch stay lost.
Mervin turned and glanced at the fine ranch home he'd built, realizing Claire should be coming out any minute. Over the years he had tried to let the wounds heal, let go of the pain and disappointment, all of it, and he had succeeded to some degree, but as if fate had a hand in it, Carl's boys had gone to Manhattan Christian, a private school in the little village of

Churchill with a solid basketball program and an endless supply of good players, while Mervin's girls went to Willow Creek, a school that had difficulty finding six or seven boys for the team and who hadn't won a game in recent memory. And every year, in their cool and restrained relationship, he and Carl bet five dollars on the game. It wasn't the five dollars, but he was sick and tired of being beaten by his big brother and the two annual games between their teams only rubbed salt in old wounds and reminded him that he lost again, lost Maggie, lost the life he planned, lost the goddamn John Deere "D."

Claire came out of the house dressed in her Sunday best and waved as she got into the gray Ford Fairlane. Mervin checked his watch and hurried to the car. They were picking up the exchange student at the airport outside Bozeman. They had conceived and raised four daughters, and after a quartet, they had given up both the hope and any further attempt to hatch a male Painter in their antimasculine fluids. They accepted the town's basketball heritage with a resolute grit and no little amount of guilt at not producing any boys to lift Willow Creek's banner out of the manure. Their daughters excelled off the land, and two of them had become exchange students, one spending a year in Spain, one a year in Brazil.

Being the fair-minded soul Claire was, she felt obliged to volunteer as a host family for some youngster who wanted to visit the U.S. for a year of study and cultural shock in Willow Creek. Thus a boy from Norway, Olaf Gustafson, would cross the Atlantic and most of the United States to spend the school year on the land where three generations of Painters had taken a stand to carve out a livelihood by raising cattle in Montana's auspicious and fickle bosom. Mervin thought it was the least they could do now that their daughters were married and scattered all over the country.

They had exchanged letters and received a bundle of information about Olaf—age, health, scholastic record, hobbies, everything, including a picture of him standing alone in front of his house in Oslo. Claire said he looked kind of skinny and they'd have to put some meat on his bones. But neither Claire nor Mervin, nor anyone in the school office, paid any attention to information given in metric numbers or tried to translate them into U.S. equivalents.

His flight touched down on time, and the gleaming Northwest 727 rolled smoothly to the concourse gate. Claire shared her anxiety as she shifted from foot to foot and fidgeted with her hands.

"What are we getting into?" she said. "What if he is unhappy and loud and impolite? What if he causes trouble and drinks liquor and gets into fights?"

Passengers began streaming from the concourse: men, women, children, all kinds of ordinary-looking people. Claire clutched the identifying snapshot as she clung to a nervous smile, the lines in her round porcelain face apparently cracks from that perpetual expression, a smile Mervin took for granted, knowing it was Claire's way of facing the uncertainties of life, knowing she could come with her right arm mangled in the baler, still bearing that sunbeam smile.

"What if he missed a connection?" she said.

"There's still a few coming," Mervin said.

Then, ducking through the gate with wide blue eyes and straw-colored hair, Olaf came bearing a duffel bag and a bright, boyish grin.

"The bed!" Claire said. "What will we do about the bed?"

They stepped forward as he came through the roped-off passenger area.

"Olaf?" Claire said with a voice of disbelief.

"Ya, hello. You are the Painters?"

"Yes," Claire said.

Mervin just stood there like a stump, with fantastic possibilities roaring through his head.

"Happy I am to be here . . . to meet you," the boy said.

He held out his hand to Mervin. Mervin looked up at him without moving a muscle.

"How tall are you?" Mervin managed to say.

"Two hundred and eleven centimeters, ah . . . what you call . . . six foot and eleven inches."

Mervin couldn't keep from smiling while he vigorously shook Olaf's hand. Immediately, his brother Carl came to mind.

CHAPTER 5

Diana Murphy hung the long, colored chart of dinosaurs on the right edge of the blackboard. After stepping back and studying the effect, she untacked the chart and fastened it on the left. She was in a rush to ready her classroom with last-minute details, and she reprimanded herself for her inability to make a decision. There was no right or wrong, she told herself, either would do at this point. She recognized she had tiptoed through life, overly cautious, always afraid of making the simplest mistake.

She walked to the window, then looked down at the children in the schoolyard, where they chased and yelled and mingled in the early September sunlight. Amidst this crowd, Diana spotted two small girls, probably first graders, holding hands and approaching the building timidly. She suddenly felt a heaviness in her stomach, an overwhelming sorrow that left her breathless, and she tried to attribute it to first-day jitters.

She hadn't been here for the first day of school last year, arriving instead in January to replace a teacher on maternity leave. Diana remembered how she'd found the opening on the Montana Education Association's newsletter: a general science teacher at the elementary and high school level with experience in health, P.E., and some coaching. She remembered how she finally found Willow Creek on the map—after some serious nose-to-the-table squinting—and how she had a feeling this was the kind of place she had been searching for.

But then she arrived at Willow Creek and she couldn't deny the second thoughts that overwhelmed her. The blacktop highway curved into town and led to the first and most impressive building on Main Street: the Blue Willow Inn, a bright, blue two-story wood-frame building with white trim and a boardwalk porch across the front. Though not the geographical center of town, Diana discovered it was undoubtedly the social center, open throughout the day as a gathering place for rumors and gossip as well as for serving meals in its historic dining room and dispensing beer and hard liquor from the tavern side of the establishment.

And when she looked for a supermarket, a filling station, or even a convenience store, all she found, besides the Blue Willow Inn, was a quaint little art gallery and a tool store. If she needed a loaf of bread or a tank of gas, forget it. But if she needed a watercolor or a radial-arm saw in a hurry, well she was in the right place. Or if she needed a bull. Willow Creek had a reputation for producing the best Hereford bulls in Montana or, depending on whom you talked to, in the country. Diana realized that in Willow Creek—a town with no drug store, no doctor or dentist, no police, no variety store, no hardware store—the Blue Willow was it, sink or swim.

But then again, in Willow Creek, if an old brown dog slept in the middle of Main Street, everyone drove carefully around him.

The Painters' gray sedan pulled up in front of the school and Diana snapped out of her reverie. A blond-headed boy unfolded himself from the passenger seat like a Swiss army knife, and when he straightened himself up he towered over the car. Diana blinked. From the second-story window it was hard to tell just how tall he was, but he was *tall*. The boy sheepishly made his way toward the front door as the kids stopped their playing and stared. They made way for him as though he were royal blood or Freddie Krueger from *Nightmare on Elm Street*.

Diana bolted for the hallway and ran the stairs two at a time. Sam had to see this.

SAM WAS THUMBING through a dictionary when Diana burst into his classroom.

"Sam, there's a surprise for you downstairs you've got to see!"

He regarded her from behind his wire-rimmed aviator glasses but showed no excitement. Aside from conversing across tables at the Blue Willow when they happened to be eating at the same hour, Sam and Diana hadn't had much social contact.

"I think I've already seen him."

"You have?" she asked, disappointed. Diana wanted to be the first to show the coach his incarnate dream.

"Peter Strong, Grandma Chapman's grandson, right?"

"Wrong. C'mon, this'll be fun." She ran out the door.

Sam reluctantly pushed away from his desk and followed, finally catching up to her at the stairs.

"What's this little surprise got to do with?" he asked.

"I'd say it's a coach's pot of gold." She laughed.

When they rounded the landing to the second floor, they saw the Painters' exchange student talking with Bess, the office secretary. Diana and Sam had stopped two steps above the second floor and the boy was at about the same level they were.

Diana stepped down and introduced herself. From ground level the boy seemed to be seven feet tall.

"Hello, I am Olaf Gustafson. From Norway I am coming."

Students filed past to their classrooms, gawking.

"It's nice to meet you and we're glad you're here in Willow Creek," Diana said.

Sam stood on the stairway as if he were nailed to the spot.

"And this is Mr. Pickett. He teaches English and coaches the basketball team," she added.

Sam slowly walked down the stairs and shook Olaf's huge hand. "Yes, nice to meet you, very nice, but I don't coach the team anymore."

"You *don't?*" Diana felt crushed. After bringing these two together, she thought for sure Sam's heart would be clicking its heels. She turned to Olaf. "Do you play basketball?"

"Play basketball? No, at sports in my country I am not playing."

"Have you ever played basketball, just a little?" she asked, probing for some sign of hope.

"No, at soccer I am playing when I am younger, but without the coordination I am becoming."

Bess said she needed Olaf in her office and Sam started up the stairs.

"Sorry, Sam, I thought your prayers had been answered," Diana said.

"No. Wrong prayers, but thanks for the try."

On her way to her room, Diana exchanged good mornings with Mr. Grant, and she wondered what on earth Sam Pickett's prayers could be.

CHAPTER 6

A hopeful undercurrent trickled through the faculty and student body, spilled over into the community, and collected into the Blue Willow Inn, where speculation ran rampant as to what good fortune the Norwegian giant would bestow on the town. Not to be outdone, Grandma Chapman didn't allow them to forget about her grandson who, she boasted, had a few gifts himself. What had started as an undercurrent had strengthened into a tidal wave of such dimensions that one needed a wet suit and scuba gear to escape from drowning in the unprecedented optimism and promise.

On the second day of school, Diana caught Olaf as he was leaving her biology class. She hadn't avoided the overwhelming hope that had spread like the epidemic, and she felt compelled to see what she could do to help bring salvation to this knock-kneed little village.

"Could I talk to you a minute?" she asked.

"Oh . . . ya, sure."

The sky-scraping boy stepped aside to let several students scurry out. When they were alone, she hesitated.

"How was the class? Did you understand everything?"

"Ah . . . some I am not understanding."

"Maybe after a few days it'll get better," she said.

"Ya. A few days."

She looked up into his boyish eyes and smiled. "Don't they play basketball in your country?"

"Some play. More and more it is coming."

"I'm surprised you didn't play, being so tall. I'd think you'd be quite good at it."

"No . . . too fast I am growing," he said and shrugged as though it were his fault.

"Are you still growing?"

"Ya, still growing." He smiled. "In the athletics I am not taking part. All elbows and kneecaps I am my father says."

"Well, we sure could use you on the team and I think you'd have a lot of fun. You'd learn the game and make good friends with the other boys. Playing on a team can bring you closer to others. It'll be a great way for you to assimilate with your American peers and have fun, win or lose. But I suppose you've been hearing that a lot around here," she said with some apology in her voice.

"Ya, Mr. Painter tells me the basketball I must learn while I am here. For me he has been praying for many years, but I don't understand. Me he's not knowing until last week." Olaf flashed a puzzled smile.

"Well, you think about it. I think you'd enjoy it," she said.

"Ya, think about it," he said and he ducked through the doorway.

THE FOLLOWING DAY, after twenty-four hours of brooding over how he had the chance of a lifetime slipping through his fingers, Sam went to get his mail at about noon, something he avoided and did only once or twice a week. Willow Creek's post office was across the Blue Willow Inn at the entrance of Mavis Powers' modest two-story apartment building. The post office was so small it couldn't keep five people out of the rain, and Mavis, with curlers perpetually in her peach-colored hair, was the postmaster. Sam came out of the government outpost, thankful his only contact with the outside world was junk mail.

From his worn-down wicker chair on the porch of the Blue Willow, old Rip called. "Hey, Coach!"

Though his name was Henry Van Winkle, the rawboned man was fondly referred to as "Rip" because of his ninety-two years. Sam crossed the street, then paused in front of the inn.

"Hello, Rip. Holding down the fort?"

"Ya seen the Norwegian kid?"

"Yes."

"I've waited all my life for this," Rip said with a gummy smile. He kept his dentures in his pocket, except when he ate; Rip claimed it was because they fit poorly.

"He doesn't play basketball," Sam said.

"I heard you wasn't going to coach anymore."

"That's right. I'm through coaching."

"You quit one year too soon."

Sam nodded and laughed. "Or four years too late. See you later." He walked up Main Street toward school.

"You quit one year too soon!" the old man called after him. "The kid'll play!"

His words caught in Sam's mind. Though there were a few diehards like Rip in the ranks of Willow Creekians, they were generally regarded as quaint or sentimental in their blind allegiance. Every community had fans like that. But most people in Willow Creek regarded these diehards with tolerance and humor because, maybe, secretly, within the most cynical of Willow Creekians, there was a hope that still flickered. Someday they would win a basketball game. Sam recognized that flame somewhere within his being, as well, hidden under a pretense of indifference. Others assumed his cynicism had been hammered into his spirit by eighty-six losses, but his coldness had been there long before Sam ever heard of Willow Creek.

Now it seemed fate had mistakenly blinked for an instant and allowed a shaft of good fortune to shine down upon him. Perhaps guardian angels could no longer bear silent witness to this test of human fortitude and endurance. Maybe they finally had cast their miraculous attention on this creaking Western town with no visible means of support where, through years of utter bravery and silent heroism, these unathletic boys laced on their game shoes and showed up on the court only to be battered and run off the floor.

By the time Sam reached school he had squelched the urge to tamper with the winds of fate that whistle through the open heart of loss.

SAM HURRIED DOWN the outside steps and cut across the basketball court in front of school, where he found several kids were taking turns heaving a scuffed-up basketball at the metal backboard and rim. It had been a good day for Sam, a day filled with classes and work, without a moment's pause.

"Sam! Sam!"

He turned and saw Diana leaning out a second-story window. She waved. "Wait a second, I'll be right down."

He paused at the edge of the court, slung his corduroy sport jacket over his shoulder, and wondered what this was about. Curiosity clashed with a growing anxiety in his chest. Although he thought others might consider her face plain—she never wore makeup and it was often hidden under long, maple-sugar hair—Sam had seen her in gym clothes on more than one occasion and tried desperately to obliterate that sensual image from his memory. But he couldn't deny that his primitive brain stem vibrated at the sight of her, his Paleolithic DNA began a mating dance, and he'd had the notion that that was the path he should take, lose himself in as much carnal pleasure as he could find. Immediately guilt and its many henchmen had shut down all further response, shaming him with Amy's memory. So he appreciated the fact that at school Miss Murphy dressed as conservatively as a nun.

"Sam," she called and bounded down the front steps. She hurried across the schoolyard in a full denim skirt and a blue, loose-fitting cotton blouse. "Thanks for waiting," she said. She paused to catch her breath.

"What can I do for you?" he asked, then smiled.

"I hope I'm not sticking my nose where it doesn't belong, but I talked with Olaf today and I think he's seriously considering playing basketball."

"What gives you that impression?" Sam picked up on the excitement in her voice and he couldn't help but notice the natural little pout of her lower lip.

"I don't know exactly. It was something in his tone. I think he's just afraid of looking clumsy, right when he's trying to get to know some of the kids. I can sure identify with that. I mean, who wants to be laughed at?" She met his eyes. "Anyway, he's a little on the defensive, with good reason, but I think he'll play."

"Even if he decides to play, he's never touched a basketball. He can't learn enough to help much in just ten or twelve weeks," Sam said.

"Okay, it's a long shot, I grant you, but take a look around." She gestured at the town's old buildings along Main Street. "Look where we're standing for God's sake. What else have you got to do? How often in a lifetime do you think you'll have a seven-foot center to coach?"

"I'm not coaching."

"I know. And what are you going to do about *that*?" She gazed into his eyes, as though she could see into his heart. Sam ducked from her encroachment by turning to the kids behind them. She took a hold of his arm and squeezed gently. "I hope I haven't been a busybody, but I just couldn't let it go without talking to you. Forgive me if—"

"No, it's all right. Thanks for your interest."

"I've got to run," she said. "See you tomorrow."

She hurried across Main and drove away in her black Volvo while Sam stood alone, his thoughts and feelings muddled beyond sorting. From the far edge of the court he smiled at Megan Riley, a sixth grader. She hugged the basketball to her chest.

"Ya want a shot, Mr. Pickett?" Megan asked.

"Sure."

She tossed him the ball. Sam caught it with one arm and threw his sport coat to the ground. He rolled the scuffed old ball in his hands, took aim, and let it fly. Swish.

"Awesome shot, Mr. Pickett! That'd be a three-pointer for sure," Megan said with pure adulation in her voice.

"Aw, that's nothing," Carol Rudd said. "He's the *basketball coach*."

FRIDAY AFTERNOON, AFTER the students had boisterously left the building, Sam approached Truly Osborn's office and found the superintendent at his desk in his typical vest and shirtsleeves, earnestly digging earwax with a paper clip. He hesitated, then knocked on Truly's open door.

Truly twirled in his wooden chair and recovered quickly into his professional posture. "Yes, what is it, Sam?"

Sam thought Truly to be a sad man, a white dwarf, a star whose light we still see streaming toward us in the night sky long after it has lost all energy. Truly managed the proper manners of a school administrator on the surface while inside, Sam suspected, he had given up on life, had burned out and died. It scared Sam, and he worried he'd share the same fate twenty years down the institutional highway.

"Since I talked with you a couple weeks ago," Sam said, "I've been thinking about the basketball team."

"The basketball team?"

"Yes. I was wondering if you'd talked to Mr. Grant about coaching?"

"No, I haven't gotten around to it yet. It's not as though there's any hurry, with all this to take care of." Truly waved the back of his hand at the files and papers stacked on his desk, stacks that had a familiar haphazardness, leading Sam to suspect they were decoys giving the appearance of busyness.

"Well," Sam said, "I've changed my mind, if it's all right with you and the school board. I'd like to coach for another season."

"You'd what?" Truly snapped up straight in his chair, startling Sam back a pace. "Why on earth would you want to do that?"

"Ah . . . I figure I know the routine and all, and the boys . . . it would be all new to Mr. Grant."

A haggard grin materialized on the superintendent's sallow face. "All this nonsense about the Norwegian boy getting to you?"

"I need something to fill those winter months. I don't know what I'd do with myself around here without the basketball program."

Truly leaned forward and spoke softly. "If you don't mind my being a little personal . . ."

Sam nodded, glancing into Truly's dark little eyes.

"I've wondered about you, Pickett, what you're doing in this outpost, never having any female companionship, a young man like you in your prime. Hell, you could hang around here for fifty years and never find a lady for yourself. Except for our Miss Murphy, there isn't an eligible woman for you in a hundred square miles."

"I like the peace and quiet here, away from . . ." Sam paused.

Truly glanced into the hallway and then leaned across his desk. "You do *appreciate* the ladies, don't you Pickett?"

Sam nodded and then caught himself, wishing he'd shown no response to Truly's inquiry. A flush of anger swept the smile from his face. "I need something to do, sir. Olaf, the exchange student, doesn't play basketball. He needs to learn. I'm familiar with the program, driving the bus and all the rest. I enjoy the boys. And like I said, it fills up my winter."

The superintendent leaned back in his chair and swiveled to the window. He didn't speak for a full minute. Sam held his breath. He prayed his superior would allow him another year of anguish, coaching the hapless team. He worried Truly would say no, snatching from him some intangible absurdity nesting in his heart.

"Very well. It'll save me from persuading Mr. Grant to stick his head in the noose."

Truly swiveled back and regarded Sam, then twitched his pointy nose. "Are you sure about this, Pickett?"

"Yes."

"There's no more money than last year."

"That doesn't matter. Thanks, Mr. Osborn."

"Don't thank me. It is I who should thank you."

Sam turned and hurried down the hall before his superior could change his mind.

"Good luck, Sam!" Truly shouted down the hall.

AFTER A RESTLESS weekend in which he could think of nothing else, Sam cornered Olaf after English class.

"Would you like to learn how to play basketball while you're here?"

"Learning do you think I could be?" Olaf asked, giving Sam a glimmer of hope.

"I think I could teach you. It's something to do around here in the winter."

"Doing well I'm afraid I would not be. Anything poorly my father is not happy for me to be doing. I am . . . how would you say . . . clumsy."

Sam pressed. "You could do it just for the fun of it."

"Thank you for giving kindness," Olaf said, "but foolish I think I would be."

"We could try it, just you and me, after school in the gym."

"After school in the gym, ya, seeing me no one will be?"

"No one, and we won't tell anyone you're giving it a try."

"Giving it a try I would like to be while I am in America."

"We haven't won a game here for a while so I can't promise you much, but you could learn about the game. If you don't like it you can let it go and no one will know."

"No one will know." Olaf's large blue eyes widened and his face brightened. He gazed down at Sam. "Then trying I will be. But feeling foolish I do not wish to be."

"You don't have to worry about that. Around here we all feel foolish when it comes to basketball."

CHAPTER 7

After sneaking in and locking the door behind them, Sam and the new exchange student stood in the shadowy gymnasium. With some inner voice cautioning him against this dangerous investment of the heart, Sam tossed the ball to Olaf. The boy caught it stiffly.

"Are you right-handed?" Sam asked.

"Right-handed, ya."

"Place the ball in your right hand and flip it at the basket with your fingers."

Olaf carefully positioned the ball in his right hand and tossed it at the basket. It hit the backboard and bounced, the sound echoing in the empty arena. Olaf awkwardly retrieved it and moved closer to the basket.

"Again, with your fingers."

Sam demonstrated, his hand fanning the air. "Flip the ball—fingers and wrist, fingers and wrist."

After a dozen more attempts, the ball finally kissed off the backboard and swished through the net. The Norwegian boy's face lit up.

"Good," Sam said and clapped. "That's the reward, that's the joy. It says 'perfect.'"

Sam's state of expectancy soared as he gently directed the boy through numerous drills and exercises. Standing on the court with this towering Scandinavian had an overpowering effect and led to instant illusions of grandeur. "That's great. Good, good. That's very good. Yes, yes, super!"

When he jumped, Olaf rose so close to the basket it was startling. Sam felt himself growing more excited.

"See this area right under the basket that's painted blue," Sam said. "That's what we call *the paint*."

"The paint?"

"The paint! When we're on offense, when we're trying to make a basket, you can only be in that painted area for three seconds at a time."

"Why is that?"

"So big guys like you can't stand under the basket and score a hundred points. It gives little guys like me more of a chance. If you're in the paint more than three seconds, you have to give the ball to the other team. That's called a turnover."

Olaf cocked his head, his expression one of confusion.

"Only once for three seconds I am allowed in the paint?"

"No, no, you can move in and out of the paint all the time, you just can't stop and stand in there for more than three seconds. See, like this."

Sam slid into the painted area, stood there crouched for nearly three seconds, and then slid back out. He repeated the move several times and then had Olaf imitate him.

After nearly a half hour, Sam called a halt for fear of overdoing it.

"Good, good, that's enough for now. Do you think you might like it?"

"Like it? Ya, I think so. But very excellent is what I want to be."

"One last thing," Sam said. "Here." He tossed the ball to Olaf. "Stand right under the basket and see if you can jump up and throw the ball down through the net."

Olaf took the ball in two hands and tried to stretch to the rim.

"No . . . try it first with one hand."

The graceless boy took the ball in one hand and dropped it as he attempted to jump. Sam lobbed it back to him and nodded. On the fourth try Olaf went up on his toes, and with a slight jump, flung the ball down through the net. He turned to Sam with a puzzled smile.

"That is allowed?"

"Oh, yeah, that is very much allowed. It's called dunking the ball."

"Dunking?"

"Dunking . . . you just dunked the basketball. Was it fun?"

"Fun? Ya, fun. Are you given more points for the dunking?"

"No, but it scares the other team."

Sam locked the gym door as they exited.

"One more thing. We don't want anyone to know about this until you make up your mind whether or not to join the team. Otherwise you might feel foolish if you want to quit."

"Not feel foolish, oh, ya, good."

"You can tell the Painters I'm helping you after school, and that I'll give you a ride home."

"Ya, a ride home. But about the ball playing, I won't be speaking."

"Good."

A FEW WEEKS LATER, Sam stepped outside after school for a minute of fresh air before he was to meet Olaf in the gym. The blustery fall afternoon lifted his spirits as he looked about. A bunch of kids were shooting a basketball on the outdoor court while waiting for the bus, Curtis Jenkins among them. Sam decided it was as good a time as any to talk to the shy sophomore.

He knew that the boy's whole life was laid out in front of him with virtually no room for choice. Tall, plain looking, moderately intelligent, Curtis seemed resigned to his life, one in which he'd undoubtedly follow in his father's footsteps: working the land, growing hay and tending cattle, with nothing to look forward to after high school but the repetitive routines of the ranch. The oldest of four children, he would be expected to step in beside his father. If he married, he and his bride would pull a double-wide onto the home site and set up housekeeping a hundred feet from his parents. Accepting, reticent, congenial, he would follow the life he found himself born to, maybe never winning at anything, slowly mired in the sadness, never finding the joy.

Sam ambled toward the court where Curtis had little trouble snatching rebounds from the shorter kids, three of whom were his younger sisters. He remembered the humiliating evening Curtis went through the year before when he had been thrown into a game at Twin Bridges and managed to turn the ball over the first three times he touched it. Sam noticed that the boy had grown taller over the summer and he hoped his coordination had kept pace.

"Curtis!" Sam called.

The boy glanced over at Sam and then took a shot. The ball hit the rim and came off into the frenzy of little rebounders. Curtis stepped toward Sam.

"Mr. Pickett, did you know a cockroach can live nine days without its head before it starves to death?"

The boy had the habit of starting conversations with bizarre facts, and Sam didn't want to get sidetracked. "No, I didn't know that, Curtis. Have you been practicing over the summer?"

"No . . . not really. My dad keeps me pretty busy."

Sam felt a nervous flutter in his chest. In the past he simply announced when the first practice would be and then waited to see who showed up. This year he had hopes for a real team.

"Are you going to play this year?"

Curtis squinted at him for an instant and then watched the boys and girls scrambling after the basketball. Sam held his breath. Was the boy remembering the embarrassment last year?

"Yeah, I guess so."

"Good," Sam said, exhaling. "You'll be a starter this year."

The taciturn sophomore seemed to brighten for a moment and then a darkness clouded his face. "I don't think Tom is going to play," he said.

"It's going to be better this year, I promise you," Sam said. "Have you seen Peter Strong shoot? He'll be a big help."

"He says he's not going to be here."

The ball skidded over to Curtis and he picked it up and bounce-passed it to one of his sisters as the bus pulled up in front of the school.

"We won't even have five unless we get Scott to play," he said as he turned for the bus.

"We'll have enough, don't worry. We'll have enough!" Sam yelled, but Curtis had deposited a tumor in his coach's belly. Sam had heard the rumor and he knew he couldn't put off talking to Tom Stonebreaker much longer. But right then he had to give his full attention to smuggling Olaf into the gym past the vigilance of Carter Walker and Louella Straight, who followed the exchange student's every move.

Carter Walker had set her cap for Olaf the first day she laid eyes on him, but almost at the same moment, so had Louella Straight. Carter felt she had the better qualifications, being a sandy-haired, buxom girl who stood 5'10" in her stocking feet. But Louella, standing barely 5'1" on tiptoe, declared unequivocally that disparity in height made no difference in matters of love.

Carter and Louella were the female half of the senior class. Friends since second grade, each secretly believed they were being rewarded by destiny for suffering so long without a boyfriend when the enormous, fair-haired Olaf Gustafson arrived there. Their infatuation with the boy was immediate.

SHORTLY AFTER OLAF's arrival, the two of them sifted through all conversation and information about him in search of any hint of a girl-friend back home. After exhaustive efforts, Carter found a way to confirm the fact that he had no sweetheart pining for him along the fjords: she asked him. When he said no, she knew it was fate.

The first time Carter thought she had him all to herself, having invited him to a movie in Bozeman, he naively asked Louella along. Then the first time Louella sat him alone for a hike along Willow Creek—the town's namesake—Carter happened along in time to share their excursion as well as their lunch.

Since then, it had become a holy triad. Together, like happy triplets, they provided an active—if sometimes bizarre—social life for the boy, who had a busy schedule already, what with school work and clandestine basketball sessions. Fortunately, the Painters welcomed the girls, recognizing they were in a common effort to help Olaf beat back his homesickness and make him feel loved.

THE COTTONWOOD LEAVES had turned orange and were already falling when Sam finally gathered the gumption to mention basketball to Tom Stonebreaker during lunch one Friday. Sam had put off approaching the veteran player as long as possible, sensing how troubled the boy was and fearing a negative response—a blow that would dismantle Sam's pipe dream of coaching a competitive team.

Though most of the Willow Creek kids dressed in typical American teenage fashion, Tom found his identity with Western attire, and at times could pass for a drugstore cowboy, the only difference being he lived on a ranch. Tom Stonebreaker gave the impression he had been conceived in cowboy clothes. Sam had never seen him without his thick leather belt—with large oval silver buckle—upholding his jeans, his first name tooled on its back and a wire cutter and bale knife attached.

In his J. Chisholm–handcrafted diamondback boots—wearing them only when the weather was dry—Tom always seemed more confident, appeared to walk taller. He earned the four hundred and fifty dollars he paid for the boots breaking horses and he bought them a size too big so he wouldn't outgrow them. He wore them like courage and always padlocked them securely in a locker when he played ball. Every student in the school, down into the grades, knew you didn't mess around with Tom Stonebreaker's diamondback boots.

Tom often came to town on horseback, having ridden from the west of town where he lived with his mother and father, a man known for his drunken fits of rage. The boy had come to school occasionally over the years with bruises on his face and dubious stories of how he'd gotten them. For someone so young, Sam sensed a presence about him, an intangible blend of rebellion, uncertainty, and bluff. Sam figured that though all the young girls hoped to marry Rob Johnson one day, all the younger boys wanted to grow up to be like Tom Stonebreaker. Sometimes Sam thought he, too, would like to grow up to be like Tom Stonebreaker.

After playing basketball for three years under Sam's direction and never winning a game, rumor had it that Tom had had enough and was hanging up his jock strap.

"We'll have a much better team this year," Sam said, standing next to the table where Tom sat eating his lunch alone.

"My dad says I have to work, that basketball is a stupid waste of time," Tom said, "that hell will freeze over before we ever win a game."

"You can work the rest of your life, Tom. Do you really have work to do?"

"Naw, there isn't that much for me to do during the winter, at least so long as he stays sober. He's just pissed, says we're a bunch of losers."

"Maybe we'll surprise him. I don't have to tell you how good Rob will be, and though I haven't seen him actually play, I think Peter could be as good as Rob."

Peter Strong's notoriety had flourished during the fall, spread about the community by Grandma Chapman, and Sam hoped Tom had gotten wind of it.

"Pete says he won't be here for the basketball season."

"But what if he is? Think of it, two guards like Rob, and if you play, we'll have three solid players," Sam said.

"Yeah, but then there's Curtis and Dean who can't play diddley-shit. We won't win a friggin' game."

Tom finished scraping a small bowl of chocolate ice cream.

"Anyway . . ." He rubbed his right knee. "Hurt my knee last summer, Ennis Rodeo. I don't think it'll let me play anymore."

"Don't you *want* to play?"

"Used to, but I'm tired of losing, getting it stuck to me by other players. You're not out on the floor, you don't hear it. When I go into Bozeman and see kids from other teams, it's embarrassing."

"You always played hard, Tom, you always did your best."

The 6'4" senior looked up at Sam with piercing eyes. "I don't just want to do my best—I want to *win!*"

Sam fell silent for a moment. A slumbering fierceness deep inside of him identified with Tom's despair and his passion. He pushed his glasses up on his nose and slid around onto the bench, moving close to the husky senior.

"If I could convince you that we *will* win this year," he said in a confidential tone, "and if your knee is all right, would you play?"

Tom regarded him with a puzzled expression. "How you gonna do that?"

"Would you play?"

"I'd love to beat the crap out of those smart-asses who stepped in my face for three years."

"Stepped in *our* faces," Sam said. He remembered how Tom had almost come to blows on the court several times last season. "Okay, wait for me in my room after school. You'll have to miss the bus, but I'll give you a ride home. Will that work?"

"I guess so, but it sounds weird to me."

"Don't mention this to anyone. I'll see you after school, and, Tom, we're going to win."

"That'll be the day."

As Sam left the lunchroom and walked down the hall, the specter of Tom's father rose in his mind, a brutal and violent man, the personification of everything Sam had been hiding from for all these years. He knew that he would have to work to avoid any confrontation with the volatile man.

CHAPTER 8

Thankful for an excuse not to go home after school, Tom Stonebreaker sat on a desk in Mr. Pickett's classroom with his wide-brimmed black hat beside him. Sometimes he'd drive over to Cardwell after supper, hoping that Ellen would be glad to see him. With her you could never tell. He already knew some turkey in her class in Whitehall was after her.

He gazed past the railroad tracks to the broad landscape of the Tobacco Roots, where the early snow blanketed their peaks and high ridges. Nowadays, the tracks only carried the talc train from the mine at Cameron to the plant in Three Forks, and the main lines through here were long abandoned and forgotten; Tom knew what that felt like.

He looked forward to the coming rodeo season, his only source of excitement, appreciation, and applause. He was too ashamed to tell Mr. Pickett that it was his father who stuck it to him the most when they lost, calling the team the Geldings and calling his son a loser. More than anything, Tom wanted to show his dad he was wrong, although at times he caught himself believing that maybe his dad was right.

Mr. Pickett broke Tom's trancelike posture when he entered the room. "Are you ready?" the teacher whispered.

"Ready for what?"

"What you're about to see is a secret, Tom, and I want it clear that whatever you decide, you won't tell anyone."

"Okay, okay. I promise."

They walked down deserted halls and stairways, and Tom thought Mr. Pickett looked like a burglar who was about to empty out the school safe. At the gym door, the teacher glanced behind them and paused, listening. He unlocked the door and they hurried in. Mr. Pickett quickly relocked the door.

"What're you locking the door for?" Tom asked, feeling his skepticism grow.

"To keep the secret." Mr. Pickett grinned.

The gym floors creaked and the fading afternoon sunlight filtered weakly through the narrow frosted windows. The aroma of sweat and floor wax blended with faint flavors from lunch hour.

Tom stood in his diamondback boots and his black hat, his hands were at his hips. The coach walked to the bleachers and took off his sport coat.

"Why don't you take off your jacket, Tom? We can shoot a few baskets."

"You got me in here to shoot baskets?" He pulled off his Levi jacket and threw it on a bench.

Big deal.

Coach Pickett picked up a basketball and tossed it to him.

"You've seen me shoot before," Tom said. He dribbled several times and lifted a halfhearted shot at the basket. The ball hit the rim and came back toward him. Tom caught it.

"How'd that feel?"

"I missed. Did you get me in here just to see how it would *feel?*"

"Yes! But I also brought you here because we'll need you if we're going to win this year."

The coach turned toward the boys' locker room and hollered.

"Olaf!"

Tom glanced at the doorway as Olaf appeared, all knees and elbows, a scrawny scarecrow with long, lean arms, spindly legs, wearing gunboat Adidases, economy-size boxer shorts, and a T-shirt that read PARTY ANIMAL.

"What are you doing?" Tom said.

"Hi, Tom," the Norwegian said with a smile plastered on his face. Olaf began skipping a spliced rope. He had mastered it enough to jump rapidly for almost half a minute before hitting a snag. When he untangled himself, he looked as though he was imitating a plucked flamingo.

"Son of a bitch, is he going to *play?*" Tom said, tipping his hat back.

"All right, Olaf, that's enough for now," the coach said. "Let's use the ball."

Olaf tossed the rope aside; his straw-colored hair was tousled and his chest heaved from the exertion. Tom flipped him the ball. Olaf snapped a two-handed pass to Mr. Pickett. While they tossed the ball around, Tom fumed.

"You turkey, you told us you didn't *know how* to play!" He turned to the grinning English teacher. "That was the first thing we all asked him."

"That's the secret. He's learning and he needs lots of help. He has a long way to go in a short time, but he's willing to work hard, and that's what it will take from all of us, gut-wrenching hard work."

The coach caught the ball and kept it.

"I can't promise you anything, Tom, and Olaf can't promise you anything. But I think we've got one of those extraordinary opportunities you have to grab before it slips away forever. If Olaf keeps working the way he has and improving as much as he has, we'll have four players, including you."

Mr. Pickett nodded, and Olaf moved into the paint just in front of the basket. The teacher lobbed a high pass to him. Without a dribble, Olaf jumped, turned in the air, and slammed the ball down through the net. He looked at Tom with a big grin on his face.

"That is allowed."

Tom stared in disbelief and the upcoming season loomed in his mind, how he'd watch the opposing teams swallow their tongues and piss their pants when the Jolly Green Giant in a jockstrap lumbered into view.

"You can jam it," Tom finally said.

"Yam it? Ya, yam it," Olaf said.

"No—Jam! Jam!" Tom shouted.

Mr. Pickett picked up the ball and tossed it to Tom.

"You try it."

Olaf moved into the paint and Tom fed him a high pass. The awkward kid turned and hammered the ball down through the netting and left a hollow echo booming off the gym walls. Then, smiling as though they'd just won the lottery, Olaf and Mr. Pickett turned to Tom for his response.

"Now, do you think any player from Twin Bridges could prevent Olaf from doing that?" the coach asked.

"*Hell* no," Tom said.

"Could anyone from Gardiner stop Olaf from doing that?"

"*Nooo* way!"

"Do you think you would enjoy helping Olaf rain basketball leather down upon the brows of those opposing teams?"

Tom held his breath for a beat and he stared at the other two grinning faces. "I've dreamed of that day," he said.

They traded high fives, laughing and hooting. Soon they fell silent, looking into each other's eyes. Tom felt a vow had been taken, a bond formed, and they paused for a minute, letting it sink in. He knew he'd have to buck his dad about this, but he couldn't wait for the season to begin, when he could start kicking ass.

Willow Creek had four basketball players.

CHAPTER 9

The blacktop highway goes to Willow Creek to die.

During her stay in Willow Creek, Diana had sensed an invisible flag of surrender fluttering over the town. Though there were more than a few well-off and even wealthy ranchers on neighboring land who coffeed and socialized in Willow Creek, a dark pessimism had firmly entrenched itself into the daily lives of its citizens like ticks. Here, people resigned themselves to a mediocre life, to an uneventful, aimless existence.

For every house that was maintained, one had been left to the whims of sun and weather. For every yard neatly trimmed, one had gone to seed. For every trailer house spruced up with pride, there was another surrounded by discarded junk decaying and forgotten.

Some people had journeyed here only to see their carefully woven dreams unravel, their once bright hopes fade or rust. Others, who had already given up on living, migrated to Willow Creek to settle into the dust, a place at the end of life, a place where their personal abandonment and isolation could be fulfilled.

Diana wondered if Sam Pickett was one of these. Perhaps he was secretly drowning, up to his ears, struggling but losing, soon to become another Willow Creek casualty. As for herself, Diana believed she knew what she was doing. She was in Willow Creek for a brief detour on her personal journey of healing and regaining her balance. But try as she may she couldn't ignore the graveyard crouched across the tracks to the west like a predator facing the withering herd, watching and waiting.

After rummaging for half an hour into cupboards and a near-empty refrigerator and finding only a reluctance to cook after a long day at school, Diana drove from the old farmhouse she rented into Willow Creek. Traveling directly into the falling sun, she flipped the visor down and slid on her sunglasses.

Suddenly, out of the blinding glare, a large rabbit appeared on the road. *Oh God! Brakes! Don't swerve! Don't swerve!*

At the last second, the rabbit bolted to safety and the Volvo skidded and squealed to a dead stop. Diana's hands were tightly locked on the steering wheel. Her face, her whole body, was damp with perspiration. She could feel her heartbeat in her temples and she struggled to catch her breath.

Oh, God, she thought, it's just a rabbit, happens all the time, just let it go. Her leg was locked rigid, her foot still jammed on the brake pedal. Her arms and hands trembled on the wheel and she forced herself to breathe deeply, a trick she'd learned to calm herself just this past year. She glanced in the rearview mirror for any cars or trucks. Then she slowly moved her foot onto the accelerator and crawled down the road, trying desperately not to lose it altogether.

When she entered the Blue Willow's dining room, Axel took one look at her and came barreling over.

"Are you all right, girl?" He pulled out a chair at an unoccupied table and she dropped into it. "You look kind of pale. Are you feeling okay?"

"I'm all right. I just about hit a rabbit on the highway and it scared me a little." Diana hadn't planned on telling anyone; she scolded herself and didn't want to give her fear any power.

Axel laughed. "Don't give it a thought, happens all the time around here. If you nail a nice big jack, haul it in here. We can always cook up some *road kill.*"

His words cut her like a razor. She felt queasy and faint.

Vera, Axel's wife, pushed him aside. "You leave her alone, you old coot. Can't you see the girl is upset?"

Vera sat with her a few minutes and gabbed about the gossip of the day. When Diana first met Vera, the wrenlike woman's nose was flushed as if she had a cold. But after a month, Diana realized it always looked like that. After calming down and chastising herself for not doing a better job of hiding her feelings, Diana convinced Vera she was fine and ordered a taco salad.

Vera scooted off with her order and Diana exchanged chitchat with some of the people she knew. She soon found herself wishing Sam had been eating at this hour, imagining how she might invite herself to sit at his table.

Axel Anderson, a balding barrel of a man in his late fifties, lived upstairs above the kitchen and dining room with his high-strung wife, Vera. They took over the Blue Willow with the hope of making the inn prosperous, much like the former owners, who themselves had hung on as long as possible before succumbing to the predictable fate of businesses alongside dead-end highways. Axel had a gnarled ear and the left side of his neck had a rugged scar traveling down under his collar. He spit and polished anything connected with the property as though a spotless and inviting restaurant off the beaten path would have the power to draw hungry customers out of thin air. As owner he was also bartender, waiter, dishwasher, cook, janitor, and anything else it took to keep the ship afloat. On any given day you'd never know whether that ship was sinking.

One of the relics Axel and Vera inherited with the place was the aging bicycle built for two that sat on the front porch throughout the year. Diana had found that the locals were protective of the old bike's history and it was often difficult for a stranger to get an answer regarding the bike's origins. The peculiar bike had become almost sacred in the eyes of the townsfolk, a trademark of the town, leaning there against the wall on the porch of the Blue Willow Inn, to be borrowed by whoever would like to take a turn around the town.

The story went that one day, many years ago, a happy young couple rode the tandem bicycle from Bozeman on an all-day outing, and stopped at the Blue Willow for lunch. Local people were touched by their affection, by the look of their gentle faces as they gazed across the table and held hands.

Then, something came up between them.

One of them revealed something—people who tell the story are uncertain here—and the young man, it was said, stood up abruptly, knocking over plates and spilling water all over the tablecloth and onto the dining room floor. He stomped out of the inn, and soon afterward the lovely young woman quietly followed. In their anguish and hurt, they both ran off and left the bicycle leaning on the porch. For days people hoped the couple would make up and then, back together again, would remember that neither had taken the bicycle. Weeks went by, summer became fall, and finally, when the winter snow dusted the seats of the bike, the townspeople began losing hope.

That was over twenty-five years ago and still the bike rested there as though the community expected that the couple would forgive each other and come back for it. Successive owners of the inn kept its tires inflated and replaced as needed and all parts in working order. Since neither of the lovers ever returned for it, the common sentiment was they never got back together, coloring the local legend with the bittersweet shades of a tragic love story. But Diana figured that tourists who noticed the timeworn bicycle would just assume it was decoration, like the many antiques inside the inn.

She'd lost her appetite and gently pushed her half-eaten salad away. Just when she felt determined enough to dare the drive home, Sam Pickett walked in, wearing his running outfit. On his way to the back counter he nodded and smiled.

She settled back in her chair and thought about how she'd see him running out the gravel road that curved past the graveyard, how she always got the impression he wasn't jogging for fitness but trying to outrun something. She had tried running but it gave her too much time to think, so she preferred her excursions into the woods and river bottoms where she could lose herself tracking and observing.

Sam came to her table and held a can of Mountain Dew.

"Have a good run?" she asked.

"Yeah, I got five miles in." He wiped the arm of his sweatshirt across his sweating face.

"Would you like to sit down?"

"Oh, no thanks. I'm dripping and the aroma might kill your appetite." He backed a step away.

"Well maybe some other time," she said, and clearly felt his reluctance to get too chummy on any social level.

"I better get out of here before Axel comes with a deodorant spray." He laughed and she sensed a warmth in his smile she'd never noticed before.

"I hear you're going to coach another year."

"Yeah, thanks for your input."

"Input?" she asked, baffled.

"About coaching, and what a once-in-a-lifetime it is to have a seven-footer."

She laughed. "I guess I got caught up in that rush of excitement over Olaf. I didn't mean to stick my nose in."

"No, I needed another perspective. And I really need something to do around here all winter." He gulped the soda down.

"Maybe it was bad advice. It looks like you won't have a seven-footer after all."

"I know," he said, then quickly frowned. "But we'll have to make do with what we have, as usual."

He backed another step from the table and she felt a strange sensation shiver through her. Something in his expression leaked the smallest hint of something else, something she couldn't name but had an inkling of joy; it made her want to smile.

Sam glanced at a man exiting the bar and staggering to the front door. All the warmth drained from his face. George Stonebreaker stopped in his tracks when he spotted Sam.

"Hey, Pickett, you gonna coach that bunch of losers again?"

The voice of the huge, unshaven man in bib overalls, a denim work shirt, and a sweat-stained cowboy hat boomed for everyone in the Blue Willow to hear. Diana suspected he'd been at the bar four or five beers too long.

Sam nodded and faced Stonebreaker across an unoccupied table.

"Well, my boy ain't playing, that's for sure. He's wasted enough time stumbling around with those other pansies. He show up, you tell him he ain't playing this year."

"I can't do that." Sam spoke so quietly, Diana thought his voice had a quiver in it. "You'll have to tell him," Sam said.

"He don't pay me no mind anymore, got his nose up his ass. You tell him."

Stonebreaker pointed a meaty finger at Sam and he squinted. Diana could feel the tension in the hushed restaurant.

"If he plays with those geldings you'll answer to me, ya hear." Stonebreaker slammed a fist on the table, rattling silverware and salt and pepper shakers. "To me!"

Axel came from the kitchen in his white apron and rolled up sleeves. "You get on home now, George. Let these folks enjoy their meal."

Stonebreaker glanced at Axel and then turned back to Sam.

"I don't want him playin', Pickett."

Axel stood next to Sam. "That's enough, George," Axel said in a soothing voice. "You head on home."

Stonebreaker abruptly stomped out and banged the screen door behind him. Only then did Diana see the baseball bat Axel held at his side under the long apron.

The Blue Willow immediately went into a buzz and Axel, wiping sweat from his bald head with a hanky, apologized to the customers. Then he turned to Diana and Sam. "I'm not letting that man drink in here anymore. He's a mean bastard and a sorry excuse for a human being. He can go do his drinking somewhere else."

When Axel headed for the kitchen, Sam set the can of Mountain Dew on the table.

"Who said things were dull in Willow Creek?" he said and flashed a thin smile.

Diana saw how the soda can shook in Sam's hand. "Can't somebody do something about him?" she asked.

"I feel sorry for Tom," Sam said.

"Will Tom play?"

He peered out into the darkness. "I don't know."

CHAPTER 10

It came after Sam that morning.

Was it his confrontation with George Stonebreaker that had unearthed it? Was it because of that terrifying moment when he teetered between cowering under a table or ripping the man's throat out with his bare hands? This feeling somehow always manifested, just when he thought he was doing well. He gobbled breakfast and hurried to school, but no matter how hard he concentrated on the students and lesson, it stalked him in his classroom, staring out from unoccupied corners, rising in the shadows, sucking the breath from his lungs.

He force-fed his mind with pointless details and jabbered to his class like a nervous wreck. And when his mid-morning free period arrived, he fled from the building to the school yard, where a fresh, balmy southwesterly wind gushed across the mountain flanks and barnstormed through town.

Sam spotted Dean Cutter chasing Helen Bates during recess. For years Sam had thought of Dean as a frisky grade schooler who, peering out of his thick lenses and habitually wearing a dog-eared maroon Kamp Implement cap, seemed to regard life in a happy-go-lucky way. Now the squat kid was a freshman and played an integral role in the expectations Sam was guardedly inventing. He didn't know much about the family; Dean was the only Cutter in attendance. He had an older sister, but she had been born with cerebral palsy and didn't come to school. In his class that fall, Dean had shown little interest in academics but exuded a rough-and-tumble zest for life.

Sam spotted Diana on the far edge of the playground like a homesteader's wife. He waved and she waved back, as though they conspired to display warm affection for each other from a safe distance, and at close quarters had to be on guard, polite, and restrained.

A United Parcel truck pulled up and the young suntanned driver hollered toward Sam. "You know where the Skogan place is?"

"Yeah!" Sam shouted. "You have to go back to the fork north of town and go west until you hit 287, then southwest about four miles."

"Thanks!" the driver waved a hand as he roared off.

On the wrong road, Sam thought, maybe his first day.

Oh, God. It avalanched over him and he couldn't hold it off. The lunatic had been *lost*. The outraged husband went to the *wrong* Burger King. His estranged wife worked at a Burger King four miles east on the same street. With the shotgun hidden under a long coat, he demanded to see his wife and when they told him she wasn't there he went berserk and started shooting. It should never have happened, not there. It was a *mistake*, all a mistake.

Sam tried to rid his brain of that voice. He clapped his hands over his ears and bent forward. Sweat immediately soaked him and he fought for breath. He had to escape, knowing his sanity hung in the balance, how he hung in the balance, entertaining the thought to just blind his pony.

When he got up and turned around, Diana was there, close, looking into his eyes.

"What's the matter? Are you hurt?"

"Oh . . . no. I was . . ." He tried to laugh, to hold her off.

"Is there anything I can do?" she asked with a tenderness in her voice.

"No, thanks. I actually came out to talk to Dean."

He turned abruptly, then hurried toward the children. He retreated from the reflection in her eyes. He fled from the currents threatening to drown his soul.

"Dean!" he shouted.

The scruffy, nearsighted boy skidded to a stop and regarded Sam.

"Could I talk to you a minute, Dean?" Sam wiped his face with a handkerchief.

The boy glanced at his playmate with a shrug and walked hesitantly toward the English teacher.

"Hi, Dean. I'm coaching the basketball team again this year and I hope you'll be coming out."

Relief spread across the freshman's face, as though the teacher hadn't found out what he'd done. And then, just as quickly, he bunched up his face. "I'm no good," he said in a high-pitched voice known throughout the community.

"We're going to need you, Dean. We'll practice a lot and you can learn."

"I stink." The boy squirreled up his nose as if he could actually smell his inability.

"Do you think you'd like to play, if you learned how?"

"I can't dribble or nothing. Scott's better than me."

"I've seen you running around school. You run pretty fast. If you practice hard every day, you'd be surprised how quickly you can learn."

"Would I have a uniform?"

"Yes, of course. And you'll get out of classes."

Sam fished, wondering what bait would be needed to convince this country boy to lay his self-esteem on the line and step onto the varnished hardwood. He knew how disgrace was still a stark reality for any kid who dared put on the Willow Creek jersey.

"We'll travel to other towns and eat at restaurants."

"McDonald's!"

"Yes."

"Bodacious!"

Sam caught his breath. He'd pulled the correct dry fly from his fishing vest.

"When we go to Bozeman, Mom always says we can't afford to eat at McDonald's."

Sam noted the boy's patched jeans and faded flannel shirt.

"Do you think you'd like to give it a try?"

"I stink."

"Listen, Dean. Why don't you come out for a few practices. See how it feels." He ought to say, See how it smells. "If you don't like it, you can let it go."

"Think we'll win a game this year?" Dean asked.

"I know we will, if you come and help us. What do you say?"

Sam regarded the athletically-challenged schoolboy. Dean screwed up his face and tugged at his hat.

"Okay. I'll try, but I stink."

"Great. I'll let you know when we'll have our first practice. Thanks, Dean."

The bowlegged boy dashed back to his friends while Sam found his bearings and caught his breath. He hurried through the town toward the Blue Willow in hopes of being distracted and lost in conversation for the remainder of his free period. He knew he would have to find something that Dean could do well and build on that. Dean Cutter was definitely not a boy with great self-confidence when it came to basketball, but after all, look where he grew up.

PETE STRONG SHUFFLED into the front room, having slept in until ten. He found his grandmother doing aerobics along with the *Bodies in Motion* gang on TV. The parrot hunched on the bar from its hanging cage and Tripod gazed from one eye while curled beneath the coffee table.

"Glad . . . to see . . . you're still . . . alive," she said. "I'll . . . whip up . . . some breakfast . . . in about . . . fifteen minutes."

"Up your ass," the parrot squawked.

"Grandma, did you *hear* that?" Pete said.

"What a gas . . . what a gas," Grandma said as she kicked to the left, then kicked to the right.

By the time Pete had washed in the makeshift bathtub shower and dressed, Grandma was flipping pancakes in the kitchen with Tripod at her feet. Pete crossed the living room and the parrot cackled.

"Piss your pants."

"Hear that?" Peter said.

"Certainly, he said, 'Miss the dance.'"

"Grandma, I think you're hearing is shot."

Pete pulled up a chair at the kitchen table.

"Nonsense. I can hear a meadowlark down on Cooper Road." She flopped a pancake on his plate.

Shaking his head, Pete poured maple syrup over the first pancake. After chewing a heaping forkful, he spit it back onto his plate.

"Yhaaaacck! What's in the pancakes?"

She doubled over with laughter. "Should've seen the look on your face!"

"What's in these?" Pete wiped his mouth with a paper napkin. "It tastes like soap."

"Just a little Joy. Thought you needed a little in your life," she said, taking the plate and giving him a clean one.

"Hairy old bitch," the parrot said.

"Merry old witch," Grandma said. "His favorite name for me, merry old witch. Here's a real pancake, now that you've had your morning Joy."

Pete, learning fast, cut a small portion from the pancake and slipped it to Tripod. The cat gobbled it down and Pete noted the absence of bubbles drifting from Tripod's nostrils and mouth. Satisfied that the pancake was safe, Pete covered it with maple syrup and began again to chow down.

"Well, the Montana Education Association left you with a few days on your hands, huh?" she said, pouring another pancake onto the large iron skillet.

"Yeah, no school till Monday."

"What're you going to do?"

"Carter's dad is putting a new floor in their machine shed. We're all going out and watch the concrete set."

"You getting to know the kids?"

"I know every kid in the high school," he said with his mouth full.

"Sounds like you and Trilobite are getting along. You're not grinding second gear anymore." She slid another pancake on his plate.

"That's an awesome bus. I had the whole senior, junior and sophomore class in it the other night. I wish I had it at home."

"You lonesome for home, boy?"

"Yeah. For Kathy and my friends." He covered the pancake with syrup.

"Real bad, huh?"

"Yeah, the kids here are cool, it's just . . . so different. They'd roll up the sidewalk at eight-thirty if they had one. Where does everybody go?"

"To bed, I guess."

"I started my letter to Kathy yesterday with 'Greetings from the end of the universe.'"

She flipped another pancake onto his plate. "How many more for the bottomless pit?"

"A few." Pete grinned. He was continually surprised at how well she managed with only one hand.

"Going to Billings for a couple days next week to see a dear friend, Jean Mack. You be all right here alone?"

"Yeah. I'll play basketball. Mr. Pickett said I could use the gym whenever I wanted."

"Stay off that phone. Don't want to find a twenty-three-page bill from US West in my post office box next month. A half hour Sunday night, right?"

"Right."

He finished a pancake and washed it down with milk.

"Mom never told me how you lost your hand."

"Well, one day I just lost the circulation in it. Nothing they could do but lop it off." Her voice softened.

"You do so good with your . . ." Pete said and came up short.

"Stub? Yep, the fastest stub in the West."

"Do you miss Grandpa?"

"Nope. Never could be myself around that man. Don't miss him for a minute, though sometimes he shows up like one of Willow Creek's ghosts."

"Up your ass," the parrot said.

"What a gas is right. I've had a gas ever since he died."

She glanced at Pete and he caught a pained look on her face.

"You're old enough to know how it was and you deserve to know how it was." She sighed and delivered another pancake. "When I married your grandfather he had another lover, a mistress he'd carried on with for years."

She glanced into his face and he felt awkward, didn't know what to say, talking about that kind of stuff.

"Her perfume betrayed him. I could smell her on his breath, on his clothes. I think he tried to stop but she'd always seduce him back."

She slid the sizzling iron frying pan into the dishwater.

"Your grandpa started as a connoisseur of liquors and then, in his passionate love affair, became a rummy and a lush. It was like living with a demon of a thousand faces and never knowing which one you were dealing with."

Numbed by this picture of a grandfather he never knew, Pete fumbled for words but couldn't find any.

"Your mom ever tell you?"

"No . . . she never said anything about him."

"Your mother never had a father, and that probably has something to do with you ending up without one."

"You're full of shit," the parrot said.

"You pull a ship?" Grandma said. "Your grandpa used to be in the Navy. Always asking the parrot if he pulled a ship."

"Did you have the parrot then?"

"It was his parrot. Called him Pistol. That's why I just call him Parrot, I don't want to remember those times. Bird must be sixty years old, refuses to die." She whispered, as if the bird could understand her, "Tempted to give him rat poison more than once."

She gazed toward the front room and the bird.

"You finish up now, and we'll run to Bozeman. Got some shopping to do."

Pete took stock of his peculiar grandmother with that crazy brown hat atop her gray head like a chef in a city flophouse.

"Where'd you get that hat?" Pete said.

"Don't you like my hat?"

"Yeah, sure, it rocks. All the kids think its cool."

"Got it last summer in Billings. Saw it in the window of some swanky men's store. Should've seen the look on the salesman's face when I put it on and walked out. His mouth opened like a sardine can. Think he figured I was buying it for my husband."

"Why did you buy it?"

"Was an important day for me, maybe the most important of my life."

"What happened?" Pete said.

"I decided to be me."

Pete didn't understand. "Who were you before?"

"Someone I was expected to be. Since then I haven't given a fiddler's fart about what people think. It's wonderful. Wish I could've done that a long time ago."

It sounded good, but how did you find out who you are? He didn't dare ask.

CHAPTER 11

With the word out that the gigantic Norwegian wasn't going to play after all, the familiar pessimism loomed again in Willow Creek. Grandma Chapman polished off a hearty lunch at the Blue Willow and felt it was her duty to shore up the eroding optimism for the coming basketball season for Peter's sake, if for nothing else.

Though basketball seemed of little consequence to many, Grandma had come to realize that for these small Montana towns in the grip of winter, when nights are long, when wind chills are deadly, when ranch work has slowed to a standstill, basketball was their heartbeat. It was their lifeblood, something to unite them and uphold them and get them through till spring. They lived it, they breathed it. Residents could tell you the score of the last game they won six or seven years ago, how many seconds were on the clock when the winning shot fell, and the name of the boy who made it. No matter how desolate or disheartening things were, when the water line to the stock tank froze, when snowdrifts closed the road, and when the battery in the pickup went dead, there was always a Friday night game to look forward to. And nothing warmed their hearts and took the chill out of their bones like a win by *their* basketball team.

If your team lost, or worse, lost consistently, winter became unbearable. In Willow Creek, the winters had become interminably bleak and unending.

After finishing their lunch and their daily dose of Paul Harvey's golden-voiced state of the world—during which time the high-ceilinged dining room hushed like a cathedral and Vera, the perpetually hustling waitress, tiptoed around the tables—the subdued locals sipped coffee and tried to think of something no one else in town had heard when deliveryman Bobby Butcher swung in the front door with Pepsi and Mountain Dew canisters.

Rip Van Winkle would have been on the front porch in the wicker rocking chair to greet Bobby, but the cutting north wind had driven his brittle ninety-two-year-old bones closer to the fire.

"Hey, Rip. You folks planning to scrape up a basketball team this year?" the lanky Pepsi man shouted.

"Damn tootin', by God, an' we'll kick the shit out of Christian," Rip said, his voice rattling in his hollow rib cage.

"It's a miracle Willow Creek still has *one* fan left standing," Bobby said.

"What're you mumbling about, boy? I'm a fan," Grandma Chapman said. She sat beside Mavis Powers, who was still wearing her curlers in her peach-colored hair. "And so is Hazel."

Hazel Brown, in an Orange Crush sweatshirt and enormous jeans, moved through the front door like a sumo wrestler. She had just finished her shift as cook for the school lunch program, first grade through senior at eleven-forty every school day. She slumped next to Grandma, who caught a whiff of Hazel's cheap perfume.

"I'm a fan, but I'm not blind," Hazel said. "They won't win a game this year either."

With short, curly black hair and small green eyes peering over her chubby cheeks, Hazel had doubled in size since she'd come to Willow Creek, so much so that one chair could scarcely shore up her proliferating body. She confessed to Grandma once that she didn't know for sure but she thinks she got fat to keep her mother's boyfriends from going after her after her one and only legitimate boyfriend ran off with her savings.

"I don't know why we even have a team," Axel said, busying himself around the red and white checkerboard tablecloths. "They've never won a game since I've lived here."

"Well, I can remember beating the bejesus out of Christian, Sonny," Rip said, smacking his toothless gums. "In seventy-one the Gilman kid had twenty-seven points and we licked 'em in their own backyard fifty-eight to forty-one."

"Don't forget the night the Kilmer boy made two free throws after time had run out and we won by a point," Mervin Painter said from a corner table, where he ate with his wife, Claire.

"And we'll do it again," Rip said.

"Yeah," Grandma Chapman said, "and my grandson, who is a cracker-jack player, will help them do it."

Amos Flowers, wearing a mountain-marinated Tom Mix hat, drifted in and glided to the far end of the bar, acknowledging no one, always appearing as though he'd just driven a herd up from Texas.

"There are some of us who support our boys no matter what," Vera said. Her red nose looked as though she'd had a sneezing fit.

She'd been plum amazed at the things some of the tourists asked when traveling through this back country. Her all-time favorite was the spiffy-dressed lady from New York City who ate lunch with her distinguished-looking husband. A few miles up the interstate there was a sign designating a state monument, MADISON BUFFALO JUMP. These New Yorkers had seen the sign and were somewhat interested.

"What time do the buffalo jump?" the lady asked in her Northeastern dialect.

"Gee, Hon," Vera had said, "I think the last time was about two hundred years ago."

Finished with his delivery, Bobby picked up two empty canisters and headed for the door. "Well, your grandson will need a lot of help. We have a better team this year than last, and if I remember correctly, we walloped you twice last year by about a hundred points." The Manhattan Christian enthusiast laughed his way to his truck.

"Smart-ass," Rip said, his weather-beaten wide-brimmed hat sagged around his ears.

No one knew where Rip had come from. Some twenty-odd years ago, he bought a small house in town and became a popular figure on the front porch of the inn. When he'd fall asleep there, strangers, stopping for a meal or a beer, took him for one of those carved figures once popular a hundred years or so ago. The chiseled features of Rip's face and hands kept locals from laughing at these tourists; he very well could have *been* carved from cedar or cottonwood.

The most popular story about his origins concerned a Dutch family who fleeced him out of his holdings, leaving the old man to drift into town. Rip would never say, and after a while it didn't matter. He cashed two government checks monthly, one from the Veteran's Administration, one from Social Security, the total of which could hardly feed a medium-sized dog.

"I heard the big Norwegian boy is going to play," Axel said.

"Rutabagas! Have you seen him walk? Of course he can't play," Hazel said, dumping sugar in a cup of coffee. "Couldn't catch a basketball in a washtub."

Mervin Painter sat upright, raised a hand and started to open his mouth as though to disagree when his wife put her hand on his arm and he settled back.

"We ought to stand behind the boys no matter what," Mervin said, and Grandma saw something hopeful in his eyes. Mervin wasn't a diehard fan. He didn't show up at every game and grumble with the rest, but she'd noticed how he never missed a game with Christian.

"Elizabeth, I'll bet you here and now we don't come within twenty points of another team," Hazel said.

"Bet you!" Grandma said, tugging at the brim of her brown fedora as she always did when her dander was up. "I don't want to take your money so easily. I'll bet you we *win* a game."

Hazel laughed and jiggled like a bucket of Jell-O. "Let's make it ten bucks."

"Done!" Grandma shouted. She tipped her hat back and finished her coffee. "With my grandson and Rob Johnson, we have two dandies, and then there's Tom Stonebreaker who's no daffodil on the basketball court."

"Not playing this year," Hazel said with a thick smugness, up to date on all school scuttlebutt from the serving counter.

"Not *playing*?"

"Hurt his knee riding a Brahma in Ennis," Hazel said.

"Isn't he a little young for that?" Mavis Powers said, keeping one eye peeled on her post office door across the street.

"You mean there's a sane age for climbing on the back of an enraged bull?" Vera said.

"He's probably just tired of losing," Mavis said.

Axel grunted. "Tired of being embarrassed."

"Speaking of being embarrassed," Mavis said, "is Mr. Pickett going to coach again this year?"

"I heard Mr. Grant is," Vera said.

"Mr. Pickett is coaching again," Grandma said. "Already worked with Pete on some things."

Grandma liked Sam Pickett. She felt sorry for him. He'd been helplessly caught in the void when Willow Creek lost its last coach. Without the common sense to refuse the assignment, he demonstrated a dogged courage by taking the flack and criticism of the community for five long years. And though no one had ever heard him raise his voice, they had on occasion caught a glimmer in his eye and noticed a catch in his throat when he shared a favorite author or poem with his class. His quiet tenderness endeared him to most of the students. But sometimes he acted strangely distant, as if he were looking right through you, as if you were a ghost.

"Let's face it," Hazel said. "Basketball is deader than a doornail in Willow Creek."

No one replied, not even Rip, and Grandma Chapman could find no words to patch the damage.

Steeped in the community's long-standing gloom, the townspeople had wallowed in defeat for too long. It had soaked into their bones, weighing them down into a slouching posture, turning their eyes to the ground. Losing had become so normal, so ingrained, that the students didn't even seem to notice; they had no idea of how long it had been since their Broncs trotted off the court with a victory, and they no longer considered the possibility of a basketball win.

For the numbed townspeople who still showed up at games, the lopsided contests had evolved into a social event at which one joined the other locals in the bleachers without paying much attention to the game, like attending a movie you'd seen before and knew how it would come out. The likelihood of winning was never approached. One talked about rural things: spotted knapweed, rainfall, beef prices, and occasionally clapped when one of the hometown boys managed to score. It was hard to remember when it felt good to be a Willow Creekian.

"Well, if there's no hope for the basketball team, maybe we'll have a mild winter," Hazel said. She giggled and trudged her massive body toward the front door. "I think I'm getting arthritis."

To make things worse, Hazel passed John English on his way in, the practical, hard-headed rancher who sat on the school board and did his best to convince the other members to make basketball players an extinct species in Willow Creek.

"Morning, Vera, how's it going?" John tipped his bone-colored Stetson and clomped toward an unoccupied table.

"Not so good, Hon," Vera said from behind the pie counter. "We've been wondering if the boys'll win a game this year."

"Ha!" John said as he sat with his back to Grandma Chapman. "They'll win a game the day Rip there runs a four-minute mile."

Because of John's outspoken opinion of Grandma Chapman—he thought her a ridiculous old coot who embarrasses the town as much as the basketball team—she and John not only did not speak, but neither of them acknowledged the other's presence.

"Don't care what they say, by golly," Rip said. "Willow Creek is comin' back, wait and see."

John, in his spiffy Tony Lama boots, studied the menu while the others kept their thoughts to themselves. The old man's banality seemed a pathetic reflection of all their tattered hopes and dreams.

Grandma Chapman had failed to shore up the town's optimism for the coming basketball season, and worse, she'd found her own run into the ground.

CHAPTER 12

Sam had driven himself to exhaustion, often falling asleep in his stuffed chair while watching videos and taking notes on coaching basketball. Amy appeared in his dreams less and less, although he'd still waken in a sweat, calling her name, then remembering she was gone.

On the news, he'd seen how one of the powerhouse colleges kicked off their basketball season by holding a practice session one minute after midnight on the first day the team could officially work out. Over three thousand students and fans showed up in their field house to celebrate the start of another season. Sam had hoped that emulating such a high-flown optimism wouldn't seem ludicrous.

THE SHIVERING BOYS gathered in the locker room and hustled to get their uniforms on—Rob Johnson, the senior veteran; Peter Strong, the import from Saint Paul; Tom Stonebreaker, against his father's orders; and the quiet sophomore, Curtis Jenkins. Lastly, Dean Cutter, the 5'5" freshman, seemed more than a little uncertain about this endeavor, peering at Sam through his heavy lenses with magnified brown eyes.

Rob's golden shirt bore the number 10 he had worn through three years of defeat. Tom's familiar number 18, which had hung from his neck last year like an anchor, looked as though the gold had faded along with the team's reputation.

Sam reflected on the boys and what he was asking them to do. The team was like a youngster Sam had sent to the door of a pretty girl to ask for a date. When she came to the door, the boy asked. She said, "No." The next night Sam asked him to dress and go to the door and knock again. When the boy asked for a date, she laughed in his face. The following weekend he asked the boy to dress and go knock on the door. When he asked for a date, she slammed the door in his face. The next night Sam sent him again, up to the porch to knock on the door. Her father threw him off the porch.

The pretty girl enjoyed the boy's mortification. Sometimes she'd have girlfriends watching in the window and giggling when he would come to the door. Sometimes the father would beat him up. Eighty-seven times he had sent the team out to knock on the door. Eighty-seven times they were belittled, beaten up, and thrown off the porch in dishonor. And now he had it in his foolhardy head not only to ask them to go back on the porch and knock on the door, but to ask for the girl's hand in marriage!

It was five minutes before midnight. He hoped the absurdity of a team who hadn't won a game in half a decade waiting up until midnight to start another season wouldn't be as obvious to others as it was to him. In their right minds, they'd put off the first practice as long as possible. But he wanted to begin with a flare, just once, even though he feared becoming laughable.

"Men, I'm glad to see you here tonight. In one minute the basketball season will begin."

Sam looked for any hope in their eyes, any fire, but found only confusion and uncertainty.

"I believe that this season will be different from what you're used to. I want it to be a season you'll stick in your scrapbook."

The boys shuffled their feet and glanced into one another's faces.

"I don't have a scrapbook," Dean said.

"Oh, well . . ." Sam coughed. "I meant it would be something you'd like to remember."

"I'm sure trying to forget the last three," Tom said.

"You got that right," Rob said.

"I know what you mean," Sam said. He checked his watch. The loud blaring of the Notre Dame fight song, the school's adopted battle hymn, reverberated from the gym.

"I hope you're ready to have more fun than you've ever had. Okay!" Sam clapped his hands. "Once around the floor and then shoot layups."

He handed Rob the ball. The boys charged out into the gym, clapping and shouting. They hesitated a beat in turn when they saw the assembled towns-people in the bleachers, as though astonished that any sane person would be sitting along the unheated basketball floor in the middle of the night.

Sam came through the door behind them in shirtsleeves and tie, topped off with a new Acme whistle around his neck. He hoped his attempt to muster the town's support would not turn out as tragicomic as Truly Osborn had said this silly spectacle would be. Sam had promised those he invited that he would have a surprise for them.

Besides Scott Miller, the chubby freshman who would be the team's manager and who had played the fight song at exactly twelve o'clock, there were ten people in the cold stands. With Tripod peering from her partially unzipped coat, Grandma Chapman hooted and cheered as the boys lined up and ran layups. Rob's parents, the ever-faithful Ben and Alice Johnson, were there. The quiet and unassuming Painters, who were known as faithful fans, raised no suspicions by appearing at this ridiculous hour of the morning. Massive Hazel Brown was present to see if her ten-dollar bet was safe. And bleary-eyed Axel Anderson, who made every attempt to support local functions without expressing how laughable he thought they might be, sat in the bleachers with all the excitement of a tree stump.

Andrew Wainwright was there, the talc plant executive and school board member who lived alone in town and almost singlehandedly had fought to keep the town from giving up on the basketball team. Truly Osborn, like a spectator at the Indy 500, was there only to witness a disaster. Rip Van Winkle, not to be left out of anything, perched in his usual seat at the top of the bleachers—four rows up—where he could lean back against the wall.

Sam had wanted the whole town out, but still thought it miraculous that there were ten. Many of the people he approached actually laughed at him when they realized he was serious.

"Come to the gym at *midnight*? For a *practice*?"

After each response, Sam lost a pound or two of confidence and almost called the whole thing off. Now, as he observed the mixed bag of spectators and the minimal team of five, he could see the comedy in it all. Dashing toward the basket with his cockeyed Kamp Implement cap pulled tightly over one ear, Dean fumbled a pass from Rob and drop-kicked the ball against the wall with the detonation of a cannon shot.

Sam intercepted the bouncing ball and halted the layup drill. He nodded at Scott Miller and the freshman shut off the fight song. The scattered band of players stood around their coach out on the court as he turned toward the bleachers.

"Thank you for coming out at this late hour to honor the team," he said. "I promised you a surprise. I thought I'd serve you all lemonade and cake . . ." Sam paused, noting several disappointed exchanges from the weary spectators and a nearly inaudible groan. "But I came up with a better idea."

He struggled to prevent the snicker dancing in his mind from showing off on his face, savoring the moment briefly. Then he blew his whistle, his new chrome Wile E. Coyote whistle. From the girls' locker room, where he'd been holed up since eleven-thirty, Olaf materialized. He was a gangling giant in oversized game shoes and a bright new jersey, number 99, striding toward the south backboard with a flimsy confidence and a glimmer of hope in his innocent blue eyes.

He dribbled once, jumped, and jammed the basketball down through the netting. He turned and regarded his audience with uncertainty.

Everyone in the gym sat gawking, silent, catching their breath. Then, breaking out of this trance, they rose, hooting and clapping and shouting in shocked surprise.

"Are you going to *play*?" Rob asked.

"Why didn't you *tell* us?" Pete said, looking up into Olaf's boyish mirth.

"Olaf and I have been working together for a while," Sam told the meager company. "He wanted to try it and see how it felt. He's never played before, he's learning. We're all going to learn to play basketball together."

Sam turned to his team.

"We're going to learn how to run together, rebound together, play defense together. Men, we're going to learn how to *win* together."

"Yo!" Rob shouted.

"Sweet!" Pete yelled.

"Bodacious!" Dean shouted, and a fresh enthusiasm lit up their faces.

"By God, we'll beat those son-bitches!" Rip shouted hoarsely, and everyone in the gym echoed his sentiments.

"All right, let's scrimmage for five minutes or so," Sam said, tossing the ball to Rob, "and then we'll all go home and get some rest." He divided them evenly, with Sam as the ref, and they played half-court. They went at each other with a fiery frivolity. Olaf dropped passes, missed shots, and stumbled around, making it evident that he had no experience with the game. But he made one deep, unexpected impression on Sam. The long-armed boy batted more than one shot away, and his reactions were quicker than Sam had hoped.

Wearing a bright, multicolored ski jacket and a Padres baseball cap, Diana scrambled into the gym looking sleepy-eyed and out of breath. Sidling up to Sam, she caught him off guard.

"I'm sorry, I fell asleep," she said. Then she noticed Olaf out on the floor. "My God, is he going to *play*?"

"That was my surprise," Sam said, feeling flushed beside her.

"*Can* he play?"

"I hope so."

"Wow," she said, then ran up into the bleachers to watch. Peter Strong, in this first glimpse, was all that Grandma Chapman boasted, and then some. If Olaf could do it—and seeing him in action for the first time gave Sam severe doubts—they would have a formidable attack that would send the opposing coaches digging through their duffel bags for their antacid.

Sam blew his whistle. An outburst of clapping came from the bleachers.

"I want to thank you for coming out tonight. Neither the boys nor I will forget your kindness. They'll change and be right out."

Scott turned on the Notre Dame fight song, a ludicrous footnote to this unlikely gathering, and the handful of players hustled into the locker room.

"I told you so," Truly said to Sam. "Didn't amount to a rat's ass."

The superintendent marched triumphantly from the gymnasium. Sam glanced up at Rip and couldn't help but wonder if all this was a divine omen of the season to come. The frail old man had fallen sound asleep, snoring loudly from his toothless mouth.

CHAPTER 13

Into the first week of practice, Sam recognized he was caught up in a newfound insanity. He was dropping into bed near midnight and he feared he was driving the boys beyond their limits like some NCAA coach obsessed with national rankings. Sam even faltered in English class on more than one occasion, standing before his students in the middle of a lecture without a notion as to where it was going.

Some things were obvious, even to a coach who had never won a game. It was critical that the boys had to stay out of foul trouble because there would be no relief from the bench. They would have to endure the whole game without substitution. And when fatigue set in, they'd make mistakes and foul more. And by the fourth quarter, the Broncs would find themselves playing against teams of ten or twelve rested players. If one of the four fouled out, there would be a glaring vulnerability that their opponents would quickly exploit. To win they would have to be in better shape, play harder, longer, and with more heart than those teams who annually used Willow Creek to blow the carbon out of their tailpipes. What could he possibly conceive and bring forth out of his fruitless and infertile life to inspire them to give in blood? And how could he convince them to believe they could win when he knew his faith in the matter was utterly impoverished?

THAT AFTERNOON AFTER five minutes of wind sprints, Sam gathered the boys at midcourt. Sweat dripped from their bodies and Olaf braced his hands on his knees, gasping.

"Men, last year we had an excuse not to succeed. We were outmanned and outgunned and we didn't believe we could win so we coached and played with no expectations."

Sam glanced at Rob and Tom.

"If we're going to succeed this year, we can no longer simply pull on a uniform and play half assed. I'm asking each of you for a new level of dedication, to give your very best every second, every minute, at practice as well as in games. I'm asking you to play hard until the final buzzer, knowing you've played your best, always."

He glanced into their eyes and was overcome by the intensity he found; they appeared to take his challenge to heart.

"Besides regular practice, I will be holding voluntary sessions for whoever can make them, watching films and going over plays. The first one will be tonight at my house, seven-thirty to eight-thirty. Try to come if it doesn't interfere with your homework or family life. No one will be penalized for missing."

Sam cleared his throat. "Thank you for your hard work. I'm happy to announce that you all made the first cut."

He paused as the boys shared amused glances.

"That means you're all officially Willow Creek Broncs. It also means you'll have to maintain your eligibility. In order to participate with the team, you have to be passing in every subject at each two-week grading interval. Poor grades can beat us as surely as Gardiner or Twin Bridges. So hit the books. As members of the team it means no tobacco—including chewing, Tom—no alcohol, and most importantly . . ." Sam looked kindly into Dean's magnified eyes, ". . . no wild women. Got that Dean?"

The unassuming freshman, his cap cocked over one ear, gawked at the coach with the most confused expression Sam had ever seen.

"Yeah," the boy said in his squeaking falsetto.

They laughed and Tom gently swatted his abbreviated teammate. Sam sensed that the hard-bodied country boy was strong for his age, probably working like a man on the ranch since he was old enough to see over the tailgate.

"You're fast, Dean," Sam said. "You're going to help us a lot."

The sturdy boy puffed up slightly. "Are we going to eat at McDonald's?"

"Yes, when we travel."

"Bodacious!" Dean said with a bright smile.

"Burger King," Tom said. "Better burgers."

Sam flinched. His heart skipped a beat. He glanced at Tom then looked back at Dean, fighting it off.

"Don't you find it awfully hot wearing your cap when you practice?" Sam asked.

"It makes me run faster," Dean said.

Sam paused, and the boy gave no indication that he was joking. "All right, then. Everyone have a good shower and a restful night . . . after ten laps around the gym."

"Yeeehaaa!" Rob shouted and took off running.

The others followed with rekindled enthusiasm except for Tom, who trotted behind.

IN THE MODEST whitewashed locker room Peter shouted and bantered with the boys while they scrambled for the four showers and dressed. It was as though a large 0–93 were stenciled in bloody red on the wall and everyone averted his eyes.

"That was the toughest practice we've had in four years," Rob shouted.

"That would just be a warmup at Highland," Pete said.

"Who's got a towel?" Tom hollered.

"I do," Dean said.

Tom took one look at the tattered towel and hooted. "That's not a towel, Dean, that's a rag. That wouldn't absorb snot."

"I don't think they're going to get any easier," Rob said. "Mr. Pickett has changed. He has a look in his eye."

"It's about time someone had a look in his eye around here," Tom said. "We practice our balls off but never win."

"You did good today," Rob said and slapped Olaf on the back.

"Dying I am thinking," Olaf said, drooping on a bench.

Tom pulled on his J. Chisholm boots and looked at Pete. "How big is the school you go to?"

"Around twenty-one hundred."

"*Kids?*" Tom said.

"No, ninja turtles."

"Shit, that's bigger than Three Forks," Tom said.

"Would you have started on the varsity this year?" Rob said.

"I don't know. When I go home after Christmas I'll find out."

"You can't go home now, dude," Tom said as he nudged Pete aside by the small mirror. "We need you, man."

"You got that right," Rob said.

The other boys chimed in.

Pete combed his hair and enjoyed the unexpected affection he felt from being wanted.

"You don't have to look pretty," Tom said. "Your girl's in Minnesota."

"Yeah, but I want to look nice for all the cows and sheep and horses I'll meet walking home on Main Street."

Tom laughed and slapped him on the shoulder. "Don't forget to say howdy to the pigs."

As always, Sam checked the gym before leaving, making sure the school was locked up. When he finished checking the boys' locker room, he noticed a sliver of light draining from the girls' locker room. He knocked on the door and asked if anyone was there. Hearing no response, Sam stepped in, reached for the light switch, and was struck dumb by a vision he couldn't immediately comprehend. Diana stood, naked and with her eyes closed, toweling her wet hair.

For a moment he couldn't move or speak, couldn't take his eyes off her firm athletic body. She bent forward and vigorously dried her long, almond colored hair. Her body consumed him like fire, sucking the air out of him.

When she opened her eyes and saw him, she gasped. Their eyes met for a second. Then, she whipped the towel around her torso and Sam turned around.

"Oh, gosh, I'm sorry," he said, gazing at the scuff-marked concrete floor. "I didn't know anyone . . . I was just . . . I saw the light and . . . I'm really sorry."

He darted out the door without another glance.

Late that night, after all the boys—except Tom—had come and gone, Sam tried to diagram plays on a notepad, but frustration plagued him in every attempt to concentrate. That accidental vision of Diana had so routed him from his path that he found himself addled and disoriented.

He'd been celibate in the five years following Amy's murder, but after witnessing Diana he was hopelessly overcome. No matter how hard he tried, he couldn't erase her from his energized mind. Her image was a like grass stain he couldn't wash out.

The following night, after a tortuous practice, when he had lingered in his classroom an appropriate length of time, he made his way back to the gym to lock up. With rampaging anticipation, he had dreaded finding a seductive light beckoning from the girls' locker room, terrified that she might be nakedly awaiting his return, yet at the same time, agonizing to catch another glimpse of her, a whiff of her soapy dampness. There had been no light.

CHAPTER 14

S am was running, puffing, and breaking a sweat, pushing himself past the Blue Willow Inn and onto the gravel road. Dawn blushed bleakly in the gray overcast. Awake early, he was driven from his bed by a new drive, desperate to change the direction of his life before it was too late.

Gasping and hurting, he fell back into a slow walk. The landscape came into focus with the arrival of daylight, and Sam told himself he was doing this for the team. But he knew he was lying. Somehow he suspected that this sudden drive to run harder and farther had something to do with Diana.

He crossed the old single-lane bridge over Jefferson River, where the turkey vultures nested west of town. Though the birds were rare in Montana, they chose the town of Willow Creek to haunt as though they were on to something. Sam checked his watch and turned back, hoping to go a little farther next morning. Halfway back he came upon Ray Collins, the unvarnished propane man and member of the school board, standing by his pickup with his yellow Lab. Wearing his dark green gabardine uniform and cap, he greeted Sam with more enthusiasm than usual.

"I hear the big Norwegian is going to play."

After several minutes of exuberant speculation regarding the upcoming season, something that Sam tried to avoid early in the conversation, Ray explained that he was training his dog to stay away from livestock with a shock collar. His teddy-bearlike fat strained his uniform and his shirttail hung out the back.

"I run him near the cattle and horses. If he takes after 'em, I zing him with this doodad." He displayed the remote-control transmitter he held in his hand.

"Watch." He grabbed a stuffed canvas training dummy from the bed of his blue Chevy pickup. He wound up and heaved it as far as he could toward several white Simmental bulls that grazed on the far side of the pasture. The dog sat at heel, every nerve and muscle straining, aching for Ray's command.

"Fetch," Ray said.

The Lab exploded from the road, leaped the barbed-wire fence, and sprinted across the browning pasture. When he noticed the massive animals, he veered toward them at a run. Ray called. "Poke! Come, Poke!"

The retriever didn't heed his master's voice until a second later when Ray pushed a button on the transmitter and shouted. "Poke! Come!"

The Lab instantly swerved from his course and dashed back toward the men. The Lab's tongue hung from one side of its mouth like fresh liver and he sat obediently at Ray's feet, panting. The collar had a round four-inch cylinder attached and two prongs that touched the Lab's neck.

"I don't want him messing with any animals. Could get himself shot."

"What if the shock doesn't turn him?" Sam said, wiping his forehead with his sleeve.

"Then you just turn this little doodad up." Ray pointed at a small dial on the transmitter. "All the way up and it'll just about knock him down."

Ray sent the dog out again for the scented decoy. "So how come you stuck with the coaching job? The board wanted to give you a break."

"I need something to do all winter. I thought it would be better this year."

The Lab glanced at the massive bulls as he sniffed for the decoy, but he made no move toward them.

Ray squinted at Sam. "Do you really believe we'll win a game this year?"

"I think we have a good chance to win a few."

Poke came up to Ray and sat eagerly at heel with the canvas dummy in his mouth.

"Good dog, good dog," Ray said.

"That really works," Sam said. "Amazing."

Thankful for the excuse to rest, Sam pushed off toward town for another day of school and practice. He would continue to duck any face-to-face encounter with Diana. After a shower, he gazed in his bathroom mirror to see if his run had diminished his stomach by any stretch of the imagination. Even then, all he could visualize was the white outline of a bikini on Diana's flat belly.

OPTIMISM SOARED AT the Blue Willow. Word spread like weeds, and stories of the foreign exchange student's abilities grew to outlandish heights. Rumor had it—amid doughnuts, coffee, and sticky sweet rolls— that he had played on an international all-star team in Europe and could dunk the ball with either hand. The few true witnesses to the unveiling of the Norwegian phenom spread their gospel efficiently until the burdens of hope and promise and potential victories were hefted on Olaf Gustafson's young back.

Sam tried to simmer down these starry-eyed proclamations of Olaf's talent whenever the opportunity arose, but for a handful of diehards, the fire was already lit. And for the first time in years, a growing number of townspeople were actually looking forward to the basketball season. But knowing better than to dismiss the hardened skepticism standing guard at the entrance to their hearts after years of emotional pain and disappoint- ment, they were looking forward cautiously, daring only to allow hope onto the back porch in its muddy shoes.

One patriot who was trying to avoid being sucked into the anguish and punishment that loyalty to the Willow Creek basketball team exacted was the balding, barrel-chested St. Bernard who piloted the Blue Willow Inn. That night, Sam ate a late dinner alone, wavering between the hope that Diana would show up and fearing that she might. He also feared George Stonebreaker would show up; Sam stared at the Inn's front window just to make sure. He imagined a terrifying scene over and over: Stonebreaker pulling a shotgun from out of a long coat and depopulating Willow Creek. Twice that day, at totally unexpected moments, he'd heard Amy's voice.

Axel pulled up a chair and flopped his hands onto Sam's table as if he were a fortune teller. A perpetual bead of perspiration glistened on his fore- head above his pug nose. Sam had wanted to ask Axel how he got that dis- figured ear and gruesome scar on his neck, but figured everyone had old wounds they wanted to forget, even the ones that didn't show. In Axel's warm, wide-set eyes, he revealed something like the vulnerability of a child who wanted to know once and for all if there was a Santa Claus. He leaned close and spoke confidentially, though there weren't a half dozen people in the place.

"Are we going to *win* a game, Sam?"

Sam paused and considered an answer but Axel went on without him.

"I don't think I can take anymore of this. I get too involved for my own good. Even when you're down by twenty you get more and more pissed, what with the other fans yelling against your boys and the ref screwing them. Soon you're pulling for little victories, you know what I mean, Sam? When the only thing you can cheer about is a good play, a shot made, a steal, something you can thumb your nose at the other team with because they're beating the crap out of you and you start taking it personally."

He wiped his glistening forehead with the back of his hand.

"Hell, when they're ahead by thirty they keep calling for blood, wanting to run the score up like a goddamn feeding frenzy, trying to rip the flesh off your heart, and you start praying that the boys will hold it at thirty—"

"Or keep them from scoring a hundred," Sam said, hearing Axel evoke the agony Sam thought was his alone.

"And they drop passes, kick the ball," Axel said, "step out of bounds, try to dribble through two guys, and your heart just gets beat to hell. I decided during the summer that I wasn't going to let myself get emotionally involved this year. I can't take it anymore. But now with the Norwegian kid and all, I get to thinking maybe it's our turn. Maybe old Willow Creek is going to kick some ass this year, and I feel myself getting sucked in again."

"I decided last summer that I wouldn't coach another year."

"What made you change your mind?"

"Mental illness. Dementia. Lunacy, you name it."

Axel's face brightened like a Coleman lantern. "Why do you think we get so wrapped up in it?"

"I don't know," Sam said. "I've wondered about that a lot."

Sam felt an affinity with the thickset man, knowing that, win or lose, like it or not, Axel was already in the susceptible soup.

"I guess it's just wanting to win at something," Axel said and Sam detected a note of defeat in his voice.

"How's it going with this place?" Sam said. "You making out okay?"

Axel leaned closer and spoke in a hushed tone.

"I don't think we'll make it, Sam. I had high hopes when we came here, but . . . well. The last place I tried, a gas station outside Boise, went under.

Before that, a convenience store, and we were doing fine until an Albertson's supermarket went up two blocks away."

Amos Flowers walked in and Axel nodded at him.

"I don't know, Sam. I don't know what I keep doing wrong. My life has been one long string of losses."

It was as though a curtain had been pulled aside for an instant and Sam caught a glimpse into Axel's soul.

"The wife and I thought it would be different here, but I don't know how long we can hang on. We're eating up our savings . . ." His voice trailed off and he sat in silence for a moment, gazing at the checkerboard tablecloth. Then he stood and squeezed Sam's shoulder. "Thanks for your ear, but please keep this under your hat."

Axel tugged at his suspenders, put on his everything's-just-great face, and headed for the corner table where Amos Flowers had settled. Sam recognized his own hiddenness in Axel's, and he couldn't answer the question of why he was getting wrapped up in this again, but he desperately cautioned his heart against it.

Amos Flowers was a wizened loner of unknown age who came from the foothills of the Tobacco Roots and had adopted Willow Creek as his social center, which meant the townspeople saw him once or twice a month. Rumor had it that though he had a bundle, he never paid taxes, had no mailing address, and was a fugitive from the IRS, which made him somewhat of a local folk hero. More than one person had confided to Sam that Amos kept his money in the Sealy Posturepedic Savings & Loan. Sometimes he'd ride his horse into town and tie it up in front of the inn, a big gray gelding whose color matched Amos's handlebar mustache.

Sam had greeted him on occasion and Amos had only nodded distantly, as though Sam were a treasury agent or worse. How did a person end up like that in life, so estranged and solitary? With a rush of fear, Sam realized that on his current path, he might well find out.

Worldly matters never seemed to interest Amos much, and he was never one to notice a basketball score, but the newborn enthusiasm among the Blue Willow bunch dry-gulched him. He listened to the mushrooming reputation of the unproved exchange student from under his oil-treated duster and his oversized roan-colored Tom Mix hat that rested on his eyebrows and large ears.

It always appeared as though Amos had been born in and grown down out of his hat, like a snail out of its shell. The seasoned, sweat-stained wide-brim with a Montana crease seemed to have a life of its own and the thin, gnarled, tobacco-colored cowboy simply lived in it. No one had ever seen him without his trademark and no one could ever remember hearing Amos say, until now, that he thought he'd come over some night to see the boys play.

And as winter poked around the edges of the valley, Sam felt an expectation thickening the air like pollen, and he saw how people found it easier to smile.

CHAPTER 15

Diana realized it wasn't by chance that she hadn't crossed paths with Sam since he stumbled upon her stark naked in the girls' locker room, but she wasn't sure why he was avoiding her. In a school that size he had to be a magician to have pulled it off that long. She admitted she liked the man; there was something warm and inviting about him in spite of his obvious unwillingness to get better acquainted. Did he have a girlfriend somewhere? Was he attracted to women? It was just as well . . . but she was confused and she warned herself to keep her distance; she didn't want to stockpile any more freight in the storehouse of unbearable sorrow.

Because it was a small school and because she was trying to keep one eye on Olaf and see that he was adjusting well to his new environment, she had stumbled on another drama, being acted out among some of her favorite kids.

Carter Walker and Rob Johnson had been friends since they were in diapers, their family ranches sharing fence lines, hay baling, and branding parties before Carter and Rob could walk. Carter and Louella Straight, being good old country girls, had fallen on the common subject that had been tickling their curiosity for weeks—having grown up amid the magnificent thrusting bulls and obliging heifers in heat.

Daring, finally, to share it as girlfriends, it got them no closer to the truth and only seemed to compound their frustration and feed their fantasies. Carter approached Rob with their riddle, and Rob listened with a mask of serious concern. What the girls had been wondering since day one was— and Carter found it difficult to confide in Rob—were all of Olaf's parts that enormous? With a frown of dedication on his face, Rob promised he would find out.

A few days later, when Olaf, Carter and Louella were eating in the lunchroom and visiting with Diana, Rob hollered over the bustle and din from a table away. "Hey, Olaf! Carter and Louella want to know how l-o-n-g . . ."

The two girls sprang from the table, scattering their half-eaten lunch, and almost maimed each other dashing through the door as Rob continued.

". . . the *nights* are in Norway."

From then on, when least expected, as the three of them might be walking in the halls, Rob would amble up behind and inquire with full voice, "Olaf, Carter and Louella were wondering how b-i-g your . . ." at which time the girls would shriek to cover ". . . *hometown* is?"

It was usually the most exciting thing that happened all day for the two girls, and as abashed as they were to think that Olaf might figure out they actually wondered about such things, he seemed oblivious to what was going on, laughing at their fickle flight and always answering Rob's questions with seriously considered facts and figures. Unintentionally, Rob was learning a whole lot about Norway, but unfortunately the often-embarrassed girls were learning nothing new and startling about Olaf. And Olaf had his own questions about life in the United States on the order of, Why did so many Americans sell their garages? or How did they manage to sell their yards?

FRIDAY NIGHT, SAM studied basketball videos with a vengeance. His recurring dream had startled him and driven him from his sweat-soaked sheets. He turned on every light in the house and paced from room to room, choking back the sobs and trying to breathe. To drive all memory from his brain, he turned on a basketball video, with the volume so loud it sounded as though the game were taking place in his living room. He hoped the neighbors wouldn't be awakened.

In the dream, he was always in a car and Amy was entering a building, sometimes a Burger King, sometimes a supermarket, a movie theater, or a shopping mall. He tried frantically to stop her, to warn her. He tried to open the car door but it wouldn't open. He'd try to roll down the window but there was no handle or switch and so he'd try to break the door open with his shoulder or smash the window out with his fists. He'd try to yell but nothing would come out of his mouth and Amy would disappear. No matter how he tried he couldn't save her. He was afraid to go to sleep.

And into the muddle of his life—his struggle to claw his way out of the past and into some portion of the present—came Diana Murphy. As difficult as it was in a high school of eighteen students, he had managed to duck any direct encounter with Diana, afraid that he would blush an array of shades if he had to look into her eyes. She was often gone, off to visit Ellie and Randolph Butterworth, a couple she had met who ranched over toward Cardwell. Part of him lived in terror of the moment when they would finally speak of how he had seen her that night. Another part of him longed for it, that intimate confidence shared, something intriguing and mystifying, something breathing a carnal and scary possibility.

The door rattled. Sam looked away from the TV for a moment, listening.

The knock came again, more distinct. He put his notepad aside and left the taped basketball game running.

The light bulb on his porch had burned out weeks ago and he opened the door without immediately recognizing her in the gusty darkness. In a gray, quilted down coat and a crimson matador hat she held in place by the brim, Diana stepped into his house, her wind-kissed cheeks flushed and glowing.

"Hi, Sam, it's really howling out there."

She pulled off her hat and shook out her hair.

"I saw your light. Am I interrupting anything?"

"Oh, uh . . . no." Sam nodded toward the television. "Just basketball."

Diana entered the living room and settled on the sagging sofa amid books, magazines, and stacks of videos. She watched the game in progress.

"Is this on now?"

"No. I've got it on tape."

Sam turned down the volume and picked several newspapers and magazines off the carpet, trying to cover his dirty dinner plate before she noticed it. He tripped and knocked a stack of books off an end table.

"Sorry about that. I wasn't expecting anyone."

He sought refuge in his tattered upholstered chair, praying that she wouldn't ask to use the bathroom. Thankful for a diversion, he picked up his notepad, glancing at the TV with a businesslike manner.

"I wanted to catch you at school," she said. "But you seemed to disappear all week."

He loved her throaty voice.

"Yeah, I know," he said, catching a strong scent of Diana's lavender soap. "I'm watching a lot of basketball."

"I'd like to help out. You don't have enough players to scrimmage. I played basketball in college and I could play defense or whatever you needed, I'd be another body."

Sam feared he visibly shuddered at the "B" word and he had difficulty finding his voice. Another *body*. How could he concentrate with her promenading her shapely anatomy around the gym floor while he tried to instruct his boys on a give-and-go? How could any of them? *Here, Tom, you move up and screen Miss Murphy and try not to notice her sumptuous proportions as she rubs past you.* He'd have to put Tom's eyes out first.

"Well, that's good of you to offer. Maybe . . . now and then . . ." Sam said, trying to avoid her stare.

"Why don't you ask a few other people? I'm sure there'd be some who'd like to help and give the boys a team to practice against. I'll bet some of the recent players would, if they weren't working."

"Not many kids stay around here after high school," Sam said. "No work." He nodded at the game. "See that? A back pick on the center and Olaf rolls free for a backdoor slam." Sam reversed the tape and they watched the San Antonio Spurs spring David Robinson for an easy slam.

"That's what I mean," she said. "You need some *bodies* out there if you're going to practice five-man basketball."

She put on her matador, tilted in an alluring manner. "I'll be at practice Monday. I think you've got something here. I can see why you're excited."

"Wouldn't you like something? A Coke? Some coffee?"

"No, thanks. It's late." She laughed and glanced around the littered room. "What are you doing, passively defying Superintendent Truly?"

"No, my mother."

"I tack up posters off-centered," she said, "just to see him grit his teeth."

She walked to the door and opened it, ushering in southwesterly squalls into the stuffy house. Sam followed her to the door and halfway out she paused, her face shadowed under her tilted hat. "Oh, and I'll try to remember the lights in the girls' locker room."

Sam caught his breath and tried to study her eyes in the darkness for signs of a rebuke or understanding. He caught them for an instant in a small shaft of light. He felt hot blood flowing through his face and ears.

She smiled. "The shower out at my place is a joke."

When she left, he paced through the house again, stepping around and over things, forgetting all about the basketball game. He could hear the barren lilacs tapping Morse code on the faded siding and unwashed window panes. He stood motionless, listening. He'd never interpreted the signs correctly; he'd never heard the Muses clearly.

Dousing the TV and lights, he fumbled out of his clothing and felt his way to the haunted bed. The wind rocked the house to sleep as he lay awake, and he heard the tapping on his soul. He couldn't detect if it was a warning against hope or the dancing lilacs in Diana's inviting garden.

⇆ CHAPTER 16 ⇆

In class, Sam was utilizing the film *Man of La Mancha* to spark his students' interest in Cervantes and his absurd hero, Don Quixote. Among the many posters on his classroom wall was one that advertised the film, depicting the lunatic knight attacking a windmill. The entire junior and senior class, eight of them, watched the video on the TV Sam propped up on his desk.

Some of his students had shown only mild interest at the beginning, occasionally whispering to each other during the movie. But now, viewing the second half of the film, most of them quietly watched. Sitting off to the side, Sam observed their faces. As the story concluded, the kids hardly seemed to breathe, caught up in the drama of the peculiar old man following his quest with his fat little squire, Sancho.

Aldonza forces her way in to see Don Quixote in his deathbed. He is failing and confused and Aldonza pleads with him. "You spoke of a dream. And about the Quest!"

"Quest?" Don Quixote whispers.

"How you must fight and it doesn't matter whether you win or lose if only you follow the Quest."

"The words. Tell me the words," he says.

Aldonza speaks in time with the music.

"To dream the impossible dream . . . But they're your own words.

"To fight the unbeatable foe . . . Don't you remember?

"To bear with unbearable sorrow . . . You must remember!

"To run where the brave dare not go—"

Don Quixote remembers and stammers.

"To right the unrightable wrong."

"Yes," she says.

"To love, pure and chaste from afar," he says with a stronger voice.

"Yes."

"To try, when your arms are too weary. To reach the unreachable star!"
Aldonza takes hold of his hand. "Thank you, my lord."

"But this is not seemly, my lady. On thy knees, to me?" He tries to rise in
the bed and she holds his hand.

"My lord, you are not well!"

"Not well? What is sickness to the body of a knight-errant?" he says and
sits up in the bed. "What matter wounds? For each time he falls he shall rise
again—and woe to the wicked!" He shouts, "Sancho!"

Don Quixote stumbles out of his deathbed and calls for his sword and
armor.

Tom held up a fist and shouted, "Yeah!"

Sam turned on the lights and raised the window shades. No one spoke.
Then Tom broke the spell. "Did that dude really live?"

"Did he ever," Sam said. "A soldier who was seriously wounded, Cervantes spent five years in Africa as a slave, wrote over forty plays that never
were successful, was imprisoned by the Inquisition and spent several terms
in prison. After all this—and this is the good part—when he was old and
sick and a complete failure to the world, he wrote what many have considered the world's greatest novel, which he finished in 1615. He died a year later
and no one knows where he was buried."

The kids gazed at Sam, moved by the story of this rusting, whimsical
hero.

"Does this remind you of anyone else in history?" Sam said.

The students thought for a moment.

"Mozart?" Louella said.

"Yes, many similarities," Sam said. "Unsatisfying success while living,
never giving up, dying a pauper, a failure in his own mind, dumped in an
unmarked grave, his genius recognized years later."

"Shakespeare?" Mary Shaw, the strawberry blonde junior, said.

"Strangely enough, Shakespeare and Cervantes died within ten days of
each other," Sam said. "Anyone else come to mind?"

"The Willow Creek basketball team," Tom Stonebreaker said, his hawk-
like eyes brimming with resolve.

"You got that right," Rob said.

The bell rang and the other students flashed puzzled glances at each other, having no clue what Tom and Rob were talking about.

Sam did.

"KEEP THE BALL above your head!" Sam shouted at Olaf as they practiced bringing the ball upcourt with only four players. Scott, the ungainly freshman manager, and Sam played defense while Dean and Curtis did most of the running.

For lack of a better name, Sam called the tactic "volleyball." The boys lobbed high passes to Olaf who, keeping the ball in the stratosphere, passed it to an open teammate and then ran upcourt to set up again for a high lob.

"If you bring it down they'll take it away from you!" Sam shouted.

Olaf caught the ball on the center line as Curtis tried to leap and knock it away. Sam blew his whistle.

"Okay, hold it right there. Look at where your feet are, Olaf. Don't set up until you're in the front court, otherwise you're going to get called for over-and-back. Okay. Let's run it three against five. Pete, you come on defense."

They ran hard. Rob, Tom, and Olaf attempted to bring the ball upcourt against five defenders, over and over, switching everyone around except Olaf. He wanted them to feel normal four against five, confident, expecting it. The boys went at each other on the court, and Sam racked his brain for every possible situation they would encounter, every possible scene he'd witnessed in his five-year history of being outclassed and outmaneuvered.

While Sam was absorbed in the scrimmage, he suddenly caught sight of Diana as she appeared from the girls' locker room. He blinked, then sighed with relief. As if she had anticipated his worst fears, she showed up in baggy gray sweats that made her look boyish, except for the long dark brown hair she held in place with a gold headband.

Sam worked the team on offensive plays, making Diana, Dean, and Scott play defense. He paid little attention to Grandma Chapman and Hazel Brown when they entered the gym and clambered into the bleachers, followed by the hobbling cat, Tripod. Pete acknowledged his colorful grandmother with a smile and wave.

"Here are two more players," Diana said with a lowered voice.

Sam paused. "You don't mean—"

"Why not? They can stand, can't they?"

"I'm not going to ask them to—"

"I will," Diana said, and she trotted over to the bleachers.

"You want *me* to play basketball?" Hazel Brown said.

"Come on, they need us," Grandma said.

Sam frowned as the two women—a white-haired, one-handed grandmother in brown fedora and Reeboks and her fortyish, Volkswagen Beetle–sized friend in tentlike pants and bright orange sweatshirt—walked onto the court waiting for instructions.

"Put Hazel on Olaf," Diana whispered.

The boys exchanged sideways glances and rolled their eyes. Diana was one thing, but *this* was downright mortifying. With Grandma and Hazel it became five on five, of sorts.

Though Sam admitted that desperation breeds insanity, it wasn't a bad idea. For a half hour, they walked through offensive plays. As the boys rolled off picks at half speed for layups, Grandma Chapman batted the ball out of Pete's hands as he attempted a shot.

"Hey, no fair!" Pete shouted.

"Enough of this monkey business," she said. "Let's play ball."

With some trepidation and Grandma's egging, Sam had them try it at full speed. He was shocked to discover that the older, unathletic women suddenly mutated into emotional, competitive jocks who took this scrimmage very much to heart. Grandma resembled a mother hen defending her eggs against marauding predators, clucking and huffing about with wings flapping.

Hazel Brown—amazingly graceful and light on her feet for her bulk—was a load to handle and was possessive of the paint. Olaf tried to get into position, but after Sam's instruction to shove him around, Hazel proved as tenacious as any opposing player Olaf was likely to run up against. Sam noticed that the more Hazel sweated, the more pungent her cheap perfume became. Because he allowed more contact than a legitimate ref would, the volunteers got away with murder.

"Oh, excuse me," Olaf said after bumping into Hazel.

"Don't you worry about being polite, boy," she said and knocked him four feet out of the paint with a single heave of her belly.

These makeshift, patchwork defenders in street clothes, baggy sweats, and house dresses took it all very seriously, shouting to one another and rapidly developing a highly competitive esprit de corps. Their enthusiasm far outdistanced their conditioning. Though quicker and more agile, the boys were taking their lumps in this strange combat with elbowing and clawing misfits.

Sam was hoping no one else in the human race would witness this bizarre sideshow when, sure enough, Truly Osborn showed up along the sidelines. After almost ten minutes at full throttle, Sam blew his whistle with a sudden dread. He'd noticed Tom was favoring his knee. He thanked the recruits and sent the team to work on free throws.

Grandma turned to Sam.

"When do you want us back?" she asked, avoiding Hazel's frown.

"Oh . . . I don't know. Maybe if you could come around four tomorrow?" he said without much time for thought.

"We'll be here," Grandma said, as Tripod rubbed against her leg. She bent and scooped up her cat.

"I don't know about tomorrow," Hazel said, red-faced and trying to catch her breath. "I must have lost ten pounds."

"What do you think of the Norwegian?" Grandma said as the two women shuffled to the bleachers to retrieve their coats.

"Well, he's clumsy," Hazel said, wiping her brow with her shirt sleeve. "But he's slow."

"Ha!" Grandma said.

Truly marched over to Sam. He spoke out of the side of his mouth without a pause in his step or a hint of dissatisfaction on his narrow, expressionless face.

"You gone completely out of your mind?"

Sam sputtered for a reply, but Diana saved him, approaching the two with a look of concern.

"Tom's limping a little," she said.

"I noticed," Sam said. He watched Tom on the free-throw line.

"Oh, Mr. Pickett," Grandma called. "We have a mascot."

She held Tripod high in the air. Sam nodded and then drifted toward the boys. His team practiced against a candidate for Weight Watchers and a woman old enough to be in any hospital's geriatric ward, and now they were a team with a three-legged cat for a mascot. *Perfect.*

"Your knee hurting?" Sam asked Tom as he shot free throws.

"A little."

Tom swished a free throw. Curtis bounced the ball back to him.

"Did you have a doctor look at it?"

"No. My dad wouldn't pay a nickel for a doctor. Said I'd have to pay for it myself 'cause I hurt it riding rodeo. I told him I'd walk it off."

Tom took aim.

"I want you to go to a doctor I know in Bozeman."

"It'll be okay."

Tom swished another. Curtis flipped the ball back to him.

"Don't worry about the cost, that'll be covered. We have to find out what's been damaged."

Tom took aim. "It's just a little sore."

"Something like that could be serious," Sam said. "We don't want to make it worse or do permanent damage."

"I hate goin' to doctors."

"He's just going to look at it." Sam frowned. "No more practice until you do."

Tom missed.

CHAPTER 17

Tom arrived at the end of Monday practice. With the bull rider missing, it had felt like the team was diminished by half. His appointment with the doctor had been scheduled for two-thirty, and when he appeared in the gym in his long duster and black wide-brimmed hat, everything stopped: balls ceased dribbling, words were left half spoken, and steps froze. Tom hobbled onto the court. The little drove of hope Sam had herded together in his chest stampeded in all directions. Dread gripped him by the throat. He caught his breath and forced his words past his thumping heartbeat.

"Did you see the doctor?"

Diana and the boys gathered around.

"Yep," Tom said without meeting Sam's eyes.

"What did he say?" Sam said.

The answer was already broadcast in the expression of pain and disappointment in Tom's face. "I don't know how you're going to take this, Coach."

"Tell us. What did he say?" Diana asked.

"Said I'd need arthroscopic surgery."

The faces and postures of all present sagged, the air in the gym crystallized.

"Then," Tom continued in a monotonous voice, "maybe a year of rehabilitation before I could play on it." He paused. "Sorry, Coach."

The despair engulfed them. No one spoke. Sam couldn't bear to look at anyone. They were waiting for him to speak, to say something that would make it all right, but his spirit seemed utterly void of optimistic, encouraging words.

Then Tom grabbed the ball from under Rob's arm and went charging across the floor, dribbling like mad and shouting. "Just kidding, you wimps!"

Before he got to the far basket for a layup, the boys broke from their stunned paralysis and were on his trail. They hit him coming back the other way. Rob took him low, Pete hit him high, crashing him to the floor. Then in a wild, spontaneous release of anxiety and disappointment, eight of them mugged Tom at center court, pounding him with affectionate relief and happy, joyous blows.

When they finally untangled and rolled away like kids off a playground hog pile, laughing, hooting, and catching their breaths, Diana spoke first.

"What did the doctor *really* say?"

"It's a medial collateral ligament on the inside of the knee," Tom said. "Says it's been strained, overstretched, but it's not torn. I can play."

The boys cheered.

"He said icing it would help when it hurts," Tom said.

"You pull anything like that again and I'll ice you," Sam said.

"I probably shouldn't run much on it at practice."

"Aw, sure, trying to chicken out of wind sprints," Rob said.

"He said it heals slow. It'll probably hurt a lot if I play." Tom glanced at them and then focused on Sam. "I told him it would hurt a whole lot more if I didn't."

That silenced them. Sam's eyes blurred as he sat there in the middle of the basketball floor with this peculiar gathering: a scrubby-looking bunch of players, his intimidating female cohort, a jolly little manager, and a misplaced cowboy who wanted to take his stand with them. They remained there for a moment, catching their breaths, and in that instant, something in Sam's heart warned him that he was moving out onto thin ice.

"We thought we'd have to go on without you," Diana said.

"That'll be the day," Tom said.

Truly Osborn entered the gym, paperwork in hand, and hesitated under the south backboard. "Can I see you a minute, Mr. Pickett?"

Sam sprang to his feet and hurried to the superintendent. Truly's brows furrowed, and he stared at the team lounging in the middle of the court.

"You have the strangest practices I've ever seen," Truly said.

"We're stretching our medial collateral ligaments."

"Is that important?"

"It's the most important part on our team."

LYING IN BED that night Sam tried to visualize a medial collateral ligament, figuring he'd never heard of that body part. It had a musical ring to it. *Medial collateral ligament.* It would be like buying himself an early Christmas present, the doctor's bill, and he'd pay it with a cheery "ho ho ho." But it sobered him to realize how his heartstrings were subtly becoming more and more entangled with the boys, and maybe even a little with Diana.

As sleep approached on softly padded feet, his mind kept slipping from the medial collateral ligament to other body parts: up her limber thigh to her supple hip, her soft belly, her willowy waist. After falling asleep, he awoke to a faint swishing sound outside, passing his window, and he realized he'd heard it other nights, mysterious and yet strangely familiar. Before he could sleep in his rumpled bedding he heard it again, but when he hurried to the window he could see nothing in the town's faint light. Maybe one of Willow Creek's ghosts?

AXEL SHOWED UP at practice the next afternoon. "I heard you needed players," he said.

He had confided to Sam that he had played football with a vengeance during his school days and, without ever letting on at the time, had yearned to play basketball. However, his lack of agility and the dramatic proportions of his body dictated against it, so Axel never made the team. Now he could fulfill the dreams of his bygone youth by roughhousing with these Willow Creek lads. Sam instructed Axel, with his brawny, knockabout manner, to work on Olaf inside. The Blue Willow's proprietor proved to be as immovable in the paint as a fifty-five-gallon drum of hydraulic fluid.

The team practiced long hours over the Thanksgiving weekend. George Stonebreaker, who had the reputation of a hand grenade even when he was sober, came and jerked Tom out of Friday's practice, claiming that their cattle were out on the road. And though Tom was reluctant to go, Sam made no protest at losing his power forward because he was unable to tell if George had been drinking or not.

Sam had a close call with Thanksgiving dinner. Grandma Chapman had invited him to eat with them, and Diana had done the same only minutes

before. While enjoying a sumptuous meal with Grandma, Peter, and
Hazel, Sam learned that Grandma had invited Miss Murphy, but she
left early and told Grandma that she had commitments for the day. He
found himself imagining what being her *commitments for the day* would
be like.

CHAPTER 18

Peter Strong was watching television at two in the morning when Grandma appeared. He sat in the dark with the volume low in hopes she wouldn't discover him. On her nightly visit to the bathroom she turned the light on in the hallway ever since Pete had greased the toilet seat with margarine, nearly causing her to dismount abruptly onto the linoleum when she plunked her fanny down in the dark.

She had short-sheeted his bed sometime after he planted a dead mouse in the toe of her Reebok after she had turned off the hot water at the water heater while he was in the shower after he had somehow snuck a handful of white popcorn kernels into her bowl of pancake batter just before she poured it into the hot skillet, scaring the hell out of her with exploding gobs of pancake splattering all over the stove and kitchen, and so forth, an inheritance of pranks whose history traced itself back to the detergent in the pancake batter—they were acting like kids at summer camp whose counselor was off necking on the beach.

After snapping out the hall light on her return from the bathroom, she must have caught a glimmer in the darkness of the living room.

"What're you doing up at this hour?" she said, sleepily shuffling into the room in her NFL-monogrammed nightie and furry bear-paw slippers.

He lay in the worn, upholstered chair. "I couldn't sleep."

She glanced at the program on TV: a cheesy old western where cowboys piteously shot at each other and the camera speed increased during the horse chases. She perched on the sofa, facing him.

"Something botherin' you, boy?"

"No. Just couldn't sleep."

"Does this have something to do with basketball practice?"

"I'll go to bed when this is over."

"What do you think of the coach?" she asked, attempting to keep him talking.

"He's cool. Kinda funny. He knows his basketball and he doesn't yell at us like our Highland coach."

"He yell a lot?"

"Yeah, thinks he's Bobby Knight or something."

Tripod stalked across the hardwood floor and leaped onto a small magazine-littered table. He eyed Parrot's cage, a few feet from him, and he crouched in anticipation. Parrot, anxiously rustling about in his confinement, seemed to sense Tripod's presence. Tripod leaped for the cage. The three-legged cat tried to grab hold of the fitted cloth cover with one paw, but he fell to the floor and miraculously landed on his padded feet.

"Kathy said she wanted to go out with another guy while I'm away," Peter finally said.

"That was the letter you got today?"

"Yeah."

"'Dear John.'"

"What?"

"A Dear John letter. You're too young . . . it's when a girl wants to tell her boyfriend good-bye."

"She told me she loved me. We planned to get married when we got out of high school."

"Sorry, boy. Don't mean to give advice, but a boy your age should be going out with lots of girls, trying all the lollipops. Might be surprised at the flavors you'll find, and the flavors you'll like before you go making up your mind."

Peter's eyes widened. "What? Grandma, I love Kathy."

"Of course you do! And you'll love a half dozen more before you're through."

"Kathy's the only one I want."

"I know how you're hurtin' but it's not good when you get too serious at your age. I did, and I ended up on the wrong train most of my life. Life is big and wide open and we go lifting iron anvils on our young backs that grind us into the dust."

The cowboys had the desperados trapped in some big boulders and gun smoke hung in the air. Tripod made another grab for Parrot's cage, rocking it sideways before dropping to the floor, bringing forth angry croaks and squawks from the besieged bird.

"Guess it's a good thing I saddled up with your grandfather, though. You'd have never showed up if I hadn't."

Forgetting the Beverly Hills cowboys and their formula blank-cartridge drama, they watched Tripod try to figure another route to the birdcage.

"One day I found your grandpa comatose, lying right on this sofa." She gently patted the cushion beside her. "He'd taken a handful of pills with his booze and left me a note. All it said was don't send for help. That's all, after forty years together. Don't send for help."

"What did you do?" Peter asked.

"He was still breathing when I found the note. All my life I'd been trying to save him, but he never changed. Oh, he always claimed he would when he'd sober up and feel bad about himself. I was scared to death." Grandma slowly shook her head and looked at Peter.

"Picked up the phone and started to dial 911, but I put it down. Must have done that a dozen times, checking on him, going back to the phone. I cried and screamed at him, beat my fist on the wall. I was so scared and so angry. I wanted to get in the car and drive for hours, pretending I'd never found him or the note. Instead, I sat down beside him and held his hand while he finished the job."

Grandma wiped a hand across her cheek. "Don't know why I'm telling you this, never told a soul. It was the one time I could've really saved him and I didn't. Guess I thought it was best for him, that his life had become unbearable and that he honestly wanted out. I sat with him for half an hour before he quit breathing. They could hang me for murder."

The room took on a heavy silence despite the faint gibberish from a television ad, something about calling a 900 number to talk with a gorgeous woman if you were lonely, two dollars for the first minute and seventy-five cents a minute thereafter. Grandma watched for a moment, the flickering hues off the screen giving her jutting chin and furrowed face a somber cast.

"Should've called an ambulance . . . wish I had." She sighed. "You know, I had a mind to have his last words chiseled on his tombstone: Don't send for help."

Peter couldn't think of anything to say, though he wished he could. They both watched the persevering cat, perched on the windowsill, measuring the distance to the parrot's cage, calculating how far he could leap and what he would do with only one paw if he made it.

"I turned out like the cat," Grandma said.

Peter had no idea what she meant.

When she shuffled off to her bedroom, he sensed they had traded wounds. He wanted to say something to her, some offering, anything that might absolve her, but he came up empty.

"Good night, Grandma." She didn't respond.

When he turned off the TV, leaving the house in total darkness, he heard the cage squeak on its spring and the three-legged cat hit the floor.

CHAPTER 19

December blew into the broad valley between the Tobacco Roots and the Madison Range, dumping so much snow onto Willow Creek that the weather became the only topic of local television coverage and coffee-cup conversation.

The world took little note of the all-consuming preparations of six boys and their win-less coach. Actually, there were two coaches now, since Diana had appointed herself assistant and showed up every practice. She proved to be extremely helpful: scrimmaging on the court with the players, chasing, rebounding, whatever was needed.

Most important, Diana introduced the team to a stretching program so as to prevent injury. Sam realized he had been lax in that matter for the past few years, but it seemed ludicrous to stretch before going out and getting the mothballs beat out of you, like a caught-in-the-act rustler wanting to do his neck stretches before the vigilantes hung him. Diana checked their feet, knew how to properly tape a sprain, covered hot spots with moleskin, and recognized problems before they became serious. Her large first-aid box was crammed with tape, Tuf-Skin, Cold Spray, an ice pack, Tylenol, Rolaids, elastic wraps, spare mouth guards, extra socks, shoelaces, and even a spare jockstrap, anticipating youth's forgetfulness. Sam was grateful. He knew that an injury to one of his players would render their chances to win next to none, and it was comforting to have someone around who knew what she was doing.

GRANDMA CHAPMAN SAW Denise Cutter in the red pickup parked in front of the D & D grocery store in Three Forks. Grandma climbed out of her VW bus and knocked on the partially frosted passenger window of the battered Ford. "Hello, Denise. Your mom shopping?"

The girl turned her head and stared at Grandma with her summer-blue eyes. A thin string of drool hung from the corner of her mouth and soaked a spot on the shoulder strap that held her upright. She wore a brightly colored stocking cap and an oversized insulated jacket. Grandma opened the door and patted Denise's mittened hand.

"It's nice to see you. You look beautiful this morning."

Denise made a sound in her throat and Grandma nodded.

"I'll catch your mom inside. See you later, sweetheart."

Grandma shut the truck door and cautiously shuffled across the icy sidewalk. She found Sally Cutter in the produce section and noticed the skimpy purchases in her basket. The aroma of ripe bananas hung in the market.

"Morning, Sally."

Sally hadn't seen Grandma coming and glanced up, wide-eyed. "Mornin'. Didn't expect to see anyone today. Roads out our way are a fright."

"Talked to Denise. She looks so pretty today."

"Can't leave her home alone."

Grandma noticed Sally's weary face and realized she'd never seen this woman smile. Sally held on to the grocery cart and Grandma put her hand on Sally's arm.

"You doin' all right? Is there anything I can do?"

"No, thank you. Nothin' anybody can do."

"Is it terribly hard for you taking care of Denise?"

"It's not the caring that's hard."

"Is it the worry?"

Sally looked into Grandma's eyes with a plea for understanding. "It's God's way of punishing me."

"What on earth do you mean?"

"My girl is God's way of punishing me."

Grandma moved back a step. "If he'd wanted to punish you, he'd have put *you* in the wheelchair."

"Ooh, nooo." Sally's face twisted. "Don't you see? It's much worse if it happens to your children."

"Why, I wouldn't have anything to do with such a God," Grandma said.

"Don't you believe that the father's iniquity is passed down to the children and the children's children?"

"Not the way you're meaning it."

"That's what the Bible says."

"Sally, you can't believe that God struck down that precious child to punish you."

Sally Cutter gazed into Grandma's eyes as if out of a torture chamber, a woman being consumed in the furnace of her own guilt.

"I know exactly what I did," the woman said, "and my baby has to pay for it."

A young woman with two bundled children in her shopping cart pushed down the narrow aisle. Grandma stepped aside and lowered her voice as the shopper and jabbering youngsters passed.

"Well, I think you've got it all wrong. No one's paying for anything here. That little darling is God's gift to you, to all of us. You think about that. I won't hold you up any longer; that little lamb will be freezing out in the truck."

Grandma squeezed Sally's arm. She walked down the aisle and for a moment had forgotten what she had come for. All she could think of was what Sally could have done to believe she'd brought down that insufferable life sentence on her daughter's head as well as her own.

"PLEASE DON'T TELL anyone about Kathy's letter," Peter said one morning before school.

"I wouldn't do that, sweetheart," Grandma said. "It's nobody's business. Besides, she could change her mind again this afternoon."

"I just don't want the kids to know." He picked up his basketball, then hurried out the door.

Grandma held the door open and sent Tripod out. "Go on, catch up to him."

The tomcat bounded from the step and, in a lurching scamper, followed Peter in the morning's reluctant light. In the front room, Grandma lifted the cover off Parrot's cage.

"Hairy old bitch," he squawked.

Peering up the street in the half-light, she could still see them halfway to school, Peter dribbling the basketball, left hand, right hand, left hand, right hand, with the three-legged cat draped on his shoulders. It was as though all the people Peter loved had Dear Johned him one way or another. It would be too painful to have his classmates know, to see him abandoned as though he were lost baggage no one came to claim. He assumed a sweetheart in Saint Paul gave him some measure of value in their eyes and therefore a scrap of self-respect in his own. And so her grandson went off to school to fake it with his peers and pretend he still had an affectionate and devoted girlfriend languishing for his return to Minnesota.

Grandma turned from the window. She had faked it all of her life: that she was happy, that her life was in order, that it all meant something. And all this changed when she saw that brown fedora in the window and walked into that men's store and bought it. She pulled it on her head and never again valued herself by the opinion of others. She only wished that she had been strong enough to live her whole life that way.

She recognized the anger that drove Peter to pour himself lock, stock, and barrel into basketball. Whether he was on the way to or from school, cold or warm, he was always seen dribbling a basketball. And when he wasn't dribbling, he tucked it under one arm. She calmed her worry with the hunch that once her grandson released some of that anger in a basketball game and showed the town his skill, he wouldn't need any other credentials in the eyes of his peers, or in his own.

Wise enough to respect the wild forces of young love and old enough to fear that any minute her grandson might impulsively hop a Greyhound going east, Grandma suggested to Carter and Louella with deliberate subtlety that Peter might not be as taken as they were first led to believe. Dating a boy a grade below you was something to avoid in general, but Grandma suspected that Peter's sorrowful blue eyes might draw their affection like a sponge.

As the days passed, she encouraged Peter to take Trilobite out more often and do things with the juniors and seniors of Willow Creek High, grasping that a teenage boy is seriously hurting when he'd rather dribble a grubby leather ball than drive around in a cool VW bus with a bunch of spirited teenagers. She worried a little less one morning when she couldn't get the eggs out of the tray in the refrigerator door, breaking two in the process. She finally discovered Peter had set each of them on a drop of Krazy Glue the night before while she was absorbed in a *Waltons* rerun.

BOOK II

At five minutes to four, the team was loaded in the stumpy carrot-colored bus, a vehicle that appeared as though some enterprising mechanic had taken an acetylene torch and cut the back three fourths off an ordinary school bus and slid the rear axle forward. Rolling along the highway, it gave the impression that some kids were playing school. Besides the team and three cheerleaders, Grandma Chapman and Hazel filled out the roster, with Sam driving. The sixteen-passenger GMC was full, due to the fact that Hazel and Olaf each filled space designed for two.

Strapped in the driver's seat, Sam closed the doors. A chill slid down his spine. For the first time he was driving out to a game with a chance to win . . . no, it was more than that . . . he was daring to expect to win. He started the engine, revving it several times and the passengers let out a cheer.

"Be off, Rozinante, O great steed!" Sam shouted.

No one seemed to pick up on the name of Don Quixote's cadaverous horse, and they all remained silent. Diana sat directly behind Sam and she leaned forward to his ear.

"Nervous?"

"You ever read *Fear and Trembling*?" Sam said. "Kierkegaard wrote it just before he took his basketball team on the road."

Diana sat back and laughed. Sam wheeled a U-turn and headed out of town, honking as he passed the Blue Willow. Rip waved and shouted from the front porch rocker, camped beside the bicycle built for two, but Sam couldn't hear what he yelled with all the noise the bus made. As they headed north up the narrow highway, the Old Yellowstone Trail where pilgrims ventured generations ago, a tempest developed in Sam's stomach. With his young green horses, he was off on the adventure into the forest, off to do terrible combat with unknown forces and unexpected foes.

Behind him, Louella and Carter tutored Dean in the basics of English and algebra in an attempt to keep their one substitute eligible to play. Dean's enthusiasm for basketball had mushroomed while his interest in class work remained a dead seed in barren ground. Amid the hum of conversation and the girls drilling Dean, Sam caught Rob's voice above the others.

"Olaf, Carter and Louella wanted to know how *thick*"—Carter and Louella screamed and tried to reach back and prevent Rob from continuing—"the malts are in Norway."

"There are two hundred and ninety-three ways to make change for a dollar," Curtis informed them, out of the blue, as he was accustomed to do with information that had absolutely no bearing on the present conversation. Everyone but Olaf was laughing.

Nearly an hour later, darkness shrouded the valley as they left it behind, crossing the Bozeman Pass, descending into another valley, a little bus sallying forth, down into the dark uncharted night.

THE TEAM STRETCHED and warmed up in the Big Timber Civic Center, an all-purpose concrete building, where a basketball floor had been crow-barred in between the back wall and the stage. Front row bleachers, which ran along both sides, meant sitting with your feet on the playing floor, and where inattention could mean a trip to your orthodontist or chiropractor. Close to a hundred curious and buzzing spectators witnessed the Broncs displaying their power center. The six boys seemed terribly vulnerable in their faded gold and blue uniforms and distracting mixture of playing shoes, even though Olaf dunked the ball each time he approached the basket, to the utter amazement of the wide-eyed Reedpoint players.

Reedpoint was a small village much like Willow Creek, bypassed by the world's traffic out on the interstate, but they had accumulated several athletes from the larger Big Timber school district, boys who for one reason or another were moved by their families to the smaller Reedpoint system with its exemplary reputation. They had ten boys in uniform, six of them with several years experience, though their tallest was only 6'3", and their strong suit was a front line of three husky sandy-haired boys, Olson, Olson, and Olson, two brothers and a cousin, who could rebound and score.

A small covey of Willow Creekians gathered behind the players bench: the Johnsons, the Painters, Andrew Wainwright, and Curtis Jenkins' mother.

Axel complained that he couldn't get away from the inn on Friday night, so these few, with those in the bus, made up the total visiting delegation in this valley where the Boulder and Sweet Grass rivers give up their souls to the Yellowstone.

"All right, men, we're starting a new tradition tonight," Sam told them as they gathered at the bench. "After you shake hands with the other team at the end of the game, win or lose, we huddle up. I always felt bad last year when we straggled off alone. We're a team, and regardless of the outcome, we're in this together, and at the end of the game we walk off together."

AS SAM HAD asked, they walked off together—sweat-drenched, exhausted, and beaten. Again.

Sam stood at the far end of the civic center, waiting for the boys to shower and dress. He attempted to maintain his composure and manifest a posture that didn't give away the fact that he felt like an engineer who'd designed a prototype car that in its first public showing not only had the wheels come off, but the doors, the hood, and the roof as well.

On the ride home the cheerleaders attempted to coin small tokens of good humor. The game had been a colorful party balloon with a slow leak. Reedpoint had beaten them, 76 to 60, a score that looked much better than it was, with Olaf fouling out in the middle of the third quarter and only Rob and Peter keeping it respectable with their outside scoring. Still, they were going home again with the same tedious results, their flag in the road tar.

"I told you so," Sam had heard Hazel say to Grandma as they walked to the bus.

Crestfallen, Sam felt worse than he had over any of his long history of defeats because, for the first time, he had dared to believe. But they'd been thrown off the porch again, and this time he took it personally, as if he'd been thrown off with them, and this despite the effect he warned himself to stay detached. It was his job to send them up on the porch but not allow his heart to go with them. There were good signs, he reminded himself, as he guided their battered chariot along the freeway, and after all, it was only the first game for this newly molded team.

The highlight of the evening was Dean, leaping pell-mell to block a shot and landing on the stage behind the backboard. He slid out of sight under the heavy curtain. The crowd roared with delight and then went deathly silent as Dean failed to reappear. Sam guessed the boy was too humiliated to show his face when suddenly the stubby little freshman hustled out from behind the curtain and jumped down onto the court, an exasperated expression on his young face. The crowd applauded and the game went on.

Sam didn't want to admit it to himself, but Olaf, the linchpin of their hope, had been the shattering disappointment, not because of his performance as much as Sam's and everyone else's expectations. Sam made the same miscalculation that the whole community had: that merely because he was such a towering specimen he would be able to do well on the hardwood even though they all knew the fledgling had no previous experience with the American game.

Sam sighed. Now he had to ask them to turn around tomorrow and drive back to Big Timber to play Lavina, a team that had little height but several fast, experienced boys who loved to press you all over the court. Sam wondered how in less than twenty-four hours he could rebuild the scaffolding around Olaf's crumbling confidence—a confidence that he'd been nurturing for over three months. The somber exchange student brooded in a backseat and no one, not even Carter or Louella, attempted to break in on his solitude.

"We were diseased," Pete said.

"You got that right," Rob said.

"At least the score was close," Mary said. "That's a lot better than last year."

"Big deal, close is for losers," Rob said. "We lost."

"That's ninety-four in a row," Tom said. "Maybe we should go for a hundred."

Glumly visualizing a fresh dent in their already tarnished shield, Sam pulled off I-90 at Bozeman and parked at the Golden Arches supper club in hopes of feeding the team some McCheer and McLaughter.

Dean came out of a doze and realized where they were. "McDonald's!"

Sam turned to the subdued company and smiled as brightly as he could manage. "I believe it's time for some nourishment. And remember, men, we're out here to have some fun."

"So lighten up," Diana said.

"Bodacious!" Dean yelled and leaped from the bus when Sam swung the doors wide. It appeared that at least one warrior had forgotten their defeat, at least for the moment. Still enamored with America's fast-food champion, Olaf came out of his glum shell enough to add generously to the BILLIONS SOLD sign out on the Golden Arches. Miss Murphy sat next to Sam in a booth and the cheerleaders raised their eyebrows, elbowed each other, and giggled. Hazel ordered two Happy Meals and giggled. Sam felt exhausted and wished he could order a McMurphy to go. Tripod had a cheeseburger.

"Dean, where did you learn that impressive word?" Diana said.

"What word?"

"'Bodacious,'" Diana said.

"In fourth grade Mrs. Martin had us all pick a word from a list and said it would be our own very special word," Dean said. "She said we'd remember it all our life, and she was right."

"You haven't lived your whole life yet," Curtis said.

"What does it mean?" Carter said.

"It means 'outstanding and bold and remarkable,'" Dean said.

"Well you sure are remarkable, Dean," Diana said.

"That's what Mrs. Martin said," he responded. "It's the only thing from her class I remember."

"Can I borrow your word, 'bodacious,' some times?" Sam said.

"Sure . . . anytime you want."

ON THE LONG journey home, Sam felt all his energy drain away.

"Are you awake?" he said to Diana.

"Yes . . . fine, how about you?"

"I'm falling asleep, will you drive?"

"Oh . . . no . . . I couldn't drive this thing," she said, alarm in her voice.

"Sure you could, it's just a fat car. You just sit a little higher."

"I'll drive," Tom said.

"I don't doubt you could drive this contraption better than I, Tom, but I can't allow it," Sam said. "Has to be faculty."

"Drive, Miss Murphy," Louella said.

"No, no, please, I can't," Diana said. "Here, let me wake you up."

She moved up on the edge of the seat behind Sam and began massaging his neck and shoulders. It felt so wonderful he almost let go of the wheel in a swoon, never suspecting there was so much tension stored in those muscles. Her touch was so erotically therapeutic, another muscle began to stir.

"Does that help?" Diana said.

"Oh, God," Sam whispered, "I may just drive to Seattle."

Her hands worked wonders all the way to Three Forks, and as he turned off the freeway, he glanced in the wide rearview mirror to see that everyone but Diana was asleep.

"Thanks," he said. "That was great." And then, with his guard down added, "I haven't had a woman touch me in six years."

He caught himself and held his breath, not daring to glance into the rearview mirror and chastising himself for slipping. When at first Diana didn't respond, he looked up at her face in the mirror.

"Maybe we can do something about that," she said, a smile in her dark brown eyes.

CHAPTER 21

Sam had fallen into bed emotionally drained and physically exhausted and awoke Saturday morning at nine, thankful for a long, dreamless sleep. He found his cupboards bare when he tried to manufacture a breakfast of sorts and he knew he wasn't up to facing anyone at the Blue Willow, where optimism had sprouted like winter wheat. He felt as if he were sneaking out of town when he drove to Three Forks to replenish his meager supply of groceries.

When he came out of D & D grocery store with a bag of frozen TV dinners in arm, he spotted George Stonebreaker slogging toward him from across the street. His mind wanted to do a one-eighty back into the store but his body got tangled with indecision and caught out in the open. On the few occasions Sam had seen this hammerhead shark who preyed on lesser fish, Sam had always felt a tremor of fear. From what he'd heard and what he'd seen, George Stonebreaker was the personification of the madness, as if with purposeful intent it had found Sam hiding in this remote encampment.

Under a plaid wool cap and steel wool eyebrows, the surly man projected a contentious hostility that was as accommodating as a coil of barbed wire. From George's trajectory it appeared he had come from the bar across the street.

"Well, if it isn't our hotshot basketball coach." An old scar curled across Stonebreaker's upper lip.

"How are the Geldings doing down at the glue factory, Pickett? Win any games lately?" the hulking rancher roared out of his soiled sheepskin-lined Levi jacket. Sam caught a whiff of beer.

"Not yet," Sam said and attempted to continue on a beeline to his car. Stonebreaker cut him off.

"Not yet? not yet? Not *never*, Pickett! Don't you think you've wasted enough of my boy's time? He could be doing something worthwhile, like helping me put bread on the table."

"Tom told me that during the winter there wasn't—"

"Tom'd say anything to get out of a little work."

Stonebreaker crowded Sam back a step, and naked fear seized him by the throat. Stories of the men Stonebreaker had put in the hospital blinked like a neon sign in Sam's imagination.

"If you're not the lead sled dog, the view's always the same, Pickett, and you and your horseshit team are always looking at someone else's asshole."

With a meanness on his burnished-leather face, Stonebreaker backed Sam against the storefront. His only chance would be to get a knee to Stonebreaker's groin before the man made his move.

"You know my boy has a bum leg, could do permanent damage playing that damn game. You going to be responsible for that, Pickett? You going to pay the medical bills?"

Sam opened his mouth to explain, but the bully gave him no chance.

"I think it's time you tell my boy he can't play anymore, Pickett," he said, jabbing an ironlike finger into Sam's chest to emphasize each word, "or I'm holding *you . . . personally . . . responsible.*"

"You and Tom have to—"

Andrew Wainwright squealed to the curb in his white Lincoln Town Car and slid out quickly. As though he sensed Sam's predicament, he stepped up to George Stonebreaker and smiled with the confidence of a man who has a cocked .357 under his tailored topcoat.

"Morning, George. Hello, Sam."

He never took his eyes off Stonebreaker, sliding between the two of them and pressing the rancher back a step.

"You two look like you're having quite a discussion."

Sam was overcome with relief and gratitude, though he attempted to appear unshaken.

"Don't butt in, Wainwright," George said, "this isn't your—"

"I'm making it mine, George."

Stonebreaker puffed his chest and turned his eyes on Wainwright like the bore of a double-barreled shotgun. Andrew never blinked, revealing a cold steel side of himself Sam had never seen. He was surprised at how well

Andrew stacked up against Stonebreaker. He'd never considered the well-dressed executive's physical size, though he now realized it must be at least 6'2" and a leanly packaged two hundred pounds.

"You see, I don't take kindly to anyone crowding one of our teachers," Andrew said, with the menacing smile anchored on his face and his eyes riveted on Stonebreaker's. For a terrifying immeasurable interim the two men stared at each other unblinking, in a silence from some page out of the Stone Age, and Sam, unable to breathe, shrunk from the force field of their potential violence. Amid the terror Sam was impressed; Andrew stood like a man who had looked down the barrel of fear before. Finally, when Sam felt the atmosphere stand still—expecting the virulent explosion of human rage and fury, thudding skulls and cracking teeth—Stonebreaker backed off a step, then two. He paused and glanced at Sam.

"Remember what I said, Pickett."

Then he snorted and stomped off like an angry rhino.

Andrew put a hand on Sam's shoulder. "Are you all right?"

"Yeah, I always appreciate a madman getting my blood pumping to start the day," Sam said, attempting to smile.

"What did he want?"

"He wanted me to tell Tom he couldn't play basketball anymore, wants him to work or something."

"Well, don't worry about it. I'll take care of Stonebreaker."

Andrew half turned and glared up the street.

"Thanks, I'm really glad you came along."

"The boys didn't do too well last night," Wainwright said with a mock frown.

"I never realized you had the gift of understatement."

"Do you think there's any hope for the Norwegian kid?"

"I don't know," Sam said. "There's so little time and there's so many fundamentals he doesn't get."

"It really hurt when the boys scored from outside and it got nullified because he was camped in the lane."

"Yeah, and that's just for openers," Sam said.

"Well, you go get 'em tonight. I'll be there, and hopefully they've shaken the moths out."

"Or the butterflies," Sam said, realizing his stomach fluttered with a newly hatched swarm.

Andrew went into the grocery store and Sam scurried to the safety of his Ford. He kept an eye peeled for Tom's father while despising the garments of cowardice he wore, yet knowing he could easily give in to the madness and unleash the vengeance stored in the arsenals of his rage. He started his car and hightailed it out of Three Forks. For a fleeting moment he thought of buying a gun. *No, never give in to it, never.* It was Amy's voice he heard, clear and strong, and he felt ashamed.

SATURDAY NIGHT AT the Big Timber tournament had been more of the same. Diana massaged Sam's shoulders and neck on the way home before he could suggest she drive. Olaf and Curtis had fouled out and, playing four against five, Willow Creek fell to Lavina, 61 to 50. She sensed the disappointment in all of them, but more acutely in Sam, and as was her habit, she tried to make things better. When they were locking up the equipment late Saturday, she suggested they go out to eat Sunday night.

"Oh . . . ah . . . that would be nice," Sam said.

"How about the Land of Magic in Logan? I'd like to get away."

"Sure, that sounds fine."

"Okay, pick me up around seven. Do you know where I live?"

"Of course."

She turned his *of course* over in her mind on the way home. Was it the response of people who live in a small community and know about each other, or was it the response of someone who took a personal interest in someone? She caught herself hoping it was the latter.

SUNDAY NIGHT, SAM's headlights raked the deteriorating barnyard. He pulled up to the house and stopped, a once-thriving ranch site that had been left behind in the wake of modern expansion, the house a casualty, farmed out as rental property. Before Sam could get out of the car, Diana came bounding out of the house and into the front seat. She wore a white sweater and red skirt under her unbuttoned down coat, and beneath that crimson matador hat, her hair flowed freely over her shoulders, begging him to touch it. She planted herself next to him and smiled. Sam swallowed hard and was sure he caught a whiff of lavender soap.

"I'm starving," she said. "I could eat a horse."

"Well, good . . . let's go find a place that serves horse Wellington."

"Horse Cacciatore."

"Corned horse and cabbage," he said.

"Horse Newburg?"

They laughed and he drove out of the yard.

The Land of Magic was a renowned restaurant in the valley, sitting in the little village of Logan, a once-thriving community now bypassed by all but locals, sheltered in a rock gorge along the Gallatin River that was only frequented from the outside world by passing freight trains on their journey to somewhere else. The brown-stained log building hardly stood out among the other dozen or so dwellings along old Highway 10, once the main artery across southern Montana between Chicago and Seattle.

At a candlelit table along the log wall, they ordered dinner.

"This was my idea, the treat's on me," Diana said.

"Oh, that's good of you, but you don't need to do that."

"Is that hard on your male genes?"

"I don't know, I haven't had a woman offer to buy my dinner lately." He tried to laugh.

When the waitress left with their order, Sam said, "The shrimp here is terrific, some special batter."

"I love shrimp," she said as Sam relished the natural pout of her lips and the seduction of her throaty voice.

"Why didn't you order it?"

"I refuse to eat them."

"Why?" Sam tried not to stare.

"The shrimpers of our country refuse to use devices in their nets that would prevent the drowning of sea turtles. They say it's too much bother. It's my way of identifying with sea turtles, while they're still around. I'll never *bother* to eat anything that has shrimp in it until they *bother* to stop the unnecessary killing."

Her voice carried a weight he'd not heard from her before.

"Good for you, I think that's great."

Sam pushed his aviator glasses up on his nose and turned toward the kitchen.

"Ma'am!"

The middle-aged woman in a long Western dress and apron scurried to their table. She raised her eyebrows on her aiming-to-please face. "Yes?"

"I'm sorry to bother you, ma'am, but I'd like to change my order. Hold the shrimp. Give me, ah, the rib eye, medium well . . . no make that medium rare. Thank you."

The woman nodded and headed for the kitchen.

"You didn't have to do that," Diana said.

"I wanted to, I admire your stand."

"I've gotten seven people to quit eating shrimp."

"Eight," he said.

Throughout the meal he tried to concentrate on what she was saying and keep his eyes on her natural, unpainted face when they wanted to tippytoe the outline of her sumptuous orchard or trace the nape of her supple neck. She was ravishing in her soft, white sweater, and being with her sent testosterone mainlining through his body; he felt intoxicated, brave and strong and strangely happy.

" . . . and the birds are the only living descendants from the dinosaurs," she said as Sam caught up with the conversation.

"Have you seen the vultures?" Sam said.

"Yes, there were two more nests this summer." She nibbled on a radish. "Dean told me about them just north of his place."

"Are we going to keep him eligible?"

"I don't know," she said. "It'll be close all winter, but I'd sure miss him on our trips."

"Isn't he God's green creation?"

She nodded with her mouth full.

Sam finished the last slice of his steak. "You'll have to learn to drive the bus, those long trips—"

"No, I can't drive that thing," she said and laughed.

"Sure you can, there's nothing—"

"No! I don't *want* to drive it." She laid her fork on the table and looked into his eyes. "Do you understand? And please don't ask me to drive in front of the kids, it's embarrassing."

"I'm sorry, I didn't realize you felt so strongly about it."

"It's all right," she said, her voice calming. "It's just something I have to get over. I'm sorry I can't help with the driving."

Sam was puzzled, she drove her Volvo all over the country. But he recognized the worm holes in his own peculiar history and he let it go.

WHEN SAM PULLED into the unused barnyard he floundered in the ambivalence of his emotions. He wanted to prolong this time with her, dreaded saying good night and going home, and yet feared giving in to his attraction to her and becoming involved. Before he could turn off the ignition, she rescued him.

"Would you like to come in?"

"Ah . . . yeah, thanks."

Inside she took his coat and he began browsing through her front room. Her little farm house was a revelation: bookshelves crammed with volumes on birds and flowers and stars and insects and fish and mammals, a depository on nature, a museum of the earth's creatures, with dolphins and humpback whales and passenger pigeons adorning the walls. Sam moved from shelf to shelf, from painting to poster, completely astonished and deeply impressed with this biology teacher who had come out of nowhere to teach in Willow Creek, Montana.

"Now I see why you're always disappearing into the fields and woods," Sam said, perching on the edge of her deep-cushioned sofa.

"I didn't know anyone noticed."

She regarded him with the warmth of her dark eyes. Sam felt his face flush and he glanced away. She turned on her television and slipped a cassette into a VCR.

"You might like this," she said, settling on the sofa beside him. For nearly an hour Sam was fascinated by the documentary on the plight of the sea turtle: coming back to the beach where they were born after thirty or forty years to bury their eggs; the newborn, coming out of the shell and struggling for two days up through the sand, then racing across the beach for the ocean, instinctively knowing it was their home. Sam found tears blurring his vision as the little hatchlings, about the size of a silver dollar, touched wet sand and scrambled like Keystone Kops for the surging waves, swimming out into the vast ocean, going where? A species that has survived for millions of years was presently being slaughtered for food, jewelry, wallets, and knickknacks, their existence threatened and their future in doubt.

When the documentary was over, Diana put on a cassette, Mozart he thought, and she lit several candles, dowsing the lights. They sat on the sofa facing each other, Diana with her shoes kicked off and her legs folded under her red skirt. He'd fallen into his most farfetched fantasy. He pulled off his shoes and they swapped chapters of their stories like cross-legged traders at a Turkish market. With the scene meticulously set in flickering shades of possible passion, Sam—sweating out this delectable perplexity like answered prayer—hadn't a clue as to what was expected of him. His mouth went dry.

"Why are you teaching in Willow Creek?" he said.

"I'm an endangered species, hiding out in the backwaters of America. I'm not sure what I'm hiding from." She laughed. "But it feels right." She shook her hair back over her shoulder. "How about you?"

"I thought it would be . . . different, and I wanted to see the West."

Sam had long ago come to the conclusion that all of them had stepped out of the mainstream, into the calm, quiet backwaters of Willow Creek, to find refuge and healing, to lick their wounds and find some peace, to hide from life's capricious whims, to save their souls. But he kept it to himself.

"Ever been married?" she said.

"Once, a long time ago."

"What happened?"

"It didn't work out."

"I know about that," she said.

"You been married?"

"Yes . . ." She paused. "For six years."

"Any children?"

"We had a girl." She picked at a fingernail.

Sam sensed he'd touched a nerve but pushed on. "Is she with her father?"

"She died when she was four."

"Oh, God . . . I'm sorry . . ."

Diana cleared her throat. "Do you think there's some way we can get it into Olaf's head about the free-throw lane. I've looked at the stats and if we eliminated sixty or seventy per cent of his turnovers, we'd have won both games."

Glad she changed the subject, Sam said, "You're right, I've thought about that all weekend, his walking with the ball, three seconds in the paint—"

"And fouling," she said. "If he caught on to those three, he'd be some player. Right now he's a liability."

"That's it," Sam said. "How do we get it into his head in just a few days or weeks?"

"Brain implant," she said and he sensed she'd fended off a darkness.

He had the impulse to reach over and take her in his arms, to hold her closely and protect her from some self-inflicted wound he sensed she continued perpetrating in her mind. At the door she took him by surprise once more and leaned against him, zeroing in with dark liquid eyes.

"I've enjoyed being with you, you're different, I like you."

Sam swallowed hard and attempted to find something to say in the dizzy motion of his mind. Tentatively he put his arms around her waist. She brought her warm pouty lips to his. He pulled her close for a moment, feeling her breath in his mouth, her belly and breasts against him. Then, as the fierceness threatened to break loose within him, he stepped back as though some unseen hand had tapped him on the shoulder, warning him of three seconds in the paint.

"Thanks," he said. "I better go."

"See you tomorrow."

Sensing they had traded lies, Sam made his getaway, an owl gliding into the night who understood that the birds were the only living descendants of the dinosaurs. He lay in his bed that night, scared, muddled, confused, frightened to death that he could become deeply in love with this woman, the way he was with Amy. So deeply in love that he'd be utterly destroyed if he ever lost her.

CHAPTER 22

Monday morning Grandma Chapman felt the defeats seep into the daily routines of the townspeople like arctic drafts through worn-out weather stripping, bringing a chill to the bones, frost to the heart.

The hard-core pessimists of Willow Creek, those who had steeled themselves against any expectation of victory, accepted the weekend losses as part of nature's unremitting cycle, where winter winds eat snow, blow away topsoil, and bury dreams; where short bleak days and long lightless nights suck heat from the body, joy from the spirit; and where—as a part of this ceaseless tide—the basketball team limps through its foreordained itinerary of loss. These defectors dismissed the teams's failure with a few snide remarks about the games, and Olaf, the Norwegian oaf, and then summarily moved on to more significant matters such as government subsidies, subsoil moisture, and the price of heating oil.

But those townsfolk who had willingly or unconsciously allowed themselves a glimmer of hope caught themselves hurting again, having dared to believe: children standing along the siding, waiting for the circus train, hearing that it had been rerouted another way because of a washout and wouldn't be stopping here after all, the earned coins languishing in their pockets. Already tasting cotton candy, smelling roasting peanuts, and following elephants along the street in their minds, they had to turn for home and try to swallow the dried saliva of their expectations.

At the Blue Willow, Hazel strutted her prophecy to Grandma Chapman with I-told-you-so's, but after the ponderous woman had worked so hard at the scrimmages and personally identified with the team—misplacing over twenty pounds somewhere in the modest gym—Grandma Chapman recognized the note of hurt in Hazel's braggart voice and the disappointment in her nearly hidden hazel eyes. Leaning against the pie counter and bending Axel's ear, John English, who raised his ireful voice at obviously appropriate times, let all eavesdroppers know that if the school board had listened to him they wouldn't be going through the torture of another humiliating winter.

With her peach-colored hair in curlers that resembled the jet engines on a 747, Mavis Powers, who kept one eye on the post office through the front window, got in her two cents worth.

"One of these years we'll have a bunch of boys coming up through the grades."

"We should live so long," Hazel said.

"One of these years cows will fly," John said loudly.

Amos Flowers, who had furtively roosted in a corner of the bar, glided toward the front door under his inseparable Tom Mix hat.

"Well, the boys are getting good exercise," Mildred Thompson, a retired teacher, said in her sophisticated manner, as everyone casually noted Amos's passing, "and they're staying out of trouble."

"If we don't win this year," Grandma said, "we never will, with them about to shanghai our kids off to the Three Forks High School."

She watched as Amos momentarily hesitated by the door, squinting out into the street. Then he shuffled back through the dining room and said something to Axel, who nodded toward the kitchen. Behind the serving counter Grandma could see Amos's hat drifting through the kitchen until it went out of sight, apparently out the back door. Grandma turned and gazed out the front window. Nothing unusual. Only a green four-door sedan she didn't recognize across the street. She shrugged.

"This is the year, by God," Rip said with his toothless mouth.

"This is the year of lunatics," John English said from his leathery, suntanned face.

He cast an accusing glance at Rip and Grandma. Then he stomped out in his black going-to-town Tony Lama boots.

EVEN THOUGH THE losses were treated like relatives in the penitentiary, the stink of defeat drifted through the school hallways, contaminating any attempt at frivolity and lightheartedness. Sam bumped into Dean as the boy rushed up the stairs to the second floor before first bell.

"Good morning, Dean."

"Hi," he said.

His face glistened with sweat and damp ovals spread from the armpits of his faded flannel shirt. Sam couldn't help but wonder if that's what the exuberant freshman was referring to when Sam talked him into playing basketball, when the boy insisted that he stunk. Maybe it was glandular. It wasn't glandular that Olaf hung around after English class, and when they were alone, approached Sam with a pensive face.

"The basketball I am not playing," Olaf said firmly.

"Oh, I think you're doing well; you've come a long way. Those two losses don't mean much, we'll start winning."

"No, the basketball I am not playing."

"What do you mean?" Sam said, gazing up into the boy's remorseful expression. His blue eyes pooled with disillusionment.

"Myself a fool I am making; many mistakes I am making. Angry my father would be."

"That's no reason to quit, all the boys make mistakes. I made some lulues during the game. Heck, that's part of playing."

"In my country the word 'oaf' we are having."

"Okay." Sam paused. "Why don't you make them eat that word by the way you play."

"Making the fool I am not liking; I am, how you say, disgrace. The oaf I am at playing the basketball. Finished I am with it."

Sam slumped in his chair, dumbfounded, as Olaf ducked out of the room.

It was all coming unraveled, the vision he had seen, the hope he was tentatively considering to embrace, and his disappointment seemed bottomless. Had he misinterpreted the wink in destiny's eye, made too much of his quiet inklings, the silent whispers within? Had he been tricked into hoping again by the darkness?

In three short days this venture onto the high road had detoured hell-bent-for-leather into a bog. Sam's daring leap in the dark was slowly sinking into that familiar quagmire where losers try to spit the mud from between their teeth. His stomach felt like it had the time his stump-fingered neighbor started describing in vivid detail how he got his hand caught in the garbage disposal.

How would he face the team? Would Tom follow Olaf's desertion in light of Sam's bargain with him? He shuddered to think what would happen when the word leaked out—the Norwegian exchange student had given up his number 99 and wouldn't be suiting up for the Broncs, leaving the paint unguarded, exposed to enemy penetration and despoilment. Sam wanted to cry but he didn't dare open the head gate to that seething reservoir, and he had no outlet for the grief and sadness that washed over his heart. Without the Scandinavian hammer, his impossible dream turned into lutefisk.

THE BOYS STRAGGLED into the gym after school and, as was their routine, began shooting free throws until practice formally began. Grandma, Hazel, and Axel weren't due for another hour. Olaf's absence wasn't immediately felt, and when Diana appeared in the drab, untailored sweats that camouflaged her sweet but deadly arsenal, Sam gathered the team at midcourt, their expectations soggy yet still afloat.

"Olaf has decided to quit basketball."

Their startled faces and disbelieving eyes wounded Sam and he had to look toward the varnished bleachers for cover. Recouping slowly from the unforeseen blow to their sense of mission and team unity, they blurted their incomprehension.

"*Why?*"

"What happened?"

"How come?"

Sam glanced into Diana's face and found his own hurt and confusion reflected there.

"He doesn't seem to be able to handle the failure," Sam said, "making mistakes that are so glaringly obvious. He's much more sensitive than I realized. He's a stranger here among us and he's trying very hard to fit in, do his best. He just can't handle being laughed at or blamed for our losing. He heard someone call him an oaf."

"Screw those people," Tom said. "We want him on the team."

"We need him," Rob said with confusion gathering in his face.

"You might tell him that when you see him," Sam said. "Try not to be upset with him."

"Without him, we're toast," Tom said.

"You got that right," Rob said.

Sam pushed the glasses up on his nose and regarded Tom, whose anger and disappointment paraded nakedly in his face.

"I know you decided to play because of Olaf. We'll understand if you decide to give it up now."

The brawny senior held Sam's gaze for a moment. Then he glanced at his teammates. His chest heaved with a deep sigh and his eyes smoldered when he turned back and looked down into Sam's face. "I'm stickin'."

CHAPTER 23

That night Grandma Chapman steered clear of the kitchen while her tortured grandson suffered through the unbearable fires of young love. From her ripened vantage point she could write it off as puppy love, most likely one of many to come, but she understood that from his adolescent stance he faced the howling void of eternity alone. It was all she could do to keep from rushing headlong to his side and encompassing him in her scrawny arms, begging him to let go, to let it all go in this flow of life where we are altogether powerless to dictate outcomes.

She stared at the television and attempted to block out his impassioned pleas, his hanging on with shredded, bleeding hands, his heart laid out on the kitchen table as an offering, a sail left too long in hurricane winds. She could hear his desperate attempts to anchor himself to something shifting and fluid, unable or unwilling to give up his last fleeting connection with love and tenderness on the vessel that was his life where someone had given the order for all hands to abandon ship.

"If I come back for the second half?" Pete said. "That's just a month away."

He was quiet for a long stretch in the utter silence of rejection in which his girl undoubtedly gave reasons and explanations for the uncharted and illogical courses of the heart. Grandma felt the burning ache in her chest as though she were being forsaken, calling up buried apparitions of her own passage as a castaway.

"But I *can,* I can talk to Mom," Pete said.

A cold emptiness enveloped the kitchen as though the planet were hurtling out of orbit away from the sun and all living things were turning to ice. She leaned toward the kitchen with an ear that hated the human race at that moment, and she heard the last beseeching words.

"Please, Kathy . . . *please.*"

That wrenching appeal cut Elizabeth with the edge of a razor, a million

million voices supplicating in a swelling chorus down the thoroughfares of desertion, where the stench of burnt clothing and flesh arose as numbed fingers clutched at the rear bumpers of fleeing lovers over the blacktopped fields of love. It was the howling emptiness she remembered from her youth, when she loved Josh Kowalski more than life itself.

Josh was a year older in high school, played on the Brainerd football team, and she had loved him for a year before he ever asked her out. They went out twice. He never called her again, though she saw to it that she ran into him at school as often as possible. If he acknowledged her with a "Hi" she had enough to go on for another week. Then word leaked out that Josh had gotten Doris Wilson pregnant, and as horrible and disgraceful as that was back then, she'd never admitted to anyone how she wished it had been her he'd gotten pregnant, cried bitterly that it hadn't been her. Josh took off, leaving the school, Doris, and the town in the lurch. It took Elizabeth over a year to get over him. The only rumor she ever heard was that he'd been killed in Italy during World War II.

Grandma didn't hear Peter speak for more than ten minutes and figured he'd hung up or been hung up on. Finally she heard him move, pushing back a kitchen chair. When she stepped into the kitchen, she found her grandson fumbling on a jacket halfway out the back door with a basketball under one arm.

"Going out?"

"Yeah . . . I'm going to run."

She knew what was asked of her: to wrap her arms around him and rock him with all the love she had until dawn healed them both, but she couldn't make her legs move; she couldn't cross the worn black-and-white linoleum, and she despised her cowardly words of negligence. "Don't catch cold."

Peter ran into the grinding teeth of his inconsolable grief and Grandma hurried to the door and hollered.

"You're a tough, brave kid, Peter Strong!"

He had already gone too far and the wind hurled her words back in her face, unheeded.

FRIDAY NIGHT, WITHOUT Olaf in the lineup, Sam watched the team warmup for their first home game against Sheridan. At first Olaf wasn't even going to go to the game but the Painters, in their calm and comforting manner, convinced him there wouldn't be many there other than the students anyway, and they were right. You could throw a brick into the stands and not hit anyone.

Besides a smattering of local fans and the students, several carloads had come from Sheridan, a picturesque mountain town south of them where most of the boys came off well-established cattle ranches. And come they did. With an enrollment of around a hundred, the Panthers filled both their varsity and JV's with a full squad. Most of these schools suited up twenty to twenty-four boys between their varsity and JV's, and they had mixed feelings when they saw Willow Creek come up on their schedule. Though it meant an easy win, it also meant there would be no JV game for the younger boys.

Hazel Brown ran the scoreboard and clock and Mavis Powers, with her hair in curlers, kept the official game book.

Without Olaf dominating the paint, Sheridan employed a straight man-for-man defense, often double-teaming Rob and Pete and allowing Dean to run free once they assessed the freshman's inability. Pete played as though they had killed his dog. It wasn't that the other boys weren't going hard, but Peter was trying to beat them single-handedly. Sam was puzzled because he didn't regard Pete as a kid who was out for personal glory.

"C'mon, we gotta beat these guys," Pete shouted during a timeout.

"Work a play out there," Sam said and looked into Pete's dripping face. "I haven't seen one good pick, one good screen. Don't forget what we've practiced, and have some fun out there."

At halftime, Rob played the drums and Curtis the trumpet as the band entertained the spectators with a peppy march and the Willow Creek fight song, to which no one sang along. Sam had cringed when the band—comprised of more grade school kids than high school—played the National Anthem before the game, out of key, faltering, pausing at times as though someone had run off with their music.

The way the band played turned out to be an omen of how the game would go. At times it seemed as though the Willow Creek fans had been hit with an epidemic of narcolepsy. The cheerleaders tried to create noise by example, urging the team on with straining vocal cords and youthful enthusiasm, making more racket than all the spectators combined. There wasn't what you could call crowd noise but rather sporadic bursts, singular eruptions of support and encouragement, recognizable voices over the nominal noise of the game, though at times they got together on a bad call. When your team's been losing there are lots of bad calls.

"Get your cataracts removed!" Rip shouted.

Axel Anderson, who had managed to slip out of the inn for the second half, rooted on his adopted boys with a cannonlike voice along with the Johnsons and the somewhat inhibited Painters. Amos Flowers had appeared, and he hung from his Tom Mix hat in the stands with a confused expression, as if all that talk about a giant Norwegian had been a cock-and-bull story.

Truly Osborn, who felt it his duty to appear at home games to monitor the behavior of his faculty and students but deemed it a waste of his valuable time to travel to the remote mountain towns to witness the slaughter, remained properly reserved in the bleachers, considering it uncultivated to shout and cheer and make a spectacle of himself. Andrew Wainwright, both proper and cultivated in his designer jeans and sports jacket, shouted and cheered loudly without making a spectacle of himself, personally identifying with the team as much as any of them.

In the fourth quarter, after Dean fouled out, Peter picked up his fifth foul, and Willow Creek finished this game of attrition three against five, saddled with their ninety-sixth consecutive loss.

The teams formed their customary lines and walked past each other, shaking hands in a display of sportsmanship in what had become the final effigy of disparagement for the Willow Creek boys. Sam hurt more than he would have expected, again politely accepting the winning coach's *Nice going, your boys played hard.*

In the locker room Sam slapped the boys' sweaty backs and assured each of them they had done their best. As luck would have it, on his way out, he met Olaf near the doorway to the locker room, the overgrown foreign student gathering poise to say something to the team.

"Did you see them out there!" Sam said. "Those boys aren't afraid of making mistakes."

A primitive anger arose from his belly and found its voice.

"You know, Olaf, it's far better to try and end up looking like a fool, than it is to sit on your ass in the bleachers. Do you know *how long* some of those boys have been trying? Can't you see the floor burns on their hearts? Don't you see, it's when you quit trying that you become the oaf. I'm proud of those boys. *They* never quit."

"Ya, good they are doing." Self-reproach clouded Olaf's pale face as he gazed silently out of troubled blue eyes.

Sam stomped away feeling the heat in his nostrils. It felt good, and he suddenly experienced a renewed pride in his boys. With only five players and with Dean and Curtis starting, they made a game of it for a while against a good Sheridan team. But, like the famous Dutch boy, Dean had to hold his finger in the dike all night long and it was asking too much of him, the water pressure too great, and finally the sea came, washing them away, only a Norwegian arm's length from dry ground.

THE LAST TO leave the school, Tom, Pete, and Sam dragged up the middle of Main Street through the slumbering town like warriors leaving a field of battle where their army had been soundly thrashed, their horses killed, their weapons lost, bearing the wounds and defeat of the day. They slogged the four blocks to the Blue Willow with vague hopes that they might find balm for their bruised spirits and a word of cheer at the inn. Sam had tried to put the menacing threat of George Stonebreaker out of his mind, but he caught himself keeping one eye peeled for the brutish man's pickup.

Inside the teenagers gravitated to a table where Rob and Mary sat glumly with Carter and Louella. Sam made a quick check of the half-filled watering hole in hopes he'd find Diana, but she wasn't there. Just as well. After condolences from a few of the faithful, he found a small table on the tavern side and sagged into a chair.

Damn! They were right where they were last year, and the many years before, 0–3.

He considered having a beer, but he didn't like it that much and he wanted to respect the training rules of his underdogs, so he had a Mountain Dew on the rocks. He'd drink alone.

John English stood at the bar with a few men who hadn't been at the game. "Who won the game?" the middle-aged rancher called over to Sam.

Sam regarded him calmly and didn't answer. *Screw you.*

John knew who won the game. Just because he's on the school board Sam didn't have to take his crap. What could he do, fire him?

"Sheridan," Axel said from behind the bar, picking up on John's sarcasm, "in a damn close game that we almost won with only three players."

"Is that our motto this year, 'Damn Close'? Last year it was 'Almost' and the year before it was 'We're Toast.'"

The gang at the bar laughed and Sam looked away, into the dining room where three of his boys were licking their wounds. He didn't notice Grandma coming up on his blind side. She leaned close to him with one arm propped on his table, one around his shoulder, and her eminent chin close to his ear.

"Don't pay those turncoats any mind," she said. "I want to thank you for keeping the faith with these boys. I have a message for you."

Like a lover she clandestinely shoved a folded piece of paper into his hand. Then she stood, throwing out her chicken-bone chest.

"Axel, how do you stand the sewer gas building up around that bar?"

She pulled the brim down on her hat and swaggered back to the dining room. The men at the bar rumbled and muttered unintelligible responses. Sam wasn't sure if he should reveal the secretive note in the presence of others. He left his coat and drink and stepped out onto the front porch where the bicycle built for two rested against the wall in the shadows. Unfolding the cheap tablet paper and holding it out to catch the light, he read the pencil-scrawled note aloud.

Even youths shall faint and be weary,
    and young men shall fall exhausted;
but they who wait for the Lord shall
    renew their strength,
they shall mount up with wings like eagles,
they shall run and not be weary,
they shall walk and not faint.

Sam folded the note and tucked it into his pants pocket, gazing down the deserted blacktop toward the school. What did that mean, how do you wait for the Lord?

Wasn't ninety-six losses in a row waiting enough?

⮜ CHAPTER 24 ⮞

Sam woke with a bad taste in his mouth that had nothing to do with the failure of his Crest toothpaste or last night's loss to Sheridan. It originated from the knowledge that he—like most of the Willow Creek community—had laid the blame for that defeat, as well as the first two, at the feet of the polite, unassuming visitor from across the Atlantic.

He fumbled with his razor and removed the night's silent increment, but he couldn't remove the nagging truth that reflected back at him from the water-spattered mirror. He had used the exchange student, or attempted to, in pursuit of his unspoken yearning to turn his life around, the coinage to buy a pittance of satisfaction and triumph. He pulled on his sorry running shoes and knew he had to right the wrong, to make amends. In the snow-sodden gravel he ran almost two miles before gasping to a walk across the rusting iron bridge, rehearsing his contrition both going and coming.

SAM PARKED IN the farm yard. On his way to the house, he spotted Olaf and Mervin out behind a machine shed and he turned toward them through the trace of snow. They were unloading railroad ties from a flatbed and stacking them against the shed, their yellow cotton gloves blackening with creosote. Olaf was a caricature of a homeless refugee, appearing gaunt in a bulky, oversized brown canvas coat, its sleeves halfway up to his elbows, a brown wool cap with ear flaps flopping, high-water overalls shrunk halfway up his calf, and huge mud- and manure-caked galoshes. Mervin, in his usual garb, noticed Sam first and paused with their work.

"Mr. Pickett, what brings you out this way?" Mervin said, removing his right glove and shaking Sam's hand.

"I'd like to speak to Olaf for a minute, if it's okay."

Olaf looked perplexed, as if he expected another improbable assault from his former coach. Sam caught the mixed aroma of wet gravel and creosote.

"You two go right ahead. We need a break," the rancher said. "If I had the brains I was born with I'd have hauled these in my dumpbed, wouldn't have had to manhandle 'em."

Sam noticed a gamesmanship among these people where they would put themselves down, a casual banter depreciating themselves, either as a true reflection of their own lack of self-worth or as a subtle way to beat anyone to the punch who might find fault with them. Mervin, without the brains he was born with, nodded at Sam and footslogged toward the house, his unlatched overshoe buckles clicking rhythmically.

Sam paused and regarded his former player. Olaf patted his gloves together nervously and shifted his weight from foot to foot, avoiding any eye contact.

"Olaf, I've come out here to apologize to you. I had no right to call you a quitter. You agreed to try basketball and if it didn't work out to let it go. That was the deal, and you stuck to it." Sam tried to find Olaf's eyes, hidden behind the visor of his cap, his head turned to the ground. "I was mad at myself and the team—no, not the team—the *losing*, the sorry-ass losing, but I took my anger out on you. That was wrong. I'm sorry."

"It is good . . . okay. The team I am helping by not playing. Without me last night good they are doing."

"Anyway," Sam said, "thanks for giving it a try. I'm sorry it didn't work out."

Sam offered his hand. Olaf took it in the creosote-stained glove and they shook hands. With a glance, Sam found sorrow drifting down from the boy's face like house dust in a shaft of sunlight.

"How do you like working on the ranch?" Sam said as he stepped back a pace, wanting to soothe Olaf's grief but feeling helpless.

"Working? Oh, adventure sometimes it is. The tractor I am driving and the bales loading when the cattle we are feeding."

Sam smiled up at the overgrown kid, his straw-colored hair splayed from under the ear-flapped cap, his boyish blue eyes peering from his perplexed face, a stranger in their land making his way the best he knew how, and Sam let him go. He climbed off the young Norwegian's shoulders and climbed into his car. Without looking back he drove away, a weight of sadness in his chest. Out on the highway he found creosote stuck on his hand.

He drove west with no destination in mind and tried to hold off the memory that visited him mercilessly whenever he suffered a loss. He'd attempted to erase it from his brain cells since he was a kid but it had been indelibly imprinted, and without his permission, at the worst of times, it reared its horned head.

Since he was a boy he believed that somehow he got off on the wrong foot in life and could never quite get back in step. And it always seemed to be epitomized by that fateful day in August when he was ten, as though it were the gods' way of foretelling him what to expect down the pike, a landmark event that colors all that follows, an undeniable motif in the pantomime that his life had become.

They were at the state fair, and after tagging along behind his parents for what seemed like hours through machinery displays, food and craft exhibits, and 4-H stock, Sam had to pee with great urgency. He'd been well trained to never use the word "pee," nothing that crass allowed in the Pickett family household, although "urinate" seemed to be acceptable with a minor frown. Sam let them know he had to "go to the bathroom" in a hurry. In the midst of long rows of gaming booths and food tents, they spotted several of those temporary green fiberglass outhouses sitting in the blazing sun.

"Don't use those filthy things," his mother said. "Wait until we get to the Horticulture Building where they have decent bathrooms."

But Sam insisted he couldn't wait and with his father's support was given permission to relieve himself. He always wondered why he chose the one he did, as if at that point he still had some free will over his destiny. With his bladder about to burst, he stepped into the first one available, latched the door, and unzipped his pants. It was ten or fifteen degrees hotter inside and the foul odor swarmed up and all but strangled him with its humid, suffocating reek. The cesspool was nearly full and that disgusting deposit starkly visible. He held his breath and, with the pressure of a young horse, finished in seconds. He shook off his penis and was tucking it in when the world tipped over!

A beer truck backed a foot too far, felling the fiberglass privy like a tenpin. In an instant Sam was flung backward onto the door, which was now flat on the ground, and onto him, as though in slow motion, came sloshing a great tidal wave from some vile sea of human excrement, washing over him and clinging to him with its nauseous stinking slime.

Terrified, he began spitting and gasping, trying to get up but slipping and sliding on the human filth that drenched him from head to foot. He kicked and pounded on the side of that putrid coffin in which he was sure he would die. In the eerie green light the sun projected through the fiberglass, he pulled off whatever was sticking over one eye, a bloodied gauzelike thing he didn't recognize as anything more than the gore of the human race.

Bystanders finally rolled the tomb on its side and Sam flopped out, kicking and retching like a rotting fish, a Lazarus who had spoiled. He sprang to his feet with toilet paper and all manner of filth clinging to his clothes and skin and he couldn't stop throwing up.

He'd never forget the loathing horror in the eyes of the people around him, their hands over their mouths and noses, the voice of the teenage girl who kept shrieking, "Oh, gross! Oh, gross!" as they backed away. Nor would he ever forget the humiliation hurled on him by those who joked and laughed.

His mother stepped toward him to help and at once backed away with her hands held up in front of her in fluttering indecision.

"Oh, Samuel, you've gotten it all over yourself."

His father took his hand and, with the Hamm's Beer truck driver—from the land of sky blue waters—led him across the street, away from the nauseous crowd. The driver found a hose behind one of the fair booths, and with Sam standing over a sewer grate beside the curb, shivering, the two of them hosed him down, the cold water washing the world's shit out of his hair and ears and pockets, back into the world's cesspool.

"I'm really sorry, kid, I'm really sorry," the delivery man kept saying. "I have an accident-free record, I don't know what the hell happened."

Sam felt at fault somehow, standing there being publicly cleansed, as though he'd done something wrong, as though he should have picked a different outhouse or waited as his mother had urged, silently chastising himself that there was something he could have done to prevent this. He lived his childhood like that—when he hadn't done anything wrong, still afraid his parents would find out, ever vigilant, always on guard. To this day he realized there was a kid in him who still accused and denounced him for being so stupid.

All of it didn't wash off that day, down the sewer. Something stuck to him and he carried it with him still, though he could never quite identify what. As he grew up he would catch himself, when something went wrong in his life, thinking, If only I hadn't gone in that goddamn shithouse. From that day on, he became a boy who—like primitive homo sapiens listening for a snapping twig—always kept one ear cocked for the howling transmission of a backing beer truck. He remembered wondering as a boy, *Who* had sent that truck? and he didn't mean someone from Hamm's Brewing Company.

A few days after he lost Amy, the memory of the fair came crashing in on him late one night. From then on his nightmares were not only occupied by maniacs with shotguns, but, in those insane shrouded scripts, vile and tipping outhouses.

With the detachment time brings, Sam tried to remember the whole incident with humor, to defuse its curse. What the hell, so he was in a latrine when it got knocked over, big deal. Most people would respond to his story with laughter, what a joke, hooray for the truck driver!

But sometimes, like now, driving through the Jefferson canyon, when he tried to regain his balance after a setback or dared to entertain dreams, he could subtly smell the obscenity of that August afternoon, vaguely sense a beer truck backing.

They had two games coming up fast, with Christmas vacation beginning Friday. Tuesday they played at Harrison, a small town twelve miles south that also depended on far-flung ranch sites for the survival of their school and team. Thursday they took on the Lima Bears at Willow Creek. He would knuckle down and do everything he could to prepare his five players. With hard work and a lot of luck, they might win a game yet.

He attempted to let it go, feeling better about the whole incident with Olaf Gustafson, yet wishing he had never talked him into trying, never seen the towering boy dunk a basketball, never allowed himself to get his hopes up and dare to dream such lofty thoughts, but he couldn't prevent those images of the young gangling giant from lapping up against the shore of his memory, couldn't wash the creosote off his heart.

Inexplicably, even in the face of the Norwegian's desertion, Sam heard a faint refrain of promise somewhere in his head. Hope, like a creditor, held him by the lapels of his soul and wouldn't let go.

CHAPTER 25

Olaf picked at his food and only spoke in response. He ate Sunday dinner with the Painters in the neatly cluttered dining room amid the knickknacks, frillery, and fine bone china that Mrs. Painter obviously hadn't found at a flea market or one of Hazel Brown's yard sales. Pieces with the names Lenox, Pickard, and Royal Albert overran their home, causing him to wend his way cautiously through the front rooms, narrowly avoiding catastrophic probabilities.

Olaf enjoyed amazing the female-producing couple with the quantity of food he packed into his tall, narrow frame, but today, with a seasonal chinook—a warm snow-eating wind—humming overhead, he had no appetite and the Painters eyed him with concern.

"You mustn't let basketball get you down," Mrs. Painter said. "We're used to losing around here and everyone will soon forget all about it."

"To me, says my father: A thing do not be doing if excellent you cannot be. Expecting the top grades, one hundred per cent."

He glanced into Mrs. Painter's soft, motherly face.

"My father I am not telling the basketball I am playing. Am I winning he would be wanting to know."

"I think the boys around here want to play for the fun of it," Mrs. Painter said in her melodious voice as she subtly nudged the gravy toward Olaf. "Goodness knows they don't do very well, but we've all accepted that. We want them to win, but we know they won't, and life goes on just the same."

"The quitter I am not wishing to be, but making them to be losing the game I am."

"Don't you fret about it," Mrs. Painter said. "In a few weeks they'll forget you ever tried. You get back to enjoying your time here. Have some more potatoes."

But Mr. Painter wouldn't leave it lying there on the dining room table.

"I have an older brother who ranches over by Churchill. We get together every Monday at a cafe in Manhattan with some other ranchers and when the basketball season comes, my brother always suckers me into betting on the games between Manhattan Christian and Willow Creek. I don't want to but I always do, praying for a miracle. Then, the next Monday, after we've gotten the stuffing kicked out of us, everyone in the café laughs and makes fun of Willow Creek."

Mr. Painter paused and Olaf caught a glimpse of pain in the rancher's weathered face.

"I have to sit there and take it. I pretend not to care, but it gravels me, especially when my big brother jabs his finger in my face like he used to when we were kids. I just sit there and try to smile, but I *hate* it!"

Mr. Painter snatched the linen napkin out of his lap and threw it down on the table.

"I sit there and pray that somehow, some day, Willow Creek will stand up and beat the shit out of Christian."

"Mervin!" Mrs. Painter held a hand over her mouth.

"Beat the *shit* out?" Olaf said. "Oh . . . ya." He couldn't prevent a smile from elbowing into his gloomy mood.

A knock on the kitchen door startled the three of them. With the constant drone of the wind they hadn't heard the crunch of gravel under tires in the driveway. Mrs. Painter dropped her napkin on the table and scurried out of the dining room. After a minute she came back beaming.

"Olaf, there's someone to see you."

He didn't move.

"Who is coming?" he asked, figuring it might be Louella or Carter or both.

"I guess you'll just have to come and see," Mrs. Painter said with a giddy grin.

Reluctantly Olaf unfolded himself from his chair and ducked through the doorjamb on his way to the kitchen. Immediately he started, stumbling back on his heels and nearly wiping out a shelf crammed with china cups and saucers. He had been partially right: Carter and Louella stood in the large white kitchen wearing happy smiles, but along with them was the entire student body of the high school, eighteen strong, including Susan Bradley, who had the flu, out of her bed to make it happen. Beholding the sea of laughing eyes and animated faces, Olaf, astonished and bewildered, lost his tongue in either language.

Rob stood in the front line as their spokesman, his curly black hair tousled from the wind. "We want you back, Olaf, we need you, we can't do it without you," he said, and then everyone chimed in: "Yeah, we miss you, we want you on the team!" "Yeah, please come back!" "We don't care how good you play!"

They paused, and the jammed kitchen fell silent. Tears streamed down Olaf's cheeks and he quickly attempted to wipe them away.

"Wanting me you would be when I am losing the games?"

"Yeah!" they hollered in chorus. "We want you back."

"Stick it in their ear!" Tom shouted.

"*You* don't lose the games," Rob said. "We're a *team*."

A silence wedged itself between Olaf and the students for an awkward moment. Then Carter ventured into the emotional vortex. "We love you even if you play like an oaf," she said, tears in her puppy-dog eyes.

They stood facing each other for a long, uncomfortable pause, Carter's words hanging in the air. Mr. and Mrs. Painter fretted mutely beside him as Olaf glanced into the expectant faces of his classmates. He realized that they cared about him for more than what he could contribute to the team. They were inviting him to be a part of their lives. They knew he played very badly and they didn't care. That was something brand new for him, something fresh and bright. He struggled to swallow the sentiment clogging his throat, and forced the words out into the utterly silent kitchen.

"At the basketball then I could be playing."

"Does that mean you'll play?" Rob asked.

"Translate, translate, you crazy Norwegian," Pete said.

"Ya, I be playing."

"*Yeeaaahhh!*" the students erupted, jumping up and down, hugging one another and trading high fives. The team members started it, but the other students caught on quickly, and the chant went up through the kitchen ceiling, out through the cedar shake roof, carried by the mountain winds across the valley and beyond, warning all who would pay attention that their flag had been unfurled and was rippling in the winter gusts once again.

"Oaf! Oaf! Oaf! Oaf! Oaf! Oaf! Oaf!"

Olaf felt the warmth of their acceptance and affection, and he raised a fist high into the air, knocking a figurine of a man on a horse crashing to the floor.

"Oh, so sorry," he said and he stooped to pick it up.

Having a shorter distance to go, Mrs. Painter beat him to it and retrieved the broken porcelain, now in two pieces. The rider had lost his horse.

"It doesn't matter, it's a dime-store piece," she said, carefully placing her broken Royal Doulton on the counter. "How would you all like a dish of ice cream?"

THE WHOLE SCHOOL—EXCEPT Susan Bradley, who went out and threw up in Carter's pickup—ate ice cream at the Painters' Sunday afternoon, demolishing a three-gallon tub of butterbrickle. Mervin examined the horseless rider and thought it was a sign: the Norwegian hammer would knock others from their horses. Mervin grinned and thought of his brother.

SAM SHOVED FROZEN Tombstone pizzas in the oven and made a perfunctory effort to straighten the front room in anticipation of the arriving team. He had called a voluntary session, determined to do everything in his power to prepare them for their next combat with the hope that they could still win a game or two during the season.

He was glad when Tom arrived first because he'd been anxious to ask him about his father ever since their confrontation in Three Forks. When they had settled in the cluttered front room, Sam leaped into the momentary silence.

"Ran into your dad Saturday. . . . Seemed pretty steamed about your playing basketball."

"He's usually steamed about something. He'd have booted me long ago if he didn't need me to get the crop in this spring."

"Does he make it hard for you at home?"

"Sometimes. You can never tell what mood he'll be in. I avoid him most of the time. If I see his truck, I don't go home. He's out drinkin' a lot. Don't worry about him. I'm really on my own and there's no way he can stop me from playin'."

Sam's imagination ran wild when he thought about what George Stonebreaker might be capable of doing. In some measure Tom was playing in defiance of his volatile father, and it had little to do with Sam's attempts to motivate him with lofty visions of what the team might accomplish.

The other four boys arrived together, extremely cheerful and boisterous, causing Sam to wonder if they didn't care that they had lost their first three games—not to mention all realistic expectations of winning any others—and had succumbed to the infection of failure. He served up pizza and Pepsi, and pick-and-rolls on the television screen, sensing a preoccupation with the boys, a lack of concentration, as though they watched halfheartedly when he pointed out individual moves for each of them.

"Rob and Tom, see this: they isolate on the side. Tom, you come up and put a body on Rob's man. Now, see that, see that."

Sam rewound the tape and showed it again, Magic Johnson and James Worthy running the pick-and-roll.

"You play it by ear. If they switch, Tom, you back off straight for the hoop and Rob fires you the ball for a layup you've got them no matter what they do. Watch it again."

Sam reversed the tape and ran it again, becoming irritated with their lack of focus. Damn it, didn't they have any heart for it left? He noticed the boys exchanging glances as though they knew the house was on fire and he didn't.

Heavy knocking sounded at the door, and Sam stopped the tape and flipped his clipboard onto the floor. He regarded the boys, who were smiling slyly and ducking their faces. He pushed himself out of the chair, upset that someone had disturbed their concentration and interrupted their practice session, especially when the boys were already unfocused.

On his way to the door an alarm went off in his stomach. George Stonebreaker! Could it be that brute standing at the door looking for Tom? When he inched the door open, Sam was startled. It looked like Olaf standing on the darkened porch, and Sam blinked at this Norwegian apparition, thinking at first it was a figment of his imagination.

"Olaf!" Sam said, unaware that the team had moved to the door behind him.

"Ya, hello."

"What are you doing here?" Sam said.

"Dunking the basketball I am coming for. That is allowed."

"Yeah!" the team shouted.

"You're going to *play*?" Sam said.

"Ya, yamming I am thinking to do."

"Jamming! *Jamming*!" Tom shouted, "you seven-foot cob."

Sam stood with astonishment catching in his throat, stunned into a momentary immobility. Then he gathered his senses and capitulated to a giddy lightness of spirit.

"Come in, come in, we have a lot to do before Tuesday."

Sam shut the door and followed the six boys into the front room. "Gee, if I knew you were coming, Olaf, I'd have bought five more pizzas."

They huddled around the TV in earnest, a joyful glow in their young unshaven faces reflecting a common warmth in their hearts. They were back together and they had dreams to chase.

⌒ CHAPTER 26 ⌒

Diana was surprised by Andrew Wainwright as she poked around in the grocery store in Three Forks. She had been trying to decide between a frozen TV dinner or throwing together some stir-fry, but realized her heart wasn't in either.

"I saw you through the window," he said, looking elegantly out of place in his gray three-piece worsted suit and tasteful soft orchid tie. "What are you up to?"

"Oh . . . just trying to decide on something to fix for dinner. I'm like a kid in a candy store. Some day I'll starve to death in a supermarket making up my mind."

"I was on my way to Bozeman for a steak. Why don't you join me?" He smiled warmly, and his invitation caught her completely off guard.

"Oh, no. I . . . maybe some other time."

"I'm going to eat alone and you're going to starve, so it's fate." He held his hands out in a supplicating gesture. "Come on, a steak and some good conversation."

She glanced down at her embroidered muslin skirt and bulky white Angora sweater under her open gray quilted down coat as if to recall what she was wearing. "I'm not dressed . . ."

"From where I'm standing you look good enough to go anywhere and stand them on their heads."

"Well . . ."

"Good, now all you have to decide is rare, medium, or well done."

He opened the passenger door of his white Lincoln for her and she slipped into the leather interior. As he drove out of town, she felt like Dorothy, suddenly no longer in Kansas, in a whirlwind swooped from the D & D grocery store, flying down the freeway in a luxurious Town Car with one of the most gorgeous eligible men in five states, and she hadn't a clue as to what was expected of her.

When he told her to buckle up, she pulled the seat belt across her lap and slipped the metal tongue into her purse. She didn't notice what she'd done until halfway to Bozeman and was too embarrassed to correct it, hoping he'd never notice. She managed a calm front while her stomach was doing a song and dance.

He was as calm and at ease as she'd always found him in their brief social exchanges, and she realized she'd never been alone with him, not even for a minute. A mixed aroma of leather and something she couldn't name embraced her, a sensuous, male scent. Whatever it was, she decided someone ought to market it.

"I insist on going Dutch," she said, checking him out as he drove, his graying temples, strong, square jaw, and obvious self-confidence.

"If that's what you want. But I'm on the school board and I know what you're making and I see nothing wrong with taking our underpaid assistant basketball coach to dinner for a little encouragement and good cheer." He laughed lustily with a deep resonance from the center of his chest.

"Well, we could all use some of that. Losing last night at Harrison was so disappointing, so exasperating."

"We came close," he said.

"Coming close is even more maddening. I don't know what got into Pete."

"He had a lot of turnovers," he said, glancing over at her in the dark interior of the Lincoln.

"Turnovers, forced shots, unfocused . . . not the kid I've seen in practice for a month."

"When Olaf fouled out I figured we were out of it, but the other boys really put up a scrap."

Traffic on the freeway was sparse and the lights of Bozeman grew brighter at the east end of the valley.

"That's our real problem: getting Olaf out of the paint in three seconds and teaching him not to shuffle his feet. If we could do that we'd be winning games."

"And keep him in the game," Andrew added. "He's too gung ho on defense, tries to block every shot. I imagine it's really frustrating for you when you see the potential in that kid."

"Yes . . . I think it gives Sam nightmares."

She winced when she thought of Sam and felt a twinge of guilt. What would he make of this? Better still, what did *she* make of this? Just a friendly dinner between two adults or something with deeper overtones? She was flattered that this attractive, mature man wanted her company. Did he want more?

They were seated at a cozy table at the Black Angus Restaurant and she felt an immediate intimacy with him, separated from other guests by smoked glass partitions and classical music softly blending with the candlelight.

Andrew helped her decide on the type of steak, rib eye rare, and the waitress regarded them as though they were lovers when she poured the red wine. Diana handled the small talk well enough and couldn't help but notice Andrew's hands, appearing strong yet gentle, hands that told her they had worked hard and experienced much of life, hands that had learned to touch lovingly. She sensed he was a warm, kind, caring man, and though he was a generation beyond her, she was taken by his understanding. She felt he would have been able to handle her terrible failure, that he was the kind of man who would have been there for her no matter what she had done.

Halfway through the meal she tiptoed out on fragile ground.

"If you don't mind my saying so, you're a real surprise in Willow Creek." She quickly laughed. "What on earth are you doing there?"

He looked at her calmly. " I found the kind of a job I wanted with the talc company, and I looked around for something within driving distance: Bozeman, Manhattan, Butte. Then one day by accident I followed the little blacktop that meandered by the plant. I found Willow Creek and I immediately felt at home. Strange, huh?"

"No, not so strange, it's just that there's nothing there."

"There's more than you think."

"Maybe, but you don't fit the mold."

"Do you?"

"Touché. But don't you want more of a social life than following the Willow Creek Broncs around?" She didn't give him time to answer. "Have you ever been married?"

He finished the last of his wine and set the glass down carefully, staring into the glass as though it contained old memories.

"I lost someone . . . a long time ago. Before the war."

"Vietnam?"

"Ha!" He broke the trance with a booming laugh. "What war do you think, World War II? Don't be making me any older than I am, girl."

"I didn't mean to pry."

"Pry away, my closets are empty," he said, embracing her with forgiving eyes. "I was married, long time ago, and I wanted it to work, gave it my best shot, but I wasn't any good at it, my fault . . . my fault, God knows."

"That's refreshing," she said.

"What?"

"Someone taking the blame for a failed marriage. I don't hear that very often, usually just the opposite."

"It's true. I couldn't give her what she needed. We had two great kids, a boy and girl, who're off in the world finding their own lives."

"Well, do you ever want to have someone, to be married again?"

"I've tried with other women from time to time, but it was never any good."

"Given up?" she said softly.

"I guess you'd have to say I still cling to a very battered and trampled hope, but—"

The young waitress interrupted him, asking if they wanted anything more. He waved her away.

Diana recognized a hunger in his eyes she'd seen in other men, and she also knew her body had a power to draw men, caught them drinking her in, and she dressed to counter that to some degree. Did he want to be her lover or was this nothing more than he'd claimed, a little cheer for the assistant basketball coach? She tried to pay for her meal, as if that would neutralize their time together, but he convinced her it was not important and she relented.

She was thankful they could jabber about the team on the way home and that he hadn't asked her why she was in Willow Creek.

"Thanks for being a good sport," he said as he turned off the freeway at Three Forks. "I'm glad we got better acquainted."

"Yes, thanks for the lovely dinner and for saving me from my indecision." She spoke more rapidly than usual and hoped he didn't pick up on it.

"Well," he said, "if you ever need someone to spend time with . . . or help with your indecision . . ."

She didn't know how to respond and tried to sort out the ambiguity in his words. She considered asking him if he'd like to stop at her place on the way home, for coffee or something, but then asked herself what she was doing. Had he touched a longing in her she didn't want to admit? She thought of Sam.

Andrew pulled in beside her car in front of the deserted grocery store. Out of the Lincoln quickly, he came around to open her door. She stood beside him and unlocked her car. Her hand trembled. Her throat went dry. She turned toward him and he stepped closer.

"Thanks, Andrew. I'm ready to take on Olaf and the boys again." She tried to laugh. "Thanks for the encouragement and cheer."

She felt an excited warmth rush to her face and hoped in the dimly lit street he wouldn't notice. In that moment she felt this solitary man's loneliness and was on the verge of offering to comfort him.

"Maybe we'll do it again some time," he said lightly and he held her door.

She slid into the car, catching her breath. He leaned toward her. "Good night, Diana."

He shut the door and stepped back. She started her car and drove away, watching him in the rearview mirror as he stood in the street. An avalanche of feelings overwhelmed her, frightening her. Driving the narrow blacktop toward Willow Creek, she watched for his headlights behind her, but they didn't appear. She felt like a grade school girl on the playground with a high school boy showing interest, but she had the strange intuition that he wasn't available, except maybe for a brief affair, and that his heart was irrevocably taken.

When she turned in her gravel road, she was confused to find tears in her eyes. She thought of Jessica and began to cry. She sat in the Volvo in front of the dark, lonely house and sobbed loudly until she could sob no more.

CHAPTER 27

D rained physically, as though he himself were out on the basketball floor, Sam agonized through another game Thursday night.

In addition to their eleven-man team, a few carloads of parents and students had traveled the hundred-and-forty-some miles from Lima, a small town that hung its hat in a high, expansive valley in the southwestern tip of Montana. But being a weeknight, the gate on both sides of the court was thinner than usual.

Kneeling in front of the bench, he caught himself vacillating between a cool detachment from probable loss to supplicating the gods for victory. And then quickly, Willow Creek climbed back to within three points with just over a minute to go. The scant weeknight crowd held its collective breath. Sam fought back hope that kept rearing its head, unwilling to set himself up for the disappointment he was used to.

Earlier, with three minutes to go, Olaf punched a ball into the bleachers when Joe Kelly tried to put one past him, and the ref called a foul, Olaf's fifth. Dean looked as though he wanted to crawl under the bench rather than go out on the floor and entertain the crowd with his glaring blunders and miscues, and Olaf folded his frame onto the bench beside Miss Murphy. He had played fiercely but was still a liability, in the paint more than three seconds many times and shuffling his feet while handling the ball. Sam cringed when, twice, Olaf dunked the ball only to have it waved off because he traveled.

Now, down by three, with one minute left, Sam watched as the Bears brought the ball up and Garth McDonald, with Pete's hand in his face, missed a jump shot from the side. Curtis grabbed the rebound and threw a perfect down-and-out to Pete as he raced along the sidelines. Grandma Chapman's pride and joy streaked to the backboard and laid it in as Troy McDonald collided with him from behind.

One-shot foul, down 78 to 79.

Sam knelt in front of the bench, chewing on his ballpoint pen. Inflamed by the boys' grit and fanned by the cheers of the cheerleaders, the hometown faithful were on their feet. Peter Strong toed the line, took a deep breath, and flipped the ball with fingers and wrist into the utter silence. Like the Prodigal, the ball remembered the way home. Tie game! 79 to 79.

The loyal Willow Creek crowd inhaled with an audible gasp, which was followed instantly by noisy cheering. Then, as if all sound had been sucked from the universe, the hometown supporters stood inanimate, limp, as the Lima team hustled into the front court, sure to deliver the doom that always befell Willow Creek in similar circumstances.

Sam knew they'd go to one of the McDonald boys, but so did Pete and Rob. The Willow Creek guards overplayed the Lima sharpshooters, preventing them from getting the ball until finally, out of desperation, Glenn Turly, an angular forward, got off a shot from the side. The ball rimmed the iron and spun out, then was grabbed up by Rob Johnson.

Eighteen seconds.

Rob dribbled the ball upcourt and looked for an opening, but the Lima boys stuck to him like gumbo.

Ten seconds.

Rob started a drive to the basket, pulled up short, and lifted a jump shot over the frantic reach of the defender. The ball seemed to hang in midair. No one in the gym took a breath. Caroming off the backboard, the ball glanced down onto the rim and came off.

Four seconds.

Tom went high to snatch the ball above the others and descended to the floor in a crouch. Without hesitation he exploded back through frantically thrashing outstretched arms to kiss the ball off the glass. The leather Spaulding sphere, obedient to the natural laws of the planet, descended at the proper angle through the iron hoop and nylon netting just as the time drained off the clock.

The nerve-jarring resonance of the buzzer—which had been the signal of merciful relief for so many years—was the first voice to proclaim the unthinkable. The scoreboard followed suit, displaying an astonishing rarity in the record books of recent history: VISITOR 79, HOME 81.

The miracle had happened! Willow Creek High School had won a *basketball game* after ninety-eight tries. Sam exploded from his prayerful crouch and raced onto the floor, embracing his exhausted cowboy forward as though he were a father welcoming a son home from war. Rob converged on them, and the two seniors nearly crushed Sam between them. They seized each other, pressing their foreheads together and emitting animal sounds, bellowing, howling, releasing four years of frustration and bitter disappointment, ending four years of indignity, shame, and humiliation. They were like grizzlies after a long winter's hibernation, young eagles leaping from the nest in first flight, wolves reunited after years of separation.

Then the trio was engulfed by the team and student body and those staunch townsfolk who rushed onto the floor to join in the mugging celebration. Diana found Sam and hugged him with abandon.

"We did it! We did it!" she shouted, and in the midst of this spontaneous outpouring, he felt her tantalizing firmness against his chest.

The teams shook hands in line on the court and exchanged brief recognition and comments, which were good-natured, if sometimes forced. The Willow Creek boys, with bright happy faces, huddled on the floor with their coaches, chattering and praising one another.

Hazel happily forked over the locally famous ten bucks by slapping it into Grandma Chapman's hand, these two women a part of the small loyal bunch that had witnessed the seemingly insignificant victory of one small-town school team over another. Undoubtedly others would raise an eyebrow when the score appeared in the *Bozeman Daily Chronicle* the next day, thinking it typo.

Truly Osborn caught Sam heading off the floor. "Well done, Sam, well done! Now that we've won a game, we can get back to some semblance of sanity around here."

"Thank you, Mr. Osborn." *But you ain't seen nothin' yet.*

Sam walked into the noisy locker room, and amid the moist odors of sweat, tape and exhaustion, he could smell the rare sweet fragrance of triumph. The boys, unlacing their dissimilar shoes and stripping off their soggy uniforms, had for the first time tasted the pure, intoxicating nectar of victory. Sam hoped they would soon become incurably and absolutely addicted.

THE CELEBRATION MOVED down Main Street to the Blue Willow where Sam could see Axel was visibly upset that he had missed the unexpected triumph, sure he'd have to wait another three or four years for the next. The inn buzzed with an uncommon energy as the team ate and jabbered about every aspect of the game as they each remembered it, laughing and savoring the heady flavor of winning on their virgin palates. Dean laughed the hardest at his field goal attempt when, running wide open, he drop-kicked the ball off the scoreboard. Sam, holding the squat boy's arm high like a victorious prizefighter, officially dubbed him the "Dutch Boy" who saved his town with his finger in the dike.

At a table with Hazel and Mavis, Grandma looked across at John English who stood at the bar.

"Hey, English, who won the game?"

John turned in reflex and then, catching himself, returned to his conversation, ignoring her.

"I believe I just saw a cow flying by!" Grandma shouted, and although John gave no indication he heard her, he certainly heard the laughter that followed.

Rip fell asleep in a chair next to the red player piano that Olaf pedaled with unrestrained joy, giving a beat to the spontaneous celebration that had been five years incubating and which most of the Willow Creek community—probably Christmas shopping in Bozeman—would only hear about when they awoke to a new day.

In the midst of the merrymaking, Grandma dragged Peter outside to take a turn on the bicycle built for two. Others followed out onto the porch in the mild winter night and they made a game of it, seeing who could ride down past the grain elevator, around the block, and back to the porch in the shortest time.

Though it looked easy, they soon found out there was more to it than riding single. Grandma and Pete did it in two minutes and eleven seconds, according to Axel's second hand. Tom and Olaf took a turn, wobbling and weaving down the faintly lit Main Street with everyone on the porch howling and shouting, Olaf behind Tom like a grown man on a child's trike, his knees higher than the handlebars, a grasshopper trying to stay upright on a quaking blade of grass. They made the circuit in two minutes and forty-two seconds, having fallen over twice. When Tom got off, Hazel shoved her way through to the bike before Olaf could dismount.

"Let me take a round with you."

"You can't ride that thing," Grandma said.

"Just watch me," Hazel said, giggling as she hoisted her heavy body onto the tiny bike seat in front of the startled Norwegian.

The spectators on the porch exchanged incredulous glances while the two pushed off and teetered down the blacktop, the tires all but flattened by their weight, veering from side to side, nearly flopping to the left, then pitching to the right. They glided through the shadows like circus performers, the fat lady and the thin man on a tandem bike, out of sight past the elevator and onto the gravel.

"I wonder if the lovers will ever come back for their bike?" Axel said as they waited.

"Yep," Rip said without hesitation. "One a these days they will, sure as shootin'."

Back down First Street, nearly sideswiping a parked pickup, Hazel and Olaf rode, heading for home, bobbing and weaving toward the rowdy spectators, reaching the finish line in three minutes and seven seconds. Rob and Pete inspected the tires as Hazel puffed up the steps. She settled heavily in the rickety wicker rocker and nearly destroyed it.

Curtis and Dean took a turn and everyone could hear the Dutch Boy's shrill whoops and hollers all around the block. Rob and Mary had the slowest time and were accused of parking on the far side of the block. Andrew Wainwright convinced Amos Flowers to climb on the contraption and it appeared as though the Tom Mix hat was driving.

When nearly everyone had taken a turn on the bike, Diana pulled Sam by the coat sleeve. "Come on, we can beat that time."

Sam climbed on the back for power and Diana up front for navigation. They were off to a fast start with the roar of the gang behind them. They swooped and swayed and careened around the corner.

"We shouldn't be doing this together," Diana called.

"Why not?" Sam said, floating in the joy of this rapturous moment.

"They say that couples who ride this bike will have a falling out."

"Do you believe in folklore?" he said as they took the third turn.

"You're the English teacher, I stick to biology."

Oh, how he'd like to stick to biology with the biology teacher!

They pitched around the corner and came to a faltering stop in front of the inn. Axel clocked them at two minutes and four seconds. They had won together on this night of winning. Sam mused over the legendary bike to which some attributed magical powers. Would it adversely affect his budding relationship with his assistant coach? They couldn't very well have a falling out before they had a falling in. At least, if the bike held any enchantment at all, he could look forward first to the falling in.

As Diana put on her ski jacket she caught Sam who was still out on the porch.

"I'll be leaving in the morning." She smiled. "Why don't you come out for a while if you can break free."

"I'll try."

The look in her eye and the invitation in her voice sucked all the oxygen out of his lungs.

CHAPTER 28

S am checked his watch: ten-thirteen; it wouldn't seem unrea-
sonable. He gathered the boys and told them it was time they
headed for home, that they would practice tomorrow afternoon with no
letup. They didn't protest, not even Tom, which surprised him.

He attempted to look nonchalant as he bid some of the other celebrants
good night and worked his way out the door. Main Street was deserted
except for a balmy mountain wind, and he quickened his pace, somewhat
giddy with this strange and wonderful night. A new moon beamed a thin
smile at him, lying on its back near the rim of the Tobacco Roots. Stars
glimmered in the cloudless sky and animals scurried in the darkness ahead
of him in a town of wild creatures.

Lima had a decent team in a conference where some coaches had to work
miracles with baling wire and chewing gum, but teams like Twin Bridges
and Gardiner and Manhattan Christian were another matter. Nonethe-
less Sam would savor this exhilarating experience and unparalleled feeling
while it lasted; he'd deal with the other in turn. He felt an unfamiliar surge
of pride, and he jumped high enough to click his heels. He wanted to tell
someone about what they had done that night, but he didn't know who.

I'm doing better, Amy, I'm doing better.

He banged through the front door and snapped on the lights as conflict-
ing voices competed in his head: *Got to take a shower, shave, change clothes.
Don't go out there, just turn on the TV and get to bed early. Hurry, she may
go to bed thinking you aren't coming. You're not ready for this! Tell her you
were too tired. There's danger out there, you know what can happen. Are you
mad, turning down an invitation to Eden?*

As though his fate were determined by some unseen hand, he hurried
toward the magnetic vision of Diana standing naked in the locker room. A
navy shower, pull on some clothes, no clean underwear, forget the underwear, a clean pair of jeans and his sexy soft cotton Levi shirt. Hurry, run the

electric shaver over his face, splash on aftershave, hurry, brush hair, brush teeth, socks, forget socks, pull on loafers, out the door.

Sam drove up the blacktop in his Ford Tempo and as he passed the Blue Willow, Grandma's VW bus had pulled up at the back and the brake lights were on but not the headlights. Grandma? Peter? He checked his watch. Nearly eleven. Strange. But as he rounded the curve and headed north he discovered the voices were waiting for him in ambush.

DIANA STRIPPED OFF her clothes and showered the moment she got home, feeling hot and sticky from the night's excitement and exertion. She kept asking herself why she'd invited Sam out. What would he think? Could she tell him, being that she was leaving in the morning for San Diego and Christmas with her parents, that she just wanted to have some time alone with him to talk and unwind? Why *did* she invite him out? Out of the shower, she pulled on a pink terry-cloth robe she'd never worn, and it felt sensuous against her tingling skin. Should she get fully dressed, jeans and sweater? She combed her hair and avoided eye contact in the mirror as if her own eyes would accuse her.

"We'll just talk," she said aloud. "Keep it light, nothing serious, a friendly good-bye. Offer him something to drink—I think there's some wine—and we'll just spend a nice quiet hour together and then he'll go home . . . maybe a kiss at the door, and I'll be safe on my way to California in the morning. Or, if we do make love, it's just a physical thing, a basic need, that's all, nothing to take seriously, people do it all the time."

She hesitated, standing before the mirror in the bathroom. Was that the door? Just her imagination. *Relax, nothing serious, keep it light, stay cool.* She snapped off the light in the bathroom and hurriedly lit several candles in the living room. Then she blew them out. Too much. She turned on all the lights, stood there a moment, relit the candles and turned out all the lights.

She peered out the window for headlights. Maybe he wouldn't be able to get away; after all it was their first win in almost six years. He was probably still celebrating at the Blue Willow. Though she hadn't been very aggressive, he did have a knack for avoiding her whenever they might spend some time alone. But she'd felt his passion the night they went to dinner and embraced at her door. Sometimes she caught him looking at her. Had she read him wrong? Damn! She wasn't ready for this. She lit several lamps and blew out the candles.

ON THE DRIVE out of town, Sam couldn't deny Amy's memory, and he knew that one of the voices in his head was hers. He knew she wanted him to live his life fully, with gusto, with passion, but he was terrified of falling in love again, afraid of needing someone like that again, someone who could be snatched away in an instant.

"Not going to fall in love, not going to fall in love," he said aloud, in rhythm with the yellow highway strips flying past on the blacktop. "Not going to fall in love, not going to fall in love."

Maybe she just wanted to talk, to say good-bye when they were alone. He could turn around; she'd never know he came this far. *Keep it light, don't get serious, don't get involved, you're not ready for this.* His hands trembled on the steering wheel when he turned on the gravel road to her farmhouse. She'd see the lights by now, too late to turn around. Maybe we'll just neck on the sofa, friendly like, just for the fun of it.

He pulled the Ford to a stop in front of the house and doused the lights. Damn, the house was almost dark, she was probably already in bed. He'd taken too long. He stumbled onto the porch and was about to knock when the door opened and she was standing there in a terry cloth robe, barefoot, and the room behind her was aglow with candles.

"Hi," he said, his throat going dry.

"Hi."

"I almost didn't come."

"Me too," she said softly.

She backed into the house and he followed, tentatively, shutting the door behind him, his breathing quickening.

"You want to talk?" he said.

"Yes . . . talk . . ."

He stood in the flickering light for a moment and fire mainlined through his body and face. He could smell her, soapy and sweet, see her in the dull glow with the pink robe's sash tight around her small waist, the cleavage of her breasts slightly visible. The next moment they flew into each other's arms and kissed with a primitive hunger.

"We're not getting serious," she said between kisses. "Nothing serious."

"Nothing serious," he said with his mouth tasting the skin of her supple neck. "Just some fun." And with his last rational thought he told himself, *I'm not going to fall in love.*

CHAPTER 29

With the lights off, Peter guided the old VW bus around to the side of the Blue Willow, moving stealthily even though the village appeared deserted. A few vehicles lingered in front of the café, like weary horses tied at the rail. The night was unseasonably warm, more like April than December, a balmy wind gusting from the southwest.

Tom and Pete crept to the building's back door with the bearing of burglars, leaving Olaf in the bus, a getaway driver. Through the windowed door they could see Axel mopping the room. Tom knocked lightly and the brawny man looked up, momentarily startled. Then he waved them in.

"What are you guys doing up?" the innkeeper said. "You're supposed to be resting."

"We need some paint," Tom said.

"*Paint!* At this time of night?"

"Yeah, do you have any around?" Pete said.

Axel cocked his sweat-glistened bald head and regarded the two boys suspiciously, his hand holding the mop handle like a meat cleaver.

"What are you fellas plannin' to paint?"

"We have to fix something," Tom said. "Do you have any?"

"We don't have a water tower." Axel paused. "A bridge?"

"No, nothing like that, honest," Pete said. "Don't you have any?"

"Yeah, I got paint. I'm always touching up something around here. What color you need?"

"Anything but red," Tom said.

Axel set the mop aside and led them to a neatly kept back room. He swung open a cupboard and revealed a dozen or more cans of paint in a variety of colors and sizes, none of which was more than a quart.

"We need a gallon or two," Tom said.

"A gallon or two!" Axel shook his head slightly. "What are you going to paint, the talc plant?"

Tom glanced at Pete with disappointment in his face.

"Sorry," Axel said. "That's all I got."

"Would you get my grandma?" Pete asked. "We're supposed to be in bed and don't want anyone to see us."

"Sure."

Axel fetched Grandma Chapman, who was still savoring the win with a few loyalists in the dining room. She came plowing through the kitchen with worry taking root in the furrows of her face.

"What's the matter? You all right?" she asked Pete.

"Yeah, fine," Pete said. "We need to talk to you."

"What are you still doing up? Coach Pickett sent you to bed an hour ago."

"I know," Pete said. "We need your help." He nodded. "Outside."

She exchanged a "what's up" look with Axel and followed the two boys out the door.

"They need some *paint*," Axel called after them.

At the bus, Grandma noticed Olaf stacked in the back seat.

"They keeping you up, too."

"Ya, falling asleep I am."

"Have you got any paint?" Pete asked, standing beside the truck.

"Paint? Yes . . . have a couple of gallons of white; was going to paint the fence last summer, but decided there were more important things to do."

"Have you got a brush?" Tom asked.

"Yes."

"Have you got two brushes?" Pete asked.

"Yes, I have several old brushes. What are you three up to?"

Tom glanced at Pete, questioning. Pete knew his grandma and nodded at Tom.

"We're going to paint the score of the game on my dad's barn," Tom whispered as if George Stonebreaker were lurking in the shadows. "He told me we'd never win a game as long as I played, that I was a loser, that the whole team was a bunch of geldings."

Grandma stood silently for a moment, regarding the three boys. Then she looked into Tom's stubborn face. "Can *I* help?"

GRANDMA BOUNCED THE Volkswagen bus across the pasture, the vehicle's lights off. Tom sat beside her, pointing the way, while Pete and Olaf rode on the bone-jarring bench seat, shaking two cans of Sherwin-Williams outdoor latex. They stopped at a fence line and scrambled out of the bus, a quarter of a mile south of the ranch site.

"This is great," Grandma said. "Thought I'd lost any chance to do something like this."

They helped each other through the barbed wire fence, headed toward the one dim yard light, which did little to dispel the smothering darkness. The wind prodded at Pete's back as though sensing he was losing his nerve. Was he the only one with a knot of fear in his stomach? he wondered. His mother was coming to Willow Creek for Christmas and, though he felt like a traitor, he knew he could talk her into letting him go home with her.

"What will your dad do if he catches us?" Pete asked Tom, who led the way.

"He'll kill us."

Pete tried to find some comfort in numbers, but as he glanced at the shadows beside him, he found no comfort. Tom hurried ahead of them, and all at once the barn loomed out of the darkness like a great ship, casting its outline against the star-spangled sky. Passing an assortment of farm machinery, Tom led them around to the dark side of the barn, in the lee from the yard light. He stopped and swept his arm toward the towering broadside.

"There," he said.

The three of them stood gawking at the huge wall, the first story of which was constructed out of mortared field stones. Small square windows six feet above ground level ran the length of the barn like cannon ports.

"How are we going to get up there?" Pete asked.

"We've got an old ladder," Tom said, "but first I've got to see if my dad is home."

A dog barked from beyond the barn.

"That's Skipper. You wait here," Tom said, and he crept off into the darkness toward the aroused dog and the one low-watt light.

Shortly after Tom disappeared, the dog stopped barking. His three cohorts instinctively crouched and waited. Pete began wondering if this was such a great idea after all. He'd heard stories about Tom's violent father and he wished they had let Axel in on their scheme and brought the oxlike innkeeper for backup. As a million stars watched mutely from the endless sky, things were moving on the barn, creaking and groaning and bumping in the wind, as though it were a rocking vessel moored to a wharf. How would they ever know if one of the sounds was Tom's dad? Peter was able to make out more of his surroundings as his eyes adjusted to the shadows of the barnyard. The minutes stretched on until it seemed as though Tom had deserted them.

"Keep shakin' the paint," Grandma said, obviously enjoying herself.

Kneeling, the two of them were shaking the gallon cans when Pete heard a rustling coming toward them. Just as he stopped jiggling the can to listen, he was knocked flat by a pouncing animal. A large, shaggy-haired mutt licked his face and wagged its tail, greeting the other two with the enthusiasm of someone who wanted in on the caper. Tom appeared with a long wooden ladder.

"Down, Skipper, down," he said.

"Is your dad home?" Pete asked, picking himself off the ground.

"No, not yet . . . out drinkin' somewhere."

Tom hoisted the ladder up against the barn wall. It only reached a few feet above the stone.

"Damn," Tom said.

He climbed the widow-maker and stood near the top, testing his reach against the vertical one-by-ten boards. He scrambled back down.

"Olaf, will you paint on the ladder?"

"On the ladder? . . . Ya."

"How big are we going to make this?" Grandma asked.

"Six feet tall," Tom said.

"Sweet!" Pete said. "That rocks."

"That's the county road," Tom said, pointing west. "I want this big enough so you can see it from the road. Every time my dad drives in he'll have it starin' at him; all the neighbors will see it. That'll burn his ass."

"Won't he just paint over it?" Pete asked.

"Not the way we're going to do it. Olaf will paint the lower part with the ladder."

"The *lower* part?" Grandma said.

"Yeah. I'll paint the Willow Creek score higher."

"How you gonna do that?" Pete said, gazing up at the towering barn.

"With rope, to where my dad can't touch it."

They got Olaf started, painting from right to left because he was right-handed, Grandma steadying the ladder and spelling out the Lima score in reverse. He began painting a six-foot "9." Peter followed Tom to the other side of the barn, where Tom scrounged a variety of rope in some of the outbuildings, including several of his lariats and a block and tackle. On this side of the barn, the yard light cast shadows in all directions and Peter felt exposed to whatever eyes might be peering from the old two-story house.

After knotting the rope together, Tom heaved a heavy wrench tied to baler twine over the barn roof. Pete went around and waited for Tom to lower the old tool on the twine until he could reach it. Quickly he pulled on the twine until he had the attached rope in hand. Olaf had the "9" completed, and after moving the ladder, he was working on the "7." Grandma had been appointed lookout, instructed to keep one eye peeled on the road for any hint of George Stonebreaker's pickup. It was past midnight.

Tom came around the barn with an old truck tire. He tied it securely to the rope. He picked up the other can and a brush and climbed into the tire. He sat with one arm around the tire and holding the can, the other free to paint.

"Okay, hoist me up."

Pete scrambled around to the east side of the barn where Tom had the rope running through the block and tackle and snugged to a railroad tie in the corral. He began pulling as he'd been instructed, heaving Tom off the ground on the other side of the barn. In a minute he heard a whistle, the signal to stop, and he tied off the rope. He hurried around to see where he'd hung Tom. High above the white "9" Tom rode the old tire in the wind, a foot or so off the wall because of the eaves, already lining out a six-foot "1" with his slapping five-inch paint brush.

"You've got to let me down fast if my dad comes," Tom said.

The ranch road came in straight from the west, and if he glanced at the barn, George Stonebreaker would be the first to see their night's handiwork. Pete found himself squinting northwest into the darkness and manufacturing headlights in his imagination.

Both boys painted with a frenzy, slopping their brushes against the rough, weathered boards. Grandma guided their crude calligraphy from below, having them leave two-board spaces between letters. Tom could move himself along by pushing himself out from the wall with his legs and flipping the rope over the eaves a few inches at a time. But Pete would have to move it from the other side when he'd worked his way eight or ten feet laterally.

The scoreboard began to take shape. Below, Olaf had the "79" finished and was about done with the "A." Above, painting faster, Tom had finished the "K 81" and had started the "E."

"A car!" Grandma shouted.

Far to the north, headlights fluttered along the country road. Olaf scrambled down the ladder and Pete ran around to the far side of the barn, almost cold-cocking himself by running into a post of the corral. He untied the rope and was about to lower Tom to the ground when he heard Grandma calling in a whisper as she came around the barn.

"It's okay, false alarm, wasn't him."

Pete retied the rope and realized that one of these times it *would* be George Stonebreaker!

They painted with a fury, aware that time was running out. They lowered Tom and readjusted the rope over the roof twice. But the monument to their triumph was taking shape.

OW CREEK 81
    IMA 79

Pete turned with a start and found a woman standing behind them in a long coat and overshoes, staring up at the barn wall.

"Oh, ah . . . Tom," Pete said, "*Tom.*"

Tom gazed down and regarded the woman for a moment, who was hardly visible in the oblique illumination from the distant yard light. Grandma and Olaf froze in place.

"It's okay," Tom called softly, "it's okay."

Tom went back to painting, followed by Olaf. Then, at the sight of this lunatic spectacle before her, the woman began clapping, hardly audible in the friendly wind. Just stood there clapping. When she stopped, Peter glanced over his shoulder again. Tom's mother was gone.

The next pair of headlights, twenty minutes later, turned in at the mailbox, and all hell broke loose around the barn. Olaf came off the ladder in two strides and Grandma shoved it bouncing onto the ground. Pete raced through the old manure and untied the rope, lowering Tom as quickly as he dared without breaking his teammate's legs. Around to the other side of the barn, all of them cowered behind the corral fence as the pickup rattled into the barnyard and skidded to a stop near the house. Skipper barked and circled the truck.

"Will your mother tell him?" Grandma asked.

"No. If she dared, she'd be out helping us paint."

Pete had one foot pointed south across the stubble toward Trilobite. Tom's father turned off the truck lights. They could no longer see him, barely able to make out the outline of the pickup in the faint light. In the wind all they could hear was the creaking ship beside them. Had he seen the white lettering on the barn in the headlights?

"Where is he?" Pete whispered.

Then, soundlessly, the hulking form of George Stonebreaker came toward them. His silhouette grew as the four of them cowered in the dry manure of the corral.

It was time to run like hell!

"I'm glad I got my Reeboks on," Grandma whispered.

She held Peter's arm in an iron grip and he could tell she was plenty scared, too. The expanding shadow of the man moved past them to their left and into the large half-opened door of the barn. Pete felt all of them begin breathing again.

"What's he doing?" Grandma asked.

"Sometimes he goes to the barn to sleep it off," Tom whispered. "Won't admit to my mom that he gets drunk. He has blankets on some straw bales. In the morning he'll act as though he got up early to feed."

"Let's get outta here," Pete said.

"We're not finished," Tom said.

"You mean we're going to keep painting with your dad *in the barn*?" Pete said.

"Gotta get 'er finished," Tom said. "Otherwise he'll be right, we'll be quitters."

Oh, Jeez. How could they be scrambling around on the barn with George Stonebreaker right on the other side of the wall? Pete wondered. Thank God *he* wasn't the one hanging up there in the tire with no place to run or hide.

"Pete," Tom said, "you finish the top and I'll keep an eye on my dad."

OLAF HAD FINISHED the bottom line. Pete hung high above the ground in the old truck tire and worked feverishly to complete the top. Tom had sent Olaf and Grandma tiptoeing for the bus and had lugged the ladder back to wherever he'd found it. This left Peter alone, hanging on for dear life while trying to fashion the final letter—the largest in the English alphabet. Why couldn't Grandma have lived in a town with a name like Lima or Roy or Belt?

He pushed off with his legs and reached high to whiten the peak of the huge "W." The Sherwin-Williams was running low and it was hard to get much paint in the bristles. In a sweat, he slopped the brush against the rough barn boards and kept one eye on the ground below. Had Tom been waylaid and wasn't ever coming back? Then, as the wind abated for a moment, he heard something and looked down. Someone was standing directly under him. About to whisper Tom's name, he realized it wasn't Tom.

George Stonebreaker was twenty feet below him, peeing like a draft horse. Pete held his breath. His body tightened. He clung to the tire as if it could hide him. All Stonebreaker had to do was look up. The man must have consumed five gallons of beer the way he stood there pissing. The wind gently swayed Peter as he hung in the tire, and he kept his toes against the wall in hopes of remaining motionless and quiet. He carefully placed the knuckles of his brush hand against the barn to steady himself but in doing so he inadvertently tipped the can to one side. It was nearly empty, but the small amount of paint that had collected in the groove around the top began dripping to the ground.

Tom's father was fumbling with his fly when he suddenly cursed.

"Son of a bitch! Goddamn pigeons!"

He stepped back from the stone wall and started to peer up toward the eaves when Tom came around the barn from the front.

"Can't find the house?" Tom said.

"Huh . . . oh, Mother of God . . . you scared the shit outta me."

The inebriated rancher forgot the pigeon and ambled toward Tom at the corner of the barn.

"Sleepin' it off?" Tom said.

"Don't get smart-ass with me or I'll—"

"Or you'll fall on your face."

"You got that Cardwell girl in the loft?"

"No."

"You go screwing around and you'll be punished. I'm tellin' you, boy, God'll punish you sure as hell."

"I'm not screwing around."

"Then what're you doin' out here?"

"I'm painting the barn," Tom said, and Peter all but fell out of the tire.

"Huh, paintin' the barn. That'll be the day," Stonebreaker said.

They moved out of earshot around to the front of the barn and Peter realized he wasn't breathing. Would he be hanging there come morning for the whole county to see? he wondered. What the hell, he might as well finish it. After a long moment, he dipped his brush into the paint can and slopped away, completing the final letter in the message that would broadcast their victory to everyone who passed. Pete understood why Tom had to do this, and he hoped that somehow, across the sky, his father would see the barn as well.

He had barely enough paint, wiping the bottom of the can dry with his brush, but the "W" was finished. As though he'd been silently watched over by guardian angels, Peter was lowered gently to the ground the moment he was done. Tom hurried from behind the barn.

"Where's your dad?" Pete whispered.

"Sleeping in the barn."

They stepped back and gazed at the dark wall; the large white letters and numbers seemed to glow with their own light.

WILLOW CREEK 81
LIMA 79

When the tire and ropes had been stashed, Tom and Pete ran across the field. Tom would sleep at Pete's and stay clear of home for a while. They hooted and laughed as they ran, and Olaf and Grandma greeted them with high fives and clamorous glee. Peter and Tom filled them in on the hair-raising climax and they all nearly fell down laughing.

". . . and he was taking a leak right under me," Pete said, "and I was dripping paint on him."

"And he thought it was pigeons!" Tom roared.

"And he asked Tom what he was doing," Pete said, "and Tom said he was *painting the barn!*"

The boys had the evidence of their mischief on their jeans, on their hands and faces, on their Levi jackets, even in their hair.

"We'll throw all of you in the wash machine when we get to the house," Grandma said. "Good thing paint's latex."

As Pete jostled the VW bus across the pasture, he wished he could have written PETE LOVES KATHY on the side of the barn for the whole world to see. But Kathy didn't love Pete. While his heart thought she had promised with an oil-base, her promise had been written in latex, and it was washing away in the rain.

If he hurried back to St. Paul, maybe he could stop the rain.

CHAPTER 30

Friday morning, the beginning of Christmas vacation, Sam settled into a comfortable pace, rounding the curve out past the cemetery with the gravel crunching rhythmically under his running shoes. Under the cloudless sky and low-flying December sun, he tried to sort out his jumbled feelings. One part of him wanted more, wished Diana wasn't gone for almost two weeks. Another more prudent side applauded the space, time to cool off, glad she was gone for a while so he could come to his senses, realize he was playing with fire, how unwittingly he could be drawn over the edge and lost.

After a night of utter bliss, Sam was reminded of how late he slept when Ray Collins rattled by in his pickup with his yellow Lab, Poke, sitting beside him, close as a sweetheart.

On waking, Sam set off on his morning run with uncharacteristic enthusiasm. His legs possessed an unexpected strength and he found energy he didn't recognize, stretching out into a run through the mild winter day as though last night's unexpected adventures had jump-started an unknown engine in him. When he hesitantly mentioned birth control to Diana, she informed him that she started taking the pill again the day he saw her naked in the girls' locker room. He smiled easily at the thought of it.

Sam slowed his pace as he crossed the one-lane bridge and searched for the vultures in the lofty, leafless cottonwoods where they habitually hung out. Those wily scavengers had given up on Willow Creek too soon this year. Their victory was big news. The implausible win had even been reported in *USA Today* as the breaking of an astounding ninety-seven game losing streak.

Only one burr rubbed under Sam's saddle. Olaf showed no improvement in his ingrained habit of turning the ball over by loitering in the paint for more than three seconds. They had won a game, playing better every outing, but Sam allowed himself no illusions. This had been the soft part of their schedule, light skirmishes, a time to learn. Starting in January they would come up against the heavyweights of the conference, teams who actually cut players to get down to twelve, teams with six or seven real athletes. Willow Creek wouldn't survive giving away the ball fifteen to twenty times to these boys.

He turned around at the two-mile mark—the rusted body of a half-buried Model T in a creek bank—and headed back toward town. Olaf's repetitive blunders continued to irritate Sam, rubbing a mental blister that he couldn't soothe or ignore. The boy was intelligent enough, but like patting the top of your head with one hand and rubbing your belly with the other, the kid's mental coordination just couldn't keep tabs on the three seconds while he so intensely focused on catching the ball and scoring. Sam so far had been unsuccessful in reprogramming Olaf. With his towering presence in the paint, every coach in the conference would be screaming at the referees: Three seconds! Three seconds!

He jogged east into the brightening sun, his happiness clouded by this nagging frustration. The lethargic Simmental bulls Ray Collins had used to test his dog grazed near the fence. He was visualizing the handsome yellow Lab sprinting across the pasture like the lilting motif in an enchanting symphony, when an idea hit him like a particle from the sun at the speed of light.

The dog collar!

Ray Collins's beautiful Lightning Commander remote-control shock collar: fashioned around Olaf's waist, under his trunks, it could turn Olaf away from the bulls also. Someone, maybe Scott, could sit in the stands with the remote-control transmitter. When Olaf stepped into the painted area under the basket, the freshman manager would count, and if the Norwegian was still in there three seconds later, Scott could shock him—not a painful charge, but just enough to remind him. After hours of that, Olaf would do it instinctively, wouldn't he? If not, well . . . they could always turn up the charge a little.

Sam sprinted past the cemetery like Ray Collins' Lab, unable to quench his excitement, and as he panted by the Blue Willow, Rip—already in his chair on the porch—called out.

"Where's the fire?"

Sam couldn't find enough breath to reply, and he threw a wave. But after showering and calling around, he located Ray Collins out at the Avery place, filling their propane tank. Ray listened to Sam's scheme and thought it was a great idea. He not only donated his Lightning Commander but promised not to mention it to a soul, which Sam figured was like asking a child to walk around puddles. Before the team's practice, Sam had fashioned a makeshift belt that would be comfortable as well as effective and, under Olaf's huge, loose-fitting jersey, inconspicuous to boot.

At the two o'clock practice, Sam heard from Tom how he and unnamed *others* had painted the score of the Lima game on the side of his father's barn. Sam shuddered to think of the mood that would put George Stonebreaker in, but he couldn't help but laugh at their audacity.

"What did your father do when he saw it?" Sam said.

"I don't know," Tom said. "I'm staying clear of there for a few days."

Then, Sam explained the device and took several shocks on his hands to demonstrate there was no pain involved, that the faint tingle would only remind Olaf to step quickly out of the paint. The somewhat skeptical boy held the shocking device in his hand, and Sam, using the transmitter, tickled him several times, causing the lanky center to smile at the ingenuity of the thing. They fastened it on his skinny frame under his PARTY ANIMAL sweatshirt and were ready to try it out.

"Awesomely sweet," Pete said.

"Let me crank that thing," Rob said. "I'll give him an instant Afro."

"Ought to put it in his jock strap," Tom said, "then he'd remember."

"What if it electrocutes him?" Dean asked.

"Then we'll have to bury him," Scott said, revealing a sense of humor Sam hadn't seen before in the boy.

Hazel, Grandma, and Axel showed up, and Sam joined them playing makeshift defense. While moving through offensive patterns, every time Olaf stood planted in the paint too long, Scott zapped him. The Scandinavian danced out of the paint as if someone had whispered in his ear, and Scott sat with a wide grin on his face, using batteries to control this basketball giant much like a little boy running his remote-control toy car. But it worked! Olaf concentrated on scoring and Poke's dog collar took care of the paint.

CHAPTER 31

Christmas Eve anointed Willow Creek with a windless snow. Large flakes danced their way to the windowsills of the Blue Willow Inn, where only upstairs lights denoted human gatherings. A string of colored bulbs outlining the large front windows illuminated the frosted bicycle built for two, enduring expectantly on the porch. The lone figure of a rider moved past the inn on a large Appaloosa, the snow collecting on his wide-brimmed hat. The horse snorted visibly and its hooves crunched a solitary cadence.

Peter and Grandma Chapman, in her bright red holiday dress and Reeboks, exchanged gifts around their tree. He fought off a darkness that accumulated daily with the dark of winter. Parrot perched in the evergreen and slung invectives at Tripod, who attempted to climb the spruce amid the tinsel, balls, and tangled strings of lights.

"That's enough of that," Grandma said. She swooped up the three-legged tomcat and put him out the back door.

"Go find a Christmas mouse stirring."

Irene Strong, Peter's mother, had planned to join her son and mother for several days over Christmas, but her work tied her up at the last minute and she couldn't get a later reservation on any airline that serviced Bozeman. Pete and his grandma had shared their common disappointment, his much more painful than hers, and attempted to make the best of it, grilling steaks in the oven and improvising weird sizes and shapes of homemade potato chips.

"This sure beats chestnuts roasting by the fire," Grandma said.

They competed for the most original or the most grotesque, and the only thing that put a stop to potato-chip creating was the rule that they had to eat their own handiwork. Grandma deep-fried a slice she said was Amos Flowers's ear, and Pete cooked one dark that he claimed was a scab off Truly Osborn's ass. They engorged several potatoes along with the

T-bones and drank three bottles of Martinelli's apple-cranberry sparkling juice. Grandma had taped the skimpy newspaper clipping of their win on the refrigerator door.

"We won't be able to find the food by the time the season's over," she said.

With Parrot mimicking an ornament on a high branch, they settled in the front room by the tree. Grandma handed Peter a brightly wrapped gift. He had received an expensive red ski jacket from his father, and on the phone his mother promised hers would be a little late but would be the best he'd ever had.

"Go ahead, open it, open it," Grandma said.

Peter tore off the cheerful paper and opened the rectangular box.

"Wow, thanks, Grandma!" He pulled out a white high-top basketball shoe, the Reebok Twilight Zone Pump. "These really rock!"

"That's only the half of it," she said. "Those are *game* shoes. I got them for the whole team, all the same, so you don't look like a bunch of scrubs out there."

"How can you do that? These cost over a hundred dollars."

"I won five hundred dollars playing bingo in Three Forks two weeks ago. Almost died wanting to tell you. The Athlete's Foot in Bozeman sold me six for the price of five. Only hitch is Olaf's fifteen triple 'E's haven't come yet. Had to be special-ordered."

"How did you know their sizes?" Pete asked, lacing his ten-and-a-halves on.

"Coach Pickett. He's the only other person who knew, except Hazel. She was with me the day I won."

"Thanks, Grandma," Pete said, hopping in his Twilight Zone Pumps. He tried hard to look enthused and beat back his sadness, tried hard not to spoil Grandma's joy, and knew he'd never wear the game shoes with his teammates. "They're awesome."

"They ought to be good for at least a couple extra buckets a game," she said.

As he bounced on his toes he suddenly stopped and pressed his face against the window. From the back porch light he could see that a large German shepherd had Tripod cornered against the high wood fence and the wall of the garage. Its fangs bared, its jaws snapped, and it waited for an opening to dismember the crippled cat. Tripod stood his ground, his lips curled, his teeth poised, his back hunched with hair standing on end, and he faced the ferocious canine eyeball to eyeball, holding at bay the beast that was trying to kill him while gentle snowflakes cascaded like unwrapped gifts from above.

"Tripod!" Pete shouted. "Some dog's trying to kill him!"

Grandma looked out the window as Peter raced for the back door in his game shoes.

"Hairy old bitch," Parrot squawked.

Pete fumbled the door open and grabbed a snow shovel from the doorless back entryway.

"Get outta here!" He threw the shovel like a javelin and nailed the large predator in the hind quarters.

The shepherd howled, then fled around the garage with its tail between its legs. Pete squatted beside the cat as he slowly moved out of his defensive stance. There was blood on its face. Pete lifted Tripod onto his lap and wiped the smear off his ear and cheek, revealing a small gash. When Peter stood and turned around, he found Elizabeth Chapman behind him with a double-barreled shotgun.

"Jeez, Grandma, where'd you get that?"

"Never saw that mutt before. Wonder where he came from?"

"He hurt Tripod," Peter said, showing her the wound.

She regarded the cat's head carefully for a moment.

"Another scar, that's all. The world's not safe for cripples even on Christmas Eve, never was. Merry Christmas."

Tripod sprang out of Peter's arms and beelined for the house. When they had locked the door behind them, Peter noticed a drop of blood on his game shoe.

Peter had spent most of the money his mother sent him on one special gift for his grandmother. He pulled it from where he had hidden it in the basement because he knew she would cheat and open it when he was away at practice. She hefted the large box in Christmas wrapping and shook it.

"Scuba gear?" she said.

"Open it, open it."

When she tore off the wrapping and saw the printing on the box, she hooted.

"Oh, you sweetheart, you."

She opened the box and lifted one of the Rollerblades high, purple and pink and black with pink fluorescent laces.

"I've wanted these ever since I saw a kid zooming around on them in Bozeman last year. Wait'll Rip sees me flashing by the inn on these babies. Why, he'll probably swallow his dentures."

She laced them both on and tried them around the living room, swooping, careening, scaring the hell out of Tripod until the cat dove under the Christmas tree.

"Up your ass!" Parrot said.

"Whatta gas this will be come springtime," Grandma said.

Then all four of them hushed at the solid knocking on the front door. Grandma skated to the door and swung it wide. Tom stood framed in the doorway, the rim of his black hat carrying an inch of downy snow. He regarded Grandma in her red holiday dress and Rollerblades and Peter in his new Pumps.

"Just going by, wanted to wish you a merry Christmas," Tom said.

They could see his Appaloosa gelding tied to the faded picket fence.

"Why, land sakes, I thought it was old St. Nick. Come in, come in." Grandma tottered on the Rollerblades and braced herself against the wall.

"Oh, no, I was just passing by."

"You get on in here and help us eat some of this food," Grandma said. Tom took off his hat and slapped it against his leg, dislodging the accumulated snow. He brushed the shoulders of his canvas duster and strode into the house, a bright red bull rag around his neck, a figure that could have been visiting on Christmas Eve a hundred and fifty years ago.

"Up your ass," Parrot squawked, and Tripod stalked the overburdened tree as though he took the slanders personally.

She had bought a third T-bone and had thought to offer Peter more than one on this festive occasion, but the potato-chip gorging had all but left the third steak forgotten in the refrigerator. She had it grilling in the oven and the deep-fat fryer heating well before Tom finished pulling off his duster and settled in the front room with Pete. While the food cooked, Grandma—still wobbling in her Rollerblades—brought the package marked with Tom's name and set it in his lap.

"Santa stopped just before you. Did you see his tracks?"

Tom regarded the package for a moment, obviously puzzled over how Grandma Chapman came up with a present for him when she had no idea he was coming. He pulled the baling knife from his belt and sliced through the tape and paper. The sight of the pure white Pumps brought a tinge of joy to his gloomy features, and he pulled off a diamondback boot to try it on. Pete noticed he was wearing his precious boots when it was snowing. Something was up.

"You're full of shit," the green bird cackled from near the top of the tinsel-draped spruce.

"Same to you, birdbrain," Tom said.

He pulled the other Twilight Zone on. Soon, she had him sitting at the table in front of a medium rare sixteen-ounce T-bone and a production line of homemade potato chips stringing from the deep fryer. In fact, when he finished the beef, he joined in concocting his own chips and destroying two more large potatoes.

"This is a rocky mountain oyster that got caught in the baler," Tom said, getting into the swing of the game.

"What did your father do when he saw the barn?" Grandma asked.

"He's really steamed, said I have to paint the whole damn barn if I want to keep living there." Tom laughed. "That'll be the day." Then his expression turned grim. "He says he knows Pickett put us up to it. I told him he was wrong, but he doesn't believe me."

Grandma and Pete exchanged a glance that reflected their mutual fear of George Stonebreaker and fear for Coach Pickett.

THE BOYS WERE shooting baskets with the sponge rubber ball and the miniature rim hanging above the hallway door when Grandma came from the kitchen.

"I haven't missed a Christmas Eve service at United Methodist since your grandfather died," she said, no longer in her Rollerblades. "Don't intend to start. Don't matter if you're Methodist or not, don't matter what you are, something mighty peaceful about it. You boys coming with me?"

Tom glanced at Pete. Then he sat down and quickly unlaced his game shoes, tugging into his J. Chisholm diamondbacks. They slipped into their coats and, in the gently floating snow, walked the block toward the candlelit church.

"Your horse be all right?" Grandma asked.

"Yeah, sure. He'll probably leave you a few Christmas apples."

"Apples?" Pete asked.

"Horse shit, city boy, horse apples." Tom laughed. "Where'd you get the cool jacket?"

"From Kathy."

He glanced at Grandma in the wake of his fiction. She didn't bat an eye. Then she noticed Tripod tagging along, making his intriguing unpaired track. She stopped and turned to Pete.

"Would you toss him in the house? I don't want him burning down the church with the candles and all. We'll wait."

Pete scooped up the family shadow and trotted back to the house.

"You ought to bring Parrot," Tom said.

With winter's brush gradually coloring them, Grandma nudged Tom and spoke quietly. "Why aren't you with your family tonight?"

"My dad told me to get the hell out."

"Your father is a hard man. He must have a torture chamber of pain in him somewhere. Try not to take it personally."

Tom regarded her in the sparkling, diffused light.

"The whole time I was growing up I was always afraid he'd kill me some day."

"And now you're growed up."

"Now, I'm afraid *I'll* kill him."

"You can stay with us tonight," she said as Pete returned. They crunched and squeaked through the snow to the church and joined the cluster of people filing into the modest cement church.

Grandma removed her snow-speckled felt hat as they entered the narthex.

Among the townspeople were Dean Cutter, his mother, and his sister, in a wheelchair. The boys nodded at Dean as Grandma squatted in front of the young girl.

"Hello, sweetheart. You look so nice tonight."

The golden-haired girl cocked her slightly wobbling head, her eyes met Grandma, and her mouth formed a twisted smile that dangled a gleam of spittle. The boys shifted uncomfortably.

"Merry Christmas," Grandma said, patting her hand.

In her colorful winter jacket, the girl made a muffled sound and nodded. Grandma leaned out of her crouch and wrapped her arms around the girl as others entered the church. Then Grandma stood and regarded Dean's mother, the worn-down-looking woman in her worn-down winter coat.

"Merry Christmas," Grandma said.

Sally Cutter forced a threadbare smile and nodded. Grandma stepped aside and Dean, with his mother following, pushed his sister down the aisle. Grandma and the boys followed, and after passing Olaf and the Painters, they found a place for three in a pew halfway up. When Grandma realized she was sitting next to Louella Straight, there with her family, she asked Pete to move onto her other side, beside Louella, because, Grandma claimed, she couldn't see.

THE LARGE CHRISTMAS tree dominated the cozy sanctuary, hung with homemade paper angels children had cut out and colored, and the aroma of candle wax and evergreen accented the peaceful silence and uncommon hush in which they all participated. Louella and Pete shared a hymnbook, and Grandma sang the Christmas carols with gusto, until the last, when the congregation stood, holding small burning candles, and sang "O Little Town of Bethlehem." Pete noticed she wasn't singing and regarded her from the corner of his eye.

O little town of Bethlehem, How still we see thee lie!

Tears streamed down her face and though she tried to sing, her voice choked on emotion.

Above thy deep and dreamless sleep
The silent stars go by;

Pete lost his voice on the third line and his eyes blurred.

Yet in thy dark streets shineth
The Everlasting Light;

As the congregation came to the last line in the verse, none of the three could manage a sound: as though some long-repressed sorrow found its way to the surface in the safety and warmth of that hallowed moment.

The hopes and fears of all the years
Are met in thee tonight.

AFTER STROLLING HOME through tumbling butterfly flakes, and after Tom had bedded down his Appaloosa in the backyard, the three kissed the night good-bye, eating cookies and drinking apple cider around the fragrant Christmas tree.

"Do you know Dean's sister very well?" Peter asked his grandmother.

"Denise? Yes, as little as I see of her."

"What's wrong with her?" Pete asked.

"Cerebral palsy."

"What's that do to you?"

"It's a damage to the brain. You tell your body what to do but it doesn't get the message."

"Does she understand you?" Tom asked.

"Oh, yeah, she just can't let you know very well," Grandma said, sipping at her cider.

"Can she ever go to school or anything?" Pete asked as Tripod leaped into his lap.

"Her mom teaches her the best she can at home. She's bright," Grandma told him.

"How long has she been that way?"

"Since the day she was born."

Pete thought about that a moment.

"She never even had one chance," he said as he stroked the cat.

"Don't you two go writing that girl off." She regarded each of them. "Don't you know that angels always come in disguise."

Tom slept on the sofa where Grandpa Chapman killed himself. Tom preferred to keep the Christmas tree lit through the night, and the three-legged cat curled beside.

When Grandma woke early and peeked in the front room, the young cowboy had taken his leave without a sound. The open shoe box remained under the tree, but Tom's game shoes were gone. A good sign, she thought, and she went back to bed.

CHAPTER 32

Peter waited from the porch with Grandma's suitcase in hand. When Hazel rolled up in a green 1976 Caprice and honked, he yelled over his shoulder, "She's here!"

Grandma came from the house with her Rollerblades under her arm. The sun had the sky to itself, warming the earth and stirring mild breezes into hope. Grandma opened the door and tipped the threadbare passenger seat back.

"Morning, Hazel, you're late."

Grandma pitched in the Rollerblades and stepped aside as Pete slid the suitcase onto the back floor. It looked like Hazel had been raising chickens in the backseat.

"Heavens to Betsy, quit your bellyaching," Hazel said. "I'm here, aren't I?"

Grandma pulled the seat back in place and slid in.

"Now don't forget to plug Trilobite in at night, even during the day if it gets cold again. Eat at the Blue Willow so you get a square meal. I'll only be gone two days. You got enough money?"

"You ought to go see your friend every week, you've given me money three times," Pete said and forced a laugh.

"Hope it's warmer in Billings, sidewalks'll be dry; I can get some roller-blading in."

She slammed the unwieldy door and cranked down the window.

"Don't kill yourself," Pete said.

"Nonsense. You take care of yourself, sweetheart." She turned to Hazel. "Hit it, we'll miss the bus."

She waved as the old Caprice rumbled away, tilting far to port, a listing ship whose cargo had shifted during a heavy storm. A bumpersticker read IF YOU LOVE JESUS, HONK! Pete watched until they pitched out of sight around the corner beyond the Blue Willow. His chest ached. For days he'd wished he'd be getting on the Greyhound with her and staying on all the way to Saint Paul.

With a howling emptiness he turned for the house. He didn't know how long he could stick. He grabbed his ball and slammed the door behind him, dribbling up the street, left hand, right hand, left hand, right hand, a cross dribble he knew once perfected would blow him by any defensive player in the state. After practice he'd cram the VW with kids and go cruise the drag in Bozeman. Tom was staying overnight with him until Grandma came back. He wondered who would stay with him until Kathy came back.

SATURDAY MORNING, THANKFUL he'd made it through another Christmas with the help of basketball videos and sleep, Sam drove the all-but-empty blacktop to Three Forks on his way to Bozeman. Besides stocking up on groceries, he had a personal shopping list, things he'd buy for himself in after-Christmas sales. He still caught himself anticipating some unexpected gift from Amy; she always would come up with something he loved but never would have thought of. He glanced at the snow-covered Madison range and realized he was getting better. He could remember little things like that without sliding into the sadness. Amy rode gently on his mind.

That's enough, let it go.

He'd worked the boys obsessively all week and thought they all needed the weekend off. The dog collar was working and Olaf was improving. But it bothered him how often he thought about Diana, how he found himself missing her, and it frightened him. He gazed across the winter ground to her little frame house, a half mile off the highway, and his heart skipped a beat remembering their night of bliss in its cozy shelter. A familiar pickup flew past him headed toward Willow Creek, and when he glanced in the rearview mirror his heart tried to leap out of his mouth.

It was George Stonebreaker, and he was slamming on his brakes and turning around!

Sam planted the gas pedal on the floor and his four-cylinder Ford strained to outrun the big V-8 coming from behind. With one eye glued on the rearview mirror, Sam could see Stonebreaker's battered pickup hurtling at him over the frost-heaved blacktop like a heat-seeking missile. He could see the man's large, alcohol-reddened face, feel the man's rage, and by the way the pickup was veering and weaving, figured he was drunk.

Sam had whipped his Tempo up to almost eighty, racing for Three Forks, when the madman rammed him from behind. Sam's head banged against the headrest, the glove box flew open, and he nearly lost control, swerving toward the deep ditch on the right and bringing it back within inches of rolling. The blow left several car lengths between them but the berserk rancher was closing in fast. Instantly covered with sweat, Sam thought for a second it was a beer truck from the Land of Sky-Blue Waters.

Stonebreaker slammed into him again, like a great battering ram. The air bags exploded, the horn blared, the car filled with smoke. Sam bounced off the ceiling and wrestled with the steering wheel. The jolt almost carried him into an oncoming car that swerved off on the left shoulder, missing a head-on by inches. He shoved the deflating air bag out of his way and struggled to stay on the road. The windshield was shattered but intact.

As he flew past the talc plant he knew he couldn't make the curve into Three Forks at eighty miles an hour and he slammed on the brakes. With a great sledgehammer blow Stonebreaker rammed him again, going into the curve, and the little Ford bounced wide, over the shallow ditch, just missing tons of concrete blocks stacked in the brickyard, across someone's lawn, and back onto the street. Terror filled his throat and a mounting rage in him wanted to stop the car, wait for the maniac, and shoot him squarely between the eyes. But he had no gun.

In the rearview mirror Sam could see that Stonebreaker had recovered from the collision and was coming like a wrecking ball, the pickup bouncing and veering wildly on his tail. Sam swerved to the right down a residential street, pulled the automatic transmission into second gear, and floored it. He turned north again at the first intersection. If he kept turning, he'd have a chance, evening the odds against the pickup's superior power.

He wove through the small town, striking fear into more than one driver and pedestrian, hoping someone would call the sheriff. Stonebreaker narrowly missed him at several intersections and overshot. When Sam turned west on Ash Street and headed for Main, he couldn't believe his eyes. Pulled in at the Conoco station on the corner was a beautiful shiny Montana

Highway Patrol gassing up. Sam jammed on the brakes and came skidding into the station in a cloud of dust.

"There's some drunk chasing me and ramming my car!" Sam shouted as he jumped from his Tempo and pointed.

Stonebreaker came roaring down the street, aiming his truck like a gun. Just when Sam was about to leap behind his car, Stonebreaker veered up the street, swerved around the Sacajawea Inn, and headed for the freeway, not so drunk he couldn't recognize the large gold badge on the patrol car's side door.

The patrolman slammed the gas hose in its housing and jumped into his cruiser. He peeled out of the station, his lights and siren came on, and Sam, with wobbly legs, flopped back into his car. His hands trembled, his chest heaved. He was back in the Burger King, back in the outhouse, back in the berserk world of chaos and violence, and he felt his anger overcoming his terror. He sat for a while until his heartbeat and breathing returned to something near normal. He hated that bastard, that monster who could reach into his life with his rage and violence. He hoped they'd hang him.

He got out and looked at the rear of his car. Trunk and taillights and bumper all mangled, but nothing terminal enough to keep him from driving. He conjectured that Stonebreaker had run out of car insurance a long time ago and that there was no hope there. He drove for the freeway. He wanted to see if the officer caught up with that sonofabitch and hopefully, if Stonebreaker resisted arrest, shot him.

Eight miles down the freeway he was in time to see the highway patrolman shove the handcuffed Stonebreaker into the backseat of the cruiser. He pulled over and answered the patrolman's questions as the officer filled out his report. Stonebreaker had failed the sobriety test, his fourth DUI on record for starters.

"Why was he after you?" the officer said.

Sam stood beside the Ford. He shrugged. "I have no idea."

The patrolman waited as though giving Sam time to think about his answer.

"Do you know him, owe him money, do business with him?"

"I teach at the high school in Willow Creek," Sam said. "I coach the basketball team."

The officer glanced up from his metal clipboard and grinned knowingly. "That could be it, maybe he's a disgruntled basketball fan."

Sam nodded and managed to smile back. Was the patrolman serious?

Sam dared a glance at Stonebreaker in the backseat of the cruiser while the patrolman took notes on the damage to Sam's car. It seemed that the alcoholic's furious glower would melt the window glass, and Sam turned away. When all necessary information was exchanged and the patrolman told him to drive directly to a body shop, Sam drove away.

He sighed. He wouldn't have to worry about Tom's father for a while. He hoped until after the basketball season, and he tried to laugh at a joke from his college days. After hours of testing and therapy, a guy sits in a room waiting for the psychiatrist's evaluation. The psychiatrist comes in and sits behind his large desk.

"Well, Mr. Wilson, I have good news for you. You're not paranoid."

"Whew," Mr. Wilson says, wiping his brow. "I'm sure glad to hear that."

"Yes, well, the tests definitely show that the world *is* out to get you!"

Sam laughed. Then he drove home slowly, admitting to himself a strong leaning toward paranoia.

CHAPTER 33

The following Monday morning, December thirty-first, Mervin strode into the café in Manhattan with the swagger of a gunfighter who knew he could outdraw anyone in the place, having savored this moment in his mind for a lifetime. He hung his insulated canvas coat on a hook at the end of the booth and stood for a moment as the three Monday morning regulars broke off their conversation and regarded him. They didn't seem to notice his confident posture or the confident smile hovering on his face as they looked up from half-eaten doughnuts, coffee cups, and spiraling cigarette smoke.

"Well, now, seeing we're playing Willow Croak this week, I didn't think you'd show up this morning," his brother said.

Mervin regarded his big brother Carl, a rock of a man, fifty-nine years of standing up and spitting in life's face, two hundred and thirty solid pounds on his frame, a face as resolute as the land. Though his complexion appeared to be eroded out of sandstone, it was his cold, gray eyes that caused everyone to back down. Mervin slid into the booth across the table from him.

"Let's see now. You've won one game already. Maybe you ought to give me odds," Carl said. He wore a green John Deere cap that looked as though it had gone through the transmission of a John Deere tractor.

"Yeah, they beat Lima," Lute Jackson said, a heavily built, unhurried dairy farmer. One of Carl's sidekicks, he wore the solemn-eyed expression of his Holsteins.

"Oh, yeah, Lima," Carl said, taking a drag on his cigarette. "Is that the Lima Beans?"

The three men roared, getting their Monday morning kicks, as usual, at Mervin's and Willow Creek's expense.

"Say," Carl said with a serious squint, "how's the scourge of Norway's fishball league?"

The cronies laughed with big brother.

"I remember when we beat Willow Creek in the sixty-nine Divisional Tournament," Sandy Hill said, a scrawny retired railroad engineer who used to highball Northern Pacific passenger trains through Manhattan at such speeds that the travelers would miss the town if they sneezed. "Randy Whitt hit a shot from the corner with three seconds on the clock. You had a ball club that year."

"Yeah, and I remember when gas was thirty cents a gallon," Carl said. "Willow Croak hasn't beaten us since they invented plastic and they never will again."

Without uttering a sound, Mervin reached into the upper pocket of his bib overalls and pulled out a neatly folded, brand-new, one-hundred-dollar bill. He set it on the table in front of his blustering sibling.

"Well, what have we here?" Carl said.

"A bet," Mervin said, tipping his brown wool cap back on his head.

"The man has lost his marbles," Lute said.

"You want to bet a hundred dollars on the game?" his brother said.

"That's why it's on the table," Mervin said.

"Don't you think that's a little bit heavy? We always bet five dollars."

"What's the matter, you chicken?"

"We've heard about your Norwegian totem pole," Sandy Hill said. "We'll saw him down and split him up for fire wood."

"One hundred dollars," Mervin said, no longer smiling at his brother.

"I don't want to take advantage of you," Carl said, blowing smoke in Mervin's direction.

"You're not afraid of little ol' Willow Croak are you?" Mervin said.

Carl's face flushed as he studied his little brother's swagger, a demeanor he hadn't seen in Mervin.

"All right, by God, it's a bet!" Carl said. "I'll have to write a check."

He snuffed his cigarette in an ashtray.

Per tradition, Lute Jackson held the money. Then every Monday after the game, Lute would ceremoniously present the winnings to Carl in Mervin's presence, usually two five-dollar bills, while the three and whoever else was in the cafe would roast the Willow Creek team.

With that semi-annual ritual taken care of—the teams played each other twice during the season—the four men settled into their usual discussion of less important matters such as foreign trade policies, the prime rate, and organic farming. But the two brothers remained preoccupied. Mervin wanted to get the hell out of there so Friday night would come quicker. Carl was restless, baffled by this uncharacteristic confidence in his little brother, and all of it revolved around that beanpole kid from the fjords.

"How's Maggie doing?" Sandy asked Carl, and Mervin tensed, attempting to keep his face expressionless.

"Not good . . . not good."

"It's a shame," Lute said, then shook his head.

When Mervin first heard Maggie had cancer, he wanted to drive straight to their farm, throw open her door, and beg for her forgiveness. But he knew he was too late, thirty years too late.

On his way home, Mervin knew things were all tangled up, but he was glad he'd suckered that sonofabitch into the hundred-dollar bet and he knew that the bet had to do with a whole lot more than the basketball game.

MONDAY AFTERNOON THE team practiced, and Sam still hoped Diana would show up at the last minute for New Year's Eve. She had to be back soon, school would resume on Wednesday. That morning, Hazel had followed him to the Ford dealer's body shop in Bozeman to drop off his car for a week. Riding home in the '76 Caprice, Sam was assailed by the odors of a chicken coop that had been sprayed with a nauseous sweet perfume. He tried to crack the window a bit but there was no handle. Though Hazel didn't mention it, the word was that she and Mavis Powers went in to Bozeman Saturday night to see a traveling bunch of the Chippendale dancers, beautiful young men in G-strings. Hazel reportedly sat in the front row, jamming five-dollar bills in G-strings and handling the goods she found there. Sam bet she was giggling and wondered if Mavis took the curlers out of her hair for such an ostentatious event.

Sam had ramrodded the boys all week, and with the taste of victory on their palates, they responded with fire and a willing zeal, doing all that he asked and beyond. Tom didn't mention his father and Sam let it lie. Hazel, Axel, and Grandma had continued their lend-lease program, donating their bodies to whatever purpose Sam dictated on the court to the raised eyebrows of many in the community, particularly Truly Osborn. But with Andrew Wainwright and Ray Collins on the school board, Sam no longer had to concern himself with that flank.

Not only did he keep the team stretching as if Diana were there, but he began working on the floor with the boys, suddenly feeling hamstrings he didn't know he had. He arrived decked out in his new multicolored nylon sweat outfit and black low-top coaching shoes, something he'd been wanting for a long time and finally found the courage not only to buy but to show up in at practice. The boys whistled when they first witnessed their low-key mentor decked out like a high-salaried NBA coach, and Olaf attempted to compliment him by saying, "You are looking cold."

Thanks to Grandma Chapman's luck and generosity, they scrimmaged three on three in their new white game shoes, to break them in, though Olaf's hadn't arrived yet. Meanwhile, Scott worked the transmitter on the Norwegian's paint prompter. They played for almost ten minutes the first time Olaf, already dripping wet, overstayed his welcome in the paint. Scott zapped him.

"Hiiiyyyyiiihh!" he shouted, leaping as if he'd been decked by a ghost.

All play stopped in animated suspension. The boys howled and regarded their smirking manager with suspicion. Sam checked the device and found it turned up to the maximum shocking power. He turned it down to an acceptable tickle, catching a mischievous grin infecting Tom and Pete in greater dimensions than the others. But accident or not, it apparently worked miracles. Olaf danced in and out of the paint without violating the three-second rule once during the rest of the practice. Scott lost interest when he could no longer jolt him, and Olaf ended the scrimmage by making several smooth turnaround hook shots. Only trouble was that he traveled.

After more than twenty minutes of wind sprints in which Tom didn't participate, Sam gathered the breathless boys around him. He shoved the glasses up on his nose.

"Friday we travel to Manhattan Christian. Saturday we play Twin Bridges at home. We've come a long way since our first game and I've seen giant steps of improvement."

Sam glanced into Olaf's eager, sweating face.

"Now we know something we didn't know then: We know we can win. These are the big boys, as some of you well know, excellent teams that have completely outclassed us in the past. Now we have the chance to see if we can run with them."

Sam caught Tom's eyes and found a hint of doubt.

"When we started, I asked you to do your best and you have all done that. But now I'm asking you to reach deep inside and extend beyond your best. There's a word for it that I want you to memorize, to breathe, to carve on your heart. *To transcend*. If your best is to run for ten minutes, run for eleven. If your maximum is to elevate three feet, go an inch higher. When your body and mind are screaming at you to quit, go five seconds more. That's what it will take, from all of us, if we're going to go to the next level."

"Do you think we can beat Christian?" Rob asked with a note of awe in his voice, as though speaking those words aloud was so incredible it verged on blasphemy.

"We can go as far as our hearts will lead. You boys are composing your own music, you are writing the lyrics of your life, and I want it to be a song you'll come back to over and over again, smile with pride in the warm glow of memory."

"I can't sing," Dean said in a squeaking voice.

"Yes, you can, Dean," Sam said, smiling at the freshman. "You make magnificent music, as if you are singing, when you play basketball."

Completely bewildered, Dean looked at his teammates to see if they knew what in a rat's ass their coach was talking about. Dean knew he couldn't sing a note and he couldn't play basketball worth a chicken turd. The coach was always talking funny like that and he wanted to pretend he knew what the coach was saying. Maybe if he practiced harder he'd understand, and he was willing to try this *trans end* stuff, but what bothered him most was that the other boys seemed to know exactly what the coach was talking about.

CHAPTER 34

That night there was constant traffic at Sam's door, though not the traffic he'd hoped for. First, Tom showed up around nine with an uncharacteristic look on his face. Sam was halfheartedly studying basketball on the VCR and he invited Tom to join him. Sam thought he caught a whiff of beer on Tom's breath as the cowboy settled on the sofa. It had always confused Sam why the self-confident cowboy image was so intertwined with alcohol when the last thing a drinking man had was self-confidence.

"I'm sorry about my dad chasing you," Tom said, glancing quickly into Sam's eyes.

Taken by surprise, Sam's anger rose in his throat.

"Your dad tried to kill me."

"He's in jail for thirty days," Tom said.

"A man like that needs to be locked away from a sane society."

"It's the damn alcohol," Tom said. "I hate him when he drinks, the things he does. I'm glad he's in jail."

"I know it must be hellish for you and your mom."

"Yeah . . . at least he doesn't hit her."

"How about you?" Sam said.

Tom looked away and shrugged.

"Maybe the jail time will turn him around," Sam said.

"That'll be the day."

Sam fought off the intense sadness in the room. "You want a Pepsi?"

Tom ignored the offer and went on as if he didn't want to leave it at that.

"I saved my money for three years, bought a beautiful buckskin gelding—two year old. I brought him along, trained him, worked with him for hours every day. Called him Horse. He followed me around like he thought I was his daddy or something. The summer he was five my dad wanted to take him to Three Forks and ride him in the rodeo parade. Finest looking horse we'd ever had. I told him No. I knew he'd be drinking. I was only thirteen. I was down in Ennis that day baling hay with the Donaldsons. My dad took Horse to the rodeo.

"We baled until after dark and I didn't get home until around eleven. Horse was gone and I knew my dad had taken him. I took our old Chevy and drove for Three Forks. When I got to Willow Creek, there was a patrol car sitting off the blacktop just past the elevator. Its lights were twirling and there were a few people standing around. It felt like I had a horseshoe in my stomach. I thought of my dad immediately. I didn't have a driver's license yet but I pulled over and got out.

"The patrolman was trying to get the story straight. Several people had reported a pickup and trailer dragging a horse down the blacktop. I felt sick, I couldn't breathe. The patrolman turned his flashlight on the pavement. There was a bloody smear trailing off onto the gravel. No one had been able to get a license plate number or recognize the pickup and they couldn't find the carcass. I knew instantly it was my father."

"Oh, God, Tom, how awful, how horrible."

"My dad hid out until noon the next day when the alcohol would be out of his blood. Then he showed up, said it had been a terrible accident. Said he'd gotten something to eat after the rodeo and then got in the pickup and drove for home. He forgot he'd tied Horse to the back of the trailer rather than loaded him. I couldn't sleep for weeks, running along in my mind behind that trailer with Horse, through Three Forks at a trot, then speeding up out of town, trying his damnedest to keep up at a full run and, finally, falling, hitting the blacktop with his hide, screaming, forty-five, fifty miles an hour, burning the hide off him, the incredible pain, the shock, wondering why this man was doing this to him."

Sam felt his throat go dry, his heart race, the perspiration breaking all over his body. It was the madness.

"I couldn't sleep for weeks," Tom said, "reliving Horse's last minutes being dragged to death, praying he died quickly before his organs were spilling out on the highway. There was a bloody smear from just outside Three Forks, all the way into Willow Creek. I wish I'd never seen what was left of him. My dad showed the sheriff the ditch where he'd dragged him that night. I wish I'd never seen his frozen brown eye still screaming from his slaughtered head.

"The sheriff couldn't prove squat. It passed for a terrible accident. But I knew my dad was drunk. I knew he came out of some bar and drove away drunk. I hate him and his goddamn alcohol. He can rot in jail for the rest of his life for all I care. Lock him up and mail the key to the moon and the world will be a better place!"

Tom wiped at his eyes and stared into the TV. They sat there in an utter silence despite the noise from the basketball game.

Someone knocked at the door and Sam was thankful, momentarily, off the hook. His heart was fluttering on the way to the door, but he attempted to keep the disappointment off his face as Carter, Louella, Olaf, and Pete bounded into the house a little after ten, back from a movie and hamburgers in Bozeman and looking for other ways to bring in the New Year.

"Having a big night?" Sam said.

"Oh, yeah," Pete said. "We've been down at the river listening to the ice crack."

"Great," Tom said, seeming to have thrown back the horror. "Now we can go out to my place and play cow pie."

"Cow pie?" Pete said.

"Yeah. We each put a buck in the pot and pick a cow. The one whose cow shits first wins."

They talked Sam into turning off basketball and finding *A Nightmare on Elm Street 3* at which they could hoot and shriek. Sam found two frozen pizzas in his freezer, and Pete scrambled back to his grandmother's to scrounge what pop he could. Louella insisted on going along, in case he couldn't carry it all.

The new year approached and they found pots and pans and other objects with which to make noise. Another knock at the door convinced Sam that Diana had made it back from California in time. After rushing to the door, his disappointment exposed itself when he found Rob and Mary on the dark front porch.

"Saw Carter's truck. Didn't know you were having a party," Rob said as he and Mary bustled in.

"I didn't either," Sam said, closing the door and trying to keep the heartache at bay.

They brought in 1991 together, and Sam attempted to hide his loneliness and find comfort in their company.

"Olaf," Rob called from the kitchen, "Carter and Louella want to know how *hard* . . ."

Louella and Carter sprang off the sofa where they flanked Olaf and ran into the kitchen screaming.

". . . the *tundra* is in Norway," Rob shouted before the girls got to him.

They played poker, sang the school fight song—sounding like Notre Dame alumni—ate everything that wasn't locked away, and the party broke up shortly after two in the morning.

When he was finally in bed, Sam could hear the wind that had eaten the Christmas snow and had left Willow Creek bare and dry. Sam shivered under his blankets. He kept seeing the bloody smear on the blacktop all the way from Three Forks, kept trying to evade the image of George Stonebreaker attacking him with his truck. Could he ever forgive the violent rancher, the Hamm's Beer truck driver, the monster with a shotgun?

A sudden sadness assaulted him and he strained to recall the scent of lavender soap.

Diana called Sam on New Year's Day, back from San Diego. She suggested they go for a drive and made only two demands: they could not even skirt the topic of basketball, and he should bring a swimsuit and towel. He told her how Stonebreaker had put his Ford in the shop and her voice became hesitant, as though she were contemplating canceling the invitation if Sam couldn't drive.

"Would you mind driving my car?" she said in an apologetic tone, "I'm really beat from all the driving."

"No, not at all. Always wanted to drive a Volvo."

When they hung up he grew excited at the thought of being with her in their bathing suits. He scrounged through drawers, closets, and overstuffed boxes, unable to recall if he owned one or not, finally discovering a scant silk red-and-white Speedo he remembered buying a few years ago at Krazy Days in Bozeman. But though it had been a good deal for a couple bucks, he wasn't sure he'd have the courage to wear what there was of it.

Since he started running, his waist had diminished noticeably, but as he tried on the Speedo in front of the bathroom mirror he could see that he filled it completely and that it left little to the imagination. He quickly put on clothes over the swimsuit.

Diana pulled up in front of Sam's house and stepped out of the black Volvo. The car looked road-weary, with dirt and winter scum streaking its fenders and wheels. He wanted to wrap his arms around her and kiss her but she quickly danced around the car and slid into the passenger seat. He settled in the stylish leather bucket seat beside her and smiled.

Wearing jeans, a pink sweater, and a light pink-and-blue ski jacket, and with her long hair flowing free, she unsettled him to such a degree that he made a horrendous noise with the starter, engaging it when the engine was already running. She grimaced.

"Hello. How was the trip?" he asked quickly in an effort to cover his embarrassment.

"Fine up till now." She laughed.

"Sorry about that. The engine's so quiet I thought—"

"It's all right."

He drove tentatively out of Willow Creek and tried to use his memory of Amy to mortar some kind of defense. But he knew a desolate part of him ached to fall in love with this delectable woman.

"Why a Volvo?" he asked, searching for a normal heartbeat.

"It's the safest car on the road."

"That's it? No thoughts of resale value, gas mileage, affordable parts?"

"It's the safest," she said emphatically. "The other things don't mean much if you're dead."

They cruised along the grandstanding Jefferson River, through its twisting cavernous gorge, and out into the magnificent valley south of Whitehall. More and more Sam felt at home in the mountains, where their permanence gave him a sense of security.

He brought her up to date on Willow Creek's adventures while she was gone, including Hazel's raucous behavior with the Chippendale dancers, at which Diana hooted.

"They ought to lock him up and burn down the jail," she said with bitterness when he filled in the details of George Stonebreaker's berserk highway assault. "Next time he'll come with a gun."

Startled, he glanced over at her, as if for an instant she *knew*. He stared back at the highway and calmed himself.

Next time he'll come with a gun.

Thankful for the reminder, he gained his balance and got his feet back on the ground. He would not fall in love with her. Maybe they could be good friends, even lovers, but he would keep his heart out of it. Oblivious to the turmoil boiling in him, Diana seemed to be transfixed by the magnificent mountain landscapes.

Suddenly, she grabbed his arm.

"Stop! Pull over, please, quickly!"

Sam pulled the black sedan to the shoulder and stopped. She unbuckled the seat belt and got out. He watched her in the rearview mirror walking back down the highway. Then he got out and followed her. She stopped and was kneeling over something at the edge of the blacktop. It was a large jack rabbit, fluffy white in its winter coat. It lay on its side in a peaceful pose, except for the dried blood on its muzzle.

She picked it up gently and walked down into the ditch and over to a fence line where there was a thick bed of dried grass. She knelt and carefully laid the animal in a soft winter bed.

"What are you doing?" Sam asked.

"Would you leave the body of a *person* lying alongside the highway?"

"Of course not."

"We slaughter creatures such as this one without a thought," she said, gazing down at the pure white animal. "We kill them for sport, we destroy their living space and consider them a nuisance to be trapped and poisoned, and yet they're our fellow residents of this earth. Our future and theirs is irrevocably intertwined. The least we can do is to show them our respect."

She stood, glanced once more at the rabbit, then turned for the car.

Sam followed her, wondering what would be next with this woman.

Through Twin Bridges, they followed the Ruby River Valley to Sheridan and then on to Virginia City as a sallow January sun ducked behind the foothills far to the southwest.

"I think we're going to lose Peter," he said.

"Ah, ah, ah." She shook a finger. "None of that."

They stopped to eat in Ennis, and she insisted on paying for their food.

"My idea, I buy the chow."

He fumbled for his wallet and left an overly generous tip in an effort to even things up, recognizing her attempts at keeping things light, friendly, anything but a romantic date.

Out the door into the sudden winter darkness she said, "Want to go hot potting?"

"Where?" Sam's mouth went dry.

"Norris, Beartrap Hot Springs, you've never been there?"

"No."

BLEACHED WHITE FROM sun and steam, a rough wooden fence enclosed the hot spring and appeared as though it hadn't changed since the miners and railroad men soaked their weary bodies in the soothing flow a century ago. The dressing room was a wooden shack tacked on the west edge of the pool, where frayed curtains covered cockeyed doorways and one bare light bulb illuminated the interiors. Sam hurried, wanting for him and his Speedo to be in the water before Diana appeared.

When he came out, she was nowhere in sight. He stepped down the wide stairs until he was waist deep into the clear, steaming water. One low-watt spot halfheartedly illuminated the rustic bathing hole, allowing him to detect the few people who were soaking in the wooden pool, which appeared to be about thirty foot square.

He could scarcely make out a young couple lurking in the far left corner. Three middle-aged men to the right of the stairs drank beer and prattled in tones that implied an alcohol-induced loosening of the tongue. A family of five played on the left side, where a pipe shot water high into the air and allowed it to fall back into the pool like a small waterfall.

With the satin-smooth water covering him, Sam glided over the water-logged timbers and settled in the far, unoccupied corner. From there he could hardly even see the others lounging in the tingling, blissful bath, and he was left to anticipate the vision he expected to emerge from the women's dressing room.

Finally, Diana stepped out into the dim light, her bright yellow bikini stretched as snugly as her San Diego tan. Her long, dark hair spilled over her shoulders as she descended the rough wooden steps and let the water lap against her rib cage. The three men became silent, unconsciously lowering their Bud cans, gaping at her across the steamy pool. Even the male half of the couple in the corner allowed himself a direct stare.

She stepped close and half-whispered from her natural pout: "I figured I might as well wear the bikini. I mean, it isn't as though you haven't seen me before."

"It's not that." Sam swallowed. "Why don't I want other men seeing you in it?"

"I don't know, but I think I like that."

He settled on the submerged bench that ran along the edge, leaving him chest-deep in the soothing water, and she stood, between his knees now, her hands on his shoulders. With hungry eyes, he shamelessly traced her sumptuous body. Then he glanced up into her mischievous eyes, overcoming his reluctance and nervousness by allowing his hands to grasp her willowy waist.

"How long will Stonebreaker be in jail?"

He broke eye contact and glanced over her shoulder, catching the three men ogling her, men, he imagined, who were aching inside and wondering what a goddess such as her was doing with him. It was, he knew, a common male response.

Tenderly she brushed aside his damp hair and kissed him lightly on the forehead.

"Thirty days . . . ah, twenty-six now," he said with his lips on her ear.

She turned and sat in his lap, his hands still around her waist.

"A monster like that should be put away permanently," she said, leaning her head back on his shoulder so they were cheek to cheek, gazing out over the steaming pool.

"It's funny you should use that word," he said

"What word?"

"'Monster' . . . I ran into one of them a long time ago . . ."

"What happened?" she said.

"I suppose you could say he's the reason I'm in Willow Creek."

"Who was he?"

"I've never told anyone."

"Tell me," she whispered.

He held on to her, his arms tightly around her waist as though fearing he might be blown away by a sudden wind. Then something gave way in him and, soaking in that primitive hot spring somewhere in the mountains of Montana, he told Diana Murphy about Amy, about their love for each other, about her sudden, shattering death, about his flight from the sadness, about his clinging to something he couldn't name.

"I grew up with the illusion there was someone out there who would love and cherish me," he said, "in the way commercials and movies and love songs promised. After years of searching and meeting flaky people, I gave up. I realized there *was* no one like that out there. It was all a romantic illusion. Then I met Amy."

Diana didn't speak, but he felt her shudder and tremble in his arms.

"Why didn't I *know*?" Sam said so loudly some of the other soakers turned his way. "There had to be a warning of the madness as we approached that terrible force field."

"The horror," she said.

"You've seen it?"

"Yes, I've seen it."

"Why didn't I sense what was coming?"

"We can't," she said. "Don't torture yourself with that. The horror strikes when we least expect, demolishing our lives."

He felt her tummy heave with a sob. She turned, standing in the water, and cradled his head against her breasts.

"When the sadness came, I realized it had been there all along," he said, "underneath it all. Everyone tries to hold it down, deny it with the routines and busyness of everyday life, never calling it by name. Preachers sugarcoat it, teachers hide it, therapists duck it, but people in the mental wards see it. Parents never let on to their children, telling them to smile for their photos, pretending they've never caught a glimpse of it. For years I've kept myself busy, hurrying, working, reading, channel surfing, never taking my eye off the TV screen, afraid that lurking in a corner I'll notice a shadow of the sadness."

When he'd told it all, she held him. They didn't speak for several minutes, listening to the others in the pool, laughing and splashing and drinking to avoid their own sadness.

"Do you still miss Amy terribly?" she said.

"Sometimes."

"I miss Jessica terribly sometimes."

"You lost her when she was four?"

"Yes."

"That's got to be tough," he said with his lips against her collar bone.

"It's the horror," she said softly, and he sensed it was still too painful for her to talk about.

She held his head against her and whispered into his ear, "I'm so sorry . . . for you . . . for Amy. So sorry."

He lost it then, and sobbed quietly in her arms, shrouded by the steam and the night, letting his sorrow pour out of his eyes and into the pool, mixing with the water of the creek, from which it would flow to the Madison, then the Missouri, the Mississippi, and out into the Gulf of Mexico.

After several minutes, Sam looked up, and he felt released, forgiven in some way he couldn't explain or understand, suddenly free to be with this woman without any paralyzing freight from his past, to be alive and passionate and completely there with her.

Though they were less and less visible in the thickening steam and fog, he wished the others would leave. He'd even bribe them to leave—fifty bucks to everyone if they would just head out.

"Your ex-husband must have been mentally deficient, an imbecile, a lunatic, a half-wit, a congenital idiot, a simpleton, a moron, a mutant, a—"

She gently put a finger to his lips and silenced him with her eyes. She took his trembling hands and placed them on the back of her neck, pressing them against the bow of her bikini string.

"Pull," she said.

Sam glanced around, checking the others around the pool. The family was heading for the dressing rooms; he wondered if he owed them fifty dollars. The two lovers appeared to be breaking camp also, and he wondered if they could read his mind. The bullshitting, beer-drinking trio occasionally cast a lusting glance through the suspended mist and it appeared as though they were almost out of beer.

With her up to her armpits in the water, he gently tugged on the string and her bikini top drifted into his lap. He pulled her close, his Speedo straining to its stitched-nylon limits, his breath coming in such short gasps he thought he might faint.

"You know what you're always telling the boys—we're here to have some fun."

He kissed her, following his instincts and vaguely recalling from some clouded past that he mustn't fall in love.

Within minutes they were alone, the others having shuffled off to their cars. Sam and Diana were two hungry, lonely people, trying to escape the madness with their frenzied love.

Sam released a cry that carried out over the steam-blanched walls into the silent sky, and he noticed that a winter moon had been brazenly watching them.

Another couple appeared through the gate and went into the dilapidated dressing rooms. In a daze, Sam and Diana cuddled, with her on his lap. When the other couple appeared and stepped into the pool, Sam staggered toward the dressing rooms still holding Diana's hand, having forgotten for that moment that he had another life somewhere beyond these weather-scarred walls.

On the drive home through the wild, nocturnal landscape, she snuggled to him with feline softness.

"I wanted to take your mind off the team," she said.

"What team?"

Driving with one hand holding hers in her lap, he wondered how he could ever leave her and return to his solitary bed, suspecting that tonight he had passed from his familiar world of cold isolation into one of warmth and closeness.

CHAPTER 36

Elizabeth Chapman was desperate, sure that her grandson was making a mistake he'd regret the rest of his life. In her desperation, she decided the only thing that might sway him to reconsider was to tell him how she lost her hand. She'd never told his mother the truth, and no one in Willow Creek knew, but it was the only card she had to play that might derail Peter's headlong rush back to his girlfriend.

She stood in the doorway to his room while he stuffed clothing into his duffel bag.

"You promise me you'll talk to Coach Pickett before you leave," she said.

"I promise. Besides, he's not home. I've been over there three times."

"Well, you hold off your packing a minute and you listen to me, boy, and listen good."

"I'm listening, I'm listening." He threw himself onto his bed and lay there, staring at the ceiling.

"Your grandfather and I were sweethearts when he joined the Navy and went off to war. His ship fought in the South Pacific, a 'tin can' he called it, and somehow he managed to stay alive. When he came home after the war he got a job as a deputy sheriff and we got married. But like I told you, he had a drinking problem, and after a couple of years he lost his job because of it. Well, I was young and full of vinegar and I figured it was my Godgiven duty as his good wife to save him, to make him stop drinking."

Peter slipped past her into the bathroom to grab his personal things.

"Are you listening to me, boy?"

"Yeah, I'm listening," he called from the bathroom. "You thought it was your duty to make him stop drinking."

"Right," she said, raising her voice. "Well, one night he told me he was going off to the Legion Hall to get together with some of the vets, no women allowed. I knew it was just an excuse and I told him I was going with him to see that he didn't get to drinking, said that I'd even drag him out of there in front of his buddies. We got to fighting, yelling and arguing until he just picked me up and hauled me off to the garage. Your grandfather was a powerful man."

Peter scrambled back into his room and gathered his Walkman and tapes.

"Well, he still had a pair of handcuffs from his deputy days and he handcuffed my left wrist to a metal pole in the middle of the two-car garage. I couldn't reach a thing. He was laughing and said not to wait up for him, that he'd damn well do what he wanted with his life. He turned on a light, left me a jug of water, a pillow and blanket, a radio playing, and shut the door. In a few minutes I heard him drive off."

"Did you have any neighbors?" Peter said as he tucked a small bundle of Kathy's letters into his bag.

"We were living in Utah then, a ways out from town on a dirt road. I was embarrassed, humiliated, and plenty sore. I hated to admit he'd gotten the best of me and I tried to figure a way out of that mess. The floor was concrete and there was no way I was going to move that metal post. Wasn't until I'd settled down a bit that I realized he'd closed the cuff on my left hand to the last notch. It was too tight."

"Damn, Grandma, what did you do?" Peter sat on his bed.

"At first I panicked, started yelling every few minutes, just in case, and when I'd hear a car coming by I'd shout bloody murder. Hand got red and started swelling up and hurting real bad. I was scared. Poured water over my wrist and tried wiggling out of the cuffs but couldn't. After a while the pain stopped, hand turned white and I couldn't feel it much. Laid down and tried to sleep but I kept peeking at my hand. It got all blue, looked a fright and then I heard him come home. By then my voice was shot. I'd yelled until it was raw and I couldn't make a sound. I pounded the water jug on the concrete floor, hoping he'd notice I wasn't in bed and remember, but I knew he'd be drunk as a skunk. He stumbled into the house and fell asleep on the sofa, never looked in the bedroom, forgot all about where he'd left me."

"He was a mean sonofabitch." Peter scowled.

"He found me around ten Sunday morning, rushed me to the hospital, but by then my hand was black, they couldn't save it. The law wanted to throw him in jail but I told them I put the handcuffs on myself to keep me from going into town and acting foolish. Nobody believed me but there was nothing they could do."

"They should've hung the bastard." Peter pushed his way out of the room. "I'm glad I never knew him." He searched through the kitchen and came back with a sweatshirt, then stuffed it in his duffel bag. Grandma grabbed his shoulder and directed him to her stuffed chair.

"You listen to me now, Peter Strong."

She squatted in front of him.

"I wanted to leave him, but I thought I could save him, that somehow my life depended on his. So, I stayed. My decision was bad for both of us, we never should've been together. He didn't touch a drop for six, seven months, devastated by what he'd done to me. He could be a prince when he wasn't into the booze and I got pregnant with your mother during those sane months when he wasn't drinking. Lucky for you, huh?"

"Yeah," he said with a slight smile.

"But I wouldn't let him forget, found subtle ways to stick it in his face, no forgiveness. I became a real cunning bitch. That's how he went back to his faithful, forgiving bottle. It was the only way he could black out his guilt. Every time he saw my stump it reminded him. When your mother was about grown, I finally gave up my anger. I tried to forgive him, told him over and over."

Peter's face had turned ashen and she worried that she'd thrust too much on his young heart.

"Your mother doesn't know any of this, don't know for sure why I'm telling you except that it comes down to this: I squandered the best years of my life trying to make a man who didn't love himself love me, and I just don't want to see you miss your chance at something special in life trying to make someone love you." She grunted as she stood up. "That's all I've got to say."

"I just want to find out if Kathy loves me or not, that's all." Peter cleared his throat, and she could tell he was choking up. "I'm sorry about your hand, Grandma . . . and about all that stuff with Grandpa. Thanks for having me, I . . ."

He didn't finish. He pushed out of the chair and went to the kitchen door. "I gotta tell the coach."

Tripod followed him.

She knew he was making a terrible mistake, that he would be tied to some girl's skirts the rest of his life and not do what he was meant to do. But Grandma Chapman had learned, finally, that she couldn't save anyone, not even herself. She prayed Mr. Pickett could do what she'd failed to do.

WHEN SAM AND Diana pulled up in front of his house, they embraced in the Volvo.

"If I don't have you again I will cut my throat."

"We can't have you dying in the middle of the season," she said.

He watched her taillights disappear at the end of Main Street and all the old feelings came rushing back. What was he doing? Did he understand what was at stake?

Sam walked to the house and was startled by a shadowed figure sitting on the sagging front porch.

"I need to talk to you, Coach, if you've got a minute," Peter said.

Sam felt the tightening in his stomach. "Sure, sure, c'mon in."

Sam attempted to gather his thoughts as he opened the door and lit lamps in the front room. They settled in and the room seemed strangely quiet without the customary basketball tape playing on the TV screen. Peter explained his decision at some length. When he finished he regarded Sam with imploring eyes.

"I don't know what to do. I want to go back, to be with my friends and my mom, but I want to stay with my grandma and the team. I hate to leave in the middle of the season. I know how much the team needs me."

"When would you go?" Sam asked as calmly as he could manage.

"Tomorrow. I could catch a bus late afternoon."

"What does your grandmother say?"

"She says if I go now, I'll regret it for the rest of my life. She thinks I'm going back because of my girlfriend."

"Are you?"

"No . . . not really . . . I don't know. Damn it, Coach, I just don't know. She dumped me a couple months ago."

"But I thought—"

"I didn't want anyone to know."

Sam pushed the glasses up on his nose and cleared his throat.

"Pete, we come to forks in the road we can't avoid, and the way we choose changes the direction of our life forever. Life is not forgiving. We can never go back. I've got the funny feeling that this group of boys is very unusual, as though you were meant to come together for this one bright season, from Saint Paul, from Norway, from the plowed fields surrounding Willow Creek. We want you to be with us, but I don't want you to stay to win basketball games. I want you to stay because of this chance to do something you may never be able to do again, something that will prepare you and inspire you for the journey ahead. I believe you're here for a special purpose, but I could be wrong. God knows I've been wrong before. Don't you think it's strange that you ended up in Willow Creek this year?"

"Yeah. I've thought about that."

"I have a hunch I'm in the place I'm supposed to be right now," Sam said. "I've never felt that before. I have no idea how I got here. Sometimes it seems more by fluke or accident or Fate's sense of humor than my making the right choices. Somehow we've been drawn together in this common quest, and maybe, whether we know it or not, someone else has a hand in it."

Sam gathered himself.

"I know how hard it will be for you to decide." He reached over and put his hand on Peter's shoulder. "Do what you feel in your heart."

"That's the trouble. It's all mixed up inside. Whatever I decide—it seems right and wrong at the same time."

"I wish I could be more help."

The boy glanced at Sam and he had tears in his eyes.

"Say good-bye to the team for me. I can't."

"Okay, I will."

SAM LAY IN bed restlessly and fought off the images that found him there with no defenses. He'd shared the hidden place of his soul with Diana and she offered him all that was missing from his life, there for the taking if he'd dare to open his heart. But he knew the terrible danger, the terrifying possible consequences.

He came out of a shallow sleep shortly after three. That familiar swishing sound went past his window but when he got out of bed and squinted into the darkness there was nothing there. He could see a million stars. How could they go on without Peter Strong? How could he go on without Diana? He asked the stars. They winked at him mutely from an eternal silence.

CHAPTER 37

Wednesday, the first day back at school, word spread, and by the time the boys gathered for practice, everyone knew that Peter Strong had jumped ship. All day Sam had rehearsed what he could say to keep the team afloat, to make any sense for them to carry on with only five boys.

While Sam was trying to patch together some survival plan for his unraveling basketball team, his mind kept drifting back to the Beartrap Hot Springs, where he carelessly and foolishly lowered his defenses and became dangerously vulnerable. And now he missed her, felt off balance, and couldn't get her out of his head.

At practice, Diana greeted him politely and stood with the boys under the south basket. Axel and Hazel joined the group, but Grandma sat on the lower bench of the bleachers, ostracizing herself as though she bore the blame for her grandson's desertion.

The plan was simple. With Dean a starter, they would each have a specific role and they would stick to that role no matter what. They would employ a zone defense. Dean would play out front and harass the guards, using his quickness and stamina to full advantage, but he had to avoid fouling. Curtis would play the baseline corner where he would also hound his opponent with his long arms, keep a body between his opponent and the basket, and rebound. Dean and Curtis would keep moving, setting picks and screens for the other three boys. They were never to shoot unless they had a clean breakaway to the basket for a layup. Only Tom, Rob, and Olaf were to shoot the ball.

Sam went over it several times and then they went to work against the village scrubs. When practice was about over and the boys were shooting free throws, Sam caught Diana before she ducked into the girls' locker room.

"How about dinner tonight?" he asked. "I don't feel like cooking."

"Oh, thanks, that sounds wonderful, but I have so much to do to catch up I better not." She smiled warmly. "See you tomorrow."

He felt his chest ache. He turned back to the boys. "Same way every time!" he shouted. "Develop your ritual. Same way every time!"

MERVIN PAINTER ARRIVED at the Manhattan Christian gym early and staked out a seat for himself and Claire right at center court, four rows up. He usually sat down at the far end, where the whipping they took didn't seem so personal. But tonight he wanted to be smack dab in the sweat and heat of it. He was unable to remember being so ready for a brawl. His mind kept leaping ahead to Monday morning when he'd march into the café and finally lord it over that sullen bastard of a brother.

Olaf was becoming like an adopted son, and the lanky Norwegian caused more than a mild stir among the fans filling the bleachers, dunking the ball while running layups during a warmup drill with what looked like a pickup team in a refugee camp. Mervin felt a fatherly pride watching him. He knew that though they were somewhat intimidated, the Willow Creek boys relished the chance to play in this sizable gymnasium where you didn't have to pick your teeth out of the wall after a layup or trip over a fan's shoes down the sidelines.

His brother Carl bulldozed his way into the gymnasium without Maggie at his side. Mervin hadn't seen her at a game for years and for him it was just as well. Regret was an unforgetting, unforgiving traveling companion. Carl climbed up the bleachers with Lute Jackson and Sandy Hill in tow, and he entrenched himself straight across from Mervin. He wore a crisp, green John Deere cap and was undoubtedly figuring how he'd spend Mervin's crisp, green hundred-dollar bill.

Manhattan Christian was located in Churchill, a peaceful rural hamlet where the surrounding dairy farms and cattle ranches were meticulously manicured and where basketball was second only to God, or vice versa, depending on whom you talked to.

Mervin knew it was just damn luck that because of the density of the surrounding farms and the wide draw this private school enjoyed, their coach had the luxury of cutting boys to get down to the officially allotted twelve. Though Mervin understood the practicality of it, he admitted the resentment he felt over the past several years because Christian would only send out their JV's against Willow Creek, allowing their varsity to schedule two additional games with more worthy opponents and blatantly humiliate the Willow Creek boys.

Mervin anchored the small contingent from Willow Creek. Beside the diehards, Ray Collins sat with his family, mostly to see if Poke's collar had done the trick.

When the teams took their mark at center court, Mervin felt goose bumps on the back of his neck. Only he wished his Willow Creek boys looked a little sharper out on the basketball floor. They wore faded, mismatched gold jerseys and shorts. The skinny Jenkins kid looked like he could fly if he could learn to flap his mulelike ears, the bowlegged Cutter kid looked like you could fire a cannon between his legs and not touch a hair. And Olaf looked like a scarecrow with his ill-fitting uniform, long skinny legs, and enormous game shoes. They looked more like the Katzenjammer Kids, more like a comic, underfed jailbreak than a basketball team.

From the opening jump, Mervin was hovering between glimmers of hope and utter despair. The Willow Creek boys managed to stay out in front through the first half, but in the second half they were dropping passes, missing shots, and traveling with the ball. His goddamn brother was beating him up again, just when he dared to believe it would finally be different.

Mervin clung to the wooden bleacher with both hands and shouted until he was hoarse. He felt a kinship with Andrew Wainwright, the talc plant executive, who was a cut above the farm-implement caps and unpolished boots, there in his fancy tailored suit, pulling for the boys. He looked more like a banker, or worse, a lawyer. With his suit coat off and his shirt sleeves rolled up, he was leading the vocal charge, although the Willow Creek fans were outnumbered twenty to one.

Mervin wished Grandma Chapman's grandson had stayed, though in his heart of hearts he thought the kid was doing the right thing: run to your girl and hang on to her until they chop your arms off. Mervin just wished the kid had stuck one more week, until they'd knocked his arrogant brother off his throne into the maggot-infested manure of loss.

Willow Creek made a late surge. With twenty-three seconds to go and Christian ahead by one point, the little Cutter kid slapped the ball out of a Christian player's hands and Rob Johnson grabbed it and dribbled into the front court. Fans on both sides of the gym stood, holding their breath.

Stonebreaker put a bulldogging pick on Olaf's man and the big Norwegian swung into the paint. With four seconds on the clock Olaf caught a high pass from Johnson and jammed the ball in the basket.

The horn sounded!

They won! They broke Christian's long domination over Willow Creek.

Mervin exploded with joy, the ecstatic Willow Creek fans jumped and hooted and shouted, the Christian fans slumped, stunned with blank faces. But the referee blew his whistled and signaled.

The basket *did not count!*

The referee rolled his hands as though he were balling yarn. Traveling! Halfway out of the bleachers, Mervin felt a stab in the chest. The Willow Creek fans slumped back into their seats as though shot by the man in the striped shirt, and the enraptured Eagle fans erupted in cheers. Mervin led a heated chorus of booing as the referees fled to the dressing room.

Christian fans wiped perspiration from their brows and praised God for providing such a clear-eyed and honorable referee.

Mervin led Claire to their car in the darkened parking lot against a chilling wind from the north that felt like his brother's curse. Damn, the boys played their hearts out. It was far worse than losing by forty, it was more painful having had the game in their grasp, tasting it, and then having it ripped away in the final second. He felt the blood rush to his face. His brother had beaten him again, snatched the hope out of his life, and he didn't dare believe that it would ever be different.

AFTER LICKING THEIR wounds at the Blue Willow for an hour or so, Carter insisted on driving Olaf home. Olaf asked Rob and Mary along, and they agreed to ride shotgun. Because of the stick shift, Olaf had to stuff himself in on the passenger side, leaving the other two kids between him and Carter.

"It's too bad your family couldn't have seen you tonight," Carter said.

"No, I'm not wanting my father to see," Olaf said.

"But you played so well," Mary said.

"That stupid referee is blind," Carter said. "He just didn't want Willow Creek to beat Manhattan Christian."

"You got that right," Rob said. "We'd have taken them if Pete was still here."

"Yeah . . . but he's not," Carter said.

When she parked in the yard, Carter left the pickup running and walked Olaf to the house.

"Good game, Oaf," Rob called, "we'll get 'em."

"You were great," Mary said.

The lights were on in the big barn and they could hear someone hammering, which normally would have drawn Olaf to see what was going on. But right then he didn't have the courage to face Mervin, who had told him about his bet with his haughty brother. He wanted so badly to win the game for his kind and genial hosts, especially for Mervin.

At the door Carter wrapped her arms around him the best she could. "I know it hurts. I'm sorry. You played so well."

"Ya, but we are hurting together. It is okay."

Carter lingered, hugging his waist.

"You can kiss me if you'd like," she said.

"Oh . . . thank you," he said, but he had other things on his mind. He didn't speak. He stood there, hearing the hammering in the barn.

"Good night," Carter said, and then she released him.

"Good night. Thank you for giving a ride."

Carter walked to the truck. Olaf stood there, listening.

WHEN MERVIN HADN'T come in by midnight, Claire got worried and was unable to sleep without him next to her. She fixed a thermos of coffee and bagged a handful of his favorite chocolate chip cookies. She pulled on her coat and carted the offering out to the barn to see what he was up to at this time of night, to coax him to the house and to bed.

In the barn she found her fuming spouse hammering a two-by-four framework on the end of the loft wall, too upset to talk or explain what on earth he was doing. He did consent to drink the coffee and eat the cookies, and that assured her he was working through his anger on schedule and would probably slip into the warm bed beside her within the hour. On her way back to the house she wondered where all this basketball business was leading and she knew that Carl and Maggie Painter were somehow stuck in her husband's craw.

CHAPTER 38

The Twin Bridges Falcons came north like birds of prey to pick clean the bones of the Willow Creek team. They strutted into the gymnasium ready to add a notch to their already impressive win column. Thus far, they had no loss column, and it was inconceivable that the first one would come from a town that their new bus driver had trouble finding.

Peter's desertion had scattered Sam's hopes. He was teetering, losing his balance, and he knew he had to get a grip on himself for the boys' sake, for his five remaining boys, standing with him.

Only a small contingent of fans showed up from Twin Bridges, not for lack of team support, Sam guessed, but for lack of interest in watching their Falcons stomp a hapless bunch of uncoordinated boys into the varnish one more time. Thus, when the trip to Willow Creek appeared on their schedule, most of their avid fans probably thought more of saving gasoline and rented videos.

On the Willow Creek side the bleachers held only a few dozen, a big turnout for a town where the question of whether or not the band would make it through the national anthem held more suspense for the spectators than the basketball game. Little kids chased about, the three cheerleaders practiced cheers in a world of their own, and parents hobnobbed around the concession window until game time.

Diana, in a striking blue-and-gold jumpsuit, saw to it that the boys stretched properly before the game. Mervin Painter entrenched himself in the stands, top row, middle of the court, not the pew he and Claire usually occupied. His fierce posture replaced his usual mellow manner, while beside him Claire beamed at the anarchic activity around her. Not far from the Painters, John English stepped up into the bleachers and sat, the first game he'd appeared at and one he knew for sure Willow Creek would lose, adding ammunition to his efforts to abolish the basketball program.

The teams warmed up. Twin Bridges, twelve strong in matching sweats and loud banter, displayed evidence of being a contemptuous, well-trained squad. Willow Creek, with only five, found it difficult to even run a layup drill.

Sam was proud of his team. They stayed with Twin Bridges until halfway through the third quarter, holding back the inevitable avalanche they all knew was coming. Craig Stone, a Falcon center, was abusing Olaf in the paint and the referees seemed blind to it—cheap shots with his elbows, jabs to the ribs—and when Olaf retaliated he was called for the foul. Tom had had enough of it. As the teams hustled downcourt, Tom ran alongside Stone and pushed the opposing player headfirst into the second row of the bleachers, somewhere in the vicinity of rotund Axel Anderson and the more fragile Truly Osborn. Stone came out from among the shocked and delighted Willow Creek fans with his fists flailing, walled off from Tom by the referees and coaches.

Tom was tossed out of the game, banished to the locker room, and the avalanche came down on all of their heads. Twin Bridges poured it on, five against four, until Olaf fouled out. At five against three there was no mercy. The haughty Falcons used Curtis and Rob and Dean for fodder and yet the Willow Creek boys never gave up, occasionally stealing a pass and even scoring.

When it was mercifully over, 72 to 51, Jeff Long, the balding Twin Bridges coach, approached Sam out on the floor.

"Your kids are quite good," he said as he shook Sam's hand.

"They're better than that, they're excellent," Sam replied.

"You ought to clean up your act," Diana said over her shoulder as she helped Scott gather equipment.

"Ah, a bad loser." Jeff smiled at Diana. "We must set a good example of sportsmanship, right?"

Diana glared at him. "I'll remind you of that next time we play."

In the locker room, Sam didn't speak a word to his beaten athletes. He approached Tom, who was slumped on a bench at the far end of the narrow room with an ice bag on his knee. Sam stooped and embraced his strong forward, soaking his shirt and tie with the boy's grief and anger. He moved over and hugged Rob, who, counting tournament games, had absorbed his ninth straight beating at the hands of Twin Bridges. Sam looked at Olaf and saw the welts from Craig Stone. He patted Olaf on the back as well as Dean and Curtis. He hesitated at the door and turned to face the boys who were absorbing their defeat with a stoic dignity.

"Tom, didn't your mother ever tell you not to throw stones?"

Sam paused, allowing a thin smile.

"I'm proud as hell that you stood up for a teammate," Sam said. "You were the better team out there. That ought to make you feel good because they're rated number two in the state right now. They had to find a dishonorable way to win. We'll meet them again."

"Can we go to McDonald's tonight?" Dean said.

"Not tonight, Dean, but next week we'll travel," Sam said, "and then we will."

"Why did Pete quit on us?" Dean asked.

The locker room went still, no one moved. The question hung in the humid air.

"I don't know, Dean," Sam said. "Maybe it was something he had to do."

"We'd a beat them if Pete was here," Dean said.

"I know . . . we would have," Sam said.

He turned and hurried into the gym, almost knocking Diana over as she listened at the locker room door.

"We're just beginning, Coach," she said. "The boys are lucky to have you."

She kissed him quickly on the cheek, and he glanced around the nearly empty gym to see who might have witnessed their simple affection. No one.

In the smattering of stragglers, several grade-school kids were chasing a basketball around on the floor and trying to toss it high enough to make a basket. Sam wondered if they would be among those who followed in this litany of loss. He thought the kind and merciful thing to do would be to warn them before it was too late. And like Tom and the boys, he wished that Peter had been there to battle with them against the Falcons, and against the fates and the ghosts that inhabited their hearts.

CHAPTER 39

January hadn't lived up to its notorious reputation, but instead had turned mild and sheepish, with daytime temperatures in the forties and fifties. Diana called on Sunday, inviting Sam for an afternoon hike, and he eagerly met her out at the old iron single-lane bridge that spanned the Jefferson River. In her Levis, Padres cap, and weathered khaki safari jacket that was slightly too big for her, she appeared somewhat girlish and in need of protection. Sam was so happy to see her he nearly kissed her.

He expected her to drive to some remote place near the mountains, but he was surprised when she led him on foot down through the road ditch, past a senescent barbed-wire fence, and across a cattle-tracked pasture. The snow had been consumed by wind and sun except in a few isolated protected patches.

At the far side of the meadow they walked along a broad river bench that was sparsely wooded with cottonwood, juniper, and willow. A few of the giant cottonwood had given in to weather and time some years ago and their barkless bones had scattered. As though in her natural element, Diana blended with the environment, moving nimbly through brush, deadfall, leaves, and dried grass without a sound.

For Sam, the hike became a voyage of discovery in a landscape that, while jogging on this gravel road, he had paid little attention to and imagined it to be barren, void of all life and forsaken in winter's grip. Diana pointed out nests, tracks, and animal tracks. She pulled Sam to his knees and then flattened herself. With a finger over her lips, she pointed upriver. Sam, lying beside her, couldn't see anything.

She whispered, "River otter."

Twenty feet out in the water, a dark, sleek-headed creature appeared, and then another. Sam was taken with surprise at the existence of these aquatic clowns so close to his daily routine.

Diana and Sam crept further down the shore to a grassy bank, where Diana again stretched flat on the ground. Sam lay beside her and the sun warmed his back. A raven glided above them, its solitary call reminding Sam, in hazy shadows, of a time when he was a boy in Wisconsin, catching frogs and fireflies and exploring the woods with a wonder he had misplaced with his childhood. He could not recall a time since then when he had sprawled on the ground in the woods in hiding. Diana rolled onto her back and told him to do the same. She had him look up at the partially clouded sky.

"Now relax, let yourself fall back into the arms of the earth."

He let go, feeling his body mold to the shape of the ground under him.

"Take several deep breaths," she said. "Slowly . . . in and out."

He inhaled the clean moist air, held it within him for a moment, and then emptied his lungs. He repeated the ritual, hearing Diana doing the same beside him.

"Now imagine you're becoming part of the earth, that there are grasses and flowers growing out of the ground and right through your body."

He breathed deeply and visualized himself sinking further into the humus, sprouting grass and weeds and sage like a flower bed. As Diana suggested, he could feel the earth breathing under him, with him, sighing up the scents of its moist subsoil, molecules from its warm bedrock, fertilized and imprinted by its previous eons of life, energy rising from the deepest recesses of cooking creation.

The land had its rhythms, its music and motions, an ebb and flow that washed over him like surf, a vitality so essential and primary that it seemed eternal, a heartbeat, a pulse that he could reach out and touch, a soul he could feel. At that moment Sam would swear, cross his heart and hope to die, that he could hear Respighi's "The Pines of the Appian Way" coming out of the ground around him.

"Now," she said, "feel the earth rotating . . . slowly . . . turning east, moving away from the sun."

After a minute he found himself leaning very slightly to the east, sensing a movement, knowing the planet under him was turning. His eyes teared, and he was overwhelmed with an engulfing sense of peace and oneness with the earth, an acceptance he'd never experienced, a centering that he had no idea existed.

"Feel it?" she asked.

"Yeah."

He watched the clouds with watering vision, stretched out on the ground beside this mysterious woman, feeling the nebulous rotation as they rode this streaking earth ball through intergalactic space, its children at the molecular level. He wondered what it was he clung to after he saw Amy's body. Was he clinging to the earth itself to keep from falling away into the netherworld force, some nihilistic black hole? Was he clinging to some fairy tale that would one day abolish the sadness, some hope in the eventual triumph of goodness and joy? Or was he hanging on in the faith that something or someone would save him, save him from the violence and madness?

"The clouds are telling stories," she said so softly he barely heard.

"Do they have a name?"

"I hate to label them with technical names. It takes all of the mystery out of them." Diana pointed. "Those are fair-weather cumulus." She pointed another direction. "Those are stratus."

From where they stretched out on the ground, Sam could see no sign of civilization: no power lines, no fence, no road, no sound of machinery, nothing but the unspoiled creation. He pointed out over the mountains.

"How about that one?"

"Oh . . . that's a lenticular altocumulus."

"A what?"

"Lenticular altocumulus. They form over the mountains when we're in high pressure."

She rolled up onto one elbow and he caught a poignant look in her eye. She gazed at the bright, saucerlike cloud.

"I used to think they were God's skipping stones."

"Used to?"

"Now I know they are hearts that have been betrayed, sailing off to a land where those you love are never wrenched from your bloody arms."

Sam felt a shudder of sorrow as though he were watching her tattered heart making sail for another world. He had an instinctual urge to take her in his arms and comfort her, wishing he had an epoxy for her heart, or an anodyne that would enable it to overlook its fractures. In his moment of hesitation, she was up and ready to move on.

On the circular passage back to the cars they spooked two white-tail deer out of the dense underbrush. Soon after, they caught a fleeting glimpse of a red fox streaking across the meadow, one, she assured him, they had undoubtedly disturbed. Sam came out of the field with a fresh perspective of the living miracles drenching him. He came out with a sense of the fullness of the land and the incredible web of life on it, a vision through Diana's eyes of this earth and cosmos, a universe that he was part and parcel of, mingled with its sinew, blood cells, and bone marrow.

When he saw the cars he realized that she had led him less than two miles from the gym. She had taken him to a world altogether oblivious to basketball games, winning and losing. It was a much more profound awareness of just being alive, and all of this right in his backyard.

"That was really something," he said as they scrambled out of the barrow pit and onto the road.

"You ought to see it come spring. Things are popping alive so fast you have to duck."

When she drove away, saying she was off to visit Randolph and Ellie Butterworth, he lingered a while longer and looked off to the mountains to watch the distant passage of the lenticular altocumulus gliding over the Spanish Peaks.

On SUNDAY, OLAF worked in the barn with Mervin, who hammered away with a grim but unflagging resolve. Claire made several sorties with food and liquids during the day, but the two would not come to the house for their traditional Sunday dinner.

That evening, a carload of kids stopped to pick Olaf up. Outside the barn Olaf told them, in confidential tones, that he had to stay and help Mr. Painter work in the barn.

"Come on, please," Carter said.

"C'mon, you turkey," Tom called from the backseat of Louella's four-door Mercury.

"Building we are . . . a-a-ah . . . to hammer he is teaching me."

His puzzled friends drove off for Bozeman without him, and Olaf turned for the barn.

Monday morning, gray and mild, Mervin Painter nudged his 1990 4×4

Ford pickup toward Manhattan, recalling his long personal history of defeat.When he was young, his big brother Carl used to win at everything because of his size and age. And then as Mervin began catching up and would nearly beat him at something, Carl would cheat and do anything to win. When Mervin would call him on it, Carl would punch him in the stomach, hard, or in the ribs, and then, as they both got older, in the head, several times knocking Mervin out cold. One time he woke up and found himself lying on the ground in the apple orchard and the last thing he could remember was confronting Carl for stealing his money. He had always felt it dishonorable to tattle to his father about his big brother's down-home sibling brutality, as though any son worth his salt should be able to take care of himself.

Nearing Manhattan, Mervin muddled over how the same damn thing continued in his adult life, over bad luck or the unfairness that Willow Creek, the town nearest the family farm, should have the basketball team that could never win, and that Manhattan Christian, the school closest to his big brother's spread, should have the abundance of boys and the excellent program for a winning basketball tradition. Mervin attempted to disguise how deeply it incensed him with an aw-shucks, good-old-boy exterior. He turned off the interstate and approached the café as one would approach hemorrhoid surgery.

Mervin took a deep breath as he hesitated in front of the Garden Café. Then, he shoved the door open and strode in with the intent of keeping cool and taking the ribbing good-naturedly. Mervin slid heavily into the booth.

"Well, I guess you'll never learn, little brother. You wouldn't have been within twenty points if our boys hadn't been a little overconfident," Carl said.

He wore his oil-stained John Deere cap and was fortified in his customary booth with his two cronies. Lute Jackson and Sandy Hill jauntily echoed his ridicule and added some of their own.

"What was the score?" Mervin said, sitting next to Sandy and directly across the table from his big brother.

"Willow Croak lost again," Carl said, loud enough that the cook in the kitchen could hear.

With a restrained calm in his voice Mervin said, "What was the score?"

"Christian beat Willow Croak, so what else is new," Carl said.

"By *one point*. And you were damn lucky."

"We don't need luck to beat Willow Croak, never have, never will. You were lucky to even be in the game," Carl said.

Lute made a showy display of handing over the check and the crisp one-hundred-dollar bill to Mervin's big brother, and most everyone in the coffee-scented establishment, where decades ago wrestling exhibitions and boxing matches were held, clapped and hooted.

"If you had been man enough to have fathered a boy or two," Carl said, having had two boys who had played for Manhattan Christian, "maybe Willow Croak would have won a game."

That ripped it!

It was unacceptable for these ranchers and farmers to let on that they had accumulated much wealth, even though both Mervin and Carl had prospered at their inherited vocations. The hundred dollars had been straining the boundaries of this unspoken commandment; to bet anything larger in monetary sums would smack of arrogance and be a denial of their self-imposed, outwardly-frugal lifestyle.

"Let's bet on the next game," Mervin said, trembling with a controlled ferocity.

"Hell, that's four weeks away," Sandy said, tipping his cherished Northern Pacific engineer's cap. "By the way you're losing players, you better wait and see if you still have five boys standing by then."

The three men generated waves of laughter that spread until even the eavesdroppers chuckled. After all these years, Mervin was still surprised at how quickly word spread across the valley; they already knew about the Strong boy's defection.

"You giving me another hundred-dollar bill?" Carl asked.

"Something bigger," Mervin said.

"Whoa," Lute said, "the man has gone bananas."

"Bigger?" Carl said.

"The John Deere 'D'," Mervin said calmly.

"My 'D'!" Carl said. "My 'D'?"

"What's the matter? You afraid you might lose?"

"Wait a minute here," Carl said. "You want me to bet my tractor on the *basketball game?*"

"That 'D' is a rare son-bitch," Sandy said. "Wasn't that made in twenty-nine?"

"Twenty-eight," Carl said, "and only one hundred of 'em built."

"Built in Waterloo, Iowa," Mervin said. "An experimental model: two-cylinder, three-speed transmission, all steel wheels. They shipped 'em to Montana and Arizona, mainly."

"And you want me to bet my 'D' on a basketball game?" Carl said, employing his favorite tactic of repeating something a dozen times in an effort to intimidate.

"Our father bought the twenty-second 'D' from Oliver Stout Implement Company in Bozeman," Mervin said, "serial number X67522."

"Can't be many of them suckers left," Lute said.

"Only eight that anyone knows of," Carl said. "Rest gone to junk and rust, and you want me to bet the 'D' on a *basketball game?* You must be outta yer skull."

Carl eyeballed him and Mervin felt like he was ten again. Their father used the "D" for years in the field. Took care of it like it was a living, breathing member of the family. He finally stuck it in a shed, never able to bring himself to trade it in on other equipment. Shortly before he died, their father gave the cherished "D" to the eldest son—deserving or not—the sacred symbol of family birthright. The pampered "D" still ran as good as it did the day it rolled off the assembly line in Waterloo.

Mervin stuck his thumbs in his armpits and moved his folded arms like chicken wings, mimicking his brother's familiar gestures when Mervin balked at a bet.

Carl's sandpaper face became florid, veins bulging.

"That tractor's irreplaceable," Carl said.

"Don't you think your pansies can luck out again against poor little ol' Willow Croak?" Mervin said.

"And what are you putting up?" Carl asked.

"My ninety Ford Lariat, only four thousand on it."

"Yeah, and all beat to hell."

"It's in top-notch shape. Course if you're afraid you're going to *lose* . . ."

Mervin knew his brother cherished the polished green heirloom far beyond any monetary value and he also knew he had his big brother by the balls.

"All right, by God, the 'D' against your pickup!" Carl said.

"Done!" Mervin said and the two brothers glared at each other across the table as Lute and Sandy—and most of the other occupants of the café, who turned on their swivel stools to watch—held their breath at the escalating confrontation.

Mervin struggled against an old but not forgotten instinct that kept shouting at him to duck, sure he could recognize in his brother's eyes that impulse to slug his younger kin. A part of Mervin wished he would, giving Mervin an excuse to strike back with all the pent-up resentment he never got a chance to unload, using his work-hardened fist like a sledge against anvil, one thudding blow.

"We'll run you right out of our gym," Mervin said, smug with the entrapment he'd finagled.

"Ha! That lummox in a jockstrap will travel again. He doesn't know a pivot foot from a club foot."

"Hey, you two, it's only a basketball game," Lute said, trying to hold a smile on his face with the two Painters glaring at one another.

"That's what you think," Mervin said. "Should we have Lute hold the 'D' and my pickup?"

"Hell no," Carl said. "That tractor stays in the shed where it belongs."

"If Christian wins, I'll bring the pickup here Monday morning," Mervin said, "and I expect you to do the same with the 'D'."

"So be it," Carl said, slamming a fist on the table, rattling the accumulated cups and plates and everyone in the café.

Then they all sat quietly for a minute with their coffee, their baked goods, and their jangled private thoughts.

"Henry Ross got one of them new chisel-plows the other day," Sandy said, and they returned to a semblance of normal conversation, though everyone in the café secretly searched the dark wood paneling for excuses to vamoose.

The Painter brothers had bet a John Deere tractor and a brand new 4×4 Ford pickup on a *basketball game,* and folks were forfeiting half-eaten doughnuts and unfinished cups of coffee to be the first to broadcast the word. News of the unheard-of wager spread along Railroad Avenue like cottonwood seed.

Mervin drove for home, knowing this was his last chance.

CHAPTER 40

Tuesday night, Sam pulled into the Painters' yard around seven-thirty, and though light splintered from the big barn, he approached to the front door and knocked. Grandma Chapman had driven him in to Bozeman Ford to pick up his repaired car. The ride in the VW bus was an enterprise he didn't want to repeat as Grandma ramrodded the beat-up contraption with one hand, gabbing all the way. Neither of them had mentioned Peter.

Claire swung the door wide and Sam asked for Olaf.

"Oh, Olaf's out in the barn with Mervin," Claire said.

"What are they doing?"

Claire regarded him with a polite smile. "Hammering."

"Well, I thought if he had a little time I'd go over some things with him on my VCR, but if he's busy—"

"Yes, they're pretty busy," she said, attempting to be brief, which was against her God-given nature.

"Well, thanks anyway," Sam said and walked toward his car.

When Claire had closed the door, Sam snuck through the shadows, avoiding the shafts of light from the house and barn. He entered the lower level of the old structure, ripe with odors of baler twine, feed grain, and gunny sacks. He could faintly hear muffled voices. Creeping past animal-worn calf pens and rusted stanchions, he found a ladder up the wall that led to the loft. As he climbed he heard a familiar thump.

He stuck his head above the hole and found himself just behind Mervin Painter, who passed a basketball to Olaf. In sweatshirt and jeans, Olaf wheeled around smoothly, his pivot foot never leaving the floor, and tossed in a soft shot off a new fiberglass backboard. The basket jutted from a wooden superstructure fastened to the barn wall. Olaf grabbed the rebound and flipped it back to the rancher, who was decked out in bib overalls and a worn woolen cap. The Bronc center moved in position in front of the basket and Mervin shot him a pass. Again, the boy spun quickly and banked in a soft shot, his pivot foot never leaving the wood planking, though he stretched awkwardly to retrieve the ball.

"Good, good," Mervin said.

Sam watched transfixed. Inhaling barn dust and about to sneeze, he clung to the wooden rungs of the ladder and wondered how Mervin had disciplined Olaf to keep that pivot foot on the floor. After another four or five minutes, Sam found out.

"Should we try the other foot?" Mervin asked.

"Ya."

Olaf sat awkwardly on the hay-polished wood flooring. Unlacing his left shoe, he pulled his foot out of it and the shoe remained attached to the floor. He unlaced his other shoe. Mervin knelt and somehow detached the left shoe from the planking. Olaf handed him the right high-top and Mervin attached it to the pine board. Olaf stepped into it and went down on one knee to lace it. Then he stood and turned it a hundred and eighty degrees. The shoe was on some kind of a swivel; it would turn, but it wouldn't come off the deck. Sam wanted to laugh. He watched for a few more minutes as Olaf swung to his right, making short backboard shots or shooting soft swishers, pivoting, pivoting, with his foot literally nailed to the floor.

Sam pulled himself up the ladder and stepped into the cleared loft area that was surrounded by hay bales. Olaf spotted him first and stopped in mid-swing. Mervin turned to see what the boy was staring at.

"Hello. I came out to get Olaf for a while. I saw the lights in the barn."

They looked like twelve-year-olds who had been discovered with their noses in a *Hustler* magazine. Mervin tried to explain.

"We thought we'd work on that traveling business. Ever since the game on Friday I've been trying to figure out what could hurry the process a little."

He motioned to Olaf and the center unlaced his right shoe and stepped out of it. There, with a thin metal washer welded to a headless bolt, was an ingenious farmer's method of teaching a boy to keep his pivot foot on the floor. It wasn't tight; there was enough play in it to give the athlete some leeway, but though the shoe would turn three hundred and sixty degrees freely, it would not come off the floor. Needless to say, both of Olaf's practice shoes had a quarter-inch hole in the sole.

"It'll pop free with enough pressure," Mervin said, "in case he falls."

Sam smiled. "It seems to be working."

Mervin and Olaf agreed that they had "hammered" enough for now, and Olaf, folded into the front seat of the compact Ford like a carpenter's ruler, left for town with Sam.

Forgetful in his preoccupation with the rancher's inventive solution, Sam drove too fast, bouncing over the roller-coaster frost heaves and banging Olaf's head on the car's roof.

"Oops, sorry," Sam said.

Every winter, on the highway into Willow Creek, the frost heaves reappeared like acne. The natives had learned to reduce their speed considerably or risk being bounced into the deep irrigation canal that ran alongside the blacktop. In the arid climate of summer, the heaves would settle back to a fairly level surface. But in winter, it was as though the blacktop were slamming on its own brakes, digging in its heels, bucking and heaving, knowing it was approaching Willow Creek, reluctant to arrive at the dead end that awaited it there.

"Have you heard from your parents lately?" Sam asked.

"Ya, from my mother a letter I am getting."

"Have you told them about the game we won?"

"No . . . I am not writing my father about the basketball."

"He'd be proud of you. You can't imagine how much you've improved."

"He does not want for me to be playing at sports. I am not good and it is a waste of time, he says. Excel at studies, he says."

"He's wrong about you. I'm glad you got a chance to try. You have more athletic ability than you think."

"To be coming to USA I did not want."

The boy paused and Sam was surprised, always assuming it had been Olaf's idea to be an exchange student.

"I must be coming my father said. Understanding America and this language is necessary to do well in business."

"Is that what you want to do—business?"

"No. To be a teacher."

"Doesn't your father want you to teach?"

"No, to make a good living, he says, be in business and finance."

Sam rounded the curve into Willow Creek and chuckled at the irony. If Olaf grew another inch or two and kept improving at the rate he had in the past four months, he would likely, after college, make more money *playing basketball* than his father ever dreamed of making in the world of business.

During almost an hour of watching basketball, Sam noticed Olaf's attention waning, his eyes drifting off on occasion. After hurrying him home to bed, concerned that they were wearing the boy out in their eagerness to forge another win or two, Sam wondered if he was using Olaf as Mervin might be, or was he helping the boy to grow and learn and experience one of the grandest times of his life? He didn't know, and he recognized that he could never understand, truly, why he did anything. If Mervin was wagering on Olaf for a victory over his brother, what was Sam's bet?

All his hope had amounted to nothing. They were 1 and 6. Other than the one narrow victory they were right where they always were.

FOR THE REST of the week, like two children who had played with matches and nearly burned down the house, Sam and Diana shied from each other as though neither wanted to admit they had a strain of pyromania in their nature.

CHAPTER 41

When the Greyhound pulled up along Main Street in Three Forks, Peter was the first one off. With his backpack and duffel in hand, he trundled across the street to the Conoco station. He called Grandma on the pay phone, but no one answered. He realized where she was now—at the game. They were playing Gardiner that night and he would've made it with time to spare if the bus hadn't had mechanical trouble. They had to transfer onto another bus in Bismarck.

Inside the Conoco station, he asked the stoop-shouldered man behind the counter if he could leave his stuff until he came back for it with a car. The man glanced over the *Guns & Ammo* magazine he was reading and nodded. Peter crossed the street and ran through downtown, three blocks, then out the road to Willow Creek. There was a cluster of cars around each of the several bars, but nothing moving. He quickly put the five or six blocks of residential neighborhoods behind him. As he followed the curve at the edge of town out past the brick yard and talc plant, he was winded. The blacktop aimed the six miles to Willow Creek as straight as an arrow. There were no cars on the road, it seemed everyone was at the game. He slowed to a walk and held his watch up to his face. Eight-thirteen. They would be into the second half. He started running again, pushing himself. He knew he could make a difference.

Headlights appeared coming around the curve behind him. He turned, hung a friendly smile on his face and stuck out his thumb. The car swung to the other side of the highway, slowed, and went past him several car lengths before stopping. Pete ran to the passenger window, which was down.

"Thanks for stopping, are you going to Willow Creek?"

It was a woman, maybe fifty years old.

"I'm supposed to be playing in the basketball game tonight and the game's already going and—"

"Hop in," she said.

Peter opened the door and slid into the passenger seat. It was a big car, a Buick or Oldsmobile.

"So you go to Willow Creek, huh?" she said.

"Yeah. Are you going to the game?"

"No . . . just driving around, remembering . . . making my getaway."

Pete didn't understand. With only the light from the dashboard he noticed she had a bathrobe on under her winter jacket, and slippers.

"What's your name?"

"Peter . . . Peter Strong."

"I used to live around here, grew up on our ranch west of Willow Creek, the Taylor place now."

She sounded sad, really sad. Pete looked at his watch. Eight-twenty.

"How come you're late for the game?"

"I was visiting someone in Minnesota. I was supposed to be back in time but the bus broke down."

She didn't seem to hear him.

"I went to school in Willow Creek a long time ago," she said. "We had a few good teams back then, even went to State once."

"Did you win it?"

"No, didn't win a game, but we sure had fun going."

"We have a kid from Norway. He's six foot eleven."

"I've heard all about *him*. I live over east of Churchill, had two boys play basketball for Manhattan Christian."

"Yeah, I've heard all about *them*. I missed our first game against them when I was back in Minnesota."

Pete could see the meager lights of Willow Creek and he prayed he would at least make the fourth quarter.

"You know, even when my boys were playing for Christian, in my heart I'd be rooting for Willow Creek."

Pete thought of Kathy and the hurt rose up in his chest. "When you went to school here, did you have a boyfriend?" he said.

"Yes . . ."

"Did you get married?"

"No . . ." she said, "we never did."

"Why not?"

"We got mixed up and confused and lost."

Pete didn't know what she meant. "Did you love him?" he said.

"Yes."

She stopped in front of the school.

"What's your name?" Pete said with his hand on the door latch.

"Maggie."

"Thanks for the ride, Maggie."

He opened the door and got out.

"I still do," she said.

"Still do what?" he said, about to shut the door.

"I still do love him."

"I gotta run," he said, and wondered if she'd been drinking.

He shut the door and turned for the school. The car window purred down.

"I hope you win!" she called. "I hope *someone* wins in Willow Creek one of these times."

Pete dashed for the school door.

When he came through the lunch room and across one end of the gym, the action was at the other end and no one seemed to notice him. The scoreboard had VISITORS 49 HOME 37. He knew he had at least twelve points in him. In the locker room he found his jersey and trunks hanging where he'd left them as if they expected him back, as if they knew better than he that he'd return. He had no jock. He'd wear his underwear under his trunks. His game shoes were in his duffel but the shoes he had on would do. He glanced in the steel mirror to see if he was all together, took a deep breath, and ran out onto the court.

The teams were at their benches, it was the end of the third quarter. Fans in the bleachers saw him coming first and after a blink of the eyes, they were standing, clapping, and shouting. He waved at Grandma, whose mouth hung open so far she nearly fell out of the stands. The boys turned from their huddle around Coach Pickett and Miss Murphy with astonished faces, and Peter ran into their arms like the one lost sheep. They hugged him and shouted and laughed, growing wide smiles on their exhausted, sweaty faces. Coach Pickett beamed as if he'd swallowed the sun.

They needed him here, he counted for something. He thought he'd burst with the joy of it.

SAM HAD WATCHED coach Fred Sooner and his Gardiner Bruins swagger into Willow Creek. State Champions two years ago, the Bruins still wore the confidence and self-assurance such achievements breed. Sam had hoped that his five could give them a game, knowing in his head that that was highly unlikely. Denise Cutter, Dean's cerebral-palsied sister, sat in her wheelchair at the end of the bleachers, watching. He couldn't remember seeing her at a game before.

Olaf fouled out halfway through the third quarter and Fred Sooner showed his sportsmanship by having one of his players simply stand on the court in front of their bench without participating in the game, playing four on four.

In the last minute of the third quarter, with Gardiner ahead by fourteen, Curtis was called for his fifth foul. They were down to three; they were beaten. Sam felt the utter absurdity of his hopes, heard the voices ridiculing and mocking his expectations as if he were the lunatic knight in Cervantes' imagination. He conceded and sat quietly on the bench.

Then, like a Willow Creek ghost, Peter trotted across the floor out of nowhere, in uniform and ready to play. Was he dreaming?

Now they had four players, and it was four on four when the fourth quarter started, but after Peter hit five straight shots, Gardiner's sportsmanship had soured and their fifth player was no longer just standing in front of the bench. Their fifth player was double-teaming Peter, who was playing like they'd insulted his mother.

Mervin Painter, who had become one of their most boisterous fans, thundered from the bleachers, "You can't beat us man for man! You can't beat us even-Steven!"

Rob hit a nice turnaround jumper, bringing the Broncs within three. Sam wanted to believe. The Willow Creek fans were on their feet, daring to hang their hearts out one more time, but Sam couldn't join them. It hurt too much.

They lost by seven. Peter Strong had come too late. Sam praised his boys in the locker room, though there wasn't much to say anymore. They were 1 and 7. While all the other boys circled around Peter, asking about his journey to Minnesota and looking for assurances he was back for good, Sam approached Dean, who slumped on a bench and pulled off holey socks.

"You played well, Dean," Sam said, patting him on the back. "Did you have some fun?"

"Yeah, but I stunk," the freshman said, crunching up his nose.

"No, you did great, and your mother and sister were here. I hope they'll come again."

"Mom says they can't afford the tickets," Dean said.

"Oh," Sam said, taken back. "We always have some extra tickets lying around. You tell them to come. We need all the fans we can get. I'll take care of the tickets."

GRANDMA DROVE THE VW bus up the blacktop for Three Forks after Pete told her he had to get his things at the Conoco station. He sat quietly for a while, hurting over the immediate loss which seemed to magnify his greater loss.

"How'd you get to Willow Creek?" Grandma said.

"I hitched a ride with a nice lady. Her name was Maggie."

"Maggie Painter?" Grandma said.

"She didn't say."

Grandma wondered if it was indeed Maggie Painter. What was she doing driving around Willow Creek at night? Grandma had heard tell when she first arrived in Willow Creek that Mervin's older brother had stolen Maggie from him when they were young sweethearts. The latest word was that Maggie, who was pretty sick, had taken a turn for the worse.

"Well," Grandma said, "what did you find out back in Saint Paul?"

"No one wants me back there."

"Well, that's hunky-dory with me because there's lots of us who want you here."

"Kathy's going with some senior jerk. She said she was sorry."

"How about your mom?" Grandma said, swinging down Main Street in Three Forks.

"I think she has a boyfriend, she was always talking on the phone like she didn't want me to hear. I was in her way. She always had some place she had to go."

She pulled into the station and Pete threw his stuff in the back. She turned for home.

"How about your dad? Did you see him?"

"Yeah, stayed with him a couple nights, but he said it was a bad time, that I'd have to stay with you until summer."

"Well, at least you didn't lose a hand in the deal," Grandma said, trying to lighten his load, "or other body parts."

"Does a heart count?" He stared out the side window.

"Peter, my lovely grandson, you'll discover that the heart is a very resilient muscle."

"I wasn't good enough for her, or cool enough or something."

"You feeling . . . ugly?"

"Yeah, like there is something wrong with me . . . ugly."

He didn't speak again until they were almost into Willow Creek.

"Grandma, do you ever get lonesome?"

"Lonesome? Well, I'll tell you. Lonesome is a sly bugger. It crouches behind every memory, it lies in ambush in every drawer, it hangs in the closet like old clothes, ready to waylay you when you're least expectin' it. But one thing I've found, it's slow, it's sure slow. It can only grab you if you're giving in to life, sittin' around thinkin' too much. I just keep moving so fast it can never get its stinking hands on me."

She stopped in front of the house and pulled on the hand brake.

They were home.

ᏹ CHAPTER 42 ᏹ

When most of the fans had filed out of the Blue Willow, Sam and Diana remained huddled at a small table near the antique black-iron stove. The bar was busy, and a few couples danced to country and western music out of the jukebox. After they had traded their feelings from losing again, mitigated by the joy of having Peter back, Diana shared her excitement over a teaching position she had applied for near San Diego.

"They even have a course in oceanography for the high school students," she said.

"Sea turtles?"

"Yeah." Her face brightened.

Their conversation had slowly circled their Beartrap Hot Springs excursion until Sam finally jumped head first into it.

"When are we going hot-potting again?"

He toyed with the salt shaker, trembling inside that she'd say Never.

"That was a surprise," she said. "I don't know what got into us."

"Well, whatever it was, I hope it gets into us again." He laughed.

"It was good, wasn't it?" Her eyes smiled warmly.

"Milk chocolate."

"Milk chocolate?" she asked.

"Yes, you ruined everything."

"What on earth are you talking about?"

"When I was a young boy I couldn't go off our block. That was my boundary. On the other side of our block and across the street there was one of those filling stations that sold more pop, junk food, and cigarettes than gas. My parents were super strict about candy. I only got it on rare occasions like holidays or birthdays."

"Was this before you started school?"

"Yeah, maybe I was five or six. Well, there were these three girls in my neighborhood, about my age or a little older, who didn't have like-minded parents. They hauled candy out of that store like looters in a riot. We'd sit on a cement-block wall in the alley and I'd watch them feed their faces: Reese's Peanut Butter Cups, licorice twists, Milky Ways."

"Good night, you two!" Andrew called on his way out. "Great to have Peter back!"

"Yes," Sam said, and Diana waved.

"Back to our gang," she said.

"Well, at first they shared some of their candy with me. One of them, a kind of pushy little girl, always got Hershey bars, and I became addicted to milk chocolate. But it wasn't long before they figured out I never had any candy of my own and that I wasn't allowed to have any. That got them started. They'd bribe me, offering me one little square of milk chocolate if I'd do something ridiculous like roll in the dirt or sit up like a dog and bark—humiliating things."

"Would you do it?" she said, then grinned.

"Oh yeah. Boy could I do a good dog imitation. And they enjoyed this wondrous power they held over me. Then, after a while, they turned it up a notch to cruel. They'd make me run around the block. When I was finished, they'd say it wasn't fast enough, and around I'd go again, faster. They'd make me shinny up a telephone pole and when I'd slide down, full of slivers and creosote, they'd say I didn't go high enough. Up I'd go again, anything for a square or two of milk chocolate."

"Those dirty little creeps," Diana said.

"I started to hate those girls, teasing me, hoarding their glut of candy and making me beg, using me for their cheesy entertainment. One day I finally had enough. I began telling myself I hated candy, especially milk chocolate. I wouldn't take it if they gave it to me. I would repeat it over and over: I hate candy, I hate candy. And you know, I never performed for them again."

"Good for you."

"Yeah, but that's only the half of it. When I was in my teens and early twenties, girls had something I wanted—affection, sex, love, pleasure—and they wouldn't share it with me. I'd trip over my tie being nice and polite and kissing their pretty round asses in hopes they'd share their candy."

"Like the little girls in the alley," Diana said.

"Like the little girls in the alley. Women seemed to sense the power they held over me. They taunted with their big, beautiful eyes and their delicious-looking lips and their suntanned legs, like Reese's Peanut Butter Cups and Hershey bars and licorice twists."

"Ha!" Diana clapped her hands.

Sam leaned toward her with elbows on the table.

"Hey, understand I'm not your proverbial sex fiend. I admit to the lusting little hormones, but what women don't realize, or most men for that matter, is that the physical allurements aren't an end in themselves, but constant reminders of a much deeper mating, that precious oneness that exists between two people in love."

"You want anything more?" Vera called from the counter.

"Sam wants a lot more," Diana said.

"No, thanks. We're about to go," Sam said.

"Don't want to rush you," Vera said.

Sam glanced at his watch. Eleven-fifty. He looked into his assistant coach's eyes for some understanding.

"Okay, one day I realized I was back on the block with those little girls who had the candy I wanted. They had power over me again. So I did what I did then. I disciplined myself to give up wanting that wonder with a woman."

"Did it work?" Her dark eyes searched his face.

"It worked . . . until Amy. I had learned to live alone and to do without. Some people think it not normal to go without someone to love, to go without sex, that you're weird, that there's something wrong with you. Yet there are millions of people who seem fated to be incapable of matching up with. They go without love and affection for long stretches of their lives, some their entire lives, and it's not that they don't *want* it."

Sam leaned toward her and spoke with a hint of pain in his voice. "It's that they can't *find* it and they can't *have* it. And they've given up running around the block and sitting up like a goddamn dog to beg for it!"

Sam sat back and sighed, calming himself. She seemed to hold her breath with his intensity.

"I thought I had found a certain contentment without it, and now you've gone and ruined it for me."

"Ruined it for you?"

"Yes. You let me taste milk chocolate again. I'd forgotten how much I love it."

They got up to leave. Diana went over to the counter and purchased something from Vera while Sam left a tip and pulled on his coat. At her Volvo she handed him a Hershey bar.

"Here. This will have to satisfy you for tonight." She smiled.

"Will I have to sit up like a dog and beg for it?"

"Let's see how fast you can run around the block."

They laughed. She kissed him. Then she got in her car and drove away.

Eating the candy bar, Sam walked home through the sleeping town, knowing he was precariously close to the edge. With the taste of Hershey's milk chocolate on his tongue tonight, he dared to believe in the promise of tomorrow.

CHAPTER 43

In the heart of the Shields River Valley, two towns, Wilsall and Clyde Park—traditional, and sometimes bitter, athletic rivals—finally gave in to necessity and accepted the marriage of their high schools in the manner of the Hatfields and McCoys, making them a much more formidable power in the conference. It was the kind of wedlock Willow Creek dreaded, knowing that in its case, with Three Forks, it wouldn't be matrimony but a common-law kidnapping. Sam slowed the bus he now fondly referred to as Rozinante as the team approached the weather-battered town of Wilsall. Diana pointed out a small hill covered with sage and crescents of drifted snow.

"There, there, right behind that ridge," she said. "The Anzick Site, one of the oldest in North American. They found evidence of hairy mammoth hunters from over ten thousand years ago."

Sam gazed out at the murky outline of the ridge and found it hard to visualize ivory-tusked mammoths striding into Wilsall. The night before, these Shields Valley boys had upset Twin Bridges, handing that team its first loss, and though Sam felt some apprehension as to how good these local boys might be this season, he couldn't help smiling. This night he had a mammoth with him and he knew the natives had better sharpen their Clovis points lest they be trampled and find themselves limping for cover.

In the valley of hairy mammoths, Olaf beat back the Shields Valley Rebels, slapping shots away, clearing the boards, keeping his pivot foot on the hardwood, and clumping out of the paint in less than three seconds. When they tried to bring him down, he hit thirteen of sixteen free throws to completely shatter their final ploy. Olaf played his best game to date, dominating the Rebels, and Sam and Diana, somewhat overwhelmed on the bench, appreciated the creative ways their clever guards were concocting to get the Norwegian the ball: no-look passes, alley-oops for jams, and baseline bounces. Pete passed up numerous shots to deliver the ball to his center, and Olaf displayed an offensive aggression that Sam could never have taught.

Against Dean's shrill protests to wait until Bozeman and McDonald's, they ate in Livingston at Martin's Café, which was a part of the old Northern Pacific depot where, once upon a time, passengers used to get off passenger trains and eat on their way east or west. Now the enduring depot was a museum, like much of the old West, a spectator sport.

The team—"The Dirty Half-Dozen" as Tom now labeled them—along with the cheerleaders and coaches, was in a euphoric mood besides being very hungry. Diana subtly snuggled against Sam in the booth and he kept hearing the TV beer commercial that alleged "It doesn't get any better than this." The Willow Creek Broncs had taken apart Shields Valley in their own backyard. Unprecedented! Sam tried to take it a game at a time, to stay out of the future, to savor this spectacular, giddy present. They had all played well, striving to transcend ordinary efforts, given abilities. But Olaf outdid himself; Olaf transcended for thirty-three points.

When they rolled into Willow Creek close to midnight, the town was a ghost town and the Blue Willow was dark. Sam parked Rozinante in front of the school and everyone scurried through the cutting cold to their cars or pickups while he, Miss Murphy, and Scott hauled duffels of equipment into the building and locked up. With the games out of the way, Sam couldn't stand it any longer. He had to see her, had to touch her. During the week he had wondered if that night was just an inconsequential one-night stand for her, and until their conversation, he feared it might have been. While he locked the gym door, Diana had scurried across the street to her Volvo and had the engine running. He dashed to her car and rapped on the roof as she pulled out into the street, apparently leaving. When she stopped and rolled the window down part way, he had no idea what he would say, standing in the middle of Main Street after hailing a cab and having no inkling as to where he was going or what to tell the driver.

"Are you *leaving*?" he asked.

"Oh . . . yes, I assumed everyone was going right home."

She peered from the partially open window with an ambiguous expression.

"I just thought," he said, "m-maybe we could . . . you know."

He shrugged his shoulders and searched for the correct words.

Then he croaked like a teenager. "I'd like to see you."

He stood with his hand on the edge of the cold glass, shivering and feeling foolish. She hesitated, gripping the wheel with leathergloved hands and staring ahead down the dimly-lit blacktop.

"I thought it was pretty late and we'd call it a day," she said.

"If you're too tired—"

"No, get in, you'll freeze out there."

Sam scooted around the Volvo and slid into the passenger's leather upholstered bucket seat. She backed to the side of the road, killed the lights, and left the engine and heater running.

"I won't stay long. I just want to . . . see you. It seems we're never alone."

She turned toward him. "Isn't it fun when no one fouls out, when we have the five of them all the way. I had goose bumps watching Olaf, all of them—"

"And all I could think of all week was you," he said.

He reached over and took her gloved hand. "I miss you," he said.

She regarded him in the refracted light coming through the frosted windshield. Unwittingly he peeled the soft leather glove off her fingers as though it were something he had done all his life.

"I miss you, too, it's just that . . ."

Gently pulling her toward him, in utter terror, he leaned across the console and kissed her softly. For a moment only their lips touched. Then, in an eruption of desire, they grabbed each other with unrestrained hunger.

They searched through winter coats and clothing like bargain hunters at a garage sale. The windows glazed over. Their partially discarded clothing became entangled on their arms and legs and door handles in their frenzied embrace. In the cramped front compartment of the richly-appointed sedan, he thought he'd need integral calculus to get her high-heel boots and tight jeans off. Somewhere on the passenger seat in a jumble of clothing, with Diana kneeling and facing him, they found each other. He thought he would die with the joy of it.

Headlights on high beam came into town from the north, and the lovers crouched as much as they could.

"We have to get out of here," Sam said.

A familiar-looking pickup slowed as it pulled alongside the idling Volvo, and Sam recognized it through the frosty glass.

"Jeez, it's Carter. We have to get out of here."

The red Chevy pickup—probably with Louella, Pete, and even Tom if they hadn't dropped him off—went past a car's length and stopped, idling, as though the occupants were trying to decide what to do.

"Drive away," she said.

"I can't."

He tried to free himself.

She kissed him deeply, destroying his concentration.

Sam reached over with his left leg and placed his foot on the accelerator. He shoved the shift lever into drive with his left hand and grabbed for the steering wheel as the car lurched up Main. The pickup didn't move.

With one eye he peered around her cascading hair to see they were heading dead center for Willow Creek United Methodist.

"Holy Jeez," Sam said.

He was driving drunk, in a state of intoxication from the unplumbed pleasure of her. He lunged with his left foot for the brake pedal, but his pants were caught on the shift lever, pulling the car into reverse. The Volvo stopped, shuddered, and started back up the street.

"We're in reverse, we're in reverse!" Sam said.

He fumbled for the shift lever.

Only able to see to the side, Sam tried to steer, gauging where the street was by the nebulous outlines of the passing houses, realizing that she cared little whether they were going forward or backward so long as they didn't break stride.

"Their backup lights are on. They think we're coming back to talk," Diana whispered, able to peer through the fogged-over rear window.

"We can't let them see us like *this!*" Sam said.

He fumbled with the lever and jerked the Volvo into some forward gear, fearing the automatic transmission would drop onto the pavement. The weaving sedan staggered forward as he managed to touch the gas pedal. Again they headed away from the pickup, which paused in the middle of the street, idling.

"Oh God, Oh God." She moaned.

"You're crazy," Sam said.

He managed to make a slow-speed turn at the corner where the bicycle built for two observed from the shadows of the Blue Willow's porch. They zigzagged over to the only other road in town that ran parallel to Main, a dirt road someone had the audacity to name Broadway. Sam swung a wide, shaky turn onto Broadway, the eastern boundary between hay fields, cow pastures, and town dwellings. Finding a spot beside a vacant lot with no street light, he reined the Volvo over and shoved the shift selector into park, turning his full attention to the inflamed woman in his tangled lap.

Suddenly the big red pickup came roaring around the corner, spraying gravel and skidding to a stop alongside the idling Volvo.

With the window rolled down, Tom's voice came through the frigid air with a sing-song inflection.

"Miss *Muur*phy. Who you got in there with you?"

Laughter. The pickup's engine revved, followed by honking.

"They can't see through the frost," Diana said.

The 4×4 Chevy spun away and Sam figured Tom was driving. The street became instantly dark and deserted with only their rapid breath and refrains of pleasure breaking the winter still.

Soon, a horrendous banging from under the car interrupted Sam's trance. He thought the idling engine had blown up, the heater had exploded, the steaming radiator had burst. In a moment they both recognized the glow of fireworks. They surmised that the kids had snuck back and thrown a lit package of firecrackers under her Swedish sedan.

They collapsed in each others arms. Then something pounced on the hood of the car. Sam rubbed away the condensation on the windshield. It was the three-legged cat.

"See what I mean about being alone. Even the team mascot is watching us," Sam said in mock disgust. "And you! You wouldn't have noticed if the girls had gotten out and led a cheer."

"You were good," she said, still in his lap. "You were *so good*."

"I was?"

"Yes."

• • •

COACH PICKETT LATER learned that it wasn't the kids after all, at least not the kids he thought, and he might have figured it out when he saw Tripod. When the gang dropped Peter off, after the Chevy's second time around, Peter told his grandmother—who was waiting up to privately praise him for the spectacular win in the valley of the Shields—that Coach Pickett and Miss Murphy were out necking in Miss Murphy's car. Grandma couldn't pass up the opportunity, dug out a leftover package of firecrackers, and in her robe and furry bear-paw slippers, sneaked up on the Volvo with Peter. When Peter didn't have the guts to light and throw, Grandma's aim was accurate enough. Then the two of them scurried for the house, giggling all the way, and Peter guessed that both of them secretly wished *they* had someone to love.

CHAPTER 44

S am had called her several times on Sunday but there was no answer. Diana had appeared at school for all her required classes,
including basketball practice, but outside of that she became as wary as a
river otter. The gossip around school and town was that they got caught
necking after the game and therefore a winter romance was surely blossoming. Sam noticed a few giggles from underclass students, but it wasn't the
full-blown scandal he had feared. He didn't know how much Truly Osborn
had heard of the incident when the superintendent stopped him on the way
to lunch.

"There have been complaints about Peter Strong dribbling the basketball
in the halls between classes. Talk to him about it. And Sam, I know I don't
have to remind you that teachers are expected to set a good example at all
times."

Tuesday night Sam ate at the Blue Willow, hoping, by chance, that she
might do the same. He ended up eating alone, though Andrew Wainwright,
in a finely-tailored suit, came over and sat a minute with him.

"You're doing a good job with the boys," Andrew said, "real good. With
only six players, who'd have thought a month ago we'd have won two games
and scared the hell out of Christian and Twin Bridges? A year ago, well, it
would have been preposterous. You deserve a lot of credit."

"The boys have responded to everything I've asked. We're into transcending right now."

"It takes a special person to draw that out of kids. I'm sure glad you stuck
with it for another year."

Sam wanted to disagree; it was these boys that kept him going, their
courage keeping him afloat.

"So am I," Sam said. "I'm learning a lot."

"Is there anything I can do," Andrew said, "or the board can do?"

"Yes. We need new uniforms. We have every year's model out there from the past eight or ten, all with different shades of gold and blue, depending on how many times they've been cleaned. I don't think any two match. We look like a team someone just found in the attic."

"You're right. I'll talk to the others on the board. As you know, there's never enough money, but I'll get those uniforms."

He stood and pulled on his topcoat.

"Keep up the good work," Wainwright said. "I'll see you at the game Friday."

With that he went briskly out into the winter night and Sam followed his form until it disappeared in the darkness. What was Andrew Wainwright hiding from in Willow Creek? What wounds had he brought with him, what bloody smear followed him down that narrow blacktop highway into town?

"STOP AT THE post office," Grandma said as Peter gunned Trilobite Friday afternoon on their way to Bozeman.

"Probably nothing but junk," she said.

He stopped across from the Blue Willow. She hopped out and scurried into Mavis Powers's front room. In a minute she came out with a multicolored advertisement in hand and almost bumped into Axel, grunting up the steps in shirtsleeves and white apron.

"How you doin', Grandma?"

"I'm cookin'," she said. "Takin' my sweetheart to town to get him some decent socks to play in tonight."

She nodded at the bus. Axel turned and waved at Peter.

"Go get 'em, Pete! Sure glad you're back!"

On the top step he turned and glanced at the sky, his apron flapping in the wind.

"Don't stay too long. Looks like it's gonna snow."

"We'll be back for early supper," Grandma called and she climbed into the hippie bus.

Since his return, Peter had waded through a swamp of emotions that seemed to change within him by the minute, but above the confusion something felt right being here. He steered the rattling '65 VW bus along the narrow secondary blacktop.

"What happened to all your socks?" Grandma asked. "You had more than a dozen new pair."

"I gave some to Tom. He's always forgetting his, and I probably left some in Saint Paul."

"We better get a few for Dean as well. That boy's in rags half the time."

"Grandma, how come you always say you're cookin'?"

"I haven't told you my sea story?" she asked with some surprise.

"Nope."

"Well, I used to read a lot when my eyes were better, back when your grandpa was gallivanting around the world in some ship. I read sea stories, like I was sailing along with him. One of my favorites was a story by Joseph Conrad about a sailing ship that was caught in a typhoon coming around the Cape of South Africa, sails ripped, waves crashing over the deck, the ship listing and being tossed around like a cork. The men, hanging on for dear life, lashed themselves to the riggings, sure they would die at any moment. *Watch out for those cows!*"

Peter slowed for three Black Angus loose along the road, grazing on the dry ditch grass.

"Never know where those buggers will jump," she said.

"We'd be eating a lot of steaks," Pete said.

"Well, anyway, the first mate shouts through the gale to the cook and asks him if there is any water—the men had been without water for more than a day. But everything on the ship had been turned topsy-turvy. They'd even seen their trunks and blankets and clothes floating up from inside the ship and off on the sea. The first mate looked like he was heading for the galley and the cook unlashed himself and shouted back. 'Not you, sir, not you!' Then he scrambled toward the hatch, shouting into the wind, 'Galley! My business! As long as she swims, I will cook!'

"Well, the men think the cook's gone crazy. But clinging to the weather ladder with numb, frozen hands, he made his way toward the galley with the waves crashing over the deck. Before he went out of sight, he shouted at them again. 'As long as she swims, I will cook!'"

"What did he mean 'As long as she swims?'" Pete said.

"As long as the ship stayed afloat."

She pulled her hat snug as if she were in the typhoon.

"Well, the other sailors think it was a brave thing to do but didn't ever expect to see the cook again, betting that he was washed overboard. Hours pass. Nothing. Then in the middle of the howling cold of night there were voices, shouting, unclear, until each man, one by one, heard the good news. There was coffee coming. It came out of the dark in a large pot and it was *hot*. They drank right from the pot. It was a miracle. In a galley that was half underwater, with the stove flipped over on its side, with the ship pitching and lurching like a bobber, the cook had managed to do his job. He'd made hot coffee."

Peter slowed as they came into Three Forks, a town that seemed to some to be watching Willow Creek from a limb with a vulture's eye, waiting impatiently to gobble up their high school students for openers.

"We have to stop for groceries on the way back if we have time," Grandma said. "Don't want you eatin' supper too close to game time."

Peter guided Trilobite through the three blocks of downtown and headed north for the interstate.

"So you say you're cookin' like the cook on the ship?" Pete said.

"You got it. The ship eventually survived after three days and nights of that murderous storm, and the men remembered what the cook had done. He became a bloody hero to that crew and whenever they were tempted to give up while doing some tough job or back down from the hard way, they would show their grit and backbone by shouting, 'As long as she swims, I will cook!' And that's what I do. No matter how bad things seem to be, when I think I'll never get through the next day, I say to myself, As long as she swims, I will cook. As long as this old body is still kickin', I will do what I'm here to do."

Pete pulled out onto the freeway and slipped Trilobite's stick shift into fourth gear. He glanced at his unpredictable grandmother.

"What do you think you're here *to do?*"

She paused a moment, gazing out the rattling side window at the distant mountains.

"To help people along the way," she said, "to bring them hot coffee when they're cold and scared to death and hangin' on for dear life."

Peter pushed the truck a little over sixty. He didn't speak for a few minutes, thinking. An eighteen-wheeler shook the VW bus with a shock wave as it rippled past. Peter gripped the steering wheel.

"Grandma, do you believe in God?"

"Who do you think built the ship?"

"How come you hardly ever go to church?"

"There are churches and there are churches. There's the church that wouldn't bury your grandfather because he committed suicide. And there's the church who's always talking about a God of love on the one hand who will incinerate you like barbecued chicken if you don't live up to his expectations on the other."

She turned her crinkled face to regard him. "I guess I work undercover, and I suspect God works mostly undercover, too."

The '65 bus sailed along the interstate on their way to get him some decent sweat socks so he could help knock the socks off Reedpoint that night. He was glad this woman was his grandmother and he thought he wouldn't trade her for any human being on earth.

On their way home, winter's darkness caught them as they drove through Three Forks. On the edge of town there was a homegrown motel with the only indication of life a glowing red neon vacancy sign.

"What's the deal with that place?" Pete said, nodding. "I've never seen a car there since I've been in Montana."

"Don't know," Grandma said, "but you're right. I've never seen a car there either. Maybe they went south and forgot to shut off the sign."

Pete aimed the VW bus down the narrow blacktop.

"Keep an eye peeled for Black Angus, boy, they won't show up in the dark until too late."

"I feel like I have a vacancy sign on me," Pete said without looking over at her.

"I know the feeling. But one of these days you'll hang out a no vacancy sign because you'll realize what a unique and wonderful young man lives there."

Peter didn't respond until they were almost to Willow Creek.

"What if I never find someone to love?" he said softly.

"I'll tell you something you can bet on. Us gals are peculiar in this way. It's when we see a no vacancy sign hanging out there that we try to break the door down."

"But what if I never *do* find someone?" he said.

"Then you just keep on cookin'."

CHAPTER 45

Andrew was at the game Friday night. Reedpoint showed up, too, but Dean was in bed with the flu and its accompanying 103°F fever. Dean wasn't the only one missing when seven o'clock approached and a blizzard moved in over the Tobacco Roots. Tom hadn't arrived and no one knew where he was. Sam had dared to call the ranch, planning to hang up if George answered, out of jail only a day ago. Tom's mother answered and with an evasive tone said she wasn't sure where Tom was. When it came time to jump ball, Willow Creek had four players on the floor. If a team loses a player with five fouls, they can legally continue with less than five, but a game cannot start unless both teams have five players alive and standing. The referee had warned Sam twice: Come up with your missing player or forfeit the game. It was seven thirty-five and the Reedpoint players and fans were milling around like depositors at the door of a failed bank.

Caught between the dilemma of forfeiting the game or embarrassing his valiant manager, Sam scooted Scott into the dressing room.

"You don't have to do this if you don't want to," Sam said. "It's only a game."

"No, it's all right," Scott said with a wavering voice.

Sam decked him out in the best fitting uniform he could patch together: an extra-large jersey, a pair of trunks from bygone days, Scott's own brown socks and black Adidas shoes. The coach and his draggle-tailed manager trotted out of the locker room to the murmurs and snickers of the visitors and to the whoops and cheers of the hometown crowd, which was a modest increase after their unexpected victory over Shields Valley.

The referees gave Sam a quizzical look but said nothing as Scott, slightly knock-kneed, stood on the floor for the jump ball. Coach Joe Decker made no protest, undoubtedly recording an easy win in his mind. The Reedpoint boys smiled and licked their chops, and though rumor had spilled down the interstate that Willow Creek was vacating its long-occupied tomb, the Pirates swaggered confidently into town, having beaten the Broncs in December. Now, with a chubby, far-from-athletic Scott at one forward and Curtis Jenkins—who appeared as though he could hang glide with his ears—at the other, the Pirates were ready to board ship.

Olaf easily controlled the tip and batted the ball to Rob. Although Scott had helped in practice, as he trotted downcourt with the other boys he was an alien fallen on a strange planet. Sam dreaded the possibility of humiliating the ungainly boy.

"Time out! Time out!" Sam hollered, forming his hands in the familiar figure of a *T.*

When they came to the bench, Sam put an arm around the freshman manager.

"Thanks, Scott, we couldn't have played this game without you. Go in and get dressed now."

With obvious relief, the pudgy boy in an ill-fitting uniform dashed for the locker room as the Willow Creek crowd cheered.

"Four-man zone," Sam said. "Give 'em the outside stuff, but nothing inside. No second shots. Make 'em beat us from eighteen feet. Let's go! Have fun and learn something."

The team huddled for its cheer, but the fans drowned them out with their own.

"Oaf! Oaf! Oaf! Oaf! Oaf!"

The four boys moved onto the floor but Sam didn't expect the corresponding gesture of sportsmanship from Reedpoint. The Broncs had a plausible chance to win, and that so-called sportsmanship had limited applications and was much easier to flaunt by an opposing coach when he knew he would thrash you anyway. It would be four against five.

WHEN TOM WAS leaving their hardscrabble ranch for the game, his father, in one of his fitful moods, refused to let Tom take a vehicle to town. Finally, George removed the distributor cap from the old GMC pickup Tom drove.

"You can take the pickup," George said, "when you paint over that bullshit you put on the side of the barn."

"I'll miss the game."

"Then miss the goddamn game! Who cares! You'd only lose again."

Tom hurried to the pasture and called Patch, his Appaloosa. Out of the dark the gelding had come straight away, nosing for the oat bucket. A few flakes were swirling when Tom had Patch saddled and bridled. He tied on his duffel and swung into the saddle, heading out the nearly eight miles to town.

The blizzard caught him in the open with less than two miles to go and swept over him, immediately obliterating all sense of direction. He could no longer see fence lines or make out the road bed. In the murky darkness of January, the landscape had lost all contour and delineation, all human sign had been erased in one swoop of nature's brush. He tied his hat on with his bull rag, folding the brim down over his ears. He put on his leather gloves and he hunkered down in his full-length duster against the stinging snow.

He trusted Patch to feel his way, but several times they stumbled into the barrow pit, ran into fence lines, turned back and lost their bearings. He slid off the Appaloosa and slogged through the accumulating snow in his diamondback boots, leading Patch across open ground. Eventually he ran into a poorly kept barbed-wire fence and followed it. The temperature plunged. It hadn't been lost on Tom that people froze to death like this only ten yards from their back door. It was as though the weather was on his dad's side.

In THE COZY, noisy gym, where most were unaware of the sudden blizzard descending outside, the four-man home team was holding its own. Sam kept one eye on the game and one on the door, where Diana stood, going out into the raging storm from time to time. Sam tried to give his under-manned team time to catch their breath by judicially using their time outs. By rotating substitutions of fresh troops, the opposing coach was methodically wearing down the outnumbered Broncs, and they were falling behind, 39 to 31.

"GO TO TOWN!" Tom kept shouting to his Appaloosa in the shrieking storm. Though he knew his gelding might more easily find his way home, Tom figured they were within a mile or less of town and that they'd never make it back to the ranch. His survival instincts told him to find shelter, drowning out his uncompromising resolve to get to the game. Several times he managed to cut their way through barbed wire with his trusty wire cutter when a fence line impeded the direction the Appaloosa was heading.

After what seemed like hours of stumbling on foot and hobbling on horseback into the blinding whirlwind, Patch lurched up an embankment and his shoe clanked on metal. Tom rolled off with numb hands and feet. He kicked at the snow-covered ground and struck steel track with the toe of his boot. They had hit the line that carried the talc train along the west edge of town. It ran north and south and passed only a few hundred feet behind the school. They were close, if they hadn't wandered too far south. Tom knew they hadn't climbed, and that left them on the old flood plain between the foothills to the south and the Jefferson River to the north. For the first time since the blizzard closed in on him, he had some idea of where he was. In one way or another, the horse had led him east.

Tom's intuition told him they were south of town. He led Patch on foot. They moved north along the track, into the teeth of the storm's violence. Tom kept squinting into the howling darkness to his right in hopes of finding some glimmer of light from town. Repeatedly he went down off the right-of-way to check what bordered the track, searching for any recognizable landmark. Doubt and indecision wedged their way into his head as the terrifying cold and numbness hammered their way into his bones. Had he come too far north? Was the town actually south? He climbed on Patch and gave him free rein.

"Go to town!" he shouted into the horse's ear. Patch turned his rump into the assailing wind and stood, with snow caked in his mane and tail. In an escalating desperation, Tom slid off the horse and, leading the Appaloosa, continued feeling his way north along the talc line.

Like an apparition from an arctic hell, a familiar silhouette leading a horse out of the snow blast nearly passed Tom going the opposite direction along the track. It was the hat that brought Tom out of his mental stupor or he might have let them pass as the hallucination of a numbing brain. Amos Flowers, on his way to town for the basketball game, head down, never noticed Tom and the Appaloosa, though they passed within four feet of one another. Tom grabbed the startled man, who seemed to know exactly where he was. His handlebar mustache drooped with icicles and his big gray gelding loomed like the ghost of all horses killed by winter storm.

Screaming into each other's ear, Amos convinced Tom that Willow Creek was south. Hanging onto the tail of Amos's horse, Tom led Patch, trailing down the railroad bed through the swirling wind, following the strange man in his Tom Mix hat, wondering what held the damn thing on his head in this inferno and remembering with surprise that for the last half hour or more he'd been muttering a prayer that God would send help.

Miss Murphy saw the pair leading their horses through the tempest and she rushed out to embrace Tom. Amos took the Appaloosa, promising he would tie the horse on the lee side of the building.

It was halftime. The spectators let out a whoop as Tom, with nearly frozen feet and hands, stumbled toward the locker room like a survivor from Shackleton's failed Antarctic expedition. In the locker room, the team exploded in a burst of happiness at the sight of him, huddling around him in a warm, sweating embrace. Coach Pickett helped him peel off his snow-caked duster and settle onto a bench. Diana kneeled and pulled off the diamondback boots. When she gently massaged Tom's brittle feet and toes, Tom winced and jerked his feet away.

"What happened?" Sam asked.

"My son of a bitchin' father wouldn't let me take the pickup."

"Do you think you should play?"

Tom looked out of his thawing face at his coach. "If I don't play, they'll win. If I don't play, my *dad* will win. I didn't come through that hell out there to *lose*."

They guided him into a lukewarm shower and gradually made it hotter. Through the remaining halftime, while Rob and Curtis went out to play in the band, Tom stood in the comforting shower, restoring the feeling in his feet and hands.

The four players started the second half with Tom still in the locker room. They held their ground for most of the third quarter, falling back only by another four points. By then Tom was dressed and ready. When he loped out of the locker room with his J. Chisholm boots under arm, the hometown fans stood and applauded; word had spread that he had come through a blizzard. Rob noticed the commotion and saw Tom coming down the sidelines. He immediately called time out.

"Okay, we held the fort," Sam said, "and they couldn't burn it down. Now let's chase them back to their ships."

"Chase, hell," Tom said, "let's run them into the ground."

"Okay, back to regular zone," Sam said. "Be careful, Olaf, you've got three fouls. Have fun!"

Sam glanced at the scoreboard: VISITORS 51, HOME 37.

It took the rest of the quarter for Tom to recover his coordination, but he warmed up banging Reedpoint's strong front line for rebounds. With Olaf beside him, they began to take their toll. Tom crashed the boards with such intensity that Chad Olson, the husky Reedpoint boy he propelled out of bounds, looked back in shocked surprise to see what new force had exploded into the game.

The Willow Creek boys were rejuvenated, feeding off Tom's will and ferocity. Amos Flowers, perched in the bleachers with his hat dripping melted ice and snow, shouted hoarsely whenever Tom had the ball, to the amazement of those who knew the reclusive man. When Willow Creek caught the Pirates with little more than a minute to go, Sam dared to believe. But Olaf fouled out and Reedpoint won, making four straight free throws, 71 to 68.

THEY FOUND A barn in town for the two horses. Amos Flowers had increased his mystique as a local folk hero and Coach Pickett and Miss Murphy bought Tom all he could eat at the standing-room-only Blue Willow where everyone from the game, including the Reedpoint bunch, had holed up as the blizzard raged. They scrounged up blankets and pillows around town and bedded down the opposing team and its few fans in the gym, and Truly Osborn assigned Miss Murphy to take charge and oversee the night on the hardwood.

Pete and Grandma brought Tom and a reluctant Amos home to sleep with them, and Grandma figured she'd finally solve the mystery of his celebrated hat—whether or not he took it off when he slept. After everyone was tucked in and the house was dark, Grandma crept into the front room in her bear-paw slippers. The wind hummed outdoors, rattling window panes and eliciting creaks and groans from the walls. From the many drafts, she could smell the sweet, fresh snow. In a shadowed silhouette she could distinguish Amos, stretched out on the sofa. The rumor was true—he slept with his hat on.

THOUGH THE BLIZZARD was abating, only a few of those who lived close ventured out of town for home. Sam managed to kiss Diana in the hallway outside the girls' locker room before heading into the wind-driven snow, aching to bed down with her. He was startled at how treacherous it was for him, right in the middle of town, to trudge the two blocks to his house and then find it.

How on earth had Tom found his way for more than an hour through this assault? Better yet, how had Tom found his way for more than seventeen years through his father's insane asylum?

CHAPTER 46

The following day the little yellow bus slipped and skidded on ice-slick highways while carrying the team fifty-five miles south to Sheridan. Though the cheerleaders tried to pull enthusiasm out of the winter sky, the team traveled without much promise. They left Curtis behind, a victim of the flu, and by the time they arrived Rob wasn't feeling too well either, though he insisted he could play.

In the shoe box of a gym that had Panther Country emblazoned across its back wall, the Broncs gave all they had. Rob had to empty his stomach halfway through the second quarter and from then on Willow Creek played four against five and the Panthers ran them into exhausted defeat. Several carloads had followed the team despite the road conditions and weather, having seen victory against Shields Valley and daring to believe it could happen again.

The highlight of the game was provided by Dean in the fourth quarter, though the game was well out of reach by then. With the manner of an un-attended fire hose, Dean leaped for an errant pass and landed pell-mell on top of the scorer's table, touching off the buzzer as though trying to end the game three minutes prematurely and stop the carnage.

During the treacherously slow drive home the mood in Rozinante was subdued, sometimes deathly silent, as each of them brooded over his or her inner thoughts. Sam knew the boys were hurting. They had played with their hearts and been thrown off the porch again. With an inner agony that devastated him, he finally gave up on his dream. They just didn't have enough players to keep up with teams of ten and twelve. He chastised him-self for even considering such expectations. This was Willow Creek. There was a difference between appearance and reality. They were 2 and 8. In-credulously, somehow, they had *won* two games!

They arrived home past midnight and when Sam saw to it that things were put away and the building locked, he left the school and saw the Volvo was gone.

THROUGH THE WEEK, Diana became a wild creature that one senses is there but can never catch sight of. Though warm and friendly when they talked briefly between classes and at practice, she disappeared into the landscape the moment Sam turned around. He knew it wasn't coincidence. She didn't answer her phone; she wasn't at home the few times he drove out. When he asked her to dinner at the Blue Willow, she was going out to Ellie and Randolph Butterworth's.

At the end of Thursday's practice, she agreed to go for dinner and he picked her up after he'd showered at home. On the drive to Bozeman they talked basketball, seemingly a relief to both.

"You looked really down after the game Saturday," she said, "and I've noticed less enthusiasm in you during practice."

"I think I'm just tired, maybe a touch of the flu."

"Are you giving up on the boys?" she said.

He didn't look over at her. "I've learned to keep expectations down. It hurts less."

"The boys can tell when we're faking it."

"Are you faking it?" he asked.

"No, I believe they can win . . . if we could just keep all five of them *in* a game."

"Would you like to try Chinese?" he said, glancing at her.

"That'd be fine, but don't change the subject. How about Harrison and Lima?"

"My head says we should beat them, but my heart . . ."

"Don't give up on them, Sam. They're so dedicated and brave. They'd follow you through a mine field."

Her words hit him with sorrow. "Maybe that's the only place I could lead them." They were silent on the final fifteen miles into Bozeman.

Sam parked the Ford beside the Great China Wall Restaurant, and once at their table Diana ordered Chicken Lo Mein and a glass of Fuji plum wine. Softened by traditional Chinese music, the dining room had a faint aroma of fresh vegetables and peanut oil. There were only a handful of patrons scattered among the tables. After appetizers of egg rolls and fried wontons, Sam went for the pizazz, ordering the Szechuen Beef Hot Plate War Bar delivered to him on a sizzling platter.

"That not only looks delicious, it sounds delicious," she said.

Sam smiled. "Sounds like someone I know."

"How about taste?" she said.

"When I thought of you as 'Delicious Diana' I had no idea how you'd taste."

"Stir-fried. Anyway, these victory dinners are a good excuse to enjoy the local cuisine. And it's my turn to treat. I'm a coach, too, remember."

Sam couldn't get used to the lady picking up the check, but that wasn't the cause of the stressful stomach he experienced throughout the meal. After interminable small talk, he took a deep breath and stifled his terror.

"Have I done anything wrong?"

"No . . . why?"

"I don't know. I get the feeling you want to . . . avoid me?"

She regarded him and set her chin.

"You haven't done anything wrong. It's too good."

"*Too good?*" Sam said.

"What if, when you were seven, you were a rather plain little girl who no one noticed? And what if one day an uncle who lived in, um, Switzerland sent you an elegant music box that played beautiful songs when you wound it up? And suddenly other kids started noticing you, hanging around, paying you a lot of attention, even though you knew it was your gorgeous music box that they wanted to play with, to wind it up, turn it on, stroke its satin-smooth surface."

"Everyone wants to be your friend," Sam said.

"Exactly. Well, that didn't last long but I remembered how it felt. And then it happened again when I became sixteen. My body bloomed and that made gawkers out of boys who had never given me a second look, made tongue-tied boys who had never spoken to me. Just like with the music box, they wanted to wind it up."

"I know exactly how they felt," Sam said.

"I didn't know what to do. Resent them because I knew it was only my body they were interested in, or savor their attention, let them play, and enjoy the music with them."

She avoided his gaze.

"And?" Sam asked, dreading her reply.

"I let them play, at first. I basked in the attention, but eventually I knew it went against something inside me. I stopped. I only dated guys I liked, guys I thought I could get serious with. And then along came Greg. We married, we were happy. Along came Jessica and for four years it was perfect. Then Jessica died and it all unraveled. We couldn't handle it. I had failed him and he couldn't live with it."

"What do you mean you failed him?"

"I wasn't the woman he thought I was."

"How did Jessica die?"

"She . . . she just did."

Diana took a drink of water and tucked her hair behind her ear.

"I left San Diego. I was scared. My self-worth was shattered. I thought I'd never be loved again, though I had lots of boyfriends—no, I didn't have boyfriends, I slept around. I wanted reassurance that I was desirable, lovable, that someone would want me. Well, after a while that old feeling came back, that it wasn't me they wanted, only my body."

Sam frowned, trying to blur the scenes she was describing.

The waitress, a lovely Chinese woman named Jean, interrupted. "Would you like anything more?"

Sam nodded at Diana.

"No," Diana said, "thank you."

The waitress smiled, left the check, and was gone.

Diana leaned toward Sam and spoke as if she were being timed.

"Well, I began to feel ugly and unclean, I stopped altogether, several years ago, fretting over the possibility of having picked up some form of VD or even AIDS, loathing myself, distrusting all men."

"Did it work?"

"After a while. Most of those feelings went away. When I came to Willow Creek I was somewhat content with my life. I thought you were cute, absurd, straight-laced. Too serious. Dying."

"*Dying?*"

"But there was something about you that was different, something good and fresh and untouched. Now that I've gotten to know you, seen you with the boys, now that we've made love, it's too good. Those old feelings are flooding back and I'm scared. That's why I'm pulling the Cinderella-at-midnight act. I'm afraid."

"You're afraid!" Sam exclaimed. "*I'm* afraid. I've always been afraid. I grew up being afraid. I won the grade school championship for utter fear. I was all-conference in high school. I was on the all-fear team in college. I won medals, scholarships, trophies. I have a masters in fear, a Ph.D., I won the Nobel Peace Prize for being afraid."

By then Diana's smile had cascaded into a belly laugh. "And you say *I'm* crazy?" she said.

"You're the only woman I ever heard of who continues making love while her partner is ramming her Volvo down the center aisle of the local Methodist church."

She caught her breath and leaned toward him across the table.

"I'll tell you when I was scared, really scared. When I came to my senses I went to one of those places where you can have your blood tested anonymously. It took three days, I nearly died, imagining all kinds of symptoms, reading pamphlets, figuring the odds were stacked against me."

"What did it show?" Sam said with growing anxiety.

"It was clean, I was clean. God, I was relieved. I thanked my lucky stars and began a do-it-yourself sex life."

"I had to have a similar test last summer when I changed my health insurance. It came back with the rating of a celibate monk in some Tibetan monastery where it's so cold every body part is shriveled twelve months of the year and the only thing that gets hard is the ice."

They laughed.

Then, turning somber, she reached across the table to take his hand.

"I care for you a great deal. I'm afraid that if I fall in love with you, one day you'll tell me you don't love me, that I've failed you in some way, that I wasn't the good person you thought. I know this has nothing to do with you and everything to do with my history, but I need to work this out, so please have patience with me."

"Patience! I'm the definition of patience. I won the grade school championship for utter patience. I was on the all-patient team in college. I won medals for patience, scholarships, trophies. I have a masters in patience, a Ph.D . . ."

She bridled her laughter to speak. "You're not like any man I ever knew."

"Did you really get a music box from Switzerland?"

"Oh, yes, an elegant Edelweiss disc player. It has a hand-rubbed mahogany case with inlaid rosewood, came with shiny metal perforated discs and played a Bach Chorale, "O Christmas Tree," and "Oh, You Beautiful Doll." I'll let you play it the next time you're at the house."

"I hope there's a double meaning in there somewhere."

"I'll let you figure that out."

At her door he kissed her, several times, but she didn't invite him in. Though he ached for her, he felt wonderful. She liked him and she asked him to be patient with her. Oh God, could he be patient. His life had taken such dramatic turns he could hardly catch his breath. He headed for town in his faithful Ford, content to go home and sleep alone for at least one more night because Diana had at least given him hope.

But later, as he lay in bed, he felt scared, knowing that he was starting down that perilous path where one walks barefoot in the dark over broken glass. As he fell asleep, he listened for a backing Hamm's Beer truck. What he faintly heard was a Willow Creek ghost swishing by his partially open window.

↪ CHAPTER 47 ↩

Diana felt guilty for not helping Sam with the grueling three-hundred-mile round trip to Lima on Saturday. She knew it was time for her to get over her obsessive fear, but when she considered volunteering, she found her hands trembling and her breath quickening.

Friday they had been punched in the stomach again. When the two-week grades came out, Dean was failing in two subjects, English and Social Science, and he was temporarily ineligible. Sam helped the boy as much as possible, but he couldn't take Dean's tests for him. Sam had toyed with the idea of slipping Dean by for a two-week period—their basketball days would probably be over by then—but he knew the boy would know and Sam didn't want to damage Dean with the lie. They had tried to keep Dean eligible with the help of the girls tutoring on trips and even during lunch hour. The freshman had narrowly survived the last two-week grading period. Worse yet, Tom barely slipped by in Truly Osborn's U.S. history. Sam had considered forfeiting the weekend's games, saving the team and a handful of fans the long snow-packed road trip. Once more it would be five against ten or twelve.

Friday night they had played hard against Harrison at home, but the exhaustion and fouls had taken their toll. In the end, only Peter Strong hadn't fouled out, and with less than a minute to go, he was the only Bronc still on the court, only down by five points. Diana had never seen anything like it. The referee threw the ball in to Pete and he zig-zagged through several Harrison players and managed to get into the front court. Then, when it looked as though they had him bottled up, he split two defenders, went up with a shot, and buried a 3-pointer from about twenty feet out. Unbelievably, Willow Creek's one-man team had closed to within two points. Even the Harrison fans were applauding Peter. Of course the five Harrison players played keep away for the remaining time and won 59 to 57.

Diana smiled just watching Grandma's sweetheart—graceful, brash, daring, exploding to a run-off his first step and embarrassing opponents with his cross dribble. He was as cool as a riverboat gambler on defense and had a natural, unpredictable flair for the game that she and Sam knew better than to tamper with. Pete had inspired all of them. But once again, they turned for home beaten and had to find some comfort and cheer in things like their grit and doggedness and beautiful arcing shots.

RIDING IN THE seat behind Sam, Diana went over the score book on the bus trip to Lima. The cheerleaders were grilling Dean on English grammar and spelling.

"February," Louella said.

"Ah . . . f-e-b-u-a-r-y," Dean said.

"Wrong!" Carter said.

"Two-thirds of the world's eggplant is grown in New Jersey," Curtis said out of the blue, seemingly to no one in particular.

"I've noticed," Diana said loudly to Sam over the bus noise, "Olaf hasn't been called for three seconds in the paint for a while, and he's had only a couple traveling calls lately."

"Now if we can cut down his fouls," Sam said.

"Yeah . . . keep him in the game."

Diana spotted something along the road ahead.

"Sam, slow down, slow down. Stop the bus!"

He pulled over on the wide shoulder.

"What's wrong?" Tom hollered.

"Out of gas?" Rob said.

Diana stood and stepped into the door well. "No, everything's fine. It's a deer." She hopped out of the bus and walked back to the deer. It was a young doe, maybe three years old.

The bus unloaded and the kids followed her.

"Whatcha doin', Miss Murphy?" Dean said.

"Help me," Diana said.

"Road kill," Scott said.

"The poor thing," Carter said.

Diana took a hold of the doe's front legs.

"The meat might not be good anymore, Miss Murphy," Rob said.

"Help me," Diana said.

Peter and Rob picked up the two hind legs and the three of them carried the frozen deer over to a fence line where clumps of long brown grass stuck out of the snow.

"What are you doing?" Louella said.

"It's against the law to take it, Miss Murphy," Tom said.

"We're not taking it," Diana said. "We're showing respect for a fellow creature."

She guided the boys to gently lay the doe in the grass.

"It's just a dead deer," Dean said.

"Would you want to be left out on the road if you were dead, Dean?" Diana said.

Dean shrugged. She knelt and noticed the gang exchanging puzzled expressions.

"There, there, little lady," Diana said to the deer. "Go on your journey now."

There was a moment of confused silence. The wind chill cut.

"Okay, back on the bus!" Sam shouted and clapped his hands.

They raced for the bus, sliding and slipping on the snowpack. Only Curtis and Diana stood a moment.

"Thanks, Miss Murphy. That was nice," he said.

"It's the least we can do," she said, and they stepped up into Rozinante for the challenge ahead.

THE LIMA TEAM, still smarting from their earlier loss to Willow Creek—the leper in their conference—poured it on all night. They ran in fresh troops in a constant rotation, and for more than three quarters Willow Creek held them off. But Rob fouled out, and then Olaf, and the scavengers swooped in and picked their bones clean.

Lima 73. Willow Creek 59.

Explaining to Dean that there was no McDonald's on the lonely stretch of highway between Lima and Willow Creek, they stopped at the one-room schoolhouse in Dell. Once a lively small town along the railroad tracks, Dell had been pared down to a quaint little spot on the road where a handful lived and either tried to lure tourists off the freeway or hoped they'd truck on by. The sturdy brick schoolhouse with a bell tower had been converted into Yesterday's Calf-A, where patrons sat at long tables family style and shared the food with friends and strangers alike.

The Willow Creek gang filled one large table. Through the hard days of training and practice and through the long nights of travel and loss, they had become a family. Diana realized how much she'd come to care for them, all of them. Despite the loss, they held their heads up and enjoyed the food. They laughed and kidded each other, but she could tell that Sam was struggling inside. He smiled and joked, but he was drowning with pain.

She remembered her question to him in the Chinese restaurant. *Have you given up on them?* Had he? Had he given up on winning, on joy, on living? It scared her. He was becoming a Willow Creek ghost. She sat next to him and leaned close to his ear.

"Would you like to try the music box tonight?"

He looked at her and she caught his sadness.

"Yes."

SAM WOKE WITH dawn slanting in the bedroom window, buried in Diana's down-covered bed with her snuggled against him. They were naked and the warmth of her aroused him. He remembered that she'd been restless all night, burrowing around under the down quilt as if searching for sleep. She stirred in his arms.

"Are you awake?" he said.

"*Mmmmmm.*"

He pulled her more tightly against him and ran one hand over her hip and thigh.

"How are you?" he said. "You didn't seem to get much sleep."

"*Mmmmmm,*" she said.

"You're not used to having a big lug like me in your bed."

"No . . . it wasn't you. . . . I'm like that every night, I don't sleep well."

She opened her eyes and smiled. He kissed her warm lips and caught the scent of lavender.

"I feel so safe and good in your arms," she said.

He looked at the plaster ceiling and shuddered slightly. He knew he could protect her from nothing, save her from nothing, not from the sudden stroke of violence.

"You are good," he said, hoping she hadn't noticed him copping out on the *safe* part.

"No . . . no I'm not *good.*"

"What's eating you?" he said.

"Do you think one can ever right an unrightable wrong?"

"Well, I'm not sure . . ."

"I killed Jessica," she whispered as if the world were crouched and listening at the door.

"What do you mean?"

"She'd spent the day with a friend of mine who had a daughter Jessica's age. I picked her up when I was done teaching and we took a shortcut home. I wasn't driving fast, I wasn't in a hurry or anything, honest. Then, out on the highway, a raccoon ran in front of us. I swerved to miss it, overcorrected to bring the car back, and rolled several times into the ditch. I remember the car was on its side. I reached over to see how Jessica was. She wasn't moving. I managed to lift her out my window and lay her in the grass. I gave her CPR until someone came along and called for help. It didn't matter. Jessica was dead."

Sam lay horrified. He held her tightly. "I'm so sorry, Diana, so awfully sorry."

He understood so much now. Why she wouldn't drive the bus, why she didn't want to drive her car with any passengers, why she drove a Volvo. He understood the bloody smear that followed her down the highway in the rearview mirror.

She stared out the window.

"Greg couldn't handle it. He shouted his rage at me for a while. *For a raccoon! You killed our precious angel for a goddamn raccoon!* Then he went silent, didn't speak to me for weeks. We went our separate ways because down deep he couldn't forgive me for killing Jessica."

"I'm so terribly sorry, Diana."

"I've gone over it a thousand times until I thought I'd go crazy. I can scientifically explain what happened with my mind and body. I've made a study of it to see where I went wrong when the raccoon showed up suddenly on the road. My mind automatically sounded the alarm to my body out of fear and I immediately panicked. Those brain signals quickly translate into physiological reaction. My pituitary gland released adrenaline and other stress hormones to help sharpen my perceptions, and my pupils dilated to allow more light in. My breathing—"

"Don't, you don't have to—"

"No, let me finish, please," she said with desperation in her voice. "My breathing and heart rate and blood pressure increased to maximize blood flow to my limbs, and my digestion ground to a halt as my liver released sugars, cholesterol, and fatty acids into my bloodstream for energy. I was ready to react to the situation. While mobilizing all its resources, my body was able to react under pressure. And with all that working for me, I made the wrong decision. With all of that, I rolled the car and killed Jessica."

Sam wiped the tears from her cheeks with an edge of the sheet and she urgently pulled him toward her, searching desperately into his eyes for any sign of forgiveness. Without speaking he slid above her, strangely yet strongly aroused, and she opened herself to him. He entered her deeply and held very still. In that moment he hoped she understood he was offering to share her torment and agony and unbearable sorrow.

With him holding her securely, she sobbed for a time and then fell into a deep sleep.

CHAPTER 48

Friday was the day Manhattan Christian's basketball team came into town, the day everyone would find out which of the Painter brothers would end up with the John Deere "D." Diana and Sam, with colds and little energy, tried to prepare the boys for the game of attrition in which the five of them, minus the ineligible Dean, would have to slug it out with twelve well-conditioned boys from Manhattan Christian. All week they couldn't help but notice Olaf's infectious intensity, driving the practice sessions like a rampaging bull. The nervous strain on each of the players, and on Sam as well, was rising steadily throughout the day.

After school all six of them gathered in the shadowed gym, wondering if there might be something more they could do to prepare themselves, something they had overlooked. Sam came into the gym in his suit and tie.

"Okay, you guys, it's no fair if you start before the other team. Why don't you get home now and eat. Be back here by six-thirty. We'll celebrate at the Blue Willow after the game," Sam said, noting the perspiration on Dean's forehead. "And don't worry, Dean, if you study hard you'll be back with us next week."

Their faces lit up. They never had to ask the question that dogged each of their thoughts. He had insinuated a confidence into their bloodstream, into the fibers of their muscle, into the tissue of their hearts. Now all he needed was someone to insinuate confidence in him.

After the blizzard incident, Sam took no chance of losing his lionhearted forward. He would eat with Tom at the inn, removing the necessity for Tom to go home. While they ate, Sam accepted the good wishes of everyone in the place, from Vera and Axel to all the early Friday night diners. Some of the skeptics, unbelievers, and fainthearted had timidly clambered back on the bandwagon until there was hardly room for the few diehards who had never gotten off.

"How are you feeling?" Sam asked Tom after he'd demolished a chicken-fried steak dinner.

"Good . . . a little uptight."

"Me too."

"We've never beaten those cocky ass—" Tom paused. "Turkeys."

"It'll be fun. How's the knee?"

"Okay."

"Do you think your mother will come to a game?"

"No." Tom sobered. "She wouldn't dare."

"I'm sorry," Sam said, wishing he hadn't asked. He took a drink of water. "You boys keep surprising me. Know what I found when I got to school this morning?"

"No."

"Curtis. I came over early to do some class work. He was in the gym, in his school clothes, shooting from his corner. I asked him if he'd done this before. He said he had. I asked him if he didn't think I worked you hard enough at practice. He said, 'Yeah, but after Tom came through the blizzard, I just thought I could practice a little before school.' See what you've done? It's catching. That great kid, going an extra mile because you're a great kid." Tom glanced into Sam's eyes and then quickly turned away.

"You're all going to be superb tonight," Sam said. "It'll be one to remember."

Sam placed his hand on Tom's muscular shoulder and squeezed.

"How about some ice cream?"

"Yeah," Tom said, clearing his throat. "Thanks."

WHEN DIANA AND Sam brought their clipboards to the bench long before the game started, he noticed Dean's mother wheeling Denise into the gym. He'd given Dean four tickets he said were extras in hopes that the family would come. For some unknown reason he felt good that the girl was there. Mervin and Claire Painter were already camped in the bleachers directly behind the team bench. Sam stepped up into the stands and leaned close to Mervin as fans from both sides were straggling in.

"What are you going to do with the tractor?" Sam said.

Mervin tried to smile at the coach but his face seemed frozen in a mask of utter trepidation. He gripped the edge of the wooden seat with his work-hardened hands as though an unbearable disappointment might momentarily blast him to smithereens. "Do you *really* think we could do it?" he asked Sam.

"We've had a good week of practice. They're as ready as they'll ever be."

"The Cutter boy still out?" Mervin said.

"Yeah, until next week."

Mervin sighed from somewhere deep inside, a faint shadow of doom across his leathery face.

Carl Painter arrived twenty minutes before game time and sat with a flood of Eagle fans that quickly overwhelmed the bleachers and spilled over to standing room only. Some of the Christian fans slid into the few remaining seats on the Willow Creek side until the stands on both sides creaked. The small gym buzzed with the excitement and anticipation of a tournament game. The Manhattan Christian followers had brought with them an uneasy anxiety about the Norwegian beanpole—remembering their narrow victory a month ago—as well as their itching curiosity to be among the first to see who would end up with the Painter family John Deere "D."

Once the contest started, Sam flinched at the ferocity of the game. Both teams crashed the boards, banged on picks, hounded on defense tooth and nail, and neither gave an inch. They rotated three boys on Olaf from off the bench in an attempt to wear down the thin giant, elbowing and shoving him as much as the officials would allow and taking the ball to him with drives to the basket on offense.

At the end of the first quarter, Christian led, 19 to 12, and though the large hometown crowd had sustained uproarious cheers, it seemed evident that Willow Creek was back on its heels and hanging on.

"Okay, we've gotten the butterflies out," Sam said as the team rested on the bench, draped with towels and guzzling water. "Now, after we score, pick them up all over, they won't be expecting it. Tom, you'll be open if you stay out on the wing. They think Olaf has the ball."

The first time Willow Creek went into their full-court press—unheard of by a team without a substitute that wanted to protect its five starters from exhaustion—they caught the Eagles napping. Tom picked off a pass and threw a clothesline to Rob, who swished it. Immediately Christian called time out, giving the Broncs another much-needed rest.

At halftime Willow Creek led by one, 37 to 36. Olaf had three fouls. The team retreated to the locker room.

The Painter brothers clung to their bleacher seats with white-knuckled grips and the fans on both sides sighed with the relief halftime brought. Grandma Chapman and Andrew were hoarse from shouting and it seemed that Amos Flowers had appointed himself Tom Stonebreaker's personal cheering section, standing and hooting whenever Tom scored or snagged a rebound. The band, with Rob and Curtis in their sweat-sodden uniforms, played the school fight song, and many of the fans found themselves singing along with unexpected strains of hope showing up in their voices.

In the third quarter, Pete and Rob found their touch and brought tears to Grandma's eyes with graceful long-range arcs that swished the ball flawlessly through the white nylon net and added to the scoreboard in increments of three. Tom took pressure off his Scandinavian teammate by scoring from the baseline, and the Willow Creek fans rose to their feet and roared as Curtis Jenkins—left alone in the Eagles' attempt to overplay the scorers—drifted along the baseline, caught a quick pass from Pete, and nailed a layup, his first basket of the season.

With the combination of Olaf's great zeal to win and his growing exhaustion from fighting off three rotating players, he slapped a shot away but picked up his fourth foul a minute into the fourth quarter. Pete and Rob did what they could to slow the game down and stay close. With three minutes to go, Tim Volk, a knotty little guard, scored, giving Christian a six-point lead. Sam signaled for a time out, feeling the familiar doom he'd learned to expect at this point in the game. The boys huddled on the bench.

"You're playing well. Run number four, number *four*. Get Olaf the ball when he comes open." Sam looked into their believing eyes.

Diana clapped her hands. "Let's get the tractor!"

With fifty seconds to go, having closed to within one point, Olaf faked going across the paint and pivoted the other way, open for a second behind his man. Pete delivered a hard, high pass and Olaf jammed it. A whistle. Traveling! But he hadn't, in Sam's eyes. His gawky body and graceless motion had deceived the referee into a bad call. The Willow Creek stands erupted

in boos, led by the dignified and usually restrained John English, who un-
abashedly seemed caught up in the cause he had so vehemently opposed.

"Get in the game, ref!" Diana shouted, leaping up and threatening to step
out onto the court.

Christian brought the ball up the floor. Sam signaled the team to stick it
to them, but Curtis couldn't contain a quicker boy, and his man broke clear
behind Olaf and made a layup.

Eighteen seconds.

Down by three, Pete brought the ball up quickly. With a cross-dribble he
caught Manhattan's Van Dyke back on his heels and sliced into the paint,
drawing Rob's man for a moment. Pete stopped short, and without turning,
bounced the ball behind his back to Rob, momentarily unguarded beyond
the three-point line. Never blinking, Rob followed through with fingers and
wrist as the ball arced toward the basket. Heads and eyes turned with the
spinning sphere. For an instant there wasn't a sound. Sam went down on
one knee in front of the bench, and all spectators were on their feet, holding
their breath.

HOME 66. VISITORS 66.

"Yeah!" Diana and Sam shouted simultaneously, leaping to their feet and
nearly knocking Scott and Dean off the bench.

The visiting crowd fell silent, the hometown throng erupted. The contest
would go on, overtime! Sam winced as he looked into their dripping faces,
finding doggedness and exhaustion and a will of iron. He rested his weary
and breathless drove as long as possible, stalling for time in every way he
could imagine. Hazel couldn't get the time clock set at three minutes and
Sam suspected she was purposely buying them precious time. Finally the
referee came to the bench and herded them onto the hardwood.

"Have fun," Sam said, "learn something."

"And bury them!" Diana shouted.

During the overtime, while tracking the course of a loose ball, Sam
glanced into the face of Denise Cutter and was momentarily captivated
by the palsied child in the wheelchair at the end of the court, excited and
animated, pulling for Willow Creek underneath the burden of a body that
wouldn't obey, with soft blue eyes that would. For an instant nothing else
seemed to matter, no one else was present. He thought of Amy, saw her face.

No! He whipped his attention back to the contest as the Eagles continued driving into Olaf, trying desperately to nail him with that elusive fifth foul. Twice, when they surrounded Olaf, he passed to Tom who slid down the baseline and called a time out.

Twenty-two seconds were left. The Broncs had possession of the ball. Christian led by one.

"Okay, okay, listen," Sam said over the noise of the crowd. "Olaf, go into the middle. Get him the ball high. Curtis, come across and set a pick on Tom's man. Tom, cut backdoor. Olaf, if your man tries to close it, go for it."

The fans on both sides were on their feet shouting when Olaf caught Rob's high pass. He planted both feet and kept the ball above the Christian players. Tom sliced down the baseline and Olaf motioned with the ball toward him. The 6'3" Bill Dorn slid from behind Olaf, skillfully blocking Tom's path to the basket.

Only problem was Tom didn't have the ball.

The Norwegian hammer pivoted as if his right shoe were bolted to the barn loft floor and jammed the ball through the hoop with a vengeance. Hazel Brown jammed her thumb on the buzzer with a vengeance.

The game was over!

The guarded Willow Creek fans hesitated for a split second, holding their collective breath. Sam gazed at the scoreboard, still doubting.

HOME 76. VISITORS 75.

No late whistle. It was true! *They had won!*

The Willow Creek crowd erupted and swarmed from the stands, smothering the team with praise and affection. Standing on the court, Mervin Painter picked up his very stout wife and swung her around like a weightless schoolgirl.

Willow Creek had beaten Manhattan Christian, and better still, the John Deere "D" was coming home.

CHAPTER 49

After reliving the game with the boys for a while, Sam and Diana found a table on the saloon side of the Blue Willow. The place was decked out with high-rolling Willow Creekians who claimed they'd never given up on their team on its six-year sojourn through that winless wasteland. Tom and Rob seemed most intoxicated with the adrenaline of winning after three years of being personally pulverized by the Manhattan Christian Eagles. Curtis received numerous accolades for his faultless layup and the timid sophomore—in his Future Farmers of America jacket and Tom's black cowboy hat as a bestowed honor—basked in the glow of the sudden notoriety.

Olaf, with the intensity of the game still mainlining through him, pumped the player piano to the tune of "Roll Out the Barrel" and many celebrants sang along. Dean, acting as if he'd missed the Second Coming, had herded Carter and Louella into a corner table and with his social science book open, had the girls quizzing him, determined to never let another once-in-a-lifetime event get by him if he could help it.

After allowing the boys an hour of letting off steam and savoring the victory, Sam sent them home to bed and a good night's rest. With the trip to Twin Bridges only hours away, none of them balked, still feeling the sapping weight of exhaustion from the night's combat. Tom was sleeping at Grandma Chapman's with Pete, and she promised that if the hobbled forward neglected icing his swollen knee, she'd make the kid sleep in the refrigerator.

"Did you see Mervin Painter?" Diana said.

Wearing her crimson matador hat slightly tilted over one eye, she seductively sucked cranapple juice through a straw. Sam gazed from his hamburger and grinned.

"He looked like he couldn't decide what to do," Sam said. "Laugh or cry."

"He put down his wife and picked up Olaf as if he were a lollipop. I've never seen anyone so ecstatic."

"I think he's becoming awfully attached to Olaf, like the son he never had."

Hazel approached their table. "I can't take anymore of those overtimes, Mr. Pickett," she said. "I thought my heart would stop before those three minutes would ever run off the clock."

"Well, I'll tell the boys that," Sam said. "Win in regulation time. Oh . . . and thanks for the extra time to catch our breath."

"That was that nutty scoreboard, I had nothing to do with that." She winked and giggled.

"Well, thanks anyway," Sam said.

"This is the best I've felt in years," Hazel said. "Think of it. *We* beat Christian."

"Yes, and you had a hand in it," Diana told her, "with all your help at practice."

Sam nodded his agreement.

"Go get 'em tomorrow night," Hazel said, giggling, and then hauled herself toward the dining room with childlike glee.

Diana rolled her eyes. "Sometimes her giggling drives me nuts."

"Yeah, I know what you mean," Sam said. "But I tell myself that if I'd been raised the way Hazel was and if I'd gone through what she's gone through, I'd probably giggle a whole lot more than she does."

"Great game, coach!" Ray Collins called as he herded his family toward the front door.

"Thanks," Sam said and threw a little wave.

He regarded Diana.

"They're jelling as a team," Sam said. "They're coming together. You can't coach that. They're anticipating each other, running plays, playing hard-nosed defense, and more important, they've got spirit and heart. You deserve as much credit as anyone. Did you *see* them out there tonight?"

"Yes, I saw them," she said. "They were splendid. They'll beat Twin Bridges."

Sam caught Andrew Wainwright watching Diana from a table in the dining room. Sam put down his hamburger and looked into her eyes.

"I thought of Amy out there, right in the middle of the game. Do you—"

"All the time," she said with a shadow in her unadorned face. "When I least expect it I see Jessica's little face and her big brown eyes."

"I'm sorry," Sam said.

"No, don't be sorry, I think she's trying to tell me that she's all right, that I shouldn't worry about her or feel sad."

Sam felt that tightness coming on, that sense of falling. He glanced around at the crowd. The inn hummed. He picked up his hamburger.

Diana leaned toward him. "I don't know if you can see him, but Andrew is staring at us," she half whispered, peeking around Sam.

"Probably not *us* but *you*. He's a healthy single man." Sam took a mouthful of his hamburger.

"Well, he's too good looking for me. I'd never trust him."

"Oh, that's why you hang out with me? I'm ugly enough," Sam said with his mouth full and wiped his lips with a paper napkin.

"You're honest."

If she only knew, Sam thought. More and more he was aware of how often he lied about his feelings, covering up, hiding out.

"Was your ex . . . Greg, ugly?"

"No."

"If he wanted you back, would you go?"

Diana regarded him, her face grave. Sam pushed his plate away. "If he called and said he was over it, that he wanted me back, that he could forgive me, I think I would run back to him."

"I'm glad that you said that. It's always better to get involved with a married woman." Sam smiled. "Good sex, no responsibility."

"Is that what you want, good sex and no responsibility?"

"I'd hate to lose what we have together," he said and then took a swig from his Mountain Dew can.

She reached across the table and took his hand in hers. They had tears in their eyes.

"Music box tonight?" he said quietly.

A delightful smirk lit up her face. "You told the boys we all need a good night's sleep."

"Right," he said. "Concentrate on the game."

"Excuse me," Andrew said as he stopped by their table. "Don't mean to intrude, but I wanted to congratulate both of you."

Sam noticed the man casually placed a hand on Diana's shoulder.

"Wow!" Andrew said, "I'm still flying. It was fantastic."

"Thanks," Sam said.

"I couldn't help watching you two from the dining room. Pardon me for saying this, but you look very happy. Makes me feel good to see you together."

"Oh, well . . ." Sam faltered.

"We're enjoying the celebration," Diana said.

"Excuse me for butting in. Sam, they'll be here next week for sure. They promised they'd be here ten days ago. I called and leaned on them. Much longer and it'll be too late. I hope they arrive before Friday."

"Good, that'll be something," Sam said. "Thanks a million."

"You two have a nice night," he said and wormed his way through the crowded inn.

"What's that all about?" she said.

"A surprise. For you, for everyone. Wainwright has gone out of his way to back the team."

"Did you notice the look in his eye when he told us to have a nice night?"

"No."

She reached across the table and squeezed his hand. "Maybe tomorrow night," she said tamely, but her eyes whispered salacious promises.

Later, after Sam kissed her beside the Volvo, he noticed Andrew watching from his parked white Lincoln Town Car. Sam thought about it on the walk home. Could the talc plant executive be interested in Diana? No, he must be at least twenty years older than she.

He had a bounce in his step and he felt shamelessly happy—a feeling he attributed to his blossoming intimacy with Diana. Playing Twin Bridges on the road would tell them exactly where they were on their destined path as a team and Sam felt a strange optimism. As he walked he noticed the world around him, something else he did much more often since his day in the field with the goddess disguised as a biology teacher. He gazed at the waning moon, the delicate herringbone clouds with moon-light embroidered edges. There were no broken hearts sailing through. He whistled a tune from *Man of La Mancha*. They had beaten one of the best teams in the conference and though they were outmanned, they were not outplayed.

✎ CHAPTER 50 ✎

In the cottony shimmer of a lavender-scented candle, in the rumpled softness of Diana's large brass bed, Sam made love with desperate urgency, as though to beat back the long litany of loss in his life. With her own frenzied abandon, Diana joined him in a feverish attempt to hold off some dark destruction threatening to wash over her. They had forgetfully relaxed their defenses, exposing their hearts to the world. Now they staggered and faltered from the shattering blow that—finding their unspoken longings unprotected—maimed without mercy.

Like wounded partisans on a battlefield where they had no chance to win, for a moment dragging themselves to a hidden place under the rubble, they plunged headlong to clutch what comfort and safety they might find in the other, some tourniquet to stop the bleeding at their center, some pleasure to hold off the terrible truth.

When they finally collapsed beside each other in the damp bedding, trembling and gasping for air, he rolled away and pulled the sheet over him like a mummy.

"Do you want to talk?" she said, lying on her back and staring at the shadow-dappled ceiling.

"I can't."

"They played so well," she said. "They deserved to win."

Sam lay silent.

"It hurts when they play their guts out and come so close," she said. "I was so damn proud of them. How many times will that Miller kid hit a three-pointer from twenty-five feet? God!" Her voice elevated with anger. "And it went off the *backboard!* Everyone knew it was garbage. He never once used the backboard all night! Stupid luck. When we were up by seven in the third quarter I knew we would win," she said. "I felt it."

They lay quietly for a long time, then she broke the silence.

"A twenty-five-footer with two seconds on the clock . . . and it went off the *backboard*. Do you think things like this are all decided ahead of time, like, no matter what we did, we'd lose in the end?"

"I don't know," Sam said from his cotton cocoon. "No, I have to believe we could have won, it wasn't decided."

"What are you doing under there?"

"I just remembered. I used to do this when I was a kid, whenever I wanted to hide."

"Did it work?"

"It gave me the illusion it did," he said softly. "I must have been very young. I think I figured if it couldn't see me, it couldn't hurt me."

"What's *it*?"

Sam pulled the sheet off his head and sat up. "I've never been able to find out, but it's real."

He swung his legs over the side of the bed with his back to her.

"Whatever it is, it had its beastly hand in it at Twin Bridges tonight. God, did you see Tom and Olaf bang it out on the boards with Stone and Harkin and whoever else they threw against them."

"The refs didn't let Stone get away with much," she said.

"And the way Tom went nose to nose with Stone in the third quarter after Tom put him on the floor blocking his layup."

"I was sure Tom was going to punch him out and get thrown out of the game again."

"I almost wish he had," Sam said. "He just smiled at Stone."

"What a smile."

"And the way Curtis rode his man all night," Sam said. "He wore that kid out." Sam chuckled. "He was concentrating so hard he covered him one time when the kid was going out of the game for a substitution. I thought Curtis was going to sit on the bench with him."

"You told him to stay in the kid's shorts."

"I was exaggerating."

"You'd better be careful how you exaggerate. I think these boys would walk naked and blindfolded into the Jefferson River if you told them to."

She rolled onto her side, propping her head on her elbow.

"You made me cry, you know."

"I did?" Sam half turned toward her in the flickering light.

"Yes. What you said to them."

"I don't remember."

"Yes you do, Sam Pickett, because I know how deeply you believe it. You told them they might never have this kind of friendship again and how very special it was. You told them that maybe it was the last time in their lives they'd battle as a team for something, that for the rest of their lives they'd be out there fighting alone."

"I said that?"

"And when you broke the huddle after the game and reminded them, win or lose, we're coming off the floor together. You said, I would rather be coming off the floor with you and those boys after losing than any other team in the world after winning."

"God it hurts to see them lose," Sam said. "I think I could hear their hearts breaking."

"Yes."

"It was so goddamn presumptuous of me. I never learn. I actually expected to win—Willow Creek, Montana."

"It hurts to see how much you take it all on yourself," she said.

"*You* didn't lose. And neither did *they*. They played better than they know how."

Sam stood, seemingly unmindful of his nakedness in the shadow-dancing room. He shuffled to the window and stared out into the blackness.

"I like you without your glasses. Ever try contacts?"

"Never thought about it. Glasses were always a part of my disguise, something to hide behind."

"Do you have good friends?" she asked.

He thought a moment.

"You know, I think the best friend I ever had was a dog."

"A dog?"

"Yeah, Barkley. From before I could remember until I was eleven when he died. I still knew how to cry then. I cried for a month. My mother, after that first day, told me to quit that nonsense over a dog, to grow up. So I'd fake it until I could be alone and then I'd cry. God, I missed that dog."

"I'm glad you had Barkley."

"Yeah. He helped me through."

"Did you have any close human friends?"

"A few, from school days, scattered around the country. I haven't been very good about keeping in touch since Amy's death."

"How about now?"

"I've tried, with men, but we can't do it very well. We keep bumping into invisible barriers, passageways we mortared tight as we grew up to save ourselves from the beasts that stalked us. Now, when we want to break them down, we don't know how."

"What do you do?"

"We do the best we can. But we finally surrender to the fact that we can't handle being close, not really close, as though it were contrary to something in our genes. The fortifications are too thick and too well in place. Now and then we approach it, we knock out a stone or a brick and whisper to the other side, but I've never been close to anyone in the way I was with friends at school. It's as though I lost my childlike ability to trust."

"I've made a few friends since I left San Diego, but we gals are not as different from you guys as you might be led to believe."

He turned from the window.

"Would you prefer I went home to sleep?" he asked.

"What do you want?"

"To sleep here, with you."

She lifted the sheet and he slid in beside her, as if seeking shelter from the gale in the lee of her love. They cuddled into a twinning fetal position beside the dancing night light, two children afraid of the dark, longing to sail over the Spanish Peaks on one of God's safe skipping stones.

"Good night, Jessica," she whispered. "Mommy loves you."

CHAPTER 51

Like a bridegroom overcome with joy on his wedding night only to discover that his bride has run off with the best man, Elizabeth Chapman, and the Willow Creek community, was rocked by the traumatic weekend: the stunning victory over Manhattan Christian Friday followed by the crushing loss to Twin Bridges on Saturday. But there was no relapse into the habitual pessimism that once inhabited their neighborhoods and haunted their spirits. Seeing their boys standing toe to toe with one of the state's best and putting up a courageous fight sent their pride and expectations soaring, though a few outbursts of fatalism did erupt here and there.

There were only two more games in the season: two more chances for another rip-roaring win. Then on to the dreaded tournaments where their season always ended swiftly if not mercifully, and with the sour memories of defeat lingering in their subconscious, they'd try desperately to lay them aside and start to think about spring planting.

"That boy couldn't make that shot again in a hundred tries," Grandma Chapman said at morning coffee in the Blue Willow.

"It's like we're doomed," Hazel Brown said, her drooping clothes stark evidence of the weight she'd lost somewhere in undusted corners of the school gymnasium.

Axel puttered behind the pie counter.

"Maybe we can beat Gardiner or Shields Valley," he said.

"Fat chance," Hazel said. She gingerly stretched her right arm over her shoulder. "I think I have bone cancer."

"If you had one percent of everything you imagined," Grandma said, "why, you'd have been dead thirty years ago."

Rip unloaded the first volley at Bobby Butcher, the lanky Pepsi man, as he hauled two canisters in the front door. The loss to Twin Bridges took some of the joy out of it, but the handful in the inn blistered the former

Christian player with gusto, possessing the insight that it might be an opportunity that comes once in a lifetime. Bobby simply nodded and kept a polite smile plastered on his face. Before he left, he had the maturity and good sportsmanship to stop at Grandma Chapman's table.

"You lied to me, Grandma." Bobby frowned, waiting.

"What on earth are you talking about?"

"You told me your grandson was good."

"Well, he is! Damn good."

"That boy is all-world," Bobby said. "You have no idea how good he is."

Bobby winked and hustled out, catching another burst of flack from Rip on the porch. Grandma thought her chest would burst with pride, and she felt so elated she picked up the tab for everyone in the place.

ANOTHER WILLOW CREEK diehard would pick up the tab for coffee that morning. Mervin Painter caught himself speeding toward Manhattan, something he never did. His hands trembled on the steering wheel and his throat went dry. Would his brother try to squirm out of their bet the way he always did when they were boys? How could he and save face when his cronies and everyone in the café—hell, nearly everyone in the valley—knew about the bet?

When he approached the Garden Café, he scanned the area for the tractor. It wasn't in sight. He parked his pickup at the curb and hoofed it for the down-home restaurant. He could feel his heart thumping under his wool-lined canvas jacket. There was no way Carl could worm out of this one. But he'd thought that many times before and Carl always found a way.

The café, pungent with the aroma of coffee and bakery goods, was more crowded than usual for a midmorning Monday, and Mervin felt every eye trace his passage to the locally renowned booth where Carl and his cronies cowered.

"Good morning," Mervin said, trying to keep his voice normal and failing. He slid into the vacant space that the losers undoubtedly hoped would remain unoccupied that morning.

"I didn't think you were here yet," Mervin said and cleared his throat. He regarded Carl, who sat stone-faced. "I didn't see the 'D' out front."

"It's in the back," Carl said in a lowered voice.

"In the *back!*" Mervin exclaimed. "Why is the tractor out *in back*?"

Carl cringed, ducking his face from the locals, who seemed to be relishing this family soap opera. Something in Mervin told him to have mercy, knowing what it was like to lose when your soul ached to win. But another voice in him demanded he extract every ounce of justice after a lifetime of losing to his big brother, after years of ridicule and brutality and humiliation.

"You were lucky," Carl said under his breath.

"Lucky! Lucky? Hell, our coach tried to hold the Willow Croak boys back so the score wouldn't be too embarrassing."

A wave of light laughter washed across the café.

"Luck? Think what it would have been like if poor little Willow Croak had had *six* boys to play against Christian's twelve," Mervin said. "It would have been a slaughter. That's why Willow Croak cuts its team down to five, so they don't wallop the big schools too bad."

The chorus of laughter swelled as the locals, who were mostly avid fans of the Class B public school, enjoyed seeing their closest rivals lambasted by the likes of Willow Creek.

"Well," Mervin said. "Let's go find the missing tractor."

Mervin led the way and the three disgruntled Eagle fans dragged their abashed faces after him. Out the finger-worn front door, Mervin paused and fell in behind his seething sibling, who turned up the alley alongside the old creamery building and walked a full block. There on an inconspicuous side street, perched on a low-boy trailer, the classic John Deere endured in mint condition, its single stack skyward and proud, its green and yellow paint glossy, its large lugged steel wheels bright yellow—a powerful emotional symbol of authority to the Painter boys. Carl stopped and stonewalled with his arms folded across his granitelike torso. He had cranked the trailer off his pickup. Mervin hurried to fetch his pickup with the spring in his step and lightness in his heart of a young boy who had finally evened accounts with his brutal big brother.

After hooking up to the trailer—guessing that Carl hoped he'd drive directly out of town—Mervin paraded around the main drag several times, honking and flashing his lights. Then he parked directly in front of the Garden Café. He couldn't help but swagger through the door to the cheers and applause of many of the witnesses, some of whom had come out of the restaurant to inspect the impressive antique. Mervin settled in the booth where the three defeated had silently huddled.

"Coffee on me . . . for everyone!" he shouted, feeling as though he'd pop the brass buttons on his OshKosh B'Gosh bib overalls, drawing another round of applause for his generosity.

Mervin regarded his brother—who brooded fire and animosity in his cold gray eyes—instinctively prepared to duck the punch coming from out of their childhood, hoping it would come so he could defend himself by hammering his big brother into the checkered linoleum floor.

"Now that we've finally gotten things straightened out, let's drink some coffee," Mervin said, surprised at his own poise and balls.

"How long you gonna let that 'D' set out there?" Carl said.

"Until we've had our coffee and visit. What's the rush?"

A grinning waitress brought a pot and set it on the table.

"What do you think about the new weed-control deal the county is coming out with?" Mervin asked his brother.

Carl stood, dropped two quarters on the table, and shouldered his way out of the café.

"You better go too," Mervin said, glancing at Lute and Sandy, "or he'll be pissed at you. Conspiring with the enemy."

Sandy scrambled out of the booth and followed his friend. Lute picked up his cup and sipped.

"You nailed his ass," the dairy farmer said. "Never seen him so mad, but a bet is a bet. I hate to admit it, but your team played a helluva ball game. It ain't just that Norwegian kid neither. You got some ballplayers there. Too bad you don't have a few more boys. Never get far in that tournament with five or six."

After absorbing all the glory and celebrity he could milk out of the event with the tractor gleaming in the winter sunlight out front and after proudly paying the tab, Mervin drove slowly out of town and headed for Willow Creek. The John Deere "D" was going back to the place where it first worked the land, where it first lugged down and pulled through the rich topsoil, discovering the purpose for which it had been born.

With a smirk on its face, the old tractor headed home.

CHAPTER 52

At Thursday practice, Sam attempted to keep his excitement off his face without his trademark Aviator glasses. When the boys came into the gym and began shooting, they each did a double take. Sam busied himself over a practice schedule on his clipboard.

"What happened to your glasses?" Rob said.

"I walked into the locker room, caught a horrific stench and I was instantly and miraculously cured," Sam said. "Twenty-twenty vision."

"That'll be the day," Tom said.

"They break?" Scott said.

"No, I sold them to the Basketball Referees Aid Society."

Diana came from the girl's locker room in her baggy grays.

"You get contacts?" Pete asked with a smile of approval.

"Yeah, and I'll never find them again. I think they slid around onto the back side of my eyeballs."

"That rocks," Pete said.

Olaf said, "You are looking—"

"Be careful, be careful," Sam said. "This could lead to ten extra wind sprints."

". . . awe-full," Olaf said.

"Awesome, you dumb Norwegian," Tom said, "*awe*some."

"You think this is awesome," Sam said. "I had a vision last night—my fairy godmother told me not to shave again as long as the team won."

"Yeah, well I don't think they allow gorillas to teach in Montana public schools," Pete said.

The boys laughed.

"All right, listen up," Sam said. He put his arm around Curtis's shoulder. "Curtis, your layup broke Christian's heart. Just when they thought they had us stymied, you stunned them. Your basket was the winning margin. Therefore, I hereby dub you Forget Me Not. Not the flower, but the player other teams better not overlook, or, when least expected, you'll make them pay."

Sam tousled Curtis's hair.

"Forget Me Not," Sam went on. "A player never to be taken lightly."

"Forget Me Not!" the other boys shouted and Curtis turned his eyes to the floor with the color of embarrassment in his face.

"All right," Sam said, "after stretching, we're going light tonight, rest up a bit. We'll walk through some offensive sets, work on the alley-oop and volleyball, and shoot free throws. The bus leaves tomorrow at two. We have a secret weapon for Gardiner. It will blind them like a laser and we'll be able to shoot uncontested layups all night. The score will be 476 to nothing."

Sam turned to Scott, who sat on the bench with a cardboard UPS shipping box beside him. When Sam nodded, the team manager picked up the carton and trotted over. Scott opened the flaps and Sam reached into the box.

He lifted the first golden nylon jersey from the carton. It bore the number 55. They responded as one.

"Wow!"

"Olaf, I believe this will fit you."

Sam handed him the pristine uniform and then pulled out the rest.

"*All* right."

"*Coool.*"

"Awesome."

"Bodacious."

"These were supposed to be here weeks ago. I'm sorry you didn't have them sooner. Before you leave tonight, try them on, make sure they fit."

Sam paused.

"We know how good Gardiner is. They know how good we are. It will be a terrific game. When you come out of the locker room tomorrow night, I'm wearing sunglasses. Now let's get to work."

"How'd you manage this?" Diana asked while the boys examined their uniforms and draped them on the bleacher seats.

"Wainwright. I don't know how."

"Wainwright seems to have a lot of pull."

"I think he also has a lot of money," Sam said. "But he loves the team."

She squinted and regarded him.

"Contacts, huh?"

"Yeah."

"Coming out of hiding?"

He shrugged his shoulders.

"Looks good."

"Thanks."

She turned to the boys.

"Okay, on the floor!" Miss Murphy shouted and clapped her hands. All of them, including Sam and Scott, hit the hardwood to do their stretching.

THEY JOURNEYED THE 125 miles to Gardiner, a small village with a mining-town ambience that was dissected by the irrepressible Yellowstone River. The enduring settlement perched on both sides of the river's gorge like squatters hanging on by their toenails, the portion of town south of the river rumped up against the very edge of Yellowstone National Park. In fact, from the expansive, newly constructed gym, if the wind was right, one could nearly spit into that natural preserve where undoubtedly elk and bison and coyote turn an ear at the faint echoes of crowd noise wafting across the snow-glazed foothills on cold winter nights.

The Broncs came out shining in their new uniforms and Sam, as promised, wore sunglasses for their warmups.

"You going snot-nosed on us, Sam?" Fred Sooner, the Gardiner coach, said. "What's with the shades?"

"My team is so dazzling I can't look at them without sunglasses."

"Yeah, well they *do* look better," the burly coach said. "At least it won't look like we're playing the Salvation Army tonight."

Fred gazed across the floor at Diana, who fed the ball to the boys running layups.

"Tell me, Sam, how do you get an assistant coach like *that*."

"Well, first you have to lose ninety games in a row and then the heavens feel sorry for you and send a biology teacher."

The game started and the fans were into it immediately. Most of the ruckus came from the Willow Creek delegation, led as usual in delirious vocal decibels by Axel, Andrew, Grandma, Amos, and as of late, with unmuzzled emotions, John English. Sam and Diana—becoming more animated and vociferous on the bench with each game—glanced at each other out of the corner of their eyes during the first quarter when the boys played up to their new uniforms and then some, transcending all over Gardiner's new gymnasium and all over Gardiner's wide-eyed players.

They looked smooth and relaxed and disciplined, a graceful flow of gold and blue, hustling on defense and moving with a gilded fluidity that overwhelmed the skilled Bruin players. Olaf had a monster dunk and slapped a Gardiner shot into Yellowstone Park. Fred Sooner was visibly alarmed. He called a time out in a panicked effort to slow down this Willow Creek onslaught which left the home team trailing early, 15 to 6.

Gardiner gradually climbed back into it during the second quarter, finding the range from outside while the Broncs' defense shut down their two best scorers from around the paint. Fred Sooner came up alongside Sam as they walked to the dressing rooms at halftime.

"Your boys can be had, Sam," he said with a tenuous smile and hustled off with his players.

In the locker room Sam pondered Sooner's words as he tried to anticipate the opposing coach's moves. Willow Creek led 43 to 36. Three players had two fouls, including Olaf; the zone defense was working, taking the Bruins out of their usual offense.

"What's the key to this game?" Sam asked the newly eligible Dean as they huddled prior to returning to the gym.

"That we have more points than they do," the goggle-eyed freshman answered with a high-pitched enthusiasm.

"No, no, how many times do I have to tell you?" Sam said, panning disappointment on his face. "The key to this game is that you don't get your new uniforms all sweated up and wrinkled. You have to wear them tomorrow for the team pictures."

The boys laughed and lightened up.

"Keep doing what you're doing," Sam said in the team huddle. "I don't know where you learned to play like that. I taught you much worse."

Coach Sooner hadn't been bluffing. In the third quarter his boys demonstrated their great acting skills. With Glenn Tuomey, a secondstring center, they attacked Olaf. The angular 6'2" boy would work into the paint, pivot, and drive deliberately into Olaf, throwing up his arms and ball with little hope of hitting the basket. The ref called a foul on Olaf. Sam came off the bench.

"Offensive foul! Offensive foul!" he shouted, backed by the vocal dissent of the Willow Creek battalions.

At the other end, Ben McShane, the 6'3" junior, rode Olaf's back, and when the towering Bronc center made a move with the ball, the defender flopped backward onto the floor as if he'd been hit with a twelve-pound sledge. The inside ref called an offensive foul on Olaf.

"Give him an Oscar!" Diana shouted.

Sam held his head in his hands, unwilling to believe these Class C refs couldn't see through this obvious sham, while the visiting spectators poured outrage down on the referee.

The rest of the third quarter turned into a nightmare. Gardiner didn't shoot until they had a boy near Olaf with the ball, and he would take it straight at Olaf. Though the Bruins picked up several offensive fouls, had many shots stuffed down their gizzard, and lost Tuomey with five fouls, it worked. With twenty seconds remaining in the third quarter, Olaf was whistled for his fifth foul.

Sam sprang off the bench. All Willow Creekians rose to their feet, hollering their disgust.

"What are you doing!" Sam shouted as he stormed onto the floor.

"He drove into my man! My man didn't move a muscle!"

The short balding ref who made the call blocked Sam's advance.

"Get off the floor, Coach."

"You're blind! Can't you see what they're doing? What kind of a ref are you?"

The ref made a T with his hands and blew his whistle.

"Technical foul on the Willow Creek coach!"

The hometown crowd roared their approval, pointing their fingers at Sam with swooping gestures and chanting, "Oooowww! Oooowww! Oooowww!"

Diana grabbed Sam's arm and tried to drag him off the floor. The ref signaled the technical to the scorer's bench and turned back to find Sam standing at his ear. Sam spoke with a friendly tone, looking at the back of the official's black trousers.

"Oh, Jeez, there's something all over your pants."

"What?" the baffled man said, twisting to glance at his backside.

"Oh, man," Sam said softly, "I think you crapped in them."

Sam held his nose as the puzzled ref ran a hand over his rump.

"Get out of here," he told Sam with mounting anger.

Sam leaned close again, cupping a hand to his mouth in a confidential manner. "It must be your call I smell."

The ref turned and made a sweeping gesture that looked as though he were throwing a javelin into the far wall.

"You're out of here!" he shouted.

The Willow Creek followers stood and rained incensed boos down on the bald man's head, the likes of Claire Painter and Truly Osborn outdone by no one. Sam stomped to the locker room, wanting to punch someone or something. He slammed the metal door behind him. There he languished like a bad boy sent to his room, dying a slow death, able to hear the muffled roar of the crowd without any interpretation as to its significance.

DIANA RODE THE bench with Scott and Olaf, who wore Dean's grubby cap. She did what she could to keep them in the game. Without Olaf in the middle, Willow Creek became vulnerable despite Rob's leaping ability and Tom's 6'4" brawny presence. It was like a downhill ride on a streaking toboggan with the boys desperately dragging their arms and legs, hoping the time on the clock would run out before they hit the bottom and went over a cliff into the river. But Gardiner's tall back line began to overcome, and with twenty seconds to go, Willow Creek was down by five. With a cool indifference to the pressure or the wildly lunging Kenny Green, Pete buried a shot from beyond the three-point line. The quick Gardiner guard crashed into Pete after he'd released the ball. One-shot foul; down by two.

Diana called time out with eleven ticks remaining on the clock.

"Okay, Pete, miss the shot, everyone on the boards, Curtis you slide along the baseline under the basket, if any crumbs come off the table, that's where they'll be. Remember, when you get the rebound, if you don't have a put-back, try to get the ball to Rob or Pete, if you can't, get the best shot you can. Just like practice, go around Hazel Brown and can it."

With everyone in the gym standing and shouting, Pete intentionally missed the free throw, trying to carom the rebound to Tom's side. Ferociously ten boys crashed the backboard and scrambled for the ball amid flying elbows, spraying sweat, and the guttural grunts of their colliding bodies. The leather object of their passion skittered along the floor and hit Dean in the shins. He snatched it as if it were a fleeing chicken and looked for someone who knew how to pluck it. Ben McShane cornered Dean along the sideline. In desperation Dean struggled to find someone open. Drowning in panic, he bounced an obvious pass toward Tom. Kenny Green cut in front of Tom and intercepted the ball. The Gardiner faithful erupted. Green dribbled swiftly away as the Willow Creek team chased frantically to foul. Curtis dove at him but missed, sprawling across the gleaming hardwood, and the final buzzer sprung the trap door that hung Willow Creek, 68 to 66.

The homegrown crowd thundered a jubilation that undoubtedly cocked the ear of more than one nocturnal beast grazing the mountainsides. The Willow Creek fans slumped in hostile silence. The wild beast in Coach Murphy prowled close to the surface as Fred Sooner crossed the court to shake her hand.

"Tell Sam he got outcoached," Fred said.

"I'll tell him he got outreffed. See you in the tournaments, Sooner, and you better come up with something better than grade-school drama class. They have refs with two eyes up there."

IN AN ATTEMPT to avoid the anguish, Sam went out into the pitch-dark parking lot to warm up the bus. Before he climbed into Rozinante, he paused. There was something on the wind. He listened. There, across the hills to the south, coyotes howling. That chilling, solitary wail coming out of the wilderness, stirring something wild in him. He stood by the bus, cocking his ear, understanding their lament, the loneliness, the loss. It was all he could do to prevent himself from hiking off across the snow-crusted foothills and joining them—if they'd have him—all he could do to keep himself from getting down on his knees and wailing into the black Montana sky.

He cupped his hands and howled, imitating the wild creatures as best he could. Then he held his breath, listening, hoping for a reply, a reply of acceptance and healing. It came, a coyote off to his right, a barking, howling song on the wind, but Sam couldn't understand the words, couldn't translate the message. Was it a note of joy or a word of warning?

On the bus Sam noticed tears trickling down Dean's face as though his fishbowl lenses were leaking. Sam realized he had held out on the young boy, only expounding half-truths when he talked him into coming out for basketball. He had neglected to tell the fledgling about how bad you feel when you lose, and worse, how ashamed when you believe it was your fault. Sam tried to soothe the pain by announcing they would stop at McDonald's on the long trip home, but not even a Big Mac with fries would stem the young boy's sorrow. Like it or not, he was growing up.

Mervin was up early Saturday morning, tinkering with the John Deere "D", trying to find some fault with his brother's maintenance, trying to shake the residue of the Gardiner loss from his head and heart. He felt damn proud of Olaf, who had played like a warrior, only to be cheated out of a chance to win by that goddamn referee who shouldn't be allowed to work a grade school game. It had been worse than that professional wrestling on TV, the way the Gardiner boys faked being hit and flopped all over the floor. As long as they played dirty to get Olaf out of the game, Mervin wished Olaf had coldcocked one of them and got his money's worth out of his fifth foul.

He knew something else was stuck in his craw that he couldn't shake. Olaf, who was still sleeping in the house, would be leaving in a few short months and Mervin didn't know how he'd take that. He realized he'd grown to love the boy, and something more he'd never admit to a soul. He figured he loved the boy more than he'd ever loved his four daughters. Something had grown up between him and the boy, something he never had with his girls. He dreaded losing Olaf come summer, and he tried not to think about it.

He had made room for the old tractor in a back corner of the metal machine shed he had built seven years ago, a godsend in winter and bad weather days when he had to work on a piece of machinery.

Mervin had drained the crankcase on the "D" but, to his disappointment, found the oil fresh and clean. He was removing one of the steel wheels when he felt a presence in the metal shed. He turned and started! Claire was standing there in her winter coat, watching him. She wasn't smiling and he realized he'd never seen the expression on her face that she showed him now.

"I want to say something to you that I've wanted to say for thirty years," she said and she moved closer to him.

Mervin felt his throat tighten. He laid down the heavy wrench and wiped his greasy hands on a rag. Something in him wanted to run.

"When you courted me, I realized you weren't a romantic man. But I came to think it was more than that, that there was something broken inside you, muffled," Claire stepped closer to him.

"And there was something frantic in you, like you were trying to gather frogs in a wheelbarrow. I heard stories over the years, hints and slips of the tongue, people trying to be kind by whispering or dropping the subject. I learned that you loved Maggie, planned to marry her. Through the years I've realized you still do love her, always have ever since I knew you. I've never said a word, figured it would pass with time and we'd become closer. That never happened."

"I never wanted—"

"Let me finish," Claire said, wringing her hands. "I heard at the grocery store this morning that Maggie is real bad. She's at the hospital in Bozeman. She's dying. I want you to go in the house, clean up, and go see that woman before she's gone." Claire's voice broke. "I'm afraid if she dies before you see her, we'll have her ghost between us for the rest of our lives. I've never told you what to do in all our married days, but I'm telling you now. You hightail it to that hospital as fast as you can!"

Stunned, Mervin set the rag on the tractor seat and walked past Claire out of the machine shed.

In his Sunday suit and Stetson, Mervin turned onto the freeway toward Bozeman. He pushed his Ford up around ninety, and after driving forty miles in twenty-five minutes he left the car in a No Parking space, tightened his jaw, and hurried through the automatic hospital doors. A receptionist told him how to find Maggie's room, and when he got off the elevator, his heart was racing. He turned a corner in the corridor and found his brother with several other men and women in the hall outside Maggie's room. He didn't hesitate.

"Where do you think you're going?" Carl said, stepping in the way of Mervin's march toward the door of Room 234.

Mervin stepped up to Carl, chest to chest, and spoke in a low, steady voice.

"You stole her from me thirty-five years ago and now, by God, I'll have this time with her alone or I'll tear your throat out!"

Carl glared back, his cold gray eyes never blinking. Mervin figured he'd rather face a jail term for assault and battery than have to face Maggie in her dying moments.

Time seemed to stand still. Mervin clenched his fists. Carl's face flushed. Then he nodded and stepped back.

Mervin opened the door and stepped in. A nurse passed Mervin on the way out, and whispered, "She's very tired."

Mervin moved to the side of the bed and forced himself to look into Maggie's withering face, forced himself to see the tubes and tape and needles, forced himself to look into her haggard eyes. He tried to find the sweet girl he'd loved so long ago.

"Hello," Mervin managed to say, but his voice broke.

"Hello . . . what are—"

"I had to come, I wanted to come, when I heard . . ."

"Never thought I'd see you again," she said.

"I don't know what to say."

"How did the boys do last night?" she said.

"Willow Creek, the team?"

"Yeah."

"They lost to Gardiner," Mervin said and wondered how they could be talking about the Willow Creek basketball team at a time like this.

"I always pulled for Willow Creek. Always." She coughed and it scared him. "I know it always seemed hopeless, but I was a Willow Creek girl and I thought that some day they would win again."

"They've won three games this year," he said, though he wanted to get away from news, weather, and sports. He knew his time with her was short.

"Will you say hello to Peter for me?" she said.

"You know Peter? Peter Strong?"

"Yes, he's a good boy."

She coughed and closed her eyes for a moment. Mervin knew he'd never have this chance again.

"Maggie, I want—"

"I heard you won the tractor," she said.

"Yeah."

"That always should've been yours."

"*You* always should've been mine," he said.

"You gave up on me." She looked into his eyes. "Why didn't you tell me it didn't matter that I was pregnant, that I had his baby inside me? Why didn't you say that you forgave me for being a foolish young girl who was trying to make you jealous so you'd quit putting off our marriage?"

Mervin moved close to the bed and leaned toward her face.

"I'm so—"

"I just went for a ride with him, that's all he said it would be, a ride in his new pickup," she said. "He raped me. He said it would be my word against his, and how would I explain being out on the old deserted Quinn Road with him in his pickup?"

"Oh, God, Maggie," Mervin said. He felt his heart being torn out.

"I was so scared and humiliated and I didn't dare tell anyone. Who could I tell? What could I say? The night you came looking for me, that wasn't the first time. Your brother blackmailed me into going out there with him three more times after he first raped me. Each time he said once more and that would be the end of it."

"If I'd only known, if you'd have told me—"

"I was petrified. I wanted to kill Carl. I was a scared young girl who felt trapped. How could I tell you, what would you think? Well, we found that out, didn't we. You just drove away, never looked back."

Mervin sat on the edge of her bed and took her hand in his.

"I'm so sorry, Maggie . . ." He lost his voice.

"Was it my unfaithfulness that hurt you or was it that you didn't want to spend your life with a woman your brother had first? A woman your brother *knew* he had first? Was it that he got the best of you again, you and your goddamn Painter pride? Is that all you really cared about? I held my breath, praying you'd say it didn't matter, that you forgave me, that you still loved me and would marry me. You just drove away!"

"I'm sorry, oh God, I've never stopped loving you," Mervin said, feeling the mountains coming down around him.

"Your love was selfish and weak and small. All you cared about was your pride and how hurt you were, without a thought about what I was going through. Goddamn you. You threw away our love, my love and my life. Your feeling sorry doesn't count anymore, it's way too late."

Maggie closed her eyes. She was shutting him out. Mervin let go of her hand and stood.

"I'll let you rest now."

"You'll let me die now, don't you mean?" she said, opening her eyes. "Maybe you already did that thirty-five years ago."

Mervin sucked it up and picked up his hat.

"Good-by, Maggie." His voice trembled.

"Good-by, Paint."

He nearly lost his balance leaving the room and closing the large door gently. Carl stood by a window with another man. Mervin waved a hand for his brother to follow him and then he walked down the corridor away from the others. When Carl caught up with him, Mervin turned and gathered himself, straining to hold back stampeding wild horses, with every nerve ending in the attack mode, his fists swelling hammer heads.

"She told me what you did to her back then. And now it's too late to do anything about it. But hear me well, you sonofabitch. Don't ever let me catch you anywhere around Willow Creek, *ever,* or I will do to you what I would have done to you the night you raped Maggie in your pickup!"

"Now just wait—"

"You killed us, our life, Maggie and me. You are no longer my brother. May you rot in hell for what you did! I would kill you in the blink of an eye if it would bring Maggie back."

Mervin turned for the elevator and the way out. His legs felt weak and he couldn't catch his breath and the hospital corridors seemed to blur. When he found his pickup, still in the No Parking space, he fled out of town. He didn't know where he was going, the road was awash in his eyes, he feared the veins in his head would burst.

He had given up on her, he had thrown it away because he was a proud, selfish bastard. Where do you go? What do you do when you've had your chance at life and you've thrown it away and when you've seen it go to ruin and loss? He was driving away again, away from Maggie, away from his life, from his love.

He drove aimlessly. He prayed to God there was forgiveness in her last words, the affectionate nickname she used to call him.

She had called him *Paint.*

CHAPTER 54

S am arrived at the gym before anyone else on Saturday afternoon. Without turning on a light, he stood at the edge of the
shadowed court. This would be their final game in this building, and an
unexpected nostalgia engulfed him; the season had passed so quickly. From
here on they would hold off the inevitable demise that defeat would bring
to their fragile and faultless fraternity, the dissolution of their season, and
their once-in-a-lifetime comradeship. They would never play here again.

A PHOTOGRAPHER FROM Three Forks set them in a pose under
the south backboard: Olaf in the middle, flanked by Tom and Curtis. Rob
and Pete and Dean knelt in front. Sam stood on the outside next to Tom.
Miss Murphy and Scott smiled from the other side, next to Curtis. All the
players wore their bright new uniforms. They bantered and laughed as the
thin, birdlike man in an undertaker's attire fussed and aligned them with
painstaking care.

"Thanks for letting me shave this morning, men," Sam said, revealing a
slight smile on his face. He had realized the no-shaving-until-they-lost was
a short-lived and corny gimmick.

"We didn't want you looking grubby for the team picture," Rob said.

"Don't move, don't move," the photographer said. "You there, the boy on
the outside, turn your head a little to the left."

Curtis turned his head slightly, and Sam figured the man was trying
desperately to conceal Curtis's ears.

"We lost because we didn't want Miss Murphy to have rug burn all over
her face," Pete said.

"What makes you think I'd have it all over my *face*?" Diana said.

That shut them up for a while as they pondered her meaning. Sam fought
off a blush with his own interpretation.

When their uniforms were hung neatly on coat hangers and the team was ready to leave, Sam had them sit on the bench in the little rectangular locker room. Diana leaned against the cinder-block wall near the doorway.

"Get something to eat and be back here by six-thirty." He paused. "You played well last night. I'm proud of you. You didn't get beat."

Some of the boys exchanged glances.

"I got outcoached. I'll try not to let it happen again."

Sam took a breath and tried to push his missing glasses up on his nose.

"Tonight is the last game of the regular season. We've come a long way since that first game. You've all worked hard. Now there's one thing I want you to think about. What will you remember we accomplished after this team picture was taken when you gaze at it in twenty or thirty years? You have the opportunity to write that memory. I hope you write one that is wonderful and shining and full of joy."

The team spontaneously huddled around him and joined hands with both coaches and Scott.

"Win! win! win! win! win!"

Nine voices bombarding the concrete walls, seeping through the cracks out into the cold February afternoon and dispersing into thin air, like their odds of winning in the days to come.

THE SHIELDS VALLEY boys came to the wrong town on the wrong night. They'd have done better to have stayed at home. The local fans filled the bleachers on the east side of the gym and spilled over onto the west side with only a small contingent journeying from the Shields Valley. The loss at Gardiner and the losing season hadn't seemed to discourage many Willow Creek fans as in the past five years. What was it about these boys? Was it Olaf they came to see? Sam was baffled. He couldn't help but notice that Claire Painter was in the bleachers without Mervin, something else he'd never seen.

Once the game got under way it turned into a party. The fans shouted and cheered and displayed emotions that had been in mothballs for many tedious years. The team played the way Sam knew they could and though it was only by five points, the boys won their final game on the home court with class.

While Dean proudly pushed his sister around the gym, babbling to her about the game and rolling her toward the basket as though going in for a layup, Sam caught Sally Cutter pulling on her coat beside the bleachers.

"I'm glad you were able to come," Sam said. "I know it means a lot to Dean."

She nodded wearily. "Thank you for the tickets."

"Oh, that's nothing, we always have a bunch we give out to some of the players' families. Does Denise enjoy the games?"

"Oh, yes," she said, becoming more animated than Sam had ever seen her. "She loves to come and watch the boys."

"Well, she's a great fan. I hope she can come to the tournament. She brings us good luck."

"Oh, I don't think we can do that."

"Don't worry about transportation or tickets or any of that. If she's able, we want her there."

"That's mighty kind of you."

"And we'd like Dean's father to come, too."

"Oh, I don't think he will. He's kinda funny about some things."

Dean wheeled Denise to where they stood, and Sam gazed down into her disarming face and smiled.

"I'm glad you were here tonight, Denise, you helped us win. We need you."

She tilted her head and twisted her soundless mouth.

Sam had an overwhelming desire to scoop this helpless child out of her hopeless chair and wrap her in his arms, promising her that they all would win. He stood frozen for a moment. Then he knelt in front of her chair and dared to venture into her sailing blue eyes.

"We really need you," he said.

She exuded a brightness with her bearing, through her skin, as if from some light deep inside. Then her mother wheeled her away.

DIANA HAD GONE ahead and saved a table for them in the crowded Blue Willow. When Sam arrived he noticed small outbreaks of euphoria and optimism regarding their chances in next week's tournaments. It reminded Sam once more of the indestructible longing to win in the human breast.

Diana looked up from her game book as Sam slid into a chair. She'd ordered his favorite hamburger but he still couldn't eat the homemade French fries.

"How's this for balance," Diana said. "Rob seventeen, Pete twenty-one, Olaf fifteen, Tom thirteen, Curtis one, and Dean didn't score. Have you ever thought what it would be like if we had two or three more players?"

Sam set down his hamburger and wiped his mouth with a paper napkin. "Yeah, have I ever, especially now with tournaments. But they complement each other so well: Tom's muscle, Olaf's height, Rob's consistency, Pete's dash, Curtis's work ethic, and Dean's hustle. It's like they've each filled a hole in the puzzle, like they each found his role."

"But they have to play the entire game with little or no rest," Diana said.

"Yeah, that's their Achilles. We should have brought twins over from Norway."

Andrew, navigating through a constant flow of well-wishers, came to the table.

"You two deserve a tremendous amount of credit. Imagine it! We hadn't won a game in ages and tonight we've won our *fourth*."

"Thanks, but that's where the credit goes." Sam nodded at the boys, crowded around the red player piano as Olaf pumped out "Auld Lang Syne."

"How did you get the board to buy new uniforms?" Diana asked.

"There wasn't time for a formal meeting," Andrew said. "Though we've taken in more revenue from the last six games than anyone can remember. The uniforms were from an anonymous donor."

"They got here just in time," Sam said. "Thanks for getting it done."

Andrew glanced around the dining room and into the tavern side.

"Look at these people," he said, "they're excited and looking forward to the tournaments. Do you know how long it's been since anyone in this town wanted to admit there even *were* tournaments? All it ever meant was two more humiliating defeats."

"Don't forget, friend, it could still mean two more humiliating defeats," Sam said.

Andrew leaned between the two of them and regarded Sam. "Sam, do you really believe that?"

"With those uniforms, who could beat them?" Sam said, trying for a cheerful note in his voice, unwilling to admit the inbred pessimism that warned him against painful expectations.

Grandma Chapman barged through the front door and scrambled her way to the team, speaking frantically. The boys jumped up and headed for the door. Sam intercepted her in the crowd.

"What is it?" he asked.

"Parrot got outside. I can't find him, he'll die in this cold."

"Hey! Yo!" Sam shouted.

The crowd hushed and listened.

"Grandma's parrot got loose outside. It'll freeze out there. Let's go help her find it!"

He pulled on his coat and pushed through the door, followed by Diana and almost everyone in the inn. They fanned out, covering the neighborhood around Elizabeth Chapman's house. With only the few streetlights it was difficult to see. Gradually a number of flashlights began beaming into leafless trees, sweeping rooftops, and tracing power lines. People stumbled through yards and along fence lines, searching under cars and atop buildings, shouting to one another throughout the town. The temperature had fallen to below zero, and after a while, many of the searchers gave up and retreated to the warmth of the inn. Sam pushed through the front door.

"Anyone find it?" he said.

"That bird is frozen solid," Vera said.

"It couldn't last long out there tonight," Axel said.

"That thing should have died a long time ago," Hazel said.

"It's probably headed for South America," John English said.

Gradually the Blue Willow filled again, and then Grandma came in, trembling with the cold and grief.

"Anybody see him?" she said. She swiped her dripping nose.

No one answered.

"You stay in and warm up some," Hazel said. "You'll catch your death out there."

"He might still be alive," she said and turned to go.

"Let's warm up a bit," Sam said, "and we'll go at it again." Sam helped her into a chair and Axel brought a steaming cup of coffee.

"I have to get back and look," she said.

She was about to stand, when Pete and Olaf scrambled through the door.

"Did you see him?" Grandma asked, tears filling her eyes.

Pete kneeled beside his shivering grandmother and opened his coat. A familiar squawk emanated from somewhere around his chest.

"Ooooohhhh, you *found* him, you *found* him!"

She gently lifted the parrot from inside Pete's jacket and cuddled the bird to her breast. A cheer arose from the cluster that had crowded around Grandma and the boys.

"No, *we* didn't find him," Pete said when the noise subsided.

"Who did?" Grandma said.

Olaf opened his jacket and Tripod stuck his head out, content to remain next to the warm body of his Scandinavian host.

"Tripod?" Grandma said.

"Yeah," Pete said happily. "I figured he always kept track of Parrot like his lunch. So I let him out of the house and he went bouncing all over the place."

"Where was the bird?" Sam asked.

"In Bremer's old outhouse," Pete said.

Everyone laughed. Sam thought he should've known.

"Tripod led us right to him," Pete continued. "I'd have never looked in there. He must have gone in through that little moon on the door."

Applause arose from the happy group and Olaf held the three-legged cat aloft. The cheery bunch spread out, filling the tables and crowding the bar, more alive and boisterous than before. Diana, standing beside him, looked into Sam's eyes and nodded at the door.

"I'm cold. Let's go light a candle."

He leaned toward her and kissed her on the forehead.

"Coffee and Pepsi on the house!" Axel shouted.

"Up your ass," Parrot shot back.

Grandma smiled through chattering teeth. But she'd been had. Now everyone in tarnation knew how much she loved that flea-bitten, foul-mouthed bird.

Sam paused at the table, still trying to keep their love affair from the full-blown winds of Willow Creek gossip by letting Diana leave alone for home. He had come to care about these people deeply over the years, and he hoped, as he witnessed the frivolity from this night's winning, that they weren't setting themselves up for the wrenching and inevitable loss to come.

CHAPTER 55

Diana sat at a table in the Blue Willow, feeling down, something dark she couldn't name, a mood that moved in unannounced during the afternoon. She never knew where they came from, stealing in silently like low-rolling fog, but she figured it didn't help that she had heard talk about Maggie Painter's funeral. She wouldn't let the memory of Jessica's funeral elbow its way into her head, and she nervously scrutinized the sports page to ward it off while awaiting Sam's arrival for a late supper.

The boys had practiced hard Monday and Tuesday and today Sam had tapered off, going over their game plan and walking through offensive plays, hoping to rest the boys and have them strong for the coming storm tomorrow, going against Twin Bridges again, the top seed in the tournament. After surviving a normal run of slight sprains, jammed fingers, and head colds, they were all healthy and ready, focused on the tournament that would test their conditioning and endurance. As usual, Axel, Hazel, and Grandma Chapman had helped out when Sam asked. Hazel, of all people, had become addicted to the game.

"Can we come in here and shoot when the season's over?" she had asked, and Diana assured her they could.

All three days they worked on Operation Jelly Fish, a name Sam had concocted for Olaf's benefit, which the boy called Yelly Fish. They knew that the other teams' strategy was to attack the Willow Creek center with offensive thrusts and bring Olaf down under the burden of five fouls. In the last three or four games, the opposing coaches each attempted a variation on that theme, though only Fred Sooner actually pulled it off with the inadvertent aid of bush-league officiating. The opposition couldn't do much about the swift, blitzkrieg strikes of the excellent Willow Creek guards. They were far too mobile. But Willow Creek's thunderous, more stationary cannon was also the vulnerable point of their arsenal. Without Olaf in the paint, the Broncs were utterly exposed.

For three days, Sam had the boys attack Olaf with the ball. After entrenching him in the paint, Sam instructed the others to drive into him, literally, and try to put up a shot. He used the image of a jelly fish with Olaf, a pliant creature that gave way but still had its long tentacles extended. When the boys would drive into Olaf, Sam had him back off, in a receding posture, but with his arms high overhead, unmoving, forcing the smaller players to alter their shot.

In his passion for blocking shots, Olaf found it a difficult discipline to move backward a step and stand motionless. Sam had him practicing turning his back once the shooter had left the floor, positioning the big center for the rebound and dramatically reducing the chance that he would be whistled for a foul.

Sam came through the door and Diana's heart did a little flip.

"Been waiting long?" he asked.

He pulled out a chair and slid into it, laying his clipboard on the table and squeezing her hand.

"Are you hungry?" Diana said.

He had a way of making the turmoil in her life vanish like darkness at the first sweet noise of dawn. He melted her depression away with the warmth of his smile. They ordered and shared excitement over the tournament. He was holding a voluntary session at his house that night, going over plays on the videotapes with the team.

"What do you think of the paper?" she said.

"I'm glad they're not even mentioning us. Twin Bridges and Christian should be favorites."

"If we lose to Twin Bridges, we're out of it, aren't we?" Diana said wistfully.

"Not quite."

"What do you mean?" She tilted her head.

"There's always the outside chance of a challenge," Sam said.

"I keep hearing that word. What does it mean?"

"In Montana tournaments, if the team that finishes second hasn't played the team that finishes third, that third-place team can 'challenge' the second-place team. And if the third-place boys win, *they* advance."

"I've never heard of that."

"It makes sense. To take third place, a team has to win three games, even though moving up through the losers' bracket. The second-place team has only won two. It leaves a little bit of hope for all the teams who lose one, and the game on Monday night can be deadly. I've seen a lot of good teams get bushwhacked in a challenge game."

"So even though the first- and second-place teams move up to Divisional," she said, "second place isn't very safe."

"Right, except, as often as not, the second-place team has already beaten the third-place. Then there can be no challenge."

"How do you think our boy is picking up on Yelly Fish?" she asked.

They laughed.

"I don't know, I think he's catching on. I think he likes the challenge of giving ground and still swatting the ball away with his reach. The way he demolished some of those yesterday I should have called it Operation Lutefisk."

"What got into Tom and Pete today? They didn't take anything you said seriously."

"I don't know. Maybe they're scared."

She narrowed her eyes. "You know, I've never seen you lose your temper with the boys."

"Oh, well . . . I do, I do," he said, a little off guard.

"No, you don't."

"For a lot of years I stored my anger like a battery."

"You can't store it forever."

"I think I bleed a little of it off every time Rob hits a three, or Pete steals the ball, or Olaf jams one."

"I don't know if I'll ever figure you out," she said, flipping her hair out of her face.

"That makes two of us."

AT HIS HOUSE, a voice kept muttering in Sam's head that he'd forgotten something in preparing the team, some glaring oversight that would find them out, on the floor in front of thousands.

When the boys left after watching basketball videos and talking over the game—Tom never showed up—Sam found himself rattling around in his house for several hours. After unsuccessfully searching for sleep in his solitary bed, he turned on the radio. On the oldies' station in Bozeman, Sinatra was singing "I've Got You Under My Skin." It was one of his and Amy's favorites when they'd dance naked by candlelight. He could smell her perfume, taste her on his lips and tongue, hear her singing the words with Sinatra, turning and turning, until he could bear it no longer. He snapped off the radio, turned on the lights, pulled on his clothes and took to the street. He hurried as though he were trying to outrun his memories.

Eventually, he slowed his pace and caught his breath. The moonless night sighed a southwesterly that calmed his spirit. It reminded him of a boyhood wherein, after bedtime, he'd sneak into the backyard on a summer night and sit with his back to a great maple tree, listening to the nocturnal creatures and secretly wanting to join them.

He strolled up Main Street toward school, finding a soothing tranquility in the constancy of night.

Tomorrow Rozinante would carry them to Butte and the district tournament, where they would either win or die, his time with this uncommon bunch of boys over. It pained him to know that. That somewhere down the line, probably in a couple days at best, this inimitable journey would have run its course and he was powerless to stop it.

In Butte, eight teams would scramble for two seeds to the divisional tournament the following weekend in Helena. The districts were constantly being realigned as familiar schools no longer appeared on the pairings roster. The missing schools were recent prey of consolidation—that hungry shark that Willow Creek was dog-paddling upstream to avoid. In those communities, stripped of their allegiance to a team, the townsfolk had no one to cheer and no way to win in their daily experience, and winter settled in their hearts as a freighted melancholia.

Sam strolled along the deserted blacktop. Then, for an instant, a shadow caught his eye, a movement over on Broadway, the gravel road to the east that paralleled the main drag. When he turned to catch a glimpse, it was gone in the darkness. No light, no sound, yet leaving a gliding image in his mind of something sailing south. His curiosity enticed him to cut over the dirt side street past Grandma Chapman's and onto Broadway. Along the unlit street he could distinguish nothing. He let it go as pretournament jitters.

They had drawn Twin Bridges as their first opponent, and Sam recognized how difficult it would be to play them again. Sam attempted to get into the Twin Bridges coach's head and imagine what innovative pitfalls he would fashion around the paint, what ambushes he would spring from the baseline.

Sam turned his head as though struck with premonition. It passed again, over on Main Street. He wasn't seeing things, though it had been like a shadow floating through his imagination. He ran the block back to Main. Several blocks north, almost to the Blue Willow Inn, he caught a glimpse of a figure gliding through the circle of illumination under a streetlight. From the way it moved it had to be either a ghosting apparition or a person on a bike—at two in the morning?

Sam followed his curiosity toward the restaurant. The warm chinook winds had eaten most of the snow in town, and a little covey of dried leaves jitterbugged along the street beside him. At the Blue Willow he settled in Rip's rocking chair on the porch, hidden in the shadows of the totally darkened building. He waited.

After nearly ten minutes, the figure came scudding with the wind down Main again, having made a loop up Broadway several blocks and then back north past the school and toward the inn. Sam slouched into the shadows, barely breathing, as the figure skimmed closer and swooshed by within a few feet of the porch. In a dark ski cap and jacket, it was Andrew Wainwright riding the bicycle built for two.

Sam stood and was about to call out when he caught himself, hesitating to intrude on the man's solitude. Andrew disappeared around the corner past the elevator. Sam hadn't noticed that the bicycle had been missing from the porch. Sensing a drowsiness creeping up on him, Sam figured he'd hike back home and see if he could fall asleep, leaving Andrew to the serenity of the town and his own quirky pleasures.

But something pulled at Sam, coaxing him to remain, and finally, he slid back into the rocker. While the talc executive pedaled another round, Sam remained concealed. All at once he understood that it had been there in plain sight from the beginning, as obvious as the alphabet and as inconspicuous as migrating bats. It was as though he had always known it, and swiftly a heavy sorrow burrowed itself into his chest.

On his next round, Andrew drew up alongside the porch and slid off the bike, catching Sam off guard.

"Hello," Sam said softly, realizing it was too late to avoid startling the man.

Andrew jumped back a step, almost falling over the cumbersome bike. "Who the—"

"I'm sorry. I should have let you see me," Sam said.

He pushed himself out of the rocker and moved into the meager light.

"Oh, Jeez. I didn't expect anyone around this time of the morning."

"Yeah, I know. Couldn't sleep, the game tomorrow."

Andrew quietly rolled the tandem bike up onto the porch and leaned it against the wall. "I've been thinking about it myself," he said. "I hope the boys can win one or two. They sure deserve it."

Andrew sat on the top step and Sam settled beside him. Not another creature stirred along the street. He spoke in hushed tones as though not wanting to wake Axel and Vera who slept upstairs above the inn.

"Has George Stonebreaker given you any more trouble?"

"No," Sam said, unwilling to admit that only yesterday he drove over to Manhattan to buy groceries when he noticed Stonebreaker's pickup parked near the D & D in Three Forks. "I sure hope he doesn't give Tom a hard time during the tournaments. I've told Tom he can stay with me."

"You've done everything possible to get them ready," Andrew said.

"Well, they'll *look* like a tournament team in those new uniforms. Were you the anonymous giver?" Sam said in the intimacy of the hour.

"No, it wasn't me. But I can tell you it was given in moldy cash, all in fives and tens, bills that hadn't seen daylight for a while."

Sam laughed and visualized Amos Flowers keeping some of his money in the Sealy Posturepedic Savings & Loan.

He glanced at Andrew. "You do this often?"

"No, no . . . I don't know what got into me tonight, just couldn't sleep."

"I think I've heard you. I sleep with my window open," Sam said, glancing sideways at the school board member.

"Heard me?"

"A swishing sound, at two or three in the morning. I never could figure it out—bike tires on the blacktop."

"Do you think the team has a chance?" Andrew said, staring across at Mavis Powers's darkened apartment building and post office.

"It was you, wasn't it?" Sam said.

"What do you mean?"

"It was *you* who rode that bike out here with your girlfriend a long time ago, it's *you* who everybody hopes will somehow find his lost sweetheart."

Andrew didn't reply. They sat a moment silently and Sam wished he'd kept his speculation to himself, fearing he was ripping scabs off irreparable wounds.

"What makes you think that?" Andrew said calmly.

"Oh, nothing. It was just a crazy thought."

"No, really. Why would you think such a thing?"

"Oh, simple mathematics. A guy like you hanging around this end-of-the-world town. I'd guess you could make your way anywhere. What's this place got to offer a capable single guy like you?"

"I like the clean air and wide-open country."

"I'd believe you more if you told me you were in a witness-protection program."

Sam laughed weakly and his voice was swallowed in an all-absorbing silence. He held his breath. Andrew didn't speak and Sam broke the tension.

"I would take it with me to my grave."

Andrew regarded Sam.

"I came here with Sarah twenty-six years ago in June. When I ran off that day I was out of my skull with anger and jealousy about something that was over and done with. I can't bear to talk about the smallness of heart and soul that caused me to lose the love of my life."

Andrew paused and took a breath.

"In anger I went into the army, got sent to Nam, stayed alive for two years to get back to her, and when I came back I couldn't find her. No leads. She had lost her parents when she was young. None of her old friends or acquaintances knew where she'd gone. I spent almost two years trying to find her, but everything turned into a blind alley. Then, a few years later I got married, had two nice kids, did my best to make it work, stuck it out until the kids were pretty well grown up, and got divorced from a nice lady who knew I'd never had my heart in it from the beginning."

"Why Willow Creek?" Sam asked.

"It was a hair in the wind but it was all I had. It was the last place on this earth where I had been with her. I figured she might come back here, some day, if she were looking for me the way I was looking for her. It was our only common point of reference. When I saw that bicycle still on the porch, waiting after all those years, I couldn't believe it. I examined it, it was the very Rollfast Columbia we rode out here. I asked myself, Why would people keep something like that for so long? How could that happen? The tires had been replaced and were hard with air as if expecting our return. That was what convinced me. I knew it was meant to be, that she'd eventually come back as I had. So I stayed."

"Do you really believe she'll come back here?" Sam said.

"Yes."

Andrew gazed up the street. "Do you believe in soul mates?" he asked.

"I don't know."

Andrew leaned forward with his elbows on his thighs, examining his hands in the scattered light as if he might find a clue in them. Then he spoke so softly Sam could hardly make out the words.

"You know, sometimes when I'm riding in the night like this I can catch the aroma of her perfume. Am I crazy?"

"Oh, no," Sam said and gripped the porch stair.

Andrew stood stiffly and stepped into the street. "I'd better get to bed. God, I hope the boys can win, it would help me believe in miracles again."

Sam stood and stepped down beside him. "I hope you find her."

For a moment they leaned precariously close to an embrace, close to sharing their sorrow and hope. But neither could cross that infinitesimal space, and Andrew walked off, under the streetlight, into the night, alone, as if he never doubted that Sarah would come back to him in Willow Creek.

BOOK III

By a little after ten in the morning they were loaded in the sawed-off bus: team and cheerleaders, coaches and manager. Sam took the shortcut through the Jefferson's massive limestone gorge to catch the interstate at Cardwell. To look more the part of a tournament team, Sam, Diana, and Scott had coordinated their outfits under Miss Murphy's tutelage, bearing the school's colors with matching navy-blue slacks she found at the JC Penney in Bozeman and gold sweatshirts she found at the Sports Shack in the mall. Each person on that bus carried their own fears and apprehensions for a team that had not won a tournament game since flip-top cans were invented.

Though there were minor outbursts of frivolity and horseplay, the team spent the sixty-mile trip in intense silence. While Sam drove, Diana reached over the back of his seat and massaged the tension out of Sam's neck with her soothing touch. He accepted her unanticipated offering of affection and felt as tightly wound as a golf ball.

"Oh, Miss Murphy," Tom said. "My neck is a little stiff."

The team broke out in laughter.

"Yeah, my back is kinda sore," Pete said.

"I only do the driver," Diana said, continuing on Sam's shoulders and neck.

"Can I drive?" Rob said, then was immediately pummeled by Mary.

The girls pulled out several books and began grilling Dean, who was precariously close to ineligibility again, but Sam figured it wouldn't matter. After this weekend, their basketball season would likely be over.

"All right, Dean," Carter said, reading out of his English grammar book. "The student said, 'Can/May I go to the bathroom?'"

"Can I go," Dean said in his screechy voice.

"Wrong. It should be 'May I go.'"

"I always say 'Can I go' and the teacher lets me."

Those who were eavesdropping laughed with Carter.

"Well, that doesn't mean anything," Carter told him. "If you say 'Can I go?' it means do you know *how* to go."

"Well, that's stupid. Everyone knows *how* to go," Dean said.

The chubby little bus struggled up through the rocky pass, until finally the city appeared below them.

Butte was a town renowned for its long history of mining activity, inescapably caught in the predictable boom-to-bust itinerary of all such endeavors. Sam saw it as a city that had had its copper heart carved out, and now that gaping wound—the Berkeley Pit, visible for miles—was referred to by some as the armpit of Montana. Deservedly or not, it was a community that had fallen into disrepute. Groundwater was rapidly filling the hundreds of miles of underground shafts and tunnels left by the massive extraction, threatening to overflow and gush down the city's streets and alleys like a vicious baptism.

The Butte Civic Center was located off the hill on busy Harrison Avenue. Sam settled Rozinante in the parking lot where a trickle of cars and spectators arrived for the first game. The Willow Creek players and cheerleaders straggled into the looming concrete building with visible trepidation. It was high noon and Sam immediately caught the implication. It wasn't only the game with Twin Bridges, it was also coming here to the tournaments, and the throttling that lay ahead, in that spacious arena with its overhead catwalks, glimmering lights, and bright colored lines meticulously painted on the glossy hardwood.

A large, dark-haired man in a suit and tie met them in the lobby and led them down a narrow, concrete hallway to their dressing room. It had benches along opposite walls with overhead shelves and hooks for clothing, but no lockers where Tom could safely secure his diamondback boots. They stashed their gear and went to find seats in the stands. Sam figured they ought to watch the first half of the opening game between Harrison and Manhattan Christian. He well knew that if Willow Creek beat Twin Bridges, they would be playing Christian tomorrow. He sat beside Diana, who seemed quite serene and confident.

"Everything okay?" she asked.

"Everything except my stomach."

She regarded him with a smile. "I like you without your glasses. But then, I liked you with your glasses. You look like a confident winning coach without them."

"What do I look like without my clothes on?"

"Shh, the kids will hear you."

IN THE LOCKER room, after their preliminary warmups and stretching out on the court, Sam gathered the team.

"All right. We've lost to Twin Bridges twice this year—"

"Every year," Tom said.

"Yes, well, I want you to wipe that off your brain pan. Totally erase it. This is a different world up here. These afternoon games have a leveling effect, they're jinxed, they're booby-trapped. A lot of top seeds are upset on Thursday afternoon at tournaments. So let's take a shot at it."

Sam glanced at Diana.

"I want to thank you for all your hard work," he said. "You're a great bunch of boys. We've had a good season, anything more will be the frosting."

Sam paused and glanced into their faces. "Anything else?"

"Yeah, Coach," Dean said. "What's a brain pan?"

"It's another way of saying memory, Dean."

"Gosh, I never knew I had a brain pan."

They all laughed a nervous, uptight laughter.

When they linked hands and raised their cheer, it echoed against the stoic concrete and rattled out the door ahead of them. With a trembling eagerness, they scrambled down the long corridor for the court, basketballs thudding and reverberating along the runway to the arena. Diana and Scott followed. Sam stood alone for a moment, took a deep breath, and glanced in the smudged wall mirror. He didn't see a confident winning coach looking back at him. What he saw was the ghost of a man who had given in to loss.

In the sparsely occupied civic center—which could seat up to fifty-six hundred—where sound was sucked up by the yawning empty spaces, Sam groaned as the game got off to an inauspicious beginning. Both Twin Bridges and Willow Creek were trying too hard, a common thing to see in the first games at the tournament. Every boy on the floor—many of whom were awestruck by the immense building—had turned it up a notch, and the effect manifested in leaden muscles, and wobbly legs where uptight athletes dropped balls they'd normally catch, miss shots they'd usually make, and throw passes into the stands.

By using Dean, Sam took each of the starters out for a minute to give each a new perspective of the game from the sideline. This tactic seemed to work, and as each of the regulars reentered the game, religiously passing Dean's cap to the teammate he replaced, he had settled down to something closer to his normal performance. Sam instructed Dean to shoot whenever he had a shot, and the rattled freshman managed to shoot twice: one shot hit a referee in the head and did a one-bouncer onto a prostrate tuba of the Twin Bridges band, and the second hit high on the backboard and swished down through the net, making Dean the most surprised human being in North America.

At first, the Willow Creek followers appeared lost in the cavernous arena. Truly Osborn had driven a load of students and teachers, while Andrew had arranged a car pool out of the Blue Willow for anyone who wanted to come, tactfully seeing to it that Dean's sister and mother rode with him and had tickets for all the games. Under the prompting of the three cheerleaders, the Bronc boosters were doing their best to generate enthusiasm and encourage the boys, and Sam had heard Axel's "You betcha!" boom through a lull in the crowd noise.

At the half it was still close: Twin Bridges 41, Willow Creek 38. The boys were hitting their stride, but so was Twin Bridges. Sam couldn't shake the knot of dread in his stomach. He attempted to convey a face of confidence to the team and keep the halftime locker room in a light mood. Diana checked Tom's knee, which seemed to be holding its own.

Well into the third quarter the boys played heroically, beyond their talent and ability, and it tormented Sam that in his heart he'd given up, no longer believing they could win. Twin Bridges attacked Olaf with a frenzy, but it wasn't Olaf's third foul that alarmed the Willow Creek fans. Tom had picked up two quick fouls and was playing with four. Sam couldn't make up his mind. They were staying with Twin Bridges and were three points ahead. If he took Tom out, it would save him for later in the game, but if they fell very far behind without him, which they undoubtedly would, it might be too late. He gambled and left Tom in the game.

It looked like a good move. Late in the third quarter Willow Creek was up by five. Then Tom went to the boards with Craig Stone, fighting for a rebound, and Tom was called for his fifth foul.

Tom came to the bench a raging bull. Sam had guessed wrong. The five boys tried to hold Twin Bridges off, but it was over when Tom went to the bench. The fourth quarter was a massacre and Twin Bridges had the reinforcements to overcome Willow Creek's gutsy stand.

In the locker room, the boys were devastated and each blamed himself personally for the loss, as though a turnover, a missed shot, a failure at the free-throw line had alone determined the outcome. Tom stomped to the far end of the large dressing room and kicked his traveling bag against the wall. He picked up one of his J. Chisholm boots and threw it into the shower room.

"Goddamnit!" he shouted. "Goddamnit!"

He picked up the other boot and fired it into the lavatory where it splashed into a toilet. He paced from the lavatory to the shower room like a caged and crazed animal.

"I knew I had four fouls, why didn't I let the rebound go? Why didn't I play it cool? I blew it, and I can never go back. We could have beaten them! *Goddamnit!*" he shouted and he slammed himself down at the far end of the bench. He pulled off a Twilight Zone Pump and slammed it against the wall. He wanted to smash something, someone. He let that son of a bitch Stone beat them *three* times. Three times! And he'd never get another chance. Never get to play them again. He could hear his father, laughing at him, ridiculing him. For the rest of his life his goddamn father would stick it to him! He could never go home, never look his teammates in the eye.

Miss Murphy came into the locker room and told the other boys they'd done well, played hard.

God, he felt like he was drowning. He hated his father and he hated his knee that quit on him and he hated Twin Bridges.

Miss Murphy put her hand on his shoulder. "You did—"

"No!" he shouted and stood, jerking her hand away from him with such a fury that she backed up a step. He looked at all of them, scattered in the large room.

"I lost it. I let you all down and I'll never be able to change that!" he shouted. "So don't give me any of that 'You played well' crap. I lost the game for all of you, for Willow Creek, and I can't go back and do it over and I'll have to live with that for the rest of my goddamn life! So, please. No bullshit. Please . . ."

He sat back on the bench and pulled off his other shoe and threw it into a large plastic trash can. "Oh, God," he said and he put his face in his hands. His knee hurt bad, it had been for weeks. He should have listened to the doctor. He could have avoided this neverending torture and humiliation. He could see the sneer on Craig Stone's face when the ref whistled him for his fifth foul. Stone had won, again, and they both knew it.

He unwrapped his knee. It was swollen. It was throbbing and the pain ran up into his thigh. He dropped the elastic wrap on the floor. The boys were talking in hushed voices and avoiding him. They all knew he'd lost it. He had to stay in the game and he hadn't. And how could he ever face his father? How could he bear that snarling laugh, mocking him and the team?

He pulled off his damp jersey and threw it into the corner. Coach Pickett came into the locker room. He walked straight to Tom and put his hand on his shoulder. Tom felt so bad, so terrible he couldn't stand it. After all they'd done together, after all the hours of practice, he'd let them down. He buried his face in his hands. Miss Murphy knelt in front of him and gently held an ice pack on his knee.

Tom fought it as long as he could, and then he broke down and cried. He didn't notice right away, as the pain and regret poured out of him, but when he wiped his flooding eyes he saw that the team was surrounding him.

"You didn't lose the game, Tom," Dean said. "We're a *team*."

Tom wept.

Diana couldn't leave it this way. She glared at Sam, who stood motionless and looked as defeated as the boys. She got off her knees and shouted, "Yes, we're a team, and we're not through!" The boys regarded her with startled expressions, still crouched around Tom.

"Okay, listen up!" Diana said. "I'm proud as hell of you, every single one of you. I watch professional athletes on television, men who receive millions of dollars to play, and they don't give *half* of what you gave tonight! All the Birds and Jordans and Isiahs are gutless wonders and crybabies compared to you boys."

Diana gathered herself, glancing at Sam, who seemed taken aback by her spontaneous leadership.

"Twin Bridges is an excellent team," she said. "They could win the State Championship. They play nine men without much dropoff in talent. Well, by God, we play six men without *any* drop-off in heart! And if I had my choice, I'd take players with heart. Are we going to lie down and give up?"

"*Nooooo!*" they shouted, unconsciously standing and huddling around her, sweeping Tom along with their fire.

"You want to play Twin Bridges again?"

"Yeeaaahhh!"

They joined hands in the huddle and chanted, "Win! Win! Win! Win! Win!"

The door to the locker room swung open. A short, white-haired man who looked like an old prizefighter gimped in with a batch of clean towels. He regarded the boys as they trailed off with their cheer.

"Congratulations, boys. Big win, big win."

He set the towels on a bench and shuffled out. They regarded each other with surprise.

"The old guy thought *we* won," Pete said.

"No," Diana said. "He knows we're going to."

IN A DOMINO's they filled up on pizza as though it were a second chance and Dean protested. "There's a McDonald's in Butte."

The boys brought Dean around to the value of pizza and Sam figured that trying to sneak a McDonald's past Dean was harder than sneaking a sunrise past a rooster. The busload rode home in the dusk of late winter with their flag tattered and dragging in the slush. They had to return tomorrow afternoon and play Harrison in the losers' bracket, a consolation round to give the less talented teams a few more games with tournament atmosphere before they were swept aside. If tomorrow was the end of their dream, would it be over cleanly and quickly, or would it be unbearable carnage?

Around the corner and past the Blue Willow, he coasted the little bus into town. For now at least they were home, in safe anchorage, where they could bail out the ship, plug the leaks, mend the tattered sails, and prepare themselves to go back out into the storm.

"By the way, that was a terrific shot, Dean," Sam said, glancing back at the Willow Creek freshman.

The abashed boy didn't respond, as if uncertain that his coach realized it had been a miracle, and that to say anything might be to incriminate himself.

Despite their locker-room enthusiasm, Sam knew it would only be such a miracle that could save them now, and he feared he no longer believed.

CHAPTER 57

S am stared into the open refrigerator, contemplating eating something after the journey home. He wasn't hungry, but maybe food would wash the bitter taste of defeat out of his mouth. The front door slammed. Diana, with her crimson matador hat tilted and her eyes flaming, found him in the kitchen.

"You've given *up* on them!" she shouted. "You've *quit!*"

Sam was taken off guard by her fury. "What are you talking about?"

"You walked out on us, me and the boys, in that locker room before the game!"

"What in—"

"Listen to yourself. *You're a great bunch of boys, we've had a good season, anything more will be frosting.* You were announcing the season was over, for God's sake! Pardon me, but I was under the illusion that the season was still going. The boys are under the same illusion."

Diana paced in the cluttered living room.

"Yes . . . and look what happened," Sam said, feeling himself going on the defensive. "Maybe it was an illusion, the difference between appearance and reality."

"Well, just maybe the boys heard your little deathbed talk and acted accordingly, a self-fulfilling prophecy. Maybe they sensed the season was over because you were telling them it was."

"They did the best they could," Sam said.

Diana stopped pacing and, with her hands on her hips, she glared into his eyes. "All right, Sam, tell me the truth. Do you believe they can win? Do *you* believe?"

"You mean tomorrow?"

"I mean tomorrow and Saturday and all the way to Helena."

Sam paused. He stuffed his hands into his pants pockets. "No . . . as much as I want it, as much as I pray to God for it, I don't think five boys can survive in the tournaments."

"Then you've given—"

"I won't set myself up again, not like that."

"Then you've quit living, you're a ghost!" she shouted. She yanked off her hat and threw it onto the floor. "You're not a loser, Sam. You're a *quitter*. You don't deserve these boys. You can't ride on the same bus with them."

"I want to believe," Sam said. "God knows I want to believe that, in the midst of the chaos and violence and unforeseeable madness, we can win."

"Well, it has to start with the everyday risks of getting your heart broken, like daring to hope and believe in the boys who idolize you. How many times have those boys had their hearts broken? How many times? But they keep playing, playing with their hearts, the way *you* taught them."

"I know, I—"

"Have you ever seen one of them quit? You've seen them come to the bench when they were so exhausted they couldn't stand, when they were so exhausted they couldn't speak, and you've seen them go back out there, sometimes four against five, three against five, and play with every ounce of fire they can muster."

Diana flopped on the broken-down sofa amid videotapes and magazines and month-old newspapers. Her voice dropped off as if she were overcome with sadness.

"You've lied to them. You've taught them to play with their hearts and souls and you play it safe so you won't be hurt. You play chicken. I care about you deeply and it's sad to see."

She looked up at him. Sam held his breath, he didn't know what to say, how to respond to this barrage.

"Sam, you're afraid to take a chance, afraid to hope, to commit. Maybe I'll have my heart broken again and again and again, but I know I have to keep trying, like the boys, because if I don't, I've given my chance at life away. I know I might make another horrid mistake and the people I love will leave me and I'll go through that terrible black hole, that awful loneliness and sorrow, but if I don't live with my heart, if I don't live with passion, I've already died."

Sam perched on the edge of the stuffed chair across from Diana and her words spun wildly in his head and he couldn't catch up to them. He wiped the sweat off his forehead with the heel of his hand. His heart raced. He'd been found out!

"Don't you think I know that Amy would want me to live and risk it all again?" he said. "I'm just not doing very well."

"What kind of flowers did they have at the funeral?" she said.

"Amy's?" Sam asked, trying to understand.

"No, *your* funeral. You're in love with your sorrow. Your heart's at an unremitting, never-ending funeral of self-pity."

"No, no, it's *not* self-pity!" Sam shouted. "Don't you see? I know that millions of other people have had their loved ones ripped from their arms and slaughtered by monsters, torn from them by war and earthquakes and floods and tornados. That's not it! I'm terrified that if I loved someone like that again and lost her, I'd lose my mental balance, I'd go completely insane."

Diana looked away. "Well, the boys need you right now. Of course you're going to lose again. Of course you'll be crushed with sadness again. But the joy you have in the risking, no matter how short, is far greater than all the sadness."

She stood, picked her hat off the floor, and moved toward the front door, the fury of her anger blown out. Sam followed her to the front door. He caught her by the arm. She turned and looked into his eyes.

"Sam, if you're afraid of being devastated again, if you're afraid to risk loving again, you're already dead. The monster with the shotgun killed you as surely as he killed Amy, the sadness has already won."

She closed the door behind her. Sam stood there, overcome. *She cared about him deeply!* What would he do about that? This incredible woman who would always be a physical delight to him, always a bright, intelligent mate in tune with the world, always surprising him with her insight and understanding, someone to love and cherish. Was she falling in love with a corpse? He felt the urge to find Andrew Wainwright and ride the bicycle built for two with him until dawn showed its face. He knew he wouldn't sleep.

He walked slowly into the bathroom and gazed into the mirror. Staring back at him was an old man, already dead, a Willow Creek ghost.

DIANA WOKE WITH a surge of panic in her stomach, facing that familiar black, bottomless pit where she stood utterly alone, again. She realized how much she cared about Sam by how scared she was of being abandoned by him. Had she driven him away, back into hiding? She had been harsh, even cruel.

The panic followed her all morning as they went through the motions of holding classes. She found excuses to go to his classroom twice and he seemed normal, friendly. She didn't find the courage to bring up her tirade. The word had spread that the boys and cheerleaders should bring extra clothes and personal things to stay overnight. They were playing the second afternoon game in the losers' bracket. If they won that game, they would stay in a motel in Butte as a reward from the school board, saving them from rising at the crack of dawn at home Saturday morning to reach the civic center in time for a nine-o'clock game. Diana figured Andrew Wainwright was behind the motel money, and she guessed that several of the boys had never stayed in a motel. Dean's entire baggage for the overnight was a toothbrush and a comb.

When the gang gathered around noon outside school, Diana, as a token of apology, told Sam that she would drive the bus. He looked at her for a moment but recovered quickly as if to keep her secret safe. She figured she had to put her money where her mouth was, and if she expected Sam to overcome his terror, she had to start working on hers. It was a leap of faith for her. Instead of being responsible for one passenger, she bore the burden for a dozen. She strapped herself in the driver's seat and caught several of the boys rolling their eyes and crossing themselves.

The sixty-mile drive went without incident except for a few comments from the kids that if she didn't step on it, it would be the baseball season. The boys seemed normal, horsing around at times and at others withdrawn into their private thoughts.

"Banging your head against a wall uses a hundred and fifty calories an hour," Curtis said to break a quiet spell and the gang almost threw him off the bus.

"Stop the bus, Miss Murphy!" Rob called. "We have some road kill here."

"Open the doors, Miss Murphy!" Tom shouted. "We'll throw him in the ditch."

Just a joke, just a joke. Steady, steady.

Diana held course, caught her breath, gripped the wheel, and slowed.

Sam seemed his normal self, sitting directly behind her and commenting on what they'd have to do to beat Harrison. Just the sight of the civic center rattled her already queasy stomach. Was Sam right after all? That it was dangerous as well as foolish to allow hope to set you up with expectations? Maybe she'd overdone it, maybe she'd been carried away with her obsession to win, to win against the madness, to win Jessica's forgiveness.

Is *that* what this was all about, to win Jessica's forgiveness?

She pulled into the parking lot and shut down the bus. She had gotten the team there safe and on time. She sighed with great relief and realized her armpits and forehead were wet with perspiration, her hands ached from gripping the wheel. Jessica's memory momentarily broke her concentration and she tried to refocus on the present. The foreboding civic center appeared as though it would chew up and spit out their lost-looking little bunch, and she joined them as they walked into it.

THEY'D GONE THROUGH their warm-up rituals when Sam gathered the boys in the locker room.

"You're a better team, but they have more players. So it's crucial that everyone stays in the game. We can't afford to lose anyone. We'll play a tight zone, give them the long outside shot, then everyone on the boards. Have fun and learn something."

He clapped his hands and they shouted their chant.

"Win! Win! Win! Win! Win!"

The boys broke for the door and Sam glanced at Diana. She couldn't decipher what she saw in his eyes, but there was something different there.

When Diana walked into the arena, she spotted Denise Cutter at a balcony rail in her wheelchair at one corner of the stands. Sally Cutter and Andrew Wainwright flanked her in the nearly empty building. The handful of fans for either team clustered near midcourt on either side of the floor.

Both teams desperately scrambled to find their basketball legs as well as their shooting eyes. They were trying too hard. They knew that if they lost, their season was over, and the seniors knew their chance to play organized basketball was most likely over for life.

Diana lived and died with each turn of events on the floor, like an emotional yo-yo. Rob and Pete were keeping the team in the game with their spectacular outside shooting, but Pete went down with five fouls near the end of the third quarter and Dean had to fill the gap. It was the old scenario that always brought them down.

The diehard Willow Creek fans tried to energize their boys but their vocal assaults echoed hollowly in the sparsely populated arena. Sam paced in front of the bench, shouting encouragement and instructions, and Willow Creek held their own. Tom was hobbling on his bum knee. Dean never stopped running on defense. Diana caught herself holding her breath while kneeling on the floor in front of the bench.

With seconds to go and Willow Creek up by one point, a Harrison boy drove around Curtis and went up for a short eight-foot shot. Faked out momentarily, Curtis recovered in time to knock the ball away, but he fouled the boy as time ran out. The referee blew his whistle and raised his arm with two fingers pointing to the cavernous ceiling. Two shots!

The ref waved both teams to the bench. The game was over, all but the final score. The scoreboard showed Willow Creek 54, Harrison 53. A Harrison player named Jimmy Hobbs walked timidly to the free-throw lane. The ref handed him the ball and backed away. Jimmy looked small standing there all alone in his sweat-soaked jersey, gaping up at the basket and rows and rows of empty seats. He dribbled the ball three times, bent his knees, and quickly put up the shot as if he couldn't stand the tension. It hit the back of the iron and bounced harmlessly away. Harrison fans groaned softly. Willow Creek fans gasped.

Diana gulped. Willow Creek was up by one point. One more shot coming. Overtime? She realized the whole team was on its knees beside her on the court. The Willow Creek fans were deathly silent, unable to raise a sound to distract the Harrison boy.

The ref gave Jimmy the ball. The huge arena was so quiet you could hear someone coughing. Little Jimmy Hobbs took the ball, bounced it three times, bent his knees, held his breath, and flipped the ball toward the rim, a shot he probably made a thousand times in the basket at the end of his barn.

Leaning forward with every muscle, Denise Cutter fell out of her wheelchair while the ball was in the air, Diana later found out. Sam, next to her on his knees, set his jaw as if for a shotgun blast.

Seemingly floating suspended in midair, the ball descended toward the rim and net. But Jimmy Hobbs had thought about it too long, felt the pressure too heavy in his veins, and the muscles in his shooting arm went tight.

The ball hit the front of the rim and didn't have the momentum to climb over. It fell hollowly to the hardwood floor, Jimmy's prayer unanswered.

For an instant no one moved. The sound of the errant ball hitting the floor hollowly echoed through the breathless arena. *No one* in the civic center moved.

Then bedlam broke out.

Tom leaped to his feet and shouted, "Sancho, my sword, my armor!"

"Yeah, my lord!" Scott shouted back.

"For each time he falls, he shall rise again!" the boys shouted together and they danced in a joyful huddle.

The handful of Willow Creek fans joined the team in the celebration. Grandma Chapman broke into the team's huddle, appearing pale, done in by the nerve-shattering game. "Guess who was in the Harrison stands, pulling bloody murder for Harrison?"

No one had a clue.

"The whole Twin Bridges team!"

"So?" Pete asked.

"Don't you see what that means?" Grandma said excitedly. "It means they know *you're still alive* and they're scared to death of you."

"We'll be their worst nightmare!" Sam shouted. "Every time they turn around, we'll be on them like a bumpersticker!"

Diana could see it in Sam's eyes. She hoped he was back from the edge, that he and the team had stepped out of their deathbeds together and were ready to go on.

After the teams went through the line congratulating their opponents, Diana saw Sam, off with little Jimmy Hobbs, consoling the brave sophomore.

The team headed for the locker room together.

"We're playing *Saturday!*" Rob shouted.

"We're playing *twice* Saturday!" Tom shouted.

"Bodacious! We're staying in a motel!" Dean shouted.

CHAPTER 58

They checked into the War Bonnet Inn, a large motel just off the interstate on Harrison Avenue, about a mile from the civic center. After they got settled in their assigned rooms and checked out the War Bonnet, they found a restaurant near the motel and nearly overwhelmed the place. Pulling tables up to large booths, the team ravenously replenished their energy while surrounded by the loving support of their partisans, who looked more like members of a traveling road show. Andrew Wainwright told the boys to order anything in the joint, that they didn't have to worry about the normally allotted five dollars. Sam had the feeling he was back in high school, and the Willow Creek bunch jabbered and laughed and celebrated as if there were no tomorrow—or as if they knew that by tomorrow this team would be history.

"We're number one!" Rip shouted without his teeth in place.

"Great game, great game!" Axel said.

Still with an ashen tone to her face, Grandma reached across people and a booth divider to grab Peter by the cheek with her thumb and finger.

"You were peaches and cream out there tonight, sweetheart."

Then she bent over the other way and gave Olaf a big kiss on the forehead.

"You weren't so bad yourself, honey."

Olaf blushed.

By the time they were through eating—the boys putting away full dinners of steak or chicken, plus several desserts each—Rip was sound asleep in the corner of a booth. The party broke up, with most of them headed back to Willow Creek. The team and cheerleaders hoofed it to the War Bonnet Inn.

Sam decided they wouldn't watch the Friday night games. He was afraid they'd be getting too much basketball, thinking about it too much and going stale. It didn't matter who won that night, Willow Creek would be playing the loser early Saturday morning. They knew the teams well enough, and he thought a relaxing night just hanging out, filling up on protein and carbs and forgetting about the games for a while, would be a healthy tonic. He planted Tom in front of a TV with ice on his knee and told him to stay put, that the boys would bring him whatever he wanted.

THEY HAD ADJOINING rooms for the team, the four upperclassmen in one and Sam, with the dubious honor of rooming with Scott, Curtis, and Dean, in the other. Diana would bunk with the three cheerleaders. A little after nine o'clock, she walked through the open door of Sam's room to find Curtis sitting on the bed watching a basketball game on TV.

"Who's playing?" she asked.

"The Trailblazers and Sonics," the shy sophomore said, glancing at her for a moment.

"Where's Dean and Scott?"

"They went to get some pop."

"Where's Coach Pickett?"

"He went to round up the other boys."

Diana sat in the chair beside the bed and regarded Curtis.

"Are you having fun?"

"Yeah. It's scary, but I'm glad there are only six of us so I get a chance to play."

"You're doing great, you've improved so much this year."

The boy averted his eyes.

"Do you have a girlfriend, Curtis?"

He blushed. "Naw."

"Would you like to have one?"

He glanced into her eyes as if to see if she were kidding. "I guess so, but I'll never."

"Why not?"

"With *these* ears?"

Diana thought for a moment. "Have you ever seen Clark Gable?"

"Who?"

"Clark Gable, he was a famous movie star. A million women would have given their . . . well . . . would have given a right arm just to meet the guy. He had ears that would make yours look microscopic. He had ears that could pick up messages from the moon. You go get rent one of his movies sometime and check out those ears. Then you'll know your ears don't matter to a girlfriend. They're too busy looking in your eyes, and, Curtis, you've got great eyes."

The boy's face flushed as though he'd run a mile. He studied his large, bare feet. Before he had to speak, Scott came bowling into the room with several cans of cold pop, and right behind him came Dean, pushing Denise in her wheelchair. The girl was glowing, hanging out with her brother and his friends, grabbing a hold of this little chunk of life the best she could. Dean's shirt was wet with perspiration, his face dripping.

"What have you been doing, Dean?" Diana asked.

"Racing. Denise and me are racing Scott in the halls."

"Don't you think you ought to rest . . . for the game in the morning?"

"I'm gettin' in shape for the game. Denise is helping me."

Diana knew when to let well enough alone. She stood and squeezed Denise's arm.

"Thanks for all your help, Denise. We couldn't win without you."

Diana headed down the corridor knowing there was no more logic to all of this than the cow jumping over the moon. She didn't know why, but Denise made her think of Jessica. Would she want Jessica to have survived the crash and be imprisoned in a wheelchair for the rest of her life? Selfishly, she'd take Jessica any way she could get her. But what would Jessica choose?

SAM HAD TO search the sprawling motel for the four older boys who had unceremoniously disappeared. He located them, and the three girls, lounging around the indoor pool and jacuzzi.

"Coach, we should have brought our swimming suits," Rob said, he and Mary and Pete sitting with their bare feet in the jacuzzi.

"I'd rather not have you swim. Save your energy for the game," Sam said.

Around eleven o'clock, Sam tiptoed out of his room and rapped lightly on the girls' door. Diana came out quietly with her scorebook and they went down to the lobby together. They settled in deeply cushioned chairs facing each other.

"What do you think about Tom's knee?" Sam asked.

"First, I want to apologize. I'm sorry if I went too far last night—"

"No . . . you don't need to, really. You made me do a lot of thinking."

"But it's not my place—"

"It's your official place, as assistant coach, to tell the head coach when he has already taken to the lifeboats. Thanks for having the guts to tell me. I don't think you said a word that wasn't the truth."

He smiled at her and she felt herself relax.

"I wish we'd reserved an extra room," she said.

"That would be nice." Sam said, trying to hold off his aching longing for this woman. "Now, what about Tom's knee?"

"Let's pray his knee will come around in eighteen hours. We'll keep it iced off and on, but I don't know if that will do it. It must hurt a lot. We can't beat Shields Valley without him."

"They don't have anyone who can stand up to Olaf," he said.

"Wasn't he something today? Only two personals, several blocked shots, and seventeen points. And how's this for balance?" She ran a finger down her scorebook. "Pete thirteen, Rob eleven, Tom nine, and Curtis four."

"How many did Jimmy Hobbs have?" he said.

She turned her scorebook over. "Eleven."

"That poor kid won't sleep tonight. That'll be with him the rest of his life. We don't warn kids enough about the possible consequences. About what they might have to handle."

He looked into her eyes and paused.

"*Why* did Jimmy Hobbs miss both of those free throws?" he said.

"Why? Because the pressure was too much for him," she said. "Because he didn't practice enough? Because he was scared? I don't know."

"Do you ever think that—"

Andrew Wainwright came in the front door in a snappy-looking nylon sweat suit and jogging shoes.

"Hey, you two. Can't sleep either? What a game, great coaching job, just great."

Sam and Andrew exchanged a glance.

"Are you staying over?" Diana said.

"Yeah. That's half the fun. I've already got reservations in Helena for next week."

"I hope you won't be up there alone," Sam said and laughed.

"You have them ready, coach. Those poor Harrison boys never could figure out which gate our kids were coming out of next, at least until Pete fouled out."

"We were lucky," Sam said.

"Maybe yes, maybe no. We were the better team," Andrew said.

"The good teams win the squeakers. If that kid made both free throws, it would have been a tragedy."

"We were just talking about that," Sam said. "Why didn't he make those two simple free throws?"

"We'll never know that," Andrew said. "Just our good luck. Anyway, sleep well, a big day tomorrow."

Andrew hurried across the lobby.

"You too," Sam called.

"Now there's a man I can't figure," Diana said. "Why doesn't he have a woman in his life, a wife or something? He's kind, intelligent, well-heeled, and he's gorgeous."

"And he enjoys looking at you."

"At me?"

"Yep. He's single, alive, and a man. In his situation I'd be looking at you, kid." He smiled at her. "Only a blind man wouldn't."

Without hesitation she kissed him at the door to her room.

"I'm sorry if I hurt you," she said softly.

He drew her close. "No, we need to be wakened before the chances are gone, before there's nothing left but regret, before Lazarus is rotten."

He kissed her deeply.

"God, I wish we had our own room," she said.

"Me too."

She opened the door, and a chorus of male and female voices greeted her with sing-song mockery.

"Where have you *been,* Miss *Muurphy?*"

SAM FOUND NO healing for himself, waking suddenly from his recurring nightmare, covered in sweat and gasping. He was in the sawed-off school bus, parked across the street from the Blue Willow. The door was jammed and he couldn't get out. Amy had gone into the restaurant to get the French fries. A Hamm's Beer truck stood around the back and Jimmy Hobbs was practicing free throws on a basket at the side of the Blue Willow. Sam frantically called to the boy, begging him to run into the building and warn Amy, warn her to flee! But Jimmy wouldn't quit shooting, missing free throw after free throw. "I have to practice!" he called back. "I have to practice until I make two in a row."

The dull, thudding detonations went off inside the Blue Willow like the sounds of Jimmy's poorly inflated basketball hitting the backboard. Sam was shouting, "No, no . . . please!" when he woke in the unfamiliar bed and darkness. From the trace of light coming at the edges of the heavy drapes, he could see Dean, sleeping next to him in the king-size bed. For an instant he thought it was Jimmy Hobbs.

FOR PETER, THE next morning was a muddled blur and it caught him off guard. Wake early, dress, breakfast, then the short drive to the civic center before the sun came over the mountains. It was going too fast and he was scared. They were counting on him, these people who had taken him in, people who cared about him. It worried him that they might lose here and it would all be over. He wanted to win for them more than anything in the world, and he prayed he wouldn't let them down.

Mr. Painter caught him after the game yesterday, said Maggie Painter told him to say hello to Peter. She had died. Peter didn't know what he thought about dead people—did they still know what was going on here? She was a Willow Creek girl and now all her chances were gone. As he dressed in the chilly locker room, he told himself there was no way he would let them lose, but he was afraid he would.

And then the game was on top of him.

He pushed his legs and body but it seemed so unnatural this time of the morning. He had butterflies, no, lead in his stomach. He was off balance, and he couldn't find his legs. He was winded, couldn't catch his breath. It made him mad; he knew he was in good shape.

Willow Creek started cold, they couldn't hit the toilet bowl with a shotgun. Shields Valley had found their shooting eyes quickly and they were pulling ahead.

He thought of Grandma and his mother. He wanted to make them proud. These games were hard on Grandma and he wanted to give her a lopsided win. He missed his first three shots; he was pressing, aiming the ball. He tried to get the ball into Olaf and had two turnovers. He was screwing up! What was he doing? He had to quit pressing and let his game come to him.

Work hard on defense, move your feet, hit the boards.

The sweat was flowing, and with it he felt his balance coming back. He blew by his man with a cross dribble and made the layup. He was back in the flow.

They were staying even but they couldn't make up the seven points they had fallen behind earlier. Shields Valley was playing nine guys and coming at them hard, running the floor. By the middle of the third quarter he'd focused, forgetting about the mechanics and allowing his head and body to go with his instincts. He hit two shots in a row from the outside and he felt it all coming together, that natural rhythm he didn't have to think about. Shields Valley couldn't handle Olaf in close and Tom was starting to hurt them from the side. Rob picked up his fourth foul near the end of the third quarter and he promised Coach Pickett, who was about to put Dean in the game, that he'd not pick up the fifth.

Shields Valley was up by six with four minutes to go and Rob got his fifth foul, a bogus call by the ref. When Rob turned for the bench he looked into Pete's eyes with desperation, pleading with him not to let it end here in this crappy morning game. Pete looked back as if to say, No way! He would not let them lose. In that brief moment he saw Denise Cutter in the stands, Grandma, Maggie Painter, all the Willow Creek fans from the past six years. He turned back to the game.

Up the court fast, he drew the defense in to him and lobbed a high pass to Olaf. The Norwegian jammed it. Shields Valley missed an outside shot. Tom got the ball to Pete on the side and he lifted a three-pointer. Nothing but net. Exhaustion swarmed over him as he sprinted back on defense. He fought it off. Cutting into the passing lane, he stole the ball, raced down the sidelines, and pulled up behind the three-point arc. He buried it. He couldn't miss. Shields Valley missed an outside shot. Tom rebounded the ball and fired a down-and-out to Pete. He took it to the arc, stopped when he could have gone in for the layup against only one defender, and nailed it. He scored nine points in the final two minutes and Willow Creek won by eleven.

Pete leaped into Rob's arms with his last bit of energy. The team and a small group of Willow Creek fans swarmed down onto the floor. Tom wrapped his arm around Pete and held him up.

"You played a hell of a game, kid," Tom said.

"You were super sweet yourself."

"And we're still standing," Tom said.

"Barely," Pete said.

Then the happy Willow Creekians, shouting and laughing, embraced everyone within reach.

⌒ CHAPTER 59 ⌒

Tom was watching TV in the motel room, lounging on the bed with an ice bag on his knee. The others had scattered in all directions, and Coach Pickett and Miss Murphy had taken the girls to the mall. Scott burst into the room.

"Tom, Tom, they're beatin' up Curtis and Dean!"

Tom sprang up, pulling on his diamondback boots.

"Where? Who?"

"I don't know, some guys from Butte."

Tom grabbed his duster and black hat and ran after Scott.

"WHO GAVE YOU permission to walk on our sidewalk?" a tall, narrow-faced kid said. He wore a large silver cross dangling from one ear.

"No one," Curtis said, trying to hang on to his courage.

Three of them, leather-upholstered and in black bikers' boots, had Dean and Curtis backed into a littered alley between two vacant brick buildings. Curtis could feel the hatred in them, the tall, the fat, and the ugly.

"You think you hayseeds can just walk into our town and go where you please?" the fat, sullen-looking boy said from his black, chrome-studded clothes. He must have weighed way over two hundred pounds, and his bare stomach bulged out between his pants and shabby leather jacket. Curtis couldn't look into his deeply pockmarked face and beady pale eyes.

"What about you, dimpleshit? What haystack did you crawl out from under?" the ugly guy said, jabbing a finger into Dean's chest. The bully had long, oily hair stringing out from under a red bandanna.

"'We're just walking around," Dean said. "We didn't mean to make you mad."

"'We didn't mean to make you mad,'" Ugly Bandanna said in a falsetto voice, snatching the Kamp Implement cap from Dean's head.

"Gimme my cap!"

"What would you want with a piece of shit like this?" Ugly Bandanna pulled out a cigarette lighter. "I think I'll rid the world of this diseased rag."

"No-o-o-o, please," Dean said.

Fat traced the lettering on Curtis's Future Farmers of America jacket with a stubby finger.

"What in hell is a Willow Creek?"

"It's over by Three Forks," Curtis said.

"What in hell is a Three Forks?" Bandanna said.

"Why don't you let us go?" Curtis said.

"Because, dipshit, you pissed us off," Fat said. "We can't just let you cow pies come slopping all over our ground. Jesus Christ, look at the ears on this shithead."

He flicked his hand at Curtis's ear.

"He's a walking satellite dish. We could plug a TV into him and get programs from stinkin' China."

Fat stepped nose to nose with Curtis, assailing him with putrid breath. "Can you get programs from China, cow pie?"

The porky goon, who wore metal-studded leather wrist bands, slapped Curtis across the mouth. Stunned, Curtis flinched and stepped back quickly. Dean backpedaled beside him. They were inching deeper into the deserted alley.

"I'll call the sheriff," Curtis said, wiping a trickle of blood from his lip.

"He'll call the sheriff," Tall Earring said. "We ain't got no sheriff, shit brain."

"I think we oughta torch this farmer's jacket, too," the fat thug said, and he slapped Curtis across the mouth again, harder.

"Hit me, chicken shit," Fat said.

Curtis spotted Scott and Tom out on the sidewalk. Tom glanced down the alley and saw them. He came down the alley, fast. Bandanna lit his cigarette lighter and held it up to Dean's cap.

"What are you smiling at, dipshit!" Fat shouted at Curtis. "Why don't you hit me?"

"Because *he's* going to," Curtis said.

The fat one turned, too late. Tom's fist caught him on the side of the skull, a thudding blow that sounded like a fastball hitting a catcher's mitt. With a grunt he dropped to his knees and then flopped face first to the alley floor, his beady eyes wide with shocked surprise.

"Bodacious!" Dean yelled.

"Get 'em, Tom!" Curtis said.

Startled by Tom's sudden appearance, the other two turned and clenched their fists.

"Who the fuck are you?" Ugly Bandanna said.

Then, as though they'd done this a lot, they were on him like alley cats, swarming, tackling, pinning his jabbing arms. Amid the grunts and curses and broken bottles, Tom was losing ground. Every time he zeroed in on one of them, the other would punch him from his blind side. Held in a strangling hold from behind, Tom threw a crunching elbow to Bandanna's gut. Bandanna lost his grip and sagged to the ground. Dean and Curtis cowered from the violence.

The fat one staggered to his feet, still unsteady. Then he drop-kicked Tom in the groin with his heavy boot. Tom's knees buckled, he sucked for air, his eyes bulged. He doubled up on the crumbling asphalt. In a burst Curtis broke from his petrified state and leaped on the fat guy's back, his arms around that pulpy neck. Fat turned around and around and then slammed backward into the brick wall of the building, knocking the wind out of Curtis and forcing him to give up his stranglehold. Curtis slid to the ground, slumped against the wall, thinking he would die if he didn't find a breath of air immediately.

"Kill 'im, Hank, kill 'im," Bandanna said with a sleazy grin.

Curtis couldn't breathe.

Dean, wide-eyed with terror, leaped at the heavyweight and tried to tackle him. But the brawler, whose senses seemed to be returning to him, kneed Dean in the head and sent him and his glasses sprawling.

Tom forced himself up onto his knees, wobbly. Then Curtis, gasping for breath, saw Rob, Pete, and Olaf sprinting down the alley, with Scott trailing behind. The thugs heard their running footsteps and turned to see the fury in their approaching faces.

"These maggots think they can beat up on our teammates!" Tom shouted.

Dean scrambled to pick up his glasses. "Get 'em, Pete! Get 'em, Rob!" he said.

Peter Strong never broke stride, as though driving for a layup. Before Bandanna could gather himself, Pete was wailing away on his head and body as though Bandanna had insulted Pete's mother or something. Sprinting just behind Pete, Rob threw a cross-body block into Tall Earring, hurtling him backward into the dirt and rolling over him. Dean, on his hands and knees, picked up a brick and cracked it against Fat's kneecap. The jerk yowled and grabbed his knee in both hands, hopping on one leg.

Tom sprang to his feet, bringing a haymaker to the spongy, unprotected face of the fat guy. The slob dropped like he'd been shot. Olaf had a fist made up and was windmilling toward Earring as the tall one scrambled to his feet. One glance at the towering Norwegian and he took off down the alley. Never able to gather his defenses against Peter's fury of quick, solid punches, Ugly Bandanna turned and hightailed it, too, his bloodied nose coloring his filthy Levi jacket.

"Run, greaser, run for your life!" Pete yelled.

Tom lifted the blubbering heavyweight onto his feet and propped him against the brick wall.

"You want me to hit you again, you tub of lard?"

Fat shook his head, the left side of his face already swelling and coloring.

"If you ever so much as look at one of my teammates again, I'll shove your head so far up your ass you'll need a flashlight to find your way out!"

Tom shoved the jerk down the alley.

"Go find the hole you maggots crawled out of!"

The leader of the gang stumbled after the others, weaving, off balance.

"Run, you chicken shit!" Curtis yelled.

"Yeah, you chicken shit!" Dean said, pulling on his recovered cap, "you have bad breath."

"How are you?" Rob said, turning to Tom.

"I'm sore." Tom looked at his bruised right hand. "I think I broke my hand."

"You should have seen Tom *punch* that kid!" Dean shouted.

Peter shook his hands and grimaced. "I think I broke both of mine."

Curtis bent to pick up something in the alley that caught his eye. "Look!"

They all examined the upper front tooth speckled with blood. Tom felt his jaw and checked his teeth.

"You knocked his tooth out," Dean said to Tom.

"Or Pete did," Tom said. "It'll give them something to remember us by."

With Tom's arm around his shoulder, Rob helped him limp toward the street. Pete got under Tom's other arm and they took most of his weight.

"We saw you running down the street," Rob said. "We knew something was wrong. You're supposed to stay off your knee all day. Sorry we didn't get here sooner."

"It was soon enough," Tom said and smiled. "We kicked ass, didn't we?" He rubbed Dean's and Curtis's heads as they flanked the three of them. "You guys all right?"

"Yeah."

"Yeah."

"You done good," Tom said. "You done real good."

"Wow, did you ever smack him," Scott said to Pete.

"You're a madman," Rob said, looking over at Pete. "What were you doin'?"

"Cookin'," Pete said, examining his skinned right knuckles. "What did they want anyway?"

"They wanted to show they were tough shit against Dean and Curtis," Tom said. "Well, they found out no one messes with our team, right?"

"Yeeaaahhhh!" they shouted. They had gone in alone and scared. They were sore, bruised and bloody, but together. Curtis sensed that they all felt the same, that as long as they were together no one could beat them.

"Crap, we'd better get you back to the motel," Rob said. "Coach will swallow his whistle if he finds out you've been running around on your knee."

Olaf and Curtis each picked up one of Tom's legs. They carried him down the sidewalk as though they had just won the tournament, elated, happy, on fire.

"I wish *I'd* punched him," Dean said.

"Next time," Tom told him. "You'll nail him next time."

They were a team. They couldn't wait to play the consolation game that night. None of them dared mention the possibility of playing the challenge game on Monday. Who could beat them when they stuck together?

Curtis felt proud, felt good about himself. Next time he went into Three Forks, he'd see if they had a Clark Gable movie at the video store.

CHAPTER 60

S am gathered the boys in the locker room after they'd warmed up. Diana and Scott sat with them along the two benches and Sam stood at the far end. Ever since he'd returned from the mall with the girls, Sam had an uneasy feeling. The normally transparent boys seemed secretive in the motel room while they watched basketball videos that afternoon. Their stories of horseplay didn't satisfy him in explaining the marks on Tom's neck, Pete's swollen knuckles, and Curtis's puffed lip. Were those knuckleheads wrestling or playing football or something? He couldn't believe they were seriously fighting each other.

Standing in the locker room, he paused and looked into each expectant face shining up at him. They were in fate's hands tonight. They had no control over the other game. If Twin Bridges lost, their chance to challenge would be lost and their season would be over. But they did have a say in *their* game. They had to win to have any hope of playing Monday night. He cleared his throat.

"Men, we're here to fight the dragon tonight. Together. But the dragon is not Manhattan Christian—a bunch of hardworking boys just like you with families and girlfriends and pet dogs, doing their best to win for their moms and their school and their town. The dragon you face is the voice in your hearts that whispers, 'You're losers.' The dragon you face tonight is the fear in your guts that tells you to quit, to give up. It is the softness in your spirits that tempts you to surrender your dreams, to lie down and accept defeat politely. Those are the dragons that will rear their ugly heads tonight, the beasts who beguile us to be something less than we can be."

Sam paused and scanned their faces, faces longing for something he hoped he could give them.

"We're not going out tonight to beat those other boys."

"We're not?" Dean squeaked.

"No," Sam said. "We're going out to play better than we ever have before, to play beyond our physical limitations, to play above our God-given talent, to play harder and higher and longer than we ever have before. We're going out there to live not as life *is* but as it *should be!* If we each do this, every *one* of us, then it won't matter if we win the game, because we will have defeated the dragons. But I can promise you, men, that if we play that way, we *will* win the game."

"Yeeaaahhh!" they leaped to their feet and shouted. Then they huddled, with their hands held high and knotted together in the center.

"Win! Win! Win! Win! Win!" they chanted.

"Okay, let's go!" Sam shouted and followed the little herd out to the court.

He paced beside the bench while the boys took their final warm-ups. He tried to enjoy the ride, this nerve-tingling, gut-twisting ride. The cavernous building was filling with fans from Churchill, Gardiner, Twin Bridges, and Willow Creek. These small towns could never do better than partially fill the large arena, though a few fans from the Butte area who loved basketball usually added to the gate. It seemed that not many had noticed the unfamiliar contestant among the perennial favorites in the Saturday night games. In past tournaments, his boys had been shipped out by this point, and the only way a basketball player from Willow Creek could get in here Saturday night would be to buy a ticket.

He scanned the Willow Creek section behind their bench and was astonished at the numbers, finding among the throng the few familiar faithful who had been there all along. He remembered the midnight practice almost three months ago when there were only ten. Denise Cutter sat at the balcony rail above the temporary bleachers in her wheelchair, Andrew and Sally Cutter in seats beside her.

The horn sounded and the boys quickly gathered at the bench. He noted their animated faces, infused with resolve and hope.

"Give all you've got every minute you're on the floor. And remember, *they can only put five players on the floor at a time,*" the boys chorused with him.

Most of the spectators were standing as the ref tossed the ball high and two Christian defenders raced into the paint in front of their basket, anticipating Willow Creek's favorite play.

Well coached, but sorry.

Olaf tipped the ball to his right where Rob waited. The Broncs hustled into the front court and, as Sam anticipated, the Eagles took them man-for-man, with Curtis's man sagging off and double-teaming Olaf. Tom, with his knee tightly wrapped, sucked his man with him as he crossed the paint and put his nose in the ear of Dorn, who was guarding Olaf. Olaf slid high and swung around the double pick. Rob alley-ooped the ball toward the basket. Olaf went up, caught the ball in midair, and hammered it down through the net like a cannon ball. An auspicious beginning, a bell-ringer that sent a thunderous message to every heart in the arena, bringing the Willow Creek crowd to its feet cheering and leaving most Manhattan Christian followers with the wits scared out of them.

Sam settled on the bench and smiled and the boys went on playing with discipline, intelligence, and dogged determination. They did it the way Sam diagramed it; they did it the way Sam taught them; they did it the way Sam dreamed it.

George Stonebreaker walked in through the back door of the Hub Bar in Belgrade and settled on a stool. He was done drinking with those assholes in Three Forks. Some smart ass always brought up the accident with Tom's horse. Most of the people in the place were clustered as close as they could get to a radio. He needed a beer but the damn bartender had his ear glued like the rest.

". . . Gustafson comes out on the high post. . . . Dykstra and Dorn stay with him. . . . Strong gets the ball to Stonebreaker . . . back to Strong. . . . Strong comes around Stonebreaker's pick. . . . Stonebreaker slides free. . . . Strong gets him the ball. . . . Oh! Stonebreaker goes up and banks it home. . . . Willow Creek is up by four. . . . beautiful pick-and-roll . . ."

It seemed George just couldn't get away from it.

"Hey," George said. "How about some service."

The rotund bartender reluctantly moved down the bar.

"What can I do you?" he said.

"Well, for openers, will you shut off that damn radio."

"Hell, no. Those Willow Creek boys are tough nuts."

"Shit, they're just lucky. They'll lose, you'll see."

"What are you drinking?" the big, balding bartender said.

"Give me a Hamm's."

". . . Wow, Gustafson jams the ball. . . . This kid gets better every time I see him . . . Volk brings the ball up . . . over to Van Dyke . . . back to Volk . . . oohhh! Johnson steals the ball . . . quickly upcourt . . . over to Jenkins . . . back out to Strong . . . in to Stonebreaker. . . . He fakes a pass to the big center and takes it to the boards himself. . . . Count it. . . . Christian is befuddled. . . . When they cover Gustafson, Stonebreaker kills them inside . . . when they patch the hole in that screen door, Willow Creek comes in the attic window. . . . Dykstra tries a three . . . it comes off. . . . Stonebreaker rebounds. . . ."

George moved down the bar with his beer, a little closer to the radio. A rancher sat beside him, smoking a cigar.

". . . Christian goes back into their zone, trying desperately to stop the Willow Creek attack. . . . Strong takes the three . . . it's good. . . . these Willow Creek guards are tearing hinges off Christian's barn door. . . . Volk gets the ball into Dorn. . . . Dorn makes a nice move around Gustafson and goes up. . . . Holy cow . . . Stonebreaker came over and rejected that shot. . . . Jenkins grabs the loose ball. . . ."

George turned to the rancher. "That's my boy, Stonebreaker."

The rancher turned and regarded George. "No kidding?"

"Yep, that's him, hell of a ball player."

"You must be damn proud," the rancher said.

". . . Dorn just can't stop this Gustafson kid. . . . Johnson comes across midcourt . . . over to Jenkins . . . back to Johnson . . . Strong gives him a screen. . . . Johnson takes the shot from downtown . . . it comes off. . . . Holy cow, Stonebreaker goes up and tips it in . . ."

Another man sat on George's other side. Looked like a business man or lawyer or something. Suit and tie, polished shoes.

". . . Jenkins in the corner . . . he's all alone . . . takes the shot . . . makes it. . . . This kid's only a sophomore but he's hurting Christian with that shot from that corner. . . . They better send damage control out on that kid. . . . Trouble is, that leaves Dorn alone on Gustafson. . . . Volk misses from out in front. . . . Stonebreaker sweeps the boards. . . ."

George turned to the guy in the suit.

"That's my boy, Stonebreaker, hell of a player."

"No kidding." The man was impressed. Then he frowned. "Why aren't you at the game?"

"Oh, well, I had to—"

"Hell, what's the matter with you? If I had a kid like that I'd be in the front row."

George finished his beer and went out the back door.

BY THE MIDDLE of the fourth quarter Tom could hardly run the floor and Sam replaced him with Dean. The Willow Creek fans never sat down through the fourth quarter, sustaining a constant chant and roaring approval every time their boys scored. Diana iced Tom's knee on the bench, and his teammates iced the victory on the court with their unrelenting defense and free-throw shooting. When the buzzer sounded, Sam glanced quickly at the scoreboard. MANHATTAN CHRISTIAN 63, WILLOW CREEK 75.

He picked Diana off the floor. "I hope Mervin Painter bet the farm!" he shouted.

"We have to pull for Twin Bridges now!" she shouted back.

After shaking hands with the Christian players and wading through the exuberant fans, the boys passed the Twin Bridges team coming from the locker room. Craig Stone caught Olaf by the arm as they passed.

"You try that alley-oop shit on me and I'll have your balls!"

Olaf pulled his arm away and hurried past.

"What did he say?" Tom asked, hobbling behind.

"He is afraid with his balls I am going to alley-oop," Olaf said.

"He's afraid we're going to Helena, because he knows we'll beat them," Tom said, putting as little weight as possible on his tender knee.

After showering, they watched the Twin Bridges–Gardiner game. For more than a half it was nerve-wracking, with Gardiner out in front and the Willow Creek team and fans pulling vociferously for Twin Bridges. Finally, in the fourth quarter, Twin Bridges pulled ahead and won by four. The Willow Creek bunch exploded with joy. They weren't dead after all. They would play the challenge game with Gardiner on Monday night and the winner would go on to the Divisionals in Helena.

They ate at a McDonald's, at Dean's insistence, and with Andrew Wainwright escorting them, Denise and Sally Cutter joined the gang. Andrew sat across from Sam and Diana in a booth and beamed with effervescent praise.

". . . and that deal with Curtis, great, just great. What a surprise. How long have you been plotting that?"

"Oh, Curtis kind of did that on his own," Sam said, talking with his mouth stuffed with a Big Mac. "He's been practicing that shot for months without my knowing. I figured, unguarded, he could hit a few of them."

"Brilliant," Andrew said. "When they have to cover all five of us, we've got 'em."

Someone raised his voice behind Sam, angry words, shouting. Cold sweat broke out on Sam's forehead, panic gripped him. He turned. A man scolded a boy who'd dumped a shake and fries onto the floor. Realizing where he was, the man calmed down and a McDonald's employee came to his aid.

It's all right, it's all right, let it go.

"Are you okay?" Andrew said. "You look a little peaked."

"Yeah . . . I'm still recovering from all this. I kept catching myself cheering for Twin Bridges and thinking I'd gone nuts."

Andrew laughed and Diana regarded him with concern in her face.

The journey home was one of exultations and exhaustion and agonizing anticipation. Halfway home, Sam glanced in the rearview mirror and saw the entire bus was sound asleep, all except Diana, who had one hand on his shoulder. She leaned close from behind him.

"I'll leave the light on at home for you," she said, and Sam felt the world was friendly and tomorrow would be bright.

WHEN THEY HAD satiated their long-restrained appetites for each other, Sam and Diana snuggled naked under a down quilt.

"I have a strange daydream that pops into my head every so often," Sam said.

"Tell me."

"I've never told anyone."

She kissed his forehead.

"It's a secret longing to stand in a great congregation of people, thousands of people, tens of thousands of people, singing a great hymn together with such force and beauty that it shakes the earth and makes me weep."

They lay quietly for a minute.

She whispered, "Whenever I've revealed my inner feelings to someone I've always had them thrown back in my face or used against me in some destructive way."

"So have I, usually in ridicule."

"Can I trust you?" Diana said.

"Yes."

She brushed her lips softly along his shoulder.

"Sometimes I have a deep yearning to go home, an ache, just to go home, but I have no idea where that is. I know it isn't my parents' home in San Diego and it isn't this little farmhouse. I don't think it's anywhere I've ever been before. It's like I know it exists, but I don't know where, and I'm on my way but afraid I'll never find it. Do you ever feel that way?"

"Yes."

They were quiet under the spell of the fluttering candlelight.

"Sometimes," he said, "when I'm inside you, or when I'm snuggled against your breasts, I feel I'm home."

"Like now?"

"Yeah."

SAM NOTICED THE kitchen clock nudging one o'clock as he shuffled through the house. In a pleasant state of exhaustion he snapped off the light and fumbled off his clothes, feeling his way toward his cold, Dianaless bed. He always hated to get up and go into the cold night after they'd made love.

He heard rapping. It came from the back. Sam stopped in the doorway of his room, his pants down around his ankles and about to be kicked off. He listened. A moment passed. Then the rapping again. No one ever came through the back door. Sam pulled his pants up and zipped the fly, feeling on the floor for his shirt with his bare feet. He snapped on the kitchen light and pulled on his shirt. With growing trepidation, he went to the back door, at the last moment imagining George Stonebreaker standing on the other side with a shotgun.

When he jerked open the door that had swollen against its jam, he was confronted with a shadowy apparition. When Sam's eyes focused, the apparition became a misplaced person with a ratty leather suitcase in hand.

"Amos?"

"Sorry to bother at this ungodly hour, but I figured you'd do a favor."

He stood as though he'd grown there, his large ears curled down by the wide brim of his Tom Mix hat. His handlebar moustache drooped.

"Come in, come in."

Sam backed into the kitchen, and Amos followed him with his strange burden, closing the door behind him. He set the suitcase down. It had two leather straps that were buckled on top, and the handle was worn down to the metal in spots.

"I've been waiting for you to come home."

"Oh . . . well, a few of us have been celebrating."

"Them boys done good," Amos said.

"Would you like to sit—"

"No, no, only be a minute."

Sam had the impulse to ask if he could take his hat, but felt it would be like asking Amos to undress.

"May be leaving soon, want to leave something for Tom, thought you would do it for me."

"Why, yes . . . I could do that, but why don't—"

"Can't give it to him until spring, until he finishes school. Told me he was thinking of goin' in the service. What he really wants is to ride rodeo. Told him he ought to go to college and ride on the rodeo team. Said he couldn't afford it unless he went in the service first. There's some things in here of mine: bridle, lariat, spurs. There's some money, enough to help him get started in college, keep him out of soldiering, but no one can know about that except you and Tom. That mean son of a bitch that fathered him would try to get his miserable hands on it. That's the favor."

Amos stood without emotion in his eyes, the patina of worn leather on his face.

"Well, sure. I'd be glad to do that, but you could give it to him. He'd want to thank—"

"Won't be here much longer."

"Where are you going?"

"Away."

"Will you be here long enough to see the boys in the tournament?"

"That's the only reason I'm still here, stay as long as they're in it. I want Tom to know I'm there pullin' for him."

"I know how much that means to him. I've seen him look for you in the crowd."

Amos turned and dragged open the sticking door. He stepped out quickly and then turned halfway and regarded Sam.

"You'll see that he gets it?"

"Yeah, sure."

"Nobody needs to know about it, just Tom and you."

"Just Tom and me."

Amos walked out the door and melted into the darkness so quickly Sam could hardly believe it. He stood in the open door and scanned his overrun back yard. Nothing. Then the dry, leafless lilacs clacked as someone passed through.

Back inside, Sam inspected the suitcase. The initials GLH could still be recognized on a tarnished brass plate. About to leave it where it stood and hit the sack, he thought maybe he should hide it. Sam picked up the suitcase, surprised by its weight, and shoved it on its side under his bed.

Settled in bed at last, he caught the scent of her lingering on him. Try as he may, he couldn't help but wonder what was in the luggage. And how had Amos come to town? Sam had seen no pickup, no horse. He tried to fall asleep against the overwhelming temptation to open the puzzling treasure that was buried beneath him.

He was thankful the team had two days to catch their breath and rest before the Monday night game. He realized he was back in it with his unguarded heart, daring to believe they could win. It scared him. And it scared him when he thought about his feelings for Diana. In a half-sleep he sensed that whatever he'd been hanging onto so desperately these past years was not so precarious any longer, as if now, somehow, he was hanging on with both hands.

CHAPTER 61

Sunday morning Peter was lounging at the kitchen table when Grandma hustled in the back door. Tripod nested in his lap.

"Oh, shucks, I wanted to be here when you woke up. You usually sleep another hour or more when you don't have school."

"The phone woke me."

She hung her coat on a peg in the cluttered entryway but kept her brown felt topside.

"The Blue Willow is buzzing this morning. You boys have this whole end of the valley more excited than I've ever seen."

"Whata gas," Parrot squawked from the front room.

"Did you hear that?" Grandma said with an astonished expression on her face.

"Yeah. So what?"

"He said, 'Whata gas.' Imagine."

She moved to the doorway and peered at the caged bird.

"He said, 'Up you ass,'" Peter said.

"I don't believe it. After forty years that bird has changed its tune."

"I think your hearing is shot."

Grandma reached for the refrigerator door, which looked like a clippings board in a newspaper office.

"Yikes!" she yelled and leaped back a step, her felt fedora flipping off her snowy hair. "What the—that damn icebox has a short."

Pete roared with laughter.

"Just trying to keep you out of the paint. Now you know how Olaf learned so fast."

He revealed the remote-control unit of the Lightning Commander in his lap, under Tripod. When she looked closely, she found the shock collar Scotch-taped to the refrigerator door, camouflaged by newspaper clippings.

Grandma picked up her hat and stuck it on. Then she swatted Pete lightly on the top of his head.

"You! A body can never relax with you around."

"Or you," he said.

"Now then, if you'll let me in the icebox, what would you like for breakfast?"

"I've had some milk and a peanut butter sandwich."

He set the remote-control transmitter on the table in plain sight.

"Land sakes, that's no breakfast for a boy who's going to knock the cheesecake out of Gardiner tomorrow night. Let me fix you some eggs or pancakes."

She opened the refrigerator and began setting food out.

"Pull a ship," Parrot cackled.

"Hear that, boy?"

"Yeah! He said, 'Pull a ship.' I don't believe it," Pete said, looking toward the front room.

"He must be getting senile," Grandma said, "losing his memory, can't remember which are his lines and which are mine."

She broke eggs into a bowl.

"Who was on the phone?"

"Oh, the doctor's office, said you should call them. Isn't it kind of funny to be calling you on Sunday?"

"Ha! Probably wants to skin me one more time before he dies. They're always pestering me about something. You got your things packed?"

"Yeah. I'm not taking much," Pete said.

"I can't remember when Willow Creek was playing in the Monday night game. We always played Friday afternoon and then slunk home with the watermelon seeds knocked out of us."

"Not this year," Pete said and wondered what it would be like to stay another year, to graduate from Willow Creek. He thought his grandma was slowing down and she might need him. No one needed him in Saint Paul.

"You're right. Not this year." She paused and regarded him. "Are you doing all right?"

"As long as she swims, I will cook."

"Attaboy. Are you glad you stayed?"

"Yeah," Pete said, "I'm glad. I'm *really* glad."

"Listen to me, grandson. There isn't any other life but what we have right now, this minute, so live it to the hilt." She banged a fist on the countertop. "That's my word to you. Live it to the hilt every day and you'll have few regrets."

"I'm trying, Grandma."

"I know you are, sweetheart, and doing a bang-up job of it, too."

She fired up the gas stove.

"What do you think of the coach now?"

Pete thought for a moment. He wanted to say he loved him but couldn't get those words out.

"I really like him."

"That makes two of us."

"Whata gas," Parrot squawked.

SUNDAY NIGHT SAM sat at Diana's table as she set a steaming bowl of spaghetti noodles and another of homemade sauce in front of him. He had slept late into the day and now looked forward to this intimate time with delicious anticipation, trying to put the Monday night game out of mind for a while. Diana brought French bread and slid into her chair beside him.

"Are we going to win tomorrow?" she asked calmly.

"Yes. We're going to win."

"I hope Tom will stay off that leg," she said. "I still can't figure what they were up to Saturday afternoon in Butte. Pete's left hand was swollen and something hit Curtis in the mouth."

"He told me it happened in the morning game."

"Huh. He told me they were roughhousing in their room," she said. "We'll probably never know." She regarded him with a frown. "You don't think they'd fight," she said. "I mean really try to hurt each other?"

"Never, and I'd bet my life on it."

He covered his spaghetti with the garlic-scented sauce.

"This smells fantastic."

"Are you hungry?" she asked.

"I'm famished—more for you than your cooking."

They traded smiles as she helped herself to the food. "Then would you characterize our lovemaking as dessert?" she said.

"No . . . never. It's a staple, the stuff of life, the main course."

"Then we're having the appetizer?"

"I don't need an appetizer," he said, watching her suck a noodle across her lip. "Being around you all week is more appetizer than I can handle."

She broke off a piece of French bread and passed it to him. "Are you going to coach again, wherever you end up?"

Sam thought a moment. He didn't want to look ahead to a time when they might not be together. "No, I don't think so."

"Oooh, you ought to, you're so good with the boys."

"I think it's the boys who are good with me."

"You're so natural with them," she said.

"It's like the local folklore about the bicycle built for two. There'll never be another ride like we've had here—there'll never be another group of boys like these."

"Listen, you've made me see things I never saw before, you've made me laugh, really laugh. You've taught me things I'd never imagined, things I'll always remember, you can't waste—"

"Whoa, whoa." Sam put down his fork and held up both hands. "I don't like the insinuation. *Always remember?* You talk as though I'm history," Sam said. He felt his chest constricting.

"I'm not going to be in Willow Creek next year. You said you were thinking of applying in Arizona, I'm applying in San Diego, among other places. I just mean—"

"You just mean this is only a temporary relationship, a Willow Creek fling," Sam said, struggling to sound lighthearted.

"Like you're always telling the boys, we have this season, seize the present, don't worry about tomorrow."

Sam pushed his chair back from the table.

"I don't want *us* to end," he said with an ironic firmness in his voice.

The words hung there, awkward, poorly dressed, out of style, a kite without wind. She started to speak but he cut her off.

"I haven't had much experience with this sort of thing, but I know this much. I don't want you walking out of my life. I don't want to leave what we have together."

She reached over and took his hand in hers. "Sam, you sweet, gentle man. Let's enjoy what we have now, let's ride the bike with the boys and not get tangled in a future that may never be."

Her eyes projected a plea for understanding.

Sam held her hand and wished he could heal her. She was the deer that had been hit crossing the road, the mother who had killed her only child, her heart shattered there in the ditch with Jessica and all of this world's mangled and butchered victims of the madness. His throat filled. He swallowed hard and forced the words.

"I want to sit up and bark like a dog," he said, "or shinny up a telephone pole, but I can't."

"No, no, don't do that, I couldn't bear seeing you like that."

They sat facing each other beside the table, holding hands while the spaghetti cooled and the salad wilted. He didn't know what to do. There were eight hundred thousand words in the English language and he couldn't remember one. She saved him.

"C'mon."

She stood and led him to her large brass bed. They slowly removed their clothing and crawled under the bedding together as though they had both been wounded, but they didn't wind the music box, they didn't light a candle.

IN HIS SAGGING bed Sam dreamed he was running around the block to earn a few squares of Hershey bar from the nasty little girls in his neighborhood. He was a small boy again. They were sitting on the concrete wall along the alley, laughing at him, and he couldn't run well because his medial collateral ligament hurt and he was limping, afraid he wasn't running fast enough. At the end of the alley Amy was rapidly cranking the Edelweiss music box—which was playing a Bach chorale—and shouting at him. "Run faster, Sam, run faster!" He could see Diana driving off in her Volvo with Andrew Wainwright. Beside him, running stride for stride, was Tom's buckskin horse, limping also, its body full of shaved spots where thousands of stitches held the mutilated creature together.

Sam woke before he reached the end of the alley. He rolled over and tried to remember what day it was. It was still dark. He got out of bed and shuffled into the living room, squinting out the front window to see if Wainwright was sailing by on the bicycle built for two. He was exhausted but he didn't want to return to his bedding until his mind had switched to another channel. He had no idea what the dream meant, if anything, but it left a boulder of dread in his stomach. He wanted to call Diana, but there was no sense both of them losing sleep. Finally, he crawled back into his bed and lay down, trying to relax and feel the earth rotating. He realized the bed was not lined up right; it needed to be on an axis of north-south.

He scrambled out and pulled it around so that the foot was pointing south. When he went to dive back in, he stumbled over the large leather suitcase Amos Flowers had deposited in his care. He thought to shove it under the realigned bed, but hesitated. He snapped on the light, unstrapped the bindings, pushed a brass key-holed button next to the GLH initials and opened it. A lariat, leather gloves, a thin Mexican horse blanket, a bridle, spurs. Sam lifted the riding gear out and pulled back a cloth partition. There, staring up at him with rubber bands across their faces, were piles of famous Americans: Jackson, Grant, Hamilton, Franklin, enough greenbacks to go to college for ten years. With a rough count Sam figured it totaled between fifty and sixty thousand.

He carefully repacked the suitcase, buckled the straps, and shoved it under his bed, then he turned off the light and stretched out on his back. He was sleeping on a fortune! He closed his eyes and tried to sense the rotation of the earth, his head swimming over whether Amos came by it honestly. Could he be arrested for keeping it and passing it on to Tom?

Feel the rotation, slowly, silently.

Monday morning Grandma was stewing over the paper with both pairs of glasses stuck on her face when Pete shuffled into the kitchen.

"Good morning, bright eyes. I was about to come and embalm you."

"What time is it?"

"Listen to what this boob says in the paper."

WILLOW CREEK CINDERELLA STORY OVER?

The Gardiner Bruins will be favored to turn Willow Creek's amazing comeback season into a pumpkin Monday night in Butte.

"Can you imagine the nerve of that dullard? I hope you win by thirty points tonight."

"We don't have anything like a challenge game in Minnesota," Pete said.

"A lot of teams have been bushwhacked in the challenge game. There's something about playing on Monday night that ain't natural."

"Did you call the doctor?" Pete said as he slid his weary body into a kitchen chair.

"Yeah, I called him yesterday. Listen to this."

Willow Creek has nothing to be ashamed of. They've played well, beaten some good teams, and come a long way from their recent legacy of defeat.

"Played well, huh! I'm going to call this moron up on Tuesday and send him a raspberry over the phone."

"It's better if Gardiner is favored," Pete said, as Tripod sprang into his lap. "We like being the underdog."

"Well, you came to the right place if you like being the underdog. Willow Creek spawns its own peculiar breed of underdogs."

"What did the doctor want?"

"Just routine stuff, as usual."

She cut the article out of the paper and taped it to the side of the refrigerator that looked like a bulletin board. There was no longer any room on the door.

"Let's stick that up there so we can have a good laugh all next week. I think I'll get everyone in town to send the guy a pumpkin, with the score written on it."

"Yeah, and we could fill the pumpkins with bullshit, *real* bullshit."

The two of them laughed as they planned their retaliation against a poor, dense newspaper reporter. But Pete felt the butterflies gathering in his stomach. He wanted to talk to the other boys. He felt scared, but it wasn't about the game. It was something about Grandma.

CHAPTER 62

February lost its bite and people were beginning to believe that Willow Creek's basketball team had influenced the weather: heavy coats came off, dead batteries started, stock found winter grass on open ground, ice melted in river ponds, and frozen water lines thawed. Frozen hope and joy also thawed in the glow of the team's victories, pulling the community together again, bringing laughter and optimism into uncounted lives.

With the challenge game hanging over their heads, Sam sensed that the whole community had put life on hold, a town caught in amber as a fossil insect with its wings spread. The team had never advanced beyond the District Tournament.

On Monday, the gloom and cold returned in the form of mountain snow showers. Sam had sleepwalked through his eighth and ninth grade classes and was in a high state of anxiety to get on the road. In lieu of the school's fight song, Sam played the soundtrack from *Man of La Mancha* on the journey to Butte. It relaxed them, took their minds off the game, and the team sang along with the familiar score as snow flurries brought on the darkness.

Even Curtis and Dean picked up on it, and of course Scott, who had long before been dubbed Sancho. Pete came up front and knelt in the aisle to Miss Murphy, singing "Dulcinea" with his arms spread to her, and Olaf and the cheerleaders backed him up with the refrain. The music had its entertaining, soothing, happy effect, but as Sam guided Rozinante into the city, he slowed down, timing it so the soundtrack would be rendering the "Impossible Dream" finale as they pulled into the civic center parking lot. He swung open the doors, and into a swirling snow the boys came out of the bus on fire, the ultimate effect Sam was looking for.

When they were dressed and ready to go out onto the floor to warm up, Sam had them sit on the benches.

"When I was a boy we had an ice storm," he told them. "I had been looking forward to going to the movie *Butch Cassidy and the Sundance Kid* on Saturday afternoon. My mother said I had to chip the ice off the sidewalk before I could go, that we could be sued if someone fell and got hurt. It was a couple inches thick and we had a long sidewalk. There was no way around it. So I took the ice chipper and went out and chipped like a madman. But my mind wasn't on the ice. The ice was something that was in the way. As I chipped, I was already sitting in the theater, eating popcorn, and enjoying *Butch Cassidy and the Sundance Kid*."

Sam paused, glancing at each of them.

"Do you want our journey to end here in the cold?"

"*Nooooo!*" they shouted.

"Do you want to give up here on a lousy Monday night?"

"*Noooo!*"

"All right. Gardiner is the ice. The Divisional Tournament is the movie. Let's go chip ice!"

"*Yeeaaahhhh!*" they responded, and Sam opened the door, releasing them into the long concrete corridor.

Tom had run off and forgotten his J. Chisholm diamondback boots under a bench. Sam hesitated as Scott hustled after the team. Diana closed the door and turned to him. They embraced, hugging each other fiercely.

"No matter what happens tonight, those boys will be all right," she said softly, her mouth beside his ear. "You've respected them for the remarkable boys they are. Now they've come to believe in themselves. Nothing that happens out there can take that away from them."

Sam could not respond. He gave her a squeeze and released her, trying to locate his contacts in his sloshing eyes. He opened the door. They went into the arena, knowing that's where they would find their heartbeat.

The Butte Civic Center seemed colder than usual, as though someone had forgotten about the challenge game and neglected to turn up the thermostat. Sam was startled by the number of people behind the Willow Creek bench, far outnumbering the Gardiner fans, who had to come some hundred and twenty miles further. Or was it that the Gardiner faithful felt confident that their Bruins would eliminate Willow Creek as usual and were saving their gas and motel money for the Divisional Tournament? Andrew had rented two fifty-passenger buses and he had vowed he would fill them both. Scanning the crowd, Sam spotted Truly Osborn, John English, Amos Flowers, and Denise Cutter.

Neither coach came unprepared, and Gardiner jumped into a trapping zone press, attempting to force the Broncs into costly turnovers. Sam hadn't been asleep all weekend either, and he crossed up Fred Sooner's brain circuits by starting Dean at guard and moving Rob to a forward. Rob's tremendous rebounding ability would be enhanced with him closer to the basket. This also wrecked Gardiner's plan at matching up with the Willow Creek players, and Rob ended up with a forward who lacked the foot speed and quickness to stay with him. And then there was Tom, resting his knee on the bench and itching to get into the contest.

With the excellent athletes Gardiner had, the Bruins concentrated on double-teaming Olaf and crowding Rob and Pete. This left Curtis basically unattended. The gangly boy had become a seasoned player through their schedule, and he drilled his first shot.

It became a superb high school basketball game with fans from both sides cheering, groaning, and slapping high fives. Dean drove two Gardiner guards nearly batty with his pestilent pressing and the Norwegian hammer was dominating the paint. Gardiner rotated fresh men into the game and Sam tried to hold the pace down, using his timeouts judiciously and alternating Tom and Dean to keep their defense off balance. At the half it was Gardiner 31, Willow Creek 29.

The locker room was quiet. Everyone tried to swallow their fear and act normal, avoiding the terrible concept of sudden death. They iced Tom's knee and the jittery boys listened as Diana informed them of how many fouls they each had, Dean in the most trouble, with three. Sam tried to combat the mental strain by speaking quietly to them individually, praising them, instructing, calming, when inside a horrendous storm assailed his vitals. He had the sensation of being so close he could touch it and yet being so far.

The moment arrived when they had to go out and play what could be their final half of basketball. Sam searched the concrete walls for words, any words, but the pressure became numbing. Then Pete, in a high-pitched Dick Vitale whine, interrupted the silent trance.

"Coach, could you tell us what's the key to winning this game?"

Sam could have hugged him, he'd done it.

"Well, it's quite complicated, you see. The key is for us to have more points at the end than they do."

Dean chuckled, then Olaf. Smiles spread among them. The boys rose off the benches and shouted, firing each other up. Tom glared into his team-mates' faces.

"There's no way we're going to lose this game."

"Yeah, let's go chip ice!" Pete said.

"Yeeaaahhhh!"

Sam paused and allowed them to rush through the cement corridor into the unknown.

THE SECOND HALF became an accounting of time. It became a free fall in which you had no way of knowing if your parachute would open at the end, or if indeed you had a chute. Olaf slid down the lane and stuffed one and Willow Creek crept to within three. Kenny Green, their thin, quick guard, hit a jumper from the side and the Bruins were back up by five. The ebb and flow drained them all, players, spectators, and coaches, parceling out hope and snatching it back, filling them with optimism then turning it into dread, at once promising victory then flaunting defeat.

"Four!" Sam shouted. "Set it up! Four! Four!"

Dean fouled out in the middle of the fourth quarter, but with Tom and Dean alternating throughout the game, Tom's knee was rested. Tom nodded at Sam and carried his fire onto the court. Olaf, Tom, and Rob ravaged the defensive boards time after time, giving the Bruins only one shot, and Sam thought he could feel a slight shift in the momentum, a faint turning of the tide. Diana was hoarse from shouting and no one in the civic center was in his seat when Tom Stonebreaker faked his man inside and pulled up for a short jumper. Willow Creek was ahead by one with fifty-three seconds on the clock! Sam leaped from his crouch at the edge of the floor, pumping a fist in the air.

"Blow them away! Blow them away!"

Gardiner hustled into the front court and attacked the Willow Creek zone, snapping the ball around the outside.

"De-fense! De-fense! De-fense!" the Willow Creek fans roared.

A pass inside. The 6'4" McShane put up a quick shot, but Olaf rose into the air and swatted it away. Willy Lawrence, his black curly hair matted with sweat, recovered the ball and squared up to the basket from beyond the three-point line. Open for a moment, his graceful shot went home. Gardiner 68, Willow Creek 66. Thirty-seven seconds.

Gardiner gave up their zone press and fell back tight, guarding against a breakaway layup. The Willow Creek faithful hung onto one another and held their breath. Pete brought the ball up quickly. The Bruin defenders swarmed, playing it tight, forcing the Broncs out on the floor. Olaf cut across the middle, looking for a high pass, and two defenders rode him like a horse. This left Curtis alone on the side. He broke down the baseline and Pete sent a special delivery with a bounce pass. With everyone in the arena standing and shouting, Curtis caught the ball, dribbled once on his way to the basket, and hit the backdoor off the glass. Kenny Green crashed into him trying to deny the layin.

The Willow Creek crowd exploded. Tie game, with Jenkins at the free-throw line for one shot. Fourteen seconds on the clock.

"Time out when he makes the shot!" Sam shouted to Rob. "Time out when he makes the shot!"

At the line, with the Gardiner fans roaring their distraction, Curtis bounced the ball three times. He twirled the ball in his hands and spread his fingers on the seams. Looking at the ball, he took a deep breath and slowly exhaled. He flexed his knees and raised his vision to fix it on the rim. With a spring in his legs and a flip of his wrist, he propelled the dimpled leather toward the basket. It fell as true as sunlight.

Willow Creek 69, Gardiner 68.

The rabid townsfolk cheered and danced up and down, high-fiving and slapping their neighbor on the back. Gardiner called time out, and the Broncs came to the bench, drenched in sweat and eager to finish it.

"Listen up," Sam said with his heart thundering in his ears. "Tight zone, everybody moving, hands up, make them throw it from the band seats. And when they do . . ."

He paused and regarded each of them.

"When they do, we put five bodies on the boards. They only get one shot. Don't foul. When you get the rebound, clear it quickly. They'll try to foul you. They'll try to stop the clock." Sam clapped his hands. "Okay, let's punch the ticket to Helena!"

With arms out, legs slightly bent, feet moving, and eyes focused, they met Gardiner bringing the ball upcourt with fourteen seconds remaining. Swiftly, the well-disciplined Bruins moved the ball around the perimeter of the zone with crisp passing. Kenny Green came across and put a pick on Rob. Rob tried to slip around it but Willy Lawrence was open for a blink. The courageous Gardiner senior faced up and took the jump shot with nine seconds left. All eyes followed the arc of the ball; all hearts hesitated; time stopped breathing.

Though it looked true, the ball carried the burden of the shooter's doubt. It hit the back of the rim and bounced high in front of the basket. Inside his man, Rob tracked the ball with unflinching eyes, timed his leap, and elevated above the desperate tangle of outstretched arms and bodies. For an instant he controlled the ball with fingertips above the others. But rather than try to grab it, he flipped it toward the other end of the floor to the shocked surprise of everyone in the building.

Seven seconds.

The ball hit at midcourt and bounced away.

Six seconds.

The players on both teams stood transfixed for an instant with the bouncing, unattended ball draining the clock. The Willow Creek fans began to grasp the meaning of what was transpiring on the floor. Their roar came on like a wind storm. Two Gardiner players, with agony in their faces, raced after the fleeing ball as if it were their life's blood. The ball bounced and bounced and then rolled away, squandering the final seconds of their life as a team.

Five seconds . . . four seconds . . . three seconds.

Ben McShane caught up with the ball just before it rolled out of bounds. Frantically he turned and fired a pass to Willy Lawrence near the center of the court. The desperate boy caught the ball, but before he could whirl and launch a shot, the buzzer cut through the thunderous uproar.

The Willow Creek boys embraced Curtis in wild jubilation while their fans went berserk. The stunned Gardiner players held their heads in their

hands and slumped to their knees before the ashen faces of their disbelieving followers. Sam and Diana hugged each other and were swiftly smothered by the outpouring of rollicking spectators. Sam thought he caught a
glimmer of tears in Fred's eye as Coach Sooner took Sam's hand and shook
it vigorously.

"Good job, Sam. Your boys deserved it. Go get 'em at Divisional."

"Thanks, Fred. You have a fine bunch of boys."

The burly mentor plowed through the crowd, trying to keep an unper-
turbed exterior. Diana and Sam fought their way to the boys. They had
done it! They had won on Monday night and would go on to Helena. They
huddled in a tight circle, face to face.

"Hey, coach, we cleaned the sidewalk!" Pete shouted.

"For the Twin Bridges I am looking!" Olaf yelled.

"They're slamming off their radios in Twin Bridges right about now,"
Sam said. "They can't shake us. We'll be a reoccurring nightmare they can't
escape. We'll be a boil on their ass. We'll be a disease they can't cure. We'll
keep coming and coming and coming. If we can't be better than them, we'll
outlast them. We'll *never* quit. We'll *never* give up! We'll *never* give in!"

"Yeeaaahhhh!" they shouted, and the huddle bounced along the hardwood court. "Win! Win! Win! Win! Win!"

AXEL SPREAD THE word that the Blue Willow would be open
until the last dog died, and everyone hurried the sixty miles through the
melting slush to bring their bright victory home and unwrap it in Willow
Creek. By ten-thirty it was hard to find a parking place within a block or
more of the inn. Cars and pickups inundated the vacant land around the
railroad tracks. During the last part of the trip the team had given in to
their exhaustion, becoming quiet and allowing it all to sink in. But when
Sam cocked the bus door open in front of the Blue Willow, allowing them
to spill out and into the humming inn, the wild cheers and excitement that
welcomed them rekindled their enthusiasm and relit their pilot lights.

"They're here! They're here!" Grandma Chapman shouted, plowing
through the crush to her grandson. Amos Flowers slapped Tom on the back
and the two cowboys regarded each other with affirming smiles.

"I told ya, I told ya, by God!" Rip shouted.

With standing room only, the game continued nonstop through instant replay in their minds, festooned with drama and flaring color, tapes that would be stored in their memories. People stood taller. Voices rang with confidence. The unacquainted smiled and chattered and laughed freely. Celebrants patted the boys on the back and praised them, offering to stuff them with anything available on the menu. The elation permeated the inn like fresh oxygen, uplifting them, giving the timid voice, the downhearted joy. Everyone within miles of Willow Creek had clambered on the bandwagon, standing on the running boards, sitting on the fenders, clinging to the roof, boasting they'd been riding there all along.

Almost speechless, Sam sat at a table people vacated in deference to him, absorbing this rare moment. He was trying desperately to enjoy this for all it was worth while at the same time frantically praying that this wasn't the fulfillment of their quest, that they still had miles to go before they slept.

Lost in the mingling crowd for the moment, he felt numb, as though he were floating above it all, drifting, giddy, in a state of consciousness over which he had no control. For this moment in his life, he was insulated against the struggles and loss to come by the celebrating Willow Creekians and the triumph of his team. He attempted to stay in the present moment, to relish it. The sounds around him seemed far off, the milling people hazy, and time had no meaning. He was drunk. Sam Pickett was intoxicated with the true nectar of the gods, and his only thought was a plea for mercy that it would not be his only taste. For the first time he heard someone else entertain the lunacy that had recently taken root in his heart.

"If they keep playing like this, these boys could make it to State." Grandma Chapman wove through the crush toward him, heading for the door. "Good game, Coach. The boys done like you showed 'em."

Sam smiled at her. "You're not leaving already are you?"

"I'm afraid so. This winning is harder on me than losing."

Sam tracked her brown felt hat as she walked out the door. He understood.

Someone started the school song, and the cheerleaders picked up the beat and led the way with their strained and croaking voices. Many didn't know all of the words or even some of them, but they hummed along and made up their own. Diana made her way through the boisterous fans and slid in next to Sam.

"You see what you've done?" She waved her hand at the crowd.

"That's what's so strange, I don't think I have anything to do with it."

When exhaustion and the late hour finally propelled most of them toward their pillows, Axel got off his feet and dropped his body heavily into a chair beside Sam, removing his robust demeanor like an apron. He leaned close, and Sam picked up the aroma of fried onions and accrued fear. In a subdued mood, Axel spoke as though the man didn't want others to hear.

"I tell you, Sam, I'd need a night like this every week to keep it going. Once the basketball season is over, we just won't make it."

"I'm sorry to hear that. This place means a lot to the town."

"Just not enough people. We've tried to draw them from the valley, but we're off the beaten path, too far off."

"What'll you and Vera do?"

"I don't know, it's a worry, we'll try to keep it going as long as we can. Maybe something will happen." He sighed. "You know, all my life I thought something would 'happen,' something would come through. It never did."

"Well, the boys'll try to give you a few more nights like this," Sam said, attempting to lift the brawny man out of the despair.

"Thanks, that would help."

"The past few years I used to feel that way with the boys, when there was no way we could win, that we were just going through the motions on a sinking ship."

"Vera and I are scared, Sam. It's hard to get started again when you're our age. Sometimes it seems to us that that's all life is . . . just rearranging furniture and keeping house on the deck of the *Titanic*."

They sat silently for a minute. Then Axel rubbed a hand across his bald dome.

"What the hell, Sam," he said. "Here I am crying in my beer when you've just taken us to the Divisional Tournament! What more could we ask for, and by God, our boys aren't finished yet. We're going to kick ass up in Helena, aren't we, Sam? You betcha, we're going to *kick ass*."

It was after two in the morning when Sam made his way home down the middle of Main Street. With the slush from the snow squalls melting quickly, a steady southwesterly blew in his face and a williwaw of emotion whirled in his stomach. Axel's mood clung to him as premonition. By God, he wasn't going to let it go down after coming this far.

CHAPTER 63

Everyone at school on Tuesday trudged through the schedule of regular classes though their minds and spirits had already packed their bags and run off to Helena. At the Blue Willow things were no different. The inn, normally quiet during the day, was hopping, and quickly became a rallying point for the community.

Newspapers had taken note of the upstart team from the southwest corner of the Gallatin Valley. The *Billings Gazette* called them "a likeable underdog that didn't have the needed troops to survive the trench warfare at Divisionals." The Butte paper described their Monday night victory as "a courageous effort by an outmanned team that won with savvy and guts." The *Bozeman Daily Chronicle* shared its surprise that the perennial losers had ousted the likes of Manhattan Christian and Gardiner but hinted that every year there's a fluke or two.

AFTER SCHOOL SAM had several items to finish at his desk before he joined the boys in the gym for practice. He heard what sounded like two or three kids scuffling in the hall and he knew who was coming before Dean floundered through the doorway. Something was up.

"What's the matter, Dean?" Sam asked softly, standing from behind his desk.

"I got something to tell you," the boy said. He stared at his worn-down work boots. The silence began to suffocate Sam.

"What?"

"It's my fault that Tom's knee is so bad."

"What?" Sam asked.

"It's my fault," the freshman insisted, glancing hang-doggedly into Sam's face.

"How do you figure that?"

Dean shifted from foot to foot, tugging his tattered Kamp Implement cap over one ear. "I got Curtis to go with me after the game Saturday morning."

"What's that got to do with Tom's knee?"

"Well, we were supposed to go right back to the motel. I got Curtis to go to McDonald's with me. I didn't have any money."

"Dean, you're not making any sense."

"Well, if we'd gone right back to the motel them guys wouldn't have started to beat us up."

"What guys?"

"Three guys. They pushed us in an alley. Scott was catching up and he saw them. They started slapping Curtis and was going to beat us up. But Scott ran and got Tom and Tom smacked the fat guy, you should've seen it, and then the other guys came and Pete pounded one kid to pieces and Rob smashed the other kid and they beat up all three of them until they turned chicken shit and ran away and the fat kid had bad breath—"

"Wait a minute, wait a minute," Sam said. "This all happened in Butte Saturday *morning*?"

"Yeah, while you was at the mall, and Tom got kicked and Pete and Rob hurt their hands and I know that's why Tom's knee is so bad, and if I hadn't got Curtis and Scott to go to McDonald's, Tom's knee would be okay."

Sam slowly eased himself into his chair. "Why are you telling me this, Dean?"

"'Cause something bad will happen to me if I don't."

"What do you mean?"

"If I don't do right, I'll be punished, God'll be mad at me."

"Is that what you believe?"

"Yeah, He will."

"Well, you didn't do anything wrong. It wasn't your fault that those goons, whoever they were, threatened you. It wasn't wrong for you to go to McDonald's."

Dean stared out of his thick lenses at his coach, his self-reproach retreating from his face, and Sam felt a fierce hatred for the dehumanizing vicissitudes of life that offer no amnesty to unprotected children.

"You have done nothing wrong, Dean, so don't worry about it."

"Sometimes I think I'll end up like my sister."

"Why?"

"When I do something bad. Sometimes when I feel sick, or my legs hurt, I get scared. I think I'm gettin' it too."

"Dean, I don't think you can get what Denise has."

"They just say that so I won't be scared, but I know I can."

Sam rose from his squeaking wooden swivel chair and stepped from behind his desk. He put his arm around the boy's shoulders and walked him toward the door.

"Thanks for telling me about the fight. I won't mention it to anyone, but I'm proud of all of you. You are a terrific kid and I'm happy as hell that you're on the team. We couldn't win without you."

Sam stopped at the doorway and squeezed Dean's shoulder.

"You go dress now. I'll be right down. Okay?"

"Okay."

In his scruffy patched jeans and shirt, the bandy-legged hatchling lit out down the hallway. Sam watched him go. He was an English teacher. What did he know about confession and forgiveness and the love of God? Maybe the gullible schoolboy was closer to the truth than Sam. All he knew at that moment was that he loved the Cutter kid.

WITH SCHOOL OUT, the boys were relieved to arrive at practice and reaffirm—after agonizing through the day—that they could still hit a jump shot or find out if, as they feared, they had lost all ability to do anything with the dimpled leather. Sam showed up with a new curiosity in his boys, and he observed them with a growing admiration and sense of humor.

Sam had seen the boys on the brink of debilitating exhaustion Monday night and he wanted them to recharge. At practice, he and Diana had them stretch and warm up with light running, but nothing that would wear them down and sap their endurance. Tom sat and watched much of the time. They worked through offensive sets with a spirited enthusiasm, and Sam could sense a growing confidence in them, a sense that they were a tournament team.

Though Grandma said she wasn't feeling up to it, Diana, Dean, and Scott played defense, as well as Axel—who showed up in those ancient black high-tops that after forty years had come back into fashion. Sam wanted to run picks and screens that would free each of the boys to positions where they were most comfortable and most consistent shooting the ball. People began drifting into the gym and settling in the bleachers. At first it was only a handful, but the stands along the east wall began filling and the spectators began clapping when a shot was made. They cheered as though the team were playing an invisible opponent in the Divisional Tournament. Most amazing to Sam was the fact that John English and Truly Osborn were sitting there totally absorbed watching not a run-of-the-mill conference game, not a tournament game, but a *practice*. He blew his whistle and gathered the boys at midcourt.

"Get a good night's sleep, eat well, and we'll see you tomorrow in school. We've drawn Noxon for the second afternoon game on Thursday. I don't know anything about them except they have a 17–3 record, so they must know how to toss the pumpkin in the well. We're staying through Saturday night so you'll have to bring a change of underwear."

Sam glanced at each of them, their faces bursting with happiness and anticipation, and he yearned to possess some magical power that would capture this moment and make it last for the rest of their lives.

"We're going to have fun in Helena. But remember how much fun it is to play better than you can, that besides staying in motels and eating in restaurants and hanging out in the city, the only thing you'll *always* remember will be how you played. We're going to remember how we won."

"Yeeaaahhhh!" the boys shouted and the spectators applauded and cheered.

"Are there any questions?" Sam said.

"Are there any McDonald's in Helena?" Dean said.

Everyone laughed.

"Yes, Dean, there is at least one McDonald's," Sam said, "and you can have McBreakfast and McLunch and McDinner if you want."

"I want McNoxon," Pete said.

"I want a Divisional McChampionship," Rob said.

"I want McStone's McBalls," Tom said, but so quietly only the huddle at midcourt could hear him.

"Ya, the Twin McBridges I am wanting," Olaf said with an uncharacteristic steely-eyed glare. They shouted and clapped, a gesture that spread to the bleachers where soon everyone was standing and applauding with the boys. The spontaneous outpouring touched a nerve in all of them, and a chant rose against the confines of the gymnasium's block walls and wood-beamed ceiling.

"Twin Bridges! Twin Bridges! Twin Bridges! Twin Bridges!"

Sam stood observing the fervor of his team and their boosters, painfully reminded that Twin Bridges would travel to Helena, too, leaving their coach with a McLump in his stomach.

GRANDMA KNELT ON a chair with her elbows on the kitchen table. She was working a jigsaw puzzle when Pete sauntered in and slid into a chair.

"Hungry?" she said without looking up, wearing two pair of glasses.

"A little."

He picked up a piece and pressed it in place. She took off one pair of glasses and looked at him. "Get your homework done?"

"Yeah, just some fishy math."

"Fishy?"

"Every time I get close to Mr. Grant I can smell fish—even some of the papers he hands back smell fishy."

"That's all that's keeping him here: brookies, browns, and cutthroat."

Grandma got up and cautiously opened the door of the refrigerator, casting one eye to see if Pete had the transmitter in hand. She took out a half gallon of milk, poured a glass, and set it on the table.

"Thanks," he said.

"Miss the dance?" Parrot squawked from the front room.

"I forgot to cover that mangy bird. I wonder if it will ever remember its old lines?"

"Maybe he knows he's going to die and he's cleaning up his act," Pete said. He pulled his feet onto the chair with his knees under his chin.

"He'll probably outlive me and you and the whole town," she said.

She kneeled on the chair and slipped on the second pair of glasses, studying the puzzle.

"I talked to your mother today. I told her to get out here and watch you make history."

"What did she say?"

"Didn't think she could get away. I told her to call your dad. He and I never did see eye to eye. It's a shame they aren't seeing this."

She picked up a piece and tried to force it.

"Does it bother you to see the other parents at the games?"

"Naw, Tom's don't come, and Olaf's aren't here. They don't even know he's playing."

"And yet," she said, glancing up at him over her glasses, "the Painters never miss and Olaf isn't even their son."

She worked the puzzle and Pete drained the glass of milk.

"Are Tom and Dean going to stay eligible?" she asked.

"I hope so. With Tom it's just U.S. history, with Dean it's every course he's taking."

"He's not a stupid kid."

"No, he just goofs around and never studies."

She plopped the glasses on the table and stood stiffly. "I'm worn out, time to hit the hay."

She was in the front room when Pete spoke.

"Grandma."

"Yes." She paused and turned to regard him.

"It bothers me, the other parents at the games. It bothers me a lot."

She stepped back into the kitchen.

"You wouldn't be human if it didn't."

"But when I'm bumming about it, before a game, I look over at Denise and then I'm okay and I want to win for her, for all of us."

"You're a sweetheart, Peter Strong. This has been the best year of my life, thanks to you." She bit her lip and turned away.

When the lights were out and they were in bed, Pete called.

"Good night, Grandma!"

"Good night, Pete!"

Silence. Then he called again.

"Good night, Parrot."

"Good night, Parrot," Grandma said.

"Good night, Tripod."

"Good night, Tripod."

"Good night, John Boy," he called.

"Good night, Jim Bob!" she shouted.

Peter could visualize the Waltons' house going dark and hear the theme music at the program's end. He missed his father. Just once he wanted his father to run out onto the floor after a game and hug him and tell him how proud he was.

"Good night, Dad," he whispered.

Tripod leaped onto the bed and curled up beside him.

AFTER ANOTHER LIGHT practice Wednesday, Diana and Sam went to the Blue Willow for dinner. She stopped for her mail at Mavis Powers's post office while Sam got them a table, no easy task with everyone at this end of the valley hanging around the inn. He found a small one on the tavern side next to the pool table and settled there, contemplating the next opponent. He had to look up Noxon on a map, a small dot on a secondary highway along the Montana boarder with Idaho, sheltered from the west by the Bitterroot Mountain Range. He knew that northwest Montana country had a history of logging, and he guessed that many of the boys on Noxon's team had fathers with family histories of cutting down magnificent jack or red pine.

He waved at Diana when she came in looking for him. She hurried to the table, peeling off her coat and giggling like a child.

"I got the job! San Diego, they hired me! I don't believe it, the school I told you about, they have a class in oceanography. Oh, Sam, I can't believe it. Do you know how many applicants they'd get for an opening like that?"

She waved the letter in the air and glowed in a way he'd never seen, shaking her long hair out of her face and waiting for his response.

"That's terrific. I knew you'd get it."

He fought furiously to keep the dying smile on his face, and he wished he had his old glasses on to hide his eyes.

They ordered and ate. She talked about San Diego and he tried to subdue the dread and sorrow in his chest. Would it only be a season for them, too? Would he go to San Diego with her? Would she ask him to?

"Hey, you two. Hiding in a corner?" Andrew said as he approached from the packed dining room.

"Hello," Sam said, trying to regain his composure and thinking how much he and Andrew had in common, each sitting in the Blue Willow with the woman he loved and then losing her forever.

"Everything's taken care of. The team has reservations at the Colonial through Saturday night. A lot of us will be staying there, too."

"Thanks, Andrew," Sam said. "That's a pretty fancy joint."

"Nothing's too good for the team. Hell, how many times will we get this chance? Is there anything else you need?"

Sam could think of several but Andrew couldn't provide them. "No, nothing I can think of right now."

"Great, if I don't see you before, I'll see you at the game."

OUTSIDE THE INN, he kissed her at her car. She didn't have her heart in it.

"Can I come out later?" he asked.

"Oh, gosh, I think we both need a good night's sleep. Besides, I'm going to call my folks. They'll be excited, I think, and a couple friends. I hope I'm ready to go back to San Diego."

She drove away, and he knew there was something he needed much more than a good night's sleep. He had thought they were seeking some mutual stability in their lives, some firm ground in one another, when in reality they were simply cosmic specks being hurled into outer space at the speed of light. It was a familiar turn of events in his life, feeling as though he didn't matter to someone who mattered so much to him, including her in his plans when he wasn't included in hers. He noticed the bicycle built for two in the shadows leaning against the wall. He rolled it off the porch and pedaled up Main toward the school. Andrew was right. Sam caught a whiff of lavender. Could he pedal all the way to San Diego?

THE TEAM AND cheerleaders scurried to pack the bus with their suitcases and overnight bags for three nights in Helena. Everyone had arrived except Dean. With the added luggage, Rozinante was stuffed. Sam had them get aboard when he spotted the Cutters' old red pickup banking up Main from the south. The Ford rattled to a stop and Dean jumped out. He dashed to the bus, dripping wet with perspiration and hugging a brown grocery sack containing his entire traveling wardrobe. Sam nodded through the bus window at Sally Cutter and everyone cheered as the nearsighted freshman plopped into the right front seat next to Curtis. Sam closed the doors and made a U-turn in front of the school. He honked continuously as they rolled down Main past United Methodist, Willow Creek Tool, the volunteer fire barn, and the Blue Willow. People hurried out onto the porch of the inn and waved, they themselves about to lock up the town and hit the road north.

Out of Three Forks they crossed the interstate and headed up the two-lane highway for the state capitol, singing and jabbering with a boisterous, happy confidence. The Missouri River, timelessly emerging from a watery womb here at its headwaters, frolicked in its infancy alongside the highway.

There were eight basketball teams riding the highways that morning, meaning to strike it rich in the tournament's last-chance gulch, where losing meant going home.

Scott scrambled around in the aisle, jammed as it was with legs and luggage. He looked beneath the seats, behind the back row, under feet and baggage. Then he stumbled to the front and whispered in Dean's ear. The Dutch Boy leaped out of his seat.

"We forgot our balls!" Dean shouted. "We forgot our balls!"

"Okay, okay," Sam said, keeping his eye on the road. "Calm down, calm down. Is that true, Scott?"

"Yeah," Scott said sheepishly. "I forgot 'em in the gym."

"It's okay. They'll have some we can use up there," Sam said. "We can't go back for them."

"I've got mine," Pete said, holding up the ball he constantly kept under his arm.

"Good. That's one we can practice with," Diana said.

"I've got mine," Tom exclaimed.

No one said a word, turning to see if the bull rider held up a basketball. Empty-handed, he regarded them with a wry grin. Then a ripple of laughter and whispers circulated through the crammed little bus. Sam wanted to say it out loud, deferring because of the girls present, but the one thing they better not have left behind was their balls.

CHAPTER 64

Elizabeth Chapman's stomach fluttered when Hazel wheeled her '76 Caprice into the parking lot at the Carroll College Sports Center. Hazel had piloted the faded-green gas guzzler from Willow Creek with Mavis, Grandma, and Mildred Thompson hitchhiking along, not to mention Tripod. They had talked her out of bringing Parrot. Grandma hustled them through the bright, spacious lobby of the modern facility, wanting to be there in time to watch the boys warm up. They giggled like school girls as Grandma smuggled Tripod through, concealed in her jacket.

"A lady my age has strange lumps all over her body," she said.

The gym was bigger than a barn and had enough seats for their whole county. Grandma waved at Denise in her wheelchair at the end of the court as the four of them found seats in the bleachers up behind the Willow Creek bench.

Out on the floor Seely-Swan was sending Ennis into the losers' bracket. Those two schools had mustered a good crowd for the opening Thursday afternoon game while the Willow Creek and Noxon sections had people steadily filing in. They were barely seated when the buzzer ended the first game. Grandma had seen enough to realize that Seely-Swan had a cracker-jack team, a team Willow Creek would meet tomorrow night if they could get by Noxon, but she caught herself counting chickens before they hatched. She settled between Hazel, who had pinned a gold ribbon on her ample blue sweatshirt, and Mavis, who wore a head scarf over her peach-colored hair and rollers. Grandma asked her why she didn't take the rollers out of her hair and Mavis said she was waiting for a special occasion. Grandma unzipped her Minnesota Twins jacket and Tripod stuck out his head. The tomcat viewed the bustling scene calmly, a soft, warm spot on her jittery stomach.

The Broncs came trotting onto the floor in their gold and blue sweats, and Grandma's heart leaped. Rob led the way with a basketball under arm and his teammates stringing behind. The Willow Creek section rose to its feet and cheered, and Grandma recognized more starkly how thin their lines were as the mere half-dozen of them ran a lap around the court. The Noxon fans whooped it up when their team entered from the opposite end in red and white warm-up suits. There seemed to be so many more of them. Mr. Pickett, Miss Murphy, and Scott made their way to the bench with their paraphernalia in the midst of the turmoil. Rob peeled off at midcourt and headed for the west basket, went high, and nearly dunked the ball, bringing oohs and aahs from the hometown fans as the ball hammered off the iron. When Olaf, in turn, jammed it with authority, a response of awed respect rose from all sections of the arena.

The spectators settled in their seats for the warm-ups and the Noxon boys couldn't help peering downcourt at the towering athlete from Willow Creek. Miss Murphy instructed the Broncs in their stretches and Mr. Pickett paced in front of the bench with obvious jitters. Neither of them would be in Willow Creek for long, but Grandma was glad they'd been there for Peter. The coaches looked classy in their matching shirts and pants, and she thought Mr. Pickett appeared more manly, darn right handsome, without his glasses. He ought to marry that girl, those two youngsters surviving alone in this unpredictable world.

Noxon's tallest seemed to be about 6'3" and they were a clean-cut-looking bunch of boys.

"They look awful tough to me," Hazel said.

Why did she always sit with her pessimistic friend? She knew Hazel wanted to win as badly as any of them, but Hazel harped on the negative as though she wanted to beat disappointment to the punch. The Willow Creek boys shot around and Peter scanned the crowd for her. She stood and pulled off her brown fedora, waving it in the air. He spotted her and his face brightened. She pulled on her hat and wiggled her fingers down her cheeks, their sign language that his play would bring tears to her eyes. Satisfied, he went back to the business of zeroing in his shooting eye. He joked that as long as she sat next to Hazel Brown he could always locate her in the ever-increasing crowds.

The buzzer called the teams to their benches. Grandma felt a lump in her throat and her heart increased its beat. She strained her voice when they introduced her grandson, and before she could catch her breath, the teams were circled for the opening jump. The referee tossed the ball. The Noxon center didn't bother to jump, and Olaf tipped the ball to Peter. Grandma inched to the edge of her seat as her grandson brought Willow Creek up the floor into the Divisionals, into the emotional roller coaster of high school tournament basketball.

With the Noxon boys swarming around him, Olaf missed his first shot. The Red Devils sprinted upcourt with the ball, looking eager to show their stuff. They ran wide open, full throttle, almost a blur. They ran so well it was scary. Grandma was breathless just watching. They were a gambling team, often throwing a pass the length of the court, and though several went awry or were intercepted by the Broncs, just as many resulted in easy layups. Plain and simple, they were catching the Willow Creek boys a half step behind.

"We'll never keep up with this bunch," Hazel said. "We'll have tire tracks on our backsides."

Grandma hated to admit it, but the Broncs seemed tight and somewhat overwhelmed. Pete missed his first three shots, and the shorter Noxon boys were snatching rebounds, catching the Willow Creek boys flatfooted. Grandma bit her lip and clung to Tripod. She figured the Red Devils were well named, a team from hell that hounded and hustled and never stopped running.

At the end of the first quarter Noxon was on top, 19 to 13. The Broncs caught their breaths on the bench and tried to regroup. Mr. Pickett knelt in front of them, talking excitedly, scribbling on his clipboard.

"Come on, Broncs!" Grandma yelled. "You can do it!"

The three cheerleaders fired up the Willow Creek followers, but the second quarter was more of the same. Rob and Pete were hesitant with their shots, and more preoccupied with getting back on defense ahead of the Noxon riptide.

"They're gettin' away with murder on Olaf," Hazel said.

Tom tipped in one of Pete's missed shots and Curtis dove headlong into the seats to save a ball from going out of bounds. Both teams went at each other furiously. A sinking feeling grew in Grandma's chest.

"I knew I should have brought Parrot," she said.

Noxon rotated substitutes and they kept running. The Broncs were being overrun, and only Pete and Rob seemed able to keep up.

"I knew it was too good to be true," Hazel said. "Who are we trying to kid? This is the big leagues."

"It's too good not to be true," Grandma said.

She huffed and hoped and stewed on and off her seat. She flinched when Peter fell to the floor hard in a rebound attempt, groaned when Tom missed a free throw, winced when Curtis dropped a pass.

"It's not fair," Hazel said. "They're using twelve boys against our five."

"Mr. Pickett will figure something out."

"Huh, he'll have to suit us up," Hazel said. "I'd sure like a crack at those pantywaists."

Just before the half, one of the quick Noxon athletes came out tight on Pete. He crossdribbled and left the boy guarding his shadow as her sweetheart banged home the layup. Grandma leaped to her feet, almost catapulting Tripod out of her jacket.

"Attaboy, Peter, attaboy!"

When the halftime buzzer wailed, she was feeling somewhat better. Willow Creek 33, Noxon 41. Hazel went for popcorn and Diet Pepsi with the other girls. Grandma stayed to catch her breath in the stands and felt a little dizzy, as though she'd been running the court with the boys.

The Red Devils had been out shooting for a while and only one minute remained on the halftime clock when the Broncs trotted onto the floor. They shot a few layups until the buzzer summoned them to the bench.

"Look! Look at that!" Grandma shouted, elbowing Hazel and almost dumping her popcorn. "I told you Mr. Pickett would figure something out."

"What? What?"

"Dean! He's starting Dean instead of Curtis."

She was right. In the third quarter, Dean ran the floor with the Red Devils, both directions, slapping at the ball, knocking passes out of bounds, harassing, unrelenting. He looked as if on fast forward, never where he was supposed to be, and that disrupted the Noxon offense more than it did the Willow Creek defense. He didn't have the skills of the Noxon boys, but he had the lungs.

"Look at Dean, look at him!" Grandma shouted. "Mr. Pickett must have told him to skin that kid."

"He can't keep that up for long," Hazel said.

Dean became a nuisance, a pest, and though Noxon was up by ten, his disruptive play and constant ragging was taking the fun out of their party. He stuck to one of their best players like a migraine. Coach Pickett rotated Tom and Curtis and Olaf, giving them a rest on the bench, but Dean never stopped running.

"That Cutter kid is a maniac," Hazel said. "Look at him."

The Willow Creek crowd sprang to its feet when a Noxon boy lobbed the ball to the far end of the court. Dean and a Red Devil raced after it. Dean, with his knobby legs thrashing, beat the Noxon kid, snagged the ball, and hurled it back upcourt to Olaf. Olaf charged the unguarded basket and cannonaded the ball through the net.

"You betcha!" Axel roared.

Pete started upcourt, ducked back, and intercepted Noxon's inbounds pass. Only the boy who passed it in stood between Pete and the basket. He cross-dribbled twice and blew by him for the layup. Grandma knocked the popcorn out of Hazel's hand as she leaped to her feet, and the Noxon coach called time out.

"Attaboy! See that! See that!" Grandma shouted. "They're afraid of him with that fancy dribble. He faked that poor kid out of his manhood."

Willow Creek crept back to within five, thanks to Dean's freewheeling intimidation and Olaf's growing dominance in the paint.

"That Cutter kid is sand in their carburetor!" Grandma shouted. "Look at him. All twelve of them can't wear him down."

Dean gave his teammates the opportunity to hone in on the Noxon basket, and Rob and Pete began tearing out the bull's-eye with shimmering swishes. They pulled even at 55 late in the fourth quarter, and Grandma thought she was going to die. Even Hazel was starting to believe again. Dean fouled out with two minutes to go and it seemed that everyone in the building, except for the Noxon fans, stood and applauded the flinty, rockribbed freshman. He had derailed Noxon's run-and-gun express with his bulldogged endurance. Olaf got a tip-in when Pete missed from the side and Willow Creek went up by one. Grandma clutched Hazel's arm and hardly dared to watch. With a burst of slashing grace, her grandson stole a Noxon pass and the Broncs went into their four-corner stall. Noxon narrowly missed stealing the ball when Rob found Tom alone in the corner. The over-playing defense anticipated him going back out with it, but Tom put it on the floor and took it to the backboard, stunning the Noxon faithful and putting Willow Creek up by three. The hometown fans were on their feet roaring, and Grandma nearly crushed Tripod when she hugged Hazel. A gutty Noxon boy raced upcourt and heaved the ball as the Willow Creekians counted down the final seconds off the clock.

"Four! Three! Two! One! *Yeeaaahhh!*"

Noxon's desperate three-point heave sailed harmlessly into the bleachers. The buzzer embraced Grandma with the shuddering arms of joy, and the scoreboard was as pretty as a Christmas tree. She read it out loud.

"Noxon 58, Willow Creek 61!"

Grandma threw an elbow into Hazel. "Well, Miss Pessimism, what do you think *now*?"

"I think we're in the sweet sixteen and I damn near wet my pants."

Grandma sat, catching her breath for a minute, and watched the world spin around her. When the din gradually dropped away and the crowd slowly filed out of the glimmering gymnasium, Grandma saw Pete kneeling and talking to Denise Cutter. Dean, with his face aglow and dripping with sweat under that grubby cap, stood behind her, holding on to her chair like a sentinel, the unlikely monkey wrench in Noxon's hope for glory.

CHAPTER 65

Back at the Colonial Inn, a festive mood overflowed from the team's quarters. They occupied four rooms along one corridor, with Mr. Pickett having his own for the three-night stay and Miss Murphy bunking with the cheerleaders. The boys laughed and bantered loudly while getting ready for a victory dinner at Andrew Wainwright's expense.

"Stay and eat with us," Pete told Grandma.

"Thanks, sweetheart, but we have to get on the road. Mavis has to get back and Hazel doesn't like to drive after dark."

"Are you all right?" Pete regarded her with a worried look.

"I'm cookin'."

"You look a little pale."

"It's what you boys put us through before you decide to win."

"Will you be back tomorrow night?" Pete asked.

"Will the sun rise?"

"It's the seven o'clock game."

She ran her hand through his long hair.

"I like your pretty locks. When they fly around out on the floor they make you look like you're going faster."

"I am."

Happiness glowed effervescently on his face.

"Hi, Grandma," Dean said as he and Curtis blew by.

"Did you see Dean out there today?" Pete asked.

"Did I. What did Mr. Pickett put in his tank?"

"We gave him a new name, the Duracell Boy."

"He's riding an invisible horse, that's why he's so bow-legged," Tom said from the bed where he sat buffing his boots with a motel towel.

"Good game, Tom," she said. "How's the knee?"

"Feels great."

"I've got to go, the girls are waiting," she said to Pete. "You have fun tonight."

"We're going to the other games, see the competition."

"You were jim-dandy out there today, Grandson. I'll see you tomorrow when you crush Seely-Swan."

She squeezed his arm.

"See you tomorrow," he said, and she hurried down the corridor.

HAZEL DROPPED MAVIS and Mildred off in front of the post office. She throttled the grumbling Caprice up Main toward Grandma's house. It was after six and a murky dusk slid over the land.

"If you weren't a dear friend I would never ask," Grandma said from the back seat, "but could you drive me to Billings?"

"Billings!"

Hazel pulled over on the wrong side of the street in front of Grandma's house and stopped. She turned the best she could to look at her friend.

"You mean right now?"

"Yes. I have to get to the hospital."

"Oh, dear, what's the matter?"

"I'm sick, I'm quite sick."

"Shouldn't we go to Bozeman? It's much closer."

"No, please, I want to go to Billings. They know what to do with me."

"But that's a hundred and eighty miles!"

"Will you, please?"

"Of course, of course. Do you want anything from the house?"

"No, just toss Tripod in the door. No sense draggin' him along."

Hazel picked up the tomcat and hefted her freight from the car. In a moment she was back, settling into the frazzled seat and slamming the door. She pulled out and rumbled a U-turn.

"What's wrong with you, Elizabeth?"

"It's a long story. I want to sleep now."

Grandma curled up on the back seat, and Hazel headed out of town. She reached over the seat, and with a grunt or two, managed to pull a blanket over Grandma's body.

"Thank you," Grandma said weakly. "When you get to Billings Deaconess, have them call Doctor Gene Mack."

"Gene Mack, the friend you go to visit?"

"He's my doctor. He'll know what to do."

"Will you be all right till we get there?"

"I'll be all right, but don't dawdle."

Hazel filled the tank in Three Forks and kept her foot to the pedal, streaking the hundred and eighty miles across southern Montana on Interstate 90. With the speedometer bouncing between seventy-five and eighty, she prayed that the old '76 Caprice had one more run in it, and was horrified that her closest friend might be dying in the back seat.

ANDREW WAINWRIGHT HAD reserved a small banquet room at the Colonial Inn and filled the place with Willow Creekians. They feasted on a main course of prime rib and several varieties of pasta, at Diana's request.

After they were stuffed and had enjoyed reliving the game for more than an hour, Andrew loaded the team, coaches, and cheerleaders into a Hertz van, and they returned to the sports center to watch the other four teams in the evening games. They arrived in time to see the second half of the first game, in which Alberton took out White Sulphur Springs by eight points. They ducked out of the second game at halftime where Twin Bridges, looking unbeatable, was pummeling Charlo. When he pulled up in front of the Colonial lobby, Andrew left the van running and turned around in his seat.

"All grownups out," he said. "Anyone over twenty be gone."

Sam and Diana hesitated. Then Sam opened the door and the two of them stepped out of the van, somewhat baffled.

"I know a place in town where they have the biggest sundaes, banana splits, and malted milks in Montana and a million video games."

The kids cheered and Sam slid shut the van door. He and Diana stepped up onto the sidewalk at the entrance of the motel. Andrew hopped out of the van and hurried around to catch them.

"What time do you want them in bed?" he asked Sam.

"Oh, I think by midnight."

"They'll be there," Andrew said. "I figured you needed a little time off, a little time to yourself." He smiled and hustled into the waiting van.

"Who *is* that guy?" Diana asked, watching him go.

"Just a happy fan," Sam said. "Do you feel like a little time off?"

"Sounds wonderful. I'll be there in five minutes."

They headed through the lobby for their rooms.

THEY TOOK A hot shower in Sam's room.

"Wainwright is a baffling guy," Diana said, all wet and soapy.

"Not so baffling," Sam replied, standing under the spray behind her and rubbing the soap over her hips and belly.

"I get the feeling you know a lot more about him than I do."

He wrapped his arms around her from behind and held her tightly, the hot water caressing them. He didn't want to think about the sadness of Andrew Wainwright. He didn't want to look in the elephant's eye. And most of all, he didn't want to ever let her go.

She turned off the water and they dried each other with fluffy white towels. In the king-size bed they made love leisurely, gently, savoring the aroma and sight and feel of each other, a sense-inundating expedition into a succulent, undiscovered continent. He knew if he lived two lifetimes he'd never get enough of her, discover all of her, uncover the last of her secrets. He noticed the outline of the bikini on her belly had all but faded. When she had flown off in convulsing, shuddering starbursts and he had joined her with his own, Sam fell into a sound sleep.

SAM BOLTED UP in bed. "No-o-o!"

He realized he was dreaming; Diana sprung up beside him. "What's the matter?"

He flopped back into the pillows with grateful relief. "I was dreaming."

"You seemed terrified. What was it?"

"Oh . . . nothing." He caught his breath. "I was falling."

"I've had dreams like that," she said and she curled an arm over him, her warm breasts pressing against his chest. "I always wake up before I die."

"What time is it?" he asked.

She glanced at the clock on the nightstand. "Eleven-twenty."

"We better get dressed, they'll be coming back."

He pulled her to him and kissed her, praying that he'd always wake before she died.

WHEN THE GANG came rolling down the corridor and through the open door of the cluttered girls' room, they found Mr. Pickett and Miss Murphy going over the scorebook.

"What'cha been doin'?" Carter said, as the ten of them flooded into the room.

"Oh, working hard while you bums were out feeding your faces," Diana said. "Where's Mr. Wainwright?"

"He said good night in the lobby," Rob said.

"Did you have fun?" Sam asked.

"Yeah. Mr. Wainwright's a cool guy," Pete said. "He even took Dean to McDonald's."

"Not again," Diana said. "Dean, you'll turn into a McMuffin or something."

Dean chuckled, basking in the limelight.

"Listen up," Sam said. "Tomorrow, after breakfast, we'll go over some videos and talk about Seely-Swan. I know you realize that the game tomorrow is a huge leap on our journey. If we win it, we will be on the inside track to the State Tournament."

They shouted and chattered encouragements to each other.

Sam hesitated. He had dared to say it out loud for the first time to the team, unveiling the canvas he had painted with the oils of his deepest longings, hoping he hadn't irrevocably jinxed them. At first, he was surprised that no one raised their eyebrows at such a ludicrous statement, then he realized it was more of a normal thought now, here, in the semifinals of the Divisionals. It wasn't August. It was the twenty-second of February and they were no longer playing in Willow Creek but in Helena, the state capital, poised to take the next step on their implausible quest.

"You were all terrific today," Sam said. "Get to bed now. Dream that tomorrow you're going to be better."

"Yeah, and it wouldn't hurt to do a little stretching before you hit the sack," Diana chimed in. "Keep those bodies flexible."

Sam and the boys headed for their rooms after a round of good nights. After hours of celebrating, they were finally winding down. The team would have to be rested and strong for tomorrow. He only hoped that he would be able to sleep. He sensed something like vertigo of the soul, and heard a beer truck backing.

"HAZEL BROWN?"

A short, balding man in green hospital garb startled her.

She woke in an uncomfortable, undermanned chair for an hour or so in the second-story waiting room. She'd have preferred to wait out in the car and have someone come out and get her. Hospitals gave her the creeps. Though every effort was made to hide it, she could smell death right through the stainless steel, the antiseptic tiles, and the color-coordinated lobbies.

"I'm Doctor Gene Mack," the man said. "You got her here just in time."

"What's wrong with her?" Hazel asked.

"She's kept it a guarded secret. It was a good thing, asking you to bring her here. I convinced her that you'd have to know the truth. She needs someone to support her. She's a tough lady but she's human."

Hazel sensed a warmth in him, a genuine kindness in his voice and manner. "What's wrong with her?"

"She has leukemia."

"Oh God." Hazel caught her breath and covered her open mouth with one hand.

"I found it last summer. She comes in for treatment regularly. She put it off this time. I'm guessing it was because of her grandson's tournaments."

"What will happen to her?"

"Now? She'll be able to go home in a day or two, but, I'm sorry to say, she's right on schedule with my first prognosis. These things aren't precise, but she most likely won't live through the summer."

"O Jesus, Blessed Jesus." She looked into the doctor's benevolent face for some verification of the truth. "Are you sure? That woman has more energy and spunk than anyone in Willow Creek and you're tellin' me she's dying?"

"I'm sorry. She's a remarkable lady. She's learned how to take what life gives her and make the most of it."

"Do you know she's been playing basketball?"

"I wouldn't doubt it."

"Does she know about . . . this summer?"

"Yes, and that's her one burning hope, that her grandson doesn't find out. I hear she's been telling him that she's been visiting her dear friend, Gene Mack, in Billings. She says she's the only one her grandson's got and she couldn't bear it for him to know he was going to lose her, too."

"What can I do?" Hazel stood.

"You can be there for her. You can be someone who keeps her secret, someone she can talk to about it. She's carried this alone for too long."

"I'll be there, Doc. There's a lot of me to be there."

"Good," the gentle man in green said, and then he squeezed her arm.

"Can I see her now?"

"The nurse will come and get you. Elizabeth is sleeping. Would you like a cot?"

"Yes. That would help."

"I'll have someone bring one."

The doctor walked away and Hazel dropped onto the overmatched chrome chair. Her mind turned like a kaleidoscope, back over the past year, trying to sift through hidden meanings in Grandma's words or any hint of behavior that would indicate that her closest friend was dying. She could find none.

CHAPTER 66

S am couldn't sleep. He pulled on his sweats, jacket, and running shoes and ran out of the motel. Dawn glowed faintly over the eastern mountains. The streets were deserted. He could identify a high cloudiness. A slight breeze brought a mild caress from the southwest. Old crescent-shaped snow banks shrunk back on lawns and boulevards. The sidewalks were dry.

Sam pushed himself. Uphill. Panting. Time, which had been hurtling through his life of late, had suddenly screeched to a stop, as though breathless, exhausted, and now refusing to move a muscle. It seemed to Sam that they had beaten Noxon a month ago.

He sweated and racked his brain for strategies against Seely-Swan. He'd admitted to no one how good he thought the Blackhawks were. But they had to have a flaw, a vincibility, if he could only recognize it in time. And on top of that, the cache of Federal Reserve notes under his bed troubled him. He'd wanted to ask Amos about it yesterday—not indicating he had any idea of the stunning amount—but no opportunity had presented itself.

The day came on strong, invigorating him. The temperature was somewhere in the fifties. A patch of saucerlike clouds caught his attention. Diana had called them lenticular altocumulus. He smiled. She had become so much of his life. He would always remember the look on her face as she gazed skyward and first explained them to him while lying in the brown winter grass along the Jefferson. Regretfully he hadn't followed his impulse and pulled her into his arms, kissing her while the giant clouds sailed above. He would never forget their name in the same way he'd never forget the sea turtle hatchlings, the medial collateral ligament, or the Lightning Commander shock collar.

The streets were coming alive with pedestrians and traffic as Helena's citizens woke and hurried into the day. He circled back toward the motel, downhill, gliding. His body had hardened during his four months of running, his pot belly left behind in cellular increments somewhere along the cattail ditches outside Willow Creek. When he came in view of the Colonial Inn, he slowed to a walk. Someone was sprinting across the parking lot and the silhouette seemed extremely familiar. Sam approached stealthily, crouching behind parked cars until he could figure out what was going on.

With the visor of his cap pulled down over one ear, Dean came tearing across the asphalt to the near side. He stopped, took several deep breaths, and then dashed back the half block. Sam stepped into view and jogged toward his only substitute.

"Dean! Dean! Wait a minute!"

Dean turned, with surprise on his sweating face, and he stood with the manner of a boy who'd been caught shoplifting.

"What are you doing?"

"Practicin'." He wore jeans and a worn-thin navy sweatshirt that was partially soaked in perspiration.

"Dean, Dean." Sam half laughed, choked on his own amazement. "I appreciate your spirit, but it's not good to run on the day of a game. You need to rest, save your energy."

"I'm only doin' twenty-five or thirty."

"*Thirty!*" Sam shook his head. "C'mon." He put his arm around the dripping freshman and started toward the lobby door. "On game days I just want you to rest. No running, okay?"

"Okay," Dean said.

Rivulets of sweat trickled from under his enduring cap.

"Dean, where'd you ever get that cap?"

"My sister."

"Denise?"

"Yep, for Christmas. Nobody knew how she did it. She rode along with my mom in the summer to get a part for the baler. We was puttin' up hay. The guy at Kamp's saw her sittin' out in the pickup when my mom was in gettin' the part and he gave her a cap. None of us could figure how she kept it hidden so long. On Christmas she had it in a brown paper bag and everything."

"She's quite a girl," Sam said. "Is that why you always wear it?"

"Yep. It's the only present she ever give me. She told me it would make me run faster."

"I think she's right," Sam said, completely converted to Cutter philosophy. They reached the lobby door, and Sam held it open for his freshman phenomenon.

"Have you had breakfast?"

"No."

"Why don't you get Scott and Curtis and have breakfast."

"They's still sleepin'." Dean chuckled.

"Well, they'll be up soon. Is Denise coming to the game tonight?"

"I don't know."

In the lobby Sam stopped to get what papers were available. With pure astonishment he watched the ragtag boy sprint down the carpeted corridor, never doubting that his imprisoned sister's gift truly made him run faster.

HAZEL WALKED UNEASILY into the double room. She was sure she could smell formaldehyde. A bedraggled younger woman nodded from the other bed. Hazel stepped behind the curtain separating the patients and sidled up to Grandma's bed. There were two plastic bags hanging beside her, one with clear fluid trickling, and the other with plasma dripping into a tube and following a serpentine course to the needle in her arm. Elizabeth Chapman appeared tiny and vulnerable in the high stainless-steel bed.

"How are you doin'?" Hazel said.

"I'm a little tired."

"Why didn't you tell me?"

"What was there to tell?"

"That you were sick, that you—"

"Sweetheart, we're all dying, so what's the big deal. I don't want anyone crying in my beer while I'm still drinking it."

"You're some hard-assed lady, Elizabeth Chapman."

"I know how you like to gossip, Hazel, but I pray that you'll keep this secret with me until the day I die. I couldn't bear it if Peter knew. I just couldn't bear the pain that boy would have."

"But maybe he'd want to know, so he could—"

"So he could win for his *dying* grandmother. I want this to be the happiest time in his life, not a funeral. I want him to win for *himself!* This has been the best year in my life with that boy. If I die tomorrow, I'll die a lucky woman, but as long as she swims, I will cook."

Hazel shifted her weight to the other leg, wanting to lift her frail friend into her arms.

"How long have you known?" Hazel said.

"Since July." Grandma paused. "After he told me I went out and bought that felt hat to celebrate how glorious and insane life is."

"I'll stay here with you."

"No . . . thank you, but no. Go back to the game, otherwise Peter will know something serious is wrong. If you're at the game, you can tell him I have the flu. Please, go to the game, and stop by my place and get Tripod."

"Are you sure you don't want me to stay with you?" Hazel itched to get the hell out of there.

"Yes, I'll be fine in a day or two. I'll catch the bus and be home before the team on Sunday. Pete will find me at home as usual."

"You worry too much about that boy. He's tougher than you think."

"I know he is, but I want my days with him to be happy. It's the same for everyone. We take life for granted like the air in our tires. What we share today, we have forever and what we put off, we've lost."

"I'll call you tonight."

"Okay, get going. You have a long drive."

"I'll see you later," Hazel said, ready to haul her body out of there. She stepped back, about to turn.

"And Hazel."

"Yeah?"

"See that we knock the pickle juice out of Seely-Swan."

PETER AND ROB demolished a breakfast in the partially occupied motel restaurant where they could eat all they wanted. Tom and Olaf remained in their king-size beds.

"I thought Miss Murphy would have us eatin' ravioli or something for breakfast," Pete said as he wolfed waffles and pork sausage.

"She really believes in that stuff," Rob said.

"I hope they use a zone against us tonight."

"Yeah, but if they go man-for-man we can still get it high to Oaf."

"Man, I love seeing him jam that baby down their throats," Pete said.

A few tables over, Rob's parents ate like honeymooners, obviously enjoying their stay in a motel. Pete watched from the corner of his eye as Rob's father reached under the table and squeezed his wife's thigh. She leaned toward him and they rubbed foreheads over breakfast.

"What's that like?" Pete asked, nodding at Rob's parents.

"What's what like?"

"Having two parents who like each other?"

"Them? I dunno. It's just normal."

"It's not normal where I come from."

"Are your parents coming out if we go to State?"

"No. They're busy with some real important stuff."

"Will Kathy?"

"I don't think so. She's got a lotta school work and everything." Pete felt lousy for lying as his fellow guard cleaned up an onion omelette and a side order of bacon. A motherly waitress scooted to their table.

"Would you boys like anything else?"

"More orange juice, please," Rob said.

"I'd like another waffle and some more milk, if I could," Pete said.

"Of course, it'll just be a minute. I sure hope you boys win tonight."

"Are you from Willow Creek?" Pete said.

"Heavens, no. I don't even know where it is."

"Why are you rootin' for us?" Rob said.

"'Cause you only have six players against all those other boys."

She picked up their smeared plates and hurried away.

"Did you tell Kathy we're in the Divisionals?" Rob asked.

"Yeah, sure." Pete glanced over at Rob and then back at the tabletop. "I haven't talked to her in two months. She doesn't give a damn what I'm doin'."

Rob stared at him as though he were suddenly speaking in a foreign language.

"She's goin' with some jerk. She's not my girlfriend anymore."

"But you talk to her every Sunday night about all that stuff going on in your school?"

"It's all bogus, I made it all up."

"Why?"

"I don't know. I just didn't want anyone to know."

Pete shot a look at his teammate, watching Rob's face for a reaction. Rob regarded him with a slight squint and furrowed brow.

"Is that why you came back?"

"No . . . I came back because of you guys . . . and Coach."

"Man, am I glad you did. We wouldn't be sittin' here in Helena if you hadn't come back, we'd have been blasted at District."

Pete glanced over at Rob's parents. They were finishing their breakfast.

"You boys getting enough to eat?" Alice Johnson called.

"Yeah, Mom," Rob said. "We won't be able to get out of the chair."

Pete looked at Rob and spoke quietly.

"When I called my mom and told her I was back in Willow Creek . . ."

"Yeah?"

"I could tell she was relieved. She was hoping I wouldn't stay in Saint Paul."

A trace of sadness appeared in Rob's eyes for a moment. "Do you care if anyone knows, about Kathy?"

"Not anymore."

"Well, you'll sure make Louella happy. And you've already made *me* happy. We're going to State because you stayed."

Rob whacked Pete on the shoulder and then hesitated as if he'd thought of something else.

"Do you think you would have stayed home if Kathy hadn't—"

"Hadn't dumped me?" Pete said. "I don't know, I've asked myself that a lot. Sometimes I think she was supposed to dump me so I could be here for this."

Rob opened his mouth to speak and then stopped short. Pete sensed he was about to say he was glad she had dumped him but feared how it would sound. The waitress delivered the goods and Willow Creek's unlikely shooters went back to reloading.

SAM ATTEMPTED TO orchestrate a calm, restful day. The team spent the morning talking basketball, listening to Sam's quiet assessment of Seely-Swan and planning strategy while the girls went to the mall. They

all ate lunch in the motel restaurant and left the coaches to themselves in
a corner. While shopping, Diana had picked up a *Sweetheart,* a Montana
singles magazine, and she read it aloud with restrained curiosity.

"Here's another one. 'Loves long walks, candlelight dinners, watching
sunsets.' Everyone of these gals uses the same copy, which doesn't tell you
much about them."

Sitting beside her, Sam scanned some of the personal ads, flipping
through the dozens of pages, hundreds of pleas for someone to love.

"God, they're brave," he said. "Sticking their thumb out like hitchhikers
to the passing world and believing 'Mr. Right' will come along."

She ran her finger down the columns on a page.

"There are a lot of people here."

"Shopping for love at a flea market," Sam said. "It's our greatest affliction,
that unquenchable faith that there *is* someone out there for all of us. People
are starving for love, that's why it's so easy to believe."

"Well, I think they ought to lighten up, put some humor in it while they're
at it," Diana said. "I'd like to run an ad for a man who couldn't stand long
walks, went into convulsions watching sunsets, and threw up at candlelight
dinners."

"Think you'd get any takers?"

"I'll bet I would."

"Maybe, but romance works better," Sam said.

"All right, you write an ad. What would you say?"

Sam thought for a minute.

"How about this? Extraterrestrial who doesn't know who he is or why
he's here, looking for similar female companion who also missed her home
planet due to some cosmic miscalculation. Loves intergalactic travel, inter-
facing, and weightlessness. Let's match beeps for compatibility and space
out together."

"You'd get a pile of mail," she said with a smile. "I'd answer it."

"You don't need to. I've already found you." The dread in his chest swelled
and he stopped himself from venturing further. "You're getting awfully wild
on the bench," he said. "You've come close to a 'T' more than once."

"You're changing the subject."

"I know."

She let it go, as though she understood his attempt to avoid the pain, as though she agreed it was a topic much too sensitive for both of them. He had promised himself he would concentrate on their assault on the mountain top. Today they were in a base camp just below the summit. He had to keep his mind clear. It wasn't only the boys who risked the humiliation of being blown away by some excellent team. He could end up in front of that gaping crowd utterly exposed by some brilliant opposing coach, leaving his boys in disarray and scattered, caught in rock slides, and overrun in an avalanche, while he watched helplessly from the fairgrounds in his fouled clothing.

CHAPTER 67

The girls were taking advantage of the pool and Jacuzzi while the boys sat around watching and goofing off under Diana's watch. Sam suspected that Andrew had slipped Curtis and Dean a roll of quarters and the underclassmen were hanging out at the arcades. Fully dressed, Sam sprawled on the bed, rereading Friday's papers and the sparse coverage of yesterday's games. He couldn't help but note that the traditional indifference given to Willow Creek was becoming a thing of the past. The Helena *Independent Record* captioned its coverage with the headline:

SIX-MAN TEAM ALIVE.

Rising like a giant, the six-man team from Willow Creek has surprised more than a few in its surge to the semifinals at Divisional level. But to me they're no surprise. They have impressive wealth in two outstanding guards and a dominating center that no boy in the state can match up with. They have a bruising 6'4" senior forward who can go to the boards with anyone. They also have a coach, an English teacher named Sam Pickett, who has them using their talents and strengths with uncanny efficiency. If Seely-Swan takes them lightly in the seven o'clock game tonight, the Blackhawks may have to set their alarms for an early Saturday morning game.

"Yeah!" Sam cheered.
The phone rang. He reached over and picked it up.
"Hello."
"Mr. Pickett?"
"Yes."
"Hello. This is Hazel Brown."
"Oh, hello. You back in town?"
"Yes. I have a message for Peter from his grandma. She has a little bit of

the flu and didn't feel up to the trip. Would you tell him? And tell him I have Tripod with me."

"Sure, I'll tell him. I hope she can make it tomorrow. I don't want her to miss out on the fun."

"Oh, she'll probably be here tomorrow, just a little fever and nausea."

"I'll tell him."

"Mr. Pickett . . ." She gasped with a note of desperation.

"Yes."

Sam waited through an awkward pause.

"Mr. Pickett, can you keep a secret?"

She wasn't giggling and she sounded as though she might cry at any moment.

"Yes."

"I mean a *sacred holy* secret."

"Is there something wrong?"

"I have to tell you . . . just have to . . . I don't know what else to do."

"What is it?" Sam asked. He felt the fear working its way up his stomach to his throat.

"It's Grandma . . . she's real sick. She's dying."

"*What?*"

"She's dying, Mr. Pickett, and she doesn't want anybody knowing about it, but I just had to tell you with the basketball practicing and all."

"Where is she?" Sam said, finding it difficult to breathe.

"She's in the hospital in Billings. She'll be all right in a day or two, but the doctor says she won't live through the summer."

"What's wrong with her?"

"Leukemia."

"Oh, God."

"They're givin' her blood or something. She's scared to death that Peter will find out, that's why you've got to promise me you won't tell. She'll have my hide if she knew I told you. I think I'd lose her friendship and I couldn't handle that. She's the best friend I've ever had."

"Don't worry," Sam said. "You won't lose your friend."

"Thanks a million, Mr. Pickett. I thought you had to know. She shouldn't be playing basketball or anything anymore. Was I right in telling you?"

"Don't worry, Hazel, it's all right. I'll pretend everything is normal."

"You'll tell Pete she has the flu?"

"I'll tell him."

"Thank you, Mr. Pickett, thank you so much. I feel better that someone else knows, I just didn't know what to do."

Sam hung up the phone and slumped back in the bed. The world went wrong! He wished Hazel Brown had kept her deadly secret. He felt his chest would burst.

Oh God! Grandma Chapman wouldn't live through the summer.

And still she'd sent that crazy cat as though Willow Creek would be at risk without him. He heard the thump of footsteps on the hall carpet as the boys burst into the room. Peter Strong was laughing and loving his life.

PETER SEARCHED THE crowd for his grandmother as he warmed up out on the floor, even though Coach told him she stayed home with the flu. The sports center was packed, and though he recognized a lot of people in the Willow Creek section, he couldn't find Denise Cutter. He realized that sometimes when he gazed into that sea of faces he expected to see Kathy or even his father.

Seely-Swan had come blasting out and run a lap around the floor while their pep band blared their fight song. They looked classy in black and gold sweat suits. Though they had four or five guys around six foot three or four, and Pete noticed them gawking at Oaf as they warmed up. Pete's stomach felt like cement, but he turned to his teammates who were shooting around, and he immediately felt better. Seely-Swan might beat them tonight, but they'd have to do it over their dead bodies.

It all went by so fast: the national anthem, the introduction of the players, the last-minute instructions. And before Pete could catch his breath he was crouching at the edge of the jump circle. Olaf batted the ball to Rob. Pete took off down the sideline and Rob led him with the ball. He caught it, took one dribble, went for the layup, and crashed into Boyd, the stumpy 5'10" kid with a receding hairline. Both boys splattered onto the floor. A whistle. The ref pointed at Pete and put his hand behind his neck. An offensive foul. No basket. Damn!

They fell back into their zone and the Blackhawks moved the ball around patiently, the way Coach said they would. A kid with a pockmarked face hit a sixteen-footer and Seely-Swan jumped on top. Pete hustled down the floor. Seely-Swan was so worried about Oaf, they were giving Pete anything around the three-point line. Open for a second, he lifted a quick shot. The ball hit the back of the rim and bounced out high to McHenry, a lean, long-legged forward.

Damn, take your time, be more patient, be more patient.

He broke a sweat, and his chest heaved. The Blackhawks were in no hurry. They chipped away, they worked the ball. Pete pushed himself on defense, looking for a steal, but he felt logy. These guys were quick. *Watch the overloading. Move your feet, move your feet.* Seely-Swan was getting the better of it and Coach Pickett called time out. Only two minutes left in the first quarter. The game was going by fast.

"Olaf, move up to a high post. That'll open it up along the baseline," Coach told them. "You're doing good, doing good. We need to be the aggressors, go at 'em, don't hang back. You can play with these boys."

They joined hands.

"Win! Win! Win! Win! Win! Win! Win!"

On his side of the zone, Pete guarded Thomas, a wiry 6'1" kid Pete figured might be quicker than he was.

Play him a little loose, give him the long stuff, cut off his driving lane.

He could gamble some, knowing Oaf was behind him with his long, sledgehammer arms to pile drive layups into the floor drain. Pete leaped out at Thomas as he lifted an eighteen footer. The shot dropped. Pete got whistled for his second foul. Damn! Thomas rattled the free throw in.

Pete brought the ball up, starting to get into the flow. He lobbed a high pass to Oaf at the edge of the paint. The Blackhawks swarmed around him as if he were dead meat. Oaf flipped the ball back to Pete. Wide open, he squared up to the basket and let his instincts do the rest—wrist and fingers following through. It milked the net. The referee held up both hands. A three-pointer. Confidence rushed through him. They could play with these dudes, all twelve of them, and he loved it: the squeaking shoes, the grunts and shouts, the way his body ran the floor, the joy of scoring, the look in a teammate's eye.

At the end of the first quarter Seely-Swan led 17 to 14, and Coach brought

Dean into the game, giving Tom a break on the bench. Seely-Swan had good athletes, lots of them, and they kept coming off the bench fresh, hustling, until Pete couldn't keep track of them. It seemed they were all blond, 6'2" or 3", and could shoot from anywhere on the floor. Shortly before the half, Pete saw an opening. His instincts took him to the basket. He went high, banked the shot, and crashed into the 6'4" well-built Lowell Lapp. Both of them hit the floor. Whistle. Offensive foul. His third. He sprang up. Bogus call. The shot was waved off.

Damn ref.

At the half Willow Creek led by one, 38 to 37.

The huge locker room made it seem as though they had forgotten a team-mate or two out on the court.

"Keep getting the ball to Olaf," Coach Pickett said. "Don't fall in love with your jump shots, trust Olaf with the ball." Miss Murphy iced Tom's knee and read the stats to the team.

"Pete, you have to watch it. You have three fouls, Olaf, two. Rob, two. Dean, two."

Just before they went back onto the floor, Coach shouted at them, sur-prising Pete. "We're one half away from the championship game! Do you want it bad enough?"

"Yeeaaahhhh!" they all shouted and slapped hands.

"Are you willing to give everything you have?"

"Yeeaaahhhh!"

"Let's go chip ice!" Pete shouted.

Coach Pickett's strategy began to work. They kept lobbing the ball high to Oaf. He was great. He kept Seely-Swan guessing, showing how quickly he was catching on to the fine points of the game. One time he'd fake a pass to Tom and give it back to Rob for a shot. The next time he'd fake a pass back to Pete and dish it off to Tom. Then, when they'd anticipate either of those moves, he would fake the pass and pivot to the basket for a jam. Pete felt an unexpected happiness as he ran back on defense, proud as hell to be playing for Willow Creek, Montana. A minute later, when Pete stole the ball, ripped it to Tom hustling down the side, wide open for the layup, he was overcome with a rush of affection for all of them.

"Yeah!" Pete shouted under the thunder from the Willow Creek section.

"Great pass!" Tom said as he hobbled by and Pete knew they would win.

In the fourth quarter, Pete felt grooved, confident. His body was in a dance and he knew all the steps. Confounding his man, stealing the ball, getting the ball to his teammates with humming passes, leaving a kid frozen in his tracks. He was the quick, unpredictable player he knew he could be. Living it to the hilt, he gambled to intercept a pass and crashed into Thomas, his fourth foul. Thomas made the one-and-one. Their lead had dwindled to two. The coach called time out.

"We can't do it without you in there, Pete," Coach Pickett said with fire in his eyes. "We've got five minutes to go. Give a little, back off an inch. Rob, you and Pete take the three if it's there, they're giving us the long stuff and choking off the inside. Run number two. Let's go!"

They ran a play, Pete was open and he followed through. The ball had found its way home. Coach held his two arms high to symbolize the three-pointer as Pete ran by the bench. The roar of the crowd was a constant drone, surrounding him, upholding him, loving him. He set himself on defense. He could knock down as many more of those as they needed. He felt it. His instincts couldn't miss.

After grabbing a defensive rebound, Rob lobbed the ball to Oaf on the high post. Oaf faked a pass back to Rob and snapped it to Pete. Boyd leaped toward him. Pete caught it and shot it in rhythm and the shot soared, out of reach, snapping the net in a moment of almost perfect silence in his mind. Then Rob was giving him five, the referee was holding two hands over his head as though someone held a gun to his back, and Coach and Miss Murphy were dancing up and down in front of the bench. Pete glided downcourt. He felt strong, he felt the warmth of belonging, the glow of being important to someone, *to matter*. This was his ground, his game. He couldn't miss and there was nothing Seely-Swan could do about it.

He hustled on defense. They moved the ball out in front of him. Boyd poised to shoot. Pete moved up quickly, his hand in the shooter's face. The stubby kid drove to his right. Pete reacted to his left and collided with Thomas, who had slipped up behind him and set a pick. He flattened the blond boy, who seemed to go down too easily. The ref whistled the foul.

Son of a bitch!

The buzzer pointed out his screwup. He moved numbly off the court and slammed his body onto the bench. Dean timidly handed him his rag-tail cap and he jerked it on. They were up by six with three minutes and twenty-three seconds to go. Scott wrapped a towel around Pete's shoulders and offered his timid condolence with a light pat on the back. Kneeling, Coach Pickett took Pete's head in his hands and looked into his eyes.

"You put us ahead. Now we're going to win it, don't give up."

Those last three minutes clawed at his stomach. Thomas coolly made the one-and-one, cutting the lead to four. They trapped Rob and got a turnover when Dean lost Rob's pass. McHenry cut it to two with a jumper near the key, and they tied it with a minute and ten seconds on two free throws by Lapp. All the spectators were on their feet, blistering the arena walls with their roar.

"Volleyball! Volleyball!" Coach shouted.

Pete agonized on the bench and kept repeating as though a prayer, "As long as she swims, I will cook. As long as she swims, I will cook."

In the face of a press, Rob dribbled into the front court. Olaf came to the high post and Rob lobbed it to him. Oaf faked a pass to Tom and then flipped it behind his back to a surprised Curtis, who was virtually alone on the left side of the court. Forget Me Not dribbled the ball once and lifted his favorite shot from the side. Pete came off the bench as the ball rattled home.

They were up by two with thirty-six seconds.

Pete felt helpless, aching to be out there with them. He kept searching for Denise Cutter's face in the stands as though she could save them. The Blackhawks brought the ball up smartly and ripped it around the zone, down by two. With eleven seconds on the clock they got it to the quick Jay McHenry on Curtis's side. McHenry faked a shot and got Curtis in the air. The lean kid went around Curtis and pulled up for a short jump shot. Olaf got there too late. The ball was in flight when Olaf chopped McHenry's arms. The shot was perfect, tying the game, and the arena rocked. The Blackhawk forward would get one free throw with two seconds on the clock.

"Time out after the shot!" Coach Pickett shouted to Rob.

The Seely-Swan player accepted the ball from the referee. The Willow Creek fans shook the sports center with their cheers. The boys crouched along the line, arms up. McHenry bounced the ball once, eyed the basket, and shot the ball. Pete held his breath. It was flat, no arch, a brick. But it hit the front rim, hesitated as though it didn't have the strength to get over, and then rolled into the net softly.

Damn!

The Willow Creek crowd groaned, the Seely-Swan fans leaped and cheered.

Rob shouted at the ref, "Time out, time out!"

They came to the bench and Pete struggled to muster his enthusiasm. He couldn't find his voice. He tried to encourage them by offering them water, a towel, helping Scott prepare them for two seconds of life that was no life.

"We have one chance," Coach Pickett said to Pete's stunned teammates. "We've practiced this a thousand times. Olaf, set up on the free throw line. Rob, hit him with the high post pattern. Olaf, you'll only have time to catch it and shoot. They might foul you. Go do it."

The referee handed the ball to Rob. Seely-Swan had Thomas waving his arms in Rob's face and the rest were camped back under the basket. Lapp stood behind Olaf with Cooper crowding in front. The clock wouldn't start until Olaf touched the ball.

Rob fired a perfect pass the length of the floor. In one fluid motion Olaf moved to his left, went up above the reaching defenders, caught the ball in stride, and gently lobbed it at the basket as the buzzer detonated. It had a chance! Pete stood, suffering in the suddenly silent building, tracking the softly arcing ball as it hit the backboard, bounced down onto the rim, careened around the front of the iron, and fell to the side.

They had lost!

The Seely-Swan team and fans leaped and shouted and smothered one another, a lava flow of wild jubilation. The Willow Creek boys walked numbly toward the bench. Pete had no words for them. They looked at the floor and wiped their eyes. He couldn't believe it. They could have beat those guys! He kept looking at the blurring scoreboard.

SEELY-SWAN 64, WILLOW CREEK 63.

He had lost it for them. Two foolish, stupid goddamn fouls and he would have been in there at the end. He could have buried another two or three, he could have . . .

Coach Pickett came to him and put his arm around him. Pete couldn't look into his face, knowing how much the coach wanted to win. Pete had wanted to win it for him so badly, he *should* have won it for him, for his team, for the town. The dream was over. Willow Creek would be losers after all. Somehow Pete had believed he was sent here to change that. He didn't understand what was happening.

Numbly he shuffled through the line, shaking hands with the happy Seely-Swan players, accepting their crummy compliments. Then they huddled on the floor. They grasped hands in the center of their circle but no one could speak. He crossed the court with his eyes on the floor. He was glad Grandma wasn't here to see this. He wanted to tell her that he had tried to bring his teammates hot coffee in this terrible storm, but he couldn't get a fire going. The stove had been dumped over and it was under water. He hurried to the locker room to hide his face in the howling waves of shame.

CHAPTER 68

In the locker room, each endured his solitary grief. They showered and dressed, cadavers impersonating the living. Somehow the celebrating Seely-Swan team could be heard through heating ducts and false ceiling, echoing through floor drains and shower heads, the dragon's voice laughing heinously, jabbing a bony finger into their open wounds.

Fans hung around outside the locker-room door with the redeyed cheerleaders as though waiting in a hospital corridor for the doctor's word that their relative had died. Sam was shattered. Had it all been a cruel hoax, this dream of his? He was a loser after all. He could not raise his voice in the face of their utterly devastating defeat, staggering around in a daze, picking up bloody bandages, amputated arms, detached eyeballs in a dispensary for those who had been mutilated by loss. He offered an ice pack to Tom but the thrown cowboy only said, "What for?"

When Sam, afflicted beyond recognition, couldn't come up with a thought, Diana took over. She found her direction when the rest of them had been blasted into disorientation. She hurried ahead of them to the motel with Andrew and the three girls. Sam and the boys followed a half hour later, catatonic and straggling out of the sports center while the other game raged on in the arena.

Diana was magnificent under fire, magnificent when Sam went flatfooted in any attempt to glue things together. With Miss Murphy's menu and Andrew Wainwright's wallet, a quiet private room awaited the Dirty Half-Dozen when they limped into the Colonial Inn. In the lobby, well-meaning fans threw wilted verbal bouquets . . .

"You did the best you could."

"You boys played hard."

"You came a long way, further than anyone expected."

"You have nothing to be ashamed of."

. . . cliches that touched nerve endings with the subtleties of a dentist's drill. When the twelve of them were seated in the cozy and softly lit room, two waitresses began hauling in food. The clinking of silverware and the tinkle of glass dominated the glum silence, and they passed spaghetti, ravioli, macaroni, and salad.

The calm atmosphere and wholesome food helped them all slowly find their voice.

"No sense eatin' any more pasta. We're dead," Tom said.

"You got that right," Rob said. "We should've beat those guys by ten points."

Peter didn't lift his head. He picked at his food, unable to look at his teammates.

"They are having so many players," Olaf said, shaking his head slowly.

"Eat lots of pasta, boys. You'll need it tomorrow," Miss Murphy said.

"Yeah, for the losers' bracket," Tom said.

They ate in silence as if no one could think of anything to say.

"You know, elephants are the only animal that can't jump," Curtis said.

The boys groaned and Sam laughed. He felt his feet touching ground again. One of the waitresses brought Sam a note. He didn't open the folded white paper, setting it beside his plate. He cleared his throat and all eyes swept down the table toward him.

"Men, despite what you might feel right now, this is not the Last Supper. We lost a crucial ball game. We lost with all of you giving everything you had, no one can do more. I'm proud of you."

Sam's voice cracked and he paused a moment. He glanced at their despairing faces.

"I know how much you're hurting, how much we're all hurting, but there is something to be done, together, by all of us. We lost control of our own destiny tonight, but maybe it never was in our hands. All we can ever do is give our best and see where it leads. You did that tonight, and let me tell you something while your heads are hanging. We scared the hell out of every team up here. They didn't want to play us. The four teams in the other bracket were dancing because they didn't have to face us."

Sam took a drink of water and no one moved, no one blinked.

"Well, they've got us hanging by a thread, like a spider, and they're going to try to smash us between their hands. I only want to say one thing to you tonight because I know you, I know how far you've come and how much you've given, and I know how tough you are."

Sam opened the note from Andrew. It read: "Twin Bridges 71, Alberton 46." The curiosity around the table was nearly audible.

"Twin Bridges beat Alberton," Sam said.

"Aaawwww."

"Damn."

"I knew they would."

"This is what I want to say to you, this only. If you think you feel bad now, think how you'll feel if we lose either game tomorrow and Seely-Swan beats Twin Bridges tomorrow night. Think how we'll feel if the opportunity is there to challenge Twin Bridges and we're not around to do it!"

They were silent, thinking, allowing his words to sink in.

"Seely-Swan has a great front line," Rob said with some enthusiasm. "They could snuff Stone and Harkin."

Tom nodded slowly and Pete lifted his head, casting his pleading eyes on Sam.

"Rob's right. They'll match up well with Twin Bridges," Sam said, pushing his chair back from the table. "Men, it is very possible we will catch up to Twin Bridges on Monday night, but *only* if we win tomorrow. Should we go for it?"

"Yeeaaahhhh!"

"Should we let Twin Bridges know all day that we're coming up their tailpipe, that if they so much as blink on Saturday night, we'll put tire tracks on their butts come Monday?"

"Yeeaaahhhh!" they shouted louder.

"We'll never quit!"

"Yeeaaahhhh!"

"We'll never give in!"

"Yeeaaahhhh!"

"And each time he falls—" Diana shouted.

"—he will rise again!" they chorused with a rekindled fire.

"Okay!" Sam pulled his chair up to the table. "Let's finish eating and then Miss Murphy has a surprise for us."

Pete looked at all of them with fire in his eyes. "Pass the ravioli!" he said.

WITH THEIR SHOES off and their stomachs full, they flopped on the two queen-size beds—which Diana had shoved together—or on the thick carpet and watched *It's A Mad, Mad, Mad, Mad World,* a video Andrew had run down at the third place he tried. It was also part of Diana's menu. Some sat on the bed with their backs against the headboard, Tom stretched out with an ice pack on his knee, some sprawled on their stomachs with their elbows propping up their heads, and some lounged on the floor in front of the beds. Diana wanted them close, touching, a big family having fun together. And they had fun.

Sam, sitting in a cushioned chair beside the beds, watched their faces as the movie progressed. Halfway through, where Sid Caesar and his movie wife were trying to blast their way out of a hardware store where they'd been locked in, all of them were laughing so hard they were falling off the bed. Near the end of the movie, where the dozen zany characters were being catapulted through fifth-story windows by a fire truck's ladder that had gone berserk, they were all gripped in seizures of laughter, tears in their eyes.

When the movie was over, Sam smiled at Diana with a tinge of reverence. She had waved her magic wand and healed them. For over two hours they had forgotten all about their loss, they had laughed together until they were sore, and they'd never had a thought about basketball. It was almost midnight.

"Okay, men. Get a good night's sleep," Sam said, prying himself out of the chair. "I'll wake you at seven. We want to eat a good breakfast and then loosen up. The game is at nine. We will win it."

The kids stood around for a minute, hesitating to leave for their rooms, hesitating to leave the warmth of this fellowship. Dean started it, or Tom. The squeaky freshman looked up at the bull rider he admired.

"Good night, Tom."

Tom appeared to be about to pat the kid on the head, but at the last moment, wrapped his arms around him and hugged him.

"Good night, Dean."

That did it. Spontaneously, Tom turned and hugged Curtis. Dean turned and hugged Miss Murphy, and then the whole bunch went at it like repatriated prisoners of war coming off the plane. They hugged Olaf's waist, Dean's head, Carter stooped to hug Scott and Mary went up on tiptoe to hug Peter Strong. They hugged each other with affection, with an honest, open compassion that touched them all and mended their broken hearts. The feeling of belonging was the glue. Sam had to clear his throat before daring to speak.

"One more thing. I know you'll all want to know that Denise Cutter will be here for the morning game."

They cheered and applauded.

"And my grandma will probably be here too," Pete said.

They cheered again, and Sam had a knot in his chest. He clapped his hands. "All right, off to bed."

They sauntered down the hall and into their rooms, but before they closed the door, Dean called shrilly, "Good night, Miss Murphy!"

"Good night, Dean!"

That did it.

"Good night, Carter!"

"Good night, Oaf!"

"Good night, Tom!"

"Good night, Mary!"

"Good night, Curtis!"

"Good night, Louella!"

Sam walked along the corridor, shutting doors, still hearing behind him, "Good night, Coach. Good night, Rob."

Sam and Diana were alone in his room for a minute before she went to join her girls.

"How did you do that, getting Denise Cutter here before nine?" she asked.

"Andrew. He called the Cutters while we were eating, they said she could come, he drove back tonight."

"If we go much further, I think we ought to designate him an assistant coach and have him sit on the bench," Diana said.

"Good idea, and I know someone else that ought to sit there."

"Who?"

"Grandma Chapman."

"Good idea."

She put her arms around him and held him tightly. She kissed him with an intensity he hadn't felt before. He wrapped his arms around her and they held on for a minute.

"Are you all right?" she said.

"Yes, now I am. You did it tonight. I would have never thought of that. I'd have been looking at gloomy basketball videos and planning strategy."

"I got lucky," she said. "Sleep well, we're all still together."

"For another day," he whispered in her ear.

"For another day."

CHAPTER 69

By seven-fifteen the twelve of them were present around the table in their private dining room, eating a light breakfast and chattering. Sam nodded across the long table at Diana and then cleared his throat.

"Miss Murphy would like to say something."

Their eyes shifted from Sam to Diana, who was seated in the middle of the table, between Curtis and Carter.

"How come we aren't having ravioli for breakfast, Miss Murphy?" Tom asked.

"I didn't want you massacring Ennis, just beating them. You'll thank me when they sputter out of gas and you guys will be zipping up and down the court in overdrive. And that's what I want to talk to you about. Some of you may recall seeing my video on the wild dogs of Africa."

The Willow Creek seniors nodded.

"It documents how the wild dogs hunt. They run a herd of wildebeests until they spot a slower calf with its mother. Then they cut the pair out like cowboys and let the rest of the herd run off. Circling the cow and calf, they take turns dashing in and grabbing the calf by the neck or a leg. While the mother tries to fight them off by lowering her head and chasing a dog away, another springs in behind her and takes a stab at the calf."

The team went on with their breakfast as she talked.

"This would be repeated over and over for five, six, seven minutes, wearing the cow out. Three or four wild dogs lunged and retreated, until the cow could hardly stand. Then, time after time, for its own survival, the cow gives up and runs off as the dogs drag down the calf and kill it."

"I remember that," Carter said. "You showed it to us last year."

"Well, remember later on, where quite by accident they filmed the pack hunting one day, thinking it would be another routine killing. But this time was different. Four wild dogs worked their game, darting in, grabbing at the calf, retreating from the charging cow, wearing her down. Over and over, one after the other, four against one. But this mother wouldn't quit. On and on the struggle went, the dogs dashing in from all directions, the cow chasing them off."

Sam noticed no one was eating.

"The naturalists doing the filming were astounded. For five minutes, ten, fifteen, the cow, though outflanked and outmanned, wouldn't give in and leave her calf. The dogs were exhausted, their tongues hanging out, their bodies panting for breath. And still the cow stood, gasping, played out, mouth frothing, her head and horns down, waiting their next charge. It never came. To the amazement of the film crew, the dogs slunk off, giving up. The wildebeest mother watched them go for a minute and then turned and stumbled away with her calf."

"I remember that," Louella said. "I was really glad when the wild dogs didn't get that calf."

"We don't know why that animal outlasted the wild dogs. Supposedly dumb and unfeeling, she would not relent to what seemed inevitable, went against her survival instincts, and found the heart to be more stiff-necked than the dogs themselves."

Diana regarded each of the boys, slowly, deliberately.

"Now, you're wondering what all this has to do with us? I've seen that quality in each of you, many times. Right now it seems like we're surrounded and outmanned and there isn't any hope. But there is one hope. That somewhere in your hearts, like in the wonderful wildebeest mother, you'll find the strength and the stubborn, bullheaded courage that will never quit, a hard-nosed toughness that says no, that draws a line in the dirt and spits into its hands and says not one more inch. And when they run in their fresh and rested substitutes, darting and dashing, and you've had no rest, you only stiffen your necks further and lower your horns. If you call on that inner toughness today, no matter what Ennis throws at you, you'll know you've done everything possible. That's what I wanted to tell you."

A heavy silence hung over the table for a moment. Sam was overwhelmed by this curious woman who seemed to keep surprising him with another facet of her hidden self. He wanted to stand up and shout, but he realized this amazing biology teacher was trying to elicit a response from the team. Then Tom broke the spell.

"Mooooow!" he bellowed with a perfect imitation. "Let's go stomp them dogs."

"Yeeaaahhhh!" the table responded.

With laughter and renewed chatter, everyone finished up quickly and they broke camp for the arena.

THE WORLD LOVES a winner. The Carroll College Sports Center seemed deserted compared to the night before, though both Ennis and Willow Creek had several hundred fans yawning and stretching in the stands. The boys were out on the floor shooting free throws and jump shots with balls that appeared to have insufficient air pressure. It appeared as though they were unloading nail kegs. They struggled against inert bodies, rubbery legs, and what felt like embalmed arms. Sam sensed something new about them, something he couldn't put his finger on. It was the way they treated each other, not that they had ever been callous or cold, but it was as though they had discovered each other with a fresh insight, had come to respect one another in a new way, like those who have come through pain and disappointment together only to find the joy of their comradeship a much greater gift. Something magical had happened between them, something rare, an unbreakable bond to finish what they had started.

At the bench, Sam gave them last-minute instructions.

"If it's there, run, when it's not, walk the ball up, half-court offense. Work for layups until your shooting eyes get here from the motel. Olaf, keep changing, high post, low post. We give them one shot from the lobby and then we eat the ball."

During the introductions, Pete scanned the bleachers for his grandmother. Sam glanced to see if she had somehow made it. Half the team was on the floor when the announcer called Pete's number and name.

"Tell me if my grandma shows up will you, Coach?"

Sam nodded. Shouldn't he forewarn the boy to cherish his grandma while he had the chance? Then it occurred to him that Pete already did. Number 22 high-fived those left at the bench and ran to midcourt to shake hands with an opponent. But instead of then running to his teammates gathered under the west basket, Pete ran across the floor, up into the stands as though he were going home. All eyes in the arena followed him. The young athlete ran the bleacher stairs up to the balcony rail where he stopped in front of Denise Cutter. He looked into her face and gently tapped high fives on her hands that flopped limply in her lap. Then he raced down through the stands and out onto the court to his teammates. Sam watched Denise for a moment and the young girl lit up as if the sun had been born in her face. He glanced at Diana and neither of them could speak.

Saturday morning at tournaments is a torture chamber only the gutty survive. After giving everything they had physically and emotionally the night before, young athletes try to call up some energy and strength from deep within.

Ennis, in their green and white, had an experienced team that was not blessed with height. At first they attempted to press Willow Creek, and though they did succeed in causing several turnovers, the Broncs broke through for just as many easy layups. When the fast break wasn't there, Willow Creek slowed the game down and moved the ball around the perimeter of the Mustangs' scrambling zone. At times both teams appeared to be running in sand, passing a twelve-pound ham, and jumping in shoes of iron. At other times their quickness returned, their speed exploded, and their shooting eyes focused.

At the quarter Willow Creek led, 16 to 13, and Sam pulled Tom, who was limping.

"You're playing tough," Sam told them. "Dean, go after the ball out front. I know how hard it is out there, go one minute more."

They milked every second they could on the bench, until the referee came and ordered them back onto the court.

During the second quarter, the Ennis coach used several substitutes, undoubtedly hoping that by the fourth quarter he would have run the Willow Creek boys into the barn floor. They pressed all over the court, but the Broncs kept their heads. Field goals had become scarce on both ends and turnovers more prevalent than usual. While Dean harassed on defense, showing them something about running, Tom rested his knee on the bench, wearing Dean's cap. Though they often faked Dean out or caught him going the wrong way, he kept recovering, coming back, annoying, pestering, hounding, wreaking havoc in his unpredictable way. Neither side knew where he'd be next, and Sam couldn't get over how the Cutter boy would never stop running though much of his energy was misspent. Ennis's leader, Lance Hubbard, a six-foot senior guard, hit two outside shots just before the half to draw them even at 31. The teams shuffled to the locker rooms.

Sam could see the exhaustion in their faces, and he, Diana, and Scott tried to pump life back into them with fruit juices, dry towels, ice bags, and inspirational words. Olaf and Tom lay prostrate on the benches, Tom with a towel over his face. Sam couldn't ask them to give more than they already had and he noted that Peter seemed the least tired, the most energized.

"All right, Tom, move across the paint and set up on the high post, Olaf on the same side low post, we'll clear the right side of the floor and let Pete go one-on-one with Perkins. If any of you can't go another minute, give me a wave. While you're in there, spend every nickel you've got."

"I don't have any money with me," Dean said.

"He means play tough," Rob said, as if he gently explaining to a little brother.

They cleared the right side and Pete blew by John Perkins for a layup. Next time downcourt, Pete repeated the sleight of hand, but this time the defense slid quickly to cut him off. He lofted a pass to Olaf and Olaf cannonballed it with a resounding two-handed slam.

"Blow them away!" Sam shouted. "Blow them away!"

It became a standoff. Ennis couldn't handle the Norwegian hammer and Willow Creek couldn't match the Mustang's rotation of fresh players. Like the wild dogs of Africa, they came at them again and again. Both teams were weathering a searing drought in which baskets were as hard to come by as rain. With three minutes left in the game and the score Willow Creek 45, Ennis 42, Sam called time out.

Diana reminded them of what they already knew: Olaf, Rob, and Dean had four fouls.

"Tom, can you go with your knee?" Diana asked the sweating senior.

"What knee?" he said. Then the bull rider glared at the dripping faces of his teammates and said, "Let's not give 'em the calf."

Though Ennis ran at them with everything it had left, the Willow Creek boys refused to give in. They swept the boards on defense and did some running of their own. Olaf pitched a long pass to Pete, who had dashed behind the faltering Ennis defense for a layin. Rob missed a three-point attempt but Tom went up and tipped it in. Ennis had the ball, down by three, with twenty-four seconds.

The three-point attempt Hubbard got was a bad one, over Rob's outstretched arm, and when it came off the rim, Olaf caught it. When they swatted at him, the ref whistled a one-and-one. Five seconds on the clock.

With a three-point lead, Olaf gasped for air at the line. Willow Creek had used all of their time outs. In a prayerful pose in front of the bench, Sam couldn't draw a breath. If he made the front end of the one-and-one, Ennis was dead. Olaf took a deep breath, rolled the ball in his hands, and heaved it with a leaden arm toward the basket. The ball hit the front of the rim, bounced up and tapped the backboard, came down on the side of the rim.

"Yeah!" Sam shouted, leaping and pumping a fist.

The shot ignited an outburst from everyone on the Willow Creek side, filling the empty spaces in the arena with the rumble of a long-pent-up jubilation. Sam grabbed Diana and twirled her around. The team gave Olaf high fives. The referee restored order and gave Olaf the ball at the line for his second shot.

"Don't foul!" Sam shouted. "Don't foul! Don't foul!"

Olaf lifted his second shot, an air ball. Mustang ball out of bounds with five seconds on the scoreboard. Ennis ran the ball up the floor with sudden death in their eyes. Lance Hubbard hurled a desperate three-point shot into the fated atmosphere. It caromed high off the rim and the buzzer blew. Diana dashed toward the boys. Sam shook a fist in the air and leaped off the floor.

Hazel lumbered onto the floor with Tripod under arm in the happy chaos. She and Sam exchanged a glance. After shaking hands with the disconsolate Ennis players, they huddled up, shouted "Team!" and came off the floor together. They had eight hours to reload.

CHAPTER 70

The locker room was electric, though their bodies dragged and their feet ached.

"Where do you want to have lunch?"

"McDonald's," Dean said.

"Yeah, McDonald's!" they all yelled, though Sam knew most of them would prefer someplace else. He kept his amazement to himself and they had a happy lunch at McDonald's with Dean, who gleefully collected the promotional gimmicks.

It seemed there was barely time to blink. Diana had the team in bed to try for a couple hours nap when Sam's phone rang. He picked it up while stretched out on his bed.

"Mr. Pickett?"

"Yes."

He couldn't place the voice immediately.

"Grandma Chapman here. I just talked to Hazel. Way to go, Coach, we're not out of this shindig yet. Is Pete around?"

"Ah, yes . . . but I think he's sleeping."

"Oh . . ." She fell silent.

"Hold on a minute, I'll go see."

Sam laid the phone on the bed and hustled next door. Pete was lying on the bed watching television, college basketball.

"Your grandma is on the phone."

Pete leaped up and followed him to the phone.

"Hi, Grandma, how are you?"

"I'm cookin'. I hear you were wonderful this morning."

"We won. I called you last night."

"I didn't want to get out of bed."

"Are you getting better?"

"Yes, I'm feeling much better. I'll be here waiting for you when you come home."

"Won't you be here for the game tonight?" Pete said.

"No, I think I better stay home with Parrot and save up my energy for Monday. You listen to me, Sweetheart, I've seen you playing tonight and you're going to win."

"It might be too late, Grandma."

"Listen to me, Seely-Swan will take care of Twin Bridges and then Twin Bridges will be staring you in the face again, and come Monday you're going to pull the plug in their oil pan and I'll be there to see it, you hear me?"

"Yeah, I hear you," he said, feeling her enthusiasm rekindling his confidence.

"I'll be pulling for you tonight, Sweetheart, I know you'll bring tears to my eyes."

"Thanks, Grandma. Cuss at Parrot for me."

Peter hung up.

"How is she?" Mr. Pickett asked.

"Oh, she's fine. She won't be coming tonight, she wants to rest up so she can watch us bash Twin Bridges on Monday night."

"You have some kind of grandma."

"I know."

"That was a fine thing you did for Denise at the game," Coach Pickett said. "It took a lot of guts."

"It takes a lot more for her just to get out of bed in the morning."

"You're right," Coach said. "Get some rest."

"THERE'S NO WAY I can tell you how proud I am of you, and Miss Murphy feels the same way," Sam told the team, gathered in his room prior to leaving for the sports center. "The college teams that make it to the Sweet Sixteen and the Final Four in the NCAA tournament have two full days to rest between games, but they're wimps compared to you boys. You're about to play your third game in less than twenty-four hours, which makes you a lot tougher than the college boys. I'm a lucky man to be your coach."

Sam glanced at Diana. She smiled nervously. No one spoke. Then Rob glanced up. "Go, Seely-Swan."

"Ya, Seely-Swan," Olaf said. "Twin Bridges I am wanting."

"Kick ass, Seely-Swan!" Tom shouted.

"Seely-Swan! Seely-Swan! Seely-Swan!" they yelled in unison.

When they were all on their feet and about to leave, Diana stood by the door.

"If Seely-Swan was smart, they'd lose tonight," she said and smiled. "They'll go to State either way. We can't challenge *them*. But if they win, they're going to have to play us at State, and there's no way they can beat us again."

The room exploded with shouts and cheers. He followed them into the corridor. He didn't feel they were looking past Alberton. They had taken care of that in their minds and were so confident that it was appropriate to talk about the Seely-Swan–Twin Bridges game. He knew that they each faced the prospect of defeat, of the possible dead end that loomed only a few hours away, the devastating loss that would snatch away their companionship forever.

BY GAME TIME Grandma had enlisted half of the hospital in the cause of her sterling grandson and his teammates. The lame and infirm and terminally ill found it extremely appropriate to identify with Willow Creek's fortunes, and by late afternoon, the place was buzzing with hope.

Joe Page, a lanky, Pinocchio-nosed male nurse, had scrounged a good radio from one of the maintenance men and rigged it up beside Grandma's bed. The only broadcast of the game was coming out of a station in Missoula, bringing the game to its Alberton and Seely-Swan neighborhoods. But that was halfway across Montana, and Joe warned Grandma that they might not be able to bring it in.

"We need an aerial," he said and scurried out of her room.

Shortly before game time, he attached a wire to the radio and was stringing it up to the curtain rod that divided the room. Grandma tinkered with the dial and through static and a jumble of music and voices caught something that sounded like a game.

"It'll probably fade in and out," Joe said.

Grandma hushed as a voice came through the hodgepodge.

". . . Johnson brings the ball up, snaps a pass to Strong. . . . Strong dribbles to the side and back out . . ."

"That's it! That's it!" Grandma yelled.

". . . the ball goes in to Stonebreaker. . . . Stonebreaker lobs a high pass to Gustafson, the big center turns and shoots. . . . it's short, comes off to Hackett. . . . Hackett over to Potter and the Panthers go on the attack. Potter over to Kury, in to Dupree . . ."

The voice faded back into the storm of interference washing over the hospital.

"Fiddlesticks!" she said.

Joe worked on the aerial, unbending a coat hanger and attaching it to the wire. Helen Berry leaned from her bed next to Grandma, trying to pick out a word or two from the crackling radio. Nurses on their rounds began sticking their heads in the door for word. The game came in and out, always fading just as the announcer was giving the score.

". . . and Jenkins gives it back to Strong . . . he drives up the middle, dishes off to Gustafson. . . . ooooohhhh man! The big center jams the ball and the Willow Creek Broncs are coming back . . ."

"We must be behind," Grandma said, feeling her stomach lurch.

"Does that make it any better?" Joe asked as he adjusted the makeshift antenna.

"No, it's fading," Grandma said. Her ear was an inch from the speaker.

Other patients in wheelchairs, on crutches or walkers, in hospital gowns and personal robes and slippers peeked into the room, turning their ears at the crackling radio.

". . . Potter gets it inside to Dupree. . . . Dupree goes up with it, it's blocked. . . . There's a foul, let's see . . . foul called on Gustafson . . . two shots. That's the second personal on the big center and . . ."

"Rats!" Grandma said.

Joe worked feverishly on the aerial, and other patients shuffled, rolled, and limped into the double room, patients from drug rehab, maternity, and some from post-op with draining wounds. They reflected Grandma's emotions as if she wielded a baton, directing them in the excruciating notes and exhilarating beats of pulling for this unlikely basketball team. Only occasionally they'd catch a score, and most of the time they had to guess what was transpiring two hundred and twenty-four miles northwest in Helena.

". . . Dupree makes the second free throw . . . Alberton 27, Willow Creek 22 . . ."

"There," Grandma shouted, "it's better when you're holding on to it."

Joe held onto the tangle of wire and coat hangers.

". . . Johnson dribbles to the right, stops . . . over to Strong, four seconds. . . . Strong lobs the ball high to Gustafson, he drops it off to Stonebreaker who's open in the . . ."

They kept getting tidbits of information. The announcer's voice would come in for ten to twenty seconds and then melt away into the Montana night for a minute or two. Nurses were hanging around the doorway, maintenance personnel, interns, and finally a few doctors crowded around in the hallway. Willow Creek had fans that night far beyond its notion of local neighborhoods, neighborhoods of the spirit and of the heart.

". . . and Jenkins gets the ball over to Johnson, oooohhh . . . he misses the wide-open lay-up and Farr rebounds the ball. Here comes Alberton the other way. . . . Farr gets it to Kury, Kury pulls up and shoots a three . . . count it! Alberton 46, Willow Creek . . ."

"Shucks!" Grandma shouted, "everyone hold hands."

Joe took the hand of a chemotherapy patient, a man in his forties with no hair on his head, to begin the human chain. The man took the hand of a heavy woman next to him in a wheelchair who had just lost a leg to diabetes, and so on around the room, forming an aerial out of human yearning.

". . . and the Broncs rebound . . . Gustafson swoops it off the boards, over to Strong . . . up quickly to Johnson, he holds it . . . they're setting it up, over to Strong . . . on the side to Cutter . . . Cutter back to . . . a whistle . . . Cutter's called for shuffling his feet and the Broncs turn it. . . ."

"Coach has taken Tom out," Grandma said. "He's got a bad knee from riding a Brahma last summer, bothers him when he plays a lot, but we need him in there."

Grandma felt an overwhelming despair. Tom was out, Dean lost the ball, everything going against them, and she wasn't there for Peter, even if it meant to comfort him when they lost. She realized she was starting to sound like Hazel.

Doctor Mack wormed his way into the room.

"How are they doing?" he asked her.

"We don't know, the radio only gives us scraps, the blasted announcer never gives the score or when he does—"

". . . that's the fourth foul on Hackett. . . . Gustafson at the line shooting two . . . He dribbles the ball, eyes the basket . . . puts up the shot, short. . . . He'll get one more . . . looks like the big kid is tired. . . . This Willow Creek team is going with only one substitute. . . . He eyes the basket, shoots . . ."

"Hell's bells!" Grandma shouted, pounding her mattress with a fist.

"This feels like the intensive care waiting room," Doctor Mack said, surveying the curious gathering. He twisted his way to the side of Grandma's bed and took her hand, checking her pulse.

"That's not fair. I'm a little riled right now."

"You think you can go home tomorrow?" the doctor asked.

"I have to be home before my grandson gets back from Helena."

She took his arm and pulled him closer.

"I hope this isn't hurting anyone," she whispered.

"On the contrary, it will do them a world of good, take their minds off themselves for a while."

". . . Gustafson shoots, comes off the front of the rim, oooohhh . . . Stonebreaker tips it in. . . . great move to the basket . . . This kid's leg may be hurting but he is one tough cookie. . . . Willow Creek, on a 10–2 run, is up by seven as Kury brings . . ."

The room exploded with applause and cheering out of frail and wounded bodies, hoarse and hurting throats, hopeful and expectant faces, all of them seeming to yearn that there was a "winning" after all.

". . . Cutter slaps the ball and it goes off a Panther. . . . Willow Creek's ball . . . Johnson in to Strong, up to Jenkins . . . back to Strong . . . he wants to get the ball in to his big center. . . . The Alberton boys are jamming the middle. . . . Strong takes the three, count it! Willow Creek 64, Alber . . ."

"That's my grandson!" Grandma shouted. "We must still be ahead. How much time, how much time?" She looked at her watch, trying to gauge the game's length. It should be close to over. The gentle voice came over the intercom.

"For those of you following the Willow Creek basketball game, Willow Creek is ahead, 65 to 55, with two minutes to go."

Isolated chirps and bird songs could be heard up and down the hall from those constrained in their cages. She glanced around the room and regarded her merry compadres, holding hands in a chain of hope, a chain of people willing on six boys they'd never seen, willing on the blood cells, immune systems, and antibodies they'd never seen, daring to believe they all would win against greater numbers and impossible odds. She could see the team holding hands in their huddle and willing these people to win, willing that all those who were wounded and crippled, all those who were underdogs against the forces that crush them and sweep them away, would come out winners and triumph over the darkness of defeat.

"... and Potter tries a three-pointer ... comes high off the rim and Johnson climbs a ladder for the rebound.... The Panthers foul him immediately but it's too little too late.... Johnson'll shoot a one-and-one.... This Alberton team has played their best, but the Willow Creek Broncs ..."

"Yippeeeee!" Grandma shouted and her roomful of patients and hospital staff joined her in serendipitous celebration. They chattered and laughed and patted one another on the back for a job well done.

"... and with a minute to go, this one is over folks ... the cat's in the sack, the sack's in the river.... Willow Creek will have to wait to see who wins the championship game to know ..."

A sudden dread gripped Grandma. She'd almost forgotten.

"What's the matter?" Doctor Mack asked.

"Oh my land, now we have to listen to the championship game. If Seely-Swan beats Twin Bridges, Willow Creek can challenge Twin Bridges Monday night."

They all groaned. Then they set their faces and relinked their hands, ready to take their stand with Willow Creek through one more game as though their personal destiny was somehow mysteriously linked with this obscure little town and its uncelebrated team, as though if these outmanned, also-ran basketball players could win in the face of the inconceivable, *so could they.*

CHAPTER 71

I n the locker room no one seemed to know how to act. Into the happiness of winning was blended the bittersweet knowledge that this
still might have been their last game. They showered and dressed slowly.

Sam had no idea of what he ought to say so he struggled to tell them
what he felt.

He waited by the locker room, hanging back with the slowest of the
boys, putting off as long as possible suffering in the bleachers and helplessly
watching while his pure and perfect dream was being torn to shreds at the
sweaty hands of the Twin Bridges basketball team. Even with this wondrous
season, Sam, in six years, had never beaten Twin Bridges.

Rob and Pete were ready to go out and join Miss Murphy and the cheerleaders. Sam figured every Willow Creek fan who had come would be
compelled to remain for the championship game, unable to leave until the
team's destiny had been decided.

Sam was unnerved by the roar he could hear funneling out of the gymnasium. Olaf seemed to hang back, and finally, Tom, in his J. Chisholm
diamondback boots, was ready to face the hand dealt him, forced to sit in
the bleachers and watch. Sam slapped him on the back.

"You were awesome tonight, Tom."

"Thanks." The bull rider nodded and limped out of the locker room.

Olaf tied his shoes, then faced Sam.

"Something to you I am wanting to be saying," Olaf said, looking down
to Sam's eyes.

"What is it, Olaf?"

"I am wanting you to know. All the students out to the ranch that are
coming is not what is bringing me back to the basketball. I am coming back
because you are saying life is trying and not being afraid to be the oaf. You
say you cannot be a spectator to life. Coming back I am because you are
right, I am thinking."

"Thank you." Sam said. "But ironically, now we have no choice. We have to go out and be just that, spectators, to see if our life on the hardwood is over."

They walked into the arena at floor level behind the east basket. The atmosphere was electric with energy and noise, squeaking shoes and grunts and shouts under the canopy of a constant roar from the overcapacity crowd. Sam glanced out at the two teams going at each other on the court and thought how each of them had figured so prominently in shaping Willow Creek's course.

He and Olaf wended their way up into the bleachers, receiving vociferous exclamations of praise from admirers. He saw the grim apprehension on the faces of the team and fans, who were perched like the Willow Creek vultures. He wedged in beside Diana. Olaf, right behind them, found room between Carter and Rob.

The twelve of them sat huddled together in the midst of a sheltering Willow Creek throng, as though their loyal fans could shield them from the killing arrow. All of them shouted and rooted for Seely-Swan in a game where neither team was able to forge ahead by more than a point or two. By the time the scoreboard clock showed less than a minute, all of them were weak from nervous exhaustion.

Seely-Swan went up by two with eighteen seconds to go, and all spectators in the arena were standing. Twin Bridges moved the ball upcourt quickly, snapped it around outside, and then Corky Miller bounced a beautiful pass in to Craig Stone. The Falcon center spun and banked the ball in as the buzzer went off. There had been a whistle. A foul. Craig Stone had one free throw with no time on the clock. The game was tied at 67.

The Willow Creek bunch unconsciously linked hands: Sam held Diana's hand, unable to look at her; Carter took hold of Olaf's and held Dean's, the team and the cheerleaders clung to each other, as though they were about to be smashed on the rocks by an unavoidable tidal wave.

Craig Stone toed the line as the Seely-Swan crowd roared a frantic distraction, willing the ball to be sucked into the outer reaches of hell, willing the boy's arm to turn to oak and catapult a brick five feet in front of him. The sports center vibrated, the bleachers shook. The Twin Bridges athlete, standing at the line alone, bounced the ball twice. He took it in his hands, eyed the rim, and flipped the shot. It hit the back rim, bounced to the front, and rolled off. Tie game!

The three-minute overtime became an operating room for Willow Creek, watching a heart transplant in a mirror and realizing it was your bloody chest pried open and there was a good chance they wouldn't get all the parts stitched back together. Twin Bridges went ahead on a layup by Harkin, and Seely-Swan tied it with two free throws by Thomas. With a minute gone, Stone dropped a short jump hook. Halfway through overtime, Boyd, Seely-Swan's stumpy guard, hit a three, putting the Blackhawks up by one.

The Willow Creek team leaped to their feet and cheered. From then on no one sat down. Neely missed a jumper for Twin Bridges and Seely-Swan grabbed the rebound. With a one-point lead and the ball, they went into a four-corner stall, but with thirty-four seconds to go, Corky Miller picked off a pass and raced the length of the court for a layup.

Twin Bridges 71, Seely-Swan 70.

A numbing dread seized Sam. Seely-Swan moved the ball and worked for a good shot with defenders hounding them.

Ten seconds.

Boyd penetrated into the paint but Stone cut him off.

Six seconds.

The bounce passed the ball to Cooper, who was open in the corner. Without hesitating, the senior forward lifted an arcing shot. It seemed to Sam that the ball was a time-lapse exposure, a series of still shots along its crescent course toward the basket; he could see it unmoving in the air, the seams, the full-grained leather, the Rawlings label. Then, as quickly, the world returned to full speed. The ball swished. The buzzer wailed. The scoreboard glared Seely-Swan 72, Twin Bridges 71. The Seely-Swan team mobbed the shooter, and the Willow Creek bunch mugged one another.

It was resurrection day!

The hometown throng rose into the air with such a tumult, it seemed people were in danger of bodily injury. They turned and engulfed their team, a great human huddle in the stands with layers and layers of rapturous supporters around them.

"We'll never quit!" Pete shouted.

"Never quit!" the team yelled.

"Now Twin Bridges I will be playing," Olaf said.

"We'll be their undertaker!" Diana shouted.

They had been given another chance! They were back in it with both feet. Then Tom Stonebreaker, with his arms draped around several of them, shook the inner circle with his iron grasp and swept their faces with his rapacious gaze.

"I've played Twin Bridges for four years and never beat them and I'm not going to live the rest of my life with that brand on my ass!" They shouted their assent and made promises with their eyes.

When the officials had finally cleared the floor and some of the disappointed spectators had departed for their cars, the three teams gathered at the edge of the court. The Divisional Championship trophy was awarded to Seely-Swan, and most of those remaining in the arena cheered. Then the official announced that the second- and third-place trophies would be awarded after the Monday night challenge game. The Willow Creek delegation, which hadn't dwindled by more than a body or two, roared as if they'd already won the game. When the noise subsided, Olaf looked across the floor at Craig Stone, who stood disgruntled with his wilted teammates. Olaf pointed at him with his scarecrow arm and finger and shouted loudly.

"Monday night the basketball we are playing!"

Craig Stone sneered and gave Olaf the finger. Sam was glad. If there was one thing missing in his Viking center, it was the killer instinct, to put a team away.

"He gave you the finger, Olaf," Rob said.

"Ya, I am seeing."

"That's a huge sign of disrespect, Oaf," Pete said.

Tom slapped Olaf on the back. "He's laughing at you."

"Give 'em the finger," Dean said.

"On Monday night something for him I have," Olaf stated defiantly, still staring across into the face of Craig Stone, and if the Twin Bridges veteran didn't get the message, the Willow Creek boys did.

BACK AT THE Colonial Inn, exhaustion kicked in, and the team dragged around like a convention of catatonics. They had pizza delivered to the girls' room, but they didn't eat half of what they ordered. Some of them seemed too happy and too tired to eat. A meditative mood engulfed them as the past twenty-four hours sunk in. Sam gave the boys permission to swim in the motel pool, and Diana and he found themselves alone with a few uneaten pizzas.

Sam blushed, embarrassed that he had doubted it all when they lost on Friday, when it seemed so impossible. It was so easy to slip into skepticism and despair.

"Let's see what they're up to," she said.

"No, let's just sit here and breathe."

"C'mon."

She extended her hand and pulled him out of a stuffed chair.

They came into the tiled recreation room. Only the girls were swimming. Sam walked to the pool side.

"Where are the boys?" he asked Carter.

"Right there," she said.

They crept up behind him and, with Diana's help, picked him off the floor with shouts and cheers. Then, respectfully and lovingly, they tossed him into the water. Sam gasped as he came up for air, finding himself chest deep in the pool.

"That's your victory dunk!" Pete shouted and everyone applauded.

Dean giggled and Curtis appeared somewhat shocked.

"It's supposed to be Gatorade!" Sam said.

He flopped into the water and backstroked around, remembering in his other life he would have given up everything for this moment. And then, without warning, they grabbed Miss Murphy—who had conspired with them to get Sam to the pool—and chucked her screaming into the pool. When she came up sputtering, her long hair plastered to her face, Sam gently steadied her and laughed. She brushed her hair aside and laughed with him. She pointed an accusing finger at the girls and boys around the pool.

"You rats! You traitors!"

"What goes around comes around," Sam said.

He put his arms around her and pulled her close in her waterlogged sweatshirt and blue slacks. They stood waist deep in the water holding each other affectionately for the first time in front of the kids. Peter started it and then they all followed, applauding and whistling their approval. Sam knew he loved them all. He wanted to stay. He didn't know how long he could. He understood what life would be like without her, but what would it be like without the boys?

CHAPTER 72

After sleeping until almost noon and then eating a large brunch, the weary Willow Creek team arrived home in front of the school close to three in the afternoon. Pete grabbed his duffel and ball and sprinted the two blocks home. He barged in the front door and found Grandma at the kitchen table scrutinizing the Sunday paper with two pair of glasses.

"Grandma, how are you?" He dropped his bag and ball.

"I'm cookin', sweetheart," she said and stood to greet him.

She gave him a hug and a peck on the cheek.

"Are you all well?"

"Yes, yes, land sakes, it was only a flu bug. I knew you'd do it all along, I just knew it. I listened on the radio but it didn't come in so good. The announcer would never give the blame score."

"Pull a ship?" Parrot cackled.

"Are you hungry?"

"No," he said, peeling off his jacket and sliding into a chair. "Just thirsty."

Grandma pulled a half-gallon of milk from the papered refrigerator and set it with a glass on the table.

"This place was a ghost town. I was the only one here I think, 'cept for the dogs and skunks. Why you would've thought the world had come to an end."

Pete poured a glass and chugged it.

"I sure wish you could have been there," he said. "I looked for you last night."

"Well, wild horses couldn't keep me from being there tomorrow night when you wipe out Twin Bridges. I can't wait to see them get their berries picked, and then it's off to Bozeman and the State. Oh, it plain gives me the willies."

"You look a little pale," Pete said.

"Well I didn't eat for a while, but I'm as fit as a fiddle now, and I've been readin' about you: nineteen Saturday morning, twenty-four Saturday night, and I *know,* I *know,* like Coach Pickett says, 'It's the teamwork that wins games.'"

"Yeah, he's right. I wouldn't have twenty-four if the other team wasn't wettin' its pants over the Oaf, or trying to stop Rob."

"Listen to this," she said, rapping a knuckle on the paper.

WILLOW CREEK WON'T GO AWAY. Coach Jeff Long of Twin Bridges must be looking over his shoulder and shaking his head this morning. Faced with a challenge game on Monday night, the excellent Falcon team—who've beaten Willow Creek three times this season—should make it four. The second-ranked team in the State has too many guns for the 'Half-a-Dozen Squad' from Willow Creek. But I have a feeling it will be close and I realize I could be writing on Tuesday morning, 'Willow Creek won't go away.'

She pulled off the outer pair of glasses and looked over at her grandson.

"Thank heavens we have a challenge game. Twin Bridges only won two games while you boys won three. It's only fair that you should get a crack at them. This way no one sneaks by in a weak bracket. Whoever thought it up was one smart cookie."

WHEN ALL THE equipment was in its place and everyone else had scattered, Diana and Sam walked to her car. She surveyed the sky and took a deep breath.

"Let's see what's happening," she said.

"Where?"

"Out there."

She nodded toward the mountains and the vast country beyond the meager boundaries of the town.

"You mean right *now*?" Sam said, gazing toward the Tobacco Roots.

"Yeah."

"I have a lot to get done before—"

"Like stew and fuss and worry."

Sam regarded this sprightly woman who had moved into his heart with all of her mysterious baggage and he recognized the little girl sparkling in her eyes.

"You're right. Let's go."

"I have to change," she said. "Half hour?"

"I'll pick you up," Sam said and turned for his house.

He changed into his sorry running shoes, old jeans, and Levi jacket, then he pulled into her castaway ranch yard. She bounced down the steps in her field jacket and Padres cap. She directed him down gravel roads to a different place along the Jefferson River. They parked and scrambled over the rusted barbed wire. He followed her through brush and rose thorn and sage into a towering cottonwood stand where a few juniper and aspen were competing for space and sunlight. He loved to watch her forging on ahead of him, knowing just where to step.

From time to time she pointed out animal tracks and signs, magpie nests, a blue heron rookery, coyote scats, and the other unending evidence of the ongoing life around them.

"Of course this will all be buried in snow at least once more," she said.

Sam followed her meandering course along the wooded river bench until they came to a small meadow covered with knee-high brown grass.

"Look," she pointed at a place where the grass was trodden down in several faint oval shapes. "Deer bedded down here today." She felt the ground in one of the matted places. "Maybe we spooked them."

"Can we do it here?" Sam said.

She smiled enticingly. "Do what?"

"Lie down and feel the earth turn."

"Oh . . . sure."

She knelt in one of the deer beds and stretched out on her back, her feet pointing south. Sam lay beside her.

He slid an arm under her head and she snuggled on his shoulder. Then they were quiet, their arms out to the side, watching the clouds and trying to sense the planet's rotation. The sun, mostly hidden in the multilayered sky, was mincing toward the rim of the Tobacco Roots. They were the only people in the universe. What would it be like to mate here in this hidden meadow like the deer?

"Feel it?" she whispered.

Sam tried to refocus on the earth beneath him, lying there with her in his arms. He breathed deeply. They were quiet for several minutes. A breeze whispered in the grass.

"Yeah, I got it, I can feel it."

He imagined himself falling back into the rotating earth, and a centeredness faithfully returned to him, an underlying balance that he faintly recognized from some unremembered time.

"We'll do this some clear night when it gets warmer," he heard her say. "It's easier to feel the rotation when the stars appear to be moving west."

Sam gazed at the clouds and a great sense of awe gripped him, a shivering instant in which he wanted to tell her about Amos and Andrew and Grandma and how afraid he was that she would leave him.

Finally, it dawned on him. What in *hell* was Sam Pickett worried about? Life was only found *here,* in the present. And it was tragic to poison this miraculous moment by allowing the pain and regret of his past or fear of the future leak all over it. He breathed deeply and allowed himself to cherish this wondrous interlude, letting all else fall away, to cherish the air and the earth and the warm woman lying beside him in the winter grass.

SAM ATE HIS noon meal before gathering the team. The high school kids had Monday off, game day, and at the Blue Willow it seemed that everyone else had followed suit. When Grandma slid into a chair next to him, Sam prayed that he could pretend to be totally oblivious to the cataclysm and shipwreck of her life.

She startled him. "Well, you gonna tell me I look pale like the rest of them?"

"No, no!" Sam overdid it. "You look great to me."

"Never saw the likes of it. Have a touch of flu and they try to bury you," she said with a genuine disgust on her face.

He accepted her effusive praise and they rehashed the games for a minute.

"Will you be stayin' when this is all over?" she asked.

"No . . . I'll be leaving this summer." He caught his breath. "It wouldn't be the same around here without . . . without the boys . . . without Diana."

"I know what you mean. I'm going to miss Peter something fierce." She glanced into his eyes. "Are you leaving with Miss Murphy? You're so good for each other."

"She is for me."

"And you are for her. I've seen it in her eyes. It would be a crime if you two don't up and get married."

"That sounds nice, but she's taking a job in San Diego."

"So? They don't need English teachers and top-notch coaches in San Diego?"

"I think I'll stick to English from now on. It wouldn't be the same with the basketball."

"You're right," she said wistfully, as if for a moment the garment of her courage had slipped, revealing a glimpse of her heart. "This has been something else. Things are never the same. We gotta dance before the orchestra goes home."

Sam sighed with relief when Grandma scooted off to another table, immediately aware of how strained he'd been emotionally. How in the hell do you talk to someone you know is dying but who thinks you don't? Maybe the way one should talk to everyone. They were all dying.

The chair hadn't cooled when Axel dropped in and leaned an elbow on the table.

In a hushed voice the proprietor of the bustling inn said, "Sam, there was a guy in here this morning asking about a Granville Hamilton. He never showed a badge or anything, but I think he was some kind of a cop."

"Hamilton? I don't know any Granville Hamilton. Never heard of anyone with that name around here."

Axel leaned closer and whispered, "The guy kept talking about weather and things and then would come back to this Hamilton guy, like wondering if he stopped in here now and then. It was spooky. After awhile I found myself lying!"

"Lying? Why?"

Axel's forehead gleamed with perspiration, the scar below his ear flamed, and he whispered so quietly Sam could barely hear him in the droning dining room.

"Because the guy was describing Amos Flowers!"

Oh, Jeez, I knew it, I knew it!

Sam tried to swallow the portion of lasagna he had just shoveled into his mouth and felt a deep-dish concrete form in his stomach.

Now it was Sam who was whispering.

"Amos! Are you sure?"

"Yeah, he described him to a tee except for the hat. Said he always wore a black hat, but it was Amos he was talking about."

Sam tried to disguise his fright. The hidden suitcase bulging with cash loomed in his mind as though it had spilled all over the table in the Blue Willow. He glanced around the inn to see if any strangers were watching. "Well, I hope it's nothing serious," he said. "Have you seen Amos today?"

"No, but we better warn him. He doesn't have a phone and no one knows exactly where he lives. I don't know what to do."

"Well, when he shows up we can tell him. He'll probably be at the game tonight."

On his way up the blacktop toward school, where he would walk through some offensive sets with the boys before heading for Helena, he leaned into the robust southwesterly that was indigenous to Willow Creek. He wanted to stop at the house and hide the suitcase in a less obvious place. What had he gotten himself into? He caught himself looking over his shoulder, no longer for George Stonebreaker, but for some mafioso in a black pinstriped suit who wanted his money back. Going past his house, he acted as though he'd never seen the place before.

He couldn't help but notice the fanfare of clouds, surging and swelling in the extravagant sky.

An unfamiliar car came into town from the south, and he ducked into the school as if out of some blazing spotlight of guilt. But Amos and his satchel of cash instantly faded from his mind in the glow of the bright apple faces waiting for him in the gym.

CHAPTER 73

D iana had never seen the boys that eager, that fired up to play a game, their last shot at Twin Bridges forever and forever. As they warmed up in the Carroll College Sports Center, she kept one eye on Olaf. The kid had improved so much in the past few weeks it seemed that his coordination and confidence, like younger brothers, were catching up to his sprawling dimensions. She watched him shooting free throws and she could see that the boy had a look in his eye that had never been there before, a look neither she nor Sam could have put there, a look that had its seeds back in the long lineage of fearsome Vikings.

At the bench for introductions, the boys were like sled dogs straining at their harnesses, challenging one another and slapping palms. She and Sam needed only to stand aside and turn them loose. The announcer welcomed the whittled-down Monday-night crowd to the challenge game and began the introductions.

"For Willow Creek, starting at one forward, number eighteen, a 6'4" senior, Tom Stonebreaker."

Rugged, dear-to-her-heart Tom, their rock, their anchor, yet a boy terribly unsure of himself, struggling to understand the pain in his life. Diana recognized a fierceness in him at times that frightened her.

Tom hurried off the bench and scrambled through the high fives of his teammates to the free-throw circle while the Willow Creek followers hooted and cheered. Diana didn't like the way Tom moved, definitely favoring his knee.

"For Willow Creek, starting at the other forward, number 44, a 6'2" sophomore, Curtis Jenkins!"

She smiled. Shy, quiet Curtis. Forget Me Not traded high fives with them all and trotted onto the court.

"For Willow Creek, starting at center, number 55, a 6'11" senior, Olaf Gustafson!"

Olaf, the adorable giant. Unselfish, overly conscientious, expecting too much of himself, wanting to win so badly for his teammates and coach. His adopted hometown fans roared their support and admiration for the polite visitor from across the Atlantic.

"Oaf! Oaf! Oaf! Oaf! Oaf! Oaf! Oaf!"

"For Willow Creek, starting at one guard, number 22, a 5'11" junior, Peter Strong!"

Precious Pete, fiery, playful, trying to live up to his name, trying to cope with wit and a sense of humor, channeling his confusion and loneliness into the discipline of basketball. He ran off the floor to the far end of the gym to give Denise Cutter a high five and then sprinted back to join his teammates on the court.

Finally, only Dean and Rob and Scott remained on the bench.

"For Willow Creek, starting at the other guard, number 10, a 6' senior, Rob Johnson!"

She smiled. Darling, clean-cut Rob, their bright all-American boy, happy, eager, surrounded by the safety and affection of his family and girlfriend. The senior, with a rocklike expression chiseled on his face, slapped hands with them at the bench and then joined his teammates on the court. They looked sharp, circled around Olaf in their Twilight Zone game shoes and their sparkling new uniforms.

"And the head coach for Willow Creek, Sam Pickett."

Diana whistled and clapped loudly as Sam looked out at his team on the floor. She wanted to throw her arms around him and kiss him, there for the whole world to see.

The team hustled to the bench and huddled around Coach Pickett, who was down on one knee.

"All right, men. We know this team. We've seen everything they've got and it ain't enough. Have fun and let's put a trophy in our trophy case."

Sam glanced at Diana and nodded.

"I'd like to go shopping in Bozeman next weekend, boys," she said.

"Yeeaaahhhh!" they shouted.

Then they were out on the floor, poised, staring in fortune's face with the hope and faith more common with the young.

From the opening whistle it became a war zone. She went through the elation and anguish, the ebb and flow of the combat, a contest that had come down to the sweat, saliva, and blood of ten young athletes doing what they had been honed to do so well. She found the longings of her heart entangled with the boys' gutty resolve and Sam's deepest hopes, blended into one heartbeat in the teeming, roaring arena where it was decreed that only one team could win. She couldn't help glancing at Sam, where the conflict was mirrored in the reflections of a human eye, etched in the lines of a human face. Like an aroused bear he prowled the sideline, shouted plays to the boys, and tried to influence the flight of the ball with body English.

Their rotating zone didn't give the Falcons spit and five golden jerseys rushed to the defensive boards like firefighters rescuing their mothers. But the lurking smile on Diana's face was the surprise Sam had for Coach Long and his arrogant twelve-man team. Sam called the play on the Broncs' third possession. Tom and Curtis set a double pick at the side of the paint, shoulder to shoulder. Olaf quickly slid around it, leaving Craig Stone, the 6'4" veteran center, momentarily caught behind the barnyard fence. Olaf caught a high pass from Rob and canned a soft seven-footer over Curtis and Tom.

"Bury them!" Sam yelled. "Blow them away!"

Coach Long employed the same strategy he had used to beat them three times that year: rotating nine boys, keeping them fresh, wearing down Willow Creek so they could be dry-gulched in the fourth quarter. But tonight it was the first quarter Coach Long needed to be concerned about.

Tom and Curtis kept meeting together along the edge of the paint, and when Stone frantically fought his way through the double pick, Olaf slid the other way and stuffed the ball. Gary Harkin, the Falcon defending on Tom's side, cheated all he could, but when he did, Olaf dropped the ball off to Tom and Tom knew where to put it. Stone and Harkin were consistently getting tangled in the double picks. Coach Long called time out with a minute left in the first quarter. Willow Creek 19, Twin Bridges 12.

"All right, you've got them confused," Sam said. "Now, Rob, you join the picnic with Tom and Curtis. Pete, you've got to guard the bank. The others will be tangled in the traffic jam." He smiled at his big center. "Olaf, clean out their refrigerator."

"Where's their refrigerator?" Dean asked and the boys swatted him gently and laughed.

The second quarter started like a street fight under the Twin Bridges basket. Rob set a triple screen with Tom and Curtis. Harkin and Stone scrambled to stay with Olaf as he slid around and between and behind his teammates. They bumped and grunted in teeth-jarring collisions. Olaf traveled, picked up two offensive fouls, and missed several shots, but in the scramble around the paint, he nailed fourteen points to the score-board, one a resounding alley-oop slam from Rob. And he made them pay with his free throw shooting when the frustrated Falcons hacked and battered him.

Near the end of the second quarter, Olaf came around a pick and went high with an alley-oop. When he stuffed the ball, Craig Stone fought his way through the picks and cut Olaf's legs out from under him while he was in midair. He came down like a load of fence posts. All elbows and knees, the unprotected boy slammed his back and head solidly on the hardwood, his mouth guard flying out like unglued dentures. All spectators in the sports center were on their feet.

"Flagrant foul! Flagrant foul!" Diana shouted. "Throw the jerk out of the game!"

Sam rushed toward Olaf. Tom went for Craig Stone, and in the moment's emotion, Diana hoped the bull rider would flatten him. Only Rob and Pete and a referee prevented Tom from taking the kid's head off. Sam and Diana stooped beside Olaf, who was sitting on the floor, slightly dazed.

"How are you?" Sam asked.

"Angry," he said, shaking his head lightly.

The referees sent both teams to their benches. When the smoke cleared, Olaf was awarded two free throws, making the first, missing the second. Still, Willow Creek got the ball because of the flagrant foul. Diana could sense the tension out on the court and wondered if Tom would be able to contain his wrath. That didn't turn out to be the main problem, because at halftime, Tom could hardly hobble to the locker room. They were up 40 to 36.

Sam didn't have to come up with anything inspirational. In fact, he fed off the boys' fire and confidence. Olaf got up twice and started for the door when Sam had to tell him it wasn't time yet.

"Tom can't play anymore," Diana whispered in Sam's ear.

He looked at her. She shrugged.

"Okay," Sam said. He stood in front of his team. "They're all trying to crash the party under the basket. When the ball comes in to you, Olaf, pop it right back out. We've been delivering our packages on foot. Now let's send them air mail. Rob and Pete, you ought to be open. When it's there, take it."

Sam looked at his gutsy forward.

"I have to take you out, Tom."

The Willow Creek cowboy didn't protest. Diana shared the anger and bitter disappointment in Tom's unyielding eyes, knowing then to what extent the pain had invaded his heart, to what extent the pain invaded all of their hearts as they fought and scrambled with everything they could lay their hands on in their stores of courage and endurance.

"Dean takes Miller," Sam said. "Rob, you play Tom's position. Dean, you hound Miller wherever he is on the floor. Stay in his face, ride in his jock, stick to him like sweat. The rest of you stay in the zone."

"If anyone can stick to him like sweat," Pete said, "Dean can."

"You got that right," Rob said.

And he did. Dean never stopped running, causing the Twin Bridges boy to shove him away in frustration once—Dean missing the front end of the one-and-one. With Tom on the bench wearing Dean's slightly-singed maroon cap, Twin Bridges pulled ahead. But Dean held Corky Miller, their best outside scorer, to one field goal, fouling him twice in the first few minutes of the third quarter.

"Get 'em, Dean!" Diana yelled.

They battled against nine other boys who were being rested and coming into the game fresh. In the absence of his powerful teammate, Olaf elevated his game and began hurting them inside, first going to his right, then to his left, eyes ablaze. On one lunge to the basket and a resounding stuff, he unintentionally caught Stone in the head with an elbow.

"Yeah!" she hollered, leaping up with a fist in the air, her scorebook skittering onto the hardwood. "Nail him!"

Coach Long had the paint clogged in the second half. Curtis and Dean kept loitering beside the paint and passing the ball high to Olaf. Rob and Pete began knocking blades out of the windmill with their outside shooting, twos and threes winging resplendently overhead while the Falcons were preoccupied trying to bottle up Olaf.

Then, scaring the wits out of them, Olaf picked up two quick fouls and Sam had to take him out. With fire in his eyes, Tom threw his warmup jacket aside and charged onto the court. With Olaf's inside threat parked at the curb and Tom hobbled, Twin Bridges could concentrate on Willow Creek's two hot-handed guards. Showing their experience and maturity, the gifted Falcons went on a 12–3 run closing the third quarter.

Down by four, Sam didn't know how far he could let them extend the lead before returning Olaf to the game. Olaf steamed on the bench, begging, promising he wouldn't foul out. With Dean and Curtis on the floor, Willow Creek couldn't match up with their well-coached opponents, and Twin Bridges exploited the Broncs' weaknesses. Sam called time out. They were down seven with just under four minutes. He could wait no longer.

Sam took Olaf by the shoulders. "You're going in the game. *Stay* in there."

Sam turned to the boys, who were guzzling water and toweling their dripping bodies.

"Get the ball to Olaf if it's there. Tight zone. Make them shoot from the pasture. No foolish fouls! Olaf, watch for the long outlet when you get a rebound. I think you can catch them asleep, if it's there, run!"

It was there. Miller missed a fifteen-footer over Curtis and Olaf snatched the rebound. He fired a strike down the floor. Rob caught it on one bounce and put the quarter in the jukebox.

Curtis picked up his fourth foul, but Harkin only hit one free throw. Later, Pete lofted a flawless alley-oop for Olaf. Olaf went up and hammered it through the rim, bringing a thundering roar from the crowd. But when he came back down, he landed on Stone's foot and turned an ankle. He grabbed his foot and his face was lined with pain. The referee stopped the game. Olaf struggled to his feet as Sam and Diana met him on the floor.

"How is it?" Sam asked.

"I must play," the wincing boy said, tenderly stepping on his right foot. Diana examined the ankle.

"It's going to swell," she said.

"To the bench I am not coming," Olaf said, and he hobbled away from the startled coaches and referee.

The official signaled Twin Bridges' ball out and the game resumed. Down by four, Olaf slapped Stone's turnaround off course. Rob picked it out of the air and hit Pete streaking down the floor, catching the Falcons flat-footed. Pete went high and deposited the ball gracefully with a finger roll. Corky Miller arrived too late and was whistled for the foul.

"In their face!" Diana hollered, "In their face!"

Pete went through his ritual on the line, and Sam could see that he was talking to himself. Then he rattled home the free throw with thirty-seven seconds left. They were down by one. Sam called time out. While Diana taped Olaf's ankle in a stopgap manner over his sock, Sam yelled fiercely over the crowd noise.

"We go into our zone press. If they get it across midcourt, go man-for-man and get on them tight. They'll try to burn the clock, so if we don't get a steal in the first ten or twelve seconds, foul!"

The cheerleaders had the crowd roaring.

"Go, Broncs, go! Go, Broncs, go! Go, Broncs, go!"

The arena shook. All spectators were standing. Twin Bridges fought through the trapping press and got the ball into the front court. Willow Creek picked them up all over the floor, hawking the ball. Corky Miller looked one way and then passed the other, a tendency Pete had picked up on. Pete gambled, left his man, and slashed into the passing lane, picking off the ball. He sprinted downcourt with Miller and Neely in desperate pursuit. With the grace of a gazelle, he went high and made sure. A soft bank off the glass that cranked the scoreboard to read WILLOW CREEK 74, TWIN BRIDGES 73. Twenty-six seconds.

The stands shook with elation, but the Falcons came winging swiftly, cutting, setting picks, weaving around the Broncs' barricades. With eight seconds on the clock, Travis Neely faked a shot. Rob and Pete lunged toward him, leaving Corky Miller open. Neely bounced the ball to his teammate, and the stocky senior guard poised to shoot. Olaf hobbled out at him. Miller dished it off to Stone who was momentarily alone under the basket. With Tom coming on desperately, Stone went up sure-handedly and canned the layup.

Twin Bridges 75, Willow Creek 74.

With the team momentarily stunned, Tom had the presence of mind to shout at the official.

"Time out! Time out!"

The clock stopped with three seconds.

Stone shook a fist in Olaf's face and grinned with the dragon's smile. The Willow Creek fans fell deathly silent, crushed under the foot of a fate they could never seem to escape, refugees in a high-fenced compound along the border where they could see into the land of victors but would never have the proper credentials to be admitted. Their last hope was gone.

The boys staggered to the bench. There were no more chances, no more challenges. Their dream had three seconds to live. The team slumped on the bench, devastated. He went down on one knee in front of them, a furnace of anger roaring inside of him.

"*Listen* to me! *Listen* to me!"

He shook Tom by the shoulders, swatted Rob on the thigh.

"Damnit, listen to me! It's not *over!* Are you going to lie down and quit? You going to give up? Fight it, fight it, don't quit!"

Pete crouched on his knees in front of them and pounded the floor, shouting.

"Listen to him, damnit, listen to Coach! If there's one chance in a million, we've got to go for it!"

They came out of their slouching surrender and looked to their coach, daring to entertain hope for the infinity of three seconds.

"All right," Sam said with a measure of calm. "We'll run that out-of-bounds pick play we've practiced. Remember? Rob you take it out. We can only pray that they'll try to hassle you."

The buzzer blared.

"Pete, don't set the pick until the ref gives Rob the ball," Sam said. "*Don't* let the kid see you."

The referee came to the bench. "Bring 'em out, Coach."

"Rob, if they don't fall for it, if they don't guard you, throw the ball to Olaf. Olaf, catch and shoot, catch and shoot."

They huddled up and shouted, "Win! Win! Win! Win! Win!"

Diana prayed that they would put a man on Rob and that the ref would have the moxie to call it. The Willow Creek followers stood, ashen, unable to breathe, bracing themselves.

The Broncs took their positions on the floor. Rob was at the far end with

a referee, standing out of bounds to the left of the basket. Pete loitered non-
chalantly around the free throw circle. Obviously in pain, Olaf planted himself on the free-throw line at the opposite end. Tom in one corner, Curtis in
the other. The Falcons surrounded Olaf except for Travis Neely, who trotted
to the other end of the court to guard Rob, ready to harass him when he
tried to inbound the ball. Diana felt a tingle of hope—they were falling for
it! The official blew his whistle and handed Rob the ball. Rob whacked the
ball with his right hand, starting the play. Just inbounds, crowding Rob,
Neely waved his arms in the air.

Fear grabbed Diana by the throat. Pete moved swiftly up to the baseline
to Neely's right. Coach Long, seeing the play, stood screaming at Neely, but
in the volcanic roar the boy never heard his coach's warning, focusing te-
naciously on Rob. Rob took a quick step to his right. Neely reacted, taking a
quick step to his left to stay in front of Rob, his arms waving in the air. Then
Rob took off running to his left along the baseline, still out of bounds. Neely
instantly sprinted after Rob. He never saw Pete, who stood just inbounds
with his feet slightly spread, facing the Falcon defender. Neely smacked into
Peter like a stampeding bull hitting a wire fence, flattening Peter and crashing on top of him.

The referee hesitated, caught off guard.

Call it, call it, have the guts!

Then a whistle, the arm signal, the foul called.

The bewildered Willow Creek fans broke out of their despair with an
escalating uproar. Sam leaped from his crouch with a fist in the air.

"Yes! Yes!"

Travis Neely picked himself off the floor with an expression of utter
shock. The Twin Bridges section went deathly silent. Without taking a second off the clock, Willow Creek was shooting a one-and-one.

The Falcons called time out. At the bench, neither Diana nor Sam could
look Pete in the eye. They realized what unbearable expectations they had
placed on their splendid guard—the overwhelming pressure that singled
out Peter Strong. No one could help him now. He was absolutely alone. They
would win, tie, or lose by how he stared back into the callous, unforgiving
face of that pressure.

"After the free throws," Sam said, as calmly as he could, "everyone fall back quickly into a tight zone. They'll have to pitch it from the outhouse. Don't foul. No matter what, *don't foul.*"

Pete toed the line and took his time. He went through his ritual and silently mouthed several words. Then he flipped the ball into the hope-drenched atmosphere. It fell as faithful as moonlight. 75 to 75.

The Willow Creek crowd enjoyed a moment of pandemonium and then quickly hushed as Pete got set for the back end of the one-and-one. The Twin Bridges fans, in total shell shock, tried ineffectually to muster a disrupting noise. Pete turned and glanced to the other end of the court. It would appear he was conscientiously checking to see that Rob and Curtis were back, guarding the house. But Diana discerned that he was gazing into the face of Denise Cutter. With Tom and Olaf crouched along the lane, Pete took a deep breath, exhaled, moved his lips as if he were talking to himself, and turned the ball loose. It rotated unflinchingly through the noise and hopes and dread of those watching, disdaining the iron rim and nesting in the nylon arms awaiting perfection.

Willow Creek 76, Twin Bridges 75.

Diana erupted from the bench. "We did it! We did it!"

The unexpended three seconds still languished on the clock. With panic in his face, Corky Miller heaved a rainbow toward Harkin and Stone. Olaf slid in front of the two Falcons. The ball descended and he outreached them for it, having caught fifty similar passes every day at practice. Olaf held it high and the buzzer blared. The Willow Creek bench and fans broke into a frenzied celebration. Diana stood dumbfounded for a moment, until the outpouring crowd swept her away.

CRAIG STONE STOOD in the paint, stunned, his face pale. Olaf turned to him.

"You could beat us, you turkeys were thinking?" Olaf shoved the ball into Stone's hands. "*This* is a basketball!"

Stone slammed the ball on the floor and formed a fist as Tom limped up beside Olaf.

"Try it, dipstick!"

"I could whip both of your asses," Stone said.

"That'll be the day," Tom said, curling his own fist.

Then, quickly the cascading throngs washed Stone aside, and the bull rider embraced his limping teammate and shouted, "I love you, you big crazy Norwegian!"

In an instant, the team was swept away in an unending flow of the euphoric and redeemed denizens who claimed allegiance to the flag of Willow Creek, Montana.

CHAPTER 74

On the journey home, Olaf rested his leg up, across the bus aisle, with his ankle wrapped in ice. A seat up, Tom's knee was receiving the same treatment. Fans, diehards old and new, piled in their cars and trucks and followed the little carrot-colored bus.

They were going to the State Tournament!

In some strange way he'd known it all along and yet now, when it was fact, he found it hard to grasp. The incredible win over Twin Bridges tempted him to believe that—though he knew he'd be credited with brilliance under fire—they were on a course guided by some mysteriously benevolent hand. But, by all indications, Olaf's sprain was severe. It blew up when they removed the shoe and tape, even though they immediately iced it. He couldn't put weight on his right foot and Andrew had rounded up crutches, the tallest he could find. Still, Olaf had to bow toward the earth to make them fit.

At the Blue Willow Inn, Axel carefully set the second-place Divisional trophy on a high shelf above the glass pastry counter where everyone could see the shining brass basketball player, like an Oscar, holding a basketball high in one hand. It outshone the many dull and tarnished antiques displayed throughout the inn. Sam observed the celebrating people. They couldn't squeeze one more body in the building, and yet the grateful fans made ample room for Olaf and Tom to keep their painfully strained limbs up on chairs and properly iced.

The Willow Creekians couldn't get over the extraordinary win. They reminded Sam incessantly that he had clearly outcoached Jeff Long—there never should have been a Twin Bridges defender anywhere near where he could potentially foul.

He was praising Peter again for his two flawless free throws when Grandma fought her way through the mob. "I wanted to ask you what you said just before you shot the free throws?" she asked Peter.

"'As long as she swims, I will cook,'" he said.

"What a sweetheart. Well, you were sure cookin', Grandson. I never saw two prettier shots in all my born days. I don't know how you did it with all the people and noise—"

"And hurricane sea?" Peter said. He paused and glanced at Sam. "I owed them hot coffee after Friday night."

Sam had no idea what they were talking about, but sensed it might be something to do with her illness, and he didn't dare remain longer to find out. With a nod at them both he escaped into the swelling assemblage of delirious camp followers.

Diana checked the ice packs from time to time, removing them at intervals. She wormed through the crush and settled in Sam's lap for a few minutes, as though announcing to the community what they already knew. Sam thought he would burst like a balloon with sunshine.

The Painters sat near Olaf and were as proud of "their boy." Sam heard talk that Mervin Painter was trying to convince Olaf to go to college at Montana State University in Bozeman and continue living with them. Sam watched the kid in a giant's body, at the center of Willow Creek's universe and taking it all in. He had become the fearsome offensive weapon that Sam always believed he could become. The unpretentious school boy had undressed Craig Stone, had poured thirty-five points down Stone's throat like cod liver oil. Sam only hoped that someone on the opposing teams at State would stick an elbow in Olaf's ribs or worse, if in fact Olaf could play with that ankle. But if this was his last game, he had done it in bronze.

Amos sat beside Tom for a spell, one arm around the back of the bull rider's chair, listening to Tom and Rob and Pete exuberantly relive the game with expressive faces and excited voices. Then, by chance, Sam caught the roan Tom Mix hat ducking out the kitchen. Sam pushed his way through the boisterous crowd and met Axel by the serving counter.

"Did you talk to Amos?" Sam asked.

"No, no." Beads of perspiration glistened on his balding head. "Never got a chance."

Sam hurried through the narrow kitchen and out the back door. The darkness blinded him. He stood a moment, peering across the field behind the inn. After a moment he could vaguely distinguish a distant figure moving west toward the tracks.

"Amos!" he called. "Amos!"

Sam ran cautiously through the dried weeds and grass, nearly tripping over an old car engine, but Amos had disappeared. He stopped and scanned the back side of town. There was the abandoned concrete one-room jail off to the south, and then Harrington's house on its own gravel road down a block. But north and west there was only open ground to the tracks and beyond, except for the cemetery with its rows of evergreen sentinels. Sam continued west.

"Amos, it's Sam," he called. "I need to talk to you."

When he hit the railroad bed, he stopped.

"Here," Sam heard to his right.

He turned to find Amos standing beside the tracks.

"Oh, good, I thought I'd missed you."

Sam scrambled up the slight embankment.

"Axel wanted me to warn you. There's been a man asking about you, or someone like you, a Granville Hamilton. Axel thinks he's a detective or something."

Amos sighed. "Only a matter of time."

"Who is he? Is he looking for you?"

Amos squatted wearily and sat on the rail. Sam settled beside him.

"Do I have to worry about the money . . . I mean . . . the things you left for Tom?"

"Did ya have yerself a little peek?"

Sam's natural tendency was to lie, to deny any wrongdoing, but Amos's question had none of the guilt-laden righteousness Sam had been used to. He went for honesty.

"Yes, I did, is the money . . . stolen or anything?"

"Don't have to worry 'bout it. It's clean."

"Who's after you, Amos? Or is it Granville?"

"It's the feds, the Internal *Rev-e-nue* Service."

Holy cats! Under my bed.

"Been gone a month ago if it weren't fer Tom. Be worth it if the boys'd take all the marbles over in Bozeman. God, I'd love ta see that, go quietly if I could see *that*."

"Why are they after you?"

"Quit payin' taxes."

Amos said no more, or Granville, as though it were enough of an explanation. You don't pay your taxes they come and get you.

"Why?"

"Had a nice spread in Wyoming, then my wife ran off with a trucker. Had one boy, he and me was workin' the spread by ourselves and gittin' by jest fine. One day they tell him he has to go in the army. Tell him the government of this here country needed him to defend itself against comm-u-nists in some country we didn't even know where it was. He believed 'em. They sent what was left a him home in a shoe box."

Amos fell silent.

"That must have been terrible."

"Buried him out on the place. Resta him still scattered somewhere over there—he called it 'The Nam.' After I buried him I got a letter from him, slow in coming, was kinda spooky. Had a picture, said it was of one of them comm-u-nists, a picture of a little slanteyed kid sitting in my boy's arms, like he's carrying a pumpkin. My boy was smiling, had a good smile. When I pitched the last shovelful of dirt on his grave, I promised on my soul I'd never give the government another dime to send boys away to die."

"That's when they came after you?"

"When I quit sending in ma taxes, they sent me letters and notices and finally a dude comes out and tells me I'm being investigated, even reads me ma rights and all." Amos spat. "So, sold everything I had, the spread, cattle, everything. Turned it all into cash and vamoosed."

Amos picked up a chunk of crushed rock from the railroad bed.

"Where did you go?"

"Tied up around Smiths Ferry, Idaho, fer a spell, Greenhorn, Oregon, a few years, Pagosa Springs, Colorado, after that and then Willa Creek, always moving on when I feel the hackles on the back a ma neck setting up."

Amos tossed the rock into the ditch.

"Felt 'em a month ago but didn't want ta leave. They'll put me in jail fer a spell, but they'll never git a *dime* outta me."

"Well, I—"

"Don't you worry none 'bout it, Pickett. That money is money hard earned. I jest never paid no taxes on it and I'll rot in jail 'fore I'd give 'em another cent. Don't tell 'em about the money, Pickett, please. They'll jest use it to blow young boys to smithereens."

Sam felt dumbfounded and angry and sad. All this time he thought he knew something about Amos Flowers. God—he didn't know *anyone!* And now Amos was risking his freedom and would probably spend time in jail because he wanted to see Tom win.

"Is that your whole wad?" Sam asked.

"Nope. Got money hid out in other places."

"I'll see to it that Tom gets the suitcase," Sam said. "No one else will ever know about it, I promise."

"Thank ya."

Amos nodded and spat into the ditch. Then he rose with a grunt and searched the dark horizons. The Blue Willow lay off across open ground to the east, where a gilded light and the faint sounds of rejoicing were still splintering from its cracks.

"Better mosey on outta here fer now."

He turned and offered Sam his hand. Sam took it and they shook.

"You did one helluva job tonight. By God, at the end there I wouldn'ta give Willa Creek a chance in a million."

"Maybe that's all any of us needs," Sam said.

Amos moved over the tracks and down the other side of the roadbed. He disappeared across a squeaking barbed-wire fence into the nightscape. Sam wanted to shout to him, wanted to tell him he was sorry about his son. He heard a horse whinny. Sam stood motionless, holding his breath, listening. Then he heard it. Hooves across the land, muffled, thudding, a horse running into the night.

CHAPTER 75

When Grandma opened the door, Sam was standing on her porch, as nervous as a suitor.

"I didn't know if you heard my knock . . . with the wind and all."

"Drag your body in here."

Sam stepped in and she closed the door.

"I was doing aerobics with those yahoos in Hawaii, thought I heard something. Why aren't you at school, something wrong with Pete?"

"No, no, it's my class break. I have something to ask you."

"Well, if you're not going to ask me to marry you, let's go in and camp at the kitchen table."

She led the way in her jeans, sweatshirt, and Reeboks. Her felt fedora wasn't on her head.

"Whatta gas," Parrot squawked.

Sam rapped a finger on the cage in passing. "Been in any interesting outhouses lately?" he said.

In the kitchen she nodded at a chair and went to the sink.

"Coffee?"

"No, thanks, I can't stay but a minute. I'm taking Olaf in to see the trainer at the university before practice and I've a lot to get done."

She swigged a glass of water and then settled in a chair at the table.

"You read the *Gazette*?"

"No . . . I've been running late all morning."

"Listen to this." She pulled on a second pair of glasses.

WILLOW CREEK TO STATE TOURNAMENT.

In one of the most incredible games that will ever be seen in high school basketball, Willow Creek, down by one point with three seconds on the clock and the ball to inbound, found a way to win, sucking Twin Bridges into a pickplay foul and a one-and-one free-throw opportunity, both of which the marvelous guard for the Broncs, Peter Strong, coolly made, lifting the unheralded six-man team past the second-rated team in the state, eliminating Twin Bridges from the championship show, which starts in Bozeman this Thursday.

Grandma pulled off her outer glasses and plunked them on the table.

"I still can't believe what happened, we were *dead,* we were in our coffin. Where'd you learn something like that?"

"Watching the NCAA Tournament last year on TV."

"It was bug-eyed brilliant."

"We were lucky. I didn't like putting that pressure on Pete, but someone had to shoot the free throws."

"It's a cryin' shame that neither of his parents saw that."

"*You* saw it," Sam said, tiptoeing out on thin ice. "You mean an awful lot to him."

"What did you need to ask me?"

"We've been given five passes for our coaches and assistants at the field house. Miss Murphy and the boys and I want you to sit on the bench with us."

"*Me! On the bench!* Land sakes," she exclaimed, "what would I do on the bench? Why I—"

"Help us win."

Grandma put one hand over her heart as though she were short of breath and regarded Sam with astonishment. She was about to cry. Sam struggled to fight the emotion he felt betraying him. Blinking back tears and clearing his throat, he attempted to chuckle and failed miserably, coming out with a teen-age croak.

"As you know, there's lots of room on *our* bench."

"Can I bring Tripod?"

"Sure, if you've got some way to hide him."

"No problem, right inside my jacket. He's been to more games than I have this year, what with that dang flu."

"Then you'll do it?"

"I guess so. I'll be a mighty sorry sight on the bench."

"One thing," Sam said.

"What's that?"

"I can't put you in the game."

She laughed. "That'd be the day. What'll I wear?"

"Anything you want." Sam stood.

"When do you want us up there today?"

"Oh, that's one of the things I wanted to tell you. We won't be needing you to scrimmage anymore, since we have too many banged-up boys. Most of our practice the next two days will be in our heads, besides a little shooting. Olaf can't stand on the ankle at all and Tom needs to stay off that knee and—"

"You don't want me settin' picks or—"

"No . . . there'll be no more scrimmaging for any of us."

Grandma put her hand to her mouth. "You *know*."

"What?"

"Did Hazel tell you?" she asked with a plaintive note.

Sam slid back into the chair. He stared at the sports page upside down, filled with their happy news. He tightened. She was going to make him look into the elephant's eye.

"Poor Hazel," Grandma said, "I don't blame her. I wish she'd never had to know." She reached across the table and touched Sam's hand. "You know, don't you, Sam?"

Sam nodded.

"Oh, I'm sorry, I'm so sorry," she said as though it were Sam who was terminally ill.

He could not speak. He looked up and across the table, into her gentle eyes, a small boy in line to ride the elephant, hearing his mother shouting, *You get on and ride. I paid good money.* She patted his hand.

"It's all right. It will all turn out all right, don't be sad. I'm the luckiest woman on God's earth."

Sam looked into his lap and tried to gather himself.

"I don't want anyone to know. Did Hazel tell anyone else?"

"I don't . . . I don't think so."

"Can I trust you with it?"

Sam regarded her and nailed the words.

"To my grave."

She smiled slightly.

"To mine will be enough."

At that moment he wanted to embrace her and ask her to set stone cairns on the shores of eternity so he could find his way, but he dared not. He gripped the sides of the chrome and vinyl chair.

"You're a helluva woman."

"You're not so bad yourself, Sam Pickett."

"I know where Peter got his steel," Sam said.

"That boy has come up with some of his own. Wasn't he a sweetheart last night, weren't they all? I'll be honored to sit on the bench with them."

"It'll be ours to have you there."

ON HIS WAY back to school Sam tried to shake the sadness insulating his excitement. How much longer could he glue the wings on? Two days to practice, to prepare, to heal. And then they faced the Wibaux Longhorns. All Sam knew was that they had compiled a 20–4 record. Had they ever faced the likes of Olaf? Their center sat in each class with his foot up on a chair and pillow, their hopes and destiny fermenting in the multicolored fluids cooking between his strained tendons and ligaments.

DURING SAM'S BREAK Wednesday morning, Truly stuck his head in Sam's classroom.

"Do you have a minute, Sam?"

"Yes," he said, rising from his chair with a tremor of dread.

Truly signaled for him to follow. They descended the stairs and went out the front door into a mild sunlit morning, where grade schoolers were enjoying recess with jackets open or strewn on the ground. Truly walked briskly in his all-business manner to the little carrot-colored bus parked in front of the school. When they reached the stubby vehicle, Sam saw that the hood was covered with a green canvas tarp. The superintendent walked to the front of the bus and stopped, taking a hold of the heavy tarpaulin.

"Something wrong with the bus?" Sam said, relieved that it was nothing to do with the boys.

Truly stood posed, as though he were launching a ship, holding on to the edge of the canvas, his nose twitching.

"Sam . . . I haven't always been . . . well . . . helpful this year. I wanted to do something for you and for the team."

Truly choked up. He pulled the tarpaulin from the bus. There, in large glistening black letters, was Truly Osborn's gift to Sam, professionally painted along both sides of the hood.

ROZINANTE.

Sam was momentarily overcome. Both men stood there without the wherewithal to speak, teacher and superintendent, employee and boss, stranger to stranger. Sam swallowed hard and managed to find his voice.

"How did you know—"

"I have my ways," Truly said, still holding the corner of the canvas in one hand.

"Thank you, it will mean a lot to the boys, it means a lot to me."

"I regret I wasn't more supportive while you and the boys were struggling so hard. I hope you bring that championship back to this one-horse town. It'll be the biggest miracle *I've* ever seen."

Sam gazed at Rozinante, the name of Don Quixote's faithful horse, and felt he'd just seen one.

"The school board and I have been negligent," Truly went on, "expecting you to drive the bus when you have so many other more important things to be thinking about. They've agreed to have Harold drive you to the games this week. It won't interfere with his regular schedule and you can leave that worry to him."

Sam was overwhelmed by Truly's gesture and sentiment, but something didn't feel right about having Harold Bottoms, the route driver, take them to the games. "Thank you, but I'm kind of superstitious. I'd rather not change anything at this point in our season, I really don't mind driving the bus."

"Are you sure?" Truly twitched his nose.

"Yes. Thank the board for thinking of it, but let's stick with what's working for us. Besides, Rozinante might not take to another rider."

Truly smiled thinly. "Very well, Sam, you carry on the way you feel is best."

The superintendent folded the tarp neatly and Sam inspected the perfect lettering more closely. Then Truly, with the tarp under arm, looked at Sam with his head slightly cocked.

"You know, when you came and told me you wanted to coach for another year, I thought you'd lost your marbles. I thought you were crazy." He laughed. "Now I see . . . crazy like Einstein."

CHAPTER 76

With its name emblazoned proudly on its stubby hood—to the delight and surprise of the boys—Rozinante carried them along the interstate Thursday morning. Besides the team and Scott, Diana and Axel were aboard. She wore a bulky peach-colored sweater, a gray full skirt, and her crimson matador hat. Axel tested the seams on a navy blue suit he'd long past outgrown. Snow on the Spanish Peaks reflected the morning sun to the south, and Sam was trying to keep the cap on it, the excitement, the blood-pumping thrill of it. They were going in to work out on the Montana State University field house floor, to be given a locker room, to get the feel of the place.

The team was scheduled to work out from nine-thirty to ten-thirty. The first game would be at two. When they finished, it would be better to drive back the thirty-six miles to Willow Creek and relax on home ground rather than have the boys rattle around Bozeman all day in their jittery bones and nervous stomachs. Gus Holland, the MSU trainer, had examined Olaf's ankle on Tuesday and proclaimed it "playable." He assured Sam that Olaf wouldn't damage the ankle by playing but it would probably hurt a lot. It had responded to treatment, and Olaf could put weight on it now, though Sam had him stay on the crutches. He decided he'd have Olaf sit out this morning and not test the ankle until they warmed up before the game.

"Are there any of you who haven't been in the field house?" Sam asked as they approached Bozeman.

"I haven't," Dean said.

"Me neither," Curtis said.

"How about you, Olaf?" Sam asked, glancing at him in the rearview mirror.

"No, I have not been going there."

"I've never been there," Pete said, "but I've been in the Metrodome in Minneapolis."

"I've been to the rodeo there," Tom said.

They navigated through Bozeman and parked in a lot beside the field house where hundreds of students' cars and pickups shined in the shards of sunlight. It was nine-fifteen. As they entered the outer lobby, the boys carried their duffels with one hand and their golden, freshly dry-cleaned uniforms with the other. A large athletic-looking young man hurried across the concrete toward them. He wore an MSU blue and gold sweatshirt, blue sweatpants with bobcats printed down one leg, and white running shoes.

"Are you the team from Willow Creek?"

"Yes," Sam said.

"Welcome to MSU. I'm Greg Morris, I'll show you your locker room and get you set up for tonight."

"Thanks," Sam said. "I'm Sam Pickett, the coach. This is Diana Murphy and Axel Anderson, part of our staff."

"Nice to meet you," the tall, well-built student said and nodded at each of them. He regarded Olaf, who didn't appear quite as imposing when hunched over the metal crutches. "Ankle?"

"Ya, sprained."

"Will you be able to play?"

"I am playing."

The boys stood gazing at the photos of former MSU players and the dozens and dozens of trophies displayed around the large lobby. Their welcoming guide seemed in no hurry. He stood, noticing the boys' interest.

"You boys going to take one of those home?"

"Yeah," Pete said without balking. "The big one."

"That's the attitude to have," the young man said.

Then they stood there. No one knew what more to say. What were they waiting for? Sam checked his watch. Greg Morris checked his watch. They should be getting on the floor. Finally Greg spoke up.

"Ah . . . will the rest of the team be here soon?"

The boys looked at each other and smiled.

"This *is* the team," Dean said, about to giggle, his Kamp Implement cap riding sidesaddle.

"This is *it*?" the dumbfounded athlete sputtered.

"That's right," Sam told him. "We're all here."

Greg scratched his head and made a quick mental count, sizing up knotty little Dean in magnifying glasses, skinny, lop-eared Curtis, and the bewildered-looking Norwegian on crutches. Then he spoke with a note of awe in his voice.

"How did you get this far?"

The boys glanced at one another.

"We never forgot our balls," Tom said without smiling.

"Yeah," Dean said with his screeching voice, "we never forgot 'em."

The somewhat baffled student led them through large doors into the yawning hollow.

"*Wow,*" Dean said, "this is *big.*"

Under the arcing dome of the field house, the boys swept the cavernous space with their gaze.

"Fifty-two thousand square feet," Greg informed them.

They shuffled toward the court like astronauts who had just landed on one of Jupiter's moons. The lights weren't on, but daylight filtered through the frosted glass windows just under the dome, giving the arena a shadowy, phantasmal ambiance, as though it were in a perpetual twilight. Permanent seats swept up on two sides from a balcony rail about fifteen feet high. In front of the balcony, wooden bleachers cascaded down to the edge of the floor and large bleachers were set up the width of the court behind both baskets.

"Seats eight thousand," Greg informed them, with a touch of pride in his voice.

The hardwood court was nestled in a basin of seats that would soon become a mass of humanity.

"This is *big,*" Dean kept repeating as the gawking boys walked to the edge of the floor.

They had played in several large gyms, but this was another level: there were no walls, no popcorn machines, the backboards seemed to be suspended in midair, and the rims were like Saturn's rings drifting through empty space.

"Are we really going to play here?" Dean said.

"It looks a lot different from down here," Rob said.

The other boys stood silent, as though reality were slowly sinking in. The awesome, overwhelming, tooth-rattling fact was that in a little over ten hours they would be stepping out on that court and playing basketball in front of a whole lot of people. Sam wondered if the mystery that brought them to the State Tournament would bring them this far only to lose, or if simply *getting this far* was the triumph, the victory, and what happened from here on didn't matter.

"Let's change and get on the court," Sam said.

It was time to drain some of the awe out of it.

"Follow me," Greg said. He led them into a concrete hallway under the permanent stands. The boys changed into their practice grubs in the spacious concrete locker room where they could leave their uniforms and bags for that night's game. Diana and Olaf went to find the trainer to go over proper taping procedures for the ankle.

After some free throws on the now illuminated court, they ran offensive patterns for a while with Sam, Axel and Scott providing light-hearted opposition. Then Sam turned the five of them loose to horse around, shooting, dribbling, playground stuff to help them relax while at the same time mentally measure the dimensions of this arena.

Sam and Axel sat on the bench along the side of the court. The thump of basketballs and the boys' voices echoed hollowly under the great suspended dome. Scott fed rebounds to Rob and Pete at the west basket.

"Rob's getting his eye," Axel said, nodding.

Scott rebounded a shot and tossed it back to Rob. Rob dribbled once, sprung into the air, and popped a fifteen-footer. *Swish.*

"The big question is in the trainer's room," Sam said. "Without Olaf at seventy, eighty percent, we're sunk, it could be embarrassing. I keep having the feeling that someone is going to knock the outhouse over."

"Huh?"

"Oh . . . nothing, an inside joke."

"Why do people want to win so badly?" Axel said, scrunching up his pug-nosed face. "Last night I watched a NCAA game. It was crazy—guys painting their bodies and faces with their team colors, wearing basketballs on their heads, everyone, men, women, screaming, going bonkers. I mean these people live or die with the team." He paused. "I live or die with this team. Why?"

"I don't know." Sam said. "Maybe after so many losses along the way we all need to win at something."

"Maybe that's it," Axel said, watching the boys shoot.

Olaf and Diana returned. With their time on the floor about up, Sam blew his whistle and gathered the boys at the bench. He stood in front of them, out on the floor several steps, regarding each boy. A few college students were moving around in various latitudes of the field house, preparing for the afternoon games. Sam collected himself.

"Men, we're going for three. We're not here to make a showing. The people of Willow Creek have had to duck tournament news like a bright sun, to watch this world go by, the other teams advancing to glory year after year, leaving them out. Not this time! You're going to bring them a star, the moon, the whole ball of wax. You're going to give them back their pride. We're not going to be afraid to say it out loud, we're not going to take it one game at a time, we're going for three. We're a little nicked up but we're used to that."

Sam turned his gaze on Olaf.

"Olaf, you're the most dangerous center in the tournament, I would hate to have to coach against you. You are a Maalox Moment for all opposing teams. Undoubtedly Wibaux saw the papers about our game with Twin Bridges and they probably have something on their bulletin board about an all-out effort to stop Gustafson. After your thirty-five points last game they'll be on him like flies on a picnic ham. Let's hope so, because tonight Olaf will be our bait. While they're trying to keep him from coming through their front gate, Tom will be knocking down the backyard fence."

Sam nodded at Olaf and regarded Tom.

"Tom, you're the strongest forward in Montana. There's nobody who can outmuscle you on the boards or move you out of the post. Tonight they're going to see that you are just as damaging on offense. We're going to put Olaf out on the high post and have you slide in on the low."

Sam nodded at the bull rider and then turned his gaze on Curtis.

"Curtis, you're the best invisible man around. Every team that has overlooked you has paid the price. You have personified the name Forget Me

Not far beyond anything I could have hoped for. Without you we wouldn't be here. Tonight, when they finally catch on that Tom is in their backyard and go after him, you'll be able to help yourself to the apple tree."

Sam regarded Rob and Pete, sitting in their cutoffs and grubs.

"Rob and Pete, you're the two best guards in the state. Alone, you'd start for any team, but together, you become a murderous combination that keeps opposing coaches walking the floor at night and kicking their dog. If Butch Cassidy and the Sundance Kid could've shot as well as you, they'd have died in a nursing home. Tonight, when Tom has knocked a hornet's nest out of the tree in their backyard, you'll be setting fire to the roof shooting Roman candles from the street."

Sam came to Dean, forbearing in this vaulted cavern in his unvarnished youth, gazing back at Sam out of a magnificent innocence. Unmatched socks draped out of his shoes around his gnarly legs.

"Dean, you're the toughest sixth man I've ever seen. You've kept your finger in the dike and saved us from being washed away many times. There's no boy in the state who plays harder or gives more. Tonight you're going to be a crocodile in their swimming hole. When they're diving into the water to get away from the hornets and burning roof, you'll make them wish they'd learned how to walk on water."

"What hornets?" Dean said, and the boys buffeted him gently.

Sam held out both hands and they quickly huddled around him.

"Win! Win! Win! Win! Win! Win! Win!" they shouted together, but their affirmations of faith were swallowed up swiftly in the great, indifferent spaces of the empty field house.

CHAPTER 77

Thursday night pounced on them. The field house vibrated with a crowd that far exceeded anything they'd experienced at Divisionals. Sam found himself caught up in the anticipation. For once they were playing in the night bracket of opening day, no more dog-paddling through sluggish afternoon contests. The Wibaux Longhorns ran a flashy layup drill in their royal blue and gold sweat suits. The spectators had watched Rocky Boy edge Highwood, 94 to 88, in a firehouse game of run-and-gun. Now they stretched and swarmed the concession stands in anticipation of the Wibaux–Willow Creek game. A general curiosity grew over the six-man team and its chances, where Reason and Sentiment each had its favorite.

Gus Holland, the Montana State University trainer, had taped Olaf's ankle, and after testing it several times, Olaf said it felt good. Sam watched his center's eyes for hidden reflections of pain, knowing the Scandinavian would play on a bloody stump at this point; they all would. On the ride to Bozeman the boys tried to get Olaf to pronounce their opponent's name correctly. "Wybox" he would say. No, "Wee-bow" they would correct him. Either way, the Wibaux County High School brandished twelve dashing, weaving boys who came off ranches that endured on the arid, wind-swept plains of eastern Montana. They had two players listed at 6'4", but Sam noted that only one of them started. The Broncs ran layups against a background that had been dramatically transformed from that morning. The bright, vaulted space had become a giant animated amphitheater of human energy and expectancy.

Sam had had some anxiety over their lack of accuracy in the morning workout, but now, with the boys out on the floor in their freshly cleaned gold and blue, it seemed their stray shooting eyes were at least considering coming home. Grandma and Axel resided on the bench in gold sweatshirts and blue slacks, seemingly overwhelmed at the center of this humming throng.

Axel surely looked the part, but Sam figured Grandma, in her brown fedora, would be the center of speculation at least until the game started. Tripod poked his head from a gym bag under Grandma's chair. Hazel had turned down Sam's offer to pose as an assistant coach, though he sensed she wanted to in the worst way. Denise Cutter would remain up on the balcony rail. Sam had given the remaining pass to her, forming a coaching staff—in the ticket-taker's eyes at least—of a barrel-bodied bouncer, a hatchet-faced granny, and a palsied girl in a wheelchair.

They all trotted to the dressing room for their final words. Tom assured Sam and Diana that his knee felt strong. Olaf said that, though his ankle felt stiff with the tape, it didn't hurt much. Sam briefly reminded them that the bull rider would be the point of their attack, the ball-peen hammer of their offense, while Wibaux was marshaling their defense against the alien giant who had landed in their midst. When they were about to return to the arena, Dean stopped Sam in his tracks.

"I'm scared."

Sam was taken aback.

"Thanks, Dean, for having the guts to say it," Sam said. "I'm scared, too." Sam paused and glanced at the other boys.

Rob said, "I'm scared."

The boys regarded one another. Tom nodded, then Peter.

"It's okay to be scared," Sam said. "It'll make us play harder."

Diana said, "But think how scared *they* are after seeing *you* guys."

Tom stood and roared, "What are wounds to a knight errant! Sancho!"

"Yes, my lord!" Scott shouted.

"My armor and sword . . ."

The boys shouted and ran through the concrete runway that led to the court. Sam followed, so tight he thought he was about to pop rivets. They seemed so few, so very few, in the jaws of this numbing, nameless crowd in which they and their followers were swallowed into insignificance. The cheerleaders rallied the townsfolk as the boys took a few final shots and then the team stood at the bench for introductions.

Peter ran off the floor and up the bleacher steps to give Denise Cutter high fives when he was introduced. Many in the crowd watched curiously as this young athlete singled out the small girl in a wheelchair with a bright blue ribbon in her golden hair. Olaf tried not to hobble out when they announced his name, hiding his vulnerability from the wild dogs who were stalking the herd. The news coverage during the week kept harping on the fact that a six-man team in this day and age had little chance in a state tournament. When the boys returned to the bench for last words and their huddle, they looked tense. Sam managed a smile.

"You worked hard, men, you deserve to be here, now it's time to have some fun."

"And learn something?" Dean shouted.

"Yes," Sam said, patting the top of Dean's cap.

They joined hands with everyone on the bench, including an overwhelmed Grandma and Axel, and shouted, "Team!"

The players circled the referee. Sam crouched in front of the bench, gripped with such an intense anxiety he thought he might faint. The Broncs and Longhorns went at each other with a strangling aggressiveness, chewing nails and spitting fire. The Willow Creek boys tried to fight off the early jitters like a man trying to pull on his long johns while fleeing from a bear. Curtis let a pass go through his hands, Tom knocked a sure rebound out of bounds, Olaf traveled, and Pete missed a layup.

"Run a play," Sam hollered, holding up one finger. "One! One!"

Wibaux seemed more settled and was hitting a respectable percentage of their shots, gradually pulling ahead. But by the end of the first quarter the Broncs had the long johns on and the bear hadn't caught them.

"Okay, we've got the jitters over with," Sam told them. "Now run a play, run a play, do what got you here."

In the second quarter, they found their footing and settled down. Their game plan began to work. They repeatedly got the ball to Olaf out high and the Longhorns surrounded him. The boy guarding Tom was skinny, almost as skinny as Curtis, and a portion of his attention was drawn to the towering Norwegian. Tom got excellent position in close against the lighter boy and Olaf got him the ball. Methodically the Broncs pulled even as the bull rider began killing them inside: layins, short jumpers, getting his man in the air and going around him to the constant chorus of Axel's "You betcha!" and Grandma's "Attaboy!" Olaf ran the floor quite well on the ankle and he was devastating on defense. They attacked him with a frontal assault, running expendable substitutes into the game, but Olaf had become too adept at avoiding contact while reaching over the shorter boys and swatting their hope away.

At first the cheerleaders were overwhelmed, trying to get the crowd to follow their particular cheers, realizing that this ocean of people didn't know the words nor could they follow their lead. By the second quarter they had whittled it down to basics and appeared thunderstruck at the noise they orchestrated.

"Go, Broncs, go! Go, Broncs, go! Go, Broncs, go!"

The earth shook and all neutral fans were swinging to Willow Creek's side. The crowd followed the cheerleaders' fist thrusts into the air and created more noise than the poor girls had ever imagined. Sam could see the team coming together, shaking off the awe of being on the floor before thousands of people, becoming totally focused on the game. Though the half ended with Willow Creek only up by three, 39–36, Sam sensed they could take Wibaux. Tom had played fiercely and had seventeen points.

In the third quarter, Willow Creek turned on the bear. Finally realizing it was Stonebreaker who was ransacking their team, Wibaux tried to play a more balanced defense, concentrating less on Olaf. It was a fatal mistake. Sam turned Olaf lose. His fake passes to Tom were taken seriously, leaving Olaf with one defender between him and the basket, and Wibaux quickly discovered that one wasn't enough. With a swooping pivot one way or the other, Olaf stuffed the ball, making a soft turnaround, or banking a shot from the side. When he missed, Tom was often there to put it back. With Olaf's intimidating defense inside, Wibaux's outside shooting was all that kept them in the game. But Rob and Pete, with quickness and resolve, disrupted the shooters, making them hurry, making them miss, making them mad.

Wibaux, in frustration and confusion, took bad shots, turned the ball over, and found themselves falling behind. Steve Nelson, their hard-nosed little guard, wouldn't quit, and their lanky 6'4" big man, Andy Adams, wouldn't admit the tide was turning. But it was, and Willow Creek hit its stride as the quarter ended.

Willow Creek 49, Wibaux 40.

"Don't let up," Sam said. "You're playing great. Work for the good shot, be patient, don't let up on defense."

They started the fourth quarter in the manner they had finished the third. They foiled Wibaux's zone press by using "volleyball" with Olaf to bring the ball up. Rob hit two remarkable shots, one a three, and they were on a 9–1 run. Sam held his breath. Once when everyone was covered, Olaf dribbled the ball into the front court himself and dribbled behind his back once before catching the ball and passing off. The crowd cheered with delight and Sam saw it not as hotdogging so much as the intense Norwegian having fun under these pressure-filled conditions.

Wibaux wouldn't quit. They were trying desperately to get back into it when Pete slashed out and batted a pass away. Curtis dashed after the ball, leaped into the air, and batted it back into play before crashing over the Wibaux bench and players. Rob, racing downcourt, found the ball coming to him like a lonesome dog. He dribbled once, went high and dunked it, bringing a roar from the audience. The six-foot senior who had lost for three insufferable years had finally dunked the ball in a game, a triumphal statement and emotional release.

"Stuff it!" Diana shouted.

Curtis got to his feet and returned to the floor. Wibaux hurried the ball upcourt, and Sam notice a pained expression on Curtis's face. But the lean-fleshed sophomore got into his defensive position and seemed to move all right. Steve Nelson, their fiery little guard, let go with a three-point shot and missed. Tom snatched the rebound and the Broncs broke for the front court. Curtis was holding his right wrist. Sam shouted to Pete, who was dribbling out of a trap as he crossed midcourt. Pete called time out.

Curtis came to the bench, and Diana sat him down and looked at the wrist. Scott handed her an ice wrap out of the cooler. She glanced at Sam and then told Dean to take off his sweats and report to the scorer's table. With terror in his face, Dean passed his cap to Curtis and fumbled off his warmup jacket.

"Don't let up," Sam said. "It's not over, don't let them get anything going."

"Have you looked at the score, Coach?" Tom asked.

"Forget the score!" Sam said. "Play hard every minute you're out there. When Curtis is ready, I'm going to pull Olaf to rest that ankle, then maybe Tom. Have fun, and learn something."

They huddled, shouted their team cheer, and stepped back onto the court with a bounce of confidence in their manner. Diana leaned close to Sam.

"I don't think you'll be resting Olaf. Curtis is hurting."

Sam watched his team win the first round at the State Tournament with a clutch of dread hatching in his gut. Dean got his feet wet running the field house floor and he tickled the house when he took Nelson, the startled Wibaux guard, into the bleachers behind the basket coming pell-mell too late. The greater part of the huge crowd stood and cheered as the last few seconds blinked off the scoreboard clock. Willow Creek 69, Wibaux 54.

They followed all the proper rituals after the game, congratulated the Wibaux boys on a hard-fought game, iced the damaged body parts, and planned to eat with some of the Willow Creek parents and fans at J.B.'s Restaurant. Diana and Axel took Curtis to the hospital for X-rays. Sam and the boys ordered food, but he couldn't muster an appetite. He had taken one tasteless bite out of his clubhouse sandwich when Curtis came toward him past the salad bar.

His arm was in a cast!

Sam almost swallowed the mouthful whole. He heard Diana's words from weeks ago, *If no one goes down.* He glanced over a booth, where the Dutch Boy jabbered with the team, his frazzled Kamp Implement cap pulled tight, unaware that he had just been thrown into the North Sea.

NEWS OF CURTIS'S broken wrist spread from table to table like food poisoning. Curtis was heartsick; he would no longer be able to help them fight their way to the castle. Sam went over to the booth where Curtis's parents sat with Alice and Ben Johnson and Sally and Denise Cutter. The Jenkins were Grant Wood caricatures, quiet, reticent, withdrawing, molded out of the silent seasons and rhythms of the land, polite, respectful, undemanding, expecting nothing.

"I'm sorry about his wrist," Sam said. "I hope it will heal all right."

"That won't amount to nuthin'," Albert Jenkins said, his narrow, weathered face carrying no anxiety in its leathered lines.

"I don't know what we'll do without him," Sam said, riding an ambivalent merry-go-round of joy and shock.

"We want to thank you for what you've done for our boy," scrawny little Elsie Jenkins spoke up, a rarity for her. "He was so shy, didn't have any friends, thought of himself as a lop-eared no-account. You made him feel important, Mr. Pickett. He'd never go anywhere, just hang around the place. Now he isn't afraid to go out and do things and meet people. Why, there isn't anything that boy doesn't think he can do."

"He's a great kid," Sam said.

"I'll never know how you got him to work so hard. He got an old backboard at Hazel Brown's garage sale and put it up in our hay shed. After supper he'd go out there night after night, no matter what, and shoot that basketball for an hour or more. I came out one night when it was bitter cold and he was shooting that old ball with mittens on."

Sam felt his throat constricting.

"I don't know how you do it either," Sally Cutter said. "I never can get Dean to do anything. But every morning he gets up a little early, and before the bus gets there, he runs full throttle between the corral and the pump house, back and forth like his pants are on fire, rain or shine, snow, cold, doesn't matter. Said you told him he was a good runner."

No wonder Dean was always sweating, Sam thought.

"They're right," Alice Johnson told him. "I don't know how you get the boys to be so dedicated. Rob got himself one of those dumbbells—"

"Barbells," Ben said.

"Barbells, and he hoists that thing over his shoulders and then does knee bends, squats he calls them. It weighs a ton. He must do fifty or sixty every day no matter how tired he is. I never saw a kid work so hard. Sometimes, when he's come home dog-tired, I've sent him to bed early and told him to forget the exercising. You know, I could hear that thing rattling from his dark bedroom."

Sam tried to find a response. Claire Painter, eavesdropping from the next booth, leaned in to add her amazement.

"I don't know how you do it either, Mr. Pickett. Olaf says he's going for a walk. But I see him circle back to the barn. He'd go up in the loft and shoot the ball, over and over and over. I'd sneak out to the barn sometimes. If he heard us coming, he'd go out the high side of the barn and come back from his walk and we'd never say a word. That sweet Carter would call and call and he'd rather be practicing basketball."

"Haw!" Grandma said, sitting next to Claire. "My grandson dribbles the ball up stairs, down steps, behind his back, between his legs. He sleeps with the ball. He talks to it like it's alive, and sometimes, when I see what it will do for him, I believe it."

Utterly speechless, Sam held up a hand, signaling that he would be right back. He shoved himself through the bustling restaurant and out into the crisp night air. It was the last moments of February; at midnight March arrived. He gazed down the blurring strip of blazing signs, beckoning the traveler into motels, filling stations and fast-food places. He felt the flood of tears coming like a great tidal wave from deep inside.

All his life it had seemed he hadn't noticeably influenced any of his students, and now this: this extraordinary affirmation and effusive gratitude toward him as a person. The unexpected praise from these parents and the unimaginable loyalty of these boys overwhelmed him utterly, redeemed him, healed him with tears of joy. He stood for a moment as the traffic thinned along Main Street. He would have to go back in and face them, face these people he had unknowingly come to love. But not just yet. He shuddered and allowed a sob to fall, wiping his eyes and nose with his handkerchief. Someone came up behind him. It was Diana. She put her arm around his waist. "Are you all right?"

"Yeah . . . I'm okay."

"Can we do it?"

"Yes," he said, without doubt in his voice. "Let's go in."

They walked back into the restaurant, staggered but undaunted, to take their *five*-man team into the semifinals.

CHAPTER 78

S am ran out the old road into the March morning. A sharpness in the air brought him fully awake. He couldn't sleep past six and he didn't know what to do with himself. The tumultuous experience of the previous night—not only playing in the State Tournament, but *winning*—had left him drained, which was compounded by the incalculable loss of Curtis. With little Dean starting and with a bench impoverished of any support, Sam had severe doubts about their chances to advance any further. Add to that the frightening fact that tonight they went up against Rocky Boy, the fire-engine team from the reservation, and doubt seemed all that was left to the sane.

The reservation was an uncompromising parcel of wind-swept land portioned out to the Chippewa-Cree as well as a mixture of other tribes and nations. They were boys caught in an environment where drug addiction, alcoholism, unemployment, and hopelessness stalked them with the cold perseverance of a wolf pack, and through the long, wind-borne winter the only game in town was throwing a round ball through a hoop on the wall of the school gymnasium. Needless to say, some of them could do it blindfolded, in their sleep, with one hand tied behind them.

It occurred to Sam that maybe Rocky Boy needed to win more than Willow Creek, but he quickly recycled that sentimentality when he stopped to realize that Rocky Boy had a proud winning tradition that needed no charity, asked no quarter, was consistently on top year after year with many Divisional Championships and regular appearances in the State Tournament. From an enrollment of eighty or more, they never had a lack of boys who wanted to play, supporting a twelve-man varsity, a JV squad, a "C" squad and a freshman team, talented boys whose basketball careers, lamentably, ended with high school. Though many of them would be welcome additions to college and university teams, Sam had learned that seldom did any of these boys go on with the white man's institutional notion of education.

Sam found himself running hard across the old iron bridge as he envisioned the trial to come. Rocky Boy would attempt to consume Willow Creek in the twin furnaces of their trapping defense and their unrelenting run-and-gun offense, to run them and run them and run them, and finally, fry them in their own exhaustion. He wished there was some way he could go out on the court and take his stand with the boys.

AT THE BLUE Willow, dozens of excited fans were waiting in their vehicles when Axel opened the doors, as if the inn were serving underdog dreams for breakfast. Emphasizing words for dramatic effect, Grandma read the *Billings Gazette* aloud as though it were news from the front.

WILLOW, WHITTLED TO FIVE, ADVANCES
With an answer for everything Wibaux threw at them, the dogged Willow Creek Broncs made believers out of many in the state.

A cheer arose from the breakfast tables.

Tom Stonebreaker, their husky 6'4" forward, led the charge in the first half, nearly unstoppable inside. When the Longhorns made adjustments to stop him, the other Broncs took over, led by their towering 6'11" center, Olaf Gustafson, and their two excellent guards, Peter Strong and Rob Johnson.

More cheering and clapping.

At the end, Willow Creek had outclassed and outshot the courageous Longhorns but lost their starting forward, 6'2" Curtis Jenkins, midway through the fourth quarter with a broken wrist, leaving the Broncs without a bench. With only five players left standing, their chances against the firestorm basketball of Rocky Boy seem dismal. But don't count them out. We've made that mistake all season. Their bench won't be empty tonight in the Brick Breeden Field House. It will be occupied by Courage and Character and Iron Resolve, and by a masterful coach who has brought his six boys through the District and Divisional trenches and has them well prepared for the tournament wars.

The inn exploded with applause and Axel banged on an empty pan from the serving window. Grandma passed the paper around, the article becoming smeared with maple syrup, bacon grease, and coffee stains. People kept showing up, those who had never come in for breakfast, until the Blue Willow bunch was lost in the happy smorgasbord of fans. Grandma scanned the crowd. One of them was missing. Amos's weather-sautéed hat was nowhere in the inn.

At three they gathered in the gym. The cheerleaders, Scott, and Diana stood in for the Rocky Boy players as they went through offensive sets in their street clothes. Curtis languished on the sidelines with a cast that had been autographed by half the population of the county. Dean was jittery at finding himself on the starting five. When they had gone over a few new plays, they sat in the stands and Sam attempted a matter-of-fact demeanor.

"They'll play eight to ten boys, they run to keep you unsettled, off balance." He glanced at Pete. "We must keep our cool. They can't match up with Olaf. We'll use him to bring the ball up at our pace, control the tempo of the game, work our half-court offense, and eat the clock. Remember, they can't run if they don't have the ball."

When Sam finished, Tom pulled on a beat-up Kamp Implement cap he'd concealed under his jacket. Dean lit up and quickly felt his head to see if *his* cap was in place. It was. Then the other boys brought similar caps from out of hiding and pulled them on with the visor over one ear. They all laughed and cheered.

"Where'd you get them?" Sam asked, somewhat dumbfounded.

"Kamp Implement doesn't have this kind anymore," Rob said. "They're like three years old, so my dad called around and found them. We figured now that since Dean's a starter we all ought to look alike. It'll make us run faster."

Dean brightened like a full moon, and Sam shook his head at the unending surprise of these boys.

The team had an eager, confident manner as they strolled down the blacktop toward the Blue Willow where Axel and Vera, with Grandma's help, had a pregame dinner set for them. The Dirty Half-Dozen ate calmly at the festive table that was decorated in blue and gold. The inn was closed to the public, who were all in Bozeman anyway, and the low-lit, peaceful ambience was just what Sam wanted. Diana had requested pasta salad and Axel had insisted on some red meat for the boys, serving them ten- to twelve-ounce tenderloins along with fruit and juice.

When they were nearly finished, Sam pushed his chair back and stood up. "I'd like to tell you a story."

The boys went silent and all eyes focused on him.

"I've always been haunted by the Indian legend I first heard when I came to Montana. Crow Indians were camped along the Yellowstone River near present-day Billings. Warriors, returning from a long hunting trip, found the camp decimated by smallpox, their wives, mothers, children, all dead. They were so overcome with grief, sure they would join their loved ones in another life, that they blindfolded their ponies and rode them off a sixty-foot cliff."

Sam paused. No one spoke.

"I've always been amazed at the incredible confidence of those Indians. They had no doubt that they would join their loved ones and they probably went over that cliff shouting. What courage, what faith. They believed!"

Sam glanced at their faces, hanging on his words, and he hoped his words were worthwhile.

"That's what I want to say to you tonight. Believe. Go for it. Make that leap of faith. Believe that you will play the best basketball of your lives and shout as you go over the cliff."

They finished their meal in hushed conversation and Tom explained to Dean what the coach was talking about. Then Tom added, "If we don't win this game, we'll feel like we went over a cliff." Then Sam announced it was time to leave. They would arrive in Bozeman in time to watch the first half of the Roberts–Seely-Swan game. The boys headed out the door, out of the serenity of their little town, into the unrelenting inferno of fast-break basketball.

THE PREVIOUS NIGHT, Diana had watched the kids from Rocky Boy shoot the lights out of the scoreboard while scoring ninety-four points, and now, as she watched them warm up in maroon, gold, and white uniforms that didn't quite fit, they appeared ragged, shooting the ball from all haunts of the floor without form. But she remembered Cervantes and the problem of appearance and reality and she wouldn't be conned by appearance. Ninety-four points in a thirty-two minute game is a pace of scoring that would send college and NBA teams sneaking out the alley door. Playing Rocky Boy would be like stepping in front of a locomotive just beyond where you'd greased the tracks. There were only two possibilities. Either your game plan would stop them, leaving them harmlessly spinning their wheels, or you would be run over and flattened like a penny on the track.

For the last game of the semifinals, the field house was nearly filled, well over six thousand—partly due to the fact that the media had spread the word that a five-man team would be trying to survive against the run-and-gun Northern Stars. The drama of a team without substitutes had gripped the hearts of many, and they had given up other Friday night plans to witness this extraordinary confrontation. Seely-Swan had knocked off Roberts in the first game, but Diana couldn't afford a moment's concern about something as far-flung as tomorrow.

Dean Cutter was the first Bronc introduced. After slapping hands with the team and coaches along the bench, Dean rambled out across the floor with his knotty legs and cock-eyed cap and intrepidly ran the steps of the bleachers up to the balcony, where he gave his wheel-chaired sister "five," and then scampered back to the court. Tom also ran the bleacher stairs and gave Denise Cutter "five," though he left his cap at the bench.

CHAPTER 79

The boys huddled around Sam at the bench.

"All right," he said. "Stick to our game plan, don't let them rattle you, that's *their* game plan. Keep your poise. We give nothing inside, five rebounders on defense. I'll get a timeout when you're hurting. Have fun and learn something. Let's go!"

They cheered and the five of them stepped out onto the launching pad. Sam felt as though he might break, as though an arm would snap off or an eyeball pop out. John Two Horse lined up to jump with Olaf. The 6′4″ Native American boy appeared overweight and without the manner of an athlete. The spectators roared, the referee tossed the ball into the air, and Olaf easily controlled the tip, flipping it to Rob on the side. Rob one-armed a long bounce pass between several Northern Stars that kissed the floor at the free-throw line and found Peter's hands at the instant he left the hardwood. He soared through the colored space and rang the bell.

Under the peal of the crowd's applause, Willow Creek backpedaled swiftly into their zone. The Northern Stars, with their galaxy of shooters, came headlong, wide open, finding the Olaf-anchored defense blocking their path to the backboard, ripping the ball around the perimeter until Little Dog snapped a shot so quickly Sam had to blink. It hit nothing but net, the kind of shot you feel a kid could never do again, a metaphor for the first half, and the game quickly turned into Sam's most dreaded nightmare. The Broncs, with Dean Cutter starting, were following Sam's game plan perfectly: playing excellent zone, avoiding sloppy fouls, giving nothing inside, allowing no offensive rebounds, and making them shoot from downtown. Trouble was, Rocky Boy *could* shoot from downtown; there *were* no rebounds! Rocky Boy hit its first seven shots, three of them three-pointers, seventeen straight points before a miss, and when the torrid first quarter ended, the Broncs panted on the bench, down 25 to 16.

"Okay, okay," Sam told them. "Let's not panic. You're playing well. Stick to the game plan, work for the good shot." He glanced at Diana who was checking the tape on Olaf's ankle. "What are they shooting?"

"Almost seventy percent," she said, shaking her head.

"How about fouls?" Sam asked.

"Dean one, Rob one . . . pretty clean."

"Good, play our game. No team can continue to shoot seventy percent," Sam said, attempting to sound convincing. "When their tires cool, we'll still be on their back bumper and we'll go by them like smoke."

Rob asked, "Should we go out on them?"

"No," Sam said, gambling. "Let's sit in our zone for a while longer."

They linked hands, Grandma and Axel included, shouted their cheer, and stepped back on the tracks where the Northern Stars locomotive was steamrolling them. Sam hoped that the quarter break would cool off the incredible shooting of the boys from the reservation who had—for lack of much else to do—made a vocation of tossing bull's-eyes from anywhere in the yard. Rocky Boy's coach started the second quarter with three substitutions and they picked up Willow Creek in a zone press. The Broncs broke the press repeatedly, getting several easy layups, but it was costing the boys in energy spent and the break hadn't tempered the Northern Stars eagerness for lighting up the scoreboard.

Little Dog had a square, ungainly body, bowed legs that would challenge Dean's, long black hair held in a pony tail, and Sam had never seen a boy shoot like this kid. When he caught the ball he was already in his rhythm to shoot. The boys were playing well, doing everything he had asked of them, but when they limped to the locker room at the half, the score was Willow Creek 32, Rocky Boy 50. The majority of the fans had been taken out of the game by Rocky Boy's uncompromising express. From the Land of Sky Blue Waters, a beer truck was backing over them.

The boys caught their breath and were ministered to by Sancho and the "coaching staff." Sam prowled the locker room like a trapped animal, searching in his head for an ounce of dynamite to blow a wheel off the Rocky Boy freight train. He knew there had to be something if he could only lay his hands on it before the game was irretrievably lost. It kept hitting him in the chest like a box car. They were behind by *eighteen points!*

He gathered them a minute before they had to return to the inferno.

"I know you boys," he said, glancing into their grim faces. "If Rocky Boy thinks the picnic is over, if they're already hoisting their flag, we're going to shoot it down."

He found Diana's eyes and felt her willing him the words that would rally them, but seeing also that the burden of the huge deficit seemed too great for dreams, an unbearable weight that stomped its boot on fairy tales.

"I've never knowingly lied to you," Sam said, clearing his throat. "Exaggerated a bit maybe, asking you to do things I didn't think you could. But then you went out and *did* them."

He paused.

"My wife was murdered six years ago."

Sam glanced from face to face, allowing it to sink in.

"When that happened, I quit believing in anything; in winning, in God, in life. I was afraid to bet my heart on anyone because I didn't think I could stand being shattered again. But right now I believe in you boys; right now I'm betting my heart on you. I believe as surely as I'm breathing that if we give everything we have, somehow we will win—some crazy, unbelievable way, we will win. I'm asking you to *believe,* to give everything you have, and to *believe.* We're not going to let it end here."

Grandma and Axel stood somberly off to the side, and the boys riveted their attention on their coach. Sam turned to Diana.

"How are we doing with fouls?"

"Dean two, Rob and Olaf one, Pete and Tom none."

"Good, good," Sam said with a rush of emotion in his voice. "Pete, you take Little Dog man-for-man. The rest of you in a four-man zone. Pete, with or without the ball, I want you not only in his face but in his head, in his imagination; I want him to think he's grown a Siamese twin, I want him to think he's in a house of mirrors, I want him to think you two are married. Wear him out physically, wear him down mentally. If you let the air out of his tires, we can beat them home."

"They're killing us, they're running over us!" Tom shouted. "Is this what we worked so hard for, to get our asses whipped?"

"No-o-o-o-o!" they responded, standing and huddling around Sam. They were veteran actors, wearing their masks and playing their roles, willing to go out for the third act in front of a packed house when they knew the stage was on fire.

OLAF CAME AROUND a double screen Sam had diagramed, caught an alley-oop from Pete, and jammed it to start the second half. The Willow Creek followers rose to their feet with a revitalized rumble.

When Little Dog got the ball racing upcourt, he found Pete in his socks, sticking to him like yesterday's gum. He had to pass off to a teammate. The Willow Creek boys dug in. Pete stalked Little Dog wherever he went, frustrating the dead-eye. They hadn't wilted as Rocky Boy might have expected, and the teams traded baskets as the quarter wore on. Then, trying to get the ball to their premier shooter, Rocky Boy became careless. Peter cut off a pass and went coast to coast, scoring an uncontested finger roll. Again the crowd exploded, looking for a thread of hope to cling to, gazing at the clock with growing dread. Willow Creek was down by fourteen.

Little Dog got loose for an instant around a screen, something Rocky Boy did little of with their run-and-gun offense. Peter reached around and grabbed the shooter's arm. The ball sailed harmlessly into the bleachers and Little Dog was awarded two free throws. To Sam's surprise, he missed both and a light came on in Sam's head. Double-teamed, Olaf dished off to Tom at the other end and he banged home the buck. Rocky Boy took the ball out. Rob dashed back and intercepted the long inbounds pass they were in the habit of throwing. He took two dribbles, squared up, and rattled home a three. The crowd erupted. Curtis stood hollering, "You can do it! You can do it!"

They were down by nine when the quarter ended.

The boys fought off fatigue on the bench. The fans stood, hurling their vocal support and encouragement.

"Go, Broncs, go! Go, Broncs, go! Go, Broncs, go!"

The field house shuddered, and the team was visibly puzzled at the overwhelming outpouring.

"They're all cheering for us," Pete said.

Olaf wiped his dripping face. "Why are so many yelling for us?"

Tom gazed out at the thousands. "They're not from Willow Creek."

"They are in their hearts," Diana said.

"Why are they pulling for us?" Rob asked

"Because you're outnumbered," Sam said. "Because you're the underdog, because they want you to win for them."

"Because they like us," Dean said, and they all regarded the grinning fourteen-year-old. Tom rubbed his hand over Dean's sweat-drenched head.

"Yeah, you're right," Tom said. "They like us."

They had found their fire. Rob held up a fist and shouted. "We can take these guys!"

"Kill 'em on the boards!" Pete yelled.

"Listen up," Sam said. "We're going to gamble. When they're working the ball for a shot, foul them, but do it before they're in the act of shooting. No three-point plays, wrap them up, let's see if they've done their homework."

The first time Rocky Boy came racing downcourt, they snapped the ball to Robert Stands Alone. He squared up for his jump shot and Tom whacked him across the arms before he could shoot. The thin 6'1" forward missed the front end of a one-and-one and Olaf controlled the rebound. Time became the sixth man against them. Pete dribbled swiftly into the front court. He blew by his man with a cross dribble and Two Horse slid over to stop him. Pete tossed the ball high above the rim and Olaf rose to drive it home. They were down by seven.

It was like a home game; the roaring crowd belonged to Willow Creek. Rocky Boy came on the attack, still running as though they were behind. Walking Feather missed a three-point attempt but Two Horse grabbed the rebound and went back up with it. Olaf hammered the ball away but was whistled for a foul. The deceptively good Rocky Boy center made the first but missed the second. Rob went high and snatched the rebound. On a play they had practiced when the opposing center is shooting a free throw, Olaf sprinted downcourt on his stiff ankle, took the pass from Rob, and with only 5'11" Walking Feather to stop him, glided to the basket and stuffed it, rattling the foundations, bringing the crowd back into the game with both feet. Willow Creek was down, 68 to 62. Three minutes and eleven seconds. Rocky Boy called time out.

"You've got two fouls to use," Sam shouted, looking at Olaf and Tom.

"Use them. They may try to stall before long. If they do, foul Stands Alone or Two Horse immediately."

The running and gunning Rocky Boy athletes could shoot the ball from any angle, from anywhere on the floor, so long as they were *moving*. But when they stood still at the free-throw line with no one's breath in their face, they faltered. The Northern Stars attempted a stall, but Willow Creek fouled quickly and Rocky Boy couldn't unwrap the gifts at the charity line. When Tom grabbed the rebound of a missed free throw with fifty-two seconds remaining, Sam called time out.

Rocky Boy 71, Willow Creek 67.

"All right, all right!" Sam shouted. "Get the ball to Olaf. Olaf, watch for Tom backdoor, plenty of time, then go man-for-man. Cross them up." Sam clapped his hands. "One more minute!"

The field house reverberated with the uproar as Willow Creek brought the ball into the front court. Rob got the ball high to Olaf and set a pick on Pete's man. The dauntless Scandinavian held the ball over his head and faked a pass toward Tom. The Rocky Boy defense bit for a moment but as it shifted toward Tom and surrounded Olaf, Olaf spotted Dean alone on the weak side, completely unattended by the Northern Stars. Olaf bounced the ball behind him into Dean's startled hands. With a reflex he had practiced a thousand times, the nearsighted boy flipped the ball up against the backboard and it banked in. The field house shook, Sam stood dumbfounded, Diana pounded his back, and the scoreboard blazed: ROCKY BOY 71, WILLOW CREEK 69.

"Yeah!" Sam shouted. "Bodacious!"

The Broncs picked them up man-for-man as the Northern Stars inbounded the ball. Seconds peeled off the scoreboard clock. *Thirty-one, thirty, twenty-nine, twenty-eight.* Little Dog fought to get free of Pete. The Broncs overplayed, gambled, stuck to them relentlessly. *Twenty-three, twenty-two.* Two Horse came out high and set a pick for Little Dog. The Rocky Boy guard squeezed past his teammate. Pete tried to cut behind. The guard ducked back, took a pass from Walking Feather, and flicked the prettiest shot Sam had ever seen, rotating like the earth itself, breaking Sam's heart.

Rocky Boy 73, Willow Creek 69.

"Time out!" Sam called, "Time out!"

It was their last. The boys came to the bench, their faces drained, with little more to give and only eighteen seconds in which to give it.

"Okay, okay, clear the right side," Sam said. "We'll go one-on-one with Pete and Walking Feather. Pete, if you can't get the layup, pull up and take the ten-footer. Rob, the minute they take it out, foul, you only have three. We should still have eight or nine seconds to work with. Let's go, let's do it!"

They caught their breath and dragged their spent bodies onto the court, uplifted by the sustained roar of the standing thousands. Tom attempted to camouflage his pain but Sam could see it in the way he moved. Willow Creek took the ball out and Rocky Boy pulled back, not wanting to risk fouling in the backcourt. Rob fired it to Pete and the Broncs shifted everything to the left side. Pete cross-dribbled several times until Walking Feather was back on his heels, guessing. Pete dashed by him. The surprising Two Horse moved quickly to cut Pete off. Instinctively, Pete lobbed the ball high to Olaf. Stands Alone and Little Dog were there to clog the paint. Hesitating only a second, Olaf lofted a push shot from the free-throw line as Stands Alone leaped to block it. Sam gasped until he saw the ball fall sweet and clean. A whistle. Olaf was fouled. One free throw. The clock stopped at nine seconds, 73 to 71.

The crowd hushed. With the Rocky Boy fans trying to distract him, Olaf took a deep breath and flipped the ball leadenly at the hoop. It hit the front rim, paused an instant, and with a will of its own, crawled over the iron and fell through.

The field house rocked. Down by one, 73–72, with nine ticks on the clock. When Stands Alone inbounded the ball to Walking Feather, Rob was there to foul him. Only one second had elapsed. The crowd stood roaring and Walking Feather readied himself at the line. Sam knelt at the bench; Diana held Scott's and Curtis's hands; Grandma Chapman muttered a prayer. As if the pressure were too much to bear, Rocky Boy's senior guard flicked the ball without hesitation.

It swished.

Willow Creek 72, Rocky Boy 74. *Eight seconds.*

Walking Feather again accepted the ball from the referee and tossed it quickly. It hit the backboard and glanced off the rim. Olaf snatched it. He found Rob on the side and both teams streaked into the front court. *Six seconds.* Rob pulled up his dribble and was open for a moment from sixteen feet. He squared up to shoot as two Northern Stars flew toward him. Then, at the last instant, surprising everyone in the arena, he fired a pass to Pete out beyond the threepoint line. Little Dog, having left Peter alone, was rushing frantically for Rob.

Three seconds.

Without hesitation, Peter dribbled once and lifted his shot, a continuous flow of rainbow and grace, of miracle and magic, a dimpled leather ball that carried the character and courage of the shooter as well as the breath and heartbeat of his teammates and thousands of followers, arcing perfectly on its long journey home.

Swish!

The buzzer pitchforked the Northern Stars in the chest and launched the majority of spectators into a frenzied ride over the moon.

Willow Creek 75, Rocky Boy 74.

They had bootstrapped themselves from eighteen down! They had endured without substitution. They had stopped the locomotive before it crushed them on the rails. They were going to play tomorrow night for the championship. Sam was lost in the swarm of exhausted boys and ecstatic fans. He found Dean in his sweat-smeared lenses and bear-hugged him off the floor.

"Great shot, Dean! Great shot!"

"I didn't know what else to do!"

Amid the chaotic celebration and milling confusion on the court, Sam caught sight of Little Dog heading for the locker room. Sam shoved his way through the boisterous fans and grabbed the somber boy by the arm.

"You're the best shot I ever saw!" Sam shouted.

Little Dog nodded and walked away.

CHAPTER 80

Sheltered from the frenzy in the arena, the locker room became subdued, as though each of them realized they were in the very shadow of their elusive, long-sought-after quest. Tom and Olaf limped badly, using ice in an attempt to stave off the swelling and hoping they'd be ready for one last game. With the scorebook in hand, Sam sat in the locker room somewhat numb and emotionally exhausted while the boys showered and dressed. He glanced at the totals: Tom had scored sixteen, Olaf nineteen, Rob fifteen, Pete twenty-three, and Dean, with the biggest bucket of the night, had *two*. The tough little freshman had run with Rocky Boy stride for stride without substitution, never giving an inch.

There was a knock on the metal door. Sam gathered himself and opened it slowly. Amos stood in the hallway. A stranger in a dark gray suit stood off a pace, watching.

"Can I talk to you fer a minute?"

"Sure, sure," Sam said, then stepped back. Amos nodded at the man and slid into the locker room. Sam closed the door. The moment the door latched Amos lit up like an excited kid.

"Ya did it, by God, ya did it!" Amos whacked Sam on the back. "Thought we was dead and buried six foot under there fer a spell."

"Who's the guy in the suit?"

"Oh . . . they nabbed me," he said. "Have a warrant for my arrest."

"When did they get you?"

"Just now, after the game. Musta been watching it the whole time."

"What are you going to do?"

"Begged him ta let me stay till tomorra night. He's a decent feller. Has two boys hisself. Sez he can catch me tomorrow as well as taday. He's so riled up about the team hisself I didn't have ta do much persuading. We's going ta stay in a mo-tel tonight."

"Will you be going to jail?"

"Don't know. He's real polite and everything. Sez there's got ta be a trial, unless I give 'em the money. I figure they'd druther wheedle the money outta me than slap me in jail."

"What did you tell them?"

"Thoughta giving it to 'em, but I seen how Tom stood battling out there on only one good leg and I sez, 'What money?'" Amos looked for a place to spit. "Can I see Tom fer a minute?"

"Yes, he's getting dressed."

"Don't want him knowing about this till the games is over."

Sam turned to call him.

"Hey, boy," Amos said, "that was a helluva game you played, nearly lost my liver I's yelling so hard."

Tom pulled on his Levi jacket and limped over to his peculiar friend. "Thanks."

"How's that knee?" Amos asked.

"It'll be ready. If it isn't, I'll play without it." Tom grinned.

"Have a favor ta ask ya," Amos said. "Promise me ya'll check with Mr. Pickett here 'fore ya sign any papers ta go in the service."

Tom looked confused. "Yeah, sure, okay, I will. Will you be here tomorrow night?"

"Remember the blizzard?" Amos said.

"Yeah."

"Thar ain't nuthing that'd keep me from watching you pluck the feathers outta Seely-Swan and tote that trophy home, nuthing."

Amos leaned awkwardly toward the strapping boy as though he were about to hug him. "You're a helluva kid." Then, clearing his throat, the fugitive slapped Tom on his shoulder. "I gotta git."

"See you tomorrow," Tom said.

"Tomorra," Amos said.

He nodded at Sam and opened the door. The man in the gray suit was waiting as Amos stepped out and closed the door.

EVERYONE WAS SETTLED in bed, Tom on the living room sofa, when the banging nearly popped the screws out of Elizabeth Chapman's front door hinges. In her NFL-monogrammed nightie and her furry bearpaw slippers, Grandma worked her way toward the door, hoping the ruckus wouldn't wake the boys. She snapped on the hall light, muttering to herself. "Hold your horses, I'm coming."

When she unlocked the door and swung it open, she found the hammerhead shark planted on the porch, looking mean and drunk. She immediately tried to slam the door, but the brutish man stuck a large workboot in its path, stopping it halfway closed.

"I'm here to fetch Tom."

"He's sleeping. Come back tomorrow!"

"He's coming home tonight. Can't be sleepin' all over town like some bum."

Grandma pushed against the door but it wouldn't budge. "Tom's sleeping here tonight. He needs to rest his knee for the game tomorrow."

George Stonebreaker slammed his fist against the door, knocking it wide open.

"Ain't going to be *no game tomorrow*. I come to get my boy and I'm taking him home if I have to drag him by the throat."

"Like you dragged his horse to death?" Grandma said.

The old scar curled across his upper lip, the ox of a man stomped into the house, and Grandma backpedaled, bumping into Tom. Garbed only in his Levis, Tom moved in front of Grandma and confronted his father with clenched fists.

"Get your clothes on. You're comin' home."

"I'm not going home and there's no way you can make me."

"We'll just have to see about that," the man snarled. "You got a barn to paint before any more playing."

Peter, in nothing but his undershorts, shouldered next to Tom, fists clenched. George hesitated for a moment, catching his balance.

"There's *two* of us," Pete said.

"Get out of the way, you little gelding, or I'll break your back. This isn't one of your chicken-shit basketball games."

They squared off, Tom's father brandishing a pair of anvillike fists. The boys moved back a step, crouching, into the darkened living room.

"Up your ass!" Parrot squawked, startling the inebriate.

"Who's that?" he said with a slur, appearing confused.

"You're so drunk you're hearing things," Tom said.

George lashed out with his boot, sending Grandma's wooden rocker crashing across the room.

"You're coming home with me now, by God, or I'll break your arm."

"You're full of shit!" Parrot said.

In the shadowed room, George spotted the cage hanging immediately to his left. He jabbed it as though it were a punching bag, sending it careening to the floor with Parrot cackling bloody murder. In the confusion and without warning, George kicked at Tom's right knee with his heavy boot. Tom danced back, narrowly avoiding the blow, only to bump into Grandma, who slid beside him clutching her double-barreled shotgun.

"There's two more of us here, George," she said evenly, raising the barrels to chest level, "and if the right one don't get you, the left one will."

George froze in his tracks, not so drunk he didn't recognize the deadly persuasion in Grandma's hands.

"Hold on there, you old coot." He held a hand up in front of him.

"You ease on out of here and don't take too long at it because my trigger finger is mighty unstable."

George didn't move. He glared at Grandma. "You'll be sorry, old woman. I'll get you."

"Try that on someone else, I've dealt with drunks all my life."

He turned his glare to the boys, who were still crouched in a fighting stance.

"You're not going to win any championship, hell, you'll get the shit kicked out of you and come dragging your losing asses home like always."

"Move!" Grandma poked the muzzle toward him.

George turned sideways and shuffled out onto the porch, keeping one eye on Grandma. Teetering, he stopped at the far edge of the porch and faced them through the open door.

"You boys are a joke . . . couldn't whip your own—"

"You should be ashamed of yourself," Grandma said in a softened tone. "Your boy is playing his heart out to win the state championship and you don't even have the decency to come and watch. Why—"

"His basketball got nuthing to do with me."

"Well, for land's sake, *who* in tarnation do you think he's trying so hard to win it for?"

The night went utterly silent; no one moved. George Stonebreaker's hands gave up their fists. Tom swallowed hard and looked at the floor. Grandma lowered the shotgun. They stood motionless for aching moments that were stretching into lifetimes.

"You ought to be ashamed of yourself, a grown man like you carryin' on like that, treatin' your boy like trash." Grandma lowered her voice and spoke with a note of sadness. "You ought to be ashamed."

George Stonebreaker turned abruptly and broke for cover as if he were.

✄ CHAPTER 81 ✄

S till in his damp sweats from running, Sam picked up the phone
with inklings of dread, tabulating time somewhere in his head
to make it to eight-thirty that night without losing another of his stallions.
Mentally he cocked an ear, knowing there were such things as backing beer
trucks, and he kept hearing his father at the state fair repeating helplessly,
"Things happen."

"Were you sleeping?" Diana's voice slid into his brain.

"Are you kidding? This will be the longest day of my life."

"Let's go see the dinosaurs."

"Dinosaurs?"

"Yeah. Want me to pick you up?"

"No, no, I'll be out as soon as I shower. Are we going to dig up some
bones?"

"No. They're still in them."

They drove west toward the Jefferson gorge with the unsullied spring
sky stretched on tiptoe above them in its morning blue, tempting Sam to
toss his anxiety into the ditch as useless baggage. The day caressed him
with a crisp and stimulating freshness that encouraged him to inhale it
like bliss. The mountains rolled color down on them, brindled earth-tones
out of creation's morn. Turning off a gravel road onto rocky grassland and
sage, she pointed out a faint two-track that a coyote couldn't follow. After
a half mile she directed him to swing onto cropland, where she opened the
sagging barbed-wire gate.

They drove across an alfalfa field, through a small cottonwood and juniper grove, and parked at the edge of a field of stubble. Far out in the center
stood an old abandoned two-story house that had long ago seen the last of
its paint, glass, and shingles. Diana, in jeans and her bulky jacket, paused
at the edge of the field, gazing intently at the former homestead, and he
remembered how much he loved her. The Jefferson carved its way through

gnarled limestone a half mile to the west, and sagebrush had taken over the land beyond the field south, spreading up to the bedrock cliffs like migrating lemmings.

"I've never shown them to anyone," she said.

He expected a *Tyrannosaurus rex* to come blasting out of a cave along the river.

"C'mon," she said and set off across the barley stubble. "Watch for arrowheads."

Sam found no evidence of those earlier inhabitants along the rows of stubble and sandy loam, and in a few minutes they reached the wood-frame house. It was larger than it had seemed from a distance. Several pieces of rusted horse-drawn farm equipment squatted randomly around. Scars on the land like shadows delineated where two outbuildings once stood. Diana held a finger to her lips and stealthily crept to one of the glassless windows. The sun-bleached sill pressed against Sam's chest as he peered in.

The house was littered with old plaster and lath and wind-blown dirt. From where he stood, Sam could see all of the ransacked four rooms on the first floor. Bricks were strewn around the floor from a chimney that teetered against a wall, making it hard to tell which was holding up the other. Snatches of faded wallpaper decorated the few patches of plaster that still clung to the walls, flowered patterns undoubtedly selected out of some ancient mail-order catalog that, page by page, most likely found its greatest use in the outhouse.

Diana pointed up toward an inside corner of the house. Much of the second-story floor had collapsed and he could see out through the roof in a few places. Sunlight splintered through the shadowed interior. Sam searched where she directed but could only distinguish rafters and rough roofing boards hung with the webs and deposits of creeping, crawling things. He shook his head.

She tiptoed around the side of the house, over fallen siding and shingles, and stepped up into what appeared to be the back door, a small porch and steps collapsed beneath it. Sam followed her carefully onto the uncertain floor, seeing that there were spaces where the decaying boards had broken through. No matter how hard they tried, their shoes crunched plaster, lath, and a variety of debris from someone else's life.

Without sound, it cannonballed out of the shadows, through the streams of daylight, and vanished out a second-story window like a phantom. Completely surprised, Sam only caught a glimpse of the plummeting creature. Diana froze where she stood, turning to him quickly with a finger over her lips, pointing up toward the corner from where the shadow had come. Sam's heart quickened. He had no idea what he had seen. Diana took another cautious step, cringing at her own noise. Sam followed, trying to find a place on the cluttered floor that wouldn't broadcast his approach.

Suddenly it came—a huge, grayish blur, swooping through the dappled air and out into the bright March sky. Diana grabbed Sam's arm and dragged him without caution across the rubble to a window.

"Quick!" she shouted. "There!" She pointed.

Gliding out across the stubble, with only a few powerful strokes of its enormous wings, the large bird flew, swiftly, over the sage at the end of the field and down into a draw to disappear.

"Did you *see* him? Did you *see* him?"

"Yeah. It was big. What was it?"

"The dinosaurs that are still with us."

She turned her gaze from the spot where they last saw its image.

"I hate to disturb them," she said. "They're great horned owls."

She pointed out the little dry piles of fur, feathers, and bones the owls had regurgitated, remnants from the raptor's menu. They would nest in the rafters in May and raise young dinosaurs to continue their habitation in the old homestead, having a lineage in this valley that watched the first natives learn to survive more than ten thousand years ago.

Sam and Diana settled out on the front porch of the weather-ravaged house. The serenity of the old homestead encompassed the land, and the natural rhythms of the day seemed no different from what they would have been a thousand years ago.

Sam sat with his back against the house, his knees pulled up, and she sat in the same pose between his legs, leaning back against his chest with her head against his shoulder and cheek. He enfolded her in his arms. They remained there without speaking for what seemed like hours, Sam nuzzling her long, fragrant hair that reflected reddish strands in the play of light. Then he broke the spell.

"I wonder who the people were who lived here?"

"Homesteaders, a man and woman who were wondrously in love and who never left each other," she said without hesitation. "They raised their children here and died of old age in each other's arms."

"You've thought about it before."

"Every time I come here," she said, "Ellie and Randolph Butterworth."

"*This* is the family you visit?"

"Yes, I found their names on the abstract at the county courthouse."

Sam kept his utter amazement to himself.

"Sometimes I sit here like this and I can hear them calling to each other across the land, laughing, talking in their work, hauling water from the river, putting up hay. I hear the children playing and screaming happily at twilight, I hear them singing songs and hymns together, and sometimes, when I'm very still for a long time, I can hear them making love."

Sam listened. The wind gently exhaled, and he imagined he could hear a distant child's voice calling. Was it from his past or from this sacred ground where others lived out their lives? He gazed off to where the great horned owls flew out of sight.

"Will they come back, the owls?"

"I've waited hours, but they seem to know. They'll probably come back at dawn tomorrow."

"Dawn tomorrow," Sam said.

"Are you afraid?"

"Only for the boys, they've come so far. I can't bear to see how much they'll hurt if they lose tonight."

"They would say exactly the same about you. They want to win for a lot of reasons, but mostly they want to win it for you."

Sam glanced at his watch, the sublime present torn from his grasp.

She asked, "We need to go?"

"Pretty soon."

They stood and brushed off their jeans, about to go back to what faced them in the championship game. As though she'd assessed that the land had not healed the terrible fear in him, she took his hands in hers and smiled calmly into his face.

"They'll be here tomorrow, the owls, all this will be."

He swallowed. "Will *you* be?"

"Yes."

CHAPTER 82

Grandma slipped off to Three Forks to pick up a few groceries. She knew she'd need another half-dozen eggs with Tom there for breakfast and that the boys would probably sleep until noon. She chuckled when she remembered the flabbergasted look on both of their faces the night before. After she had shut the door on George Stonebreaker, she had opened the breech of the double-barreled shotgun, revealing the two empty chambers.

"The gun wasn't loaded?" Tom had asked.

"Never invite a drunk and a loaded gun to the same party," she had told them.

When she came out of the D & D grocery store with an armload, Sally Cutter was parked beside Trilobite in her red rattletrap of a pickup. Grandma slipped the groceries onto her bus seat and stepped back to the sidewalk to visit. She waved at Denise, who was strapped in beside her mother. Sally said something to Denise and then climbed out and closed the door. In a faded green scarf and what looked like one of her husband's work jackets, Sally joined Grandma in front of the store.

"Land sakes," Grandma said, "did you ever think you'd breathe again after last night?"

"That was something," Sally said with a flicker of enthusiasm.

"Denise must have been proud as a peach the way the boys ran up to her like that. It made me bawl, and that basket Dean made, you must be mighty proud."

"I'm happy for the kids. It's been—"

Both of them glanced up to see George Stonebreaker coming along the sidewalk. Grandma puffed up her chest and gritted her teeth, preparing for the assault. But when George looked up and saw them standing there, he spun on a dime and headed the other direction as though he'd spotted someone he owed money to.

"Huh! I guess I put a dent in his fender last night. Look at him skedaddle."

Sally watched George hurry away and spoke without turning to Grandma. "Did you have trouble with him?"

"Came to the house, pounding on the door, wanted to drag poor Tom home, wasn't going to let him play today, drunk as a skunk. I got out old Salt and Pepper and put the run on him."

"Don't be too hard on him," Sally said, still tracking his retreat.

"Why, I won't allow that big bully to—"

"It wasn't you that turned him around," Sally said softly.

"Well something sure did."

"It was the girl." Sally glanced into Grandma's face.

"Denise?" Grandma said.

"He's her father!"

"*What?*"

Grandma exhaled as though she'd been kicked in the stomach.

"She's his daughter, Tom's half-sister," Sally said, gazing down at her fidgety hands as she spoke. "We were in love seventeen, eighteen years ago. He was married a couple years and knew he'd made a bad mistake. We were together every chance we got—where nobody would see us. He was different then, gentle, kind, full of life. Then I got pregnant. I went to him and told him." Sally sighed and gathered herself. "He said he loved me dearly, always would. But he was Catholic and he could never get a divorce."

Grandma took hold of one of Sally's hands.

"I nearly died with the heartache." Sally rushed on as if she stopped she'd never be able to muster the courage again. "But I told him good-bye. The next night I was out with Delbert Cutter. He always took a shine to me. In three weeks I convinced him to run off and get married. Seven months later Denise was born with the palsy."

"Did Delbert know?"

"Never said a word. He took Denise as his own, but he can count. He didn't want any more kids. Dean was an accident."

Sally looked off toward the mountains and bit her lip.

"George can't bear to see the girl," she went on after a moment. "He knows God is punishing us both. It's funny, we were so much in love. I don't sleep with Delbert, and George hasn't slept with his wife since then. He didn't want the same to happen to another child. Tom was already born."

"Did you ever . . . see him again?"

"No, I've never been with him since I said good-bye. But I think he still loves me. So don't be too hard on him, Grandma. Don't think too harshly of him."

Grandma felt ashamed and foolish and angry with herself for forgetting that everyone was making his way the best he could.

"Do you still love him?" she asked and squeezed Sally's hand.

"That don't matter. I try to make life as good as I can for Denise."

Grandma hugged Sally.

"Sally, you're a brave woman, brave as I've ever known. I'll never tell a soul."

For a moment more, Grandma held on for dear life. Then, emotionally overwhelmed, she turned and slid into the VW bus. With her eyes blurring, she waved over at Denise. Then she backed out into the empty street and drove away, praying that she wouldn't catch sight of George Stonebreaker, the man she used to despise.

SAM AND DIANA pulled up in front of the Blue Willow around one. There were no other vehicles besides Axel's pickup and car in their usual ruts around the side. Like a traveling carnival it seemed the little town had pulled stakes and moved off to Bozeman.

"I didn't know if they'd still be open," Sam said.

They got out of the Tempo and climbed the two steps onto the porch. Someone had plastered a large hand-lettered sign on the front door: open all night after the game in honor of the Broncs. Inside, Axel and Vera were bustling around the place, decorating with gold and blue crepe paper, ribbons, and balloons.

"Oh, I forgot to put up the Closed sign," Vera said.

"Looks like you're planning quite a celebration," Diana said.

Axel laid aside a stapler and a roll of gold crepe and turned to them. "The biggest Willow Creek ever saw," he said. He winked at Sam. "We're stocked like an ocean liner."

Vera scooted to the door and turned the sign around so that the CLOSED faced the street.

Sam said, "We thought we'd get some lunch, but if you're—"

"Sit down, sit down," Axel said, pulling out a chair for Diana. "We've plenty of time, plenty of time. With that woman we could decorate the field house by game time. Besides, if I don't keep busy I'll go crazy."

"I know the feeling," Sam said.

"Where you two been?" Axel said as Vera careened into the kitchen.

"Out to see the dinosaurs," Sam said.

"Yeah, I hear there are lots of their bones around here," Axel said, rubbing his meaty hands together. "Well, that's nice, take your mind off the game."

"It did until you reminded us." Diana laughed.

They ordered and ate turkey, Swiss, and sprout sandwiches on whole wheat while Axel and Vera hung the place in blue and gold.

Sam finally made himself say, "What if we don't win?"

"That won't matter," Axel said, "won't matter a bit. You and the boys have done us proud, one of the top two teams in the *state of Montana,* and come hell or high water, we're going to celebrate tonight no matter what."

"Tell 'em about the lady," Vera called from the kitchen.

"Oh, yeah. Had a funny thing happen here this morning," Axel said, up on a short stool with his back to them, stringing balloons above the antique-bathtub salad bar. "Tall, slim lady came in around eleven-thirty. Snazzy-looking gal, big pretty eyes."

"Sad eyes," Vera said.

"Said she wanted to sit at that table over there." Axel nodded with his head, tying balloon strings with both hands.

"What's so strange about that?" Diana asked.

Axel stepped down off the stool and turned to face them. Invigorated by their journey in the field and still feeling its serenity, Sam had found his appetite and was in the process of destroying his sandwich.

"Well, we had three tables open, but she waited until the Harringtons finished."

"I've done that," Diana said. "When I eat out, I wait for a spot I'd like."

"Tell 'em about the bike," Vera called while scooting back to string ribbon.

"Well, she wanted to know about the bicycle built for two, you know," Axel said, "why it was sittin' out there on the porch and all. Vera told her a little bit about it."

"Next time I came into the dining room, she asked me if it would be all right if she rode it," Vera said.

Sam bit the side of his cheek.

Vera said, "I told her, 'That's what it's there for.' In that lovely silk dress and all. I thought it was kinda funny."

"Did she ride it?" Sam asked, tasting blood inside his mouth.

"Yeah, by golly," Axel said, stretching an uninflated balloon in his hands. "When she paid up—left Vera a five-dollar tip—she went out and rode the bike down toward the school. I watched her for a minute, kinda wobbly at first, but she got the hang of it, looked kinda pretty ridin' that old thing all alone."

Sam dropped the remnants of his sandwich on its plate. "Did she give you her name?" he said.

"No," Vera told him. "Never did, said she was passin' through and had lived around here once."

"Did you see her car? Her license plate?" Sam said.

"What is it, Sam, who is she?" Diana asked with a frown.

Axel said, "I checked out her car after she went ridin' the bike. Connecticut plates, a white sports car, not sure what. They all look the same nowadays."

"Sam, what's wrong?" Diana asked.

"Nothing, nothing, did she say where she was going?"

"Yeah," Vera said, tying a gold ribbon on the post between the tavern and the dining room. "Said she'd gone to the University in Missoula and was going up there to look around for a few days, said she'd stop by again on her way back. I think she liked the food."

Sam wiped his mouth with his napkin and pushed back from the table. He looked into Diana's puzzled face. "Listen, I have to run, we're meeting the boys at school around three, we'll go over the game plan before we eat, okay?"

"Yeah, okay, but where are you going?"

"I have something I have to get done before then. Everything's great for tonight. See you at three."

Sam turned and dashed out the front door. Outside, he realized Diana didn't have her car. He hurried back in. "You take my car, I can walk."

He tossed her the keys and spun out the door. He raced up Main Street like Dean Cutter, as if his pants were on fire, though he knew the fire was in his heart. Past the Volunteer Fire House and Willow Creek Tool, past United Methodist, then he swerved east, around Grandma Chapman's picket fence, down the dirt road where he'd first glimpsed Andrew on his shadowed ride. He cut through the vacant lot where he and Diana made love in the Volvo and turned south on Broadway, past Bremers' abandoned outhouse, where Tripod led the boys to Parrot that bitterly cold night.

Harrington's hound Bonzo joined him as though something was up, and Sam dashed along that graveled road with an unbearable joy in his bursting chest, sprinting, the lop-eared hound bounding alongside. At the far end of town, where the fields and trees surround and take hostage the few houses, he turned into Andrew Wainwright's drive and raced to the door of the newer ranch-style home. Up on the step he pounded with both fists as though attempting to knock down the door of the world's sadness—to tear away the vermin-infested curtains and cobwebbed sorrow that shrouded Andrew's heart, allowing love's bright warmth to stream in; to break into that land where young elephants and sea turtles are free to live their lives, where wildebeest calves have mothers who never give in to the wild dogs; to break into that place where kids leap out of their wheelchairs to run and dance, where people shed the grinding, incapacitating burden of loneliness, and where basketball teams with only five players win championships.

Then, with Harrington's hound kangarooing and barking excitedly, he noticed the attached garage was empty, the white Town Car was gone. There was no one home.

THEY HAD GATHERED in the gym at three o'clock, all of them waiting when Sam hurried through the door. In street clothes they walked through offensive sets and talked strategy, allowing Tom and Olaf to rest their wounded limbs in the bleachers. Axel had come, and Grandma, and with Scott and Curtis they stood out on the floor impersonating Seely-Swan defenders. Sam had a few new wrinkles for the team that had beaten them a week ago, a fact he accepted as Willow Creek's advantage. They not only knew the team they were about to face, but they were also favored by the psychology of the underdog, where overconfidence can erode the concentration of the team who previously won. Sam kept track of the time, wanting to stay on schedule right up to the tip-off. Before they left the gym, Sam huddled them out on the floor.

"This could be the last basketball game Willow Creek High School ever plays," he said calmly. "Let's make it a great one—a game that will always make you and the people of Willow Creek proud. Have fun and learn something."

"Why do we have to learn something?" Dean said. "It's our last game."

"For the rest of your lives," Sam said.

No one spoke for a moment as they all seemed to reflect on Sam's words. Then Tom broke the spell with his perfect imitation of a cow.

"Moooooooow!"

"Let's go chip ice!" Pete shouted.

"Yeah!" the boys responded, and they linked hands.

"Win! Win! Win! Win! Win! Win! Win!"

In the lengthening daylight of early March, they strolled up Main Street to Sam's house, where Diana and the cheerleaders were preparing food. The landscape surrounding town, alive with promise, lifted Sam's spirit. With their choice of any movie they wanted to watch, Sam had suspected there wouldn't be much discussion, and while they sprawled around the rummage-sale living room watching *Man of La Mancha,* the girls kept a steady stream of pizza coming from the oven, to be washed down by fruit juices. At the end, when Cervantes and his squire, Sancho, climbed the stairs of the dungeon to face the Inquisition, the boys headed out the door for Rozinante to face the last team in the state who stood in the road to their underdog dreams.

CHAPTER 83

Sam guided the carrot-colored bus along the interstate. He glanced over at Dean and Curtis jabbering in the right front seat. Curtis had his arm in a sling and both of them wore their inspirational caps pulled over one ear. Curtis was giving his younger, less-experienced teammate tips on playing defense, insights that come from trying to compete with and outwit conspicuously more-talented boys.

"When he goes by you," Curtis said, "reach around and slap the ball from behind him."

Sam could see Bozeman on the far horizon, the silver dome of the field house barely visible in the twilight. He figured that, win or lose, Olaf would be selected on the All-State team along with Peter and Rob. Tom would most certainly be second-team, and if they won, possibly first-team. But who should be on the All-Courageous team? It was one thing for boys with athletic ability to work hard and receive praise for playing well, but it was quite another to go out there weaponless, without quickness or coordination, and take a stand against boys with all of those attributes.

He considered Curtis and Dean. None of this could have happened without their bravery and grit, and though they would never be talented basketball players in the true sense of the word, which boy had shown the greater courage? Would it be Olaf with his gigantic height and reach and heart, or Peter with his skill and grace and bravado? Would it be Rob with his natural athletic gifts, or Tom with his muscle and agility? Or was it Dean and Curtis, who had to go out naked each night with dull swords and crooked arrows, exposed in the bright light of their inability and hamstrung by their gracelessness, yet standing there on the battle line, doing what they can to help the team win. Were these not the truly heroic, who would never make an All-State Team, never be recognized with distinction by the public or press, but who had come the furthest and given the most?

Sam turned to them again and smiled. "How's the wrist?"

"Okay," Curtis said, "I wish they'd let me play."

"I wish they would, too," Dean said.

"You'll do great tonight, Dean," Sam said. "You're the best runner in the state."

Sam turned Rozinante off the interstate and into Bozeman. They drove through town unnoticed, this unlikely, whittled-down team in their un-likely, whittled-down bus, on their last journey together. Their coach trem-bled somewhere inside, never forgetting he bore Andrew Wainwright's reprieve in the vest pocket of his heart.

THERE WAS NOTHING Sam could have done to prepare the boys for what greeted them when they ventured out into the arena to warm up. They had gone directly to the locker room on arrival and had no inkling as to the proportions of their celebrity. Word of the crazy little basketball team from Willow Creek had been broadcast like thistle seed on the winds of radio, television, newsprint, and word-of-mouth to such a degree that not only were there no seats available in the field house, but the standing-room-only crowd had pushed the gate to well over ten thousand.

Ten thousand who generated the roar of a great ocean breaking against the land when they recognized the Willow Creek players in their cock-eyed caps loping out onto the court—Tom and Olaf, like gimpy cowboys, going directly to the basket while the other *three* ran a lap around the court. Sam was astonished at the noise when the coaches and Scott made their way to the bench with their gear. Seely-Swan came dashing twelve strong, cir-cling the floor in their black and gold, and the spectators calmed and settled into their seats.

The five of them shot layups and free throws, and Sam noticed a new addition to their bench. Under her chair in a satchel, Grandma had that motley parrot, its head sticking out like a hood ornament, the last piece of luck in her medicine bag. She also had a small radio, and its earphones protruded from under her brown fedora.

The cheerleaders had painted some signs after their frustrating attempts to coordinate the crowd the previous night, and he could see that they'd kept it simple. Carter and Louella sorted the placards, which each had only one or two words, in bold blue and gold:

DEFENSE! GO BRONCS GO! FIGHT TEAM FIGHT!

With five minutes till game time, the tiny Willow Creek contingent left the arena, winding their way through the hundreds standing at ground level at the corners of the court. When they were all inside, Sam closed the locker-room door, shutting out the tempest and finding an eddy of calm. The boys sat along one bench with Sancho. Axel and Grandma had opted to stay out in the arena with the cheerleaders, as though they felt they would be infringing on this special moment that belonged to the nine of them.

"There's so many people," Rob said.

Pete settled on a bench. "And they're rockin' for us."

"They like us," Tom said and smiled at Dean.

Then, with Diana standing beside him, Sam felt their eyes come to him in the numbing, tingling silence, expectant, hopeful, and hungry.

"I wanted a moment with you before the game." Sam regarded each of them, carefully, finding there the focused steel of five boys.

"We've come a long way. I only want to remind you that you already have everything you need to win. You've worked hard. You've earned the right to be here, and I want you to have the fun you deserve tonight. But we've learned that nothing comes easy. I want you to go out and play as hard as you can play, give as much as you can give, for as long as you can stand, so that one day, when you look back, you can smile proudly. That's the best kind of fun and it will last you a lifetime."

Sam's throat filled and he fought to finish.

"If I could have one wish tonight, other than winning, it would be that I could be out on the floor playing beside you."

Sam nodded at Diana.

"I want to thank you boys for the ride," she said. "It's been the most fun I've ever had, and like Coach Pickett, I'd give my right arm to be out on the court with you. But remember, we are, all of us, Scott and Curtis and all the people from Willow Creek, we're out there beside you and that's why we're going to win!"

"Yeeaaahhhh!" the boys shouted, leaping to their feet. Neither coach could say more and Sam extended his hands. They quickly huddled around him and lifted their cheer.

Weaving their way through the standing crowd, they found the court, enshrouded in a galaxy of human faces. A volcanic roar erupted when the fans spotted the Willow Creek boys trotting across the court. The Seely-Swan team was shooting baskets at the far end as the horn sounded, calling both teams to the bench for introductions.

Dean was the first Bronc announced, and after slapping palms with everyone on the bench, he dashed across the floor and up into the bleachers to his undaunted sister. He gently laid high fives on her dancing hands. Then he carefully fit his cap on her golden-crowned head to work what magic she and the cap could still muster at the gate to the castle. The crowd noise dropped considerably as the spectators observed this unexpected ritual and then increased dramatically as Dean raced back down the stairs and stood at the west free-throw circle, his unruly brown hair looking as though he'd been struck by lightning.

The introductions went swiftly and each Bronc was knighted by the tumultuous vocal support bestowed on them by the exuberant fans. Each boy in turn gave those on the bench high fives and then ran the bleacher stairs to do the same with Denise Cutter before joining his teammates in the exclusive circle of camaraderie on the court. Sam spotted Andrew sitting beside Denise, but Andrew's reprieve would have to wait until after the game. That didn't seem long; Andrew had endured for more than twenty years. For now, Sam had to wipe all else out of his mind and concentrate on the game with every cell of his body. He would *not* be outcoached. They announced the coaches and the teams broke for their benches through a great storm of noise.

Sam knelt in the middle; the five circled him, and Axel, Grandma, Sancho, Curtis, and Diana formed a protective shelter around them.

"Go hard!" Rob yelled.

"We didn't come this far to lose," Tom said.

"Go, Oaf!" Pete shouted.

They linked hands in the huddle and gave one shout in unison.

"Team!"

When they broke the circle, the four of them laid their caps on the bench. Then five of them walked onto the court together. The field house vibrated with the electricity of human emotion. Lowell Lapp, Seely-Swan's 6'4" center, faced off with Olaf at the center jump circle. The referee blew his whistle and lofted the ball into the air.

CHAPTER 84

Diana held her breath, almost unable to watch. Olaf controlled the tip and Willow Creek swiftly unsheathed its weapons. Their classy opponents, whose obvious objective was to strangle anything in the paint, dropped back into a smothering zone. The Broncs moved the ball around the outside until Pete got a high pass to Olaf in the low post. The Blackhawk defense collapsed on him like a wet tent. Diana couldn't fault the opposing coach for concentrating his troops to stop Gustafson and Stonebreaker inside, but that had become the unforgivable sin against this Willow Creek team. Up to his armpits in Seely-Swan players, Olaf snapped a pass back out to his momentarily unattended teammate. Peter promptly knocked down the open shot, and the multitudes came to their feet in an oceanic roar, and Willow Creek was on the board.

With a cocksureness in their faces, Seely-Swan came storming with their shooters: Thomas, Boyd, Cooper, and McHenry. Rob played the wing where Curtis usually scrambled, and Dean chased the ball out front with his fire-alarm intensity and his barbed-wire endurance. Diana was so proud of them she could hardly bear it. She was torn between trying to enjoy this magnificent moment and her desperate hope that the boys would win, feeling like a stowaway witnessing a great sea battle, helpless to influence its outcome.

The outlandish gang on the bench were a sight to behold: a perspiring, balding man, shaped like a fire hydrant, in a tight blue suit; a skinny, lop-eared sophomore with his arm in a sling and wearing a shopworn cap; a chubby freshman with a matching cap; and a gnarly, snow-haired woman with a brown fedora on her head, a three-legged cat in her jacket, and a parrot in a gym bag under her seat.

The cheerleaders wore blue pleated skirts and gold jerseys and, with the help of their placards, had thousands volleying to their lead.

"Go, Broncs, go! Go, Broncs, go! Go, Broncs, go!"

Both teams played in-your-face basketball, showing a stonelike determination that would not back down, displaying grace and quickness and athletic moves that even surprised Diana. Rob and Pete were making Seely-Swan pay by arcing glorious long-range bull's-eyes overhead, while the Blackhawks were preoccupied in a shadow dance with Olaf. Diana would have been giddy on the bench had it not been for the fact that Tom was hurting badly. He couldn't move well laterally or jump well, and though he tried to conceal it, his knee appeared to be punishing him unremittingly.

At the quarter, Willow Creek led, 19 to 16. The players caught their breath on the bench, and Diana iced Tom's knee. Sam hadn't used a timeout, deciding instead to save them.

"Rob, Pete," Sam shouted, "keep burning them until they loosen up on Olaf." He looked into Olaf's eyes. "How's the ankle?"

"I am not feeling the ankle."

"All right, be patient," Sam said. "Your time is coming." He regarded the others. "You're playing perfectly. How did you get so good?"

"We didn't forget our balls," Dean said.

Sam smiled and shouted above the din, "You're right, you guys never forgot your balls! Have fun!"

In the second quarter it became a classic game between two teams who could run if the opportunity was there and play excellent half-court basketball when it wasn't. They had done their homework and they put on a clinic of disciplined teamwork: bodies colliding and banging in the paint and shooters coming free around picks and screens to demonstrate their fine-tuned touch and flawless eyes.

The deadeyes Thomas and Boyd were keeping Seely-Swan close from outside while Olaf was making life miserable for Lapp around the basket. McHenry, their lean, quick forward, was beginning to have his way against Tom as though he knew the infuriated bull rider couldn't stay with him any longer. With gnashing teeth, Tom was conceding the sixteen- to eighteen-footer and the gifted McHenry began hitting. But as the Seely-Swan coach released his guards to come out on Rob and Peter, who were killing them softly, Olaf set up housekeeping inside. With room to move, he sucked Lapp into immediate foul trouble and the 6'4" center had to retreat to the bench with three. Sam burned a timeout with less than three minutes in the quarter. Tom wouldn't make it to halftime without a break.

"You want to sit out for the last few minutes?" Sam asked Tom.

"I can't. They'd slaughter us," Tom said.

"Yes, you can," Sam said. "We can play four-man zone."

"We can hold 'em," Pete shouted.

That Tom would even consider it gave Diana some understanding of the exorbitant price the knee was exacting. Tom glanced at his teammates and paused. The horn sounded. They all regarded Tom.

"You guys just want to have all the fun," he said. "I can wet-nurse my knee the rest of my life!"

The boys held their ground with deliberate execution and defense. Olaf rejected Lapp's turnaround and Dean found the castaway ball in his hands. Before he could pass off to a teammate, Cooper clobbered him, trying to steal it back. With great deliberation at the foul line, Dean aimed through his sweat-smeared prisms and rattled in a garbage shot. The sea roared. His second attempt hit the backboard and came high off the rim. Somehow Tom outmuscled McHenry for the rebound and banked it down the well. When time ran out in the first half, the court shook with the adulation of the standing thousands. Together, the Broncs hauled their four-point advantage to the locker room.

Halftime became an emotional storm of expectation and dread. Diana applied the ice and the boys jabbered excitedly about what was working against Seely-Swan, their confidence swelling along with Tom's knee. Grandma, with Tripod's head poking out of her Twins jacket, moved among the boys with praise and encouragement. Following her instincts, Diana nodded at Grandma.

"Would you like to say something?"

She paused, glancing around at the boys. Then she bent slightly with her hands on her knees and squinted into their faces.

"This is no time for generosity. You got to give 'em Biblical law." She shook a fist. "An eye for an eye and a tooth for a tooth." She straightened and pointed her hatchetlike chin. "That trophy belongs in Willow Creek and if it doesn't get there tonight, it never will forever and ever, amen."

"Let's get it!" Rob yelled.

"Okay!" Sam shouted, "we're one half away. Let's finish it!"

They rallied and shouted and some of them loped back to the arena. Some of them limped.

Time accelerated in the reverberating field house, the atmosphere dripped humid with hope. Diana felt as though she would be swept away with the heart-pounding exhilaration. Seely-Swan came with four rested substitutes and they attempted to get a running game started. Willow Creek played them an eye for an eye and a tooth for a tooth and effectively throttled the ploy by dominating the boards and not allowing them to get out running. The fresher Blackhawks had obviously been told to be more aggressive on offense, driving slapdash into the zone and looking for the whistle. It worked to a degree. Olaf and Rob slapped away several attempts, but Pete and Tom each picked up their third foul. Gauging the weariness in their faces, Sam burned a timeout in the middle of the quarter, leaving two in the bank.

"Get your bodies in front of them," Sam shouted, "and don't slap at the ball, they're trying to put you on the bench."

Late in the third quarter, Dean didn't see a pick and collided with Thomas. It was his fourth foul. But the boys demonstrated a seasoning and savvy that made Diana smile with pride, slowing the pace, circulating the ball outside the Blackhawks' fence line, patiently looking for the good shot while subtly milking the clock. In the closeness of their daily work, she had missed how very good they had become. Despite Dean's precarious state, she couldn't prevent confidence from seeping into her pores and bloodstream. When the boys came to the bench at the end of the third quarter, they were up by seven and were controlling the game.

"You're playing great, you're playing great!" Sam shouted as they flopped in the chairs.

They dried their faces and sloshed water. Sam knelt in front of Dean and gently took the kid's face in his hands.

"You have to lay off. Watch out for the picks, play it loose. We need you in there, okay?"

Dean nodded. "I'm not scared anymore," he said.

"Good, that's good," Sam said. "All right, we're one step from home, I can see the light in the window!"

Diana could hardly breathe as the fourth quarter began. Seely-Swan, with the well-rested regulars, jumped on them with their zone press. But the Broncs expected it and with disciplined finesse repeatedly used Olaf to break it. Peter hit a scintillating jumper from the paint and Rob put back an Olaf miss.

"Run 'em off the floor!" Diana screamed.

In the breathtaking ebb and flow, Willow Creek held a seven-point advantage.

"Go, Broncs, go! Go, Broncs, go!" the crowd pealed.

Olaf was hobbling and Tom limping, and seconds seemed to hang to the clock. Boyd outquicked Rob. Pete slid over in his driving lane. The Black-hawk guard went for the layup. In the collision, Pete was whistled for the foul, his fourth, and Diana's stomach moved up a notch toward her throat. Boyd canned both free throws.

With the Broncs on the attack, Tom slipped to the floor reaching for Rob's bounce pass. McHenry grabbed the ball and heaved it upcourt to Thomas, sprinting along the sideline. Dean raced to plug the leak.

"Let him go!" Diana shouted. "Let him go!"

Thrashing like a runaway penguin and using most of the speedometer, Dean intersected Thomas's line of trajectory and went up with him, trying to block the shot. He took the Seely-Swan guard tailspinning into the first row of bleachers, and the ball sailed into the crowd. The ref blew his whistle and pointed at the scrappy freshman. It was only then that both Dean and the roaring partisans realized the consequences.

It was his fifth foul! Dean was out of the game.

All the oxygen seemed to be sucked from Diana's body.

CHAPTER 85

The buzzer belched its note of disaster like a delinquent foghorn to a ship already on the rocks. The scoreboard showed a bloodied "5" next to Dean's number "32." With three minutes and twenty-nine seconds on the game clock, Willow Creek, leading by five points, would have to continue with only four players.

Sam called timeout as the Cutter boy, his chest heaving, came off the court dripping with the despair of his soul-searching innocence. The spectators throughout the field house stood roaring, a tumultuous tribute to the intrepid little freshman. Sam patted him on the back as he dropped onto the bench. He was crying.

"You played great!" Sam shouted to him. "You got us this far and we're going to win it!"

The huge audience remained on their feet, humming over what was transpiring in front of them. The boys sagged on the bench. Sam crouched.

"Okay, we've practiced this a million times," Sam yelled, attempting to remain collected. "Bring the ball up with 'volley ball,' four-man zone on defense. Remember, *we've* got the advantage, you're used to playing four on five, they've never done it. Be patient, use your heads, and just when they think *they've* got *us,* we'll shove them in the well."

They joined hands in a circle and shouted "Team!"

Then Tom said, "Each time he falls . . ." And the rest of them chanted, ". . . he shall rise again!" Then the four of them turned into the face of what remained.

GRANDMA CHAPMAN PRESSED Tripod to her breast as a wave of sadness attacked her. They had worked so hard, had fought their way through the woods to get here, and then *this* happens. Everything was going against them, Hazel had been right, it was too good to be true. Despair squatted on her with the weight of her good friend, who was somewhere behind her in the stands. Just off to the right of the bench and back a few rows, she had heard loud voices shouting nonstop for Gustafson and Stonebreaker. Finally she turned to see who it was and was startled to recognize Craig Stone and Gary Harkin, along with several other Twin Bridges players, athletes who had made their road so tough, shouting their guts out for Willow Creek. She feathered the volume up on her radio.

". . . can hardly hear ourselves think with the noise of this crowd as the four boys come back on the floor. . . . It's deafening, this field house is rocking, folks. . . . The teams line up at the free-throw lane. . . . Thomas will have two shots with his team trailing, 56 to 51. . . . This boy has played a hell of a game and his seventeen points have kept Seely-Swan close. . . . He bounces the ball and gets set . . . oooh, it's in and out . . . the crowd goes crazy, most of them flying Willow Creek's banner now. . . . He'll get another. . . . Thomas sets himself, shoots the ball . . . count it. . . . Seely-Swan has pulled to within four, 56–52. . . . and here we go, four against five. Wow . . . let me tell you, fans, I've never seen anything like this in a state tournament. . . . Johnson gets the ball to Gustafson, Gustafson holds the ball high in the backcourt, looking for a teammate against the zone press . . . gets the ball to Strong . . . Strong dribbles up the side . . . Thomas and McHenry trap him, there's that lob back to Gustafson just over the midcourt line. . . . They've broken the press all night with their big center. . . . Gustafson gets the ball to Johnson . . . Johnson wings it over to Strong . . . three minutes and seventeen seconds."

Grandma turned up the volume and hugged Tripod to her breast.

"The Blackhawks are swarming, double-teaming, but the Willow Creek boys are using the clock and at the same time avoid being trapped. . . . Strong guns it down the side to Stonebreaker . . . he whips it cross-court to Johnson. . . . Willow Creek is moving without the ball, back cutting and going four corners, always moving, no one standing still. . . . Their coach is only a few feet from us here at the table and I can feel the sparks coming from the man. . . . Johnson dribbles up high . . . bounce passes into Gustafson . . . he pops the ball back out to Strong. . . . The two Willow Creek guards are frustrating the Blackhawks with their speed and ball handling. . . . Johnson gets it high to Gustafson in the paint, they collapse on him . . . the big center sends it back out to Johnson . . . he's open, takes the shot. . . . Holy cow! . . . He nails it! . . . The field house is going crazy. . . . Willow Creek 58, Seely-Swan 52, with just under three minutes in the game."

Grandma jumped up, almost flipping Tripod out of her jacket.

"The Blackhawks bring it in quickly . . . the Broncs fall back into a four-man zone . . . looks like a one-two-one with Gustafson on that bad ankle directly in front of the basket. . . . Man oh man, this is an unbelievable championship game. . . . Thomas gets the ball to Boyd. . . ."

"De-fense! De-fense! De-fense!"

Sam could feel the pulse of the crowd with every missed shot, every rebound, every turnover, a legion of voices and faces on the edge, hardly able to breathe, while five boys tried to overrun four. They swung the ball just beyond the boundaries of Willow Creek's reach and the Broncs staked claims around the paint, conceding the outside shot. It seemed to Sam that Seely-Swan sensed they'd already won, moving in for the kill like the wild dogs of Africa, confident that they could wear them down and finish them. But they were overeager, extremely excited, over passing, out of sync. Impatient for the kill, Boyd took a quick fifteen-footer from the edge of the key. He missed. Olaf, Tom, and Rob went to the boards with bared teeth. Rob picked off the rebound. The rumbling sound cascaded off the walls of the field house and swirled like a firestorm.

With single-minded toughness etched on their faces, the Broncs chiseled their way up the floor, whittling seconds off the clock. Olaf grunted out position in the high post and Rob got him the ball. Completely boxed in and stumbling with fatigue, he threw a leaden pass toward Pete. Boyd cut it off and streaked upcourt for an uncontested layup. Sam felt as though someone had punched him in the stomach. The congregation of the hopeful, still on its feet, sagged and hushed. The Blackhawks had pulled to within four, 58 to 54, and there were still two minutes and twenty-one seconds to play.

Willow Creek embezzled as much time from the clock as they could while trying to escape the gambling Keystone Cop defense the Blackhawks threw at them. Growing frantic, Seely-Swan hounded relentlessly with larceny in their eyes. Pete ran a pick-and-roll with Tom and Tom broke free toward the basket. Olaf saw Tom coming and screened Lapp from Tom's path. Pete delivered the ball and the bull rider went up and nailed it, bringing a seismic tremor from the leaping and ecstatic host. Sam threw his fists at the ceiling.

Axel bearhugged Dean off the floor.

Willow Creek 60, Seely-Swan 54. Two minutes and eight seconds.

Sam saw the weariness in their faces and he wanted to call time out, but they only had one left. The Seely-Swan coach saved him; he stopped the game to calm his flustered players. The four Broncs came to the sidelines soaked in sweat and they slumped onto the bench. The noise in the arena became a tornado, willing on the gutty quartet, sustaining them, nourishing them.

"How's your knee?" Sam asked Tom.

Tom ignored the question and Sam had his answer.

"One more minute and I'll call time out," Sam said.

They nodded, still sucking for air, seemingly too exhausted to speak.

Then Tom said, "Let's not give 'em the calf!"

When the four of them went back onto the floor, the roar washed over them like a great tidal wave. In their black and gold, Seely-Swan flowed swiftly into the front court. They moved the ball to the least guarded section of the court, looking for the perfect shot. Boyd was open in the corner—the vulnerability of the four-man zone—and Tom lunged to get on him, too late. The boy snapped the net with a superb three-point shot and the arena gasped from the blow.

One minute and fifty-three seconds. Willow Creek 60, Seely-Swan 57.

Within three points, the Seely-Swan boys turned the screws on their zone press. McHenry and Thomas trapped Pete along the side before he could get his lob back to Olaf. Unable to pass the ball, Pete bounced it off McHenry's leg and out of bounds. Willow Creek's ball. Rob lobbed the ball in to Olaf and they hedge-hopped their way into the front court. Pete dribbled along the side and zipped a pass to Olaf. He looked for a teammate open and held the ball too low. Cooper got his thieving hands on the ball and tied him up. The possession arrow favored the Blackhawks.

The Black and Gold hurried the ball downcourt as the crowd droned with an uneasy noise. Sam looked at the clock.

One minute and thirty-two seconds.

He could soon give them another break with their last time out. Seely-

Swan had uncovered the weakness in the four-man zone. Move the ball around to one side and then a quick cross-court pass to the other side. They were picking on Tom's corner, knowing he couldn't get out to cover the shooter. Everyone in the field house could see what was coming. The bull rider did all he could to cover the ground between him and the shooter, but the steady McHenry hit the open jump shot, a three-pointer, bringing a gasping silence to most of the arena. The Seely-Swan section erupted with joy.

Seely-Swan 60, Willow Creek 60.

One minute and thirteen seconds.

Sam waited until Willow Creek had worked the ball into the front court and then shouted to Rob.

"Time out! Time out!"

They came to the bench with sixty-eight seconds left in their life together. It seemed that their unyielding adversaries had stolen the momentum, as though the crowd had sensed the miracle had fallen short. The Seely-Swan players were celebrating at their bench, exchanging high fives and shouting as though it were over, as though they had Willow Creek in their jaws and had only to shake the life out of them. Sam patted each of the four on the back and allowed them a minute to catch their breath, dry their arms and faces and guzzle water. The ludicrous bench crew huddled around them. Then Sam kneeled in front of them.

"Okay, you can relax. You don't have to go back on the floor."

The four regarded each other with puzzled expressions.

"It's over, look." Sam pointed at the Blackhawk bench. "They figure they've won it, they're just waiting for someone to give them the trophy."

The boys gazed at the celebrating Seely-Swan boys. Sam could see anger color their faces, tightened their jaws, narrowed their eyes. It was his last hope—that when they were drained beyond all physical endurance, they could reach back and find something to go on, something spiritual, the intangible grit of a wildebeest cow.

"Well, I'm going back on the floor, by God," Tom said.

"Let's blow 'em out of the water!" Rob shouted.

Pete stared across the floor. "Stuff it down their throats!"

"They shall mount up with wings like eagles, they shall run and not be weary!" Grandma shouted, startling Sam.

The buzzer sounded. The boys threw off their towels and stood.

"Listen," Sam said. "Get the ball to Olaf, get the ball to Olaf. Olaf, go for the shot."

The four came onto the court and the fans rallied behind them, freight trains in the sky. Sam looked up into the blur of faces and knew that, though these people had come to watch an athletic contest, it had become much more than that now. They were hoping to find out if their deepest longings—the fairy tales they clung to like a teddy bear from childhood—would ever come true. They stood and cheered for four boys they didn't know, who represented the misspent lives within themselves, the dreams they'd never realized, four boys who stood for the shattered hopes and lost loves that would never return, and they cheered because in those four boys, for this one glorious moment, they would all *win!*

With the game tied and a minute and eight seconds to find their way home, Rob got the ball inbounds to Pete. The Blackhawks swarmed around Olaf. Elbow for elbow, Olaf battled for position in the low post. Tom slid to his usual spot on the right side. Rob and Pete dashed and ducked to get free and keep the ball moving between them. Without looking, Pete ripped a high, hard one to Olaf, who had worked open for a split second, moving in and out of the paint as though Ray Collins's Lightning Commander shock collar were attached to his belt. He caught it over his head, planted his left foot as though it were nailed to the barn loft floor, and pivoted to the basket. Lapp, Cooper, and McHenry converged. Olaf rose for the shot and the three defenders went up with him, arms extended, desperately trying to prevent him from scoring. And they did. The ball hit the backboard and came off the side of the rim. Tom, who had hobbled unattended to the basket along the baseline, exploded above them all, and tipped it in. And he was fouled.

You wonderful son of a bitch!

"Take us home!" Sam hollered, "take us home!"

The building trembled as the fans erupted. Strangers hugged each other, pounded one another on the back and exchanged high-fives. With the Broncs up 62 to 60, Tom accepted the ball from the referee. He disciplined himself and went slowly through his ritual. Exhaling a deep breath, Tom catapulted the ball, and though slightly off the mark, it scooped the rim but had enough of the shooter's finesse to fall back soft and true.

Willow Creek 63, Seely-Swan 60.

Sam and the Willow Creek bench clung to each other, unable to shout, casting their eyes above to the scoreboard clock. Forty-nine seconds! Sam couldn't breathe, his heartbeat pounding in his throat, while Diana shouted and shook him by the arm.

"They're going to do it! Oh God, they're going to *do* it!"

Reeling from the blow, Seely-Swan immediately called time out. The outnumbered boys came to the bench with hope in their eyes. Tom winced when he bent the knee to sit. No one high-fived or demonstrated. They went about the business of nourishing themselves for the last mile of the journey. Without a word Sam sensed they all realized it was within their grasp and still on the other side of the moon.

"They'll try to foul quickly when we have the ball," Sam told them. "Take care of the ball. Make the free throws and they can never catch us."

The buzzer summoned them.

"Whatever happens, I am damn glad I got to be your coach."

"I'm damn glad I got to be here!" Pete exclaimed.

They shouted and broke the huddle. Diana squeezed Sam's arm as the boys made their way to the court. With forty-nine seconds to go, the ref blew his whistle and Seely-Swan came pell-mell upcourt. They moved the ball to one side and then across court to the open man. Pete lunged to block Boyd's shot. The ball bounced high and came off, but Peter was whistled for the foul.

It was his fifth. He was out of the game with forty-one seconds remaining on the clock!

The outhouse had tipped over.

CHAPTER 86

The fans were on their feet, jabbering and pointing like witnesses at the scene of an accident. Pete strode to the bench under a resounding acknowledgement of praise. His face carried the anguish of a young, exhausted soldier with a leg shot off, fiercely willing to give the other to stay at the front with his brothers.

"I blew it!" he said and flopped onto the bench with his head in his hands. "I *blew* it!"

Sam knelt beside him and shouted above the deafening noise, "You got us here! You did everything possible and we're going to win it!"

Sam stood and patted his inconsolable guard on the back. Dean, beside Pete on the bench, handed him one of the caps. Glancing at Curtis and Dean to see which ear they had theirs cocked over, Peter pulled his on. Sam shrugged his shoulders at the referee who looked to the Willow Creek coach as if they might have a kid hiding under the bench.

The tenacious Boyd toed the line. The three Willow Creek defenders crouched along the paint. The kid took a deep breath and bounced the ball once. A riptide of noise broke over his head. He tossed up the shot. It hit the rim, caromed around, and fell in.

Willow Creek 63, Seely-Swan 61.

The referee delivered the ball and the stumpy guard gathered himself again. The distracting uproar continued. With a fierce intensity carved in his face, Boyd bounced the ball and flicked it into the air. Perfect. Seely-Swan was down one, 63 to 62 with forty-one ticks on the clock.

Rob grabbed the ball, stepped out of bounds, and lofted the ball to Olaf. The Blackhawks swarmed, trying desperately to tip the ball without fouling. Keeping the ball high, Olaf managed to fire it to Tom, who was immediately surrounded and trapped. Staggering, the bull rider lobbed the ball back to Olaf, who hadn't made it over the center line. Unable to get the ball to either of his well-covered teammates, Olaf tossed it into the front court before the allotted ten seconds was up, keeping the clock running. Thomas and McHenry frantically dashed after the unattended ball. Sam glanced up at the clock.

Twenty-nine seconds . . . twenty-eight . . .

SCOTT HAD TEARS streaming down his cheeks, watching his friends battling out on the floor and aching because he couldn't go out there and fight with them. He wished God had given him the ability to run and jump and shoot a basketball. He wiped the tears from his face and realized that this was probably as close as he'd ever come to winning anything, and that he'd probably end up like Hazel Brown.

With a chance to take the lead, Seely-Swan hurried the ball into the front court. The Willow Creek boys guarded the paint. Out in front, Thomas ripped the ball over to Boyd. Rob came out and covered him. Boyd gunned it back to Thomas. Rob chased, but as Thomas anticipated that the Willow Creek player would come all the way to him, he tried to bounce pass the ball back to his wide-open teammate. Rob darted into the passing lane and batted the ball downcourt. The three players broke for the loose ball and Scott's heart leaped in his chest. With Rob's great quickness he scooped up the bouncing ball, dribbled twice on the way to the basket, and with two wild Seely-Swan boys a stride behind him, flew to the rim and laid in a beautiful finger roll.

Willow Creek 65, Seely-Swan 62. Twenty-one seconds.

Everyone on the bench was going crazy. The field house shook. Scott tried to shout Rob's name but nothing would come out of his throat.

ROB, GASPING FOR air, hurried downcourt to join his teammates at the leaking dike. Sam raised both fists and shouted at the three of them.

"Blind your ponies!"

With their faces grim and their confidence shaken, the Seely-Swan athletes raced into the front court. Frantically they moved the ball around the fragmented zone while the Willow Creek boys harassed them like three jailers trying to guard five doors. Rob chased the ball while Olaf and Tom tried to protect the basket. Thomas whipped the ball to Cooper, who was wide open about twelve feet out on the side. The wide-eyed forward took his shot, but Olaf leaped out at him and got a piece of the ball, sending it sideways into the key. The spectators roared as Boyd recovered the ball.

Fifteen seconds!

Dean, Curtis and Peter were on all fours in front of the bench, paralyzed. Grandma and Axel clung to each other and Diana held her head.

Forced to go for three, Boyd snapped the ball to Thomas behind the three-point line. Their shooter took his shot. The air in the field house stilled for the rotating leather sphere. No one moved, not in the stands, not on the floor, hearts on tiptoe. All eyes followed the ball's arc toward the basket. It hit the side of the rim, went up on the backboard, and came off the opposite side where McHenry grabbed the rebound.

Nine seconds!

The desperate forward almost put back the easy layup but caught himself in time. He bounced it out to Boyd beyond the three-point line, but Rob was in his face, arms up, shouting. Desperately Boyd dribbled away and fired it to Cooper, who had dashed out beyond the three-point line. He turned to shoot, but Olaf, realizing the paint no longer mattered, had followed Cooper out. Olaf's gigantic wingspan loomed in Cooper's face. The gutsy Black-hawk senior faked the shot, getting Olaf off his feet, and dribbled around him. Wide open, Cooper took his shot in a blink, his instincts and hundreds of hours of practice guiding the ball. It was a beautiful shot that stopped hearts and knocked the breath out of the crowd. Swish!

The field house shuddered. The overhead scoreboard flashed WILLOW CREEK 65, SEELY-SWAN 64!

Was it a mistake? In that torturous instant Sam had missed it, along with most of the spectators. Cooper had stepped on the threepoint line. Olaf had done just enough to change his shot. It was a two!

Neither team had a timeout. Three seconds. Tom grabbed the ball and stepped out of bounds. Quickly he lobbed a high pass to Olaf and before they could foul him, Olaf tipped the ball into the unoccupied front court as if to a Willow Creek ghost. Sam watched the digital lights above him telegraph their victory as the desperate Seely-Swan athletes frenetically chased the elusive ball.

Three . . . two . . . one . . . !

The horn sounded, barely audible above the crescendo in the field house. But Sam could see the scoreboard clock blink out four zeros and he knew the page had been written and the book closed.

Willow Creek 65, Seely-Swan 64.

Holy cow! It was over, they had won, they were champions!

The three Willow Creek boys held each other up in the paint, hardly able to stand. The stunned Seely-Swan boys held their heads, some kneeled, some lay prostrate, like the wild dogs of Africa. Sam leaped and bounced and bounded across the floor.

He reached the three boys before anyone else and wrapped his arms around their sweat-soaked bodies.

"Son of a bitch! We didn't give 'em the calf!" Tom exclaimed.

Then they were submerged in the flow of enraptured fans that came to them like a great surf.

CHAPTER 87

Several people tried to hoist Tom to their shoulders, but he happily fended them off, clinging to his teammates. Others tried to lift Olaf above the turmoil, but he managed to keep his ground, hanging onto Sam. Then Pete fought his way through, with Dean and Curtis. Sam hugged Dean and shouted in his ear, "Your free throw beat them!" A newborn pride danced in the youngster's magnified eyes. Shouting to each other in the chaotic revelry, the six of them embraced Sam and lifted him onto their shoulders. Spontaneously the swarming fans parted and the boys marched around the court, bearing him aloft.

Sam could feel the earth shaking while the mass of humanity stood cheering, like a great choir singing. Tears came with a shuddering release, an outpouring of the failures and unfulfilled dreams of a lifetime, and the thunderous tumult became a trancelike soundlessness; time stood still. The boys bore him on their shoulders the length and breadth of the court as the Montanans cast their bouquets of admiration and praise. Then, in the midst of his euphoric spell, Sam spotted the parrot, loose, barnstorming over the crowd. He burst out laughing, breaking the bubble of his rapture.

When they finished the course, the boys, drained of all energy, set him down. Immediately Mervin Painter and Axel manhandled Olaf up onto their thick shoulders. Amos Flowers and the stranger in the gray suit hoisted Tom into the electric atmosphere, and the crowd quickly lifted the rest of the Broncs overhead. John English and Ray Collins took Dean. Hazel Brown and Truly Osborn shouldered Scott. They paraded the boys around the floor and the hundreds on the court joined in the promenade. Sam caught sight of Andrew in wilted suit pants and vest, his shirtsleeves rolled up to the elbow. He fought his way through the jubilant mass and grabbed Andrew by the arm. When Andrew saw Sam, he shouted into the pandemonium, "It's a miracle, an honest-to-God miracle!"

"She came back!" Sam yelled. "She came back!"

"I know! I know!" Andrew hollered. "And we'll take that trophy home for good!"

"No, *she* was in Willow Creek today, *she* came back!"

"Who?"

"Sarah! Tall, slim, large eyes, about the right age, she rode the bicycle and asked all about it!"

"Oh God, are you sure?"

"Yes!"

"Where—where is she?" Andrew shouted, sheltering Denise in his arms.

"She went to Missoula, said she went to school there."

"Yes, yes, that's right—"

"She said she was coming back to Willow Creek on her way through!" Sam shouted as the processional with the team had nearly circled the court.

"Oh, my God, I can't believe it!" Andrew said with joy flowering in his face.

CLAIRE PAINTER STOOD in the stands, watching Mervin and the others celebrating, smiling and clapping her hands at the spontaneous festivities. Land sakes, she never thought she'd live to see the day. In the swarming throng, she spotted Mavis Powers and almost didn't recognize her. Mavis didn't have rollers in her peach-colored hair. Then Claire spotted Miss Murphy and Mr. Pickett, those two she had always hoped would fall in love. They were arm in arm, with shining, happy faces, turning to music no one else seemed to hear.

In the raucous rejoicing, Axel found them and gave each of them a bear hug, lifting first Sam and then Miss Murphy off the floor. When he put her down, Miss Murphy went up on tiptoe and gently kissed Axel.

IT WAS TEN minutes before the officials, pleading over the loud-speaker, restored some kind of order. The Willow Creek bunch gathered around the team at their bench as the tournament ushers managed to clear a portion of the floor. Dean stood behind his sister's wheelchair and Tripod nestled in her lap. Amos Flowers stood beside Sally Cutter. The crowd applauded when the third- and second-place trophies were awarded, recognizing how far Rocky Boy and Seely-Swan had come. But when they called the Willow Creek team forward to receive the championship trophy, the deep rumble came through human voices as though down through time from creation's first oceans and storms and earth's upheavals, deafening, unimaginable.

Sam and Diana remained at the bench. The boys—all in their caps but Dean—hesitated, gesturing for them to follow. Sam waved them on. It was their trophy. They had not only run until their lungs burned, until their legs gave out under them, and given their sweat and blisters and blood, but they had faced the dragons and won.

Rob and Tom turned and held the golden prize high. With an armload of gold-and-blue nylon jackets he appeared to pull out of thin air, Andrew Wainwright met them as they came back toward the bench. He handed them out to the boys, whose surprise and delight lit up their faces. Across the back in blue letters was stitched MONTANA STATE CHAMPIONS 1991. Then, below a large golden basketball, the words: WILLOW CREEK, MONTANA.

There were jackets for Scott and Diana and Sam, and for the cheerleaders. On the front, over the heart, their names were embroidered. Not their proper names, but Dutch Boy, Sancho, Forget Me Not. When they had all pulled them on, there were several left. He handed one to Elizabeth Chapman. Her eyes lit up. Andrew handed a jacket to Axel, one to Hazel. Then, a jacket remained, a small one.

Andrew walked over and stooped in front of Denise Cutter's wheelchair. He held up the jacket. Over the heart DENISE was stitched in gold, and Sam loved Andrew Wainwright. With her brother's charmed cap on her golden locks, her joy and excitement fought their way through facial expressions and guttural sounds she could not command. Dean helped her get into the bright, satiny jacket. It fit perfectly. Even Hazel's fit, and on the front over the heart it read: HAZEL BROWN, JV'S.

Then the team and their loyal partisans moved reluctantly across the floor and out of the arena, through the cheering crowd.

CHAPTER 88

In the locker room they were encompassed by a numbing serenity, moving slowly in the embrace of an inner peace that seemed
to touch them all. Tom and Olaf loitered in the steaming shower as though
they never wanted to come out. With his body drained and trembling, Sam
sat quietly and allowed a satisfied smile to ease onto his face.

"Now my father I will be telling the basketball I am playing." Olaf gingerly pulled a sock over his tender ankle. "One hundred percent excellent
we are doing."

They waited until everyone was ready: Curtis with his arm in a sling,
Tom limping, Olaf favoring his heavily taped sprain, all wearing their
championship jackets and auspicious caps. Then they left the field house
together, their last moments as a team. Tom and Rob, the two who had suffered the indignity of losing the longest, carried the trophy between them
as though it were the Holy Grail. The others surrounded them, escorting
the symbol of their triumph to its permanent home in the little brick school
building in Willow Creek. Grandma, Diana, and the girls met them in the
lobby where many of the townsfolk still waited, including Denise and her
mother. Axel had sped off for the inn to prepare for the onslaught.

"Can we take my sister on the bus?" Dean asked Sam.

"Sure, if it's okay with your mom."

"That would be nice," Sally Cutter said. "Denise would enjoy that."

In a group they came out of the front entrance and headed for the parking lot, accompanied by the Willow Creek bunch and Dean wheeling his
sister. Preoccupied in a cloud of elation, they suddenly realized something
was wrong. The huge parking lot was still glutted with cars. How could
that be? The team had lingered in the locker room for more than a half
hour after the presentation, savoring what they had done, in no hurry for
endings.

"Man, look at all the cars," Tom said, hobbling in his diamondback boots.

"I can't hardly see," Dean said, squinting into the glare of headlights that illuminated the acres of vehicles.

When they reached the bus, they found it draped with gold and blue streamers that were attached to every conceivable surface, ROZINANTE on both sides of the hood still clearly visible. They climbed aboard and found their accustomed seats. When the occupants of the closest cars saw them, they began honking their horns, and soon the entire parking lot was in an uproar. Pete lifted Denise into his arms and Dean set her chair in the aisle, at the back of the bus. When they were all settled, Sam started the engine and turned on the lights.

"Looks like nobody went home," he said.

"It's more than that," Diana said. "Looks like some are still coming."

Sam began inching the bus toward the street. The kids opened some of the windows and waved to the well-wishers, overcome by this clamorous blare of acclaim and the blazing headlight tribute. When they reached the street, a Bozeman police cruiser and a highway patrol car sat poised in front of them, their colored lights flashing. A highway patrol officer strode to Sam's window.

"Follow me. We'll escort you home!"

"How come?" Sam said.

"Because you're the gutsiest team *we've* ever seen and we're all proud as hell. And besides, we're going to have the biggest traffic jam this state ever saw if I don't."

"Yelly!" Tom shouted. "Yelly!" And Olaf swatted him affectionately.

The officer snapped a smart salute and Sam, without thinking, returned the gesture.

"*All riiight!*" Diana shouted, sitting behind Sam.

With lights flashing, the two official vehicles pulled ahead slowly, and Sam followed. Cars and trucks flooded behind them, pouring out of the parking lot in an endless stream of light and sound. At the first intersection, two more squad cars joined the others, their colors whirling.

The bus traveled through the university campus, its inhabitants overwhelmed by this unexpected homage from those lining the streets, waving, shouting, and cheering as the clamor of horns and vehicles increased behind them.

"We're in a parade!" Dean shouted.

The escorts led them through the residential streets between the university and downtown. At every intersection more cars waited to join the caravan, their lights flashing, their horns tooting, their occupants waving and cheering. There were pickups with people standing in the beds, there were motorcycles, and people running from their houses as the motorcade moved past, some in robes and slippers, not wanting to miss this procession of the lionhearted.

"Do they do this every year?" Pete asked.

"Land sakes, no, sweetheart," Grandma said. "This is a once-and-forever, and it's for you gorgeous boys."

When they reached Main Street downtown, the patrol cars turned west. Two abreast, vehicles of every description streamed out Main behind them.

Sam watched these well-wishers in their all-consuming happiness. They would in all likelihood return to their rutted lives on Monday. But they'd remember this day, remember how good they felt tonight, how happy they were because three Willow Creek boys stood against all the odds and won, like the overwhelming joy one feels when a wildebeest cow won't quit and outlasts the wild dogs. And they'd remember that it does happen, the miracle when you least expect it. Sam glanced over and spotted John English, standing on the curb, waving his bone-colored Stetson in the air.

The patrol cars led them out past the mall and into the countryside, gradually increasing speed. The kids shut the windows as the chilled night air rushed in, and they turned silent. Thousands of strangers who had never been to Willow Creek were shepherding them home, these unidentified people identifying with their victory, claiming it for their own, awakened from their sleep of surrender and mediocrity to the hope of miracles and winning.

Sam turned to Grandma, who sat behind Dean and Curtis.

"How are you doing, Grandma?"

"I'm having the ride of my life, thanks to you."

"No, thanks to *you*," Sam said with his eyes back on the road. "You brought us luck."

"That was Tripod and Denise."

"How are you going to get your parrot?" Diana asked her.

"Oh, I'll come in tomorrow, when he's done showing off and gets hungry. He'll come and sit on my shoulder."

When they climbed the hill on the secondary blacktop that would take them through Churchill, they were utterly astounded. They could see all the way back to the town behind them where the stream of headlights was still unbroken, *six miles long,* a multitude who wanted to be fed by the loaves and fishes these boys had shared with those who had come to believe. They silently regarded one another in the glare of the lights from behind. They smiled. Sam's heart felt as though it would burst. He gazed ahead at the red and blue flashing lights leading them. Axel would sell every bottle of beer, every can of pop, every morsel of food in the place, keeping the ship afloat for a while longer. He glanced into the rearview mirror at Denise and was touched with joy.

It was like the ride on the bicycle built for two with your one true love. It only comes once in a lifetime, but it is given to enjoy and cherish and you must tuck it safely in your soul. It had changed him, a lot, all of them. As long as they lived, they'd never forget this ride, this journey of the heart; they'd never be the same.

They were bringing home the boon, and though he wasn't sure of everything that meant, he knew it had to do with pride and self-respect. The people of Willow Creek would walk tall for a long time to come, and Sam Pickett would no longer think of himself as a loser. It meant a lot of changes. Most of all, he would miss the companionship of these boys. They had taught him to fight, to find his fierceness, to never give up on life. He wished they could drive all night, that the earth would rotate away from them at such a rate that they would never reach Willow Creek, that what he felt was enough for all of his life; there was no one else he would rather be with.

This journey had been one of many, one part of a grander journey, and nothing in life makes sense if in the end there is not a winning. Good happens, every morning that the sun rises, every night that the moon shines, every moment that the earth turns. And if you're brave enough to look in the elephant's eye, you see, finally, that behind the sadness there is joy. And suddenly Sam knew, as if he always had known, that whatever it was he had been clinging to for so long, had all along been holding on to him.

Diana put her hand on his shoulder. He glanced into the rearview mirror. He could see her lovely face, the shine of tears reflecting off her cheeks. She raised her gaze into the mirror, into his eyes, and smiled.

"I can't bear for it to end," she said.

"I know. . . . I feel so helpless," he said, staring ahead at the glowing highway. "I'm going to try to enjoy the celebration, but I know when I wake up in the morning this will all be a memory."

"I don't mean the team, the games," she said.

"What *do* you mean?"

"I mean us."

"What are you saying?" Sam said.

"I don't want *us* to end, I know how good we are."

"Are you sure?" Sam held his breath.

"No, no, I'm not sure," she said, "but I know we have to go for it even if it's only one chance in a million. Are you willing to take a chance?"

"Take a chance! I was the baby most likely to take a chance on the maternity ward, I won the preschool take-a-chance contest, I set a record for taking chances in grade school, I was on the All-Take-A-Chance Team in high school, I won the Vince Lombardi Trophy for taking chances at the University of Chicago . . ."

Rozinante hurried for home. On the back of the bus someone had fixed a bumper sticker: WILLOW CREEK, MONTANA, HOME OF CHAMPIONS. From the glare of the headlights you could see a cat in the back window. It appeared to have only three legs.

BLIND YOUR PONIES

Finding Willow Creek

Questions for Discussion

FINDING WILLOW CREEK

by Stanley Gordon West

PEOPLE TOLD ME that if I wanted to meet a nice gal I should take country-western dance classes. I was living alone, middle-aged, and yes, I wanted to find a nice gal to share life with. So, I signed up for dance classes at Montana State University in Bozeman where I lived. I showed up for the first class along with about fifty other people. The instructor assured us that he'd make it fun as he paired us off in a big circle.

And yes, right off there was a very attractive gal who caught my eye. The only problem was that she came with a tall cowboy. At the teacher's command we'd switch partners, the men moving up one space, and before long I got a chance to dance with her. She was down to earth and lovely, and she warmed me with her smile. There would be ten lessons; ten Tuesdays when I'd be hoping she'd arrive alone. But the tall cowboy didn't miss a beat, and I figured there was little hope for me with the nice gal I met in the country-western dance class.

On the seventh Tuesday, once class was over and the dancers were heading out the door, I just about bumped into her, so close I could hear her saying to another gal, "I can't find my brother."

I turned on a dime and blurted loudly, "Your BROTHER?!"

By the time her brother found us, I'd found out she was single and had no current boyfriend—and I had her phone number. I waited two days before calling, not wanting to seem overeager. She accepted an invitation for dinner, then dancing, trying out our new skills on the dance floor. She lived out of town, about forty miles away in the foothills of the Tobacco Root Mountains.

I felt a long-forgotten excitement as I turned down a narrow blacktop highway. It was nearly dark as I approached the softened lights of the quiet little village, a place I'd never been before, a place I'd never heard of— Willow Creek, Montana.

She lived in Willow Creek, worked at the Blue Willow Inn, the social center of the town, and had a boy who played basketball on the high school team. So, besides dancing, I went to games with her. None of the loyal fans who turned out for these games seemed to notice that they hadn't won a game in over five years. Five years! But the six or seven boys they could muster to carry the Willow Creek banner played every one of those games as if their life depended on it.

I was fascinated! It didn't matter if they were behind by fifty points with a minute to go; they played every second of that last minute. It didn't matter that they had only four players still on the court. It didn't matter that the opposing team had wiped the floor with them physically and emotionally and—the strange thought came to me—*spiritually*. Don't get me wrong, I'd seen plenty of favorite teams lose before. But this was different. The more games I went to the more I realized there was something unique going on here that I simply didn't understand. What made these Willow Creek boys play like that?

The romance didn't last, but I was hooked on the team and the town to which she had introduced me.

I was being drawn into the story of the team and of the village. I was enticed by the town's legendary mystery—a bicycle built for two—and the legend of the Crow Indians, whose desperate plight resonated deeply with these townspeople. When I first heard that legend I was haunted by it. I still am.

I no longer had a country-western dance partner, but I had an obsession that engulfed me. I had to know where a town and its team got so much heart. For a time I became a fixture in the life of that team. At times, at the coach's request, I even donated my body to play defense with a few other volunteer adults so the team had live bodies to practice against. It was much more tiring than country-western dancing.

I followed the team over Montana highways in the dead of winter to far-flung outposts and cracker-box gyms to find an answer to a single, driving question: Why do they carry on in the face of utter and certain defeat?

QUESTIONS FOR DISCUSSION

1. How is the town of Willow Creek and its basketball program different from other Montana towns?

2. Why does Sam think he can help the team have one last winning season? Is it for the town, for the players, or for himself?

3. What roles do the novel *Don Quixote* and the musical *Man of La Mancha* play in this novel?

4. How are Sam and Diana similar or different in the way they react to the world after the death of people close to them?

5. What does Grandma Chapman mean when she says, "As long as she swims, I will cook"? Who else in Willow Creek has a similar philosophy?

6. Why is the bicycle built for two so important to the town of Willow Creek? What do you think it represents?

7. How does each player of the Willow Creek team overcome a personal obstacle both on and off the court?

8. Does your opinion of George Stonebreaker change after Sally Cutter's revelation? How?

9. Throughout the novel, Sam's faith in his team waxes and wanes. Why is he so hesitant to believe completely in his team?

10. Why does Peter lie about his relationship with Kathy? What does this say about how much Willow Creek's basketball team means to him?

11. How are the fathers of Peter, Tom, Olaf, and Dean similar? How are they different?

12. At what point does the town of Willow Creek believe in the team? Why are some citizens more supportive than others?

13. What does Denise Cutter mean to the team?

14. What do you think will happen to Willow Creek after the end of the basketball season? And to Sam?

15. Would you have chosen a different title for this book? Why or why not?

16. How do you think Peter and Olaf have been affected by the time they have spent in Willow Creek?

17. If you imagined a sequel to this novel, which characters would you most want to see included, and what would happen to set the plot in motion?